Niccolò Machiavelli

The Works of Nicholas Machiavel

Translated from the originals: illustrated with notes, annotations, dissertations, and

several new plans on the Art of war. Vol. 1

Niccolò Machiavelli

The Works of Nicholas Machiavel
Translated from the originals: illustrated with notes, annotations, dissertations, and several new plans on the Art of war. Vol. 1

ISBN/EAN: 9783337410643

Printed in Europe, USA, Canada, Australia, Japan

Cover: Foto ©Andreas Hilbeck / pixelio.de

More available books at **www.hansebooks.com**

THE

W O R K S

O F

NICHOLAS MACHIAVEL,

Secretary of State to the Republic of FLORENCE.

Tranflated from the ORIGINALS;

ILLUSTRATED WITH

NOTES, ANNOTATIONS, DISSERTATIONS,

And feveral New Plans on the ART of WAR,

By ELLIS FARNEWORTH, M. A.

Late Vicar of Rofthern in CHESHIRE,

Tranflator of the Life of POPE SIXTUS V. and
DAVILLA's Hiftory of the Civil Wars of FRANCE.

THE SECOND EDITION, CORRECTED.

IN FOUR VOLUMES.

VOL. I.

LONDON,

Printed for T. DAVIES, Ruffel-Street, Covent-Garden; J. DODSLEY,
Pall-Mall; J. ROBSON, New Bond-Street; G. ROBINSON, Pater-
nofter-Row; T. BECKET, T. CADELL, and T. EVANS, Strand.

MDCCLXXV.

SOME

ACCOUNT

OF THE

LIFE of NICHOLAS MACHIAVEL.

THOUGH writers in general afford but very scanty materials to the Biographer, yet it might have reasonably been expected, that Machiavel would have proved an exception to this observation; for, exclusive of his active spirit and the perpetual agitations his country laboured under at that period, he was frequently employed in public characters, and consequently became, in some degree connected with the history of those times.

His fame also as a writer of extraordinary abilities, which was never called in

A 3 question

queftion till feveral years after his death, might have induced fome perfon of the fucceeding generation to collect the memoirs of his life, a circumftance that has fallen to the lot of many authors of inferior genius. But either the confufions of the times, and the little attention paid to literary merit, or the calumnies which fome years after his death were thrown upon his character and writings by feveral religious Orders, have deprived him of this honour. Even his cotemporary Paulus Jovius, that profeffed collector of anecdotes, has given himfelf no trouble on this fubject, and records little more than the falfehoods and invectives of the Ecclefiaftics.

Niccolo Machiavelli, the fon of Bernardo, and Bartolomea the daughter of Stefano Nelli, was born at Florence the 3d of May, 1469; both his parents were defcended from noble families, who had filled with dignity the firft offices in the ftate; and as his father followed the profeffion of the law, it

is

is probable that he intended his fon for the fame employment. But as young minds are frequently captivated with the fplendor of a military life, and as the profeffion of arms at that period was attended with great ho-nours and emoluments, princes becoming fre-quently tributary to generals and partizans, it is fomewhat more than probable that he fpent his earlier years in the field, where he acquired that profound knowledge in the art of war, which he has difplayed in his very ingenious treatife on that fubject. We may alfo conjecture that his poems and plays were fome of his firft productions; and alfo the Marriage of Belphegor, which, in point of ftyle, humour, and invention, is efteemed at leaft equal to any of the novels of Boc-cace, and is a proof of his powers in this fpecies of writing. His comedies are very elegant, the language pure, and the dialogue fpirited; but the many indecencies they contain, is a great abatement of their merit: they were, however, frequently exhibited,

A 4 and

and even at Rome by the particular command of the pope, which is a ftrong proof
of the corrupt tafte of the age. It is very
probable that the liberty our author took
with the Ecclefiaftics in his play called
Il Frati, was in a great meafure the occafion of that virulent perfecution his works
fell under feveral years after his deceafe, and
which terminated in the condemnation of his
Prince in 1592.

His poetical performances are hafty incor-
rect compofitions, but interfperfed with
many ftrokes of genius.

The diffenfions which the republic of
Florence at this time laboured under, rendered it no difficult matter for a perfon of
Machiavel's parts and active fpirit to advance
himfelf in the ftate; accordingly we find
him, in 1502, employed in an embaffy to
duke Vaventine; and it is a ftrong proof of
his great penetration and abilities, that he
con-

conducted his negociations both to the approbation of the factious Florentines, and alfo
that of Cæſar Borgia, the moſt baſe and in-
ſidious man of that age. Our author has
been cenſured for having an intimate connection with this prince, and for being a
friend to his principles and deſigns; but his
letters, during this employ, ſufficiently clear
his character from theſe inſinuations, and
prove him to have been ſuperior even to the
artifices of Borgia.

In 1503 he was ſent in a public character to the court of Rome, in which he conducted himſelf with great addreſs, and his
letters on this ſubject are looked upon as fine
models for public buſineſs. In this year he
was alſo ſecretary to the council of ſtate, and
conveyed their inſtructions to Tebalducci Ma-
leſpini, commiſſary of the Florentine troops
employed againſt Piſa.

In 1504 he went ambaſſador to the court
of France.

In

In 1505 he was fent by the republic to fo-licit Gianpaolo Baglioni to take upon him the command of their troops which had been defeated by the Pifans in the preceding campaign.

In 1506 the republic fent him ambaffador to Rome, and he attended Julius the Second, in his expedition againft Perugia and Bo-logna.

In the years 1510 and 1511 we find him in the office of fecretary of ftate, in which he acquits himfelf with great elegance and precifion ; and his letters, during this employ-ment, fhew his difpofition in a very different point of view from that which is collected from his political writings; for he here ap-pears to be a perfon of the utmoft candour, moderation, and integrity of heart.

From the above period to his death he was probably out of favour with the reign-ing faction in the ftate ; and, retiring from publie

public life, employed himſelf in writing the
Hiſtory of Florence, the Prince, and the Political Diſſertations on the Firſt Decad of
Livy, which remain laſting monuments of his
abilities.

In the Hiſtory of Florence, his violent an-
tipathy to a monarchical government is ſuppoſed to have induced him ſometimes to
ſwerve from truth; and thoſe diabolical
maxims which have been ſo frequently and
ſo juſtly cenſured in his Prince, undoubtedly
had their origin from the ſame powerful
principle, and ought to be conſidered rather
as an exaggerated portrait of the princes of
that age, and as an incitement to his countrymen to be zealous in the defence of their
liberty, than as a ſyſtem of policy for the in-
ſtruction of future princes.

His Political Diſcourſes are the moſt correct and elegant of his works; and though
they contain ſome exceptionable paſſages, yet
they

they abound with deep refearches and moft excellent inftruclions.

Though our author was one of the firft perfons of the age both in literary and political acquirements; and though he was frequently employed in confiderable departments in the ftate, yet he neither met with the countenance and fupport of the great, nor received any confiderable reward for his fervices, of which he very pathetically complains in one of his dedications. He died in very low circumftances, July 22, 1527, in the 58th year of his age.

THE

TRANSLATOR's PREFACE.

THE generality of Readers, efpecially thofe of a volatile turn, are apt to over-look Prefaces, as nothing more than lumber and rubbifh; or at beft, but as Offices and Out-houfes to the main Fabrick: and per-haps, if any fhould by chance caft their eyes over this, they may fee no great reafon to al-ter their opinion. There are fome other pre-fatory Difcourfes, however, at the head of the feveral parts of this work, collected and tranf-lated from different writers and languages, which are not only very curious and intereft-ing, but abfolutely neceffary to be read by thofe that would have a clear comprehenfion of the enfuing Treatifes; and as fuch, the Editor begs leave to recommend them to perufal of every one defirous to be tho-roughly acquainted with the fcope and te-nour of Machiavel's writings. A fhort Pre-amble, therefore, and that chiefly relative to the execution of this, and fome other Englifh verfions of his Works, may fuffice at prefent.

In the year 1588, his feven Books of *the Art of War* were *fet forth in Englifh* (as the Tranflator calls it) by one Peter Withorne, or Whitehorne, who ftyles himfelf *a Student at Gray's Inn:* a fample of which performance is prefixed to the beginning of thofe Dialogues in the fourth Volume of this Tranflation; and

and therefore, it is not neceſſary to ſay any more of it in this place, than that there is not ſo much as one Note throughout the whole, nor any Plan that is intelligible; and that the language is ſo obſolete, that nobody can now form any judgment whether it was well or ill tranſlated, after making all reaſonable allowances for the Idiom of the times.

The next piece that is neceſſary to be mentioned here, is *a Tranſlation of the Political Diſcourſes upon Livy, by E. Dacres, printed at London, in the year* 1636; in which there is here and there a Note, though ſeldom much to the purpoſe: the moſt pertinent of them are inſerted in this verſion, and ſet down in their reſpective places to the Author's account. But as there was an interval of no more than forty-eight years betwixt the publication of this piece, and the other juſt now mentioned, there ſeems to have been but little improvement made in our language, during that period; to ſay nothing of its other defects.

For the ſame reaſon, much more cannot be ſaid in this reſpect, (though ſomething indeed) in behalf of an Engliſh Tranſlation of all Machiavel's proſe writings, firſt publiſhed at London, in the year 1675; which was afterwards reprinted in 1680, and again in 1694, without the leaſt alteration or amendment (though full of errors and other faults) and without any body's name to it. At the concluſion of it, there is a Letter addreſſed to

Zanobi

Zanobi Buondelmonte, faid to be written by
Machiavel himfelf, in vindication of his writings and principles; which is a moft bitter
invective againft the Clergy, and at the fame
time, a bold ftroke at Monarchy : but as it is
not to be met with, either in any Italian Edition of his works, or foreign tranflation of
them, and feems not only to be of more modern date, but calculated by fome atrabilair
writer, to ferve certain particular purpofes in
the laft century, one may juftly be allowed, I
think, to reject it. Upon which account, it
is omitted in this verfion : for in a Performance, intituled, *A Tranflation of Machiavel's
Works*, it muft have been a fhamelefs thing
to infert a Piece as tranflated from Machiavel,
by a perfon who never faw the Original himfelf,
nor never heard of any other man that did.

But to fpeak a little more particularly of
the Tranflation of all Machiavel's profe
works, juft now faid to be firft publifhed at
London in the year 1675. The language in
general, is poor and jejune, full of vulgarifms,
quaint fayings, and what the Italians call *il
modo baffo*, or low-life expreffion. But that
is not the worft of it : for the meaning of the
Author is very often grofsly miftaken; of
which the Reader may take the following inftances in the Hiftory of Florence, out of numberlefs others in every part of the work. In
the fecond book of that Hiftory, the Author
fays, " I Fiorentini dopo quefta rotta Sforza-
rono le loro torri all intorno, et il Re Robert
Mando

Mando per loro Capitano il Conte di Andria, detto il Conte Novello; per i portamenti del quale, overo perche fia naturale a i Fiorentini *che ogni ſtato rincreſca*, & ogni accidente divida, la Citta, non oſtante la guerra haveva con Huguccione, in amici & nemici del Re fi divife:" which the old Engliſh Tranflator has erroneouſly rendered in this manner. "After this difaſter, the Florentines fortified at home as much as they could, and King Robert ſent them a new General, called Count di Andrea, with the Title of Count Novello. By his deportment (or rather by the genius of the Florentines, whofe property it is *to increaſe* upon every ſettlement, and to fall afterwards into factions upon every accident) notwithſtanding their prefent war with Uguccione, they divided again, and fome were for King Robert, and fome againſt him." But furely it might have been more properly thus tranflated. "After this overthrow, the Florentines began to fortify all the towns and caſtles round about them, and applied to King Robert for another General: upon which he ſent them the Count di Andria, commonly called Count Novello; whofe behaviour, added to the impatient temper of the Florentines (which is *foon tired* of any form of government, and ready to fall into factions upon every accident) occaſioned the City to divide again, notwithſtanding the war they were engaged in with Huguccione: fome declared for King Robert, and fome againſt him."

Again,

Again, in the fourth Book, Machiavel fays,
" A chi ricorreranno eglino ora per aiuto ? A
Papa Martino, ftato a contemplazione di Braccio ftraziato da loro ?" " To whom (fays the
old Tranflator) will they now addrefs for fupplies ? To Pope Martin ? *Braccio can be witnefs
how they ufed him before.*" Which fhould have
been rendered in this manner, or fomething
like it : " To whom will they now have recourfe for affiftance ? To Pope Martin, whom
they have fo vilely abufed, only to gratify
Braccio da Montone ?" *A contemplazione* being
an Italian phrafe, which fignifies *for the pleafure, gratification, or fatisfaction of any one; on
account of, or in confideration of fuch a perfon
or thing.*

The laft inftance I fhall quote, is, from the
feventh Book of the fame Hiftory, where the
following paffage occurs. " Carlo Vifconte,
perche s' era pofto piu propinquo alla porta,
& effendogli il Duca paffato avanti, quando da
i Compagni fu affalito, non lo potette ferire
d'avanti ; ma con duoi colpi *la Schiena* & la
fpalla gli trafiffe :" which is thus tranflated,
" Carlo Vifconte being placed nearer the
door, the duke was paft him before he was affaulted, and therefore he could not ftrike him
before he was dead: however, he muft do his part,
and with *a Schine* gave him two deep wounds
upon his fhoulder." Now, what in the name
of wonder is *a Schine?* one would be apt to
think it was fome dreadful murdering wea-

pon like a Butcher's Cleaver, or fomething of
that kind. Tremble not, gentle Reader, it is
no fuch matter. Indeed, I believe it is nothing
at all : for the word *Schine* is not to be found
in any Dictionary. The meaning is plainly
this : "Carlo Vifconte, who ftood nearer the
door, and by whom the Duke had paffed before he was attacked by his accomplices, not
having an opportunity of ftriking him *in the
fore part of his body*, gave him a ftab *in the back*,
and another in the fhoulder." Miftakes and
unwarrantable liberties of this fort, are to be
met with in almoft every page : fo that it
would be not only an endlefs but unneceffary
talk to collect them; as any Reader muft be
pretty well fatisfied already with thefe fpe-
cimens.

In the prefent Tranflation, the Editor may
truly fay, that no pains have been fpared to
make it acceptable to the Public : for which
reafon, he is not altogether without hope it
will be looked upon with candour. The ftyle
of the Author, indeed, (notwithftanding the
encomiums which have been beftowed upon
him in that refpect by fome writers) is generally fhort, broken, fententious, and difficult
to connect in common periods : his tranfitions
are fudden ; his meaning often deep, abftrufe,
and intricate ; his argumentation clofe and
fevere. But great care has been taken to elu-
cidate his meaning, to explain dark and difficult paffages, to connect his periods, and to
give

give his arguments their full fcope by the addition of Notes, Differtations, and Plans, where they feemed neceffary; as well as of feveral other pieces tranflated from different languages, and never before publifhed in the Englifh tongue; of which fome mention has been already made: and if the Tranflator has now and then indulged himfelf in a moderate and reafonable ufe of circumlocution, it is hoped it will be excufed; fince it would otherwife have been impoffible to do the author juftice.

As to the further merit, or demerit of the Author, little needs to be added here: the Reader will find what has been faid both for and againft his Writings, fairly and impartially laid before him elfewhere, and is left to judge for himfelf. Nothing has been either palliated or aggravated: it is true, where his Principles are liable to exception (as in fome places they certainly either are, or at leaft feem to be fo), they have been combatted *pro virili*, and an antidote attempted for the poifon: in others, where he is blamed, though not juftly blameable, his Character has been vindicated. Much cenfure, indeed, and great applaufe, have been, and ftill aré, beftowed upon him; which (how much foever they may tend to influence the living) can have no effect upon one who has now been dead above two Centuries, and far out of *the uncertain found* of both trumpets. His Tranflator, who is ftill within

diſtance, and ſubjeſt to human feelings, does
not pretend to be indifferent to either : and
though he is ſenſible how ſlender a title he has
to one, he would willingly, if poſſible, eſcape
the other.

1762.

MACHI-

MACHIAVEL's

DEDICATORY EPISTLE

T O

POPE CLEMENT VII. *

HOLY FATHER,

A S your Holinefs was pleafed to lay your commands upon me, to write a Hiftory of Florence, long before your Exaltation to the Pontificate, I accordingly applied myfelf

---

* This Pontif, whofe Name was Julio de' Medici, was fon to Juliano, killed at Florence, by the Pazzi, in 1478. *See* *Book* VIII. *of this Hiftory.* He was a Knight of Rhodes, afterwards made Cardinal by his Uncle, Leo X. and fucceeded Adrian VI. in 1523. His Pontificate was diftinguifhed by feveral confiderable Events. All Germany was divided about the new Doctrine preached by Martin Luther; and Clement, dreading the power of Charles V. having entered into a league with the French and Venetians, wrote in very haughty terms to that Emperor, who anfwered him in the fame ftyle. But the Colonni, who were of the Imperial party, rifing againft the Pope, cited his Holinefs to appear before a general Council, which Charles intended to call at Spire, and forced him to retire into the Caftle of St. Angelo, in 1526. The next year, Charles of Bourbon, the Em-

to

to it with the utmoſt care and attention, and with all the abilities which Nature and Experience have afforded me, that I might ſhew my readineſs to obey you in every thing. But after I had brought it down to the time when the death of the illuſtrious Lorenzo de' Medici gave a new turn to the affairs of Italy, and found the Events which afterwards happened, grew ſo intereſting and important, that they de-

peror's General, took and plundered Rome, and obliged the Pope to pay 400,000 Ducats for his ranſom ; to raiſe which, all the veſſels of gold and ſilver that belonged to the Churches were melted down and coined, and the vacant Cardinal's Hats ſold by public Auction. Beſides other conceſſions, it was likewiſe agreed, that his Holineſs, and thirteen Cardinals, ſhould remain priſoners in the Caſtle, where they were to be confined till the money was paid, and afterwards go to Naples, or Gaieta, till the Emperor's further pleaſure was known. In the year 1529, he made a peace with that Emperor, by a marriage betwixt Alexander de' Medici, created Duke of Tuſcany, and Margaret, Charles's natural daughter ; which alliance was afterwards confirmed by the marriage of Catherine de' Medici to Henry II. King of France. During theſe tranſactions, Henry VIII. of England, divorced his Wife, Catharine of Auſtria, and was excommunicated by Clement for ſo doing : upon which, he declared himſelf *Head of the Church in his own dominions*, and promoted the Reformation, which he had, till then, oppoſed. *Platina, continued by Sir Paul Ricaut.* It was ſaid of this Pope, whilſt he was in priſon, *Papa non poteſt errare.* Though Machiavel was much eſteemed by him, he at laſt incurred his heavy diſpleaſure, on a ſuſpicion of being engaged with the Soderini in a conſpiracy againſt him ; concerning which, the Reader will meet with ſome other anecdotes in the courſe of this work.

ſerved

ferved to be related in a higher ftyle, and
more fpirited manner, I refolved to prefent what I had already digefted, in one
Volume, at your Holinefs's feet; that fo
you might have a tafte at leaft of the fruit
which you yourfelf planted, and an earneft
of my endeavours to bring it to maturity.

In the perufal of it, your Holinefs will
fee to what havock and diftractions our
Country was expofed for many ages after the
declenfion of the Roman Empire in the
Weft; how often it varied its form of government; and to how many different People
and Princes it became fubject. You will
fee how the Popes, your Predeceffors, the
Venetians, the Sovereigns of Naples, and
the Dukes of Milan, by turns came to bear
the chief rule in this Province. You will
fee your native City, after it had fhaken off
the yoke of the Emperors, labouring under
continual difcords and civil diffenfions, till
the government of it happily fell into the
hands of your family.

But as your Holinefs (equally defpifing
flattery, and efteeming juft praife) ftrictly
enjoined me to avoid all kind of Adulation,
when at any time I fhould have occafion to
mention the names of your Anceftors, I
am afraid I fhall feem to have tranfgreffed
that command, when I extol the virtue and
liberality of Giovanni, the prudence of Cofimo, the affability of Pietro, the magnifi-

cence

cence and wisdom of Lorenzo de' Medici.
For which, and all other passages that may
appear in any wise fulsom or offensive, in
the course of this work, I most humbly
intreat your Holiness to admit my Apology,
when I say, that it was not possible to avoid
it.   For as I found all the Memoirs of those
times full of their merit and praises, I should
justly be accused either of deviating from
truth, if I represented them in any other
light, or of extreme envy if I passed them
over in silence.   And if there was any private or ambitious view concealed under
their glorious endeavours to serve their Country, as some have not scrupled to hint, I
do not think myself at liberty to say so;
as that has not appeared to me.   Indeed,
it may easily be perceived, that in all other
parts of this History, I have never endeavoured to throw a veil of Honesty over
a foul deed, nor to calumniate any one
that was worthy of praise, by meanly insinuating that it was done to serve some
vile purpose.   How little I have been guilty
of flattering any one, will more particularly appear in the speeches and harangues to
the public, and in my private reflections
and observations; which are always delivered without restraint or reserve, and in a
manner consistent with the actions, character, and temper of the person that speaks,
or is spoken of: and I have at the same

time

time ftudioufly endeavoured to avoid all odious names of diftinction and party difference, as unbecoming the dignity of Hiftory, and of very fmall account in the fupport of truth.

No one certainly, therefore, who reads this hiftory with candour, will upbraid me as a Sycophant and Time-ferver; efpecially when he finds that I have made but little mention of your Father: for, indeed, he was fnatched away from us at fo immature an age, and when his Reputation was but juft beginning to fpread itfelf amongft mankind, that I might otherwife have been thought too partial to his Virtues. Neverthelefs, if he had had nothing elfe to boaft of, the Glory alone of having given your Holinefs to the world, is fufficient to balance all the fplendid actions of his Anceftors, and will add many more ages of Fame to his memory, than the malevolence of his Deftiny fo envioufly cut off years from his Life.

I have endeavoured, Holy Father, as much as I could (without doing violence to truth), to fay nothing that might offend any one ; and yet perhaps I have pleafed no one. And, indeed, I fhall not be at all furprifed, if that fhould be the cafe : fince it is almoft impoffible for a man to write a Hiftory of his own times, without giving offence to many. However, I come boldly into the Field : for as I have been honoured with your Countenance,

and

and preferred by your Bounty, I am not without hope, that I ſhall likewiſe find ſhelter under the ſanction of your favourable opinion
and great wiſdom. In this confidence I ſhall
purſue my Undertaking with the ſame ſpirit
and alacrity that I have proceeded thus far, if
life and health continue, and your Holineſs
ſtill vouchſafes to ſupport me with your protection.

ADVER-

ADVERTISEMENT to the READER,

Concerning the Hiſtory of FLORENCE.

From the French Tranſlation, publiſhed at the Hague, 1743 *.

AS the bare title of *The Hiſtory of Florence* may appear a little dry at firſt ſight, to thoſe that are not acquainted with its merit, it ſeems neceſſary in ſome meaſure to premiſe, that the intereſts and concerns of that Republic were ſo intimately connected and interwoven with thoſe of the reſt of Italy, that it was impoſſible to ſpeak of one, without frequent mention of the other. For here we ſhall find many things that relate to the Popes, the Republic of Venice, the Dutchy of Milan, and ſeveral other conſiderable States ; which altogether make almoſt a complete Hiſtory of Italy, during a period that has not had much light thrown upon it, though very fertile in remarkable events.

With regard to Florence alone, the Reader would have no occaſion to complain of being neither improved nor entertained by the Hiſ-

---

* There had been ſeveral Editions of this French Tranſlation before. The Tranſlator's name was Tetard, a French Refugee and Phyſician at the Hague. He was a native of Blois, and of the Family of Monſieur Tetard, a Miniſter there, who made a good deal of noiſe in the French Synods, at the time of the Controverſy concerning *Univerſal Grace*, at Saumur.

tory

tory of it, if he met with nothing more than a detail of the conduct by which the Houfe of Medici, from a mercantile condition, at laft exalted itfelf to fovereign grandeur and authority.

But there are many other admirable Leffons to be learnt from it, which may be of great ufe to fuch as are called to the government of Republics. They will fee what means are moft expedient to preferve the Liberties of a free State, and to fruftrate the attempts of Ambition to fubvert them. They will find thofe wiles expofed to the world, which defigning men have practifed for that purpofe: and this may be fo far of ufe as to deter others from treading in the fame Steps, when they perceive, that the Mine is already fprung, and thefe dangerous Artifices now clearly feen through by every one. They will learn from the proceedings of the Florentines, to judge of the views and inclinations by which the feveral degrees of mankind are actuated. For as the government of their City was fucceffively in the hands of the Grandees, the Nobility, the Commoners, and the Plebeians, the predominant paffion of every one of thefe different Governors will plainly appear to be the fame ; and that whatfoever may be the rank or condition of thofe that are at the helm of fuch States, the form of Government will always degenerate into infupportable Tyranny, if they are not reftrained by good Laws, and

thofe

thofe Laws maintained in their full force and vigour.

As the Author abounds with political reafonings and reflections in all his other works, he has not been fparing of them in this, efpecially in his Harangues; of which there are many that may ferve for excellent models, in the like circumftances, to fuch as are employed in the adminiftration of public affairs, and have fometimes occafion to avail themfelves of Eloquence in moving the paffions and affections of men. And though this Hiftory may poffibly be thought too limited and circumfcribed by particular perfons, the very name of Machiavel will ftill be fufficient to recommend it to the notice and efteem of the public. Great Mafters always ftamp fuch marks of Genius upon their works, as diftinguifh them from all others: and if the Facts that are related in this, fhould not be deemed fufficiently interefting to any other people on this fide the Alps, yet the judicious manner in which they are collected and digefted, by a man who fo well knew how both to chufe himfelf, and point out to others, what was moft ufeful and worthy of obfervation in Hiftory, will always make it appear in a refpectable light.

Whofoever then fhall carefully and attentively read the prefent, which relates the Tranfactions of a wife and perfpicacious people, may reap as much advantage from it, in my opinion, as from almoft any other whatfoever.

foever. But as to such as relish no sort of
Books, except those in which a quarter of the
world at least, is dragged upon the theatre at
one time, they may better amuse themselves,
if they please, with reading Gazettes, or A-
bridgements of Chronology, where sudden Revolutions and Downfalls of great Empires,
and such astonishing Events, occur in every
page: from which they will receive just as
much satisfaction and improvement as those
ignorant people who sit wondering at the
strange gesture of puppets upon a stage (as
well they may), whilst they know nothing of
the secret springs that put them in motion.
Our author, indeed, is not altogether so sen-
tentious as Cornelius Tacitus; but yet he enters so deep into matters of fact, and lays open
the remote causes of them with so much per-
spicuity, that the Reader himself will naturally draw proper conclusions. And perhaps
this may be the better way of the two to form
the judgment: for such remarks and reflections as seem to be the result of our own rea-
soning, commonly please us more, and make
a deeper impression, than those that are ob-
truded upon us by others.

There may be some, perhaps, who will
think many circumstances in this History
might have been omitted, as trifling or super-
fluous. But every one is not capable of dif-
tinguishing what are the most proper materials for such a composition; and those that
really

really are, will pay great deference to the
Judgment of an Author, whofe Abilities and
Underftanding at leaft have never been called
in queftion. Others, very likely, who are
ready to allow him thefe endowments, will
not fo eafily be prevailed upon, to make the
fame conceffions in regard to the goodnefs of
his heart: but as the Reader will find that
Matter more amply difcuffed in the Preface to
his Political Difcourfes, and other detached
Pieces of this Work, let it fuffice at prefent, to
give a remarkable proof of his integrity and
love of truth, in fpeaking fo boldly of the
Pontifs, through the whole courfe of a Hiftory, dedicated to one of the moft powerful of
them, who was of the Houfe of Medici too,
and had been his great Patron and Benefactor.
For, not content with relating many of thofe
horrible truths with which the Lives of the
Popes abound, he fays, in his firft Book, after
a recital of the miferies and diftractions his
Country had already groaned under, "that all
the wars which Foreigners afterwards made
upon Italy, were chiefly owing to the Popes,
and moft of the feveral inundations of Barbarians that poured themfelves into it, in a
great meafure occafioned by their incitement
and inftigation : which practices being continued *even to this time*, have fo long kept, and
ftill keep Italy weak and divided." This was
but an aukward manner, fome may think,
of paying court to fuch a Pontif as Clement

ment VII. and especially in so great a Politician as Machiavel. Even our common Parochial Clergy of Paris, would have behaved with more politeness. They say finer and handsomer things in their addresses to their Archbishop, than perhaps they would do to Our Saviour himself, and his holy Apostles, if they were now upon earth.

What I would infer from this Stricture is, that a Man, who dares to speak the whole truth in such delicate circumstances, cannot be suspected of either suppressing or disguising it upon any other occasion, out of pusillanimity or private interest : so that how deficient soever he may appear to some people as a Courtier, he certainly deserves great applause from every one, as an Historian who has written with strict impartiality and regard to truth.

THE

AUTHOR's INTRODUCTION.

WHEN I firſt reſolved to write the Hiſtory and Tranſactions of the Florentines, both at home and abroad, it was my deſign to have begun with the Year 1434, at which time the Family of Medici, by the merits of Coſimo, and his father Giovanni, had acquired a greater degree of authority than any other in Florence; imagining that * Leo-

---

* Leonardo Aretino was one of the moſt learned men of the fifteenth Century, and the reſtorer of the Greek Tongue in Italy. Pope Innocent VII. made him Secretary of the Briefs, merely on account of his merit: which office he diſcharged with great credit, during the Reign of that Pontif, and the four next. He attended Pope John XXIII. at the Council of Conſtance, in 1413, and was afterwards Secretary, or, as ſome ſay, Chancellor to the Republic ef Florence, by which he amaſſed great riches. A catalogue of the books he wrote, which were many, may be ſeen in Geſner's *Bibliotheca*, and in Baretti's *Italian Library*, a very uſeful work, publiſhed by the Author at London, in 1757; in which he ſays, it was reported, that this Leonardo had found a *piece* of Tully, intituled, *De Gloria*, that he made uſe of it in ſome of his Latin works, and then deſtroyed it. The Florentines were ſo pleaſed with his Hiſtory of Florence, that when he died, they buried him with a chaplet of laurel round his head, and a copy of that book laid upon his breaſt. There is ſtill a marble monument to be ſeen over his grave, in the Church di Santa Croce at Florence. It is ſaid, that a copy of his Letters was found ſome years ago amongſt the manuſcripts of the public Library at Oxford, in which there are forty that have never yet been printed. He died at the age of ſeventy-four, in the year 1444. The inſcription upon his mo-

nardo d'Arezzo, and Marco Poggio *, two excellent Hiftorians, had given a particular ac-

nument does him great honour. It is as follows: "Since
the death of Leonardo, Hiftory is in mourning, Eloquence is
become mute, the Greek and Latin Mufes are in tears." *Mabillon Iter. Ital.* p. 165. *L'Enfant's Poggiana*, tom. i. p. 11.

* Some call him Bracciolino, or Brandolino Poggio. He
was fecretary to Pope Eugenius IV. Nicholas V. and fix
other Popes, as he himfelf fays. From Rome he was recalled
to Florence, at the age of feventy-four, to fucceed his friend,
Leonardo, in the office of Chancellor to that republic. He had
been very intimately acquainted with him during his life,
and wrote a critique upon his works. His learning was confiderable, but his genius fatirical, as appears from his invectives againft Laurentius Valla, and his Hiftory of Florence
is not looked upon to be either candid or exact. Whilft he
attended the Council at Conftance, he and Mabillon (as the
latter fays in his *Mufæum Italicum*, tom. i. part. i. p. 211.)
difcovered feveral old manufcripts, in the Abbey of St. Gall,
about twenty miles from that City, and particularly a perfect
one of Quintilian's works; the news of which was received
with great pleafure by the *Literati*, as they had no complete
copy before. Though it is faid, there is one in the Bodleian
Library above 500 years old, and feveral of very ancient date
in the French King's. In his travels through Germany, he
tranfcribed the books of Tully *De Finibus & de Legibus*, which
had not been feen in Italy before that time. Many other works
he publifhed; and died in the year 1450, at the age of eighty.

It is faid, this Poggio fold a Manufcript of Livy's works,
very fairly tranfcribed with his own hand, for 120 crowns, to
the celebrated Panormita, Secretary to Alphonfo, King of
Naples. Upon which, the Secretary, in a letter to his Majefty, fays, "I intreat you, of your great wifdom, to let me
know, whether Poggio or I act the more prudent part; he
in difpofing of Livy, to purchafe a farm near Florence, or I,
who fell an Eftate to buy that author, in his hand-writing.
Your goodnefs and modefty encourage me to afk you this familiar queftion." *Gallois traite des Bibliotheques*, p. 154, 155.
This Alphonfo was a lover of Letters, and gave Poggio a
large fum of money for a tranflation of Xenophon's Cyro-
pædia.

count

count of all the events which happened before that period. But afterwards, having
carefully perufed their writings, to fee in what
method and order they had proceeded, that fo
I might recommend my own by imitating
them, I found they had been very accurate indeed in their relation of the wars which the
Florentines had been engaged in with foreign
Princes and States : but that they were either
totally filent concerning their civil diffenfions
and domeftic animofities, and the confequences of them, or had touched upon them
in fo curfory and fuperficial a manner, that
the Reader was neither in the leaft profited
nor entertained by it; which, I fuppofe, they
did, either becaufe they thought thofe occurrences rather trifling and infignificant, than
worthy of being recorded ; or out of fear of
offending the defcendants of fuch as they fhould
have been otherwife obliged to mention with
difhonour. Both which reafons, if I may be
allowed to fay fo without offence, feem to be
altogether unworthy of fo great men. For
whatfoever is either inftructive or entertaining in hiftory, principally refults from a clear
and circumftantial narration of Facts. If any
reading can be of fervice to fuch as govern
Republics, it muft be that chiefly which lays
open the firft caufes of difcord and divifions in
them ; by which they may grow wife at the
expence of others, and learn to preferve peace
and unanimity at home : if examples drawn

b 2   from

from foreign communities are apt to affect
mankind in fome degree, furely thofe that are
deduced from their own, muft naturally be
more ufeful and make a deeper impreffion;
and if the Factions that ever exifted in any
State, were worthy of notice, it is certain, thofe
that have diftracted Florence are ftill much
more fo. For whereas moft others that we
know any thing of, have only been divided
into two, which have fometimes added ftrength
to, and fometimes been the deftruction of
them, that City has been fubject to many. In
Rome, as every one knows, there arofe a conteft betwixt the Patricians and Plebeians, after
the expulfion of their Kings, which continued
till the utter diffolution of that Republic.
The fame happened at Athens, and in all the
other Common-wealths that flourifhed in thofe
ages. But in Florence, the firft diffenfion was
amongft the Nobility; the fecond, betwixt the
Nobility and the Citizens; and the laft, betwixt the Citizens and the People, or Plebeians. In all which, one Faction had no fooner
got the upperhand, but it divided itfelf into
two: and the confequence of thofe divifions
was fuch a feries of affaffinations, executions,
banifhments, and difperfion of families, as is
not to be paralleled in the hiftory of any people that has defcended to our times. And,
in my opinion, nothing demonftrates the
ftrength of our City fo clearly as the effects
of thofe Divifions, which were fufficient to have
                                        fubverted

fubverted almoft any other in the world. But ours, on the contrary, feems to have gathered frefh vigour, and to have rifen ftronger from them. For fuch was the Virtue and Patriotifm, and fo powerful the good genius of the Citizens, that fome who efcaped thofe evils, contributed more effectually by their courage and conftancy to the exaltation of themfelves and their country, than the malignity of Faction had done to deprefs them, though it had fo grievoufly harraffed the one, and diminifhed the number of the other. And, indeed, if fuch a form of Government had fortunately been eftablifhed in Florence, as would have kept the Citizens firmly united together, after they had fhaken off the yoke of the Empire, I don't know of any Common-wealth, ancient or modern, that could have been deemed fuperior to it, either in Military power, or the arts of peace. For it is well known, that after the Ghibelines were banifhed the City in fuch numbers that all Tufcany and Lombardy fwarmed with them, the Guelphs and thofe that remained in poffeffion of it, were able to raife an army of twelve thoufand foot and twelve hundred heavy-armed horfe out of their own Citizens for the expedition againft Arezzo, which was in the year before the battle of Campaldino. And afterwards, in the war with Philip Vifconti Duke of Milan, when they were obliged to truft to dint of money and Stipendiary forces (as their own were

then

then very much reduced), the Florentines expended three millions and five hundred thousand * Florins during the courfe of it, which lafted five years : and it was no fooner ended, but, diffatisfied with the peace, and defirous of making a further difplay of their ftrength, they marched out with an army and laid fiege to Lucca.

I can fee no reafon, therefore, why the caufes and progrefs of the civil Diffenfions which happened in this Republic, fhould not be thought worthy of a minute and particular relation. And if thofe noble Authors were deterred from it only by the fear of hurting the memory of fome whom they fhould neceffarily be obliged to fpeak of, they widely miftook the matter, and fhew they were not fufficiently aware of that latent ambition which is naturally implanted in all men, and their defire of having their own names and thofe of their Anceftors tranfmitted to Pofterity. Nor did they recollect that many, who never had any opportunity of fignalizing themfelves by virtuous and laudable atchievements, have endeavoured to perpetuate their memory by the moft flagitious and deteftable means †. Neither did they confider that

* A coin firft ftamped by the Florentines. That of Palermo and Sicily is worth about 2s. 6d. Sterling ; that of France 1s. 6d. of Germany 3s. 4d. of Spain 4s. 4d. of Holland and Poland 2s. of Savoy 3d. half-penny; of Gold 5s. The laft is moft probably meant here.

† As Eroftratus, who burnt the Temple of Diana at Ephefus, which was reckoned the moft magnificent ftructure in

tranfac-

tranfactions which carry an air of greatnefs along with them, fuch as thofe of States and Governments, ftill reflect more honour than infamy upon the Actors, what ends foever they have had, or in what light foever they are reprefented. Thefe confiderations prevailed upon me to alter my firft Plan, and to begin my Hiftory from the very foundation of our City. And fince it is not my intention to tranfcribe what has been already publifhed by others, I fhall relate fuch things only as happened *within* the City to the year 1434, taking no further notice of foreign tranfactions than what will be abfolutely neceffarily for a better underftanding of what occurred at home : after which period, I fhall give a diftinct account both of one and the other. And that the Reader may have a clearer and more extenfive profpect both ways in this Hiftory, before I come to treat of the affairs of Florence, I will fhew by what means Italy became fubject to thofe Princes who governed it that time : all which will be included in the four firft books. The firft fhall contain a brief recital of the principal events that happened in Italy from the declenfion of the Roman Empire to the year 1434. The fecond, a general account of affairs from the foundation of Florence to the

---

the world. A great author obferves, that, " the love of riches and pleafure is not fo predominant amongft mankind, in general, as the thirft of fame."

war

war that was commenced againſt the Pope,
after the Expulſion of the Duke of Athens.
The third will conclude with the death of
Ladiſlaus King of Naples: and in the fourth
we ſhall arrive at the year 1434. After which
we ſhall give a particular narrative of all proceedings, both within and without the City,
till we come down to our own times.

THE

THE

HISTORY

OF

FLORENCE.

BOOK I.

ARGUMENT.

The Roman Empire ruined by inundations of Barbarians. The Weſtern Goths the firſt invaders of it. Rome taken and ſacked by them under the command of Alaric. The Huns invade Italy, take Aquileia under the conduct of Attila, and advance to Rome ; but retire at the requeſt of the Pope. The firſt reſidence of the Roman emperors at Ravenna. Odoacer cauſes himſelf to be ſtyled King of Rome, and is the firſt of the Barbarians that thought of fixing in Italy. The Empire is cantoned out into ſeveral diviſions. Theodoric invades Italy, kills Odoacer, calls himſelf King of Rome, and holds his reſidence at Ravenna. His great actions and death. Beliſarius appointed General for the Emperor Juſtinian. He is recalled and ſucceeded by Narſes, or Narſetes, an Eunuch. Longinus changes the form of government in Italy. The Lombards invade it under their King Alboin, who is afterwards aſſaſſinated by Almachild, at the inſtigation of his own wife. The Biſhops of Rome begin to extend their authority. The Eaſtern Empire ruined in the time of the Emperor Heraclius. Charlemagne exempts the Pope from all human Juriſdiction, and is choſen Emperor of the Weſt. The original of Cardinals. Oſporco being elected Pope is aſhamed of his name, and changes it ; which cuſtom is followed by ſucceeding

VOL. I.   B   *Popes.*

Popes. The original of Pisa. The state of Italy in the year 931. Pope Gregory V. is driven out of Rome, but returns thither. He deprives the Romans of the power of chusing their Emperors, and confers it upon Six Princes of Germany, who are afterwards called Electors. Nicholas II. deprives the Romans of their right of approving the Popes when elected, and reduces the election to the suffrages of Cardinals only. An Antipope is set up, which causes a schism in the Church. A quarrel betwixt the Emperor Henry IV. and the Pope gives rise to the Guelph and Ghibeline Factions: The original of the Kingdom of Sicily. The first Crusade against the Saracens promoted by Urban II. Why so called. Another Antipope. The penance enjoined Henry II. King of England, upon the complaints made about the murder of Thomas Becket, Archbishop of Canterbury. The orders of St. Dominic and St. Francis instituted in the year 1218. The title of King of Jerusalem transferred to the Kings of Naples. The House of Este become Lords of Ferrara. The Guelphs side with the Church, the Ghibelines with the Emperor. The first mention made of Pope's Nephews. Celestine V. resigns the Pontificate to Boniface VIII. The Jubilee instituted by Boniface, and at first appointed to be celebrated every hundredth year. Clement VI. removes with his Court into France in the year 1036. The Visconti, a great family in Milan, become Princes of that city by the expulsion of the Torri. The first Duke of Milan. The Dukedom falls to the Sforzas. The original of the Venetians. Candia ceded to them by the French. Nicolò di Lorenzo, under the title of Tribune, makes himself the chief Magistrate of Rome. The Jubilee reduced to fifty years. Avignon given to the Pope by the Queen of Naples. Gregory XI. returns with his Court to Rome, after it had resided seventy-one years in France. Clement VII. Antipope. Great guns first used in the war betwixt the Genoese and the Venetians. Three Popes at one time. The Queen of Naples calls in the King of Arragon to her assistance, adopts him, and

makes

*makes Braccio de Montone her General. The state of
Italy at that time. A character of the several Princes
and chief Commanders.*

THE people who inhabit the Northern parts
that lie beyond the Rhine and the Danube,
living in a healthful and prolific climate,
often increase to such a degree, that vast numbers of
them are forced to leave their native country, and
go in search of new habitations. For when any one
of those provinces begins to grow too populous, and
wants to disburthen itself, the following method is
observed : In the first place, it is divided into three
parts, in each of which there is an equal proportion of the Nobility and Commonalty, the rich and
the poor. After this, they cast lots ; and that division, which the lot falls upon quits the country, and
goes to seek its fortune, leaving the other two more
room and liberty to enjoy their possessions at home.
These demigrations proved the destruction of the
Roman empire : to which the emperors themselves
also did not a little contribute. For when they abandoned Rome, the ancient seat of their government,
and went to reside at Constantinople, the western
parts of the Empire became weak and defenceless,
being far removed from their inspection, and consequently more liable to be plundered both by their
own substitutes and the incursions of foreign enemies.
And indeed, if the indolence and pusillanimity of
the Princes, the perfidy of their Ministers, the fury,
strength, and obstinacy of the Invaders, had been
in any degree less than they were, an Empire so
powerful, and founded in the blood of so many
brave men, could not well have been subverted :
since it was not till after many of these inundations
that its ruin was finally accomplished.

The first of these Northern nations that invaded
the empire, after the * Cimbri (who were subdued

* These people, according to Cluver, at first came from the extremity of the North, and then possessed the whole of that large

by Marius a Roman Citizen) were the Vifigoths,
that is, the Weftern Goths, to whom the Emperors,
after fevcral battles fought upon the confines of the
empire, at laft affigned the country that extends itfelf along the banks of the Danube for their habitation; of which they maintained the poffeffion for
a great number of years. And though they afterwards often invaded the Roman Provinces at different times and upon various occafions, they were as
often repelled by the power of the emperors. Theodofius, to his great honour, was the laft that defeated and entirely reduced them to obedience: after which, they did not chufe any other King of
their own to reign over them, as they ufed to do before, but voluntarily fubmitted to his government,
received his pay, and fought under his banners.
But when that Prince died, and his two fons Arcadius and Honorius were left heirs to the crown, tho'
not to the valour and good fortune of their father,

peninfula which extends itfelf into the German ocean, formerly
called Cimbria Cherfonefus, and now Jutland. And this opinion
is confirmed by the teftimonies of Velleius Paterculus, Eutropius,
and Orofius. They left this angle about the year 639 of Rome, or
3940 of the world, either becaufe the fea had encroached upon it,
or that it was not any longer capable of fuftaining fo vaft a multitude of inhabitants, who, as fome fay, amounted at that time to
above 500,000, befides women and children; and joining with the
outcaft of feveral other nations, they over-ran all Germany, Iftria,
Sclavonia, the country of the Grifons, and Switzerland: from
whence they fell into Dauphiné, Languedoc, and Provence, and
laft of all into Italy. The Romans being aftonifhed at fuch fwarms
of Barbarians, fent out their armies againft them, which were often
defeated: but at laft Marius beat them near Arles in the plains of
Camargue, and afterwards gave them a total overthrow betwixt Aix
and St. Maximin. The monuments of which victory are yet to be
feen upon the fame road, where the Romans erected pyramids in
memory of this decifive battle, fought in the year of Rome 652,
and 102 years before the Chriftian æra. Some authors fay the
Cimbrians firft invented drums: but that, if it is worth their while,
is left to the difquifitions of the curious. Strabo fays, they ftretch-
ed the fkins of animals over their open chariots in time of war, and
beat them with fticks at the beginning of the fight. They were a
very fierce and warlike people, large of ftature, and ufed to rejoice, fays Valerius Maximus, over any of their relations or friends
that fell in battle, and to make great lamentation over thofe that
died of ficknefs; looking upon the one as a glorious and happy
death, the other as infamous and difhonourable.

the

the times, like the Emperors, began to alter for the
worfe.

Theodofius had appointed three Governors to prefide over the three parts of the empire, Ruffinus
over the Eaft, Stilico over the Weft, and Gildo over
the South; but, after his death, they all refolved
to drop the title of governors, and affume the fovereign dominion over thofe provinces themfelves.
Gildo and Ruffinus were foon fuppreffed: but Stilico concealing his ambition with more artifice, endeavoured to infinuate himfelf into the favour and
confidence of the new Emperors, with a defign,
however, to perplex and embarrafs their affairs, that
fo he might afterwards the more eafily fucceed in
his attempts.   To ftir up the Vifigoths againft them,
he advifed the Emperors to retrench their former
pay; and left that nation alone fhould not be able
to raife a rebellion in the empire, he likewife incited the Burgundians, Franks, Vandals, and Alans,
(Northern people like the others, and already in motion to feek new habitations) to invade the Roman
provinces.

The Vifigoths, therefore, feeing their ufual fub-
fidies reduced, determined to redrefs themfelves.
For which purpofe, they made Alaric their King,
under whofe conduct they invaded the empire, and
after many enterprizes, not only took and facked
Rome itfelf, but over-ran all the reft of Italy.   Not
long after thefe victorious atchievements Alaric died,
and was fucceeded by Ataulph, who marrying Pla-
cidia, fifter to the Emperors, promifed them, in confequence of that alliance, to march with an army to
the relief of Gaul and Spain, which provinces were
then much harraffed by the incurfions of the Vandals, Burgundians, Alans, and Franks.   The Vandals who had feized upon that part of Spain called
Betica, being now hard preffed and reduced to extremities by the Vifigoths, were called over by Boniface, (who at that time governed Africa in the
name of the Emperors) to come and fettle there:

for

for as he was then in open rebellion himfelf, he was afraid of being called to account and punifhed for it by thofe Princes. The Vandals, therefore, willingly embarked in this enterprife, for the reafons abovementioned, and under the banners of Genferic their King made a defcent upon the coaft of Africa.

In the mean time Theodofius, the fon of Arcadius, fucceeded to the empire; but as he gave himfelf little trouble about the affairs of the Weft, thefe new intruders began to think of eftablifhing themfelves in their acquifitions. Accordingly, the Vandals foon made themfelves mafters of Africa, the Alans and Vifigoths of Spain, and the Franks and Burgundians not only over-ran Gaul, but gave names to the places of which they had refpectively poffeffed themfelves, calling one part of it France, and the other Burgundy. The fuccefs of thefe adventurers inviting others to invade the empire, the Huns feized upon Pannonia, a province on this fide the Danube, and gave it the name of Hungary, which it retains to this day. And what ftill increafed thefe misfortunes, was, that the Emperor feeing himfelf attacked in fo many different places, began to treat, firft with the Vandals, and then with the Franks, in order to leffen the number of his enemies, which very much diminifhed his own power and authority, and at the fame time added confiderable ftrength and reputation to the Barbarians. Nor was the ifland of Britain, now called England, exempt from its fhare in thefe troubles. For the Britons beginning to grow apprehenfive of the people that had conquered Gaul, and feeing the Emperor not able to protect them, called in the Angli, a German nation, to their affiftance. The Angli, accordingly, under Vortiger their King, undertook to defend them, and for fome time behaved like faithful allies, but afterwards drove them out of the ifland, and taking poffeffion of it themfelves gave it the name of England. Being thus expelled their country, and become defperate by neceffity,

ceffity, the Britons refolved to invade fome other,
though they had not been able to maintain their own :
and with this refolution having paffed the fea, they
poffeffed themfelves of that part which lies upon the
coaft of France, and called it Bretagne, or Britany.
The Huns who, as we faid before, had feized upon
Pannonia, joining with divers other people, as the
Zepidi, Eruli, Turingi, and Oftrogoths, or Eaftern
Goths, put themfelves in motion once more, and, went
in queft of frefh quarters. But not being able to
force their way into France, which was then bravely
defended by the Barbarians, they penetrated into
Italy under the conduct of their King Attila, who
not long before had murdered his brother Bleda ;
by which he rid himfelf of all partnerfhip in the
government, and became fo powerful that he reduced Andaric King of the Zepidi, and Velamir
King of the Oftrogoths, into a fort of fubjection to
him. And having thus got footing in Italy he invefted * Aquileia ; before which place he continued
two years without moleftation, and during the fiege
not only laid wafte the whole country round about
it, but totally difperfed the inhabitants, which, as
we fhall relate in its proper place, firft gave rife to
the city of Venice. After he had taken and demolifhed Aquileia and many other cities, he advanced
towards Rome, which he fpared however out of reverence to the † Pope, whom he held in fo great
veneration, that at his interceffion only he withdrew
out of Italy into Auftria, where he died ‡. After

* The capital of Friuli, formerly a city of great eminence, but
now very much decayed. It is at prefent fubject to the Houfe of
Auftria, though the Patriarch is appointed by the Venetians.
† Leo I. commonly called St. Leo ; he enjoyed the pontificate
from the year 440 till 461.
‡ He was called *the Scourge of God,* fince there was hardly any nation
in Europe that did not feel the weight of his arms. The peace
which he made with Theodofius the younger was very difhonourable
to that emperor : for he obliged him to advance fix thoufand pound
weight of gold in ready money, and promife to pay him a thoufand
pound weight every year for the future. So that the eaftern empire,
notwithftanding the fpecious name of penfion, which was given to

B 4   his

his death, Velamir King of the Oftrogoths, and
fome chiefs of the other nations took up arms againft
Tenric and Euric the fons of Attila, one of whom
they killed, and drove the other with all the Huns
over the Danube again into their own country : upon which the Oftrogoths and Zepidi eftablifhed
themfelves in Pannonia ; and the Eruli and Turingi
continued upon the banks of the Danube.

After Attila had left Italy, Valentinian then Emperor of the Weft, refolved to attempt the reftoration of that empire to its former greatnefs and fplendor ; and that he might be enabled to defend it
with more eafe and convenience againft the irruptions of the Barbarians, he chofe Ravenna inftead
of Rome for the place of his refidence. Thefe calamities which the Weftern empire fuftained, had
often obliged the Emperor who refided at Conftantinople to give the government of it to other peo-

this exaction, in fact became tributary to the Huns. Maimbourg,
Hift. de l'Arianifme. Tom. iii. p. 4. The fame author fays, Hift. de St,
Leon. l. iii. p. 220. that Attila having feen a picture at Milan, which
reprefented an emperor fitting upon his throne with Scythians in
chains under his feet, ordered it to be removed, and another to be
put up in its room, wherein he himfelf was drawn, fitting upon a
throne furrounded with emperors loaded with bags of filver and
gold, which they came to empty at his feet in a very fubmiffive
manner ; intimating by this, that as he had obliged Theodofius feven or eight years before to pay him tribute, he would force the
Emperor Valentinian to do the fame, in order to fave his life and
the miferable remains of the empire. It is faid he defigned to have
eftablifhed his own language in the empire upon the ruins of the
Roman. Alcyonius in his Medices Legatus introduces Giovanni
de' Medici fpeaking in the following manner, " There is preferved
in our Library a book written in Greek by an unknown author,
concerning the wars of the Goths in Italy. I remember to have
read in it, that King Attila, after his victories, being refolved to
propagate the Gothic tongue, publifhed an edict to prohibit all perfons from fpeaking Latin, and fent for teachers out of his own
country to inftruct the Italians in the Gothic language." This fort
of ambition feems to have been common to moft conquerors. The
Greeks, Romans, Turks, Moors, Normans, and many other nations attempted it, and fome of them with fuccefs. The French in
thefe times are extending their language at a great rate, and endeavouring by all manner of artifices to make it become general
throughout Europe at leaft. This Prince was either fuffocated by an
eruption of blood from his nofe, as fome fay ; or murdered by his
bride, according to others, on his wedding night.

ple,

ple, as a charge attended with too great trouble and expence. Indeed the Romans themselves, when they saw they were thus slighted and abandoned, often created Emperors to defend them, without his permission to do so: and sometimes private persons, availing themselves of their own interest or authority, usurped the Imperial dignity: as it happened after the death of Valentinian, when Maximus, a citizen of Rome, seized upon it, and forced his widow Eudoxa to marry him; who being of royal extraction and disdaining the embraces of a private citizen, in revenge for so violent an outrage, secretly encouraged Genseric, King of the Vandals, and at that time master of Africa, to invade Italy, by representing how easy and glorious the conquest of it would be to him *. That Prince accordingly, being animated by the hope of so great an acquisition, made a sudden descent upon Italy, and finding Rome deserted, he sacked it, and continued there fourteen days. He likewise took and plundered many other towns, and having glutted both himself and his army with spoil, returned into A-

* Petronius Maximus, Grandson to Flavius Magnus Clemens, was at first a Roman senator. He had a very beautiful wife, with whom Valentinian III. fell in love, and endeavoured, though in vain, to debauch her. But that Emperor having won all the money that Maximus had, and his ring besides, one night at play, sent the ring as from Maximus himself, for his wife to come to the palace, where he however ravished her. Maximus however dissembled his knowledge of the fact, and concealed his resentment till he had an opportunity of revenging himself, which he did not long after, by causing the Emperor to be dispatched in the Campus Martius: after which, he seized the empire, married the Empress Eudoxa by force, created his own son Cæsar, and married him to Eudoxa the Emperor's daughter. But having told the Empress one night, that it was for the love of her that he had killed the Emperor, she was so incensed at it, because she knew the contrary, that she sent to intreat Genseric King of the African Vandals to deliver her from the tyrant who kept her as his wife by force. Genseric came, according to her invitation, and Maximus fled from Rome, but was pursued and stoned to death by the people, or killed by a soldier as some say, and afterwards pulled to pieces by the Empress and her servants and thrown into the Tiber. But she herself and her daughters were carried away prisoners by the conqueror. Procop. de bell. Vandal. l. i. p. 15.

frica.

frica. Upon his departure, Maximus being now dead, the Romans returned to the city and made choice of one Avitus, a Roman, for their Emperor. After this and many other revolutions both within Italy and without it, and after the death of feveral Emperors, the empire of Conftantinople fell into the hands of Zeno; and that of Rome, by intrigue and underhand practices, to Oreftes and his fon Auguftulus. But whilft they were making prepara-tions to maintain it by force, they were invaded by the Eruli and Turingi, who, as we have related, had repaffed the Danube after the death of Attila, and fettled themfelves again in their former habita-tions on the other fide of that river. Thefe nations having confederated themfelves afrefh, under the command of Odoacer, for this expedition, left their own country to the Longobardi, or Lombards, an-other northern nation, who took poffeffion of it un-der the conduct of Godoglio their King, and were the laft that invaded Italy, as fhall be fhewn here-after.

Odoacer having entered Italy, not long after de-feated and killed Oreftes in a battle near Pavia ; but Auguftulus made his efcape. After this vic-tory, Odoacer changing the title both of the gover-nor and the government, abolifhed the name of Emperor and Empire, caufed himfelf to be ftyled *King of Rome*, and was the firft chieftain of thofe nations which then over-ran the world, that refolved to fix in Italy : for all the reft before him, either out of an apprehenfion that they fhould not be able to maintain a territory that might fo eafily be fuc-coured by the Emperor of the Eaft, or for fome other private reafon, had contented themfelves with ravaging and plundering it, and then always retired to feek fome other country to live in, which they thought more tenable.

In this manner then, the ancient Roman empire was cantoned out under the following princes and people. Zeno refiding at Conftantinople, governed

the

the whole empire of the East: the Ostrogoths were
poffeffed of * Mœfia and Pannonia: the Vifigoths,
Suevi and Alans of Spain and Gafcony: the Vandals of Africa: the Franks and Burgundians of
Gaul: and the Eruli and Turingi of Italy.   The
Kingdom of the Oftrogoths was devolved upon Velamir's nephew Theodoric, who being in amity with
Zeno, the Eaftern Emperor, wrote to him, " That
his Oftrogoths being fuperior in valour to all other
nations, thought it hard and unjuft to be inferior to
them in extent of territory and command ; and that
it would be impoffile for him to confine them within
the narrow limits of Pannonia: that as he was confequently under a neceffity of complying with their
defires, and of fuffering them to take up arms, in
order to provide themfelves with larger and more
convenient territories, he thought fit to give him
timely notice of it ; that fo he might avert the danger if he pleafed, by voluntarily affigning them fome
country, where, by his favour, they might live
with more comfort and reputation." Zeno therefore, partly out of fear, and partly out of a defire
of driving Odoacer out of Italy, gave Theodoric
free leave to march againft him and wreft it out of
his hands if he was able.   This offer he accepted,
and immediately quitting Pannonia, where he left
his allies the Zepidi, he entered Italy, killed Odoacer and his fon, and after his example, not only
called himfelf *King of Rome*, but took up his refidence at Ravenna, for the fame reafons that had before prevailed upon Valentinian to do fo.

Theodoric was a great and excellent Prince both
in the arts of war and peace : in the former he always came off victorious, and in the latter, was
continually doing good to the cities and people that
were fubject to him.   He diftributed his Oftrogoths
through the feveral towns, and fet chiefs over them,
to lead them in time of war, and to adminifter juf-

* Now called Bofnia and Servia.

tice

tice in the intervals of peace. He enlarged Ravenna, repaired Rome, and reftored all its honours and privileges, except its military difcipline. He kept all the Barbarian Princes, who had cantoned out the Empire, in due bounds, without the noife or tumult of war, merely by his own wifdom and authority. He built feveral towns and fortreffes betwixt the extremity of the Adriatick and the Alps, to obftruct any future incurfion of Barbarians into Italy. If fo many great virtues had not been fullied by fome cruelties he was guilty of towards the latter end of his life (amongft which may be numbered the putting Symmachus and Boetius to death, though virtuous and innocent men, out of a fufpicion that they were confpiring to depofe him) his memory would have been every way unblemifhed and worthy of being held in the higheft honour. By his valour and goodnefs, not only Rome and Italy, but all the other parts of the Weftern Empire, were freed from the continual devaftations to which they had been fubject for fo many years, by the repeated irruptions of Barbarians, and at the fame time reduced into good order. Certainly, if any times were ever to be called wretched in Italy and the other provinces that were thus over-run, they were thofe that intervened betwixt the reigns of Arcadius and Honorius, and that of Theodoric: for if we confider the calamitous confequences that generally enfue upon a change of Prince or form of government either in a kingdom or commonwealth, when effected, not by external force, but by civil diffentions, (in which, experience has fufficiently fhewn us that the leaft alterations have proved fatal to fuch ftates, though exceeding powerful) we may eafily conceive how much Italy and the reft of the Roman provinces muft have fuffered in thofe days, when they were forced to change, not only their Princes and form of government, but their laws, cuftoms, manner of living, religion, language, habit, and even their very names. To reflect only

upon

upon any one of thefe circumftances, is enough to
make the ftouteft man tremble, much more the feeing and enduring them all.   But if they proved the
deftruction of fome cities, they likewife occafioned
the foundation and augmentation of many more.
In the number of thofe that were deftroyed, we
may reckon Aquileia, Luni, Chiufi, Popolonia,
Fiefoli, and fome others: amongft thofe that were
new built, were Venice, Siena, Ferrara, Aquila, and
many more, both towns and caftles, which, for the
fake of brevity, I fhall here omit.   Thofe that from
fmall beginnings became great and refpectable, were
Florence, Genoa, Pifa, Milan, Naples, and Bologna : to all which may be added, the ruin and in-
ftauration of Rome, and feveral other cities, which
were demolifhed and afterwards rebuilt.   Thefe devaftations and reiterated incurfions of new people
produced new languages, as appears from thofe now
ufed in France, Spain, and Italy, which, being com-
pounded of that of their invaders and the ancient
Roman, are very different from what they were before.   Not only provinces, but rivers, feas, and
men, likewife loft their names : France, Italy, and
Spain, being full of fuch as are altogether unlike
the old ones.   To omit many others, we fhall only
inftance the Po, Garda, and Archipelago, in the
firft cafe : and with regard to the proper names of
men, inftead of Cæfar, Pompey, &c. thofe of Peter, John, Matthew, &c. now took place.   But
amongft all thefe revolutions and changes, that of
Religion was of the greateft confequence : for the
cuftom and prefcription pleaded by Paganifm againft
the Miracles of Chriftianity, produced very great
tumults and diffenfions amongft men, which yet
would not have been fo fatal if the Chriftian Church
had continued united.   But the Greek and Roman
Churches, and that of Ravenna, being at variance,
and the Hereticks and Catholicks fiercely oppofing
each other, occafioned infinite confufion and mifery
in the world : as Africa in particular can teftify,
               ,   which

which fuffered much more from the Spirit and Effects of Arianifm (a doctrine efpoufed by the Vandals) than from their natural ferocity, or any oppreffive difpofition peculiar to that people. Whilft men lived expofed to fuch dreadful perfecutions, the terror and dejection of their hearts were legible in their countenances : for befides the numberlefs afflictions they otherwife endured, many were deprived of all recourfe to the mercies of God, the fureft refuge in adverfity and diftrefs : for as they were uncertain to what Being they ought to addrefs themfelves for protection, they miferably died without any hope or comfort.

· Theodoric therefore deferved no fmall return of thanks, as he was the firft that gave them any refpite from fo great Evils, and reftored Italy to fuch a degree of Grandeur, during the thirty-eight years which he reigned there, that hardly any thing was to be feen of its former defolation. But when he died, and the government devolved upon Athalric, the fon of his daughter Amalafontha, its evil deftiny being not yet fatiated, it foon relapfed into the fame miferable condition it had been in before. For Athalric dying not long after his grandfather, the kingdom reverted to his mother, who was betrayed, and put to death by Theodate, a minifter whom fhe had employed to affift her in the government of the ftate. After which, he feized upon the kingdom himfelf, to the infinite difguft of the Oftrogoths ; a circumftance that encouraged the Emperor Juftinian to attempt the difpoffeffing him of Italy. For which purpofe, he appointed Belifarius his commander in chief for that Expedition, who had already driven the Vandals out of Africa, and reduced it to its former obedience to the Empire. That general accordingly, in the firft place made himfelf mafter of Sicily ; from whence he tranfported his army into Italy, and there recovered Naples and Rome. Upon which, the Goths feeing the havock he daily made amongft them, laid hands on their King Theodate,

date, and having put him to death, as the author and occafion of it, they fet up Vitiges in his ftead ; who, after feveral fkirmifhes, was at laft befieged and taken prifoner in Ravenna by Belifarius. But the latter not having gained a complete victory, was recalled by Juftinian, and fucceeded in his command by Johannes and Vitalis, two generals fo much inferior to him both in valour and conduct, that the Goths recovered their fpirits and made choice of Ildovadus, at that time governor of Verona, to rule over them. That Prince being killed foon after, the reins of government fell into the hands of Totila, who routed the Emperor's forces, regained Tufcany, and ftripped the Imperial generals of almoft every ftate that Belifarius had recovered. Juftinian, therefore, thought fit to fend him back again into Italy : but as he came only with an inconfiderable force, he rather loft the reputation he had acquired before, than made any addition to it. For, whilft he lay with his army at Oftia, Totila befieged Rome and took it, as it were, before his face : but, confidering he could not well maintain it, and that it would be dangerous to leave it behind him in the condition it then was, he demolifhed the greater part of the city, difperfed the citizens, carried the fenators along with him, and making little account of Belifarius, advanced with his army into Calabria, to cut off the fupplies that were coming out of Greece to reinforce him. Belifarius, however, feeing Rome abandoned in this manner, refolved to attempt fomething that might re-eftablifh his reputation ; and having once more taken poffeffion of that city, ruinous as it was, he rebuilt the walls with the utmoft expedition, and then fent to invite the inhabitants to return to it. But fortune did not favour fo meritorious an undertaking : for Juftinian, being at that time invaded by the Parthians, was obliged to recall him. So that in obedience to the commands of his fovereign, he
quitted

* quitted Italy, and left that province to the mercy of Totila, who retook Rome, but did not exercife the fame rigour upon it that he had done before: for being moved by the entreaties of St. Benedict, (a perfon in thofe days held in great veneration for his fanctity) inftead of pulling it down again, he immediately began to repair the ruins.

In the mean time, Juftinian had made a peace with the Parthians, and refolving to fend frefh fuccours into Italy, was prevented by a new alarm from the Sclavi, another northern nation, who had paffed the Danube, and fallen into Thrace and Illyria ; fo that Totila had made himfelf mafter of almoft all Italy. But as foon as the Emperor had repelled the Sclavi, he fent another army into Italy, under the conduct of Narfes or Narfetes, an eunuch, but a commander of great experience. At his arrival in Italy, he defeated and killed Totila; after whofe death, the remainder of the Goths retired into Pavia, and made Teia King over them. On the other hand, Narfetes, after his victory, took Rome again, and then marching againft Teia, not only engaged, but routed and killed him near Nocera: by which overthrow the Name of the Goths was utterly extinguifhed in Italy, after they had reigned there for the fpace of feventy years, that is, from the time of their King Theodoric to that of Teia. But Italy had fcarcely freed itfelf from their yoke, when Juftinian died, and was fucceeded by his fon Juftinus, who, at the inftigation of his wife Sophia, recalled Narfetes out of Italy, and fent Longinus thither to

---

* He afterwards acquired great glory in the Parthian and many other wars. It is faid by Crinitus, Volaterran, and other Latin writers, that being accufed of confpiring againft Juftinian, he was not only deprived of all his employments, but had his eyes put out by that Prince in the year 551, and was reduced to fuch a degree of poverty, that he was forced to beg his bread in the ftreets of Conftantinople. On the contrary, the author of " The Mixed Hiftory of Conftantinople." Cedrenus, Alciat, and others, fay, that he had not his eyes put out, that he was reftored to all his employments the year following, and died in peace at Conftantinople, in 565.

fuper-

fuperfede him.   Longinus, after the example of his predeceffors, kept his refidence at Ravenna, but introduced a new form of government into Italy, not appointing governors over Provinces, as the Goths had done, but fetting up a Chief in every city and town of any note, with the title of *Duke.*   Nor did he make any diftinction betwixt Rome and the other cities in this reform : for abolifhing the names and authority of confuls and fenate, which had continued till that time, he yearly fent a Duke from Ravenna of his own nomination, to take upon him the government of it, which was called the *Duchy,* or *Dukedom* of Rome.   But he that prefided at Ravenna, and more immediately reprefented the Emperor, having the fuperintendance of all Italy committed to his charge, was called the *Exarch.*   This new divifion not only facilitated, but exceedingly haftened the ruin of Italy, by giving the Lombards an opportunity of poffeffing themfelves of it.   Narfetes was very much difgufted at the Emperor for depriving him of the government of that Province, which he had bravely recovered at the expence of his own blood : and Sophia not thinking it a fufficient difgrace to get him recalled, had alfo made ufe of fome taunts and contemptuous expreffions ; fending him word, *that fhe wanted him at home to fpin as other Eunuchs did* *.   At which he was fo outrageoufly provoked, that he incited Alboin, who then

---

* This general, however, though fo unworthily difgraced, and defigned for a fpinfter by womanifh malice and petulance, left many noble traces of his prowefs in Italy : of which, the following infcription upon a bridge, about three miles from Rome, may ferve as one teftimony.

> Quam bene curvati directa eft femita Pontis,
>   Atque interruptum continuatur iter !
> Calcamus rapidas fubjecti gurgitis undas,
>   Et libet iratæ cernere murmur aquæ.
> Ite igitur faciles in gaudia veftra Quirites,
>   Et Narfem refonans, plaufus ubique canat :
> Qui potuit rigidas Gothorum fubdere mentes,
>   Et docuit durum flumina ferre jugum.

See a Book, called, Infcriptionum Metricarum Delectus, publifhed in 1758.

reigned over the Lombards in Pannonia, to come and invade Italy.

The Lombards, as we have already related, had taken poffeffion of fuch places upon the Danube as were abandoned by the Eruli and Turingi, when Odoacer their King conducted them into Italy. There they continued fome time, till the kingdom fell into the hands of Alboin, a fierce and enter-prizing man, who paffed the Danube, engaged Cunimund, King of the Zepidi, a people fettled in Pannonia, and not only defeated him, but made him-felf mafter of all that country. And though he married Rofamond, one of the daughters of Cunimund, whom he found amongft the prifoners that were taken, yet fuch was the favagenefs and inhu-manity of his nature, that he ordered a cup to be made of her father's fkull, out of which he fome-times drank in memory of that victory. But being invited into Italy by Narfetes, with whom he had contracted a friendfhip during the war with the Goths, he left Pannonia to the Huns, (who, as we have fhewn, returned into their own country after the death of Attila) marched into Italy, and finding it cantoned out into fo many divifions, he made himfelf mafter of Pavia, Milan, Verona, Vicenza, all Tufcany, and the greater part of Flaminia, now called Romagna. And imagining, from the great-nefs and fuddennefs of his conquefts, that all Italy was now in a manner his own, he made a magnifi-cent banquet at Verona; at which he got drunk, and filling the fkull of Cunimund with wine, he caufed it to be prefented to Rofamond his queen, who fat over-againft him at the table, faying (loud enough to be heard by her) *that, upon fo joyful an occafion, fhe fhould drink with her Father.* Stung to the quick at fo cruel a farcafm, fhe fecretly vowed revenge; and knowing that Almachild, a noble and brave young Lombard, had an amour with one of her women, fhe prevailed upon her to contrive that fhe herfelf might have an opportunity of lying with him in her

ftead :

ftead : for which purpofe he was introduced into a
dark room, where he lay with Rofamond, fuppofing
it had been her maid. After which, fhe difcovered
herfelf and told him, it was now in his option either
to kill Alboin and enjoy her and the Kingdom, or
to be put to death by him for violating his bed.
Almachild therefore agreed to kill his matter : but
after they had perpetrated the murder, finding they
were not likely to maintain poffeffion of the Kingdom, but rather to be murdered by the Lombards,
out of the affection they bore to Alboin, they fled
with all his treafure to Longinus at Ravenna, who
received them with much honour.

During thefe troubles, Juftinus the Emperor died,
and Tiberius was elected in his ftead ; who, being
engaged in a war with the Parthians, could not fend
any relief into Italy. Longinus therefore, thinking this a fair opportunity to make himfelf King of
the Lombards, and of all Italy, by the help of Rofamond and her treafure, communicated his defign
to her, perfuading her to difpatch Almachild, and
afterwards to take himfelf for her hufband : which
propofal fhe accepted, and having prepared a cup of
poifoned wine for that purpofe, fhe gave it to Almachild with her own hands, as he came thirfty out of
the bath : who having drank about half of it, and
finding it began to operate, foon perceived what fhe
had given him, and thereupon immediately forced
her to drink the reft of the potion herfelf, of which
they both died in a few hours, and Longinus loft
all the hopes he had conceived of obtaining the
Kingdom : for the Lombards affembling at Pavia,
which they had now made the feat of their government, chofe Clefi for their King, who rebuilt Imola,
a town that had been demolifhed by Narfetes. He
likewife reduced Rimini, and almoft all the country
betwixt that place and Rome, but died in the midft
of his victories. This Clefi treated not only ftrangers, but even the Lombards themfelves, with fuch a
degree of rigour and cruelty, that they now grow-

ing

ing weary of a monarchical government, determined to have no more kings, and appointed thirty *Dukes* to rule over them.

This change of their Conftitution was the occafion that the Lombards could never thoroughly fubdue Italy, nor extend their conquefts any farther than Benevento : for as to the cities of Rome, Ravenna, Cremona, Mantua, Padua, Montfelice, Parma, Bologna, Faenza, Forli, and Cefena, fome of them defended themfelves a confiderable time, and others never came under their dominion at all. For as they had no Kings, they were lefs difpofed to war; and when they afterwards created Kings again, the tafte which they had had of liberty made them lefs obedient to their Prince, more apt to quarrel amongft themfelves, and not only checked the courfe of their victories at firft, but, in the end, was the caufe of their being totally driven out of Italy.

The affairs of the Lombards being thus circumftanced, the Romans and Longinus came to an accommodation with them : and it was agreed that all parties fhould lay down their arms and enjoy what they were refpectively poffeffed of.

About this time the Bifhops of Rome likewife began to affume a greater degree of authority than ever they had done before. The firft fucceffors of St. Peter having been held in the higheft veneration for the fanctity of their lives and the Miracles they wrought, their Examples gave fuch credit to the Chriftian Religion, that many Princes embraced it to put an end to thofe evils and diftractions which then reigned in the world. And the Emperor of Rome being converted amongft the reft, and quitting that Capital to hold his refidence at Conftantinople, the Roman Empire began to decline (as we have obferved before), whilft the Church of Rome, on the other hand, daily gathered frefh ftrength and grew more powerful. Neverthelefs, as all Italy was fubject to the dominion either of the Emperors or Kings,

Kings, till the coming in of the Lombards, the Bishops of that See took upon themfelves no other Authority than what was given them out of reverence to their learning and the holinefs of their lives : in civil affairs they were ftill fubject to thofe Princes, who often employed them as their Minifters, and fometimes put them to death for mal-adminiftration. But what gave them fomething more weight in the affairs of Italy was the refolution taken by Theodoric, King of the Goths, to remove the feat of his Government to Ravenna : for as Rome was thereby left deftitute of a Prince, the Romans were obliged, for their own fafety, to, put themfelves under the protection of the Pope. This, however, did not make any great addition to their authority : for the only point they gained at that time, was, that the Church of Ravenna fhould acknowledge itfelf fubject to the jurifdiction of that at Rome *. But after the Lombards had invaded Italy and divided it into feveral diftricts, the Pope took that opportunity of enlarging his power : for as he was the chief perfon and in a manner the Head of Rome, both the Em-

* Rome never recovered the fatal blow it received from Conftantine's changing the feat of the Empire. Glory and the love of their country no longer animated the breafts of Romans : their courage loft its vigour : the Arts funk into decay ; and nothing was heard in the place, which had been the refidence of the Scipios and Cæfars, but difputes and endlefs contentions betwixt the Bifhops and fecular Judges. After Juftinian's time it was governed by a Viceroy, under the title of Exarch, who no longer regarded it as the capital of Italy ; but living at Ravenna, from thence fent his orders to the Romans. The Bifhop indeed daily augmented his authority in thefe times of Barbarifm : the power of the Church increafed, and the Prefect of Rome was not able to oppofe the pretenfions of a perfon that were conftantly fupported by the fanctity of his profeffion. In vain did the Church of Ravenna difpute a thoufand privileges with that of Rome ; the latter was acknowledged by all the Chriftians of the Weft as their common Mother : they confulted her, they petitioned her to fend them Paftors, and whilft the City was in fubjection the Bifhop ruled abroad.
In this eighth Century, the Popes firft conceived the defign of making themfelves mafters of Rome, and faw that what would have been deemed a revolt and an ineffectual fedition at another time, might now be a Revolution excufable by its neceffity, and illuftrious by its fuccefs. See Voltaire's General Hiftory of Europe, Vol. I. p. 33, 34.

C 3   peror

peror of Conftantinople and the Lombards fhewed
him great refpect... So that the Romans, by the Intereft of the Pope, began to confederate themfelves
with Longinus and the Lombards, not as fubjects,
but as friends and equals.; and the Popes entering
into an alliance fometimes with the Lombards, and
fometimes with the Greeks, daily became more and
more, refpectable and of greater. importance.   But
the Eaftern Empire foon after fell to decay under.
the reign of Heraclius, in whofe time the Sclavi, a.
people beforementioned, invaded Illyria again ; and
having made themfelves mafters of that Country,
called it Sclavonia after their own name : the other
other parts of the Empire were likewife attacked,
firft by the Perfians, afterwards by the Saracens out
out of Arabia, under the command of Mahomet,
and laft of all by the Turks, who difmembered it
of Syria, Africa, and Egypt.   Upon which the Popes
feeing the Emperors no longer able to protect them
upon occafion, and the power of the Lombards ftill
increafing, thought it high time to look out for
new friends and confederates, and for that purpofe
applied to the Kings of France.   So that all the
wars, which foreigners afterwards made upon Italy,
were chiefly owing to the Popes, and moft of the
feveral inundations of Barbarians that poured
themfelves into it, were, in a great meafure occafioned by their incitement and inftigation; which
practices being continued even to this time, have fo
long kept, and ftill keep, Italy weak and divided.
However, in relating the events that happened betwixt thofe times and our own, I fhall enlarge no
farther upon the ruin of the Empire, but proceed
to give an account of the exaltation of the Pontifs
and other Princes that governed Italy till the invafion of Charles VIII. King of France : and fhew
not only how the Popes became formidable and revered, at firft by their Ecclefiaftical cenfures, then
by joining temporal arms to thofe fpiritual weapons,

                                                    and

and laftly by adding * Indulgences to them ; but likewife how, by making an ill ufe of that terror and
reverence, with which they had infpired mankind,
they have entirely loft the one, and lie at the difcretion and courtefy of the world for the other.

But to refume the method we at firft propofed.
Gregory III. being advanced to the Papacy, and
Aiftolphus or Aftolphus made King over the Lombards, the latter, contrary to exprefs agreement,
feized upon Ravenna and made war upon the Pope.
Upon which, Gregory feeing the Emperor of Conftantinople fo debilitated by the abovementioned
loffes, defpaired of any affiftance from that quarter :
and not daring to confide in the Lombards, who
had already deceived him more than once, he had
recourfe to Pepin, who, from being Lord of Auftria and Brabant, was become King of France, not
fo much by his own valour, as by that of his grandfather Pepin, and his father Charles Martel.   For
Charles, being Regent of France, gave the Saracens
that memorable overthrow near Tours upon the
Loire, wherein above two hundred thoufand of them
were killed † : upon which his fon Pepin, in confider-

* A perpetual tax upon credulity and fuperftition ; and an in-
exhauftible fource of riches to the Romifh Church.   The word
Indulgence, amongft them, fignifies a remiffion of punifhment due
to Sin, granted by the Church, and fuppofed to fave the Sinner
from Purgatory.   They found their notion of Indulgences upon the
infinite treafure of the merits of Jefus Chrift, the Virgin Mary, and
all the Saints ; which they fuppofe the Church has a right to diftri-
bute by virtue of the *Communion of Saints.*   The Jubilee grants a
plenary indulgence for all manner of crimes.   Their Cafuifts fay
that a plenary indulgence does not always prove effectual, for
want of complying with the conditions upon which it was granted.

It has been a common practice with the Popes to grant Indulgences for the extirpation of Hereticks.   Thus, Clement XII. in
one of his Bulls fays, " That we may ftir up and encourage the
Faithful to exterminate *this ungracious Crew of forlorn wretches* (the
Cevennois, then in arms againft Lewis XIV.) we freely grant and
indulge the full remiffion of Sins, whatever they may be, relying
upon that power of *binding and loofing,* which our Lord conferred
on his chief Apoftle)' to thofe that fhall lift themfelves in this *Sacred
Militia,* if they fall in battle."

† According to Anaftafius, Paulus Diaconus, and feveral other
hiftorians, there were three hundred and feventy, or three hundred

ation

ation of the father's bravery and his own great reputation, was afterwards made fovereign of the Kingdom. To him, as we have faid, the Pope applied for fuccour againft the Lombards, which he readily promifed, but fent him word at the fame time, " he was very defirous of firft feeing his Holinefs in France, that he might pay his duty to him in perfon." Upon this invitation Gregory fet out for France, and paffed through the quarters of the Lombards without the leaft impediment or moleftation, though he was then at war with them : fo great was their reverence and veneration for Religion at that time.

At his arrival in France, he was received with great honour by that Prince, and after fome time fent back with an army into Italy, which laid fiege to Pavia, and reduced the Lombards to fuch diftrefs, that Aiftolphus was obliged to accept of the terms that were granted him by the French, at the interceffion of the Pope, who faid, " he did not defire the death of his Enemy, but rather that he fhould be converted and live." In this agreement, Aiftolphus promifed to reftore all the towns he had taken from the Church. But as foon as Pepin's army was returned into France, he refufed to perform his engagement, which forced the Pope to make a fecond application to Pepin, who fent another army

and feventy-five thoufand Saracens killed, and but fifteen hundred of the French. But in this they have followed an exaggerated account which was fent to the Pope after the battle, by Eudo Duke of Aquitain, one of the French generals. But Father Labbè, Mezerai, Cordemoi, and the beft hiftorians, who fix the date of this battle in the year 732, fay plainly. that the Saracen army (which poured itfelf out of Spain into France at that time under the command of Abderama, governor of Spain for Ifcham, Caliph of the Saracens) confifted but of fourfcore, or, at the moft, a hundred thoufand men : that they fought till night without giving way, and were not purfued the next day, when news was brought that they had marched away a'l night. Now it is impoffible that fuch a prodigious flaughter fhould have been made in an army that ftood its ground, or fo many hundred thoufand men be put to the fword, except they fled and were purfued, and had no quarter given them. The former account therefore muft be looked upon as romantic.

into

into Italy, overcame the Lombards, took Ravenna,
and gave it to the Pope with all the other territories
under that Exarchate, and the country of Urbino
and la Marca befides; though much againft the inclination of the Grecian Emperor.   Whilft thefe
things were carrying into execution, Aiftolphus
died, and Defiderius, a Lombard, who was then
Duke of Tufcany, taking up arms to fecure the
fucceffion of the Kingdom to himfelf, follicited the
affiftance of the Pope for that purpofe, promifing
him his friendfhip in return for the future ; which
the Pope granted, and he was not oppofed by any
other competitor.   And indeed Defiderius for a
while obferved his promife with the utmoft punctu-
ality, and fairly refigned thofe territories to the
Pope which had been ceded to him by the agreement made with Pepin : nor were there any more
Exarchs fent from Conftantinople to Ravenna, which
was afterwards governed according to the will and
difcretion of the Pope alone. Not long after, Pepin died, and was fucceeded by his fon Charles, who,
from the greatnefs of his atchievements, was called
Charlemagne, or Charles the Great.

About the fame time Theodore the firft was advanced to the Papal Chair, and quarrelling with
Defiderius was befieged by him in Rome ; which
obliged him to apply for help to Charles, who, paffing the Alps, fhut up Defiderius and his Sons in
Pavia, took them prifoners, fent them to France,
and went himfelf to vifit the Pope at Rome, where
he declared and adjudged, *that his Hol:nefs, being
God's Vicar, was not fubject to any human jurifdiction :*
in return for which favour, the Pope and the People of Rome unanimoufly made him Emperor *.

* Machiavel feems to have made a miftake here in the name of
the Pope in whofe Pontificate this event happened, which was Zachary, and not Theodore the firft. Voltaire fets this matter in a
clearer light in his General Hiftory of Europe, Vol. I. p. 35. " Pope
Gregory III. fays he, was the firft who conceived the defign of
making ufe of the arms of France to wreft Italy out cf the hands
of the Emperors and the Lombards. His fucceffor Zachary acknow-

So that Rome began to have an emperor of the West again; and though the Popes ufed to be confirmed by the Emperors before that time, the Emperor now, on the contrary, was obliged to be beholden to the Pope for his Election: by which the Empire began to lofe its power and dignity, and the Church to advance itfelf and extend its authority daily more and more over temporal Princes. The Lombards had been in Italy two hundred and twenty-two years, and now retained nothing of the Barbarians, except their Name: fo that Charlemagne, being defirous to new-model Italy in the Pontificate of Leo the third, was content that they fhould not only ftill inhabit, but alfo give name to that part of it where they had been bred, and call it Lombardy. And that the Roman Name might ftill be refpected by them, he ordained that all that part of Italy which lay neareft them and was under the Exarchate of Ravenna, fhould thenceforth be called Romagna. He likewife made his fon Pepin King of Italy, and extended his Jurifdiction as far as Benevento: whilft all the reft of it was fuffered to continue under the dominion of the Grecian Emperor, with whom he had entered into a compofition.

ledged Pepin, the ufurper of the Crown of France, as lawful Sovereign. It has been pretended that Pepin, who was then only Prime Minifter, fent firft to afk the Pope, which was the worthier of the two to fit upon the throne, he who took no care at all of the Kingdom, or he who governed it with wifdom, and upheld it by his valour; and that the Pope, who ftood in need of Pepin's affiftance, determined in favour of the latter. It has never been proved indeed that this farce was really acted: but it is certain that Pope Stephen III. the next fucceffor but one to Zachary, called Pepin to his fuccour; that he forged a letter from St. Peter, addreffed from Heaven to Pepin and his fon; that he came into France and gave the royal Unction to Pepin, the firft anointed King in Europe, in the Church of St. Dennis. He likewife forbad the French, on pain of Excommunication, ever to chufe a King of any other family. Whilft this Bifhop, expelled from Italy and forced to become a fupplicant in a foreign country, had the courage to give law to Nations, his Policy prompted him to affume an authority which fecured Pepin: and that Prince, in order to enjoy what was not his right without difturbance or moleftation, fuffered the Pope to ufurp prerogatives that did not belong to him.

This Bifhop was the firft Chriftian Prieft that became a temporal Lord, and that was placed in the rank of Princes.

Dur-

During thefe tranfactions, Pafcal the firft was elected Pope; and the Parochial Clergy of Rome, on account of their being neareft the perfon of the Pope and ready at hand upon every Election, began to call themfelves * Cardinals, (in order to add fome Dignity to their power by a fplendid title) and affumed fo much authority, efpecially after they had excluded the fuffrages of the Laity, that it hardly ever happened that a Pope was elected who was not one of their Body. So that when Pafcal died, Eugenius (the fecond Pontif of that name) Cardinal of Santa Sabina, was chofen by them to fucceed him : and Italy being thus fallen into the hands of the French, in fome meafure changed its face and conftitution, by the Popes having taken upon themfelves greater authority in temporal affairs, and the French introducing the Titles of Count and Marquis, as Longinus, Exarch of Ravenna, had done that of Duke before. After fome others † Ofporco, a Roman, fucceeded to the Papacy, who being afhamed of fo ugly a name, affumed that of Sergius; which firft gave rife to the cuftom of the Popes changing their names, as they now always do at their Election.

In the mean time Charlemagne died, and was fucceeded by his fon Lewis : but after his death, there arofe fuch difcord amongft his Sons, that, in the days of his Grandchildren, the Empire was wrefted out of the hands of the French, and the feat of it eftablifhed in Germany by Ainolphus, the firft Emperor of that nation. And indeed the pofterity of Charlemagne not only loft the Empire, but their Sovereignty in Italy likewife, by their diffentions : for the Lombards gathering frefh ftrength, commenced hoftilities againft the Pope and the Romans, who, not knowing where to have recourfe for

---

* See the original of Cardinals, and the meaning of that word, in the prolegomena to the Life of Pope Sixtus V. Number V. which is too long to be inferted as a Note.

† *Bocca di Porco* ; *Os Porci* ; *Swine's Face.*

pro-

protection, were forced to make Berengarius, then Duke of Friuli, King of Italy. This encouraged the Huns, who at that time were settled in Pannonia, to invade Italy once more : but they were defeated in an engagement with Berengarius, and driven back again into Pannonia, or rather Hungary, which was the name they had given to that province. At that time Romanus was Emperor of Greece, who, having been Admiral of Conftantine's fleet, had deprived him of the Empire : and becaufe Puglia and Calabria (which, as we faid before, were ftill left fubject to the Empire) had revolted, during thefe innovations, he was fo enraged at their rebellion, that he fuffered the Saracens to invade thofe Provinces ; who having fubdued them, endeavoured likewife to make themfelves mafters of Rome. But the Romans (as Berengarius was fufficiently employed in defending himlelf againft the Huns) made Alberic, Duke of Tufcany, their General : by whofe valour their city was preferved from the fury of the Saracens, who being obliged to raife the fiege, retired from thence and built a fortrefs upon † Mount Gargano, by which they commanded Puglia and Calabria, and infefted all that part of Italy. In this miferable manner was Italy harraffed at that time, by the Huns on that fide next the Alps, and the Saracens on the other towards Naples : which troubles continued feveral years under three of the Berengarii, who fucceffively reigned over it. During which fpace the Pope and the Church were likewife continually molefted and difturbed, being deprived of all fuccour and protection by the diffentions which reigned amongft the Weftern Princes, and the weaknefs of the Eaftern. The city of Genoa and all its adjacent territories were alfo overrun and laid wafte by the Saracens : which depopulation gave birth to the greatnefs of Pifa, by the refort of multitudes thither that had been driven

† Now called Monte St. Angelo.

out

out of their own country.   Such was the condition
of Italy in the year 931.

But Otho, Duke of Saxony and son of Henry
and Matilda, succeeding to the Imperial crown, and
being a man of great reputation and prudence,
Agapetus the Pope implored his affiftance to deliver
his country from the tyranny of the Berengarii.   At
that time the feveral States of Italy were governed
in this manner.   Lombardy was under the jurifdiction of Berengarius the Third and Albert his fon.
Tufcany and Romania, under the dominion of a governor deputed by the Emperor of the Weft.   Some
parts of Puglia and Calabria were fubject to the Grecian Emperor, and others to the Saracens.   At
Rome two Confuls were elected every year out of the
Nobility, who governed it, according to ancient cuftom : to whom a Prefect was joined to administer
juftice to the people.   They had likewife a *Council
of Twelve*, which annually appointed Governors over
all the towns in their jurifdiction.   The Pope had
more or lefs authority in that city and the reft of
Italy, according as he had more or lefs intereft with
the Emperors, or other Princes that had the greateft
power there.   Otho therefore marched into Italy and
drove the Berengarii out of a Kingdom which they
had poffeffed fifty-five years ; and re-eftablifhed the
Pope in his former dignity.   This Prince had a fon
and a grandfon both of his own name, who in their
turns fucceeded to the Empire : and in the time of
Otho the Third, Pope Gregory the Fifth was driven
out of the City by the Romans.   Upon which, Otho
returned into Italy to reinftate him his Chair : and
the Pope, to revenge himfelf upon the Romans,
took the power of creating Emperors from them,
and vefted it in fix Princes of Germany, three of
whom were the Bifhops of Munfter, Treves, and
Cologne ; the other three were temporal Princes,
namely, the Duke of Brandenbourg, the Prince Pa-
latine of the Rhine, and the Duke of Saxony, who
were

were afterwards ftyled *Electors*, and their States, *Electorates*. This happened in the year 1002.

After the death of Otho the Third, Henry Duke of Bavaria, was chofen Emperor by thefe Electors, but not crowned till twelve years after, by Stephen the Eighth. Henry and Simeonda his wife were eminent for their piety, as appears from the many Churches that were built and endowed by them; amongft which is that of St. Miniato, near Florence. Henry died in the year 1024, and was fucceeded by Conrade of Suabia; and Conrade by Henry the Second, who came to Rome, and finding a fchifm in the Church, as there were then three different Popes fet up at the fame time, he depofed them all, and caufed Clement the Second to be elected, by whom he was afterwards crowned Emperor.

The ftates of Italy were then governed fome by the People, fome by Princes, and others by the Minifters of the Emperors, one of whom had the title of Chancellor, and prefided over all the reft. The moft confiderable and powerful of all the princes was Godfrey, hufband to the Countefs Matilda, who was daughter of Beatrice, fifter to Henry the Second. She and her Hufband were in poffeffion of Lucca, Reggio, Mantua, and all that territory which is now called the *Patrimony of the Church*. The Popes at that time were not a little embarraffed and diftreffed by the ambition of the Romans; for though they had made ufe of the Papal authority to rid themfelves of the Emperors; yet, as foon as the Popes had taken upon them the government of the City, and made fuch a reform in it as they thought proper, the citizens on a fudden became their enemies, and did them more and greater injuries than any Prince in Chriftendom: and at a time when the Pontifs made all the Weftern part of the world tremble at the thunder of their Cenfures, that people alone had the hardinefs to rebel; fo that each party at laft refolved to leave no endeavours untried to pull down

the

the reputation and authority of the other. Accordingly, when Nicholas the Second was promoted to the Papacy, as Gregory V. had taken from the Romans the privilege of chufing their emperors; fo *He* deprived them of their right of confirming the election of the Popes by their approbation, and confined it to the Cardinals only. Nor was he contented with this, but having entered into a treaty with the Princes who then governed Puglia and Calabria, for reafons which fhall be prefently explained, he obliged all the magiftrates that were fent by the people of Rome into places under their jurifdiction, to acknowledge the Pope's authority, and fome he deprived of their offices. After the death of Nicholas, there was another fchifm in the Church; for the Clergy of Lombardy would not pay obedience to Alexander the Second, (who had been chofen Pope at Rome) but fet up Cadolus of Parma, as Antipope. Upon which, Henry the Emperor, who could not bear to fee the Popes fo powerful, commanded Alexander to refign the Papacy, and the Cardinals to repair into Germany, to make a frefh election: for which he had the honour of being the firft Prince that was made fenfible of the weight of fpiritual weapons. For the Pope caufing a new council to affemble at Rome, deprived him both of his kingdom and empire *: and fome

---

* There refided at that time in Rome, a Monk of the Order of Cluny, lately created Cardinal; a man of a reftlefs, fiery, enterprizing difpofition, but chiefly remarkable for his furious zeal for the pretenfions of the Church, which he fometimes made fubfervient to his own private interefts. Hildebrand was the name of this daring man, afterwards the celebrated Gregory VII. He was born at Soana in Tufcany of obfcure parentage, brought up at Rome, admitted a Monk of Cluny, deputed afterwards to negotiate the affairs of his Order at Rome, and then employed by the Popes in all political concerns that required refolution and addrefs. He had the chief management of the Church under Alexander II. which led him to confider the troubles in Germany as a favourable conjuncture for ftriking a bold ftroke there. In fact, he engaged Alexander to excommunicate his fovereign Henry IV. under a pretence of its being reported that Henry fold Benefices in private, and led a fcandalous life in the company of lewd women. Upon the demife of Alexander, Hildebrand procured himfelf to be elected and inftalled by the people of Rome, without waiting

of

of the Italian States efpoufing the Pope's party, and
fome the Emperor's, gave birth to the two famous

for the Emperor's permiffion : but he foon obtained that, by promifing fealty and allegiance. Henry admitted of his excufes, and
his Chancellor of Italy repaired to Rome to confirm the election.
But he was fcarcely fettled on the Papal throne, when he pronounced Excommunication againft all thofe that accepted henefices
from the hands of Laymen, and againft every Layman that conferred them.' His defign was to deprive all fecular Patrons of the
right of prefentation to Church livings; which indeed was fetting
the Church at open variance with the Sovereigns of all Chriftian
nations. Henry, amazed at this prefumption, called a council at
Worms, by the advice of the States, in which he depofed Gregory
as a Simoniac and public difturber of the Peace of the Church and
Empire: and afterwards fent an envoy to read this decree of the
Council to the Pope, and command him to refign and ceafe to pro-
fane the Holy Chair, of which the Emperor was Guardian. Upon
this, the Pope declared in a Council of 110 Italian Bifhops, " That,
by the Authority of God and St. Peter, he depofed Henry from the
Imperial throne, and abfolved all his fubjects from their obedience."
The Emperor protefted againft this Excommunication, and the
Pope's ufurpation over his crown ; alledging the example of Charlemagne, and others, who had the power of confirming the Popes,
which feveral of them, and particularly Gregory himfelf, had
acknowledged to be the Emperor's right. But the German Prelates
and Princes, who had engaged Henry in their caufe, now deferting
him, and threatening to dethrone him, he was forced to pafs the
Alps in the rigour of the winter, with his Emprefs, his Son, and
one Gentleman only to attend him; and being almoft famifhed
with hunger, and ftarved with cold, this great Emperor, who had
been celebrated for fo many victories, was obliged to throw himfelf
at the Pope's feet, after he, his Emprefs, and his fon, had waited
three days at his gate, in the habit of Penitents, bare-footed, with
their heads uncovered, though it was then the middle of January,
and without eating a morfel of bread : after which, and agreeing
to the Pope's terms, he was abfolved. Upon this, the Princes of
Italy defpifing him as a coward, and the Pope as a Tyrant and Simoniac, confpired againft them both. The Emperor, therefore,
perceiving how much he had abafed himfelf, and difappointed
thofe Princes, who hoped for a Reformation of the Church, through
his affiftance, at laft called them together, and having accufed the
Pope, as the caufe of the ruin of the empire, he demanded their
fuccour againft him; by which ftep he regained their affections,
and afterwards kept the Pope in a manner blocked up at home.
The German rebels in the mean time, chofe Rodolphus, Duke of
Suabia, Emperor, and crowned him at Mentz, in the year 1077 ;
upon which, Henry returned into Germany, and defeated the
forces of Rodolphus, which fo terrified the Pope, that he endeavoured to make an accommodation betwixt them. But the Rebels
complaining, that he abandoned them in a caufe, wherein he himfelf had firft engaged them, he excommunicated Henry a fecond
time, confirmed the election of Rodolphus, and fent him a crown,
with this infcription upon it :

Petra dedit Petro, Petrus diadema Rodolpho.

fac-

factions of Guelfs and Ghibelines, and to thofe inteftine difcords which tore their country to pieces, after it was at laft delivered from the fcourge of Barbarians and foreign inundations.

Henry being thus excommunicated was forced by his own fubjects to go to Italy, in the year 1080, where he made his peace with the Pope, by afking pardon upon his bare knees. Not long after, however, there happened another quarrel betwixt him and the Pope, and Henry was again excommunicated : at which he was fo exafperated, that he fent his fon, whofe name alfo was Henry, with an army to Rome; where, with the affiftance of the Romans, who hated the Pope, he befieged him in his caftle : but receiving intelligence that Robert Guifcard was marching out of Puglia to the Pontif's relief, he did not wait for his arrival, but returned into Germany. The Romans, however, perfifted in their contumacy to fuch a degree, that Rome was once more facked by Guifcard, and reduced to that ruinous condition from which it had but lately emerged by the care and pains of fo many Pontifs. And as a fon of this Robert firft founded and modelled the Kingdom of Naples, it may not be foreign to our purpofe to give a particular account of his extraction and achievements.

Upon the difcords that arofe amongft the pofterity of Charlemagne, which we have already flightly mentioned, the Normans, another northern people, took the opportunity of invading France, and got poffeffion of that part of it, which from them is ftill called

Which wretched pun ferves to fhew the tafte of thofe times, and the intolerable pride of the Roman Pontif.
After this, Henry having at laft totally fubdued his competitor, called a council at Tyrol, in which he depofed the Pope, and, paffing the Alps, took Rome by ftorm, and befieged him in the caftle of St. Angelo, from whence, however, he was delivered by the Duke of Apulia, and died foon after, leaving behind him a memory dear and facred to the Roman Clergy, who inherited his pride; but deteftable to the Emperors, and every good Citizen, who confiders the effects of his infatiable ambition. See Voltaire's Gen. Hift. Vol. I. from p. 194 to p. 209. And Hiftoire d'Allemagne, par Monfieur de Prade.

Normandy *. One divifion of this people forced its way into Italy, at the time when it was fo cruelly harraffed and over-run by the Berengarii, the Saracens, and the Huns; and getting footing in Romagna, during thefe troubles, they bravely maintained their ground. Tancred, one of the Norman chiefs, had feveral fons; amongft whom were William, called Ferabar, or Fier-a-bras, and Robert, furnamed Guifcard. After the difturbances in Italy were in fome meafure compofed, and tranquillity reftored, William became their prince. But the Saracens being in poffeffion of Sicily, daily infefted the coafts of Italy in fuch a manner, that William was obliged to enter into a confederacy with the Princes of Capua and Salerno, and with Milorcus, a Greek, (who was deputed Governor of Puglia and Calabria by the Grecian Emperor) in order to invade Sicily : and it was agreed, that both the booty and ifland itfelf fhould be equally divided amongft them, in cafe they fhould make a conqueft of it. The enterprife was attended with fuccefs; for they drove the Saracens out of the country, and took poffeffion of it themfelves. But Milorcus having caufed more forces to be privately tranfported out of Greece, feized upon the ifland in the name of the Emperor, and only divided the fpoil with the reft : at which, William was not a little difgufted, but thinking it proper to diffemble his refentment till a more convenient opportunity, he departed out of Sicily with the Princes of Capua and Salerno. But as foon as they left him, to return to their refpective homes, inftead of going back again into Romagna, he made a fudden march with his army into Puglia, furprifed Melfi, and foon reduced almoft all Puglia and Calabria, in fpight of the Emperor's forces; which Provinces were governed by his brother Robert, till the time of Nicolas the Second. And as he afterwards had many difputes with his Nephews about the inheritance of thofe States,

---

* Before that time called Neuftria.

. he

he intreated the Pope to ufe his authority to compofe
them; which his Holinefs readily complied with, as
he was very defirous to make Robert his friend by any
means, that fo he might fupport him againft the
power of the German Emperor, and the petulance of
the Romans: and it afterwards happened, as we have
juft related, that upon the follicitation of Gregory
VII. he drove Henry away from Rome, and chaftifed
the infolence of the Inhabitants.

Robert was fucceeded by his two Sons, Roger and
William, who not only annexed the city of Naples,
and all the Country betwixt it and Rome, to their inheritance, but alfo fubdued Sicily, of which Roger
was made Lord.   But William going fome time afterwards to Conftantinople, to marry the Emperor's
daughter, Roger took the opportunity of invading
his brother's dominions, which he foon made himfelf
mafter of; and being elated with fo great an acquifition, caufed himfelf at firft to be called *King of Italy*,
but afterwards was contented with the title of *King of
Puglia and Sicily*; being the firft that gave the Kingdom that name and form of government, which it
retains to this day; though it has happened fince,
that not only the reigning family, but the very people have been often changed: For, upon the failure
of the Norman line, the Kingdom was transferred to
the Germans; from them to the French; from the
French to the Arragonefe; and from them to the
Flemings, who * ftill are in poffeffion of it.

* The reader is here defired to remember, that this Hiftory was
publifhed in the year 1531. Since which time, the Kingdom of Naples has often again changed its Mafters; particularly in 1707, when
the Spaniards, who then had it, were driven from thence by the Imperialifts: and at the Peace of Utrecht in 1713, Naples was confirmed
to the Emperor, and Sicily allotted to the Duke of Savoy, with the
title of King.   The Spaniards invaded Sicily in 1718, but were forced
to abandon it again, and then it was conferred on the Emperor
Charles VI. who held it till the year 1735, when the Imperialifts were
driven out of this Ifland, and all their Italian dominions; and Don
Carlos, the King of Spain's eldeft Son, by the Princefs of Parma, his
fecond Wife, was advanced to the throne of the Two Sicilies, (Naples and Sicily) whither he was convoyed by a fquadron of Britifh
men of war, under the command of Sir John Norris.   It was con-

In

In the mean time, Urban the Second had succeeded to the Pontificate : but as he was a person very disagreeable to the Romans, and did not think himself secure in Italy, on account of the disturbances there, he removed, with all his Clergy, into France, where he first laid the plan of a very noble and generous undertaking. For having assembled a great concourse of People at * Antwerp, he made an eloquent and pathetic harangue against the Infidels, which inspired them with such an ardour, that they resolved. upon an expedition into Asia against the Saracens : and this expedition was called a Crusade (as those of the same kind were likewise afterwards) because all that embarked in it bore a red Cross upon their armour and clothes. The chief commanders in this enterprize were Godfrey, Eustach, and Baldwin, Counts of Bouillon, and † Peter the Hermit, a man held in exceeding great veneration, both for his prudence and sanctity of life. Many Princes and Nations contributed to it with their purses, and numbers of private Gentlemen served as volunteers without any pay or stipend : such an influence had Religion at that time over the minds of men, animated by the example of their Commanders! This enterprize was at first very successful ; for all Asia Minor, Syria, and part of Egypt, were conquered by the Christians : and during the course of this war, the Order of the *Knights of Jerusalem* was instituted, which still subsists, and being in possession of Rhodes ‡, is the chief bulwark against the power of the Turks. The Order

firmed to him by a subsequent treaty, and still continues in his family, though the Queen of Hungary likewise claims a right to this Kingdom.

* Machiavel is mistaken in the name of the place ; it was at Clermont in Auvergne, where Urban harangued the people in the market-place. See Voltaire's Gen. Hist. Vol. I. p. 263.

† A Pilgrim of Amiens, first known by the name of Coucoupietre, or, Cucupierte. Ibid.

‡ They were driven out of Rhodes by the Turks, in the time of Soliman II. and the Emperor Charles V. gave them the Isle of Malta, when Monsieur de l'Isle Adam, uncle to Anne de Montmorency, Constable of France, was their Grand Master. And this Island has been their chief place of residence ever since.

of

of the *Knights Templars* was likewife founded in thefe times ; but their manners grew fo diffolute that it was foon abolifhed. After thefe things, many events happened, in which feveral nations and divers particular men diftinguifhed themfelves at different times and upon various occafions. The Kings of England and France, the States of Pifa, Venice, and Genoa, were engaged in this expedition, and acquired great reputation, carrying on the war with variety of fuccefs, till the time of Saladine the Saracen, whofe valour and good fortune, added to the difcord that arofe amongft the Chriftian Princes, at laft robbed them of the glory they had gained, and drove them out of a country where they had fo happily and honourably maintained their footing for the fpace of ninety years.

After the death of Urban, Pafcal the Second was made Pope, and Henry the Fourth fucceeded to the Empire ; who, coming to Rome, and pretending great refpect for the Pope, found means to fhut up both him and all his Clergy in prifon : nor could he afterwards be prevailed upon to fet him at liberty again, till he had extorted a licence from him to difpofe of all the Churches in Germany as he pleafed *.

* After the death of the Emperor Henry IV. his fon Henry V. being defirous to be crowned by the hands of the Pope, according to the ufual manner, Pafcal refufed to put the crown upon his head, except he would renounce his right to the inveftitures of Benefices. But the young Prince difdaining fuch a propofal, caufed the Pope and his Clergy, and all the principal perfons of the city of Rome to be feized, and kept them in prifon two months ; at the end of which, the Pope made his fubmiffion and crowned him. It is faid, that Pafcal, when he gave part of the Hoft to Henry, which he had confecrated at Mafs, fpoke to him in this manner: " May it pleafe your Majefty, in confirmation of a folid peace, and our mutual union, I give you the Body of our Lord Jefus Chrift, who was born of the Virgin Mary, and died upon the Crofs for us, as the Catholick Church believes." But the Cardinals condemning this conceffion in the Pope, he revoked it in a council. Hoffman fays, that having taken one part of the Hoft, and given the other to the Emperor, he expreffed himfelf thus : " Sicut pars hæc vivifici corporis divifa eft, ita divifus fit a regno Chrifti domini noftri qui pactum hoc violare tentaverit ;" that is, " May he be excluded the Kingdom of Heaven, who goes about to violate this agreement." Sigon. lib. x. But the Emperor was hardly got into Germany, when the Pope raifed the Saracens againft him, by whom he was defeated, and forced to give up the matter of Inveftitures. This

About

About this time, the Countefs Matilda died, and left all her poffeffions to the Church *. After the death of Pafcal and Henry IV. many Popes and Emperors fucceeded, till the Papacy fell to Alexander III. and the empire to Frederick Barbaroffa, a Suabian.

The Popes, in that interval, had had many quarrels, both with the people of Rome and the Emperors, which grew to a ftill greater height in the time of Barbaroffa. Frederick was an excellent foldier, but of fo haughty a difpofition, that he could not bear the thoughts of fubmitting to the Pope: yet he came to Rome to be crowned, and after that, return-ed peaceably into Germany. But this pacific temper did not continue long; for he fpeedily returned into Italy to reduce fome towns in Lombardy that refufed to obey him : at which juncture it happened, that the Cardinal of St. Clement, a Roman born, was fet up againft Alexander, and chofen Pope by fome of the Cardinals. Upon which, Alexander complained of him to Frederick the Emperor, who then lay encamped

Pope excommunicated the Bifhop of Florence, for faying Antichrift was then born. Platina. Baronius. Hen. Canifius.
' * She was Daughter of Boniface, Marquis of Tufcany, and Beatrice, the Daughter of Conrade II. She waged war againft the Emperor Henry IV. in behalf of Pope Gregory VII. who had gained fuch an afcendant over her, that by his perfuafion, fhe made an abfolute donation of her territories to the Holy See, referving to herfelf only the ufufruct during life, though Henry was her next heir, both as a relation and Lord paramount. She often led her armies in perfon againft that Prince, and got great reputation by her courage and conduct. Her enemies accufed her of being too familiar with Pope Gregory, who was her fpiritual director. He was fhut up with her in the fortrefs of Canofa, near Reggio, in the Apennine Mountains, all the while that Henry IV. with his Emprefs and Son, were doing penance at his gate, in the abject manner beforementioned. It is true, he was then fixty years old; but Matilda was a young, weak woman. The devout language which we find in his letters to the princefs, compared with the extravagance of his ambition, might induce fome to fufpect, that he made ufe of Religion as a cloak to all his paffions. However that might be, after fhe had loft Pope Gregory, fhe married the young Prince of Guelph, fon of Guelph, the Duke of Bavaria. Then was feen the imprudence fhe had been guilty of in making the abovementioned donation: for fhe was at that time but forty-two years of age, and might ftill have had children, who muft have engaged in a civil war to recover their inheritance. See Lambert, the Abbot of Ufberg, as quoted by Baronius, in his Annals: and Voltaire's General Hiftory, Vol. I. p. 201, 205.

before

before Crema, and received for anfwer, " that both
of them muft come perfonally before him, and when
he had heard their refpective pretenfions, he fhould
be better able to judge which of them was the true
Pope." But Alexander being diffatisfied with this
anfwer, and perceiving that the Emperor was inclined
to favour the Antipope, immediately excommunicated
him and fled for refuge to Philip King of France. Frederick, however, ftill profecuting the war in Lombardy, took Milan and difmantled it; which occafioned the Cities of Verona, Padua, and Venice, to
enter into a confederacy for their common defence
againft him.

In the mean time the Antipope died, and Frederick fet up Guido of Cremona in his room. The
Romans, therefore, taking advantage of the Pope's
abfence, and feeing the Emperor fufficiently employed
in Lombardy, had not only refumed fomething of
their ancient authority in Rome, during this interval,
but likewife demanded obedience from other ftates
which had been formerly fubject to them. And becaufe the * Tufculans refufed to acknowledge their
jurifdiction, they marched out in a confufed and tumultuous fort of a manner againft them : but as the
latter were fuccoured by the Emperor, they defeated
the Romans, and flew fo many of them, that after
that time, Rome was never fo rich and populous
again as it had been before.

This encouraged Pope Alexander to return to that
City, where he thought he might now be fafe enough
on account of the enmity betwixt Frederick and the
Romans, and becaufe he knew his hands were full in
Lombardy. But Frederick poftponing every other

---

* Tufculum was a little territory not far from Rome, fituated in
that part which at prefent is called la Campagna di Roma. It was
famous for Cicero's Villa, which is now in the poffeffion of the Borg-
hefe family. It is the feat of a Bifhop, who ftill retains the name of
Tufculanus Epifcopus. The town of Tufculum was deftroyed in the
time of Celeftine III. becaufe the inhabitants fided with the Imperialifts, and Frefcati built upon its ruins about 560 years ago. There are
a great number of palaces of pleafure in and about it.

confideration, marched with his army to befiege
Rome, where Alexander did not think fit to wait
for him, but retired into Puglia, of which William
was become King by right of inheritance after the
death of Roger. Frederick being driven away by
the Plague, raifed the fiege and returned into Germany : and the Lombards who had confederated
againft him, in order to diftrefs Pavia and Tortona,
towns that adhered to the Emperor's party, built another city, which they defigned to make their maga-
zine, or place of arms, during that war, and called
it Alexandria, in honour of the Pope and defiance of
the Emperor. In the mean time, Guido the Antipope died, and John of Fermo was fet up in his
room, who, by the favour of the Imperial party, was
fuffered to refide at Montefiafcone : whilft Alexander
was gone to Tufculum at the invitation of that People, who thought his authority would protect them
againft the Romans. During his ftay there, Ambaffadors came to him from Henry, King of England,
to clear their Mafter of the death of Thomas Becket,
Archbifhop of Canterbury ; of which he had been
publickly, but injurioufly accufed. To inquire into
the truth of this matter, the Pope fent two Cardinals
to England ; who, though there was no fufficient
proof of the King's guilt, yet on account of the infamy of the fact, and becaufe his Majefty had not
fhewn the Archbifhop due refpect, as they pretended,
enjoined him for a Penance, that he fhould call all
the Barons of his Kingdom together, and make oath
of his innocence in their prefence : that he fhould
immediately fend two hundred foldiers to Jerufalem,
to be paid by him, for twelve months, and follow
them in perfon thither with as great a force as he could
raife, before the expiration of three years : and farther, that he fhould not only be obliged to abrogate
all acts that had been paffed in his Kingdom to the
prejudice of the Church and Ecclefiaftical immuni-
ties, but give any of his fubjects leave to appeal to
Rome upon occafion, whenfoever, and as often as
they

they had a mind : all which conditions were accepted by Henry, and that great Prince fubmitted to a fentence which would be fcorned and rejected by any private man at this time of day *. Neverthelefs, whilft the authority of the Pope was fo formidable to foreign Princes, he had not power enough to make himfelf obeyed at home ; nor could he prevail upon the Romans to let him refide in their City, though he promifed them not to concern himfelf about any thing but what immediately concerned the interefts of the Church. From whence it feems, as if authority that fupports itfelf merely by appearances, is more dreaded at a diftance, than by thofe that are upon the fpot, and have an opportunity of looking more narrowly into the nature of it.

By this time Frederick had returned into Italy : but whilft he was making preparations to renew the war againft the Pope, all his Clergy and Barons threatened to abandon him if he did not reconcile himfelf to the Church : fo that he was forced to go and make his fubmiffion to the Pope at Venice, where they were reconciled †. But, by an article of this accommodation, his Holinefs obliged the Emperor to give up all the authority that he had at Rome, and infifted upon

---

* Still more harmlefs and ridiculous was the penance or curfe pronounced upon Sir William Tracey, who was faid to be the moft active of thofe that were concerned in this murder. He and all his pofterity were fentenced " to have the wind always in their faces, whether they travelled by land or water. A woeful curfe indeed, if it had been effectual ! From this fcrap of a Legend arofe the old foolifh proverb,
———— " The Traceys
Have always the wind in their faces."

† The haughty Pope fet his foot upon his neck, with this expreffion : " Super afpidem & bafilifcum ambulabo," &c. " I will tread upon the lion and adder, the young lion and the dragon will I trample under my feet." Pfal. xci. 13. The Emperor replying, " That power was given to Peter only ;" he rejoined, " Et mihi & Petro ;" " It was given to me and Peter too." Afterwards in his troubles, Emanuel, Emperor of Conftantinople, fent to offer him affiftance, provided he would confent to the re-union of the Eaftern and Weftern Empires; to which the Pope anfwered, " That he could not confent to unite, what his predeceffors had taken fo much pains to divide." Baronius endeavours to prove thefe ftories fabulous.

I   having

having his ally and confederate, William, King of
Sicily and Puglia, included in the agreement. After
which, Frederick, who was a warlike Prince and
hated an inactive life, embarked in the expedition
to Asia, to vent his spirit upon the Turks, when he
saw he could not revenge himself upon the Pope.
But when he had got as far as the banks of the Cid-
nus, a river in Cilicia, being tempted by the clearness of its streams, he could not resist the pleasure
of bathing in them †, by which he contracted such a
disorder, that he died of it. An accident that was of
more service to the Mahometans, than all the Pope's
excommunications had been to the Christians: for the
latter only curbed his ambition, but this entirely extinguished it.

   After the death of Frederick, the Pope had nothing to struggle with but the inveterate obstinacy of
the Romans: and, after long disputes about the crea-
tion of Consuls, it was at last agreed, that, according to ancient custom, they should have the privilege
of chusing them, but that they should not enter upon their office till they had sworn obedience to the
Church. Upon this agreement, John the Antipope
fled to Mont Albano, where he died soon after. In
the mean time William, King of Naples, died also:
and as he left no sons but Tancred, who was illegitimate, the Pope designed to have seized upon his
Kingdom. The Barons, however, would not consent
to that, but made Tancred their King. Celestine the
Third succeeding to the Papacy, and being desirous
to wrest that Kingdom out of the hands of Tancred,
endeavoured to get Henry, who was son to Frederick,
chosen Emperor, and also promised him the Kingdom of Naples, upon condition that he should re-

---

† It is worthy of notice, that when Alexander the Great came to
this river, he also was so delighted with the clearness of the waters,
that he threw himself into it, all covered with sweat and dust as he
was: by which he was so benumbed, that it required the utmost skill
of his physician to recover him. Qu. Cur. lib. iii. sect. 6. See the
story at large there, as it is a very remarkable one.

store

ftore fuch lands as belonged to the Church. And to facilitate the matter, he took Conftantia, an old maid (daughter to William the late King) out of a Nunnery, and gave him her to wife: and in this manner the Kingdom of Naples paſſed from the Normans, who had been the founders of it, to the Germans.

Henry the Emperor, having fettled his affairs in Germany came into Italy with his wife Conftantia, and a Son about four years old, whofe name was Frederick, and· without much difficulty took poſſeſſion of that Kingdom; as Tancred was now dead and had left but one Son, named Roger, who was an infant. Not long after, Henry died in Sicily, and was ſucceeded in that kingdom by Frederick: and Otho, Duke of Saxony, was chofen Emperor by the influence of Innocent the Second. However, he had no ſooner got the Imperial Crown upon his head, but he fell out with the Pope, contrary to the expeĉtation of all men, feized upon Romagna, and was preparing to invade Sicily: upon which, being excommunicated by the Pope, he was deferted by every one, and Frederick King of Naples chofen Emperor in his ſtead. This Frederick came to Rome to be crowned there; but the Pope being jealous of his power, refufed it, and endeavoured to thruft him out of Italy, as he had done Otho: at which, Frederick being much offended, went into Germany, raifed an army, made war upon Otho, and at laft overcame him.

In the mean time Innocent died, who, befides his other magnificent works, built the Hofpital di Santo Spirito at Rome. He was fucceeded by Honorius the Third: in whofe Pontificate, the Orders of St. Dominick and St. Francis were inftituted, about the year 1218. This Pope crowned Frederick, to whom John (defcended from Baldwin, King of Jerufalem, who commanded the remainder of the Chriftians in Afia, and ftill retained that title) gave one of his daughters in marriage, and the title of that Kingdom in dower with her, which the Kings of Naples have borne ever fince. Italy was then circumftanced in

this

this manner. The Romans no longer appointed Confuls, but invefted fometimes one, fometimes more of
the Senators with the fame authority. The confederacy ftill fubfifted, into which the following cities of
Lombardy had entered againft Frederick Barbaroffa,
namely, Milan, Brefcia, and Mantua, with moft of
thofe in Romagna, befides Verona, Vicenza, Padua,
and Trevigi. The cities that took part with the Emperor, were Cremona, Bergamo, Parma, Reggio,
Modena, and Trenta. The other cities and fortreffes
of Lombardy, Romania, and the Marca Trevigiana,
fided fometimes with one party, and fometimes with
the other, as it beft fuited their intereft.

In the reign of Otho the Third, one Ezelino came
to fettle in Italy. This man's grandfon, whofe name
was likewife Ezelino, becoming very rich and powerful, joined the party of Frederick, in oppofition to
the Pope: and it was by his inftigation and affiftance,
that Frederick invaded Italy, took Verona and Mantua, difmantled Vicenza, feized upon Padua, defeated the army of the Confederates, and advanced towards Tufcany; during which time Ezelino made
himfelf mafter of la Marca Trevigiana. But they
could not take Ferrara, as it was defended by Azzone
de Efte, and fome forces which the Pope had in Lombardy: in recompence for which fervice, as foon as
the fiege was raifed, his Holinefs gave that City in
fee to the faid Azzone, from whom thofe are defcended that are Lords of it at this day *. After
this, Frederick took up his head-quarters at Pifa,
being defirous to make himfelf mafter of Tufcany:
and by the diftinction which he made betwixt his
friends and thofe that oppofed him, he raifed fuch
difcords and animofities amongft them as afterwards

* This fief returned to the Church in the time of Henry IV. King
of France, who reftored it to Clement VIII. upon the death of Alphonfo II. Duke of Ferrara, in 1598, without heirs male; though it
was claimed by the Duke of Modena, a territory that was erected
into a Dukedom by the Emperor Frederick III. 1452, in favour of
Borfo d'Efte, whofe family have been in poffeffion of it ever fince.

proved

proved the ruin of all Italy : for the two factions of Guelphs and Ghibelines increafed every day, the former fiding with the Church, the other with the Emperor, and were firft called by thofe names at the City of Piftoia.   When Frederick left Pifa, he made fuch terrible havock and devaftation in the territories of the Church, that the Pope, having no other remedy, proclaimed a Crufade againft him, as his predeceffors had done againft the Saracens : and Frederick, for fear of being left deftitute, and fuddenly deferted by his own forces, as Barbaroffa and other former Emperors had been upon the like emergencies, took a large body of Saracens into his pay, and to attach them more firmly to him, and ftrengthen his oppofition to the Pope in Italy, by troops that defpifed his maledictions, he gave them Nocera, that fo when they faw they had a place of their own whither they could retreat upon occafion, they might ferve him with more confidence and fecurity.

Innocent the fourth was now made Pope ; who being afraid of Frederick, retired to Genoa, and from thence into France, where he affembled a Council at Lyons, at which Frederick defigned to have been prefent himfelf, if he had not been prevented by a rebellion that broke out in Parma : and, not fucceeding in his attempts to fupprefs it, he marched away into Tufcany, and from thence tranfported himfelf into Sicily, where he died not long after, leaving his own fon Conrade in Suabia, and Manfred his natural fon in Puglia, whom he had before made Duke of Benevento.   But Conrade coming to take poffeffion of the Kingdom, was feized with an illnefs at Naples and died there, leaving only one fon behind him in Germany, whofe name was Conradine.   Manfred therefore in the firft place, took the government of the Kingdom upon him, as guardian to Conradine, during his minority ; and afterwards giving out that the young Prince was dead, made himfelf King, and forced the Pope and the Neapolitans, who oppofed it, to acknowledge him.

During

During thefe difturbances in that Kingdom, there likewife arofe great commotions and diffenfions in Lombardy, betwixt the Guelphs and the Ghibelines there. The Guelphs were headed by a Legate from the Pope; and the Ghibelines by Ezelino, who had got poffeffion of almoft all that part of Lombardy, which lies on the other fide of the Po. And as the City of Padua had revolted whilft he was engaged in this war, he caufed twelve thoufand of the Paduans to be put to death, but died himfelf before the war was ended, in the thirtieth year of his age: after which, all the territories that had been in his hands recovered their liberty *. Manfred King of Naples, however, continued at enmity with the Church, as his predeceffors had done, and kept Urban the fourth, who then filled the Pontifical chair, in fuch continual alarm, that he was obliged to fet up another Crufade, and to retire to Perugia, till he could affemble his forces. But finding that few came in and very flowly, and that more powerful fupplies were neceffary to reduce him to reafon, he applied to Lewis † King of France for affiftance, (whofe brother, Charles of Anjou, he made King of Naples and Sicily) and exhorted him to come into Italy to take poffeffion of that Kingdom. But the Pope died before the arrival of that Prince at Rome, and was fucceeded by Clement the fourth; in whofe time Charles came to Oftia with thirty gallies, having appointed the reft of his forces to march thither by land. During the ftay that he made at Rome, the Romans, out of compliment, conferred the fenatorial

---

* Paulus Jovius fays, in his Elogies, he was one of the moft barbarous Tyrants that ever lived, killing man, woman, or child, upon the leaft offence, and fometimes without any at all. The punifhments and tortures he invented, were fuch as had never been heard of before. After he had exercifed every kind of cruelty upon mankind, for the fpace of forty years, he was wounded and taken prifoner by the confederated Princes of Lombardy, in attempting to make himfelf mafter of Milan: and being carried to Soncino, he died mad there in 1259; fo that he muft have lived much longer than Machiavel fays he did.

† Lewis IX, commonly called St. Lewis.

Dig-

Dignity upon him, and the Pope confirmed him in his Kingdom, on condition that he fhould yearly pay the fum of fifty thoufand florins to the Church: but at the fame time publifhed a Decree that neither Charles, nor any other that fhould fucceed him in that Kingdom, fhould be capable of being Emperor. After which, Charles advanced againft Manfred, whom he routed and killed near Benevento, and took poffeffion of the Kingdom of Naples and Sicily. But Conradine, to whom that Kingdom of right belonged, by his father's will, having raifed a good body of forces in Germany, marched into Italy againft Charles, by whom he was engaged at Tagliacozzo, and not only defeated, but taken, and afterwards killed, as he was endeavouring to make his efcape in difguife.

After this, Italy continued in peace till the Pontificate of Adrian the Fifth, who not being able to bear that Charles fhould continue at Rome, and rule every thing there, as he did, by virtue of his Senatorfhip, removed to Viterbo, and follicited Rodolphus the Emperor to march into Italy againft him. In this manner, the Popes, fometimes in defence of Religion, fometimes to gratify their own private intereft and ambition, were continually calling foreign Princes into Italy, to foment new wars: and no fooner had they exalted one of them, but they immediately repented of what they had done, and endeavoured to pull him down again: nor would they fuffer that province, which yet they were not able to fubdue themfelves, to be quietly enjoyed by any body elfe. So that the Princes of it were in continual dread of them, efpecially as the Popes always got the better of them, either by force or fraud, if they were not out-fchemed, as Boniface the eighth, and fome others of them, were by the Emperors, under the mafk of friendfhip.

Rodolphus being detained by a war, that he was engaged in with the King of Bohemia, was not at leifure to come into Italy, till after the death of Adrian, whofe fucceffor in the Papacy was Nicholas III. of
the

the family of Urfini, a bold and ambitious man, and
determined at all events to humble the power of
Charles: for which purpofe, he contrived, that Rodolphus the Emperor fhould complain of Charles for
keeping a governor in Tufcany, who fided with, and
fupported the faction of, the Guelphs in that province, where they had been re-eftablifhed by him after the death of Manfred. To oblige the Emperor
therefore, Charles recalled that governor, and the
Pope fent one of his Nephews, who was a Cardinal,
to take poffeffion of it for the Emperor: in return
for which favour, the Emperor reftored Romagna to
the Church, which had been taken from it by his
Predeceffors; and the Pope made Bertoldo Urfini,
Duke of Romagna. And now thinking himfelf
ftrong enough to cope with Charles, he degraded
him from his Senatorial dignity, and made a Decree,
that for the future, no perfon of royal extraction
fhould ever be a Senator of Rome. He likewife
formed a fecret defign, in concert with Peter, King
of Arragon, to deprive Charles of Sicily; which afterwards took effect in the time of his fucceffor. He
farther intended to have made two Kings, of his own
family; one of Lombardy, the other of Tufcany; by
whofe power and affiftance the Church might prevent
any more Germans from coming into Italy, and defend itfelf againft the French that were already fettled in the Kingdom of Naples. But he died before
thefe ends could be accomplifhed, and was the firft
Pope that openly avowed his ambition, and fhewed
that under a pretence of advancing the interefts of
the Church, he only defigned to aggrandize his own
family. And though no mention is made of the Pope's
Nephews, or other relations before this time, yet fucceeding hiftory is full of them, and we muft confider
them henceforth as their fons: for as the Pontifs formerly endeavoured to leave them Princes, they would
now leave them Popes, if they could, and make the
Papacy hereditary. But the principalities which they
have hitherto erected, have been of fhort duration:

for

for as the Popes are commonly old men before their
exaltation, and feldom live long after it, the ftates
which they found have not fufficient time to eftablifh
themfelves, and therefore are blown down by the
firft guft of wind, for want of ftrength and authority
to fupport them.

This Pope was fucceeded by Martin the Fourth,
who being a Frenchman born, favoured the party of
Charles in fuch a manner, that Charles fent an army
to his affiftance in Romagna, which had rebelled:
but as he lay encamped before Forli, Guido Bonatti,
an aftrologer, who was then in the town, advifed
the Garrifon to make a fally at a particular hour appointed by him, which fucceeded fo well, that all
the French forces were either taken or killed. About
this time, the defigns that had been formed by Pope
Nicholas, and Peter King of Arragon, were put in
execution : in confequence of which, the Sicilians *

* Moft writers agree, that Nicholas III. died of an apoplexy at Su-
tri, two years before this event happened. Platina, Du Chefne, Bzo-
vius, who continued the Annals of Baronius down to his own time.
Raynald. in Annal. Ludovic. Jacob. Bibliothec. Pontific. Voltaire
fays in his General Hiftory of Europe, Vol. I. p. 313. " It is the general opinion, that a Sicilian Gentleman, whofe name was John of
Procida, difguifed in the habit of a Francifcan Friar, laid that famous confpiracy, by which every Frenchman in the ifland was to be
maffacred at the fame hour in the evening of Eafter Sunday 1282,
upon ringing the bell for Vefpers. It is certain, that this John of
Procida had prepared the minds of the people in Sicily for a revolution ; that he had been negotiating at Conftantinople, and in the
kingdom of Arragon; and that Peter, King of Arragon, Manfred's
fon in law, had entered into an alliance with the Grecian Emperor
againft Charles of Anjou : but it is not at all probable that the Sicilian Vefpers (as that Maffacre was afterwards called) was a preme-
ditated confpiracy. If there had been any plot formed, it muft have
been put in execution chiefly in the kingdom of Naples; and yet not
one Frenchman was killed there. Malafpina relates, that a Frenchman, whofe Name was Droguet, was attempting to ravifh a woman
at Palermo, at the very time when the people were going to Vefpers :
the woman cried out ; the people flocked to her affiftance, and killed
the Frenchman. The firft emotion of private revenge awakened the
general hatred, and the Sicilians, excited by John of Procida, cried
out to extirpate the enemy : upon which, they put every Frenchman
they found in Palermo to the fword. The fury, which poffeffed the
breaft of every native, produced the fame effect throughout the whole
Ifland. It is faid, they ripped open the bellies of pregnant women,
and plucked out the fœtus as yet unformed; and that the very re-

maffacred all the French in that Ifland, and Peter made himfelf mafter of it, under a pretence that it belonged to him, in right of his wife Conftantia, as daughter of Manfred. Soon after, Charles died whilft he was carrying on a new war for the recovery of it, leaving his fon Charles the Second, in Sicily, where he had been taken prifoner during the courfe of that war, but was fet at liberty upon his parole, that he would return to his confinement there at the expiration of three years, if he did not, before that time, prevail upon the Pope to confirm the Kingdom of Sicily to the Houfe of Arragon. Rodolphus the Emperor, inftead of coming into Italy himfelf, to retrieve the reputation of the Imperial arms, fent a commiffary thither, with full power to emancipate fuch cities as would buy their freedom : upon which many cities ranfomed themfelves, and changed their laws and form of government, when they had regained their liberty.

After this, Adolphus, Duke of Saxony, fucceeded to the Empire, and Pietro del Murone (who affumed the name of Celeftine) to the Papacy : but as he had been a Hermit, and was wholly given up to devotion, he abdicated the Pontificate at the end of fix months, and Boniface VIII. was elected in his room. But Heaven ordaining that Italy fhould one day be delivered from the yoke, both of the French and the Germans, and left entirely in the hands of her own fons, gracioufly raifed up the Colonni and Urfini, two great and very powerful families in Rome, to bridle the Popes, and keep them within

ligious themfelves murdered their female penitents of the French nation. It is likewife affirmed, that only one Gentleman, a Provençal, whofe name was Des Porcellets, efcaped the general flaughter. And yet it is very certain, that the governor of Meffina, with all his garrifon, withdrew from the Ifland into the kingdom of Naples."

It would be no unpleafant amufement to compare thofe parts of Voltaire's General Hiftory that relate to the affairs of Italy, with this firft book of the Hiftory of Florence, which is only to be confidered as a fummary account. He illuminates thofe dark times, which are the fubject of it, with many ftriking remarks and obfervations, in his ufual manner.

due

due bounds by their authority and near neighbourhood, and to prevent them, when freed from the terror of foreign enemies, from eſtabliſhing themſelves
in the power they uſurped. Boniface, therefore, who
was ſoon ſenſible of this thorn in his ſide, applied
himſelf with great zeal and diligence to ſupprefs the
Colonni, firſt excommunicating, and then proclaim-
ing a Cruſade againſt them, which indeed did them
ſome injury, but was much more prejudicial to the
Church: for thoſe ſwords which had been drawn to
maintain and defend the chriſtian faith, and had done
great and honourable ſervice, ſoon loſt their edge and
became uſeleſs, when they were turned againſt Chriſ-
tians, only to ſatiate private intereſt and ambition:
ſo that by degrees, the Popes were left weak and de-
fenceleſs. Two of the Colonni, who were Cardinals,
he degraded: and Sciarra, the head of that family,
flying from his fury in diſguiſe, was taken by Catalan
Corſairs, and forced to row in their Gallies like a
common ſlave; but being known at Marſeilles, he
was ranſomed and ſent away to Philip, King of
France, whom Boniface had excommunicated and
deprived of his Kingdom. Upon this, Philip conſidering that in all open wars with the Popes, he had
conſtantly been a loſer, and often in great danger of
being utterly ruined, now reſolved to proceed in another manner, and to have recourſe to ſtratagem. In
conſequence of which, he pretended to ſubmit, and
entered into a treaty of reconciliation with the Pope:
but whilſt it was carrying on, he privately ſent Sciarra
into Italy, who arriving at Anagni (where the Pope
then reſided) gathered his friends together in the
night, ſeized upon his Holineſs's perſon, and made
him priſoner. And though he was ſet at liberty again
by the people of that town, yet ſuch was his rage and
indignation at this diſgrace, that he died diſtracted
ſoon after. This Boniface inſtituted the firſt Jubilee
in the year 1300, and made a Decree that it ſhould
be celebrated every hundred years *.

* It is ſaid of Boniface VIII. that he entered the Pontificate like a
Fox, reigned like a Lion, and died like a Dog, as Celeſtine V his pre-

In thefe times, the difcords between the Guelph and Ghibeline factions produced great troubles in Italy; which being abandoned by the Emperors, many States recovered their liberties, whilft others, on the contrary, were feized upon, and ufurped by different mafters. Pope Benedict XI. reftored the

deceffor, had prophefied. He perfuaded Celeftine, that he would certainly be damned if he did not refign the Papacy to fome perfon more capable of governing the church than himfelf. Upon which Celeftine abdicated, and Benedict Caietano (as this Pontif was before called) having got himfelf elected Pope, immediately fent Celeftine to prifon, where he died. Platina fays, that befides his own perfuafions, he bribed a perfon to fpeak thus to him through a hole in the wall of his Oratory, by means of a hollow cane, " Celeftine, Celeftine, dimitte Papatum, fi vis falvus fieri: negotium fupra vires elt," i. e. " Celeftine, Celeftine, refign the Papacy, if thou haft any regard for thy falvation; the burden is too heavy for thee:" which the fimple good man, taking it for a voice from Heaven, immediately obeyed and abdicated.

He provoked Philip the Fair, of France, to fuch a degree, by his haughty and infolent behaviour, that he refolved to compel him by force to appear before a council which he defigned to affemble at Lyons; and for that purpofe, fent Sciarra Colonni into Italy, with William Nogaret his confidant, and one of his generals; who having treated with the Ghibelines, entered Anagni, where he then was, and took him. Hoffman fays, that in a fynod and parliament, called by Philip, he was accufed of Simony, Murder, Ufury, Atheifm, Adultery, and underhand treaties with the Saracens. When he was taken by Nogaret, the French general, who threatened to carry him to Lyons, where he fhould be degraded by the council: he faid, " he was not to be frightened at the threats of a Paterin." Upon which, the faid general ftruck him on the face with his gauntlet, and taking him by the neck, forced him to Rome, where he died foon after, frantick, and gnawing his flefh off his hands with his teeth. Spanheim adds, that when his Bull arrived in France, in which he afferted, that he was fupreme Lord in all temporal, as well as fpiritual concerns, and that Philip held his kingdom of him; the fame was publickly burnt by order of the Parliament of Paris, and by the affembly of the States of the Kingdom that fame year, who vehemently protefted againft the Papal ufurpations and encroachments in the refervation and collation of Benefices, taxing the Clergy, &c. and that the king wrote thus to him, in anfwer to his Letter: " Philippus Dei gratiâ Francorum Rex, Bonifacio fe gerenti pro fummo Pontifice, falutem modicam feu nullam. Sciat maxima tua Fatuitas, in Temporalibus nos alicui non fubeffe, Ecclefiarum & Præbendarum Collationem ad nos jure regio pertinere, &c. fecus autem credentes fatuos & dementes reputamus." i. e. " Philip, by the Grace of God, King of France, to Boniface, the pretended Pope, little or no greeting. Be it known unto your Foolifhnefs, that we are fubject to none in Temporals, and that the Collation to Churches and Prebends belongs to us alone by our royal prerogative; and thofe who think otherwife, we account fools and madmen, &c." This Pope was a man of learning, and publifhed many works, which are ftill extant.

House of Colonni to their former dignity, and not only abfolved King Philip, but gave him his blefling. He was fucceeded in the Papal Chair by Clement V who being a Frenchman, removed his Court into France, in the year 1306 *. In the mean time, Charles the Second, King of Naples, was dead, and had left the Kingdom to his fon Robert. The Empire alfo was devolved to Henry of Luxembourg, who came to Rome to be crowned, though the Pope was not there. Upon his arrival, many commotions enfued in Lombardy : for all the banifhed perfons, whether Guelphs or Ghibelines, were returned to their former habitations, and daily confpiring to fupprefs each other ; which filled all that province with tumult and diftraction, notwithftanding the emperor ufed his utmoft endeavours to prevent it.

Removing therefore out of Lombardy, by way of Genoa, he came to Pifa, with a defign to have driven King Robert out of Tufcany ; but not fucceeding in that, he went to Rome, where he ftaid but a few days : for the Urfini, with the affiftance of King Robert, forced him to return to Pifa ; where, in order to make war with greater fecurity and convenience upon Tufcany, and to wreft the government of it out of Robert's hands, he caufed it to be invaded on the other fide by Frederick, King of Sicily. But

* At the coronation of this Pontif, in the Church of St. Juftus at Lyons, November 14, 1305, where Philip the Fair, Charles of Valois his brother, and feveral other Princes affifted, a Gallery that was overloaded with fpectators, broke down, and killed John II. Duke of Bretagne, Gaillard (the Pope's brother) and many others : the King and his brother likewife were much hurt ; the tiara fell from Clement's head ; and a jewel of great price was loft out of it ; from whence the omen-dealers of thofe times, formed a fad prefage, as it is faid, of the misfortunes that befel Italy in his reign by the civil wars, occafioned by his removing the See to Avignon, where it remained feventy years ; a period called by the Italians, " the Captivity of Babylon." Poffevin. Genebrard.

Juft fuch another prefage was formed by fome Englifh Seers, when our King Charles the Firft's ftandard was blown down at Nottingham, and the head of his cane fell off at his trial.—Sad prefages indeed, and fad prefagers ! yet thefe circumftances, trivial as they are, have not been thought unworthy of relation by fome of our hiftorians of the firft rank,

E 3   in

in the midſt of theſe deſigns, and at a time when he
had the greateſt hopes of ſuccefs, he ſuddenly died,
and was ſucceeded in the empire by Lewis of Bavaria.
About this time, John the Twenty-ſecond * was
created Pope, in whoſe Pontificate the Emperor carried on a continual perſecution againſt the Guelphs
and the Church : but King Robert and the Florentines interpoſing in their defence, great wars enſued
in Lombardy, under the conduct of the Viſconti,
againſt the Guelphs; and under that of Caſtruccio
Caſtracani, of Lucca, againſt the Florentines in Tuſcany. And as the family of the Viſconti were the
founders of the Dukedom of Milan, which was afterwards one of the five principal States in Italy, it
may not be amiſs perhaps to trace their original a little higher.-

After the aforementioned confederacy amongſt the
cities of Lombardy, for their common defence
againſt Frederick Barbaroffa, Milan riſing again out
of its ruins, likewiſe entered into that league, to take
revenge for the injuries it had ſuſtained : which put
a ſtop to the Emperor's career, and for a while ſupported the Pope's party in Lombardy. In the courſe
of thoſe wars, the family of the Torri grew very pow-

---

* After the death of Clement V. the See continued vacant above two
years : for the Cardinals, affembled at Carpentras, could not agree in
the choice of a new Pope. Philip the Long, therefore, Earl of Poic-
tiers, and afterwards King of France, by order of his brother Lewis
X. went to Lyons, to get the Chair filled if poſſible: for which purpoſe, after he had uſed all the art and addreſs he was maſter of, with
the Cardinals there, he at laſt ſhut them up in a convent of the Ja-
cobines, and proteſted he would never let them out till they had choſen a Pope. At the end of forty days, they began to be ſo tired of
their confinement, that they agreed to leave the choice to Cardinal
James d'Offa, Biſhop of Port, who immediately ſaid, " Ego ſum
Papa;" " then I'll be your Pope ;" to the general ſatisfaction of all
the reſt. He was a native of Cahors in Querci, and ſon of Arnaud
d'Offa, a poor Shoemaker; but a man well learned for thoſe times,
eſpecially in the Civil and Canon Law. It is ſaid, he left twenty-
eight millions of Ducats, and ſeventeen hundred thouſand Florins
of gold in the treaſury of the Church, when he died. He publiſhed
an Edict in 1322, wherein he declared all thoſe obſtinate Hereticks,
who affirmed, " that Chriſt and his Diſciples had nothing which they
could call their own ; and forbad all diſputes upon that point in the
ſchools." Nauclerus. Du Cheſne.

erful,

erful, increafing their reputation more and more
every day, whilft the authority of the Emperors was
of no great weight in thofe parts. But Frederick the
Second coming into Italy, and the Ghibeline faction
being reinforced by the affiftance of Ezelino, began
to gain ground in all the cities, and particularly at
Milan, where the Houfe of Vifconti fiding with that
party, drove the Torri out of that city. But they did
not long continue in that condition ; for by an agreement made betwixt the Emperor and the Pope, they
were fuffered to return thither: And afterwards,
when the Pope was removed with his court into
France, and Henry of Luxembourg came to Rome to
be crowned, he was received into Milan by Maffeo
Vifconti and Guido della Torre, who at that time
were the heads of thofe two families.

Notwithftanding this, Maffeo fecretly defigned to
avail himfelf of the Emperor's prefence to drive Guido
out of the City once more, which he thought would
be no difficult matter, as he was an enemy to the Imperial faction : for which purpofe he took advantage
of the murmurs and complaints of the People againft
the infolent behaviour of the Germans, privately encouraging and perfuading them to take up arms and
free themfelves from the yoke of thofe Barbarians.
After he had difpofed things in a proper manner for
the execution of his defign, he caufed a tumult to be
raifed by one of his confidants : upon which, the
whole town was immediately in an uproar againft the
Germans. And no fooner was the tumult begun,
but Maffeo, with his fons, fervants, and partifans
were in arms, and ran to the Emperor, affuring him
it was raifed by the Torri, who, not content to live
in a private condition, fomented thefe infurrections,
in order to wreft the city of Milan out of his hands,
by which they thought to ingratiate themfelves with
the Guelphs, and fo become Princes of it : exhorting him at the fame time, however, to be of good
courage, for they and their friends were both able
and ready to defend him at all events, provided he

was not wanting to himself. The Emperor believing every thing to be true that Maffeo had infinuated, immediately joined his forces with thofe of the Vifconti, and fell upon the Torri, who were difperfed up and down the city to compofe the tumult: and having killed fuch of them as fell into their hands, they banifhed the reft and feized upon their eftates. So that Maffeo Vifconti having by thefe means made himfelf, as it were, Prince of Milan, was fucceeded in the government of it by Galeazzo and Azzo; and they by Luchino and Giovanni, the latter of whom was afterwards Archbifhop of that city. Luchino died firft and left two fons, Bernabo and Galeazzo. Galeazzo dying not long after, left one fon named Giovanni Galeazzo, commonly called the Count di Virtù, who, after the death of the Archbifhop, treacheroufly murdered his uncle Bernabo, made himfelf fole Prince, and was the firft that took upon him the title of Duke of Milan *. He left two fons, Philip and Giovanni Maria Angelo, the latter of whom was killed by the people of Milan: fo that the government fell into the hands of Philip alone, and he dying without male iffue, the Dukedom was transferred from the Houfe of the Vifconti to that of the Sforza's; the manner and occafion of which fhall be more particularly related in its proper place. In the mean time we muft refume the thread of our narration.

Lewis the Emperor came into Italy to encourage his party and to receive the Crown: and wanting a handle to extort money from the Milanefe, whilft he was there, he pretended he would leave them to en-

* The archbifhop was much fuch another monfter as Ezelino, and the Count was very little better; yet he was called a Saint. Philip de Comines fays, Mem. l. vii. p. 451. That when he was at Pavia, the Carthufians fhewed him his body, at leaft his bones, depofited in a place near the chancel, and higher than the chief altar in their Convent, to which they went up by a ladder; and one of them calling him Saint, he afked him foftly, why he gave him that title, fince he could fee the arms of feveral Cities painted round his tomb, that he had either ufurped, or had no right to? In anfwer to which, the Friar whifpered in his ear, " in this country we give the title of Saint to all from whom we receive any benefit."

joy

joy their former liberties, and actually threw the
Visconti into prison. But afterwards, at the mediation of Castruccio Castracani of Lucca, he released
them, marched forwards to Rome, and made Pietro
della Corvara Antipope, (on purpose to create fresh
troubles and disturbances in Italy) by whose authority and the power of the Visconti, he thought he
should be strong enough to humble his enemies both
in Tuscany and Lombardy. But the death of Castruccio, which happened just at that time, put an
end to his hopes, and gave a fatal turn to his affairs .
for Pisa and Lucca immediately rebelled upon it, and
the Pisans seizing upon the Antipope, sent him prisoner to the Pope in France: so that the Emperor,
despairing of his affairs in Italy, soon quitted it and
returned into Germany. He was hardly gone before
John, King of Bohemia, came into Italy with an
army, at the invitation of the Ghibelines of Brescia,
and took possession both of that city and Bergamo.
The Pope (how well soever he dissembled it) was not
displeased at his coming, and therefore his Legate at
Bologna, privately favoured him, looking upon him
as a proper instrument to prevent the Emperor's return. These proceedings entirely changed the condition and circumstances of Italy : for the Florentines
and King Robert, seeing that the Legate privately
abetted the attempts of the Ghibeline faction, declared
themselves enemies to all such as were favoured by
the Legate and the King of Bohemia : and many
Princes without regard to either faction, associated
themselves with them, amongst whom were the families of Visconti and Scali *, Philip Gonzaga of Mantua, and those of Carrara and Este ; for which the
Pope excommunicated them all, and the King being
terrified at this confederacy, went home again to

---

* These Scali were Princes of Verona, and the ancestors of Joseph
and Julius Cæsar Scaliger, so well known to the world for their great
erudition and many admirable works. Joseph had a patent from the
French King, in which he is acknowledged the right heir to Julius,
and Julius owned as Prince of Verona.

raise

raife more forces. But at his return into Italy with a larger army, he ftill found the enterprize fo difficult that he abandoned it, and marched back into Bohemia, though much to the diffatisfaction of the Legate, leaving garrifons only in Reggio and Modena, and recommending Parma to the care of Marfilio and Pietrio de Roffi, two of the moft powerful men in that city. As foon as he was gone, Bologna likewife entered into the league, and the confederates divided the four cities that ftill adhered to the Church amongft themfelves : the Scali had Parma, the Gonzagi Reggio, the Efti Modena, and Lucca fell to the Florentines. But many differences enfued upon this partition, which, for the moft part, were afterwards compofed by the Venetians.

It may feem ftrange perhaps to fome, that amongft all the other occurrences and revolutions which happened in Italy, I have not made any mention of the Venetians before, although their power and rank place them above any other republic or principality in that country. But to put an end to their wonder, and to fhew my reafons for this omiffion, it is neceffary to look a good way back ; that fo the origin, and foundation of that ftate may be the more clearly known to every one, and what were the motives that fo long reftrained them from interfering in the affairs of Italy.

Attila, King of the Huns, having laid fiege to Aquileia, the inhabitants after an obftinate defence, being reduced to great diftrefs, and defpairing of relief, abandoned the town, and removed with as many of their effects as they could, to fome uninhabited rocks at the extremity of the Adriatic. The Paduans alfo, feeing the fire fo near them, and concluding, that after Aquileia was taken, the next vifit would be to them, carried away their moft valuable goods, together with their wives, children, and old men, to a place called * Rivo Alto upon the fame

* That quarter of the city is ftill called Rialto, where there is one of the fineft arches in Europe thrown over the grand Canal.

coaft,

coaft, leaving the young men, and fuch as were fit to bear arms, for the defence of the city. The inhabitants of Monfelice and the hills about it, being under the fame apprehenfions, likewife retired to other little iflands in that fea. After Aquileia was taken, and Padua, Monfelice, Vicenza, and Verona, facked and deftroyed by Attila, the remainder of the Paduans and the moft confiderable of the reft fettled in the marfhes about Rivo Alto; and all the people round that Province which was anciently called Venetia †, being driven out of their counrry by the fame calamities, joined themfelves with them, forced by neceffity to change their pleafant and fertile habitations for rough and barren rocks, void of all comfort and convenience. However, as their number was large, and their territories but ftrait, they foon made them not only habitable but delightful, and framing wholefome laws and ordinances amongft themfelves, lived fo happily and fecurely, whilft the reft of Italy was torn to pieces, that in a fhort time they became very powerful and refpectable. For, befides the above mentioned inhabitants, many other people reforted to them from the cities of Lombardy, who were driven away from thence by the inhumanity of Clefi, King of the Lombards: by which they grew fo ftrong, that when Pepin, King of France, at the follicitation of the Pope, undertook to drive the Lombards out of Italy, it was ftipulated in the treaty betwixt him and the eaftern Emperor, that the Duke of Benevento and the Venetians fhould not be fubject either to one or the other, but fuffered by both to enjoy their liberties. Befides, as neceffity had fixed their habitation amongft the waters, and they had not lands fufficient to fupply them with the conveniencies of life, it forced them to have recourfe to navigation for fubfiftence: by which they filled their city with fuch variety of merchandize from all parts of the world, that other people who had occafion for

† This country was formerly conquered, and fo named, by a people who came from Vennes, in Bretagne.

it,

it, repaired thither in great numbers to furnifh themfelves. For many years therefore, they had no
thoughts of any further dominion than what might
ferve to facilitate and extend their commerce: for
which purpofe, they bought feveral Ports in Greece
and Syria; and the French often making ufe of their
fhipping to tranfport their forces into Afia, gave them
the Ifland of Candia in return. In this manner, by
degrees, their name became formidable at fea, and
fo much refpected at land, that in almoft all difputes
betwixt the neighbouring States, they were called in
as arbitrators: as it happened in the differences that
arofe betwixt the Confederates about the towns that
were to be divided amongft them; which being referred to the Venetians, Bergamo and Brefcia were
awarded to the Vifconti. But growing more ambitious after a while, they firft feized upon Padua, Vicenza, Trevigi, and then upon Verona, Bergamo,
and Brefci, befides many other cities in Romagna and
the Kingdom of Naples; by which they became fo
confiderable, that not only the Italian Princes, but
thofe on the other fide the mountains grew jealous of
their power, and entered into a league againft them,
which in one day took from them all that they had
been many years in acquiring with infinite induftry
and expence. And though they have lately in our
times recovered part of their former dominions; yet
as they have not likewife regained their ancient
power and reputation, they now lie at the mercy of
others: which indeed is the cafe at prefent of all the
Italian Princes.

The Pontifical chair was filled at this time by Benedict the Twelfth, who looked upon Italy as loft;
and being apprehenfive that Lewis the Emperor
would become abfolute mafter of it, he refolved to
make all fuch his friends there as ufurped any territories that formerly were fubject to the Empire; imagining that the fear of being difpoffeffed of them by
the Emperor, would make them ready to join him
heartily in defending Italy. For this purpofe, he
pub-

publifhed a Decree to confirm all the ufurped titles and eftates in Lombardy to thofe that were then in poffeffion of them : but before this grant had time to operate, he died and was fucceeded by Clement the Sixth. The Emperor therefore obferving how liberally the Pope had difpofed of the States that belonged to the Empire, that he might not be behind hand with him in fuch fort of generofity, likewife gave away all the States which had been ufurped from the Church, to be held of the Empire by the prefent poffeffors. By which donation, Galeotto Malatefta and his brothers became Lords of Rimini, Pefaro, and Fano; Gentile da Varano, of Camerino; Guido da Polenta, of Ravenna; Sinibaldo Ordelaffi, of Forli and Cefena; Giovanni Manfredi, of Faenza; Ludovico Alidofi of Imola; and many more, of other places : fo that of all the lands belonging to the Church, there were hardly any left without a new mafter : which reduced the Church to the low condition it was in till the days of Alexander the Sixth, who, in our times, drove the pofterity of thofe intruders out of their poffeffions, to their utter ruin, and reftored it to its former fplendor and authority.

At the time of this donation, the Emperor was at Trent, and gave out, that he would come into Italy; which was the occafion of great commotions in Lombardy; where the Vifconti made themfelves mafters of Parma. Not long after, Robert King of Naples died, and left only two grand-daughters, (the children of his fon Charles, who died but a little while before) the eldeft of which, Giovanna, or Joan, according to his will was to inherit the crown, on condition that fhe married Andrew his nephew, and fon to the King of Hungary, which fhe did : but they did not live long together, for fhe put him to death, and married Lewis, Prince of Taranto, who was alfo her coufin. Upon which, Andrew's brother Lewis, King of Hungary, came into Italy, with an army, to revenge his death, and drove Giovanna and her hufband out of their Kingdom.

About

About this time, a very memorable event happened at Rome. One * Niccolo di Lorenzo, Chancellor of the Capitol, turned the Senator's out of the city, and affuming the title of Tribune, made himfelf head of that Commonwealth, and reduced it to its ancient form of government, with fo much reputation and appearance of juftice, that not only the neighbouring States, but all Italy, 'fent Ambaffadors to him: and feveral of the remoter Provinces feeing their old Metropolis exert itfelf in this manner, began to lift up their heads again, and fome out of fear, others out of hope, endeavoured to fhew it all manner of refpect. But Niccolò, notwithftanding the extraordinary reputation he had acquired, was foon obliged to quit his new office; for as he found himfelf not equal to fo great a weight, he privately retired without any compulfion, to fhelter himfelf under the wings of Charles, King of Bohemia, who, by the Pope's mandate, had been elected Emperor, in oppofition to Lewis of Bavaria. That Prince, however, inftead of affording him an afylum as he expected, fent him prifoner to Rome, out of complaifance to the Pope, from whom he had received fo great favours. Not long after, one Francifco Baroncegli, in imitation of Niccolò,

---

* His proper name was Niccolò Gabrini di Lorenzo, or Rienzi. There is a circumftantial and very remarkable narrative of this confpiracy, written in French, by the Fathers Brumoy and Cerceau, in 8vo. and publifhed in Englifh about feven or eight years ago: from the preface of which take the following extract : " To be told, that the fon of a fmall Innkeper and of a Wafherwoman, raifed himfelf to fovereign Power, muft appear ftrange : that he did this without any regular gradation, and almoft in an inftant, muft feem ftill ftranger ; that he atchieved this without any patron, and almoft without any affiftance, has yet more of the marvellous : that he did it purely by dint of parts, and fupported what was called, and in the end became really, tyranny, rather by eloquence than force, rifes higher ftill : but when it is added, that being degraded, delivered up to the power againft which he had rebelled, he fhould, by the bare exertion of the fame talents, not only efcape punifhment, but induce that power to deliver him out of prifon, and to replace him in the high ftation from which he had fallen, feems altogether incredible. The following fheets however, undeniably prove that all this actually happened, and much more : fo that in effect, though a true hiftory, it diftances in point of wonder, even the boldeft fictions in Romance."

I

pof-poſſeſſed himſelf of the Tribuneſhip, and once more drove the ſenators out of the city : ſo that the Pope, as the readieſt way to ſuppreſs him, ſet Niccolò at liberty, and not only ſent him to Rome, but rein-ſtated him in his former office : upon which, he re-ſumed the government of the city, and cauſed Fran-ciſco to be put to death. But as the Colonni took offence at his manner of proceeding, he himſelf, not long after, underwent the ſame fate, and the Senators were reſtored to their ancient authority.

In the mean time, the King of Hungary having depoſed Queen Giovanna, returned to his own King-dom. But the Pope, who rather choſe to have the Queen for a neighbour, than that King, ſo contrived matters, that the kingdom was reſtored to her, upon condition, that her huſband Lewis ſhould renounce the title of King, and be content with that of the *Prince of Taranto.* The year 1350 being come, his Holineſs reſolved that the Jubilee, inſtead of being held every hundredth year, as had been ordained by Pope Boniface the Eighth, ſhould be celebrated every fiftieth ; and having paſſed a decree for that purpoſe, the Romans, out of gratitude for ſo great a Bene-faction, conſented that he ſhould ſend four Cardinals to reform their City, and make what Senators he thought fit *. After which he declared Lewis of Ta-

---

* The Jubilee is a feſtival year, celebrated with great ſolemnity by the Romiſh Church, when the Pope grants a plenary indulgence to all Sinners that viſit the Churches of St. Peter and St. Paul at Rome. It was firſt inſtituted, as has been already ſaid, by Boniface VIII. about the year 1300, in favour of ſuch as ſhould come " ad limina Apoſto-lorum ;" and was to return only once in an hundred years, like the Ludi Sæculares of the antient Romans ; at which time, the people were invited by a Cryer, " to come and ſee a fight that no man liv-ing had ever ſeen, or ſhould ſee again." The firſt celebration of it ſo enriched the city of Rome, that it was called the Golden Year ; which induced Clement VI. to reduce the period to fifty years. Ur-ban VI. appointed it to be held every thirty-five years, that being the age of our Saviour when he was crucified : and Sixtus IV. brought it down to every twenty-fifth. Boniface IX. granted the privilege of holding Jubilees to ſeveral Princes and Monaſteries. The Monks of Canterbury had one every fifty years ; when people flocked from all parts, to viſit the tomb of Thomas Becket. They are now become more frequent ; and the Pope grants them as often as the Church, or

ranto, King of Naples again ; and Queen Giovanna, in return for that favour, gave Avignon to the Church, which was a part of her patrimony.

By this time, Luchino Visconti being dead, Giovanni, Archbishop of Milan, remained sole Lord of that city ; and making several wars upon Tuscany, and the neighbouring States, became very considerable. After his decease, the government devolved to his two nephews, Bernabo and Galeazzo : but Galeazzo dying soon after, left his son Giovanni Galeazzo to share the State with his uncle. Charles, King of Bohemia, was now made Emperor, and Innocent the Sixth, Pope ; who, having sent Cardinal Egidius, a

himself, have occasion for them. There is usually one at the inauguration of every new Pontif.

To be entitled to the privileges of the Jubilee, the Bull enjoins fasting, alms, and prayers. It gives a priest full power to absolve in all cases, even in those that are otherwise reserved to the Pope, to commute for vows, &c. in which it differs from a plenary Indulgence. During the time of the Jubilee, all other Indulgences are suspended.

One of our Kings, Edward III. caused his birth-day to be observed in the manner of a Jubilee, when he became fifty years of age, but not before or after. He released all prisoners, pardoned all offences except treason, made good laws, and granted many privileges to the people.

There are particular Jubilees in certain cities, when several of their festivals happen on the same day: at Puy en Velay, for instance, when the feast of the Annunciation happens on Good Friday ; and at Lyons, when St. John Baptist's day falls on the Festival of Corpus Christi. In 1644, the Jesuits celebrated a solemn Jubilee at Rome; that being the centenary, or hundredth year, from the institution of their Order ; and the same Ceremony was observed in all their Convents throughout the world.

Jubileus or Jubilæus, is used amongst the Romanists to signify a Religious that has been fifty years in a monastery, or an Ecclesiastic, who has been in Orders fifty years. Such veterans are dispensed with in some places, from attending Matins, or a strict observation of any other of their rules. The word is also extended to any man that is an hundred years old, and to a possession of fifty. " Si ager non inveniatur in scriptione, inquiratur de senioribus, quantum temporis fuerit cum altero ; & si sub certo Jubilæo manserit sine vituperatione, maneat in æternum"—say the Lawyers.

Petrarch, who was cotemporary with this Pope (Clement VI.) says, he was a very learned man, and makes particular mention of his extraordinary memory, which retained every thing with that exactness, that he had not so much as the power of forgetfulness : and what is still more remarkable, he says, this prodigious memory was acquired by a dangerous fall, the scars of which remained upon his head as long as he lived.

Spa-

Spaniard, into Italy, retrieved the reputation of the Church, by his virtue and good conduct, not only in Rome and Romagna, but all over Italy. He recovered Bologna, which had been ufurped by the Archbifhop of Milan; and forced the Romans to admit a foreign Senator every year, of the Pope's appointment. He made an honourable accommodation with the Vifconti. He routed and took prifoner one John Aguto, or Augut, an Englifhman, who was come into Tufcany with four thoufand forces of that nation, to the affiftance of the Ghibelines. After which, Urban the ¡Fifth fucceeded to the Pontificate, refolved to vifit Italy and Rome itfelf, where Charles the Emperor came to meet him: and, after a ftay of fome months, Charles returned into Bohemia, and the Pope to Avignon.

Gregory the Twelfth * fucceeded Urban, and Cardinal Egidius being now dead, Italy relapfed into its former diftractions, which were chiefly occafioned by a confederacy againft the Vifconti. The Pope therefore fent a Legate into Italy with fix thoufand Bretons, whom he followed in perfon, and brought back his court with him to Rome, in the year 1376, after it had refided in France for the fpace of 71 years. When this Pontif died, Urban the Sixth was created Pope; and not long after, ten of the Cardinals complaining of an unfair Election, chofe Clement the Seventh at Fondi. In the mean time the Genoefe rebelled, after they had lived quietly many years under the government of the Vifconti, and there were great wars betwixt them and the Venetians about the Ifland of Tenedos, in which all Italy by degrees became concerned: and in thefe wars the ufe of Cannon was

---

* Machiavel fays Gregory XII. but it is a miftake; as indeed there are many in all the chronological tables of the Popes: fome inferting the Antipopes, and others omitting them. There are great difputes alfo amongft the learned about the time of the choice and deceafe of feveral Pontifs. Thofe that have wrote the beft upon this fubject, are our two learned Countrymen, Dr. John Pearfon, and Mr. Henry Dodwell, in their differtations upon the Succeffion of the firft Bifhops of Rome, and in the Annales Cyprianici, written by the former.

firſt * introduced, which had been lately invented by the Germans. The Genoeſe prevailed at firſt, and kept Venice blocked up for ſeveral months; but the Venetians got the better in the end, and made an honourable peace with them, by the mediation of the Pope.

In the year 1381 there was a ſchiſm in the Church (as we have ſaid before) and Queen Giovanna took part with the Antipope. Upon which, Pope Urban ſet an invaſion on foot againſt her, and ſent Carlo Durazzo, a deſcendant of the royal houſe of Naples, with an army, into her Kingdom, who ſoon poſſeſſed himſelf of it, and drove her into France; which ſo provoked the King of that nation, that he ſent Lewis of Anjou into Italy to reinſtate the Queen, to force Urban out of Rome, and to ſet up the Antipope. But Lewis dying before all this could be accompliſh-ed, his army diſperſed and returned into France; at which the Pontif took courage and went in perſon to Naples, where he threw nine Cardinals into priſon for having ſided with France and the Antipope. After this, he was affronted with the King for refuſing to make one of his nephews Prince of Capua : but con-cealing his reſentment, he deſired he would give him leave to reſide at Nocera for a while; which being granted, he preſently fortified himſelf there, and be-gan to concert meaſures for depriving him of the whole Kingdom. But the King táking the alarm, advanced againſt Nocera and laid ſiege to it; from whence the Pope, however, made his eſcape and got to Genoa, where he put the Cardinals to † death that were his priſoners, and then returning to Rome,

---

* Larrey makes braſs cannon the invention of J. Owen; and ſays, the firſt that were known in England, were in 1535. Cannon, how-ever, he owns were known long before; and obſerves, that there were five pieces in the Engliſh army at the battle of Creſſi, in 1346, which were the firſt that had been ſeen in France. Mezeray alſo ſays, that King Edward the Third ſtruck a terror ihto the French army, by five or ſix pieces of cannon, as it was the firſt time they had ever ſeen ſuch dreadful engines.

† He cauſed them to be ſewed up in bags, and thrown into the Sea.

created

created twenty-eight new ones to ftrengthen his party.
Carlo went into Hungary, was proclaimed King there,
and died foon after, having left his wife at Naples,
and two children whom he had by her, one named
Ladiflaus, the other Giovanna.

In the mean time, Giovanni Galeazzo Vifconti had
killed his uncle Bernabo, and feized upon the State of
Milan; and not being content with having made himfelf fole mafter of all Lombardy, he formed a defign
upon Tufcany alfo : but juft at a time when he flattered himfelf with the greateft hopes of fucceeding in
that enterprize, and of being afterwards crowned
King of Italy, he died.   Urban the Sixth was fucceeded by Boniface the Ninth, Clement the Seventh,
the Antipope likewife died at Avignon; and Benedict
the Thirteenth was elected in his room.

All this while Italy was full of foldiers of different
nations, as Englifh, Germans, and Bretons ; fome of
them, introduced by thofe Princes, who, upon feveral occafions, and at various times, had been invited
thither, and others fent by the Popes when they refided at Avignon.   With thefe foreign troops the Italian Princes had, for the moft part, carried on their
wars ; till at laft Ludovico da Conto, a native of Romagna, trained up a body of Italians, and called them
St. George's Bands, whofe valour and difcipline much
diminifhed the reputation of the foreigners, and retrieved that of their own countrymen in fuch a manner, that they were afterwards almoft conftantly employed by the Italian Princes in their wars.   The
Pope, upon fome differences that arofe betwixt him
and the Romans, removed to Scefi and continued
there till the Jubilee that happened in the year 1400 :
at which time, the Romans, to invite him back again
for the benefit of their city, once more confented
that he fhould have the annual nomination of a foreign Senator, and be allowed to fortify the Caftle
of St. Angelo.   Upon this condition he returned ;
and, to enrich the Church, he ordained that every Be-
nefice, upon a vacancy, fhould pay the firft fruits,

or one years income, into the Ecclefiaftical Chamber.

After the death of Giovanni Galeazzo, Duke of
Milan, who left two fons, Giovanni-Maria-Angelo,
and Philip, that State was divided into many factions: and in the troubles which enfued, the elder of
them was killed, and Philip for fome time kept prifoner in the caftle of Pavia; from whence he at laft
made his efcape by the favour and affiftance of the
Governor. Amongft others who feized upon cities
that formerly belonged to his Father, was Guglielmo
della Scala, who being banifhed had retired to Francifco da Carrara, Lord of Padua, by whofe aid he
recovered the State of Verona, though he did not
long enjoy it; for the fame Francifco caufed him to
be poifoned and affumed the government thereof himfelf. The péople of Vicenza, therefore, who till
then had lived quietly and fecurely under the protection of the Vifconti, feeing the Lord of Padua
now grown fo powerful, put themfelves under the
wings of the Venetians, who, at their inftigation,
made war upon him and drove him firft out of Verona,
and afterwards out of Padua.

About this time died Pope Boniface, and was fucceeded by Innocent VII. to whom the people of
Rome prefented an addrefs for the reftitution of
their forts and liberties; which being refufed, they
called in Ladiflaus, King of Naples, to their affiftance. But as their differences were afterwards accommodated, the Pope returned to Rome, from
whence he had retired to Viterbo, for fear of the
people; at the latter of which places he created his
nephew Ludovico, Count della Marca, and foon after
died. Gregory XII. fucceeded him, on condition
that he fhould refign the Papacy whenever the Antipope could be prevailed upon to do the fame. In
confequence of this, at the exhortation of the Cardinals, to try whether it was poffible to reunite the
Church, Benedict the Antipope came to Porto Ve-
neri, and Gregory to Lucca, where many expedients
were

were propofed, but nothing concluded: upon which, the Cardinals on each fide deferting them both, Benedict retired into Spain, and Gregory to Rimini. Baldaffare Coffa, therefore, Cardinal and Legate of Bologna, encouraged the Cardinals to call a Council at Pifa, where they chofe Alexander V. who immediately excommunicated King Ladiflaus, difpofed of his Kingdom to Lewis of Anjou, and, in confederacy with the Florentines, Genoefe, Venetians, and Baldaffare Coffa, the Legate, fell upon him and drove him out of Rome. But whilft this war was carrying on with great fury, Alexander died, and Coffa the Legate being made Pope in his ftead, affumed the name of John XXIII. and foon removed to Rome from Bologna (where he had been elected), in order to meet Lewis of Anjou, who was come thither with an army of Provencals. After he had joined him, they marched againft Ladiflaus, engaged, and routed his army; but, through the default of their commanders, they could not purfue their Victory: fo that Ladiflaus foon rallied his forces and recovered Rome, driving the Pope back to Bologna, and Lewis into Provence. The Pope therefore, contriving new means to reduce the power of Ladiflaus, caufed Sigifmund, King of Hungary, to be elected Emperor, invited him into Italy, and had an interview with him at Mantua, where it was agreed betwixt them that a general council fhould be affembled for re-uniting the Church; that fo it might be the better able to oppofe the attempts of its enemies.

There were now three different Popes at the fame time, Gregory, Benedict, and John, which kept the Church very low, both in power and reputation. The place appointed for the meeting of the council was Conftance, a city in Germany, much againft the inclination of Pope John: and though the principal reafon, which had induced the Pope to have recourfe to a council, was removed by the death of Ladiflaus, yet, as he had obliged himfelf to go to it, he could not well tell how to excufe his abfence. However, in

a few

a few months after his arrival at Conſtance, he was
ſenſible of his error when it was too late, and endeavoured to have got privately away from thence; but
being taken, he was impriſoned and forced to reſign
the Papacy. Gregory, one of the Antipopes, alſo
renounced his pretenſions, by an inſtrument drawn up
for that purpoſe; but Benedict, the other, refuſed,
and was condemned as an heretick. At laſt, finding himſelf utterly forſaken by all his Cardinals,
he likewiſe reſigned, and the council choſe Otho, of
the family of Colonni, Pope, who took the name of
Martin V. by which the Church was re-united, after a
ſchiſm that had laſted forty years, and ſeveral different
Pontifs had reigned at the ſame time *.

* Benedict, ſays Voltaire, who had ſhewn much courage before,
and had fought both by ſea and land, was very humble and reſigned
when his ſentence was read to him, in priſon at Manheim, where the
Emperor kept him cloſe confined three years, and cauſed him to be
treated with ſuch ſeverity as rendered him more an object of compaſſion, than his crimes had expoſed him to the public hatred.
    The fathers of the Council did not meet at firſt in order to depoſe
him; their principal view ſeemed to be the reformation of the Church.
This was chiefly the deſign of Gerſon and the other deputies of the
univerſity of Paris. Complaints had been publickly made for the
ſpace of two years againſt the Annats, the Exemptions, the reſer-
vations, and the impoſitions of the Popes upon the clergy, to inrich
the court of Rome; in ſhort, againſt all the vices with which the
Church was at that time disfigured. But how did this reformation
end? His ſucceſſor declared, in the firſt place, that no exemptions
ſhould be granted without cognizance of the cauſe. 2. That the
nature of the Benefices which had been united, ſhould be enquired
into. 3. That the revenues of vacant Benefices ſhould be diſpoſed of
according to law. 4. He made an ineffectual proviſion againſt Simony. 5. He ordained that all ſuch as had Benefices ſhould be
diſtinguiſhed by the Tonſure. 6. He forbad the celebrating of Maſs
in a lay habit. Theſe were the laws made by the moſt ſolemn aſ-
ſembly in the univerſe.—Gerſon, with great difficulty, obtained the
condemnation even of the following propoſitions: That there are
caſes in which the aſſaſſinating a perſon is a virtuous action; far more
meritorious in a Knight than a 'Squire; and ſtill much more ſo in a
Prince than a Knight. This doctrine of aſſaſſination had been publickly maintained by a Cordelier, whoſe name was Jean Petit, upon
the murder of his Prince's own brother. The council for a long time,
evaded Gerſon's petition; but at laſt, they were obliged to condemn
this doctrine of murder, though without mentioning the Cordelier in
particular.
    John Huſs, and Jerome of Prague, were both condemned to the
flames by this Council, for maintaining the doctrines of Wicliff,
who had taught, that we muſt not believe any thing that was im-

Phi-

Philip Vifconti was then (as we have faid) confined in the caftle of Pavia.   But Fantino Cane (who, during the troubles in Lombardy, had made himfelf mafter of Vercelli, Alexandria, Novara, and Tortona, and amaffed great riches) dying without children, left his wife Beatrice heir to his poffeffions ; enjoining his friends to ufe their utmoft endeavours to get her married to this Philip ; by which match he became fo powerful that he recovered Milan and all the reft of Lombardy.   But forgetting all obligations, as Princes ufually do, he accufed his wife Beatrice of adultery, and put her to death : and finding himfelf now very ftrong and potent, he began to think of making war upon Tufcany, in order to execute the defigns that

poffible and contradictory to reafon : that no accident can fubfift without a fubject ; in a word, that the fubftance of bread and wine remains in the Eucharift.   He wanted likewife to abolifh auricular confeffion, indulgences, and the ecclefiaftical hierarchy.   It is remarkable, that the former of thefe two unhappy victims came thither with the Emperor's fafe-conduct.   And the latter, who was his difciple and friend, and a man of much fuperior eloquence and underftanding, (though at firft he had figned a renunciation of his mafter's doctrine) having heard with what magnanimity he had encountered death, was afhamed to furvive him ; he therefore made a public retraction, and was burnt.   Poggio, the Florentine, Secretary to Pope John XIII. and one of the firft reftorers of Letters, who was prefent at his interrogatories and execution, fays, he never heard any thing that fo nearly approached to the eloquence of the Greeks and Romans, as the fpeech which Jerome made to his judges.   " He fpoke, fays he, like a Socrates, and walked to the kindled pile with as much chearfulnefs as the other drank the cup of hemlock."

Out of their afhes arofe a civil war ; for the Bohemians, befides other reproaches, upbraided the Emperor with having violated the law of nations.   And not long after, when Sigifmund afpired to fucceed his brother Wenceflaus, in the kingdom of Bohemia, he found that, though he was Emperor of Germany, and King of Hungary, the death of two private men had precluded his acceffion to the Bohemian throne.   Their avengers were 40,000 men, whom the feverity of the Council had exafperated to fuch a degree, that they killed every prieft they met.   Their General, John, furnamed Zifka, (which fignifies blind of one eye) defeated Sigifmund in feveral battles : and having loft his other eye at laft in an engagement, he ftill continued to head his troops, giving directions to his officers, and affifting in their councils.   He ordered them to make a drum of his fkin after he was dead, which they did ; and thefe very remains of Zifka infpired the Bohemians with fuch courage, and ftruck fuch a terror into the enemy, that it was fixteen years before Sigifmund made himfelf mafter of Bohemia, and then with great difficulty.   Vide Voltaire's Gen. Hift. Vol. I. part. ii. from page 259 to page 373.

F 4   had

had been formed by his father Giovanni Galeazzo. Ladiſlaus, King of Naples, at his death, beſides his Kingdom, had alſo left his ſiſter Giovanna a formidable army commanded by the beſt and moſt experienced Generals in Italy: the chief of whom was Sforza of Contignuola, a perſon of very great fame for his valour and conduct in thoſe wars. She was no ſooner on the throne, but, to clear herſelf of the ſuſpicion of being too intimate with one Pandolphello, whom ſhe had brought up and preferred, ſhe married Giacopo della Marcia, a Frenchman, of royal extraction, upon condition that he ſhould content himſelf with being ſtyled Prince of Taranto, and leave the title and government of the Kingdom entirely to her*. But as ſoon as he arrived at Naples, the ſoldiery acknowledged him as their King; which occaſioned great quarrels and conteſts betwixt him and the Queen, wherein ſometimes one, and ſometimes the other had the better. At laſt, however, the Queen eſtabliſhed herſelf in the government, and became a bitter enemy to the Pope. Upon which, Sforza, to diſtreſs her and force her into a compliance with his own terms, immediately laid down his commiſſion and refuſed to ſerve her any longer. So that being diſarmed, as it were, all on a ſudden, and having no other remedy, ſhe applied for aſſiſtance in this extretremity to Alphonſo, King of Arragon and Sicily, whom ſhe adopted for her ſon: and to command her forces, ſhe took into her pay Braccio da Montone, a ſoldier of no leſs eminence and reputation than Sforza;

* This Giovanna, or Joan, or Jane II. (Queen of Naples) as ſhe is called by different authors, married James of Bourbon, ſon of John Count de la Marche, to her ſecond huſband; who not being able to bear that ſhe ſhould continue her familiarities with Pandolpho Alopo, a handſome young Neapolitan whom ſhe had made her chamberlain, ordered his head to be cut off, and not only deprived her of all ſhare in the adminiſtration, but kept her in a manner locked up, and very ſeldom admitted her either into his company or bed: all which uſage ſhe diſſembled with great artifice, till ſhe found means at laſt to get the upperhand of him and drive him back again into France, where he ended his days in a monaſtery. Brantome. Vies des Dames illuſtres. p. 384. 388.

and

and hated by the Pope for having feized upon and
ufurped Perugia, and feveral other towns that belonged to the Church.   After this, a peace was concluded
betwixt her and the Pope : but Alphonfo fufpecting
fhe would ferve him as fhe had done her hufband,
fecretly took meafures to make himfelf mafter of all
her fortreffes, in which, however, he was prevented;
for as fhe was a woman of great fubtlety and fufpected
his intentions, fhe was before-hand with him, and took
care to fortify herfelf ftrongly in the citadel of Naples.
Jealoufies increafing in this manner, they at laft came
to an open rupture; in the courfe of which, the Queen,
by the affiftance of Sforza, who had returned into
her fervice, got the better of Alphonfo, drove him
out of Naples, entirely difcarded him, and adopted
Lewis of Anjou in his room; which gave rife to new
wars betwixt Braccio, who was now of Alphonfo's
party, and Sforza, who was engaged for the Queen.
In the procefs of thofe wars, Sforza was unfortunately drowned in paffing the river Pefcara : by which
accident the Queen was once more difarmed in a manner, and would in all likelihood have been driven out
of her Kingdom, if fhe had not been affifted by Philip Vifconti, Duke of Milan, who forced Alphonfo
to return into Arragon.   But Braccio not in the leaft
difcouraged at his being abandoned by Alphonfo, ftill
carried on the war againft the Queen, and laid fiege
to Aquila : upon which, the Pope, looking upon
Braccio's greatnefs as likely to be of prejudice to the
Church, took Francifco, fon of the late Sforza, into
his pay; who marching with an army to the relief of
* Aquila, engaged Braccio, and not only routed his
forces, but killed him.   Of Braccio's party there only
remained Otho his fon, from whom the Pope took Perugia, but left him the government of Montone; but
he alfo was killed not long after in Romagna, in the
fervice of the Florentines : fo that of all thofe who

* The capital of Abruzzo, a Province in the Kingdom of Naples,
which borders on the Gulph of Venice.

had

had fought under the banners of Braccio, Niccolò Piccinino was now in the greateſt reputation.

We have thus brought down our narrative in a ſummary manner, almoſt to the times we at firſt propoſed; and as the remainder of that period contains nothing conſiderable, except the war that the Florentines and Venetians were engaged in with Philip, Duke of Milan, which ſhall be related when we come to ſpeak more particularly of Florence; we ſhall proceed no farther in it than juſt to give a ſhort ſketch of Italy, as it then ſtood, with regard to its Princes and military Commanders. Amongſt the principal States, Queen Giovanna the Second held the Kingdom of Naples. Some towns of Ancona, the Patrimony of St. Peter, and Romania, were ſubject to the Church, and ſome to its Vicars, or others, that had ſeized upon them; as Ferrara, Modena, and Reggio, to the family of Eſte; Faenza to the Manfredi; Imola to the Alidoſi; Forli to the Ordelaffi: Rimini and Peſaro to the Malateſti; and Camerino to·the Houſe of Varano. Lombardy was divided betwixt Duke Philip and the Venetians; all the reſt who had had any principality in that angle, being extinct, except the Houſe of Gonzaga, which governed Mantua at that time. The greater part of Tuſcany was under the Florentines: Lucca and Siena alone, lived under their own laws; the former governed by the Guinigi, the latter entirely free. The Genoeſe being ſometimes free, ſometimes under the dominion of the French, and ſometimes of the Viſconti, were of little account, and reckoned amongſt the loweſt and moſt inconſiderable States in Italy. And even thoſe of higher rank did not attend to the management of their wars themſelves, or carry them on with their own proper forces and commanders. Duke Philip confined himſelf chiefly to his apartment, and living a retired life, left all military affairs to be conducted by Commiſſaries. The Venetians, after they had began to get footing on the Continent, diſregarded their fleet, which had made them ſo formidable at

Sea;

Sea; and, like the reft of the Italian States, gave the command of their land forces to Foreigners. The Pope being a Spiritual Prince, and the Sovereign of of Naples a woman, were not fo proper to command in perfon, and therefore were forced to do that by neceffity, which others did out of weaknefs and indifcretion. The Florentines lay under the fame neceffity; for their nobility being extinguifhed by continual difcords, and their Republic governed by fuch as were bred up to a mercantile way of life, they were forced to fubmit to the guidance and conduct of others: fo that the armies of all the Italian States, were in the hands either of petty Princes, or of Adventurers, and Soldiers of Fortune, who had no eftate or dominions of their own; the former of whom accepted thofe commands, not out of any laudable ambition or defire of fame, but merely to fecure themfelves, and to live in greater affluence: and the latter having been bred up to the profeffion of arms from their youth, and confequently not able to turn their hands to any other employment, followed that way of life in hopes of gaining riches and reputation. The moft eminent of thefe were, Carmignuola, Francifco Sforza, Niccolò Piccinino, (who had been educated under Braccio) Agnolo della Pergola, Lorenzo, and Micheletto Attenduli, Tartaglia, Giaccopaccio, Ceccolino da Perugia, Niccolò da Tolentino, Guido Torello, Antonio del Ponte ad Era, and feveral others; amongft whom may be reckoned thofe Lords that have been already mentioned: to whom we may add, the Barons of Rome, the Urfini, the Colonni, and many more Lords and Gentlemen of Naples and Lombardy, who depending altogether upon war for their fubfiftence, had formed a fort of combination, or private correfpondence amongft themfelves, and reduced it into a trade, or fyftem, as it were; which was fo dexteroufly managed by them, that when two States were at war, they were both almoft fure to be lofers at the end of it: by which means the art of war at laft became fo mean and contemptible, that
any

any common Captain, who had had but the leaſt ſpark
of ancient valour, diſcipline, or experience, would
have held thoſe very Gentlemen in the higheſt de-
riſion, who were then ſo ſtupidly admired and idolized
by all Italy.   The exploits of theſe lazy inactive
Princes, and their pitiful Commanders, will be the
chief ſubject of the following Hiſtory.   But before I
proceed any farther, I muſt, according to my promiſe, in the firſt place, deduce the Republic of Florence from its original, in order to give the Reader a
clear view of its ſtate and condition in thoſe times,
and ſhew by what means that city arrived at it, after
the troubles and diſtractions in which Italy had been
involved for the ſpace of a thouſand years.

END OF THE FIRST BOOK.

Standard-bearer, appointed. The Nobility exhorted to
peace.

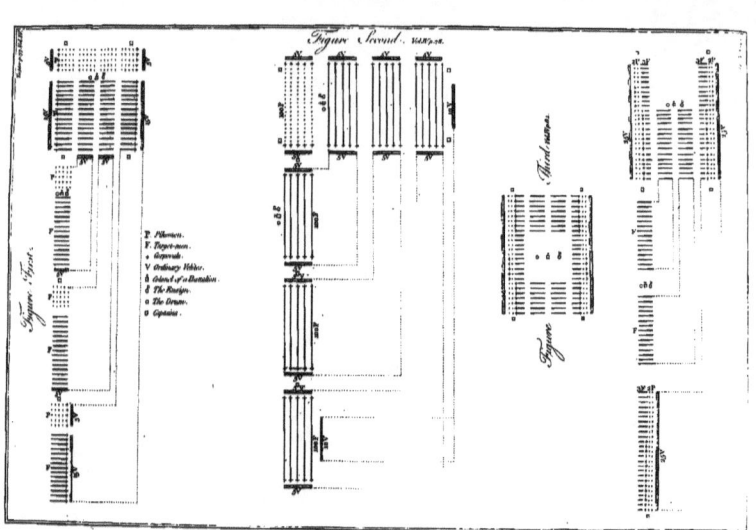

Figure Second. Vol.II.p.120.

Figure First.

P. Pikemen.
F. Bayo-men.
* Corporals.
V. Ordinary Filites.
B. Colonel of a Battalion.
E. The Ensign.
o The Drum.
D Captain.

Figure Third.

THE

HISTORY

OF

FLORENCE.

BOOK II.

ARGUMENT.

*The utility of Colonies. The original of Florence. Whence
it took its name. The first division that happened in
the City. The rise of the Guelph and Ghibeline factions. Their re-union, and the form of government
established in Florence. The institution of the Anziani,
the Captain of the People, and the Podestà. Their
forces and generosity in time of war. Manfred, King
of Naples, chief Patron of the Ghibelines. The Pa-
triotism of Farinata Uberti. Charles of Anjou called
into Italy by the Pope. A reform of the State in Florence. Fresh commotions. The government new modelled by the Guelphs. The twelve* Buonhuomini *and
the* Credenza *appointed.* Gregory X. *Pope.* Florence
under Excommunication. Innocent V. *succeeds Gregory.
The jealousy of the Popes.* Nicholas III. *Pope. The
Ghibelines return from banishment.* Martin, *a Frenchman, elected Pope. The Government reformed by the
Citizens. The institution of three* Priori *to govern for
two months, and to be chosen indifferently out of the
Citizens. The* Signiory. *Discords betwixt the Nobility and the People. A* Gonfaloniere di Giustizia, *or
Standard-bearer, appointed. The Nobility exhorted to
peace.*

peace. The fame admonitions given to the People. Another reform in Florence in the year 1298. *A great quarrel in the family of the* Cancellieri; *the occafion and confequences of it. They divide into two factions, diftinguifhed by the names of* Bianchi *and* Neri, *i. e.* Whites *and* Blacks. *Their Chiefs and Partifans.* Charles *of* Valois *made Governor of Florence. New troubles occafioned by Corfo* Donati; *fomented by the* Medici *and* Giugni. *A great fire in Florence,* 1304. Corfo Donati *condemned as a rebel; his death. Frefh divifions. The tyranny and cruelty of* Lando d' Agobbio. *The fuccefs of* Caftruccio Caftracani. *A* Council of the Signiory *to laft forty months. Election of the magiftrates by* Imborfation. Ramondo da Cardona, *general of the Florentine army; his bad conduct, defeat, and death. The Duke of* Athens, *Deputy-governor of Florence. The Emperor,* Lewis *of* Bavaria, *called into Italy. The death of* Caftruccio *and the* Duke of Calabria. *A new model of Government. The Florentines quiet at home. Their new buildings. Their tranquillity difturbed. A Captain of the guards appointed.* Maffeo da Maradi *prevents an engagement betwixt the factions in Florence, by his mediation.* Lucca *fold to the Florentines; and taken from them by the* Pifans. *The Duke of* Athens *made Governor of Florence. The fpeech of one of the Signiory to him. His anfwer. He is made Sovereign by the people. His violent manner of procceding.* Matteo di Morozzo *difcovers a plot to him. Three confpiracies on foot againft him at the fame time. An infurrection in Florence. The Duke is expelled. His character. Another reform. The Nobility turned out of their offices. The bold attempt of* Andrea Strozzi. *The Nobles endeavour to recover their authority. The people take arms and utterly fupprefs them.*

AMONGST other wife and noble inftitutions of former Kingdoms and Republics, which are difcontinued in our times, it was the cuftom to build new towns and cities upon every proper opportunity.
And

And indeed nothing is more worthy of a great and good Prince, or a well regulated Common-wealth, nor more for the intereſt and advantage of a Province, than to eſtabliſh ſuch communities, where men may live together for greater convenience, either of cultivating the earth, or of mutually aſſiſting and defending each other : and this they uſually effected, by ſending ſome of their own ſubjects to inhabit ſuch countries as they had either conquered or found unpeopled. Such ſettlements were called Colonies, and ſerved not only to beautify and meliorate the face of the country, by building new towns, but to render it more ſecure to the Conqueror, by filling the void places, and making a proper diſtribution of the people through every part of it. Thus, living with greater comfort and convenience, the inhabitants multiplied faſter, and were more able to invade others, or defend themſelves. But this cuſtom being now laid aſide, either by the ſupineneſs or bad policy of Princes and Republics, ſome Provinces are become exceeding weak, and others totally ruined. For this Order alone ſecures a Country and fills it with people. It ſecures it, becauſe a Colony planted by a Prince in a Country newly conquered, is a ſort of a garriſon to check and keep the natives in obedience. Beſides, without it, no Province could long continue properly inhabited, nor preſerve a juſt diſtribution of the people : for as all parts of it cannot be equally fertile or healthful, men will naturally abandon the barren places, and are carried off by diſtempers in thoſe that are unwholſome; ſo that except ſome way can be found to invite freſh ſettlers from the other quarters, to inhabit both the one and the other, that Province muſt ſoon be ruined; as the abandoning ſome places leaves them deſolate, and crowding too large numbers into others, exhauſts and impoveriſhes them. And ſince theſe inconveniencies are not to be remedied by nature alone, art and induſtry muſt be applied : for we ſee many countries that were at firſt unhealthful, much altered when they come to be in-

I   habited

habited by a multitude of people, the earth being purified by tillage, and the air by their fires; which, without that affiftance, nature only could never have effected.   Of this, Venice is a remarkable inftance: for though it was built in a fenny and unwholfome fituation, the concourfe of fo many people at one time foon made it healthful.   Pifa likewife, on account of the badnefs of its air, was very thinly inhabited, till the Geonefe were driven out of their territories by the Saracens, and flocked thither in fuch numbers, that it foon became a populous and powerful city.   But fince the cuftom of fending out Colonies is now out of fafhion, new conquefts are not fo eafily maintained, void places not fo foon filled, nor thofe that are too much crouded fo readily difburthened.   From whence it comes to pafs, that many places in the world, and particularly in Italy, are now become defolate and unpeopled, in comparifon of what they were in former ages; the true caufe of which failure is, that Princes have now no appetite for true glory, and Commonwealths no longer obferve the laudable cuftoms and inftitutions they anciently ufed to do.

In former times, I fay then, many new Cities were founded, and feveral that had been built before, much enlarged by Colonies.   The city of Florence, to give a particular example, was begun by the inhabitants of Fiefole, and augmented by the people they were continually fending thither.   It is certain, if Dante and Giovanni Villani are to be credited, that the Citizens of Fiefole, which is fituated upon the top of a hill, marked out a plot of ground upon the plain that lies betwixt the fkirts of that hill and the river Arno, for the conveniency of merchants; that fo their goods might be conveyed thither with lefs difficulty, and their markets better frequented.   Thefe merchants, I fuppofe, firft built warehoufes in that place to ftow their goods in, which, in courfe of time, became a fettled habitation.   But when the Romans had fecured Italy againft foreign invafions, by the deftruction of Carthage, they began to multiply exceedingly: fo

mer

men will not live any longer in want and diftrefs than they are compelled to it, by abfolute neceffity : and though the terrors of war may force them for a while to take fhelter in defart mountains, and inacceffible places ; yet, when the danger is blown over, comfort and convenience allure them back again, and they naturally return to places that are more. habitable and commodious. The fecurity, therefore, which was eftablifhed in Italy, by the reputation of the Roman arms, might poffibly be the occafion that this place increafed fo faft from fo fmall a beginning, that it foon came to be a town, which at firft was called Villa Arnina.

After this, there arofe civil wars in Rome betwixt Marius and Sylla, then betwixt Cæfar and Pompey, and laftly betwixt the affaffins of Cæfar and thofe that undertook to revenge his death. Sylla was the firft, and after him, the three Roman citizens who revenged the death of Cæfar and divided the Empire, that fent colonies to Fiefole ; all, or the greater part of which, fettled in a plain not far from the town which was already begun : fo that by this addition, the place became fo full of buildings and inhabitants, and fuch provifions were made for a civil government, that it might well be reckoned amongft the cities of Italy. But whence it took the name of Florence is not fo clearly known. Some will have it, that it was fo called from Florino, one of the chiefs of the colony. Others fay, it was not called Florentia, but Fluentia at firft, from its being fituated fo near the ftream of the Arno ; and to fupport their affertion they produce the teftimony of Pliny, who fays †, " The Fluentines are feated upon the banks of the Arno." But that feems to be an error, becaufe Pliny is there fpeaking of the fituation, not the name, of the Florentines ; and the word Fluentini is moft probably a corruption of the text, fince Frontinus and Tacitus, two writers that were nearly cotemporary with Pliny, call the

† Nat. Hift. l. iii. c. 25.

town Florentia and the people Florentines : and it is
certain, that in the time of Tiberius, they were governed by the fame laws and authority that the reft
of the cities in Italy were then fubject to. Of which
we fee a proof in Tacitus †, who relates, that the
Florentines fent deputies to petition the Emperor that
he would not fuffer their country to be ruined by
turning the ftream of the river Clanis upon it, as was
defigned : and it is abfurd to fuppofe that city fhould
have two names at the fame time. It is my opinion,
therefore, whatever might be the occafion of its original or denomination, that it was always called Florentia. It was founded under the Roman Empire,
and began to be mentioned in Hiftory in the time of
the firft Emperors : and when the Empire was over-
run by Barbarians, Totila, King of the Oftrogoths,
took and demolifhed Florence. Two hundred years
after which, it was rebuilt by Charlemagne, from
whofe time, till the year 1215, it followed the fortune of thofe that fucceffively had the rule in Italy;
for, during that period, it was governed firft by the
pofterity of Charlemagne, afterwards by the Berengarii, and laft of all by the German Emperors, as we
have already fhewn in our fummary of the affairs of
Italy.

In thofe days, the Florentines being under the dominion of foreigners, were not able either to extend
their boundaries, or to perform any thing worthy of
relation, except, that on St. Romulus's day, in the
year 1010, which the Fiefolans obferved as a folemn
feftival, they took and deftroyed Fiefole, availing
themfelves either of the connivance of the Emperors,
or the opportunity that was afforded them by the inter-
regnum betwixt the death of one Emperor and the
election of another. But afterwards, when the Popes
affumed greater authority in Italy, and the power of
the German Emperors was upon the wane, all the
towns of that province began to govern themfelves,

† Annal. lib. i. ad finem.

and

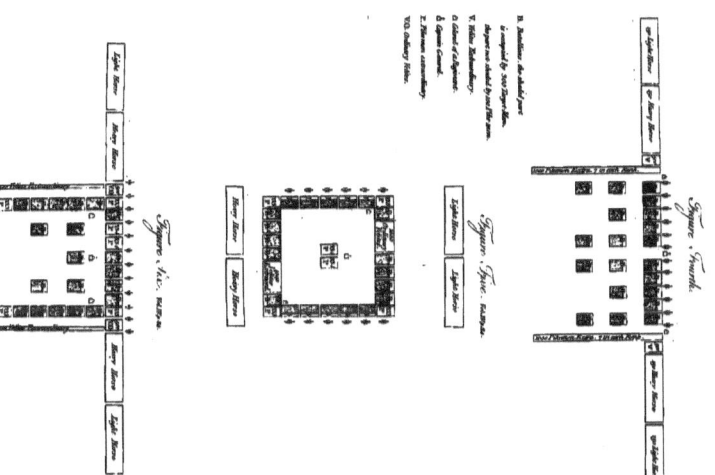

150 Light Horse

affumed greater authority in Italy, and the power of
the German Emperors was upon the wane, all the
towns of that province began to govern themfelves,

† Annal. lib. i. ad finem.

and

and fhewed but little regard to their Princes: fo that in the year 1080, Italy was in a manner divided betwixt Henry the Third and the Church. Notwithftanding which, the Florentines always fubmitting to the Conqueror, and aiming at nothing further than their own prefervation, kept themfelves quiet and undivided till the year 1215. But as it is obferved, that the later difeafes make their approach, the more dangerous and mortal they commonly are to the human body: fo the longer it was before Florence was feized by the paroxyfms of faction, the more fatal they proved when it did happen. The caufe of its firft Divifion is very well known, as it has been already related by Dante and feveral other Writers: however, I fhall give a fhort account of it.

The greateft and moft powerful families in Florence at that time, were the Buondelmonti and the Uberti; and next to them, the Amadei and Donati. In the family of the Donati there was a very rich widow Lady, who had a daughter of remarkable beauty. This Lady had refolved with herfelf to marry her daughter to Meffer Buondelmonte, a young Cavalier, who was then head of that family; but either out of negligence, or becaufe fhe thought it was yet in good time, fhe had not communicated her defign to any body: fo that before fhe was aware, young Buondelmonte had engaged himfelf to a daughter of the Houfe of Amadei, at which the old Lady was exceedingly difappointed and chagrined. But as fhe entertained fome hopes that her daughter's beauty might ftill have power enough to break the match, feeing him come alone one day towards her houfe, fhe went to the door with her daughter to falute him as he paffed by, and amongft other compliments told him, " She could not help fincerely rejoicing when fhe heard he was going to be married, though, indeed, fhe had till then kept her own daughter fingle (whom fhe prefented to him) in hopes that fhe fhould have been his Bride." The young Gentleman, ftruck with her extraordinary beauty, and confidering that

her

her family and fortune were not inferior to that of
the Lady to whom he was contracted, grew so enamoured of her, that, without reflecting upon the engagement he was under, the baseness he should be
guilty of in breaking it, or the consequences that
might ensue, he immediately replied, " Madam,
since you have reserved her for me, and it is not yet
too late, I should be very ungrateful to reject such an
offer ;" and presently after was married to her. But,
as soon as the wedding was made public, it so exasperated the Amadei and Uberti, who were nearly allied to the Donati, that after a consultation amongst
themselves and several other relations, it was resolved, that the affront was too grievous to be put
up, and could not be sufficiently attoned for, but by
the death of young Buondelmonte ; and though some
desired them to consider the consequences, Moscha
Lamberti replied, " those who considered every thing,
would never conclude upon any thing," adding the
old proverb, *Cosa fatta capá hà*, " when a thing is
once done, there is an end of it." The fact being
thus determined upon, the execution of it was left
to the said Moscha, Stiatta Uberti, Lambertuccio
Amadei, and Oderigo Fifanti. Accordingly, on the
morning of Easter-day, being posted in the houses of
the Amadei, betwixt the old Bridge and St. Stephen's, as Messer Buondelmonte was passing the river
on horseback, without fear or suspicion, (as if he
thought the affront would have been as easily for-
gotten as the match had been broken) they set upon
him at the foot of the Bridge, and killed him, close
by a Statue of Mars, which then stood there. This
murder divided the whole city, one part of it siding
with the Buondelmonti, the other with the Uberti ;
and as both the families were very powerful in alliances, castles, and adherents, the quarrel continued
many years before either of them could entirely get
the better of the other: for though their animosities
could not be utterly extinguished by a firm and last-
ing reconciliation, yet they were often palliated and

com-

compofed for a while by truces and ceffation of hoftilities; by which manner of proceeding, as new accidents and events happened, they were fometimes quiet, and fometimes at variance. In this ftate Florence continued till the reign of the Emperor Frederick the Second, who being likewife King of Naples, and defirous to ftrengthen himfelf againft the Church, and eftablifh his intereft more fecurely in Tufcany, thought it no bad expedient to join the Uberti and their party, who, by his affiftance, were enabled to drive the Buondelmonti out of Florence; and thus that city (as all the reft in Italy were before) became divided into the two Factions of * Guelphs and

---

* Machiavel fays, in the firft book of this Hiftory, that Piftoia was the firft place where thefe names of diftinction were ufed. But other authors fay that the words Guelph and Ghibeline derive their original from a fchifm which difturbed the Church in the year 1130, occafioned by the competition betwixt the two Popes Innocent II. and Anaclete. The greater part of Chriftendom acknowledged Innocent, who was ftrenuoufly fupported by the Weftern Emperor. Anaclete, the Antipope, had the countenance and affiftance of Roger, Count of Naples and Sicily, a martial Prince, defcended from the Normans, who had conquered that country. The pretence of this double election having kept a war on foot eight years together, in which Roger, for the moft part, had the advantage, the Emperor Conrade III. himfelf marched into Italy, at the head of an army of Germans, leaving his fon Prince Henry to follow him. Roger therefore, to oppofe him with forces of his own nation, prevailed upon Guelph, Duke of Bavaria, to come to his affiftance. During the courfe of this war, which began in the year 1139, it fometimes happened, tHat the Emperor's army was commanded by the faid Prince Henry, who was brought up at the village of Ghibeline in Germany, the fituation of which being exceeding pleafant made him particularly fond of it.— One day, when the armies on each fide were drawn up, and ready to engage, the Bavarians, out of compliment to their general, cried out, a Guelph, a Guelph; and the Emperor's troops, on the other hand, fhouted a Ghibeline, a Ghibeline. Thefe words feeming barbarous to the Italians that were in Roger's army, they came to Guelph to know the meaning of them, who told them, that the Pope's party were meant by the word Guelph; and the Emperor's, by Ghibeline: from whence thofe names became fo common in both armies, that the Qui vive, or challenge given by Centinels at their pofts, was generally, who goes there ? a Guelph, or a Ghibeline ? and they were appropriated to the Italians, according to their refpective fides. At firft, indeed, they were ufed only to diftinguifh Anaclete's party from the Emperor's: but afterwards, Roger having vanquifhed Pope Innocent, and taken him prifoner, he obliged him, at the price of his liberty, to erect the countries of Naples and Sicily into Kingdoms: by which treaty, Roger being taken off from the intereft of the Anti-

G 3   Ghi-

Ghibelines. It may not be amifs, therefore, to relate what families adhered to each party. Thofe that followed the Guelphs, were the Buondelmonti, Nerli, Roffi, Frefcobaldi, Mozzi, Baldi, Pulci, Gherardini, Forabofchi, Bagnefi, Guidalotti, Sacchetti, Manieri, Lucardefi, Chiaramonti, Compiobefi, Cavalcanti, Giandonati, Gianfigliazzi, Scali, Gualterotti, Importuni, Boltichi, Tornaquinci, Vecchietti, Tofinghi, Arrigucci, Agli, Sizii, Adimari, Vifdomini, Donati, Pazzi, Della Bella, Ardinghi, Teobaldi, and Cerchi. Thofe that took part with the Ghibelines were the Uberti, Mannelli, Ubriachi, Fifanti, Amadei, Infanganti, Malefpini, Scolari, Guidi, Galli, Capprardi, Lamberti, Soldanieri, Cipriani, Tofchi, Amieri, Palermini, Miglioreili, Pigli, Barucci, Cattani, Agolanti, Brunellelchi, Caponfachi, Elifei, Abbati, Tadaldini, Guiochi, and Gal'gai, to which noble families on each fide, great numbers of the commor people joined themfelves; fo that the whole city in ɛ manner was divided betwixt thefe two parties.

The Guelphs being thus forced out of the city retired into that part of the vale which lies higher uʃ the river Arno, where möft of their ftrong places anc dependences lay, and defended them as well as the could, againft the forces of their enemies. But whei Frederick died, thofe few who ftood neuter, havinʃ great intereft and reputation amongft the people thought it much better to reunite the city, if pof fible, than to ruin it by fomenting the Divifion: fo which purpofe, they at laft prevailed upon th Guelphs to forgive the injuries and difgrace they hac fuffered, and to return; and upon the Ghibelines, tɛ forget the caufe of their former animofities, and tɛ receive them. After they were reunited in this man

pope, and engaging heartily with the Church, affixed the name c Guelph to the Pope's party, and confirmed that of Ghibeline to th faction of the Emperor.
These two factions were in the height of their emulation two hur dred years after, that is to fay, about the year 1320, which was ver near the time that Caftruccio Caftracani was in his higheft profperit; Biondo. Sigonius.

nei

ner, they judged it a proper time to take fome meafures for the recovery of their liberty, and to provide for their common defence, before the new Emperor grew ftrong enough to prevent it.   With this
view they divided the city into fix parts, and chofe
twelve citizens, two to govern each ward, with the
title of Anziani, but to be changed every year.   To
prevent any feuds or difcontents that might arife
from the determination of judiciary matters, they
conftituted two judges that were not Florentines, (one
of whom was ftyled, the Captain of the People, and
the other the Podeftà) to adminifter juftice to the
people, in all caufes civil and criminal.   And fince
Laws are but of little authority and fhort duration,
where there is not fufficient power to fupport and enforce them, they raifed twenty Bands or Companies
in the city, and feventy-fix more in the reft of their
territories, in which all the youth were enlifted, and
obliged to be ready armed under their refpective colours, whenever they were required fo to be by the
Captain of the Anziani.   And as their colours were
different, fo were their weapons; fome of them ufing
crofs-bows, and others being armed with fwords and
targets.   Their Enfigns or Standard-bearers were
changed every year with great formality at Whitfun-
tide, and frefh officers appointed to command the
whole.   To add more dignity and refpect to their
army, and provide a fort of Head-colours to which
every one might repair when he was driven out of
the battle, to fhelter himfelf, and make head afrefh
againft the enemy, they ordered a large carriage, covered with red trappings, to be drawn along with it,
by two oxen, upon which a red and white ftandard
was difplayed.   And whenever their forces were to be
drawn out, this Carriage was brought into the Mercato Nuovo, or New Market, and delivered to the
Captains of the people with much ceremony.   And
for the greater folemnity in their military expeditions,
they had a bell called Martinella, which was tolled
for a month together without ceafing, before they

took

took the field, that the enemy might have time to provide for their defence: for such a spirit of generosity then prevailed amongst them, and with so much magnanimity did they behave, that though, now indeed, it is reputed laudable and good policy to attack an Enemy unprepared, it was looked upon in those days as base and treacherous. This Bell was always carried along with their armies when they marched; and by it, their signals for posting and relieving guards and centinels, and other warlike operations were regulated.

By such discipline in their civil and military affairs, the Florentines laid the foundation of their liberty; and it is hardly to be conceived, how much strength and authority they acquired in a very short time: for their city not only became the capital of Tuscany, but was reckoned amongst the principal in Italy; and indeed there is no degree of grandeur to which it might not have attained, if it had not been obstructed by frequent and almost continual discords and divisions. For the space of ten years they lived under this form of government; during which time, they forced the States of Pistoia, Arezzo, and Siena, to enter into a confederacy with them, and in their return with their army from the last city, they took Volterra, demolished several castles, and brought the inhabitants to Florence. In all these expeditions, the Guelphs had the chief direction and command, as they were much more popular and powerful than the Ghibelines, who had behaved themselves so imperiously in the reign of Frederick, when they had the upper hand, that they were become very odious to the people; and because the party of the Church was generally thought to favour their attempts to preserve their liberty, whilst that of the Emperor endeavoured to deprive them of it.

The Ghibelines, in the mean time, finding their authority so dwindled, were not a little discontented, and only waited for a proper opportunity to seize upon the government again. Seeing therefore, that

Man-

Manfred, the Son of Frederick, King of Naples, had eftablifhed himfelf in the poffeffion of that Kingdom, and fufficiently reduced the power of the Church, they thought the juncture not unfavourable for the execution of their defigns, and entered into a private correfpondence with him in hopes of his affiftance: but for want of due fecrecy in thefe practices, they were difcovered by the Anziani, who thereupon fummoned the Uberti to appear before them. But inftead of obeying, they took up arms and fortified themfelves in their houfes: at which the people were fo incenfed that they likewife ran to arms, and by the help of the Guelphs obliged the whole party of the Ghibelines to quit Florence and tranfport themfelves to Siena. There they fued for aid to Manfred, who granted it, and the Guelphs were defeated upon the banks of the River Arbia, with fuch flaughter (by the King's forces under the conduct of Farinata degli Uberti) that thofe who efcaped from it, giving up their city for loft, fled directly to Lucca, and left Florence to provide for itfelf. Manfred had given the command of the auxiliaries which he fent to the Ghibelines, to Count Giordano, a foldier of no fmall reputation in thofe times. This Giordano, after his victory, immediately advanced with the Ghibelines to Florence, and not only forced the city to acknowledge Manfred for its fovereign, but depofed the Magiftrates, and either entirely abrogated, or altered all laws and cuftoms that might look like remains of their former liberty; which being executed with great rigour and infolence, enflamed the people to fuch a degree, that if they did not love the Ghibelines before, they now became their inveterate and implacable enemies; which averfion continually increafing, at laft proved their utter deftruction.

Giordano being obliged to return to Naples upon affairs of great confequence to that Kingdom, left Count Guido Novello, Lord of Cafentino, at Florence, as deputy for the King there; who called a
Coun-

Council of the Ghibelines at Empoli, in which it was unanimoufly refolved, that in order to maintain their power in Tufcany, it was neceffary to demolifh Florence entirely, as the people were fuch rigid Guelphs there, that it was the only city capable of fupporting the declining party of the Church. There was not fo much as one citizen or friend that had courage enough to oppofe this cruel fentence upon fo noble and magnificent a city, except Farinata Uberti, who openly and boldly protefted againft it, declaring that he had not undergone fo much fatigue, nor expofed himfelf to fo many dangers, but to live quietly afterwards at home; nor was he then in a humour to reject what he had fo long and earneftly fought for, or to flight the favours which good Fortune at laft had granted him: that on the contrary he was determined to exert himfelf againft any one who fhould go about to prevent it, with as much zeal and vigour as he had done againft the Guelphs; and that if either mean jealoufy or cowardice fhould prompt-them to endeavour the ruin of their city, they might attempt it if they pleafed, but he hoped he fhould be able to defend it with the fame valour that had driven out his former enemies.—Farinata was a man of great courage, an excellent foldier, head of the Ghibeline faction, and in fo much efteem with Manfred himfelf, that his authority alone quafhed the effects of that refolution, and put them upon confidering of new ways and means to keep themfelves in poffeffion of the government.

The Guelphs, in this interval, who had taken refuge in Lucca, being defired to withdraw out of that city by the Lucchefe, at the threats of the Count, retired to Bologna; from whence they were invited by their friends at Parma, to join them againft the Ghibelines in thofe parts, and behaved fo well there that after they had conquered them, they had their poffeffions given them as a reward for their valour So that having in fome meafure recovered their ftrength and reputation, and hearing that Pope Clement had
* called

called Charles of Anjou into Italy, to depofe Manfred if poflible, they fent Deputies to his Holinefs
with a tender of their fervice, which the Pope not
only accepted, but fent them a ftandard which the
Guelphs carried ever after in their wars, and is ufed
by the Florentines at this time.

After this Manfred was not only defeated by
Charles, but deprived of his Kingdom and flain * :
and as the Guelphs of Florence had no fmall fhare in
that action, their party grew daily bolder and more
vigorous, and that of the Ghibelines ftill weaker and
weaker.   Upon which, Count Guido Novello, and
thofe that were left in commiffion with him to govern Florence, refolved to try if it was poffible by
lenity and gentler treatment, to recover the affections
of the people, whom they found they had exafperated to the laft degree by their oppreffive and violent
manner of proceeding.   But thofe favours, which, if

* This Manfred was a baftard fon of the Emperor Frederick II. It
is faid, he fmothered his father in his bed; and afterwards caufed
Conrade, fon of the faid Emperor, to be poifoned.   Conrade left a
fon, whofe name was Conradine, to whom Manfred made himfelf
guardian.   At laft he poffeffed himfelf of the kingdom of Sicily,
which he governed eleven years in conftant troubles and divifions.
He quarrelled with Pope Innocent IV. carried the war into his dominions, and routed his forces in December 1254, by the help of the
Saracens of Lauria.   Afterwards he took the country of Fondi from
the Church, and was excommunicated by the Popes Urban IV. and
Clement IV. the former of which Pontifs called Charles of Anjou into
Italy, and invefted him with the Kingdoms of Naples and Sicily, in
order to make war upon Manfred, as an enemy to the Church.   It is
reported, that he made an overture of peace to Charles; to which
that Prince returned the following anfwer: Ite & renunciate Sultano
Lucerino (fo he called Manfred, with whom the Saracens of Lauria or
Luceria had joined themfelves) me vel brevi ipfum in infernum detrufu-
rum, vel ipfum me in paradifum collocaturum.   " Go and tell the Sultan
of Luceria, that I will very foon either fend him to hell, or he fhall
fend me to Heaven."   Accordingly they came to an engagement on
the plain of Benevento, February 26, 1266; in which Manfred loft
his life, and was found covered all over with blood and dirt.   He was
thrown into a ditch near the Bridge of Benevento, becaufe he was
excommunicated, and afterwards, as a modern author fays, Pope
Clement caufed his body to be carried out of the Church-lands.
Manfred had given his daughter Conftantia in marriage to Peter III.
of Arragon, in the year 1262; and upon this match, the Princes of
that family founded their pretenfions to the kingdom of Naples.   Collenucio. Hift. Neap.

they

they had been properly applied, and before they
were extorted by neceffity, might poffibly have had
a good effect, were now conferred with fo bad a
grace, that inftead of doing them any fervice, they
only contributed to haften their ruin.　To cajole and
ingratiate themfelves with the people, they thought
it would be fufficient if they gave them back fome
part of thofe privileges and that authority which they
had robbed them of.　For which purpofe, they chofe
fix and thirty citizens out of the people of Florence,
and two gentlemen of higher rank from amongft their
friends at Bologna, to whom they gave a commiffion
to reform the State as they pleafed.　Thefe Dele-
gates, at their firft meeting, divided the city into
diftinct Arts or Trades, over each of which they conftituted a Magiftrate, who was to adminifter juftice to
all that were in his department; and to every art a
feparate banner was affigned, under which they might
affemble in arms whenever the fafety of the public
required it.　At firft thefe Arts or Companies were
twelve, feven greater, and five lefs : but the lefs being afterwards augmented to fourteen, the whole number amounted to twenty-one, and continue fo to be at
prefent.

The reformers proceeding to make other alterations
likewife for the common good, Count Guido, who
thought himfelf obliged to make fome provifion for
his foldiers, caufed a tax to be laid upon the citizens
for that purpofe, but met with fo much oppofition
in the matter, that he never durft ufe any compulfive
means to collect it.　So that perceiving all would be
loft, if he did not take fome meafures to prevent it,
he held a private confultation with the chiefs of the
Ghibeline faction, in which it was refolved to take
that back again from the people which he had fo in-
confiderately given them; and if it fhould be neceffary, even by force of arms.　Accordingly, when he
thought he had made fufficient preparations for the
execution of his defign, he took an opportunity of
raifing a tumult whilft the thirty-fix reformers were

fitting;

fitting; at which they were fo frighted that they retired to their houfes. But the enfigns of the feveral
arts being immediately difplayed, the people repaired
to them in arms, and underftanding that Count Guido
and his party were at St. John's, they made a ftand
near Trinity Church, and chofe Giovanni Soldanieri
for their leader. The Count, on the other hand,
having notice where they had pofted themfelves, inftantly advanced to attack them ; and the people not
declining an engagement, they met near a place that
is now called la Loggia dè Tornaquinci, where the
Count was worfted and moft of his party flain.
Daunted at this repulfe, and apprehenfive that the
enemy would fall upon him again in the night and
murder him, now he had fo few forces to truft to,
and thofe beaten and difmayed, he refolved to fave
himfelf by flight ; and his fears were fo violent that,
even contrary to the perfuafion of the heads of the
Ghibeline party, he retired in all hafte to Prato, with
what men he had left. However, as foon as he found
himfelf in a place of fecurity and had recovered his
fpirits, he was fenfible of his error ; and being defirous to retrieve his reputation, he marched back
early the next morning to Florence, in hopes of regaining that with honour which he had loft with
fo much ignominy. But he was difappointed in that
defign alfo ; for though perhaps it might have been
very difficult to drive him out of the city, the people
found it no hard matter to keep him out when he
was fo : fo that he was forced to draw off once more
with infinite difgrace and chagrin to Cafentino, and
the Ghibelines retired to other towns that were of their
party.

The people having thus got the upper hand, refolved to unite the city again if poffible, and by the
advice of thofe that wifhed well to the commonwealth,
to recall all fuch citizens as had been forced to leave
their homes, whether they were Guelphs or Ghibelines. In confequence of which, the Guelphs returned, fix years after they had been banifhed, the

late

late attempt of the Ghibelines was pardoned, and they were ſuffered to come back again. But they ſtill continued very odious both to the Guelphs and the people; the former not being able to forgive the diſgrace and hardſhips of their long exile, nor the latter to forget their inſolence and tyranny when they had the government in their hands: ſo that their ancient animoſities were not yet entirely extinguiſhed either on one ſide or the other.

Whilſt the affairs of Florence were in this ſituation, a rumour was ſpread, that Conradine, nephew to Manfred, was marching with an army out of Germany to invade the Kingdom of Naples: at which news, the Ghibelines began to conceive freſh hopes of recovering their former authority; and the Guelphs being no leſs ſollicitous to ſecure themſelves againſt the attempts of their enemies, applied to King Charles for aſſiſtance, in caſe Conradine ſhould actually come. This requeſt being granted, his forces immediately began their march: upon which, the Guelphs grew ſo inſolent, and the courage of the Ghibelines was damped to ſuch a degree, that they fled out of the city two days before the arrival of thoſe ſuccours. After the departure of the Ghibelines, the Florentines new modelled their city, and choſe twelve principal Magiſtrates, who were to continue in authority no longer than two months, not under the title of Anziani, but that of Buonhuomini. Next in power under them, they appointed a council of eighty Citizens, which they called the Credenza. After this, an hundred and eighty more were elected out of the people, thirty to ſerve every two months; who, together with the Credenza, and the twelve Buonhuomini, were called the General Council. Beſides which, they inſtituted another council, conſiſting of an hundred and twenty members, equally choſen out of the Nobility, Citizens, and Commonalty, which was to confirm whatſoever had been reſolved upon by the others, and to act jointly with them in diſpoſing of the public honours and of-

fices

fices of the commonwealth. Having in this manner
fortified themselves against the machinations of the
Ghibelines, by new laws, and creating magiftrates
only of the Guelph party, they divided the goods
and eftates of the Ghibelines into three parts; one
of which was confifcated for public ufes, another appropriated to the fupport of their Magiftrates and
other Officers, and the third diftributed amongft the
Guelphs, in confideration of the loffes they had fuftained. The Pope likewife, to fecure Tufcany to the
Guelph faction, made King Charles Imperial Vicar of
that Province.

Whilft the Florentines thus maintained their honour and reputation abroad, by the valour of their
arms, and at home by this new form of government,
the Pope died, and the vacancy was not filled up till
after a conteft that lafted two years, at the end of
which Gregory X. was chofen, who being in Syria
at the time of his election, (where he had refided
many years, without concerning himfelf in the intrigues of faction) and an enemy to difcord of all
kinds, did not fhew the fame partiality to the Guelphs
that his predeceffors had done. And therefore, when
he arrived at Florence, in his way to France, thinking it the duty of a good paftor to ufe his endeavours
to re-unite the city, and compofe all differences, he
prevailed upon the Florentines to receive commiffioners from the Ghibelines, to negotiate the terms
upon which they fhould return: but, notwithftanding an accommodation was concluded betwixt the
two parties, the Ghibelines were fo fufpicious, that
they would not come back again. The caufe of this
refufal was laid to the charge of the city, and enraged
the Pope to fuch a degree, that he excommunicated
it; under which cenfure it continued, as long as he
lived; but after his death, when Innocent V. was
elected, it was taken off. Innocent was fucceeded by
Nicholas III. of the houfe of Urfini: and as the
Popes were always jealous of any confiderable power
in Italy (though raifed by the favour of the Church)
and

and conftantly endeavoured to deprefs it, great commotions and frequent changes enfued. For the dread
of any one that was grown potent, occafioned the exaltation of another that was weaker than him, who
growing powerful alfo by his advancement, became
equally formidable, and was fure to be humbled in
in his turn, if poffible. This was the occafion of the
Kingdom of Naples being taken from Manfred, and
given to Charles. And when Charles was afterwards
thought too ftrong by this acquifition, his ruin was
alfo confpired : for Nicholas III. moved by this confideration, fo contrived matters, that Charles was removed from the government of Tufcany by the Emperor, and Latino, the Pope's Legate, fent thither in
his room, by a commiffion from that Prince.

The government of Florence was fallen into great
diforder and mifrule at this time ; for the Guelph
nobility were grown fo infolent, and ftood in fo little
awe of the magiftracy, that though many murders
and other acts of violence were daily committed, yet
the criminals generally efcaped with impunity, through
the favour of one or other of the Nobles. To reftrain
thefe enormities, the heads of the city thought it no
bad expedient to recall thofe that were banifhed ;
which gave the Legate an opportunity of interpofing
his authority and good offices for the re-union of the
city, and the return of the Ghibelines. This being
happily effected, inftead of twelve governors, they
refolved to have fourteen, feven of each party, who
fhould be nominated by the Pope, and remain in office no longer than one year. Under this form of
government, the city continued for the fpace of two
years ; when Martin, a Frenchman, was created
Pope, and reftored all the power and authority to
King Charles that had been taken from him by Pope
Nicholas. Upon which, the rage of faction fuddenly
blazed out again in Tufcany : for the Florentines rofe
in arms againft the Emperor's deputy, and put the
city under a new regulation, to curb the ambition of
the Ghibelines, and the infolence of the nobility.

In

In the year 1282, the companies of the Arts and Trades having for fome time had magiftrates and colours of their own, were become fo reipectable and powerful, that they got a law paffed by their authority, in which it was ordained, that inftead of fourteen citizens, three only fhould govern the commonwealth, and that for no longer than two months; who were to be chofen indifferently out of the nobility or commons, provided they were merchants, or profeffed any art or occupation: and thefe were called Priori. Afterwards, the chief magiftracy was vefted in fix perfons, one for each ward, under which regulation the city continued till the year 1342; when it was divided into Quarters, and the number of the Priori reduced to nine, which by fome accident or other, during this period, had been fometimes augmented to twelve. This inftitution, in time, occafioned the ruin of the nobility, who, upon divers provocations, were excluded, and at laft entirely fuppreffed by the people. The nobility, indeed, confented to it, becaufe they were at that time divided amongft themfelves: but by endeavouring to fupplant each other, and afpiring to the fole government of the commonwealth, they quite loft all fhare in it. There was likewife a palace fet apart for the conftant refidence of thefe magiftrates, and the meeting of the council; whereas, before, they both ufed to affemble in fome one or other of the churches. Befides which, they had ferjeants, and other neceffary officers, appointed to attend them there, to create greater reverence and refpect in the people. And though at firft they had only the title of Priori, they were afterwards diftinguifhed by the name of Signori or Signiory.

The Florentines, after this, continued quiet at home for fome time; during which, they made war upon the people of Arezzo, (for having expelled the Guelphs their city) and gained a confiderable victory over them at Campaldino. And as the City now began to grow very rich, and full of inhabitants, it was

VOL. I.   H   thought

1282.

1342

thought proper to build new walls, and extend the bounds of it, which they did, to its prefent circumfé-rence; for the former diameter reached only from the old Bridge to the church of St. Laurence.

War abroad, and peace at home, had now almoft extinguifhed the two factions of Guelphs and Ghibe-lines in Florence; and there remained only fome fparks of animofity betwixt the nobility and commo-nalty, which are incident to all Republicks; for one fide being naturally jealous of any incroachment up-on their liberty and legal rights; and the other ambi-tious to rule and controul the laws, it is not poffible they fhould ever long agree together.

This humour did not fhew itfelf in the nobility, however, whilft they were over-awed by the Ghibe-lines; but when the latter were depreffed, it began to appear, and the people were daily injured and abufed in fuch a manner, that neither the laws nor the magiftracy had authority enough to relieve them; as every nobleman fupported himfelf in his infolence by the number of his friends and relations, both againft the power of the Signory, and the Captain of the people. The heads of the Arts therefore, to re-medy fo great an evil, provided that every Signiory, in the begiining of its office, fhould appoint a Gon-faloniere di Giuftizia, or Standard-bearer of Juftice, out of the people, with a thoufand men, divided into twenty companies, under him; who were to be al-ways ready with their ftandard and in arms, whenever they were ordered by the magiftracy: and the firft that filled this office, was Ubaldo Ruffoli, who drew out his companies, and demolifhed the houfes of the Galleti, becaufe one of that family had killed a fel-low citizen in France. The Arts did not meet with much oppofition in this eftablifhment, on account of the jealoufy and emulation that reigned amongft the nobility, who were not in the leaft aware that it was levelled at them, till they felt the fmart of it; and then indeed, they were not a little awed by it foi fome time: but in a while they returned to the com-miffior

2

miffion of their former outrages : for as fome of them
always found means to infinuate themfelves into the
Signiory, they had it in their power to prevent the
Gonfalonier from executing his office.   Befides, as
witneffes were always required upon any accufation,
the plaintiff could hardly ever find any one that durft
give evidence againft the nobility : fo that in a fhort
time, Florence was involved in its former diftractions,
and the people again expofed to violence and oppreffion ; as juftice was grown dilatory, and fentence,
though paffed, feldom or never executed.   The
people therefore, not knowing what courfe to take in
thefe circumftances, Giano della Bella, a ftrenuous
Patriot, (though of a very noble family) encouraged
the heads of the Arts once more to reform the City :
and by his advice, it was enacted, that the Gonfalonier fhould always refide with the Signiory, and have
four thoufand armed men under his command.   They
likewife entirely excluded the Nobility out of that
council, and made a Law, that all acceffaries or
abettors fhould be liable to the fame punifhment with
thofe that were principals in any crime ; and further,
that common Fame fhould be fufficient evidence to
convict them.   By thefe Laws, which were called, li
Ordinamenti della Giuftizia, the people gained great
weight and authority : but Giano della Bella being
looked upon by the Nobility as the author and con-
triver of them to bridle their power, became very
odious, not only to them, but to the richeft of the
Commonalty *, who began to think his authority too
great, as they plainly fhewed on the firft occafion that
offered.   For not long after, it happened that one of
the Commons was killed in a fray, wherein feveral of

---

* It has been a common piece of policy in all Republics, to dif-
countenance and even to deprefs fuch as are remarkably eminent for
virtues of any kind whatfoever.   A brave man is fure to be brow-
beaten; and if a perfon is a little more hofpitable or charitable than
his neighbours, he is in danger of the State inquifition, left his virtues, or even the appearance of them, fhould make him popular, and
enable him to change the form of government.   Such is the envy
and jealoufy that are ufually incident to Commonwealths.

H 2   the

the Nobility were engaged, and Corfo Donati amongſt
the reſt, to whoſe charge the murder was laid, as the
moſt active and deſperate of them.　Upon which, he
was taken into cuſtody by the Captain of the people :
but whether he was innocent of the fact, or the Captain was afraid of condemning him, or whatever elſe
might be the reaſon, he was acquitted ; which ſo enraged the people, that they preſently took up arms,
and ran to the houſe of Giano della Bella, entreating
him to uſe his endeavours, that the Laws which he
had been the author of, might be duly put in execution.　Giano was deſirous that Donati ſhould be
puniſhed, and therefore, inſtead of exhorting the
people to lay down their arms, as many thought he
ought to have done, he adviſed them to complain to
the Signiory, and demand juſtice of them.　But the
people, who were incenſed to the laſt degree, thinking themſelves abuſed by their Captain, and abandoned by Giano, did not addreſs themſelves to the
Signiory, as they were directed ; but ran furiouſly to
the Captain's palace and plundered it.　A manner of
proceeding that was exceedingly reſented by the
whole city, and the blame of it being laid upon
Giano, by ſuch as meditated his ruin, ſome of his
enemies, who afterwards happened to be in the Signiory, accuſed him to the Captain, as an encourager
of violence and inſurrection.　Whilſt his cauſe was
depending, the people took arms, and aſſembled in
great numbers before his houſe, offering to protect
him againſt the Signiory and all his other enemies :
but Giano not caring to truſt to the favour of the populace, nor to commit his life to the determination
of the magiſtrates, as he feared the malevolence of
the one, no leſs than the ficklenefs of the other, reſolved to ſecure himſelf againſt the jealouſy of his
enemies, and his country from the rage of his friends,
by giving way to envy, and voluntarily baniſhing
himſelf from a city, which he alone had ſo generouſly
delivered from the tyranny of the Nobility, at the imminent hazard of his own life and fortune.

After

After his departure, the Nobility, in hopes of recovering their authority which they conceived they
had loft by diffenfions amongft themfelves, agreed to
unite, and fent two of their body to entreat the Signiory, (which they thought was in their intereft) that
they would be pleafed, in fome meafure, to mitigate
the afperity of the laws that had been made againft
them. But as foon as this petition came to be publickly known, the Commons apprehending the Signiory would comply with it, immediately rofe in a
tumultuous manner: fo that ambition on one fide,
and jealoufy on the other, at laft occafioned an open
rupture betwixt them. The Nobility were drawn up
in three bodies, at St. John's, in the New Market,
and the Piazza de Mozzi, and were commanded by
Forefe Adimari, Vanni de Mozzi and Geri Spini:
the people likewife affembled under their colours in
great numbers before the palace of the Signiory,
(which at that time was not far from the Church of
St. Procolo) and being fufpicious of the Signiory,
they appointed fix other citizens to act in concert with
them. In the mean time, whilft each party was preparing for an engagement, fome, both of the Nobility and Commons, with certain ecclefiafticks that were
in great efteem, interpofed their good offices to accommodate matters betwixt them; reprefenting to
the Nobility, " that the lofs of their authority, and
the laws that were made to curb them, were entirely
owing to their own arrogance and tyrannical government: that to take up arms in fuch a juncture, and
have recourfe to violence for the recovery of what
they had forfeited by their diffenfions and intolerable
behaviour, would be to ruin their country and aggravate their prefent misfortunes: that they ought to
confider the other party was much fuperior to them
in numbers, riches, and popularity: that their Nobility, which they vainly imagined fet them fo far
above others, was but an empty name, and would
ftand them in little ftead when they came to blows
with an enemy that had fo many advantages over

H 3   them."

them." On the other hand, they shewed the people,
" how imprudent it would be in them to carry things
to extremities, and drive their enemies to despair,
since those that hope no good, fear no evil: that it
ought to be remembered that it was the Nobility
chiefly which had gained their city such reputation by
their bravery in the late wars, and they ought not
therefore, either in reason or justice, to be persecuted
with such a degree of inveteracy: that though they
had patiently submitted to be excluded from all share
in the magistracy, yet it was an insupportable hard-
ship that they should be at every body's mercy, and
liable to be driven out of their country upon any little
disgust by virtue of the new laws: that they would
do well to moderate the rigour of them, (an assurance of which might possibly induce them on the
other side to lay down their arms) and not be rashly
hurried by too great a confidence in their numbers,
to hazard the event of a battle; since experience had
sufficiently shewn that a handful of desperate men
had often prevailed over a force seemingly much su-
perior to them." Various were the opinions of the
people upon these remonstrances. Some were for
coming immediately to a battle, as a thing that must
one time or other of necessity happen, and that it
would be better to do it now they were prepared,
than to stay till their enemies had strengthened themselves more effectually: yet if there were any hopes
that a mitigation of the laws would content them,
they should be mitigated accordingly: but such was
their pride and insolence, that it was much to be
feared they would never alter their manner of behaviour, except they were compelled to it by downright
force. Others that were more prudent and moderate,
thought an alteration of the laws could not be attended with any very bad consequences to them;
but that the issue of a battle, if unsuccessful, might
prove fatal. This opinion prevailing, it was ordained, that no accusation should be admitted against
a nobleman without sufficient evidence to support it:
and

and though both parties laid down their arms upon these conditions, yet they retained their former jealousy of each other, and began to raise forces and fortify themselves as fast as they could. The people however thought fit to new model the government and reduce the number of the Signiory, (as they suspected some of that body were too favourably inclined to the Nobility) leaving the supreme authority chiefly in the hands of the Mancini, Magalotti, Altoviti, Peruzzi, and Ceretani.

Having thus settled the state in the year 1298, they *1298.* began to build a securer and more magnificent palace for the Signiory, with a piazza or large area before it, in the place where the houses of the Uberti formerly stood. About the same time, the foundation of the public prisons was also laid ; all which edifices were finished in a few years: so that the city was never in a greater splendor nor more happy than at that time; as it abounded in people, riches, and reputation : for there were thirty thousand Citizens at home fit to bear arms, seventy thousand more in their territories, and all the inhabitants of Tuscany, partly as friends, partly as subjects, were at its devotion. And though there were some little sparks of jealousy and envy still remaining betwixt the Nobility and the people, yet they did not openly break out, or produce any bad effect, but every one lived quietly and peaceably with his neighbour : and had not this tranquillity at last been disturbed by fresh discords at home, it would have been in no danger from any other enemy ; as it was then in so flourishing a condition, that it neither feared the attempts of the exiles, nor the power of the Emperor, and could have brought a body of forces into the field able to face those of all the other states of Italy put together. The mischief, however, which foreign enemies were not able to do them, whilst they continued thus united, was unhappily effected by new divisions amongst themselves.

There were two families in Florence, the Cerchi and Donati, both very considerable for their riches,

nobi-

nobility, and dependants; and as they were near
neighbours both in the city and country, there happened several little difgufts betwixt them; yet not of
fuch confequence as to produce an open rupture:
and perhaps they might have entirely fubfided without
difturbing the peace of the public, if they had not
been revived by a ftrange and unexpected accident.—
The Cancellieri being one of the chief families in
Piftoia, it happened that Lori the fon of Guglielmo,
and Geri the fon of Bertaccio, both of that family,
being at play together, at laft fell into a difpute, and
from words proceeded to a rencounter, in which Geri
was flightly wounded by the other. But when Guglielmo heard of the quarrel, it gave him fo much uneafinefs that he ufed his utmoft endeavours to reconcile them; and infifted that his fon fhould go to Geri's
father and afk pardon, or at leaft make an apology
for what had happened. This generous fubmiffion,
however, only ferved to widen the breach: for when
Lori went to wait upon his kinfman, according to
his father's defire, Bertaccio faid, " he did not think
that was fufficient fatisfaction," but ordered his fervants (as an aggravation to the indignity) to lay hold
on him and carry him into a ftable, where they cut
off his right hand upon the manger, with this taunt,
" You may now go back to your father, and tell
him, that excufes won't do; fteel is the only remedy
in fuch cafes." The barbarity of the fact enraged
Guglielmo and his friends to fuch a degree, that they
immediately took arms to revenge it: and Bertaccio
and his dependants doing the fame; not only all that
family, but the whole city of Piftoia was engaged in
the quarrel, and divided into two parties. Thefe
Cancellieri defcended from one of the fame name
who had two wives, one of whom was called Bianca,
or Blanche; from whence that party that adhered to
her pofterity took the name of * Bianca; and the
other, in oppofition, diftinguifhed itfelf by that of

---

* Bianca fignifies white, and Nera black.

Nera.

Nera. ' Many skirmishes happened betwixt them, in which numbers of people lost their lives, and some families were entirely ruined : and as no expedient could be found to reconcile them (though both sides were heartily sick of the quarrel) they determined to come to Florence, in hopes either of putting an end to it there, by the meditation of their common friends; or if that could not be effected, to strengthen their respective parties by drawing other families into them. The Neri having an intimate friendship with the Donati, were espoused by Corso, the head of that family : and the Bianchi, to balance that acquisition of strength in their adversaries, had recourse to Veri, the head of the Cerchi, for their assistance; a man of no less power than Corso, nor inferior to him in any other respect whatsoever.

These sparks of discord, thus blown from Pistoia to Florence, soon revived the former animosities betwixt the Cerchi and Donati, which began to blaze out again with such fury, that the Signiory and others of the principal citizens were under no small apprehension that the whole city would at last become engaged in the quarrel, and hourly expected the two parties would openly attack each other. They applied therefore to the Pope, and entreated him to make use of his authority to compose those differences, which it was not in their power to do : upon which follicitation, his Holiness sent for Veri to Rome, and earnestly exhorted him to be reconciled to the Donati. But Veri pretending to be surprized, said " there was no quarrel of any kind betwixt them that he knew of, and consequently there could not be any occasion to exhort him to a reconciliation." But not long after his return from Rome, their feuds increased to such a height, that there only wanted an opportunity (which soon after happened) to make them burst out into action. In the month of May several holidays are publickly celebrated in Florence; on one of which, some young gentlemen of the Donati family with their friends, all on horse-back, stopped near

Tri-

Trinity Church to look at fome women that were dancing: prefently after, as ill fortune would have it, feveral of the Cerchi alfo arrived at the fame place, with many of their acquaintance; and being defirous to gratify their curiofity in like manner, they fpurred on their horfes, not knowing the Donati, who were foremoft in the crowd, and joftled in amongft them. The Donati therefore looking upon this as an affront, immediately drew their fwords; and the Cerchi doing the fame, a fkirmifh enfued, in which many were wounded on both fides.

This accident was the occafion of great mifchief: for the whole City, as well Commons as Nobility, divided upon it; fome taking part with the Bianchi, and others with the Neri. The heads of the Bianca party were the Cerchi, who were joined by the Adimari, the Abbati, part of the Tofinghi, Bardi, Roffi, Frefcobaldi, Nerli, Mannelli, all the Mozzi, Scali, Gherardini, Cavalcanti, Malefpini, Boftichi, Giandonati, Vecchietti, and Ariguzzi, who were followed by many confiderable families of the Commoners and all the Ghibeline faction in Florence: fo that in regard to their numbers, they feemed to have a great fuperiority. The other fide was headed by the Donati, and fupported by all thofe of the above mentioned families who did not follow the Bianchi, together with all the Pazzi, Vifdomini, Manieri, Bagnefi, Tornaquinci, Spini, Buondelmonti, Gianfigliazzi, and Brunellefchi. Nor did this contagion confine itfelf to the city alone, but infected all the country round in fuch a manner, that the Captains of the Arts, and all thofe that favoured the Guelphs and were friends to the Commonwealth, began to be very much afraid this new combuftion would throw the city once more into the hands of the Ghibelines, to its utter ruin. Upon which they fent again to the Pope, befeeching him to provide fome remedy for thefe diftractions, except he had a mind that their city, which at all times had been the Bulwark of the Church, fhould either be totally deftroyed, or at leaft be-

become fubject to the Ghibelines. In compliance with their requeft, the Pope difpatched Matteo d' Acqua Sparta, a Portugueze Cardinal, as his Legate to Florence ; who, finding the party of the Bianchi fo refractory and confident in their numbers that they refufed to liften to any propofals of peace, left Florence in a rage, and put it under an interdict : fo that it was in greater confufion after his departure than before he came thither.

Whilft the two parties were in this ferment, and ripe for an infurrection, it happened that feveral of the Cerchi and Donati met together at a funeral, where fome angry words paffed betwixt them, and from words they came to blows, though no great harm was done at that time on either fide. But after they had returned to their houfes, the Cerchi refolved to attack the Donati, and affembled all their friends for that purpofe : in which affault, however, they were valiantly repulfed by Corfo, and many of them wounded. Upon this, the whole city took up arms, neither the power of the magiftracy, nor the authority of the laws being able to reftrain the fury of the multitude. The wifeft and beft of the Citizens were in great terror : and the Donati being the weaker party, not a little doubtful of their fafety. It was agreed therefore, at a meeting betwixt Corfo, the heads of the Neri, and the Captains of the Arts, that in order to fecure themfelves, it was neceffary the Pope fhould be follicited to fend fome perfon of royal extraction to reform the city ; imagining this would be the moft effectual way to get the better of their enemies. This meeting, and the refult of it, was notified to the Signiory by the other party, who reprefented it as a confpiracy againft their liberty. So that both fides being now in arms again, the Signiory by the advice of Dante (who at that time was one of them) boldly drew out their companies, and being joined by great numbers out of the country, foon forced the chiefs of each party to lay down their arms : after which, they banifhed Corfo Donati and many of the Neri.

And

And to shew that they acted with impartiality, they
likewise banished several of the Bianchi, who not long
after were suffered to return upon one plausible pretence or other. Corso and his associates were also indulged in the same manner: and taking it for granted
that the Pope was their friend, they went directly to
Rome, in hopes of being able to persuade him to that
in a personal conference, for which they had lately petitioned his Holiness in their letters.

Charles of Valois, brother to the King of France,
happened to be then at the Court of Rome, being invited into Italy by the King of Naples to make a descent upon Sicily. The Pope therefore thought fit
(as he was so much importuned by the Florentines) to
send this Prince to stay at Florence till the season of
the year was more proper for navigation. In consequence of which deputation he went to that city: and
though the Bianchi, who then had the upper hand
there, looked upon him with an evil eye, yet as he
was Patron of the Guelphs and sent by the Pope, they
durst not oppose his coming: on the contrary, to
make him their friend, they gave him full power to
regulate the city as he thought best. He was no
sooner vested with his authority but he caused all his
friends and partizans to arm themselves; which made
the people so jealous that he intended to deprive them
of their liberty, that they also took arms, and every
man was ready to oppose him if he should make any
such attempt. The Cerchi and the heads of the
Bianchi having had the chief government of the city
some time in their hands, and behaved with great arrogance, were become generally odious; which encouraged Corso and others of the Neri who had fled,
to return to Florence, upon an assurance that Charles
and the Captains of the Arts were their friends and
would support them. Accordingly whilst the city
was thus alarmed with the apprehensions of Charles's
designs, Corso, with all his associates, and many
other of their followers made their entry into it without any sort of resistance: and though Veri de Cerchi

was

was called upon to oppofe them, he declined it, and
faid, " the people of Florence might even chaftife
them themfelves if they pleafed, as they were likely
to be the greateft fufferers by them." But that in-
finuation had no effect ; for inftead of chaftifing them,
they received them with open arms, whilft Veri was
forced to fly for his fafety. For Corfo having forced
his entrance at the Porta Pinti, drew up and made a
ftand over againft St. Pietro Maggiore, not far from
his own houfe ; and being joined by a great number of
his friends, and others that had affembled there in
hopes of a change of government, he in the firft place
releafed all prifoners, upon what account, and by
whomfoever they had been committed : after which
he divefted the Signiory of their authority, and chofe
new magiftrates (all of the party of the Neri) out of
the people to fupply their places. He then plundered the houfes of the chiefs of the Bianchi, for five
days together ; during which time, the Cerchi and the
heads of that Faction feeing the people for the moft
part their enemy, and Charles by no means their
friend, fled out of the city into fuch ftrong places as
they were poffeffed of : and though they would not
liften to the exhortations of the Pope before, they
were now forced to implore his affiftance ; reprefenting to his Holinefs that the arrival of Charles there
had been fo far from uniting the city, that it had
thrown it into ftill greater diftraction. The Pope
therefore again fent his Legate Acqua Sparta to Florence, who not only made an accommodation betwixt
the Cerchi and Donati, but fortified it by feveral intermarriages in thofe families. Neverthelefs, when
he infifted that the Bianchi fhould fhare in the chief
offices of the commonwealth, and that was refufed by
the Neri, who were then in full poffeffion of them, he
left the city with as much diffatisfaction as he had
done before, and excommunicated it a fecond time
for its contumacy. The Neri, on the other hand,
feeing their old enemies in their bofom again, were
not a little afraid they would ufe all means to ruin
them,

them, in order to recover their former authority. Thus both parties were still difcontented: and as if thefe animofities were not fufficient to enflame the city, frefh occafions of difcord continually happened.

As Niccolò de Cerchi was going one day with feveral of his friends to his feat in the country, he was affaulted by Simone, the fon of Corfo Donati, at the Ponte ad Africo. The fkirmifh was fharp and bloody; for Niccolò was killed upon the fpot, and Simone fo defperately wounded that he died the fame night. This accident threw the whole city into an uproar again; and though indeed it was altogether owing to the Neri, yet they were fkreened by the magiftracy: and before judgment could be obtained, a confpiracy was faid to be difcovered betwixt the Bianchi and Pietro Ferrante (a nobleman that attended Charles of Valois) with whom they had been tampering to perfuade his mafter to reinftate them in the government The plot was detected by fome letters from the Cerchi to Pietro; though it was the common opinion they were forged by the Donati, to wipe off the odium they had incurred by the murder of Niccolò Cerchi. However, all the family of the Cerchi, with many of their followers of the Bianca party (and amongft the reft Dante the poet) were immediately fent into banifhment, their eftates confifcated, and their houfes demolifhed: after which their party, with many of the Ghibelines who had joined them, were difperfed and fcattered up and down in different places, where they waited in hopes that fome new commotion might afford them an opportunity of repairing their loffes. And Charles having execute the defign of his errand to Florence, left that cit and went back to Rome, that he might profecute h expedition into Sicily; in which he proceeded wit no lefs imprudence and ill fuccefs than he had don in the affairs of Florence: fo that after he had lo many of his men, he returned with infinite difgrac and contempt into France.

Aft

After the departure of Charles, Florence continued tolerably quiet for some time ; though Corso Donati was still diffatisfied that he did not enjoy such a degree of authority in it as he thought due to his merits, since the government was now in the hands of the people, and conducted by those that were much inferior to him in all respects. Exasperated at this neglect, he meditated revenge : but to varnish over his defigns with a fair pretext, he accufed several citizens who had been intrusted with the public money, of embezzling it, and applying it to their own private ufes : for which, he faid, they ought to be called to account and punished. This fcandal was likewife induftriously propagated by feveral others who had the fame views ; and many were ignorant and credulous enough to believe that what Corso did, was out of pure concern and affection for his country *. But the perfons thus calumniated being in favour with the people, ftood upon their juftification : and thefe difputes, after much litigation and many proceffes, at laft grew to fuch a height that it became abfolutely neceffary to take up arms. On one fide, were Corso and Lottieri, Bifhop of Florence, with many of the Nobility, and fome of the Commons ; on the other, were the Signiory and the greater part of the people : fo that there was nothing to be feen but frays and fkirmifhes in every part of the city. The Signiory therefore perceiving themfelves in great danger, fent to Lucca for aid, and immediately all the people of

---

* The fureft way of gaining the commonalty in democratical governments, is to rail violently at the adminiftration ; and when other topics of defamation are wanting to ambitious and difcontented men, the charge of peculation and embezzlement of the public money is always at hand, which, though a very ftale cry, is conftantly liftened to with great eagernefs by the people, (whether true or falfe) whofe clamours and refentment it is calculated to excite ; as it eafily falls in with the complaints of *hard times, heavy taxes,* &c. which are ufual in every age, and under every government. The authors indeed fometimes find their account in it, under a weak adminiftration ; but the people are feldom or never the better for it under any, nor is it intended they fhould be. But it feems ftrange, that they fhould be fo often gulled into difaffection and fedition by fo trite an artifice, and the vain hopes of reftitution.

that

that city came to their affiftance: by which means,
things were accommodated for a time, the tumults
compofed, and the people fatisfied with continuing in
poffeffion of their liberty and government, without
inflicting any punifhment upon the author of this
difturbance.

The Pope had been informed of thefe broils at
Florence, and fent his Legate Niccolò da Prato thither to quiet them if poffible; who, being a prelate
of great experience, addrefs, and reputation, foon
gained fuch an influence over the people, that they
gave him a commiffion to new-model the city as he
pleafed. And as he rather inclined to favour the
Ghibeline faction, he propofed to recall all thofe of
that party who had been banifhed: but thought it neceffary, in the firft place, to ingratiate himfelf ftill
further with the people, by reftoring their antient
Companies, which added much to their ftrength, and
diminifhed that of the Nobility. When he thought
he had thus fufficiently engaged their affections, he
determined to bring back the exiles, and tried feveral
means to effect it: but was fo far from fucceeding,
that he became obnoxious to the Governors, and was
forced out of the city, which he left in the utmoft
confufion, and was provoked to fuch a degree at the
treatment he had met with, that he put it under an
interdict at his departure.

Two factions not being fufficient, the city was now
divided and fubdivided into feveral, as thofe of the
People and Nobility, the Guelphs and the Ghibelines,
the Bianchi and the Neri; and fome who wifhed for
the return of the exiles, being difappointed in their
hopes now the Legate was gone, grew clamorous and
outrageous : fo that the whole city was in an uproar,
and many fkirmifhes enfued. Thofe that were moft
active in raifing this clamour, were the Medici and
Giugni, who had openly fided with the Legate in favour of the exiles.

In the midft of thofe rencounters, which daily happened in all parts of the town, a fire broke out, to add

to their confusion, which spread from the Orto di San Michele (where it first began) to the houses of the Abbati, and from thence to those of the Capon-sacchi, which were all burnt down to the ground, together with the houses of the Macci, Amieri, Toschi, Cipriani, Lamberti, Cavalcanti, and all the new Market: from whence the flames spread to Porta di Santa Maria, which was entirely consumed; and being driven by the wind towards the old Bridge, they likewise demolished the houses of the Gherardini, Pulci, Amadei, Lucardesi, and so many others, that the number amounted to above thirteen hundred.

Many were of opinion that this misfortune was the effect of accident, and that some houses took fire by chance, whilst the owners of them were engaged in a skirmish which happened at that time. Others affirm, that it was owing to the villany of Neri Abbati, Prior of St. Pietro Scheraggio, a dissolute and abandoned fellow, who, seeing every body so busily employed, took that opportunity of doing a mischief for which there could be no remedy; and that it might succeed the better, and make him less suspected, he also set fire to the houses of his own friends, where he had a convenience of doing it.

It was in July 1304, when Florence was visited in *1304.* this lamentable manner with fire and sword. At which time, Corso Donati was the only person of any distinction that did not take up arms in those tumults: for he thought that when all sides grew tired of fighting, and inclined to a reconciliation, he was the more likely, upon that account, to be called in as an arbitrator to decide their differences. Accordingly, they soon after laid down their arms, though more out of weariness of their miseries, and that they might have time to take breath, than from any real desire of being re-united, and living in peace: for upon the whole, it was only stipulated, that the Exiles should not be suffered to return; which was agreed to by those that favoured them, merely because they proved to be the weaker side.

The Legate, at his return to Rome, being informed
of thefe new difturbances at Florence, told the Pope,
that if he had any defire of compofing them, it would
be the beft way, in his opinion, to fend for twelve of
the principal malecontents of that City, and to detain
them at Rome for fome time: for when the fomenters
of thofe evils were removed, it would be an eafy
matter to extinguifh them. This advice was fo well
approved of by the Pope, that he cited the above-
mentioned number of thofe citizens to appear before
him, (amongft whom was Corfo Donati) who readily
obeyed the fummons. But as foon as they were fet
out upon their journey, the Legate found means to
acquaint the Exiles, that if ever they hoped to return
to Florence, that was their time, as the City was then
clear of the only men that had authority enough to
oppofe their entrance. Upon this encouragement,
the Citizens that had been banifhed, drawing together
what forces they could, immediately marched towards
Florence, and not only entered the city in that part
where the new walls were not yet thoroughly finifhed,
but advanced as far as the Piazza di St. Giovanni.
It is certainly worthy of notice, that thofe very citizens, who but a little before had exerted themfelves
in the moft ftrenuous manner for their return, when
they petitioned in an humble and fubmiffive manner
to be re-admitted, were the firft that took up arms
againft them, now they faw them approach in a hoftile
manner, and joined with the people to drive them
back again, as they effectually did; for fuch was the
fpirit of patriotifm amongft them in thofe days, that
they chearfully gave up all private interefts and friend-
fhips for the fake of the publick good. Their mif-
carriage in this attempt, may chiefly be imputed to
leaving part of their forces at Laftra, and not waiting
for Tolofetto Uberti, who was advancing with three
hundred horfe from Piftoia to their affiftance; as they
imagined expedition was of much greater importance
than numbers at that time: and indeed, it is certain,
that in fuch cafes, a fair opportunity is often loft by
de-

delay; but at the same time we must consider, that precipitate enterprizes are seldom supported by a proper force.

After the Exiles were thus repulsed, the Citizens relapsed into their former distractions: and in order to deprive the Cavalcanti of the authority which they had assumed, they seized upon the Castle of Le Stinche, in the Val de Greve, which had been in possession of that family for a great number of years: and as those who were then in this Castle, were the first that were committed to the public prison which had been lately built, that edifice from thence took the name of Le Stinche, which it still retains. The next step that the governors of the commonwealth took, was to re-establish the Companies of the People, and to restore the Colours under which the Arts had formerly been used to assemble: the Captains, the Gonfaloniers, or Standard-bearers of the Companies, and the officers of Justice, were called together, and ordered not only to assist the Signiory in times of peace with their counsel, but to support and defend them by dint of arms in all exigencies and commotions. To assist the two Judges who had been constituted in the beginning of their state, they appointed an officer, called *il Essecutore*, or Sheriff, who was to act in conjunction with the Gonfaloniers, and to see their orders carried into execution, whenever the Nobility should be guilty of any enormity or act of oppression.

But the Pope dying in the mean time, Corso and the other eleven Citizens, returned to Florence, where they might all have lived in peace, if the restless ambition of Corso had not occasioned fresh troubles. In order to make himself popular, he constantly opposed the Nobility in all their schemes, and which way soever he observed the people to incline, he turned all his authority to support them in it, and gain their affections: so that in all contests and divisions, or when they had any extraordinary point to carry, they always resorted to him, and put themselves under his directions. This created him much hatred and envy

I 2   amongst

amongſt the moſt conſiderable Citizens, which at laſt increaſed to ſuch a degree, that the faction of the Neri divided and quarrelled amongſt themſelves, when they ſaw Corſo avail himſelf in ſuch a manner of the affections of the people, and join with the enemies of the public to promote his own private views: yet ſuch was the awe they ſtood in of his perſon and authority, that every one was afraid of him. However, as the moſt likely way to alienate the affections of the people from him, they gave out, that he ſecretly deſigned to ſeize upon the government, and make himſelf King; which it was no difficult matter to make them believe, from his magnificent, and indeed profuſe, manner of living, which far exceeded thoſe bounds of moderation that ought not to be tranſgreſſed by any private Citizen or Subject, and was calculated, they ſaid, to ſerve ſome dangerous purpoſe. And this ſuſpicion was not a little corroborated, when they ſaw him, ſoon after, married to a daughter of Uguccione della Faggiuola, head of the Bianchi and Ghibelines, and a man of very great intereſt and power in Tuſcany.

As ſoon as this alliance came to the knowledge of his enemies, they grew ſo bold upon it, that they took up arms againſt him; and the greater part of the people, inſtead of appearing in his defence, forſook him and joined his adverſaries; the chief of whom were Roſſo della Toſa, Pazziano de Pazzi, Geri Spini, and Berto Brunelleſchi. Theſe and their friends, with a great multitude of armed men, aſſembled at the ſteps of the Palace of the Signiory, by whoſe command an accuſation was preferred againſt Corſo to Pietro Branca, captain of the people, as a perſon, who, by the aſſiſtance of Uguccione, aſpired to make himſelf abſolute. Upon which impeachment, being cited to appear before him, he refuſed to obey the ſummons; and was therefore declared a contumacious rebel, in leſs than two hours after he had been accuſed. This ſentence being pronounced, the Signiory, with the Companies of the people under

der

der their feveral colours, went directly to apprehend him. Corfo, on the other hand, not in the leaft difmayed, either at the rigour of the fentence, the authority of the Signiory, the number of his enemies, or the inconftancy of his friends, many of whom had now deferted him, immediately began to fortify his houfe, in hopes of being able to defend himfelf there, till Uguccione (to whom he had fent word of the defperate circumftances he was in) could come to his relief. The avenues to his houfe were barricaded and guarded by thofe of his party that ftill adhered to him, in fuch a manner, that though the affailants were numerous, they could not force their way through them. Many were killed and wounded on both fides in this action, which was very fharp : at laft, the people finding they could not enter that way, got into the neighbouring houfes, and unexpectedly broke through the walls of them into his. Corfo feeing himfelf thus furrounded on a fudden by his enemies, and that there was no hope of fuccour from Uguccione, nor any other refuge left, refolved to try if it was poffible to make his efcape.

Advancing, therefore, with Gherardo Bondini, and fome others of his moft refolute and faithful friends, he made fo furious an attack upon the enemy, that he broke through them, and fled out of the Porta alla Cruce. However, as they were clofely purfued, Gherardo was killed by Boccaccio Caviciulli, upon the Ponte ad Africo, and Corfo taken prifoner at Rovezzano, by fome Catalan horfe that were in the pay of the Signiory. But as he could not endure the thoughts of being infulted, and perhaps torn to pieces by a victorious enemy, he threw himfelf from his horfe to the ground, as they were bringing him back to Florence, where he was flain by one of the guards : his body was afterwards picked up by the monks of St. Salvi, and interred without any folemnity, or fepulchral honours. Such was the unfortunate end of Corfo Donati, to whom his country, and the Neri, owed much, both of their good and bad fortune :

I 3

with-

without doubt, if he had not been of fo reftlefs a difpofition, his memory would have been held in greater honour. However, his name deferves to be ranked amongft thofe of the moft eminent men that our city has ever produced; though indeed, it cannot be denied, that the turbulency of his fpirit made both his country and party forget their obligations to him, and at laft, was not only the caufe of his own death, but brought many evils upon them. Uguccione had advanced as far as Remoli, in his way to Florence, with fupplies to relieve his fon-in-law; but being informed there, that he was fallen into the hands of the people, and imagining that all fuccour would then be too late, he thought it the moft prudent way to turn back again, as he might otherwife very likely prejudice himfelf, without being able to do him any fervice.

After the death of Corfo, which happened in the year 1308, all tumults ceafed, and every body lived quietly, till news arrived that Henry the Emperor, was come into Italy with all the Florentine Exiles in his army, whom he had promifed to reinftate in their country. The Magiftrates, therefore, in order to diftrefs him, and leffen the number of their enemies, granted a free pardon to all fuch as had been rebels, and invited them to return; exeepting fome particular perfons exprefsly mentioned. Thofe that were excluded, were moftly of the Ghibeline faction, and certain of the Bianchi; amongft whom, were Dante Alighieri, the Sons of Veri de Cerchi, and of Giano della Bella. They likewife fent to follicit the affiftance of Robert, King of Naples, but not being able to obtain it as allies, they gave him the government of their City for five years, upon condition that he would defend and protect them as his fubjects. The Emperor, in his paffage, arrived at Pifa, and from thence came to Rome, where he was crowned, in the year 1312; and being determined to humble the Florentines, he marched by the way of Perugia and Arezzo to Florence, and fat down with his army at the Monaftery

1308

1312

naftery of St. Salvi, about a mile from the city, where he continued fifty days without gaining any advantage. At laft, when he found that enterprize not likely to fucceed as he expected, he returned to Pifa, and entered into a confederacy with Frederick, King of Sicily, in order to make an attempt upon Naples. For which purpofe, he marched that way with his army ; but at a time when he thought him-felf fure of fuccefs, and Robert was fo frighted that he gave up his kingdom for loft, the Emperor died at Buonconvento.

It happened not long after, that Uguccione della Faggiuola firft made himfelf mafter of Pifa, and then of Lucca, by the affiftance of the Ghibelines ; from whence he committed great depredations upon the neighbouring ftates. The Florentines, therefore, to free themfelves from the terror occafioned by his in-curfions into their territories, invited Peter, King Ro-bert's brother, to come and take upon him the com-mand of their forces. Uguccione, on the other hand, neglected no opportunity, in the mean time, of adding to the power he had already acquired, and partly by force, partly by artifice, had made himfelf mafter of feveral caftles in the Vales of Arno and Nievole : from whence he proceeded to lay fiege to Monte Catini, where the Florentines refolved to ufe their utmoft endeavours to ftop his career, and ex-tinguifh a flame that otherwife might poffibly devour their whole country. For this purpofe, having raifed a very powerful army, they marched into the Vale of Nievole, where they gave battle to Uguccione, and were utterly defeated, after a bloody engagement, in which they loft above two thoufand men, befides their General Peter, the King's brother, whofe body could never be found. The victory, however, was not attended with any great rejoicings on the fide of Uguccione, as one of his fons, and many other offi-cers of diftinction, were killed in it.

After this overthrow, the Florentines immediately began to fortify the towns round about them, and

I 4   ap-

applied to King Robert for another General; upon which, he fent them the Count di Andria, commonly called Count Novello, whofe bad conduct, added to the impatient temper of the Florentines (which is foon tired of any form of government, and ready to fall into factions upon every accident) occafioned the city to divide again, notwithftanding the war they were engaged in with Uguccione; and fome declared for King Robert, and fome againft him. The chief of his enemies were Simone della Tofa, the Magalloti, and fome other popular families who had the greateft power in the government. Thefe perfons fent firft into France, and then into Germany, to raife men and invite officers, in order to rid themfelves of their new Governor; but unfortunately they could not procure either. As however they were determined to carry their point, and as neither Germany nor France would fupply them with a Governor, they chofe one from the neighbourhood; and having taken arms and drove the Count out of the city, they fent for one Lando of Agobio, and made him their Effecutore, or rather Executioner, with full power over all the Citizens. Lando, being naturally cruel and rapacious, went about the city with a gang of armed men at his heels, hanging up firft one man and then another, as thofe that had fent for him gave him directions, and at laft grew fo infolent, that he coined bad money with the Florentine ftamp, which no body had courage enough to oppofe: to fuch a height of power had he arrived by the diffenfion of the citizens! Miferable indeed, and much to be lamented was the condition of the city at that time, which neither the bitter remembrance of the evils produced by their former divifions, nor the dread of a foreign enemy at their gates, nor the authority of a King, was fufficient to keep united; though their poffeffions were at the fame time daily ravaged and plundered, abroad by Uguccione, and at home by Lando.

The

The Nobility, moſt of the conſiderable Commoners, and all the Guelphs, took the King's ſide, and hated Lando and thoſe that ſupported him: but as their enemies had the power in their hands, they could not declare themſelves publickly without extreme danger. However, that they might not ſeem wanting in any endeavours to free themſelves from ſo ignominious a yoke, they wrote privately to King Robert, and entreated him to appoint Count Guido da Buttifolle his Lieutenant at Florence, which he readily complied with: and the other party (though they had the Signiory on their ſide) durſt not venture to oppoſe a man of ſo eſtabliſhed a reputation. But the Count ſoon found he had very little authority in the city, as the Magiſtracy and the Gonfaloniers of the ſeveral companies openly favoured Lando and his friends.

During theſe troubles in Florence, the daughter of Albert, King of Bohemia, paſſed through that city (to meet her huſband Charles, the ſon of King Robert) where ſhe was received by the King's friends with great honour; and, upon their complaints of the miſerable condition of the city, and the tyranny of Lando and his party, ſhe uſed her good offices ſo effectually, and obtained them ſo many grants and favours from the King before ſhe left them, that the Citizens were at laſt reconciled and re-united, Lando deprived of his authority, and ſent back again to Agobbio, ſatiated with blood and rapine. After his departure, there enſued another reform in the State, by which, the government of the city was continued to the King for three years longer: and as the ſeven that were then in the Signiory were all of Lando's party, ſix others were added to them of the King's and they continued thirteen for ſome time; but were afterwards reduced to ſeven again, their former number. About this time, Uguccione was driven out of Lucca and Piſa, and ſucceeded in the government of thoſe two cities by Caſtruccio Caſtracani, a Luccheſe; who being a ſpirited young man and fortunate in all

his

his undertakings, very foon became the head of the Ghileline faction in Tufcany. The Florentines therefore laying afide their private difcords, were chiefly employed for feveral years in endeavouring to obftruct the growth of Caftruccio's power ; and afterwards, when they found that to no purpofe, in taking proper meafures to defend themfelves againft him. And that the Signiory might proceed with maturer deliberation, and execute with greater authority, they chofe twelve Citizens whom they called Buonhuomini, without whofe advice and confent, the Signiory were not to pafs any act of importance.

In the mean time the dominion of king Robert expired, and the government once more reverted to the Citizens, who again fet up the fame form of magiftracy that had been formerly inftituted, and continued united whilft they were in fo much fear of Caftruccio; who, after many enterprizes againft the Governors of Lunigiana, at laft fat down before Prato. The Florentines alarmed at this news, refolved to relieve it, and for that purpofe, having fhut up their fhops, they marched towards that place with twenty thoufand foot, and fifteen hundred horfe, but in a tumultuous and diforderly manner. And to leffen the force of Caftruccio and add to their own, a Proclamation was iffued by the Signiory, that every exile of the Guelph party, who came in to the relief of Prato, fhould afterwards have liberty to return home : which had fo good an effect, that they were joined by above four thoufand of them, and their army became fo formidable by this reinforcement that they marched with all expedition to Prato. But Caftruccio being afraid of fo great a force, and not caring to run the hazard of a battle, retreated to Lucca.

Upon this retreat, there arofe great difputes in the camp of the Florentines, betwixt the Nobility and the people. The people would have purfued him and forced him to an engagement, in hopes that a victory would have totally ruined him : but the Nobility thought it more prudent to return ; alledging, they

had

had already fufficiently expofed their own city for the
relief of Prato, which in fuch a cafe of neceffity was
unavoidable : but, now there was no manner of occafion, little to be gained, and much to be loft, it
would be madnefs to tempt fortune. After long debates, without coming to any refolution, the matter
was referred to the Signiory, which, confifting of
Commoners as well as Nobility, fell into the fame difference of opinions : and this coming to be known in
the city, a vaft number of the people affembled in
the Piazza, and threatened the Nobility to fuch a degree that they were terrified and gave way to them.
But as it was fo late before they came to fuch a refolution, and even then againft the inclination of many,
the enemy had fufficient time to retire in fafety to
Lucca : at which the people were fo exafperated
againft the Nobility, that the Signiory refufed to perform the promife they had made, by their defire, to
the exiles that came in upon the proclamation. The
exiles hearing of this, refolved on their part to force
their way into the city if poffible, and accordingly
prefented themfelves at the gates, to be admitted before the reft of the army came up : but this attempt
being forefeen and expected, did not fucceed, for they
were driven back again by thofe that were left in the
town. They endeavoured therefore to obtain by
treaty what they could not by force, and fent eight
deputies to remind the Signiory of their promife, and
the dangers they had expofed themfelves to in confequence of it, and that they relied upon their good
faith for the ftipulated recompence of their fervices.
The Nobility, therefore, having joined in that promife with the Signiory, and given their word that
they would fee it performed, thought themfelves obliged in honour to ufe all their intereft in favour of
the exiles, which they did : but the Commons being
enraged that the enterprize againft Caftruccio had not
been profecuted as they thought it ought to have
been, would not concur with them ; which afterwards
brought not only great difgrace, but alfo much trouble

ble upon the city.   For many of the Nobility being
difgufted at this denial, refolved to have recourfe to
other expedients, and promifed the Guelphs, that if
they would appear in arms before the city, they would
alfo raife an infurrection within it to affift them.   But
this defign being difcovered the day before it was to
have been put in execution, when the exiles came up
they found the Citizens ready armed, and in fuch order, not only to repel them, but to fupprefs any rifing within the walls, that no body durft offer to move :
fo that they gave up the enterprize and drew off again
without making any further effort at that time.   After their departure, it was thought fit that thofe perfons fhould be punifhed who had invited them thither : neverthelefs, though every one knew who the
delinquents were, yet no body durft fo much as point
them out, much lefs accufe them.   But that the truth
might be told without referve, it was ordered, that
any members of the general council fhould be allowed
to write down their names upon a piece of paper and
deliver it privately to the Captain of the people : which
being done, the perfons accufed were, Amerigo Donati, Tegghiaio Frefcobaldi, and Lotteringo Gherardini, whofe judges being more favourable than perhaps their crimes deferved, they were only fined a
certain fum of money and difch'arged.

From the tumults which happened in Florence upon the approach of the exiles, it plainly appeared,
that one Captain only in every Company of the people was not fufficient : it was ordered therefore, that
each Company for the future fhould have three or
four, and that every Gonfalonier fhould have two or
three other Enfigns under him called Pennonnieri, that fo
upon any emergency, when the whole Company could
not be drawn out, fome part of it might be employed
under one of thofe officers.   And as it generally happens in all commonwealths, that after any revolution
or remarkable crifis, fome or other of the old laws
are abrogated and new ones made in their room ; fo
though the Signiory at firft was changed every two
months,

months, yet the magiſtrates that were then in office, having great power, took upon themſelves to conſtitute a Signory out of all the moſt conſiderable Citizens, to continue forty months, whoſe names were to be put into a Bag or Purſe, and a certain number of them drawn out by lot at the end of every ſecond month. This method of election at firſt was called Imborſatione and afterwards Squittino.' But, as many of the citizens began to ſuſpect their names were not in the Purſe, there was a freſh Imborſation before the forty months expired. From hence aroſe the uſe of the Purſe in creating all their Magiſtrates both at home and abroad, which continued for a conſiderable time : whereas before, when the old Magiſtrates went out of office, new ones were always choſen by the council. And as this was not to be renewed till after a term of above three years, it was thought they had in a great meaſure extinguiſhed the cauſes of all ſuch diſguſts and tumults as uſed to happen from the frequent return of Elections and the number of Competitors for the Magiſtracy : ſuch was the remedy which for want of a better, they were forced to provide againſt thoſe evils, not being aware how little advantage and how many miſchiefs were likely to flow from it.

In the year 1325, Caſtruccio having ſeized upon Piſtoia, was become ſo formidable, that the Florentines beginning to ſtand in great awe of him, reſolved to attack him before he had eſtabliſhed himſelf in his new dominion, and if poſſible, to wreſt it out of his hands agian. In conſequence of which, they aſſembled twenty thouſand foot and three thouſand horſe (moſt of whom were Florentines and the reſt allies) and encamped before Alto Paſcio ; by the reduction of which they hoped to prevent any relief from being thrown into Piſtoia. In this enterprize they ſucceeded, and from thence advanced towards Lucca, ſpoiling and, ravaging the whole country : but by the ill conduct and treachery of Ramondo da Cardona, their commander in chief, they reaped but little advantage from this progreſs. For as he ſaw

the

the Florentines had been fo liberal in difpofing of
themfelves, that they had fometimes conferred their
government upon Kings, fometimes upon Legates,
and fometimes upon perfons of much inferior quality,
he thought if he could reduce them to any extremity, they perhaps would make him their Prince.
For this purpofe, he was very importunate with them
to give him the fame command in the city that he had
over their army; as he pretended he could not otherwife either require or expect that neceffary obedience
which was due to a General. But finding the Florentines did not care to comply with this demand,
he trifled away his time in doing nothing, whilft Caftruccio omitted no opportunity of taking the advantage that his indolence afforded him. For the latter
having reinforced himfelf with fupplies from the Vifconti and other Princes of Lombardy, Ramondo,
who before might have gained a victory, if he had
not betrayed his mafters, now behaved in fo un-
foldier like a manner that he could not even make his
efcape from the enemy; but whilft he was retreating
from them by very fhort and flow marches, he was
overtaken and attacked by Caftruccio near Alto
Pafcio, where, after an obftinate engagement, in
which his forces were utterly routed, and great numbers of the Citizens either killed or taken prifoners,
he himfelf alfo loft his life, receiving that punifhment from the hands of fortune, which his perfidy
and ambition had merited from the Florentines.

The havock which Caftruccio made in the territories of Florence after this victory, the depredations,
imprifonments, burnings, and every other kind of
devaftation, are not to be defcribed: for as he had
nobody to make head againft him for feveral months,
he over-ran the whole country, and did what he
pleafed, whilft the Florentines thought it no fmall
matter to fave their city after fuch a defeat. Neverthelefs, they were not reduced to fo low an ebb,
but they raifed large fums of money, affembled
forces, and fent to their allies for affiftance: but no
pro-

provilions were fufficient to ftop the progrefs of fuch an enemy. They were forced therefore, to make an offer of their government to Charles Duke of Cala-bria and fon to King Robert, upon condition that he would undertake to defend them; for as that family had been ufed to rule over them, they chofe rather to fhelter themfelves under him as their Prince, than to truft to him as an ally. But Charles himfelf being engaged in the wars of Sicily, fent Gualtier (a French-man, and Duke of Athens) as his Lieutenant, to take poffeffion of the government, who new modelled the Magiftracy as he thought fit. His behaviour, however, was fo modeft and temperate, and fo con-trary to his true natural difpofition, (as fhall be fhewn hereafter) that he gained the affections of every one.

After the wars in Sicily were over, Charles came in perfon to Florence, with a thoufand horfe, and made his entry in July 1326. His arrival gave fome check to Caftruccio, and prevented him from roving about the country and plundering it without controul, as he had done before. But, if the citizens faved any thing abroad, it was loft again at home; and when their enemies were thus curbed, they became a prey to the infolence and oppreffion of their friends: for as the Signiory were entirely under the influence of the Duke, he exacted four hundred thoufand flo-rins from the city in the fpace of one year, though it was exprefsly ftipulated in the agreement made with him, that he fhould not raife above two hundred thoufand in the whole: befides which, either Charles, or his Father, were continually laying fome heavy tax or other upon the Citizens.

Thefe miferies were ftill increafed by new jealoufies and frefh enemies. For the Ghibelines of Lombardy were fo alarmed at the arrival of Charles in Tufcany, that Galeazzo Vifconti, and other Princes of that pro-vince, by dint of money and fair promifes, prevailed up-on Lewis of Bavaria, (who had been elected Emperor, contrary to the Pope's inclination) to march into Italy with an army. In confequence of which, he came
into

into Lombardy, and from thence advancing into Tuscany, made himself master of Pisa, by the assistance of Castruccio; and having received a considerable supply of money, he marched on towards Rome. Upon which, Charles began to think the kingdom of Naples in no small danger; and leaving Philippo Saginetto his Lieutenant at Florence, he returned thither in all haste with the forces that he had brought along with him. After his departure, Castruccio seized upon Pisa, and the Florentines having got possession of Pistoia by treaty, he marched immediately to recover it, and carried on the siege with so much vigour and resolution, that though the Florentines made many attempts to relieve it, sometimes by attacking his army, sometimes by making incursions into his other territories, yet, all their endeavours were ineffectual: for so firmly determined was he to chastise Pistoia, and keep the Florentines under, that the Pistoians were forced to surrender and receive him once more for their Lord; by which he acquired great reputation; but soon after fell sick and died in the midst of his victories, as he was returning to Lucca. And as it generally happens, that either fortunate or unfortunate accidents are attended by others of the same kind, Charles, Duke of Calabria, and Lord of Florence, died at Naples much about the same time. So that the Florentines were suddenly and unexpectedly delivered from the oppression of one, and the dread of the other; and having once more recovered their liberty, began to reform the commonwealth again, abrogating the Laws and Ordinances of all former councils, and creating two new ones in their room, one of which consisted of three hundred of the Commons, the other of two hundred and fifty, of both Commoners and Nobility; the former was called the *Council of the People*, the latter, *the Common Council*.

The Emperor, upon his arrival at Rome, set up an Antipope, did many things to the prejudice of the Church, and attempted several others, which he was

I   not

not able to effect * : upon which, he left Rome with
no little dishonour, and went to Pisa, where eight
hundred German horse, either for want of pay, or
because they were dissatisfied with his conduct, immediately mutinied and fortified themselves at Monte-
chiaro upon the Ceruglio.　These forces, after he was
gone from Pisa, towards Lombardy, made themselves
masters of Lucca, and drove out Francisco Castracani, whom the Emperor had deputed to govern it ;
and being desirous to make the best of it, they offered it to the Florentines for twenty thousand florins,
which they refused to give, by the advice of Simone
della Tosa.　Happy had it been for their city, if the
Florentines had persevered in that resolution : but as
they soon after changed their mind, it was of very
great prejudice to them ; for though they refused it
when they might have had the peaceable possession of
it at so cheap a rate, they were afterwards obliged to
pay a much larger sum for it, and could not keep it
when they had done ; which gave occasion to many
subsequent disturbances and changes of government
in Florence.

　The purchase of Lucca being thus rejected by the
Florentines, it was bought by Gherardino Spinoli, a

---

* The Pope had excommunicated him in 1328, and declared him
to have forfeited the empire　Lewis, on the other hand, employed
several pens to write against the Pope, whom he stiled James of Cahors.　And not contenting himself with this, he entered Italy the
next year, and set up a certain Franciscan, called Pietro Ramuccio
de Corberia, as Antipope, by the name of Nicholas V. who crowned
Lewis, and declared John XXII. an Heretic, and that he had forfeited the Papacy.　This violent manner of proceeding offended the
Emperor's friends to such a degree, that they deserted him ; so that
he afterwards desired to be reconciled to Benedict XII. in 1336, and
to Clement VI. in 1344.　But being unwilling to submit to the conditions that were offered him, viz. That he should surrender the empire and all his estates to the Church, and hold them only at the
good will of the Pope, he was declared " obstinate and contumacious."　And at the sollicitation of Clement VI. and Philip of Valois, King of France, (whom Lewis had provoked, by siding with
Edward III. King of England against him) the Electors chose in his
room, Charles of Luxembourg, who was the fourth Emperor of that
name.　This was in 1346. Lewis died the next year of poison, or
as others say, by a fall from his horse, at the age of sixty-three. Bzov.
Annal.

Genoefe, for thirty thoufand Florins. But as it is the nature of mankind to be cool and indifferent about fuch things as are' proffered them, and eager in their defires to obtain what is difficult, or out of their reach ; fo when the Florentines heard that city was fold for fuch a trifle, they were exceedingly diffatisfied that they had it not themfelves, and angry at thofe who had diffuaded them from buying it : however, as it was now too late, they refolved to take it by force ; and for that purpofe, fent their army to make an incurfion into the territories of the Lucchefe. In the mean time, the Emperor had quitted Italy ; and the Antipope, by order of the Pifans, was fent prifoner into France.

After the death of Caftruccio, which happened in the year 1328, the Florentines continued quiet at home, till 1340, and intent only upon their affairs abroad : during which time, they were engaged in feveral wars, efpecially in Lombardy, upon the coming of John, King of Bohemia *, into that province; and in Tufcany, on the account of Lucca. They likewife raifed feveral new and beautiful edifices in their city, particularly the Tower of St. Reparata, after a plan given them by Giotto †, the moft cele-

---

* He was a Prince of great courage, and diftinguifhed himfelf as fuch in thefe wars, before which he had taken upon himfelf the title of King of Poland, and waged war againft the poffeffor of the crown there. He loft one of his eyes in battle, and going to Montpelier to try if he could find any relief from the phyficians there, a Jewifh Doctor, whom he employed, treated him in fo unfkilful a manner, that he deprived him of the other. Upon this occafion, the King of Poland, as it is reported, fent him word, that he defired they two only might decide their quarrels in a private room, with each a ponyard in his hand. But King John returned for anfwer, " that he muft firft pull out both his eyes to make the duel equal." His blindnefs did not prevent him from going to war in perfon. He went into France with fuccours to the aid of Philip of Valois, and was not only prefent, but fought bravely at the battle of Creffy, which the French loft, Auguft 26, 1346. He caufed his horfe to be faftened by the bridle to one of the beft horfemen he had, and then rufhed furioufly into the thick of the enemy, fword in hand, where he was at laft killed, as might be well expected. Charles IV. his fon, King of Bohemia and Emperor, gives a fuller account of all thefe things in the Memoirs of his father's Life.

† This Giotto was fcholar to Ciambue, and born near Florence, in the year 1276. He was a good Sculptor and Architect, as well as

                                                                a bet-

brated painter and architect of thofe times: and in
the year 1333, after an inundation of the Arno, in *1333.*
which the water rofe twelve yards perpendicular in
fome parts of Florence, carried away feveral bridges,
and demolifhed many houfes, they. repaired all with
great diligence and expence.   But in the year 1340, *1340*
new difturbances arofe.

The governors of the City had two ways of maintaining and increafing their authority.   One was, by
managing the Imborfations in fuch a manner, as always to fecure the Signiory either to themfelves or
their creatures;   the other, by getting Rettori, or
Judges chofen, who they knew would be favourable
to them in their fentences and determinations.   The
latter of which expedients, they thought of fuch importance, that, not content with two Judges, as they
had been formerly, they fometimes conftituted a third,
whom they called Captain of the Guards ;   with which
office, they had now vefted Jacomo Gabrieli d'Agobbio, and given him an abfolute power over the Citizens.   This Jacomo, under the direction of the governors, behaved with the moft fhamelefs infolence
and partiality, daily injuring or affronting fome body
or other, particularly Pietro de Bardi, and Bardo Frefcobaldi ;   who being nobly born, and men of high
fpirit, were provoked to fuch a degree, that a ftranger fhould be introduced into the city by a few of
their fellow-citizens that had the power in their
hands, on purpofe to infult and abufe all the reft,
that they entered into a confpiracy with many other
noble families, and fome of the Commoners, that
were difgufted at fo tyrannical a government, to revenge themfelves, both upon him and thofe that had

a better Painter, than his Mafter: for he began to fhake off the ftiff-
nefs of the Greek manner, endeavouring to give a freer air to his
Heads, with more of nature in his colouring, and eafier attitudes to
his figures.   His beft piece is ftill in one of the Churches at Florence,
reprefenting the Death of the Virgin Mary, with the Apoftles round
about her.   The attitudes of which Story, Michael Angelo ufed to
fay, could not be better defigned.   See Frefnoy's Art of Painting,
p. 254.

been the occafion of his coming thither. For this purpofe, it was agreed amongft the confpirators, that every one of them fhould get together as many armed men as he could in his houfe ; and that on the morning after the Feftival of All Saints, when the people were gone to Church to pray for the fouls of their departed friends †, they fhould take up arms, kill the Captain and principal Governors, and make new laws and magiftrates to reform the State. But as it generally happens, that when defperate refolutions come to be maturely confidered, many dangers and impediments occur, which damp the ardour of the Confpirators ; fo plots that are not fpeedily executed, are for the moft part unfuccefsful, as this was. For Andrea de Bardi, one of the accomplices, weighing the matter coolly, and being more effectually moved by the terror of punifhment than the defire of revenge, difcovered the whole to his kinfman Jacomo Alberti, who immediately communicated it to the Magiftracy. And as the day appointed for their rifing was very near at hand, many of the Citizens affembled in the Palace; and judging it dangerous to wait any longer, they advifed the Signiory to have the Alarm-Bell rung, and the Companies called together. Taldo Valori was chief Gonfalonier at that time, and Francifco Salviati one of the Signiory : and as they were allied to the Bardi, they oppofed that meafure, and faid it would be a dangerous thing to arm the people upon every trifling accident, becaufe it was never known that power given to the multitude, without fufficient authority to reftrain them, had produced any good effect; and that it was a much eafier matter to raife a tumult than to compofe one : they thought it would be more prudent, therefore, to enquire into the truth of the matter, and if they found fufficient reafon, to punifh

---

† This event therefore happened on the 2d of November, 134c which is commonly called All Souls Day, as the Romifh Church fet it apart *in commemorationem omnium fidelium defunctorum*, or, " Prayer for all thofe that have departed this life in the true faith."

the offenders by due courfe of law, than to run tu-
multuoufly into arms, only upon a bare report, and
proceed in fuch a manner, as perhaps might be the
utter ruin of their city. But thefe arguments were
all to no purpofe: for the Signiory were fo threatened and infulted by the other Citizens, that they
were forced to caufe the Bell to be rung; at the found
of which, all the people took arms and ran directly
to the Piazza before the Palace. On the other hand,
the Bardi and Frefcobaldi, perceiving they were betrayed, and being refolved either to conquer or die
honourably, likewife took arms, in hopes that they
fhould be able to defend themfelves in that part of
the City, which lies on the other fide of the River,
where moft of their houfes ftood. For which purpofe, they fortified the Bridges over it, and there
made head againft the enemy, in expectation that
many of the Nobility and others of their friends
would come out of the Country to their affiftance.
But this was prevented, by the people that lived in
the fame part of the city with them, who took up
arms for the Signiory: fo that when they found they
were likely to be attacked by them alfo, they abandoned the Bridges, and retired into the ftreet where
the Bardi lived, as ftronger than any of the reft, and
there made a brave defence.

In the mean time, Jacomo d'Agobbio, well knowing this Confpiracy was chiefly bent againft him,
thought his life in great danger, and was frighted to
fuch a degree, that he ran trembling to fecure himfelf in the midft of the armed men who were affembled before the Palace of the Signiory: but the
other Judges who had not been guilty of the fame
injuftice and oppreffion, were more courageous,
efpecially Maffeo da Maradi, the Podeftà, who ran to
the place where they were fighting, and paffing the
Bridge Rubaconte, undauntedly threw himfelf into
the thickeft of the fkirmifh, and made a fign for a
Parley. Upon which, out of reverence to his Perfon,
his courage, and many other good qualities, they laid

K 3 down

down their arms, and ſtood patiently to hear him, whilſt in a modeſt and pathetic harangue, he blamed the Bardi for their manner of proceeding, ſhewed them the danger they were in from the fury of the people if they did not deſiſt, gave them hopes that their cauſe ſhould be favourably heard, and promiſed that he himſelf would not only intercede for their pardon, but ſee that they ſhould have all reaſonable ſatisfaction and redreſs for their grievances: after which he went to the Signiory and exhorted them not to attempt a Victory, in which ſo many of their fellow-citizens muſt inevitably periſh, nor to paſs any ſentence upon them unheard. In ſhort, his mediation had ſuch an effect, that the Bardi and Freſcobaldi, with many of their friends, being allowed by the Signiory to leave the city, retired to their caſtles in the Country without any impediment or moleſtation.

After they were gone and the people diſarmed, the Signiory proceeded againſt ſuch only of the Families of the Bardi and Freſcobaldi as had actually been in arms: and to leſſen their power, they bought the Caſtles of Mangona and Vernia of the Bardi, and made a law that no Citizen for the future ſhould poſſeſs any Caſtle within twenty miles of Florence. Not many months after, Stiatta Freſcobaldi was beheaded, and ſeveral others of that family proclaimed Rebels. However, it did not ſufficiently ſatiate the revenge of thoſe in the adminiſtration, to have conquered and ſuppreſſed thoſe families: but, like almoſt all other men (whoſe inſolence commonly increaſes with their power) they grew more imperious and arbitrary as they grew ſtronger: for though they had only one Captain of the Guards to tyrannize over the city before, they now appointed another, to reſide in the Country, and veſted him with very great authority: ſo that any one who was in the leaſt obnoxious to the government, could not live quietly either within the city or without it. The Nobility in particular were daily abuſed and inſulted by them in ſuch a manner, that

that they only waited for an opportunity to revenge themſelves at any rate: and as one ſoon after happened, they did not fail to take the advantage of it.

During the many troubles that had happened in Tuſcany and Lombardy, the city of Lucca was fallen under the Dominion of Maſtino dell Scala Lord of Verona, who, though he was under an engagement to give it up to the Florentines, did not think fit to perform it: for as he was alſo Lord of Parma, and imagined he was ſtrong enough to maintain himſelf in poſſeſſion, he made little account of that promiſe. The Florentines, to revenge this breach of faith, joined the Venetians, and made ſo vigorous a war upon him, that he was in great danger of loſing all his territories: but they got little by it in the end, except the ſatisfaction of having diſtreſſed their enemy. For the Venetians, according to the cuſtom of all States that enter into any league or alliance with others, that are weaker than themſelves, having ſeized upon Trevigi and Vicenza, made a ſeparate peace, without any regard to the intereſt of their Confederates. Soon after, the Viſconti, Lords of Milan, took Parma from Maſtino, who finding himſelf no longer able to keep Lucca after ſuch a diminution of his ſtrength, reſolved to ſell it. The Florentines and Piſans were competitors in the purchaſe; but whilſt they were bartering for it, the Piſans ſeeing they ſhould be out-bid, as they were not ſo rich as the others, had recourſe to arms, and, joining with the Viſconti, laid ſiege to the town. The Florentines, however, were not at all diſcouraged at this, but proceeded in their bargain, and having agreed upon the price, paid down part of the money to Maſtino, and gave him Hoſtages for the reſt: in conſequence of which, Naddo Rucelläi, Giovanni Bernardino de Medici, and Roſſo the ſon of Ricciardo 'de Ricci, were ſent to take poſſeſſion; who forcing their way into the town through the Piſan Camp, were received by Maſtino, and had it delivered into their hands. The Piſans, neverthelefs, continued the ſiege, and endea-

voured

voured by all possible means to make themselves masters of the place : and the Florentines, on the other hand, were no less sollicitous to relieve it : but after a long struggle they were at last driven out of it, with much dishonour and the loss of all their purchase-money. This disaster (as it usually happens in the like cases) threw the people of Florence into such a rage against their Governors, that they publickly insulted and upbraided them with their ill conduct and administration, in all places and upon every opportunity.

In the beginning of the war, the management of it had been committed to twenty Citizens, who appointed Malatesta da Rimini Commander in Chief of their forces in that Expedition : but as he executed that charge with little courage and less discretion, they sollicited Robert, King of Naples, for supplies ; which he accordingly sent them under the command of Gualtier, Duke of Athens, who, as the evil destiny of the city would have it, arrived there just at the time when the enterprize against Lucca had miscarried. Upon his coming, the twenty superintendants of the war, seeing the people enraged to the highest degree, thought either to sooth them with fresh hopes, and take away all further occasion of obloquy, or to bridle them effectually by chusing a new General : and as they were still in great fear of the multitude, they first made the Duke of Athens Conservator of the Peace, and then their Commander in Chief, that he might have both authority and power sufficient to defend them. But as many of the Nobility had been formerly acquainted with Gualtier (when he was Governor of Florence, for Charles, Duke of Calabria) and were still highly discontented for the reasons above-mentioned, they resolved, now they had so fair an opportunity, to take their revenge, even though it should occasion the destruction of the city ; imagining there was no other way left to get the better of the people, who had so long domineered over them, but to reduce them into subjection to a

Prince,

Prince, who being well acquainted with the worth
and generofity of the Nobility and the infolence of the
Commons, might treat both parties according to
their deferts : befides which confiderations, they prefumed he would fhew them no little favour, if he
fhould obtain the fupreme Government of the city,
chiefly by their affiftance and co-operation.   To facilitate thefe defigns, they had many private meetings,
at which they earneftly perfuaded him to take the
government wholly into his hands, and promifed
to fupport him with all their intereft and power.
Several of the moft confiderable Commoners likewife
joined them, particularly the families of the Peruzzi,
Acciaiuoli, Antellefi, and Buonaccorfi, who had contracted great debts, and not being able to pay them
out of their own eftates, were defirous of getting
thofe of other people into their hands ; and to free
themfelves from the importunity of their Creditors,
were ready to enflave their Country.   Such encouragement and fo fair an opportunity, inflamed the
Duke, who was naturally ambitious, with a ftill
greater thirft of power : and to ingratiate himfelf with
the lower fort of the people by acting like a juft and
upright Magiftrate, he ordered a procefs to be commenced againft thofe that had been entrufted with
the management of the late war againft the Lucchefe :
in confequence of which, Giovanni de Medici, Naddo
Rucellai, and Guglielmo Altoviti were put to death,
and feveral others banifhed, and many obliged to pay
large fums of money for their pardon.   This fevere
manner of proceeding alarmed the middle fort of
Citizens, though it was very grateful to the Nobility
and common people, as the latter generally take
pleafure in executions, and the former were not a
little rejoiced at the fall of thofe by whom they had
been fo grievoufly oppreffed.   So that whenever the
Duke paffed through the ftreets, they refounded with
acclamations and praifes of his juftice and refolution,
whilft every one exhorted him to perfevere in his endeavours

deavours to detect the guilty and bring them to condign punifhment.

Upon this change, the authority of the Twenty began to decline, and the awe and reputation of the Duke to increafe fo faft, that every Citizen, to fhew himfelf well affected to him, had the Neapolitan arms painted over his door; nor was any thing wanting but the mere title, to make him a Prince. And being now ftrong enough, as he imagined, to attempt any thing with fecurity, he gave the Signiory to underftand, "That he thought it neceffary for the good of the city, that the fupreme power fhould be vefted in him; and therefore, as it was a thing agreeable to all the reft of the Citizens, he required them to refign their authority."

The Signiory, notwithftanding they had long forefeen the ruin of their city, were not a little embarraffed at this demand; and though they were fenfible of the danger they were in, yet that they might not feem wanting in any act of duty to their country, they boldly refufed to comply with it. Upon which, the Duke, (who out of an affectation of Religion and Humility, had taken up his quarters at the monaftery of Santa Croce) in order to give the finifhing ftroke to his wicked defigns, immediately iffued out a Proclamation, wherein he commanded all the people to appear before him the next morning in the piazza belonging to that Convent. At this proclamation, the Signiory were ftill more alarmed than they had been at his firft meffage; and having called together fuch of the Citizens as they thought moft zealous for the liberty of their country, it was refolved, fince the power of the Duke was fo great, and there was no other remedy left, to apply to him in an humble and fupplicatory manner; and try whether they could prevail upon him by entreaties, now force was infufficient, to defift from this attempt or if that could not be effected, at leaft to govern them with more gentlenefs and moderation. For thi purpofe, they deputed fome of their Members to

wai

wait upon him; one of whom addreſſed him in the following manner:

" My Lord,

" We are cóme hither to exprefs our furprife, in the firſt place, at your Demand, and in the next, at your Proclamation to aſſemble the people; prefuming it is your intention to extort that from us by violence, which, upon private application, we could not in duty comply with. It is not our defign to oppofe force by force, but rather to reprefent to you the heavinefs of that burden which you are ſo defirous to take upon your own fhoulders, and the dangers that are likely to attend it ; that ſo you may hereafter remember and diſtinguiſh betwixt our advice and that which is given you by others, not out of any regard to your perfon or intereſt, but to fatiate their own revenge and ambition. You are endeavouring to enſlave our city, which has ever been free ; for the government of it, which formerly has fometimes been conferred on the Kings of Naples, or ſome other of their Houſe, was rather in confequence of an alliance or aſſociation, than of a forced fubjeftion. Have you confidered how dear and important the love of Liberty muſt be to fuch a Commonwealth as ours ? A principle that no force can ever fubdue, no length of time can ever wear away, nor any other confideration over-balance. Recollect, Sir, I befeech you, how great a force will be neceſſary to keep ſo powerful a city in fubjeftion. All the foreign Mercenaries you can hire will not be fufficient, and the Citizens you cannot confide in : for thofe who at prefent feem to be your friends, and at whofe inſtigation you have taken this refolution, will be the firſt to confpire your ruin, in order to ufurp the government themfelves, when they have wreaked their malice upon their fellow-citizens, by your means and afſiſtance. The populace, which you chiefly truſt to, will turn againſt you upon any little difguſt; ſo that in a fhort time, you may expect to fee the whole city

6   in

in arms, which will infallibly prove the deftrution
both of you and itfelf : for thofe Princes only can be
fecure in their government, who have but few enemies, and fuch as are eafy to be taken off either by
banifhment or death : but againft a univerfal difaffection, there can be no fecurity, as it will be impoffible to guefs with any certainty, from what hand
the ftroke may come ; and whofoever he is, that has
reafon to fear every man, cannot be fafe againft
any one. For if he cuts off fome, he is fure to expofe himfelf to ftill greater dangers, by enflaming
the hatred of thofe that are left, and making them
more implacable and ripe for revenge. That time
is not able to eradicate the love of Liberty, is fufficiently evident ; fince it has often happened in States
where the citizens themfelves were not free, that
many have exerted their moft ftrenuous endeavours
to be fo, merely upon the report of the bleffings of
Liberty, which they have received from their fathers ; and when they fucceeded, and tafted the
fweets of freedom, have defpifed all difficulties and
dangers to maintain it. And indeed, if they had
never heard of any fuch thing from their anceftors,
the daily fight of the public palaces, the courts of
juftice, the colours of their militia, and other monuments of former Liberty, would naturally have infpired them with a love of it. What exploits or degree of merit, therefore, on your fide, though ever
fo confiderable and endearing, can poffibly be a fufficient recompence for the lofs of our Liberty, or
what do you think can ever make us forget the hap-
pinefs we once enjoyed ? If you was to add all Tufcany to this State, and return to the city daily
crowned with frefh victories over our enemies, the
Honour would be yours and not ours, and the citizens would gain fellow-flaves rather than fubjects,
which would only ferve to aggravate their mifery.
And though you fhould be religious, or affable, or
juft, or bountiful to the laft degree, believe me, all
would not be fufficient to gain the affections of the

people; if you think otherwife, you only deceive yourfelf; for to men that have once lived free, the lighteft chain will feem heavy, and the leaft reftraint intolerable. In a State, which has been reduced to fubjeƈtion by force, it is not poffible that the citizens fhould live contentedly, even under a good prince; and it muft neceffarily happen, if he does not conform himfelf to their defires, that either one party or the other will foon be ruined. We leave you to judge, therefore, whether it will be better for you to endeavour to ufurp an abfolute dominion over this city, and to hold it by downright force of arms, (for which the poffeffion of all the forts and guards within, and all the friends that could be raifed abroad, have often been found infufficient) or to be content with the authority and power we have already given you. We would recommend the latter of thefe two meafures to you, becaufe that Dominion only can be of long continuance, which is voluntarily conferred; and advife you not to fuffer yourfelf to be blindly led by ambition, to the brink of a precipice, where you can neither retreat nor advance, and from whence you will inevitably be thrown down and overwhelmed in the ruins of the Commonwealth."

Thefe expoftulations made but little impreffion upon the Duke, who faid, " That it was fo far from being his defign to take away their liberty, that he came thither on purpofe to reftore it: that Citizens divided amongft themfelves were no better than flaves, whilft thofe that were united might properly be called free: that if he could extinguifh private ambition and inteftine difcord in Florence, by his manner of governing, furely he might be faid to reeftablifh their freedom, and not to deprive them of it: that he did not affume the government out of any ambition of his own, but accepted it at the entreaties of many of their fellow-citizens, and therefore they would do well to concur with them in the choice they had made of him. That as to the dangers he was likely to expofe himfelf to in this undertaking, he did

not

not regard them ; as it would be mean and pufillanimous to decline an opportunity of doing good, for
fear of any evil that might enfue ; and that none but
cowards would lay afide a glorious enterprife, merely
upon the uncertainty of fuccefs. That he hoped to
behave himfelf in fuch a manner, as would foon oblige them to acknowledge they had feared him too
much, and trufted him too little." The Signiory
finding by this anfwer, that no good was to be done,
were forced to confent, that the people fhould affemble the next morning in the Piazza before their palace, and the government be transferred, by their authority, to the Duke, for the fpace of one year, upon
the fame conditions that it had been formerly committed into the hands of the Duke of Calabria.

1342   On the eighth of September, 1342, the Duke, attended by Giovanni della Tofa, with all his friends,
and many other citizens, came into the Piazza : and
taking the Signiory with him, mounted the * Ringhiera, or landing-place, at the top of the fteps before
the Palace Gate, where he caufed the Agreement betwixt him and the Signiory to be publickly read ; and
when the perfon who read it came to that Article,
where the government was faid to be given him for a
year, the people fhouted out, *for life, for life.* Upon
which, Francifco Ruftichegli, one of the Signiory,
rofe up to have fpoken, and endeavoured to compofe
the tumult ; but he was interrupted, and could not
be heard. So that the Duke was made their Sovereign Lord by the confent of the people, not for a
year only, but for ever ; and afterwards carried about
the Piazza in a chair, amidft the acclamations of the
multitude. It is a cuftom amongft the Florentines,
that whoever is appointed captain of the Palace
Guard, is to fhut himfelf clofe up in it, in the abfence

---

* As it was ufual to addrefs the people upon publick occafions from
this and other fuch eminences, the word *Ringhiera* came at laft to fig-
nify a Roftrum, Pulpit, or reading Defk. From hence, I fuppofe,
comes the Italian Verb *aringare,* the French *haranguer,* and the Englifh
to harangue.

of the Signiory. This charge happened at that time to be in the hands of Rinieri Giotto, who being corrupted by the Duke's friends, admitted him. into the palace without making any refiftance, to the great offence and difhonour of the Signiory, who returned to their own houfes, and left it to be plundered by the Duke's fervants, after they had torn the Standard of the City to pieces, and planted their mafter's there in its ftead : at which, all the good Citizens were infinitely grieved and mortified, whilft thofe that either out of malice or ftupidity had confented to this election, did not a little rejoice.

The Duke was no fooner in poffeffion of the Government, but in order to take away the authority of thofe who had been the moft zealous advocates for their liberties, he forbad the Signiory to affemble any more at the Palace, and affigned them a private houfe to meet in. He took away the colours from the Gonfaloniers of the feveral Companies ; he repealed the old Laws againft the Nobility, he difcharged all Prifoners, recalled the Bardi and Frefcobaldi from 'banifhment, prohibited the wearing of fwords or other arms, and to fecure himfelf againft his enemies within the City, he made as many friends as he could in the adjacent territories : for which purpofe, he fhewed great favour to the people of Arezzo, and all others that were in any wife dependent upon the city of Florence. He concluded a peace with the Pifans, though he had been vefted with abfolute power on purpofe to carry on the war againft them with greater vigour. He took away the fecurities and affignments from the Merchants, who had lent money to the State, in the war with the Lucchefe, and not only increafed the former taxes, but exacted new ones from the people. He entirely diffolved the authority of the Signiory, and fet up three new Rettori or Judges, Baglione da Perugia, Guglielmo da Scefi, and Cerettieri Vifdomini, who were his council upon all occafions. The impofts he laid upon the Citizens were very grievous, his judicial proceedings partial and unjuft, and that

humi-

humility and fhew of Religion which he had put on at firft, were now fucceeded by fuch an intolerable degree of haughtinefs and cruelty, that many of the Nobility, and moft confiderable Commoners, were condemned and put to death, after they had been tortured in a new and unheard-of manner. His tyranny was no lefs infupportable in the Country than in the City : for after a while, he appointed fix more Judges, to plunder and opprefs the other towns. He was jealous of the Nobility, though he lay under great obligations to fome of them, and had recalled others from exile ; as he thought they were too generous and high-fpirited to bear with his infolent manner of governing. Upon which account, he began to pay his court to the people, by whofe favour, and the affiftance of foreign forces, he hoped he fhould be able to fupport himfelf in his tyrannical ufurpation.

In the month of May, at which time the Florentines ufually celebrate many Holidays, he caufed the inferior fort of people to be divided into feveral Companies, to which he gave pay, and honoured them with colours and fplendid titles : upon which, there was nothing but feafting and rejoicings to be feen in every part of the city, one half of the inhabitants being employed in vifiting, and the other in receiving and entertaining them. And when the news of his great power and authority began to be fpread abroad many of the French nation reforted to his court, to whom he gave preferments, and fhewed more favou than to any others, as perfons whom he thought h might thoroughly confide in : fo that Florence in : fhort time became fubject not only to French mer but to the French cuftoms and drefs, every one o both fexes endeavouring to imitate their fafhions without any regard to modefty, or even common de cency. But what feemed more intolerable was, th violence that was offered by him and his followers, to all forts of women, from the loweft to the higheft The citizens therefore were provoked beyond all pa tience, to fee the majefty of their government thu

trample

trampled upon, their ordinances abolished, their Laws annulled, all honest conversation corrupted, and modesty every where despised and insulted : for those who had not been accustomed to regal pomp, could not, without infinite concern, behold the Duke parading the City, surrounded by guards, both on foot and on horseback. But as there was no remedy, they were forced to court and honour him in appearance, whilst they mortally hated him in their hearts : and they were not a little terrified at the frequent executions, and continual impositions, with which he weakened and impoverished the City. Nor was the Duke himself ignorant of the general odium he had incurred, or without fears of his own, upon that account ; tho' he affected to appear, as if he thought himself extremely beloved.

It happened, that Matteo de Morozzi, either to gain the Duke's favour, or to exculpate himself, discovered a certain plot against him, in which the family of the Medici, and some others, were concerned : but the Duke was so far from making an enquiry into it, that he ordered the Informer to be put to death * : by which manner of proceeding, he deterred every one from giving him any sort of information that was necessary for his safety, and gave great encouragement to such as conspired his destruction.

* This was acting in a manner very different from most Tyrants, and indeed from many wise States and Princes, who have always thought it necessary to encourage Informers, at least to a certain degree, upon this maxim, that if men are falsely accused, they will be acquitted when they are brought to a fair trial; and those who are guilty, cannot be punished if they are not first accused. Tully, in his oration *pro Sextio Roscio*, says, that though the Dogs that were kept in the Capitol could not distinguish thieves from honest men, yet their barking at every body that came thither in the night, was of use, as it served to alarm the people, and put them upon their guard. Thus it is the interest of the State to encourage accusers, in order to deter those who might otherwise disturb the public tranquillity. Antoninus Pius, however, would neither listen to Informers, nor suffer such to be punished as had been actually concerned in conspiracies against him: and when the Senate was very urgent with him, to make an enquiry into their proceedings, he answered, " he did not chuse to have it known, that there was any body who did not love him." Victor. in Vit. Anton. Pii.

He likewife caufed the tongue of Bettoni Cini to be cut out, with fuch circumftances of cruelty, that he died of it; and for no other reafon, but becaufe he had complained of the heavy taxes that he had laid upon the city : an act of barbarity which exceedingly increafed the rage and difdain of the Citizens, who having been ufed both to fay and to do every thing with the greateft freedom, could not bear to have their hands tied up, and their mouths ftopped in this manner.

Thefe outrages were fufficient to roufe not only the Florentines, (who neither know how to value their liberty nor endure flavery) but even the moft âbject nation upon earth, to attempt the recovery of their freedom. Many of the Citizens therefore, of all ranks, were determined either to fhake off the yoke, or to die glorioufly in the caufe of Liberty : fo that there were three Confpiracies on foot againft him, at the fame time, amongft three different forts of people, the Nobility, the Commons, and the Artificers and Tradefmen. For befides the motives arifing from a general oppreffion, each party had its particular reafons. The Commons had been deprived of the government, the Nobility were not reftored to it, and the Tradefmen had loft all their bufinefs. Agnolo Acciaivoli, who was then Archbifhop of Florence, at firft had highly extolled the actions and good qualities of the Duke in fome of his Sermons to the people, and wonderfully conciliated their affections to him : but when he faw him in full poffeffion of the Government, and exercifing his power in that arbitrary and defpotic manner, he began to think he had abufed his fellow Citizens; and to make them fome amends, refolved to put himfelf at the head of the firft and moft powerful confpiracy, in which he engaged with the Bardi, Roffi, Frefcobaldi, Scali, Altoviti, Magalotti, Strozzi, and Mancini. The principal conductors of the fecond confpiracy were Manno and Corfo Donati, and under them the Pazzi, Cavicciulli, Cerchi and Albizi. Of the third, Antonio

Adi-

Adimari was the Head, and joined by the families of the Medici, Bordini, Rucellai, and Aldobrandini. Their defign was to have killed him in the houfe of the Albizi, whither it was imagined he would come on Midfummer-day to fee the Horfe-races; but, as it happened, he did not go thither on that day, and their defign was difappointed. The next propofal was, to affaffinate him in the ftreet: but that was thought too difficult, becaufe he always went well armed and attended: and as he feldom took the fame round twice together, they could not certainly tell where it would be moft proper to lie in wait for him. Some were of opinion it would be the beft way to difpatch him in the Council: but then it was confidered that even after he was dead, they muft of neceffity be left to the difcretion of his Guards.

Whilft thefe things were in debate amongft the confpirators, Antonio Adimari communicated the affair to fome of his friends at Siena in hopes of their affiftance, told them the names of the principal perfons that were engaged in it, and affured them the whole city was difpofed to fhake off their yoke: upon which, one of the Sienefe imparted the matter to Francifco Brunellefchi, not with any defign to have betrayed the confpiracy, but becaufe he took it for granted that he was privy to it; and Francifco, either out of fear or malice to fome that were concerned, difcovered the whole to the Duke, who immediately ordered Paolo da Mazzecca and Simone da Montezappoli to be apprehended. Thefe two being examined made a full confeffion, and acquainted the Duke with the number and quality of the confpirators, at which he was not a little frighted: however, after he had confulted his friends, he thought fit rather to fummon the reft to appear before him, than to lay violent hands upon them; becaufe if they fled, the danger would be over without any further difturbance. In confequence of this refolution, he in the firft place fent for Adimari, who relying upon the number and fupport of his accomplices, boldly made

his

his appearance and was fent to prifon. After this
ftep, he was advifed by Francifco Brunellefchi and
Uguccione Buondelmonte to go to the houfes of the
others with his guards, and to feize upon them there
and put them to death : but confidering how many
enemies he had in the town, he thought he had not
ftrength fufficient to do that, and therefore took another refolution, which if it had fucceeded, would
have freed him from the moft powerful of his enemies, and made him ftrong enough to over-awe the
reft.

It had been his cuftom to call the Citizens together and defire their opinions and advice upon any
emergency ; and now having affembled as many forces
as he could, he drew out a lift of three hundred
Citizens and gave it to his ferjeants to fummon every
one of them, on a pretence that he wanted to confult with them ; defigning when they were met, either
to kill or imprifon them all. But the confinement of
Adimari, and the gathering together fuch a number
of armed men, which could not be done without fome
buftle, made many of them, efpecially the Confpirators, fo fufpicious, that the moft refolute amongft
them pofitively refufed to obey the fummons. After
the lift had been read by them all, they had a meeting, in which they encouraged each other to take up
arms and die like men with their fwords in their
hands, rather than fuffer themfelves to be driven like
fheep to the flaughter : fo that in lefs than an hour
all thofe that were concerned in the different Confpiracies, having communicated their defigns to each other,
refolved to raife a tumult the next day (which was the
26th of July 1343) in the old Market-place, upon
which they were all to take arms and excite the people to rife and attempt the recovery of their liberty.
The next day therefore, when the Bell rung for
Nones *, they all rofe, as had been agreed on, and

---

* The original is, *al fuono di nona.* The Italians begin their account of hours from fun fet, and end it at fun fet again, which in-

at

at the cry of *Liberty, Liberty*, the people likewife ran
to arms in their feveral Quarters, under the Colours
of the City, which had been fecretly delivered to
them before hand by the Confpirators for that purpofe.   All the heads of families, both of the Nobility and Commonalty, met together and took an Oath
to ftand by each other in their own defence and the
deftruction of the Duke, except fome of the Buondelmonti and Cavalcanti, and thofe four families of
the Commoners that had been the chief inftruments
in conferring the fovereignty upon him, who ran armed to the Piazza of the Palace with a parcel of Butch-
ers and others of the dregs of the people at their heels
to defend the Duke.

In the mean time the Duke, not a little alarmed at
thefe proceedings, was very bufy in fortifying the
Palace ; and thofe of his Guards that lodged in other
parts of the city, mounted their horfes and rode towards the Piazza ; but in their way thither they were
attacked feveral times and many of them killed.
However, as about three hundred Horfe had affembled there to fupport him, he was in doubt whether
he fhould fally out and face his enemies, or defend
himfelf in the Palace.   On the other hand, the Medici, Cavicciulli, Rucellai, and other families who
had fuffered moft by him, were apprehenfive that if
he fhould make a fally, many who had taken arms
againft him would declare themfelves his friends :
and therefore being refolved to prevent him from fal-
lying out and gaining more ftrength, they drew up
and attacked his forces that were affembled in the
Piazza.   Upon this, the families which appeared at
firft in the Duke's defence, feeing themfelves fo vi-

cludes a fpace of twenty four hours.   And as the fun fets with them
about nine o'clock at that feafon of the Year, their ninth hour muſt
be about fix the next morning, as we reckon time.—*Il fuono di nona*,
is alfo often ufed by Italian writers, for ringing the bell for Nones
about mid day, which is one of their ftated hours of prayer.   The
latter feems to be meant here, as the tumult was to be begun in the
Market-place, which at that time of the day might be fuppofed to be
fulleft of people.

gorouſly

goroufly affaulted, immediately changed their fide,
and deferting him in his diftrefs, all joined their fellow-citizens, except Uguccione Buondelmonte, who
withdrew into the Palace, and Gianozzo Cavalcanti
who retreated with fome of his party into the New
Market, where he got upon a table and made an harangue to the people, in which he earneftly exhorted
thofe whom he found in arms there to haften to the
Duke's affiftance. And to intimidate them, he mag-
nified his ftrength, and told them, that every man of
them would be put to death if they perfifted in their
rebellion againft their Prince. But as nobody either
feemed to regard him or thought it worth their while
to chaftife him for his infolence, after he had taken
much pains to no purpofe, he refolved not to hazard
his perfon any longer, and fneaked away to his own
houfe. The difpute was very fharp in the mean time
betwixt the people and the Duke's party in the Piazza,
and though the latter were reinforced from the Palace,
they were worfted; part of them furrendering to the
enemy, others quitting their horfes and efcaping on
foot into the Palace. Whilft they were thus engaged
in the Piazza, Corfo and Amerigo Donati with fome
others of the people broke open the Prifons, burnt
the records of the Judges Courts and publick Chamber, plundered the houfes of the Magiftrates and killed all the Duke's creatures they could meet with.
The Duke on the other hand, feeing the Piazza was
loft, that the whole city was become his enemy, and
no hopes of relief left, refolved to try if he could regain the affections of the people by fome acts of grace
and indulgence. For which purpofe he knighted
Antonio Adimari in the firft place, though much
againft his own inclination, and with very little fatif-
faction to the other: he then fent for all the reft
whom he had imprifoned, and fet them at liberty with
promifes of his future friendfhip and favour: he likewife caufed his own ftandard to be taken down, and
that of the people to be fet up again at the Palace:
all which things being done in a very ungracious
man-

manner, and out of mere neceffity, had but little effect. So that he ftill continued blocked up in the
Palace to his great mortification, when he.faw that by
grafping at too much power he was likely to lofe all,
and either to be famifhed or maffacred in a few days.

After this fuccefs, the Citizens affembled in St.
Reparata's in order to reform the Government, and
appointed fourteen perfons, one half of them of the
Nobility and the other of the Commoners, who in
conjunction with the Archbifhop fhould have full
power to new-model the State as they pleafed. They
alfo committed the authority of the Podefta to fix
Magiftrates, who were to adminifter juftice till the
arrival of the perfon whom they fhould make choice
of to fill that Office. There were many people in
Florence at that time, who had come thither to the
affiftance of the Citizens; and amongft the reft, fix
Deputies from Siena, men of great efteem in their
own Country, who endeavoured to bring about fome
accommodation betwixt the people and the Duke.
But the people abfolutely refufed to liften to any overtures of that kind, except Guglielmo da Scefi, together with his fon and Cerettieri Vifdomini, were delivered up to them, which the Duke would not confent to by any means, till the threats of thofe that
were blocked up with him in the Palace obliged him
to comply. Greater certainly and more cruel is the
refentment of the People when they have recovered
their liberty, than when they are acting in defence of
it. Guglielmo and his Son were brought out and
given up to thoufands of their enemies; and though
the Son was not quite eighteen years of age, yet neither his youth, nor innocence, nor the gracefulnefs
of his perfon were fufficient to protect him from the
rage of the multitude. Many who could not get near
enough to reach them whilft they were alive, thruft
their fwords into them after they were dead; and not
content with this, they tore their carcaffes to pieces
with their nails and teeth: that fo all their fenfes might
be glutted with revenge; and after they had feafted

L 4   their

their ears with their groans, their eyes with their wounds, and their touch with tearing the flesh off their bones; as if all this was not enough, the taste likewise might have its share and be gratified. This savage Barbarity, how fatal soever to those two, was the preservation of Ceretteri; for the people having spent their fury upon these unfortunate men, entirely forgot him, and he was privately conveyed in the night by some of his friends and relations out of the Palace into a place of security.

When the people were thus satiated with blood, the Duke and his friends were suffered to withdraw with their effects unmolested out of Florence, on condition that he would renounce all claim and pretensions to any authority over the city, and ratify his renunciation when he got to Casentino, a place out of the Florentine Dominions; in pursuance of which agreement, he left Florence on the sixth of August, escorted by many of the Citizens, and upon his arrival at Casentino, confirmed his renunciation, though with much reluctance; and indeed it is very likely he would not have done it at all, if Conte Simone had not threatened to carry him back again to Florence *. This Prince, as his actions have fully shewn, was of a sanguinary and avaricious disposition, difficult of access, and haughty in his answers. As he did not regard the affections of the people, whom he hoped to enslave, he rather chose to be feared than loved. Nor was his person less disagreeable than his behaviour was odious. For he was very low of stature,

* Livy relates, l. xxiv. c. 22. that Dionysius the tyrant used to say, " That rather than return to a private condition on horseback, he would be dragged to it by the feet." It is no wonder, indeed, that tyrants resign their power with reluctance; for when they have done so, how can they refund the sums of which they have plundered their country? How can they indemnify those whom they have imprisoned? How can they restore life to the persons they have put to death? Who will defend them against the general resentment of the people? Periander said, " it was dangerous for a tyrant to abdicate even of his own accord." Yet Sylla did it, and died a natural death, after he had shed the blood of 100,000 private men, 90 Senators, 15 of consular dignity, and above 2000 Gentlemen.

ot

of a fwarthy complection, with a long thin beard: fo that he was every way defpicable and worthy of general contempt: and the enormities of his admi- niftration in the courfe of about ten months, deprived him of that Dominion which he had acquired by the contrivance and co-operation of bad Citizens.

This revolution in the city encouraged all the reft of the towns under the jurifdiction of the Floren- tines to take up arms for their liberties; fo that in a fhort time, Arezzo, Caftiglione, Piitoia, Volterra, Colle and St. Gimignano revolted; and the whole territory of Florence, after the example of its Metro- polis, fhook off its yoke and became entirely free: in this manner, the Florentines, by the fteps they took to recover their own liberty, at the fame time taught their Vaffals to do the like.

After the Duke was thus depofed, the Council of fourteen and the Archbifhop confulting together, thought it would be better to attach their former fubjects to them by pacific meafures, than to widen the breach by hoftilities; and pretending to be no lefs pleafed with their liberty than their own, they fent Deputies to Arezzo to renounce the Sovereignty which they before had over it, and to enter into an alliance with the Citizens: that fo, though they could not for the future command them as fubjects, they might upon occafion make ufe of their affiftance as friends. This prudent refolution had a very good effect; for all the reft of the towns, except Arezzo, returned to their former obedience in a few months, and Arezzo itfelf followed their example not many years after. Thus experience fhews that fome ends are obtained with lefs danger and expence by coolnefs and indifference, than by purfuing them with paffion and impetuofity.

When affairs abroad were compofed in this man- ner, they began to fettle the form of their govern- ment at home; and after fome difputes betwixt the Nobility and the People, it was agreed that one third of the Signiory, and one half of the other Magi- ftrates

ftrates and other Officers of State fhould confift of the Nobility. The city, as we have faid before, was divided into fix parts, each of which chofe one of the Signiory; and though it fometimes happened that their number was increafed to twelve or thirteen, yet they were afterwards reduced again to fix. But as thefe fix parts were not duly proportioned, and they defigned to give more power and authority to the Nobility, it was neceffary to make a new regulation in this point, and to increafe the number of the Signiory. They divided the city therefore into quarters, and chofe three of the Signiory out of each. The Gonfalonier della Giuftizia, and thofe of the feveral Companies were laid afide; and inftead of the twelve Buonhuomini, they created eight Counfellors, four of each quality. The commonwealth being fettled upon this bottom, might have continued quiet and happy, if the Nobility could have been content to confine themfelves within the bounds of that moderation which is requifite in all republican governments. But their behaviour was quite contrary: for as they had always difdained the thoughts of equality, even when they lived a private life, fo now they were in the magiftracy they thought to domineer over the whole city, and every day produced frefh inftances of their pride and arrogance; which exceedingly galled the people when they faw they had depofed one Tyrant, only to make room for a thoufand †.

Things being thus circumftanced, the infolence of one fide, and the indignation and impatience of the other, at laft increafed to fuch a height, that the Heads of the people complained to the Archbifhop of the enormities of the Nobility and the haughtinefs with which they were treated by them; befeeching him to ufe his endeavours to bring it about that they might be confined to a certain fhare in the other offices, and leave the Signiory to be filled by Commoners

† It often happens, fays an ingenious writer, that more diforders are occafioned by confpiracies, which put an end to tyranny, than there would have been by fuffering it.

only.

only. The Archbiſhop was naturally a good man, but of a fickle inconſtant diſpoſition and eaſily moved to change his ſide : So that his acquaintance at firſt prevailed upon him to appear in favour of the Duke of Athens, and afterwards, at the perſuaſion of other Citizens, he conſpired againſt him : in the late Reformation he exerted himſelf for the Nobility, and now he was induced, by the ſollicitation of the people, to turn his back upon them ; and imagining he ſhould find other people as eaſy to be wrought upon as himſelf, he made no doubt of bringing the Nobility to comply with thoſe propoſals. For this purpoſe, he called together the *Fourteen*, who were yet in authority, and made uſe of the mildeſt and moſt plauſible arguments to prevail upon them to give up the Signiory to the People, if they had any regard to the peace of the city, or their own ſafety and preſervation. But theſe admonitions had a very different effect upon the Nobility, from what he expected : for Ridolpho de Bardi taking him up very ſharply, upbraided him with levity and perfidy in firſt coming over to the Duke, and then deſerting him in his diſtreſs ; and concluded with ſaying, " that as they had acquired the honours they enjoyed with the peril of their lives, they would maintain them in the ſame manner" : after which, he and his friends abruptly withdrew, and leaving the Archbiſhop, went directly to inform all the reſt of the Nobility of what had paſſed. Thoſe of the Commoners that were of the Fourteen, likewiſe acquainted their party with theſe proceedings : and whilſt the Nobility were raiſing what force they could, for the defence of their friends that were in the Signiory, the Commons alſo, not caring to wait till they were grown too ſtrong, inſtantly took arms and ran to the Palace, where they furiouſly called upon the Nobles to reſign all ſhare in the adminiſtration. The tumult being very great, the Signiory were deſerted : for the Nobility ſeeing all the people in arms, durſt not appear, but kept cloſe at home. Upon which, the Commoners that
were

were of the Signiory, endeavoured to pacify the Multitude, by protesting, that their Associates were good
and worthy men : but not succeeding in that attempt,
in order to protect them from further danger, they
sent them to their own houses, whither they got with
much difficulty.   After the Nobles in the Signiory
were thus deprived of their authority, the four
Counsellors of their order were also turned out of
their offices, and the remaining number increased to
twelve, which consisted of Commoners only : besides
which, the eight that remained in the Signiory, not
only made a new Gonfalonier di Giustizia and sixteen
other Gonfaloniers over the Companies of the people,
but modelled all the Councils in such a manner, that
the government was now entirely in the hands of the
people.

During these transactions, there happened a great
dearth in Florence : so that there were very grievous
discontents both amongst the Nobility and common
people ; the former repining at the loss of their authority, and the latter murmuring for want of bread
These clamours encouraged Andrea Strozzi to make
an attempt upon the liberties of the city.   For as he
sold his corn at a cheaper rate than others, it drew
such numbers to his House, that he boldly mounted
his horse one morning, and putting himself at the
head of them, called upon all the rest of the people
to take up arms : by which means he had got together above four thousand men in less than an hour,
and conducting them to the palace of the Signiory,
demanded the doors of it to be thrown open to him.
But the Signiory, partly by threats, and partly by
force of arms, happily disengaged themselves from
them ; and afterwards so terrified them by issuing out
one Proclamation after another, that the multitude
dissolved by little and little, and every man returned
to his own house, leaving Andrea alone to shift for
himself as well as he could ; so that it was with no
little difficulty that he escaped the hands of the magistrates.   The attempt was bold indeed, and though

it

it did not fucceed, (as fuch rafh enterprizes feldom do)
yet it gave the Nobility frefh hopes of recovering
their power, now they faw the inferior fort of people
fo incenfed againft the Commons.   Not to neglect fo
fair an opportunity therefore, they refolved to take
arms, and make ufe of all manner of allies to regain
that by force, which they conceived had been taken
from them with fo much injuftice.   And to infure
fuccefs, they provided themfelves with arms, fortified
their houfes, and fent to their friends in Lombardy for
fupplies.

The Commons and the Signiory on the other hand
were no lefs bufy in arming themfelves, and fent to
the Sienefe and Perugians to defire their affiftance:
fo that when the auxiliaries on each fide arrived, the
whole city was foon in arms.   The Nobility drew
up in three divifions, on this fide the Arno, at the
houfes of the Cavicciulli near St. John's, at thofe of
the Pazzi and Donati near St. Pietro Maggiore, and
at thofe of the Cavalcanti in the New Market: whilft
fuch of them as lived on the other fide of the River,
fortified the Bridges and Streets that were near their
houfes.   The Nerli took poffeffion of the Ponte alla
Carraia ; the Frefcobaldi and Mannelli, of that of
St. Trinita ; the Roffi and the Bardi, of the old
Bridge and the Rubaconte.   The Commons in the
mean time, having affembled under the Gonfalone,
or Standard della Giuftizia, and the colours of their
refpective companies, refolved to attack the enemy
without further delay.   Accordingly the Medici and
Rondinelli immediately fell upon the Cavicciulli in
the avenue that led from St. John's Piazza to the
place where their houfes ftood.   The action continued very hot and bloody for the fpace of three
hours, during which, they had great ftones tumbled
down upon their heads from the tops of the houfes,
and were terribly galled with crofs-bows below : but
as the number of the enemy continually increafed,
the Cavicciulli feeing themfelves over-powered at laft,
and deftitute of all relief, were forced to furrender

to

to the people, who fpared their houfes and effects, and were content with taking away their arms only, and diftributing them, difarmed as they were, amongft the houfes of the Commoners that were their friends or relations. When the Cavicciulli were thus defeated, the Pazzi and Donati, who had not fo much ftrength, were foon reduced; fo that the Cavalcanti only remained entire on this fide of the River, who were more confiderable both in refpect of their numbers and the ftrength of their fituation. But as they faw all the companies now advancing againft them, and their affociates had been worfted by three of them only, they fubmitted without making much refiftance. Three parts of the city out of four were now in the hands of the people; but that which ftill continued in the poffeffion of the Nobility, was more inacceffible and difficult to be ftormed than any of the reft, not only on account of the numbers that defended it, but becaufe it was fo fecured by the River, that it was neceffary to be mafters of the Bridge in the firft place, which, as we have already faid were very well fortified. A vigorous attack, however, was made upon the old Bridge, which was no lefs refolutely fuftained; and as the turrets were garrifoned, the avenues blocked up, and the barricadoe guarded by the ftouteft of their men, the people were repulfed with confiderable lofs. When they found therefore that all further attempts would be in vain at that pafs, they refolved, if it was poffible to force their way over the Ponte Rubaconte: but meeting with the fame obftructions there, they left four companies to watch the motions of the enemy at thofe two Bridges, and marched with the reft to the Ponte alla Carraia. The Nerli had the defence of that pafs, and though they behaved with great valour, yet they could not poffibly maintain it; not only becaufe there were no turrets there, but becaufe the Capponi and other neighbouring families of the Commoners attack'd them at the fame time in the rear; fo that, being over-powered by number the they were forced to abandon their barricadoes, and give way to the fury of the affailants, who, having been joined by all the families of the Commoners on the other fide of the River, then proceeded to attack the Roffi and Frefcobaldi, and foon drove them from their pofts. The only party that remained unconquered were the Bardi, who defended themfelves in fo courageous and obftinate a manner, that neither the defeat of their affociates, nor the whole force of the people combined againft them alone, nor the impoffibility of any relief, could difmay them : and they rather chofe to fee their houfes plundered and burnt down to the ground before their faces, and to die bravely with their arms in their hands, than tamely fubmit to the mercy of their enemy. With this refolution, they ftood by each other fo firmly, that though they were feveral times attacked both at the old Bridge and the Rubaconte, they as often repulfed the people at each place with great flaughter. There was an old obfcure lane that led from the Via Romana, by the houfes of the Pitti, to the wall upon St. George's Hill ; through this lane, the people fent fix companies, with orders to attack the back parts of the houfes where the Bardi had fortified themfelves : at which they were fo difheartened, that the people, in a very fhort time, got the better of them. For as foon as they heard their houfes were affaulted in that manner, thofe that guarded the Barricadoes at the Bridges, immediately quitted their Pofts and ran to defend them : fo that they were prefently forced, and the Bardi being utterly routed and difperfed, took fhelter in the houfes of the Quaratefi, Panzanefi, and Mozzi. Upon which, the people, efpecially the inferior fort of them, naturally rapacious and greedy of fpoil, began to plunder their houfes, which they afterwards burnt down to the ground, and committed fuch other outrages as the bittereft enemy to the city of Florence would have been afhamed of.

The Nobility being in this manner entirely fubdued, the people took upon them to reform the State ; and

and as there were three degrees of them, it was ordained that the higheſt rank ſhould have the nomination of two of the Signiory, the middle ſort of
three, and the loweſt of three more: and that the
Gonfalonier della Giuſtizia ſhould be choſen by turns
out of all three. Beſides which, the old Laws were
revived and put in execution againſt the Nobility;
and to reduce them ſtill more effectually, many of
them were incorporated with the other claſſes. By
theſe means they were brought ſo low, that they became abject and puſillanimous, and never durſt riſe
any more againſt the people: ſo that being deprived
of their arms and honours, their ſpirit and generoſity
likewiſe ſeemed to be extinguiſhed. After this de-
preſſion of the Nobles, the city continued in tranquillity till the year 1353, during which interval the
great Plague happened, ſo eloquently deſcribed by
Giovanni Boccaccio *, of which above ninety-ſix
thouſand people died in Florence. The firſt war with
the Viſconti likewiſe happened in this period, occaſioned by the ambition of the Archbiſhop, who at
that time was Prince of Milan; which war was no
ſooner ended, but new factions ſprung up in the City
for though the Nobility were ruined, yet Fortune found
other means to raiſe freſh troubles and diſſenſions.

1353

---

* That author has taken great pains indeed, to deſcribe this cala
mity in the moſt affecting manner, at the beginning of his Decame
rone; and it is finely wrought up.

END OF THE SECOND BOOK.

T H I

THE

H I S T O R Y

O F

F L O R E N C E.

B O O K III.

A R G U M E N T.

Animosities betwixt the Nobility and People, the chief cause of disturbances in a city. The emulation betwixt the middle sort of People and the Plebeians. Several are admonished and rendered incapable of the Magistracy. The Speech of a Citizen to the Signiory. A reformation in Florence. Pope Gregory XI. resides at Avignon, and governs Italy by Legates. Eight Citizens appointed to act as secretaries at war. A conspiracy of the Guelphs defeated. The speech of Sylvestro de Medici. The Balia, a temporary council, instituted. Another reformation. The speech of Luigi Guicciardini to the Magistrates and Syndics of the Arts, when he was Gonfalonier di Giustizia. New disturbances arise from the discontents of the Plebeians. The Speech of a Plebeian. The Plebeians rise in arms. Their Demands. Michael di Lando, a wool-comber, puts himself at the head of them, and seizes upon the government. His character. He quells the Plebeians. The popular and Plebeian factions. Apprehension of a conspiracy. Many executions in Florence. Remarkable story of Pietro degli Albizi. Another model of government. The Plebeians are deprived of all share in it. Michael di Lando is banifhed. Lewis of Anjou comes into Italy, with an army, to drive Carlo Durazzo out of the kingdom of Naples, and re-eftablifh Queen Giovanna there. The Florentines are afraid of him. His death. Carlo Durazzo is made King of Hungary, and dies there foon after. Benedetto degli Alberti is banifhed. The fpeech of Veri de Medici to the Signiory. Donato Acciaiuoli banifhed. A confpiracy defeated. The Duke of Milan confpires with the Exiles againft Florence. The Plot is difcovered. Several Families proclaimed Rebels and banifhed. The death of Ladiflaus, King of Naples.

THE bitter animofities which generally happen between the people and Nobility from an ambition in the one to command, and a reluctance in the other to obey, are the natural fources of thofe calamities that are incident to Commonwealths; for all other evils that ufually difturb their peace are both occafioned and fomented by this contrariety of difpofitions. It was this that kept Rome fo long divided. This alfo (if we may be allowed to compare a fmall Republic with one that was fo much more confiderable) gave birth to the factions which fprung up in Florence; though indeed it produced very different effects at laft in the two cities. For the difputes that firft arofe between the Nobility and people of Rome, were determined by reafon and expoftulation; but thofe at Florence by the fword. In Rome that was effected by the Laws, which in Florence could hardly be done by the banifhment and death of numbers of their citizens. The quarrels of the Romans ftill added to their fpirit and military virtue; whilft thofe of the Florentines utterly extinguifhed them. The former deftroyed that equality which was at firft eftablifhed, and introduced a prodigious difparity amongft the Citizens: the latter, on the contrary, abolifhed all fuperiority or difference of rank, and put every man upon the fame level. This diverfity of effects muft certainly have proceeded

from

6

from a difference of views. The people of Rome defired no more than to fhare with the Nobility in the adminiftration of the Commonwealth; but the people of Florence were not only defirous to have the government of the State to themfelves, but ufed violent meafures, and took up arms to exclude their Nobles from any part in it. And as the terms of the Roman people were more moderate, their demands feemed not unreafonable to the Nobility, who, therefore, complied with them; fo that after fome little bickerings, and without coming to an open rupture, a Law was made, by which the people were fatisfied, and the Nobles continued in their honours and offices. On the other hand, the demands of the Florentine people were fo extravagant and injurious, that the Nobility took up arms to fupport their privileges, and their quarrels grew to fuch a height, that numbers were either banifhed, or flain, before they could be ended; and the Laws afterwards made, were calculated rather for the private advantage of the victors than the good of the publick.

Hence it came to pafs, that the fuccefs of the people of Rome made that State more potent and confiderable: for as they were equally admitted to govern the Commonwealth, and to command their armies and provinces with the Nobility, they became infpired with the fame virtue and magnanimity; and as they grew more public fpirited, their power alfo increafed. But in Florence, when the people had fubdued the Nobility, they divefted them of all manner of authority, and left them no poffibility of recovering any part of it, except they would entirely conform to their cuftoms and way of living, and not only fubmit to appear, but to be Commoners like themfelves. And this was the reafon that induced them to change their arms, and vary their titles, and the names of their families, which was fo frequent in thofe times amongft the Nobility, in order to infinuate themfelves into the affections of the people: fo that the military fpirit and greatnefs of foul, for

which

which the Nobility had been held in fuch veneration,
was utterly extinguifhed, and not by any means to
be raifed in the people where there were no feeds of
it; by which means Florence became every day more
abject and pufillanimous.   And whereas Rome at laft
grew fo powerful and wanton by the effects of its virtue, that it could not be governed any otherwife than
by one Prince; Florence was reduced fo low, that a
wife Legiflator might eafily have new modelled it,
and given it what form he pleafed; which muft be
obvious to any one that has read the firft and fecond books of this hiftory.   As I have therefore already given an account of the original of Florence,
the foundation and eftablifhment of its liberty, the
occafion of its diffenfions, the tyranny of the Duke
of Athens, and how the factions betwixt the Nobility
and the Commons ended in the utter ruin of the former, I fhall now proceed to relate the Contefts that
happened betwixt the Commons and the Plebeians
and the feveral events which they produced.

The power of the Nobility being fuppreffed, and
the war with the Archbifhop at an end, there feemed
to be no feeds of future diffenfions left in Florence
But the evil deftiny of our City, and want of good
conduct, occafioned a new emulation betwixt the fa
milies of the Albizi and the Ricci, which produced
as fatal divifions as thofe betwixt the Buondelmont
and Uberti, and the other betwixt the Cerchi and
Donati had done before.   The Popes then refided in
France, and the Emperors in Germany: but upon
various occafions, and at different times, had fen
great numbers of Englifh, French, and German
forces into Italy, to keep up their intereft and re
putation there.   But when the wars were over, and
they were difbanded, they all united under one com
mon Standard, as Soldiers of Fortune, and levied
contributions fometimes upon one Prince, and fome
times upon another.   In the year 1353, a body of
thefe Freebooters advancing into Tufcany, under th
command of Monfieur Real, a Provençal, threw th

who'

whole country into fuch confternation, that not only
the Governors of Florence raifed forces on the public
account, but feveral private Citizens, efpecially the
Albizi and Ricci, fortified themfelves for their own
defence. Betwixt thefe two families, there was a
mortal hatred, each confpiring the deftruction of the
other, in order to engrofs the fole management of
the Commonwealth with lefs difficulty. However,
they had not as yet taken up arms, or proceeded to
open violence on either fide, but only thwarted each
other in council, and the execution of their offices.
In the mean time, whilft the whole city was ready
armed and ripe for mifchief, there unluckily happened a private quarrel in the Old Market Place; to
which all the neighbours ran (as ufual on fuch occafions) and upon enquiring into the caufe of it,
fome gave out, that the Ricci were going to attack
the Albizi, and others that the Albizi were preparing
to fall upon the Ricci; which different ftories being
immediately carried to both parties, occafioned fuch
an uproar and divifion throughout the whole city,
that the Magiftrates found it a very difficult matter
to keep the two families and their friends from coming
to a fray in good earneft; though neither fide had intended any fuch thing as was malicioufly reported.
This difturbance, though fmall at firft, and accidental, ferved to enflame their former animofities,
and determined both fides to be upon their guard,
and ftrengthen their parties. And fince the Citizens
were reduced to fuch a degree of equality by the fup-
preffion of the Nobility, that the Magiftrates were
held in greater reverence than ever they had been
before, each family refolved to avail themfelves rather of public and ordinary means, than of private
violence.

We have already fhewn that the Guelphs alone
were invefted with the Magiftracy, and had great
power given them over the Ghibeline party after the
victory gained by Charles the Firft: but this diftinction was fo far abolifhed by time and various other

con-

contingencies and new divisions, that many who were descended from the Ghibelines, had now got into authority and exercised some of the highest offices in common with the Guelphs, Uguccione de Ricci, therefore, who at that time was the head of his family, used his utmost endeavours to have the laws against the Ghibelines revived; which faction, it was supposed by many, the Albizi inclined to favour, as they originally came, though many years before, from Arezzo to settle in Florence. So that Uguccione hoped to render that family incapable of enjoying any honours in the Commonwealth by virtue of those laws; since it was enacted by them, that no person whatsoever that was of Ghibeline extraction, should presume to exercise the office of a Magistrate on pain of death. This design was discovered by Pietro, the son of Philippo Albizi, who resolved to connive at it; rightly judging, that if he made any opposition, it would be in a manner declaring himself a Ghibeline. These laws, however, though renewed to favour the interest and ambition of the Ricci, did not in the least diminish the reputation of the Albizi, but rather increased it, and were the occasion of many evils that afterwards happened; for indeed no laws can be made so prejudicial to a Common-wealth as those of retrospection, and such as look too far back into past times. Pietro therefore, having rather promoted than opposed those laws; made use of the very means to advance himself, which his enemies had contrived to ruin him: for undertaking to see them put in execution, he daily acquired fresh authority, and became the chief favourite of this new faction of the Guelphs. And as there was no certain definition of a Ghibeline laid down in those laws, nor any particular Magistrate deputed to inform against them (which rendered the laws of little effect) he got it enacted, that the Captains of the people should have power to make an inquisition into that matter, and to admonish such as were discovered to be Ghibelines, not to exercise the function of Magiftrátes; which admonition if they did not obey, they were to be put to death; and from hence all thofe that were afterwards incapacitated to fill the Magiftracy, were called *Ammoniti*, or perfons admonifhed. But in a while the Captains grew fo partial and infolent, that without any regard to principle or fufficient caufe, they admonifhed whomfoever they thought fit, accordingly as they were led by paffion or private intereft : fo that betwixt the year 1357, in which this law took place, and the year 1371, above two hundred of the Citizens were admonifhed.

By thefe means the Captains and the faction of the Guelphs were grown very confiderable, efpecially the Heads of it, Pietro degli Albizi, Lapo da Caftiglionchio, and Carlo Strozzi, who were much courted by every one for fear of being admonifhed. And though this injurious manner of proceeding gave great difguft to many, yet it was more intolerable to the Ricci than any body elfe, who had been the authors of thefe meafures, which contrary to their intentions had fo much increafed the power of their enemies and were likely to prove the ruin of the Commonwealth. Uguccione therefore, being one of the Signiory, in order to mitigate the fmart of this fcourge which he and his partifans had made for their own backs, caufed a new law to be paffed, that three more Captains fhould be added to the former fix, two of whom were to be chofen out of the lower fort of Mechanicks; and that thofe who were admonifhed as Ghibelines, fhould be certified to be fo by twenty-four Citizens of the Guelph party, deputed on purpofe to examine into the proofs of it. Thefe laws for fome time were fuch a check upon the arbitrary proceedings of the Captains, that their admonitions loft much of their terror, and were in a great meafure laid afide. The jealoufies however betwixt the Ricci and Albizi were not yet fubfided, and they ftill continued to oppofe each other in all councils, enterprizes, and other public affairs, with the utmoft degree of virulence. Thefe difcords lafted from the

M 4   year

1371.

year 1366 till 1371, by which time the Guelphs had
fully recovered their former authority.

There was a gentleman of the family of Buondelmonti, whose name was Benchi, who for his merit in
the wars againſt the Piſans, was thought worthy of
being admitted into the rank of Commoners, and
thereby became qualified to be of the Signiory.
But when he expected that honour, a law was made,
that no perſon of noble extraction, though become a
Commoner, ſhould be capable of enjoying any ſhare
in the Magiſtracy.   At this law, Benchi was ſo highly
provoked, that he joined with Pietro degli Albizi;
and after a conſultation betwixt them, they reſolved
to depreſs the lower ſort of people by admonitions,
and take the government into their own hands.   And
indeed by his intereſt with the ancient Nobility, and
Pietro's amongſt the principal Commoners, the faction of the Guelphs grew ſtill more and more conſiderable: for they had ſo ordered matters by their
new models and regulations, that the Captains and
the twenty-four being wholly at their devotion, they
began to avail themſelves of admonitions again, with
more boldneſs than ever they had done before; and
the family of the Albizi being at the head of that
faction, became exceeding powerful.   The Ricci and
their friends, on the other hand, ſpared no pains to
obſtruct theſe deſigns: ſo that every one living in
great fear and apprehenſion of ſome fatal conſequence, ſeveral of the Citizens, who were moſt zealous for the good of their Country, aſſembled in the
Church of St. Pietro Scheraggio, and having conſidered the dangerous ſituation of affairs, they went
to wait upon the Signiory at their Palace, where one
of the moſt eminent of their body addreſſed himſelf
to them in the following manner.

" Many of us have been in doubt, magnificent
Signiors, whether our aſſembling without due authority, though upon a public occaſion, might not
be cenſured as too forward and preſumptuous in
private men.   But when we conſidered that numbers
of

of other Citizens have daily cabals in fecret places, without any regard to the laws, and confer together, not for the good of the public, but how they may beft promote their own felf-interefted and ambitious defigns, we prefumed, fince thefe men have dared to do fo (only to confpire the ruin of the Commonwealth) without incurring your difpleafure, that we who had no other defign than to concert meafures for its peace and prefervation, fhould not have any occafion to ftand in fear of reprehenfion. In which cafe, we fhall not give ourfelves the leaft trouble about the opinion of others, fince they are fo indifferent concerning what we think of them. The gratitude we owe to our Country at firft induced us to affemble, and now to prefent ourfelves before you, magnificent Signiors, to complain of thofe evils which (though very great indeed already) are daily increafing upon us; and at the fame time, to offer you any affiftance to remedy them that is in our power. For how difficult foever the undertaking may appear, we don't defpair of fuccefs, provided you lay afide all private friendfhip and connection, and fupport your authority by that of the public. The common difeafe of the other cities in Italy has at laft invaded ours, and is continually eating deeper and deeper into its vitals. For after this province had fhaken off the yoke of the Emperors, all its towns, for want of due reftraint, ran into extremes, and from liberty degenerated into downright licentioufnefs, making fuch laws and inftituting fuch governments as were rather calculated to foment and fupport factions, than maintain freedom. From this fource are derived all the defects and diforders that we labour under. No friendfhip or union is to be found amongft the Citizens, except betwixt fuch as are accomplices in fome wicked defign either againft their neighbours or their Country. All religion and fear of God are utterly extinguifhed. Promifes and oaths are no further binding than they ferve to promote fome private advantage, and taken, not with any defign to obferve

them,

them, but as neceffary means to facilitate the perpe-
tration of villanies, which are even honoured and applauded as good conduct and policy if they meet
with fuccefs. From hence it comes to pafs, that the
moft wicked and abandoned wretches are admired as
able enterprizing men ; whilft the innocent and con-
fcientious are laughed at and defpifed as fools. And
certainly there is no fort of corruption that may not
be found in the cities of Italy, nor any people in the
world fo thoroughly difpofed to receive the infection
as thofe of Florence. The young men are indolent
and effeminate ; the old, lafcivious and contemptible.
Without regard to age or fex, every place is full of
the moft licentious brutality, for which, the laws
themfelves, though good and wholefome, are yet fo
partially executed that they do not afford any remedy.
This is the real caufe of that felfifh fpirit which now
fo generally prevails, and of that ambition, not for
true glory, but for Places which difhonour the poffeffors. Hence proceed thefe fatal animofities, thefe
feeds of envy, revenge and faction, with their ufual
attendants, executions, banifhments, depreffion of
good men and the exaltation of the wicked. For the
good, confiding in their virtue and uprightnefs, have
not recourfe to any bafe means, like wicked men, to
advance, or even fo much as defend themfelves : fo
that they generally fall miferable victims to the cruelty
and oppreffion of tyrants, and die in poverty and
difgrace. Such dreadful and pitiable examples, both
give rife and ftrength to parties: for the Evil will
naturally form one fide, either out of avarice or ambition ; and the Good another, out of fear and neceffity : and what is ftill more dangerous, the authors
and ringleaders of them varnifh over their pernicious
defigns with fome facred title : for being in reality
enemies to all liberty, they more effectually deftroy it,
by pretending to defend the rights, fometimes of the
Nobility, fometimes of the Commons ; fince the
fruit which they expect from a victory, is not the
glory of having delivered their Country, but the fatisfaction

tisfaction of Having conquered the oppofite party and
fecured the government of the State to themfelves.
And when they have once obtained that, there is no
fort of cruelty, injuftice, or rapine that they are not
guilty of. From thence forward, laws are enacted,
not for the common good but for private ends : from
that time both war and peace are made and alliances
concluded, not for the honour of the public, but to
gratify the humours of particular men. And if the
other cities of Italy are full of thefe diforders, certainly ours overflows : our laws, our ftatutes, and civil ordinances are made to indulge the caprice, or
ferve the ambition of the conqueror, not to promote
the true intereft of a free people ; fo that one faction
is no fooner extinguifhed but another is lighted up.
A city that endeavours to fupport itfelf by parties inftead of laws, can never be at peace : for when one
prevails and is left without oppofition, it neceffarily
divides again ; the people not being able to defend
themfelves by the ordinary laws which were at firft
made for their prefervation. The truth of this is
fufficiently confirmed both by the ancient and modern
diffenfions, that have happened in our own city.
When the Ghibelines were depreffed, every one
thought the Guelphs would then have lived in peace
and fecurity : and yet it was not long before they divided into the factions of the Neri and Bianchi. When
the Bianchi were reduced, new commotions arofe,
fometimes in favour of the exiles, fometimes betwixt
the Nobility and the people : and to give that away
to others which we either could not or would-not
poffefs quietly ourfelves, we firft committed our liberties into the hands of King Robert, then of his
Brother, next of his Son, and laft of all to the mercy
of the Duke of Athens, never fettling or repofing
under any government ; as people that could neither be fatisfied with being free, nor fubmit to live
in flavery. Nay fo much was our State inclined to
divifion, that rather than acquiefce under the government of a King, it meanly proftituted itfelf to the

                                                  tyranny

tyranny of a vile and pitiful Agobbian. The Duke of Athens indeed ought not to be mentioned, for the honour of this city: the remembrance however of his infolence and oppreffion might have taught us to behave more wifely for the future. Yet no fooner was he expelled but we took up arms again, and fought againft each other with more rancour and inveteracy than ever we had done before, till at laft the ancient Nobility were entirely fubdued and lay at the mercy of the people: and it was then the general opinion there would be no more factions or troubles in Florence, fince thofe were humbled whofe infupportable pride and ambition had been the chief occafion of them. But we now fee by experience, how little confidence is to be put in the judgment of man: for that pride and ambition which was thought to be utterly extinguifhed by the fall of the Nobility, now fprings up again amongft the people, who begin to be equally impatient for authority, and afpire with the fame vehemence to the firft offices in the Commonwealth ; and having no other way to obtain their end, but by domeftick diffenfions, they revive the antiquated diftinctions of Guelphs and Ghibelines, which it would have been happy for this city never to have known *. And that nothing may be ftable and permanent, in this world, it feems the will of Heaven that certain families fhould fpring up in all Commonwealths to be the peft and ruin of them.

---

* Schach Abas, who fat on the throne of Perfia, from 1585 to 1629, and is called one of the greateft Princes that Kingdom ever had, (though his reign was in many refpects very cruel and tyrannical) advifed his fucceffor to fow divifion amongft his fubjects, if he hoped to live in peace; that fo by putting himfelf fometimes at the head of one party, and fometimes of another, he might balance them as he pleafed, and reign in fecurity. Divide & impera. A horrible maxim, indeed ! but he had practifed it himfelf, and by various arts and means, rather worthy of a tyrant or an enemy, than the father of his people, raifed two factions in every city of his kingdom, which continued till the laft great revolution there, for which thofe divifions had paved the way. Hiftoire de la Revol. de Perfe, p. 84, 85. The fame fatal fyftem of politics has been adopted in many other countries, but with little peace to the fovereign, and infinite diftraction amongft the fubjects.

Of

Of which, our own city can produce more inflances perhaps than any other; fince it owes its miferies and diltractions not merely to one or two, but to feveral of thofe families: as firft to the Buondelmonti and Uberti; next to the Donati and Cerchi, and now, to our fhame be it fpoken, to the Ricci and Albizi. We have not enumerated our·many paft divifions, nor raked fo deep into our corruption, in order to terrify or difcourage you, but to point out their caufes, and by putting you in mind of them, tó fhew that we have not forgot them ourfelves; and at the fame time to conjure you not to let fuch examples make you defpair of providing any remedy for the prefent. For at that time, the power of thofe ancient families was fo great, and their intereft with other Princes, fo confiderable, that neither the laws nor the authority of the Civil Magiftrate were able to controul them: but at this day, when the Emperor has no power, nor the Pope any influence here, and all Italy, particularly this City, is reduced to fuch a ftate of equality, as to be able to govern itfelf, where is the difficulty? what impediment remains, why this Commonwealth, above all others, and in fpight of former examples to the contrary, may not only be united, but reformed and improved by new Laws and Conftitutions, provided your Lordfhips will be pleafed to make them: to which good work we earneftly exhort you, not out of any private pique or refentment, but compaffion to our country. We acknowledge the tafk to be very difficult, but hope you will, for the prefent at leaft, put a ftop to that madnefs, that virulent contagion which threatens us with utter ruin. You muft not impute the factions of our anceftors to the nature of the men, but to the iniquity of the times, which being now altered, afford this city fair hopes of better fortune; and our diforders may be corrected· by the inftitution of wholefome Laws, by a prudent reftraint of ambition, by prohibiting fuch cuftoms as tend to nourifh and propagate faction, and by fubftituting others

that

that may conduce to maintain liberty and good civil government. And it would be much more gracious and acceptable, if you would now do that voluntarily, and under the favour of the Laws, which otherwife you will either provoke the people to do themfelves, or compel you to do by violence."

The expediency of this advice had great weight with the Signiory, efpecially as it was very conformable to their own fentiments; and therefore, in compliance with the exhortations and authority of thofe that gave it, they commiffioned fifty-fix citizens *to provide for the fafety of the Commonwealth* *. But as moft people are fitter to preferve good order than to reftore it when loft, thefe Citizens took more pains to extinguifh the prefent factions, than to provide againft new ones, which was the reafon that they fucceeded in neither: for they not only did not take away the occafion of frefh ones, but made one of thofe that were then fubfifting, fo much more powerful than the other, that the Commonwealth was in great danger. They deprived three of the family of the Albizi, and as many of the Ricci, of all fhare in the Magiftracy for three years, except in fuch branches of it, as were particularly appropriated to the Guelph party; of which number Pietro degli Albizi, and Uguccione de' Ricci were two. They prohibited all Citizens from coming into the palace at any time when the Signiory were not fitting. They decreed, that in cafe of battery, or difturbance in the poffeffion of his eftate, any man fhould have liberty granted him, upon petitioning the Council, to accufe the aggreffor, and make him anfwer to the charge before the heads of it, who fhould have the power of compelling him to fubmit to their fentence, if guilty. Thefe provifions bore much harder upon the Ricci than the Albizi: for though they were equally ftigmatized by them, yet the Ricci were the greater fuf-

* After the manner of the old Romans, who ufed to give a charge to their Magiftrates in times of danger, to take care, " ne quid detrimenti capiat Refpublica."

ferers.

ferers. Pietro, indeed, was excluded from the palace of the Signiory, but he had free admittance into that of the Guelphs, where his authority was very great; and though he and his affociates were forward enough in their admonitions before, they became much forwarder after this mark of difgrace; and new accidents occurred, which ftill more and more enflamed their refentment.

Gregory XI. was Pope at that time, and refiding at Avignon, as his late Predeceffors had done, he governed Italy by Legates, who being haughty and rapacious, had grievoufly oppreffed feveral of the cities. One of thefe Legates being then at Bologna, took the advantage of a fcarcity, which happened at that time in Florence, and refolved to make himfelf mafter of Tufcany. For which purpofe, he not only refufed to fupply the Florentines with provifions, but invaded their territories with a great army, very early in the fpring, in order to fpoil their next harveft; hoping by that means to make an eafy conqueft, when they were in a manner both famifhed and difarmed; and, probably, his defign would have fucceeded, if the forces he employed had not been mercenary and corrupt: for the Florentines having no other remedy, had recourfe to bribery, and gave his army an hundred and thirty thoufand Florins to defift from their enterprize.

It is in the power of any man to begin a war, but not to end one, when he pleafes. The commencement of this was owing to the ambition of the Legate, and the profecution of it to the refentment of the Florentines, who immediately entered into a confederacy with Bernabo Galeazzo, and all the other ftates that were at variance with the Church: after which, they appointed eight Citizens for the management of it, whom they invefted with an abfolute power of proceeding, and difburfing money without controul or account. This war againft the Pope, notwithftanding Uguccione was dead, gave frefh courage to thofe that had followed the party of the Ricci, who, in op-

pofition

pofition to the Albizi, had, upon all occafions, favoured Bernabo, and appeared againft the Church; and efpecially becaufe all the Eight were enemies to the Guelphs.   Upon which, Pietro degli Albizi, Lapo da Caftiglionchio, Carlo Strozzi, and fome others, united themfelves more firmly together, to make head againft their enemies : fo that whilft the Eight were bufily employed in their department, and the others in admonitions, the war was carried on for three years, and did not end till the death of the Pope.   It was profecuted, however, with fuch vigour, and general fatisfaction, that the Eight were not only continued in their office from year to year, as long as it lafted, but got the title of Santi; notwithftanding they had de-fpifed the cenfures of the Pope, made free with the treafure and revenues of their Churches, and forced the Clergy to perform the duties of their function So much did the Citizens at that time prefer the good of their Country to all other concerns ; and fo zealou: were they to convince the Church, that as they hac power to defend it whilft they were its friends, fo the' were able to diftrefs it now they were its enemies having actually raifed a rebellion quite through th States of Romagna, La Marca, and Perugia.   Bu whilft they made fo vigorous a war upon the Pop they could not defend themfelves againft the captain and their adherents.   The envy and indignation wit which the Guelphs looked upon the Eight, mad them grow fo bold and infolent, that they often af fronted and abufed them, as well as the reft of th principal Citizens.   The Captains were no lefs arrc gant; they were even more dreaded than the Sig niory, and men went with greater awe and reverenc to their houfes than to the palace ; fo that all the An baffadors that came to Florence, were inftructed t addrefs themfelves to the Captains.

After the death of Pope Gregory, the city had n war abroad, but was in great confufion at home : f on one hand, the Guelphs were become fo audaciou that they were no longer fupportable ; and on tl

othe

other, there was no vifible way to fupprefs them: it was neceffary therefore, to take up arms, and leave the event to Fortune. On the fide of the Guelphs, were all the ancient Nobility, and the greater part of the more powerful Citizens; of whom as we have faid, Lapo, Pietro, and Carlo, were the chief. On the other, were all the inferior fort of people, headed by the Eight, and joined by Georgio Scali, Tomafo Strozzi, the Ricci, the Alberti, and the Medici: the reft of the multitude, as it almoft always happens in fuch cafes, joined with the difcontented party. The power of their adverfaries feemed very conliderable to the heads of the Guelphs, and their danger great, if at any time a Signiory that was not on their fide fhould attempt to deprefs them. Thinking it prudent, therefore, to guard againft fuch an event, they had a meeting, and having particularly inquired into the ftate and condition of the city, they found the number of perfons who had been admonifhed, was fo great, that they had difobliged moft of the Citizens, and made them their enemies. In thefe circumftances, they thought there was no other remedy, now they had deprived them of their honours, but to banifh them out of the City alfo, to feize upon the Palace of the Signiory, and to put the government of the State wholly into the hands of their own Creatures, according to the example of the Guelphs their predeceffors, whofe quiet and fecurity was entirely owing to the total expulfion of their enemies. This propofal was agreed to without any oppofition; but they differed about the time of putting it in execution.

It was then the month of April, in the year 1378, when Lapo judging it unfafe to defer the matter any longer, reprefented to them that delays were always dangerous, but more particularly in their fituation, conlidering that Sylveftro de Medici, who was an open and declared enemy to their party, might be chofen Gonfalonier in the next Signiory. Pietro degli Albizi was of a different opinion, and thought it better to wait a little longer, as fome forces would be neceffary to fupport them, which could not be got together privately; and to raife them publickly would be to run themfelves into manifeft danger. His advice therefore was, that they fhould have patience till midfummer day, which being one of their greateft feftivals, and at a time when vaft numbers of people refort to the city, they might introduce what forces they pleafed into it without danger of being difcovered. And to obviate their apprehenfion of Sylveftro, he propofed to have him admonifhed; and if that would not anfwer the purpofe, to manage it fo in the enfuing imborfation for magiftrates, fince the purfes were now empty, that either his name or that of fome other Candidate in his ward fhould be drawn, which would difqualify him for filling the Office of Gonfalonier. This opinion was approved, and they refolved to defer their undertaking, though Lapo came very unwillingly into it; alledging, that no opportunity could ever be complete in every circumftance, and that thofe who waited for fuch a one muft either never attempt any thing of moment, or be difappointed in it if they did. However, they proceeded to admonifh Sylveftro, but they did not fucceed in their defign of excluding him; for the Eight being aware of the trick they intended to put upon him, continued to defer the imborfation: fo that Sylveftro, the Son of Alamanno de Medici, was appointed Gonfalonier. As he was born of one of the moft confiderable families of the Commoners, he could not bear to fee the people oppreffed by a few grandees: refolving therefore to put an end to their infolence, and finding himfelf favoured by the people and fupported by feveral of the principal Citizens, he communicated his defign to Benedetto Alberti, Tomafo Strozzi, and Georgio Scali, who all concurred with him and promifed him their affiftance in it. In confequence of this, they fecretly prepared a Decree by which the laws againft the Nobility were to be revived, the authority of the Captains retrenched,

Sylvestro Medici. 1378

trenched, and thofe who had been admonifhed, admitted into the Magiftracy. And as it feemed the beft way both to propofe and have it paffed at one time, if poffible, fince it was firft to be prefented to the Colleges, and afterwards confidered in the Councils, Sylveftro being prefident (and confequently in a manner Prince of the city for a time) caufed both a College and a Council to be called the fame morning; and coming firft to the College, in which he had but few friends, he propofed the Decree to them which he had prepared : but it was thrown out as an innovation, and he could not get it paffed. Seeing himfelf defeated therefore in the firft ftep to obtain it, he pretended to go out upon fome neceffary occafion, and went away to the Council without being perceived; where, having placed himfelf in fuch a manner that he might both be feen and heard by the whole affembly, he told them, " That he thought he had been appointed Gonfalonier, not to take cognizance of private caufes, which had their proper judges, but to fuperintend the State, to correct the infolence of the great, and to moderate or alter thofe laws, which manifeftly tended to the ruin of the Commonwealth. That he had fpared no pains in either, and made the beft provifion that was poffible : but that the malice and perverfenefs of fome men was fo great, and had raifed fuch an oppofition to his good defigns, that he found himfelf incapable of doing the leaft fervice to the publick, and them fo far from being inclined to deliberate upon any thing he propofed, that they would not fo much as hear of it. That as he plainly faw it was not in his power to be of any further ufe to his Country, he knew not for what reafon he fhould continue any longer in an office which he either did not really deferve, or was thought unworthy of by others. Upon which account, he would retire to privacy, and leave the people to chufe another perfon who might either have more virtue or better fortune than himfelf." After which,

he

he got up and left the Council, as if he would go directly to his own houfe.

Upon this, fuch of the Council as were in the fecret, and others that wifhed for a change, raifed a tumult, to which the Signiory and Colleges immediately repaired ; and feeing their Gontalonier retiring, they obliged him, partly by their authority and partly by their intreaties, to return to the Council, which was in great confufion. Many of the principal Citizens were threatened and treated with the utmoft infolence : amongft the reft Carlo Strozzi was collared by an artificer, and would certainly have been knocked on the head, if fome of the by-ftanders had not refcued him with much difficulty. But the perfon that made the greateft difturbance was Benedetto degli Alberti, who got into one of the windows of the Palace, and called out to the people to arm : upon which, the Piazza was inftantly full of armed men, and the Colleges were obliged to do that by fear, which they would not come into when they were petitioned. In the mean time, the Captains of the parties had affembled as many of the Citizens as they could in their Palace, to confult what courfe was to be taken in order to prevent the paffing of this Decree : but when they faw fo great a tumult, and were informed what had happened in the Council, they all thought proper to return to their own houfes.

But whofoever he may be, that intends to make any alteration in a Commonwealth, and to effect it by raifing the multitude, will find himfelf deceived if he thinks he can ftop where he will, and conduct it as he pleafes. The defign of Sylveftro in promoting that law was only to have quieted and fecured the city ; but the thing took a very different turn * : for

---

* When circumftances of time will not admit of alterations, tho neceffary, it is much better to let things remain as they are, than to attempt a reformation ; fince the remedy perhaps may prove worf than the difeafe. It is prudent in this cafe, to imitate the practice of phyficians, with regard to certain patients, whom they will not allow

th

the people were in such a ferment, that the shops were shut up, the houses barricadoed, and many removed their goods for security into the Churches and Convents; every one apprehending some fatal consequence. All the Companies of the Arts assembled, and each of them appointed a Syndic: the Signiory called the Colleges together, and were a whole day in consultation with the Syndics how to provide some means for composing these disorders to the satisfaction of all parties; but as there was great variety of opinions amongst them, nothing was concluded. The next day the Arts drew out their several Companies; which the Signiory being informed of, and apprehending what might happen, called the Council together to consider of a proper remedy: but as soon as it was assembled the tumult increased, and the standards of the Arts, with a considerable number of men under arms, immediately took possession of the Piazza. In order therefore, to give the Arts and the rest of the people some hopes of satisfaction, and to prevent further mischief, the Council gave a full power (which the Florentines call Balia) to the Signiory, Colleges, the Eight, the Captains of the Parties, and the Syndics of the Arts, to reform the State in such a manner as they should think most advantageous for the public. But whilst they were employed in this, some of the inferior Companies of the Arts, at the instigation of certain persons who wanted to revenge the late injuries which they had received from the Guelphs, detached themselves from the rest, and went to the house of Lapo da Castiglionchio, which they plundered and burnt. Lapo himself, when he saw the Signiory at the head of this attack upon the Guelphs, and the people all in arms, having no other remedy but either to abscond or fly,

---

to take physick; because it would inevitably stir up many ill humours in their bodies, which are less dangerous in a state of coagulation than of agitation. " Expediebat, quasi ægræ sauciæque, Reipublicæ requiescere quomodo cunque, ne vulnera curatione ipsâ rescinderentur." Says Florus, l. iii, c. 23.

firſt of all took ſanctuary in the Church of Santa
Croce, and afterwards fled to Caſentino, in the habit
of a Monk, where he was often heard to condemn
Pietro degli Albizi for having put off their deſign
till St. John's day, and himſelf for having concurred
in it. But Pietro and Carlo Strozzi, upon the firſt
rumour of the tumult, only concealed themſelves, in
hopes that their friends and relations would have intereſt enough to ſecure their ſtay in Florence when it
was over.

The houſe of Lapo being thus burnt and rifled,
ſeveral others underwent the ſame fate, either out of
public hatred or private malice ; (as miſchief is generally ſoon propagated when once begun) and to go
through with their work the more completely, they
broke open the Jails, and ſet the priſoners at liberty :
after which, they plundered the Monaſtery of St. Ag-
noli, and the Convent di Santo Spirito, into which
ſeveral of the Citizens had conveyed their moſt valuable effects. Nor would the public chamber have
eſcaped their fury, if they had not been reſtrained by
the preſence and authority of one of the Signiory,
who being mounted on horſeback, and attended by
a body of armed men, oppoſed himſelf to the rage
of the multitude in the moſt effectual manner he
could. This commotion being thus in ſome meaſure
quieted, partly by the authority of the Signiory, and
partly by the approach of night, the Balia proceeded
the next morning to requalify the Ammoniti, though
with an injunction not to exerciſe any function in the
Magiſtracy during the next three years. They repealed ſuch laws as had been made by the Guelphs
to the prejudice of the other Citizens, and proclaimed Lapo da Caſtiglionchio and his aſſociates Rebels,
with many others that had incurred the hatred of the
public : after which, the names of the new Signiory
were publiſhed, and Luigi Guicciardini declared their
Gonfalonier. As they were all eſteemed men of pacific diſpoſitions, and deſirous of public tranquillity,
great hopes were conceived that there would be no
more

more tumults. However, the shops were not opened; the Citizens still continued armed, and strong guards were placed in all parts of the city: so that the Signiors were not publickly invested with the Magistracy, or with the usual pomp; but privately in the Palace, and without any ceremony. They rightly concluded, that the best and most necessary service they could do the public in the beginning of their office, would be to compose the city: for which purpose, they commanded the people to lay down their arms, the shops to be opened, and every one that had been called out of the Country to the assistance of any Citizen, immediately to depart. They planted guards in the several streets; so that if those that were admonished could have been content, the whole city was in a fair way of being quieted. But as they thought it hard to wait three years longer before they could enjoy any share in the Magistracy, the Arts having assembled again to obtain them satisfaction in that point, demanded of the Signiory that for the good and quiet of the city, it should be decreed that no Citizen for the future should be admonished as a Ghibeline, who had ever been one of the Signiory or the College, or the Captains of the companies, or the Consuls, or Syndics of any of the arts: and further, that a new imborsation should be made of the Guelph party and the old one burnt. These demands were readily granted both by the Signiory and the Councils, in hopes of preventing any further tumult. But as it seldom happens that men who covet the property of others and long for revenge, are satisfied with a bare restitution of their own, some who expected to advance their fortunes by exciting commotions, endeavoured to persuade the Artificers that they could never be safe, except many of their enemies were either banished or cut off: which suggestions being represented to the Signiory, they summoned the Magistrates of the Arts and their Syndics to attend them; and when they were assembled,

Luigi

Luigi Guicciardini, their Gonfalonier, addreſſed himſelf to them in the following manner:

"If theſe Gentlemen as well as myſelf had not
long ago been acquainted with the temper and genius
of this city, and obſerved that its foreign wars were
no ſooner ended, but diſſenſions began at home, we
ſhould have been more alarmed and more incenſed at
the tumults which have lately happened: but as things
that are familiar to us become leſs affecting, we have
borne them with ſome degree of patience; eſpecially
as we were conſcious to ourſelves that the cauſes of
them could not be imputed to any miſconduct on our
part, and had reaſon to hope that they, like all former commotions, would ſometime or other have an
end, upon our complying with ſo many and ſuch extravagant demands. But finding you are ſo far from
being ſatisfied, as you ought to be, that you are contriving freſh miſchiefs againſt your fellow Citizens,
and endeavouring to procure their baniſhment, we
confeſs we are highly diſpleaſed at the malice and
baſeneſs of your proceedings. We can aſſure you,
with great truth, that if we had apprehended the
city would have been in the leaſt danger, during the
time of our Magiſtracy, either by ſiding with or
againſt you, we would have declined that honour by
a voluntarily exile. But preſuming we had people to
deal with, who had ſome degree of humanity, and
love of their Country ſtill left, we chearfully accepted it in hopes of getting the better of your Ambition at laſt by our lenity, and readineſs to oblige
you. We have the misfortune however, to ſee that
the more we grant, the more ſhameleſs and arrogant
are your demands. And if we are obliged to tell
you ſo, it is not with any deſign to increaſe your
diſcontents, but to convince you of your error:
others perhaps may flatter you, but we ſhall always
think it our duty to tell you plainly, and without
diſguiſe, what we think is for your good. What is
there, in the name of God, that you can reaſonably
aſk more of us? you deſired to have the Captains of
the

the parties deprived of their authority: they have
been deprived. You infifted that the old Imborfation fhould be burnt, and a new one made; we confented. You wanted to have thofe reinftated in the
Magiftracy that had been admonifhed: it has been
granted. At your interceffion, we pardoned fuch as
had been guilty of burning houfes and robbing
Churches, and banifhed many of our principal Citizens at your inftigation. To gratify you, the grandees are bridled with new laws, and every thing done
that might give you content. Where then can we
expect your demands will ftop; or how long will
you thus abufe your liberty? don't you perceive,
that whilft we fubmit with patience, you fhew no moderation in your Victory? whither will your diffenfions at laft hurry this poor city? can you ever forget how Caftruccio, a private Citizen of Lucca,
availed himfelf of fuch Divifions to diftrefs it? and
how the Duke of Athens, from an inferior Commander in your fervice, made himfelf your Lord and
Sovereign? on the contrary, when ye were united,
neither the Archbifhop of Milan, nor the Pope himfelf, was able to cope with you; but, after a war
that lafted many years, were forced to fheath their
fwords with difhonour. Why then will ye fuffer your
own difcords (when ye have no other enemies) to
bring a city into flavery, which fo many powerful
princes could never reduce? for what elfe can ye expect from your divifions, what from the goods ye
have already taken, or may hereafter take from your
fellow Citizens, but fervitude and poverty? the perfons you plunder, are thofe whofe fortunes and abilities are the defence of the State, and if they fail,
how muft it be fupported? whatever is got that way,
cannot laft long; and then ye have nothing to look
for but remedilefs famine and diftrefs. We therefore command you, and, as far as our dignity will allow of it, we for once intreat you to live quietly,
and be content with fuch regulations as we have
eftablifhed; and if any thing feems wanting to give
you

you fatisfaction, that you would make it known with
modefty, and not infift upon it with clamour and
tumult : for if your requefts are reafonable, you
may affure yourfelves, they fhall always be complied
with, and no handle left for wicked and defigning
men to plot the deftruction of your Country, and
confequently of yourfelves, under the fhelter of your
own wings."

The reafonablenefs of thefe expoftulations made
fuch an impreffion upon the audience, that they humbly defired the Gonfalonier to accept their thanks, acknowledged that he had behaved himfelf like an upright Magiftrate, and a good Citizen, and promifed
to pay a ready obedience in whatfoever he fhould
command them. To make a trial of them, the Signiory deputed two Citizens for each of the chief offices, to confult with the Syndics of the Arts, what
reformations were moft neceffary to be made in them
for the good of the publick, and to report them to
the Signiory.

But whilft thefe things were in agitation, a frefh tumult arofe which was attended with ftill more danger
to the city than the former. The greater part of the
late robberies and other mifchiefs had been committed by the Rabble and dregs of the people ; and thofe
of them that had been the moft audacious, apprehended that when the moft material differences were
compofed, they fhould be called to account for their
crimes, and deferted, as it always happens, by thofe
very perfons at whofe inftigation they had committed
them. Befides which, the inferior fort of people had
conceived an hatred againft the richer Citizens, and
principals of the Arts, upon a pretence that they had
not been rewarded for their paft fervices in proportion to what they deferved. For when the city
was firft divided into Arts, in the time of Charles the
Firft, there was a proper head or governor appointed
over each of them, to whofe jurifdiction in civil cafes
every perfon in the feveral Arts was to be fubject.
Thefe Arts or Companies, as we have faid, were at

firft

firſt but twelve, but afterwards they were increaſed
to twenty-one, and arrived at ſuch power and authority that in a few years they wholly engroſſed the government of the city : and becauſe ſome were more,
and others leſs honourable amongſt them, they came
by degrees to be diſtinguiſhed, and ſeven of them
were called the *Greater*, and fourteen the *Leſs*. From
this diviſion, and other reaſons before-mentioned,
proceeded the arrogance of the Captains of the parties : for the Citizens that had formerly been Guelphs,
to which party thoſe offices were always appropriated,
had made it a conſtant rule to favour the greater
Arts, and to diſcountenance the leſs, and all thoſe
that ſided with them ; which chiefly gave occaſion to
all the tumults we have hitherto made mention of.
And, as in the diviſion of the people into Arts and
Corporations, there were many trades in which the
meaner ſort are uſually occupied, that were not incorporated into any diſtinct or particular company of
their own, but admitted into any of the others, according as the Nature of their Craft made them fit,
it happened that when they were not duly ſatisfied for
their labour, or any otherwiſe oppreſſed by their maſters, they had no other head to apply to for redreſs,
but the Magiſtrate of that company, to which the
perſon belonged that employed them, who, they commonly thought, did not do them juſtice. Now, of
all the Companies in the City, that of the Clothiers
had then, and ſtill has, the moſt of this ſort of people depending upon it ; and being more opulent and
powerful than any of the reſt, it maintained by far
the greater part of the multitude. The meaner ſort
of the people, therefore, both of this company and
the others, were highly enraged at ſuch treatment ;
and being terrified alſo at the apprehenſion of being
puniſhed for their late, outrages, they had frequent
meetings in the night ; where, conſidering what had
happened, they repreſented to each other, the danger
they were in. And to animate and unite them all,
one of the boldeſt and moſt experienced of them,
harangued his Companions in this manner :

" If

" If it was now to be debated, whether we fhould
take arms to plunder and burn the houfes of our fellow Citizens, and rob the Churches, I fhould be one
of thofe who would think it worthy of great confideration, and perhaps be induced to prefer fecure poverty to hazardous gain.   But fince arms have been
already taken up, and much mifchief done, the firlt
points to be confidered are, I fhould think, in what
manner we muft fecure ourfelves, and ward off the
penalties we have incurred.   If no one fhould give us
this advice, without doubt, Neceffity itfelf would
point it out.   You fee, the whole City is full of rage
and complaints againft us, the Citizens are daily in
council, and the Magiftrates frequently affembled.
Affure yourfelves, they are either preparing chains
for us, or contriving how to raife forces to deftroy us.
It behoves us, therefore, to have two objects chiefly
in view, at thefe confultations : firft, how to avoid
the punifhment due to our late mifdeeds ; and in the
next place, what means are to be ufed that we may
enjoy a greater degree of liberty and fatisfaction for
the future, than we have done hitherto.   To come
off with impunity for our paft offences, it is neceffary, if I may prefume to advife you, to add ftill
more to them, to redouble our outrages to rifle and
burn a great number of houfes, and artfully depend
upon our numbers for protection : for where many
are guilty, none are chaftifed.   Small crimes are punifhed, and great ones ufually rewarded ; and where
many fuffer, few feek revenge ; a general calamity
being always borne with more patience, than a particular one.   I fay again, therefore, that to redouble
our crimes, is the fureft way to procure a pardon for
what has been already done, and to obtain the liberty
we defire * : nor is there any difficulty to difcourage

---

* Monfieur Balzac fays, from Phalaris's Epiftles, " It has always
been a general opinion, that they who rife in arms againft their country, or their prince, are in a manner under a neceffity to do evil,
becaufe they find it unfafe to do good.   They dare not become innocent, left they fhould expofe themfelves to the feverity of thofe

us. The enterprize is eafy, and the fuccefs not to be doubted of. Our enemies are opulent, indeed, but divided : their difunion will give us the victory, and their riches, when we have got them, will maintain it. Let not the antiquity of their blood, nor the meannefs of our own, with which they fo infolently upbraid us, either dazzle or overawe you. All families having the fame original, are of equal antiquity * : nor has nature fhewn any partiality in the formation of mankind. Let both fides be ftripped naked, and both will be found alike. Clothe yourfelves in their robes, and them in your rags ; and then you will appear the Nobles, and they the Plebeians : for it is poverty alone that makes the real difference betwixt us. It fills me with juft concern, indeed, to hear that fome of you repent forfooth of what you have done, and out of a qualm of confcience, refolve to proceed no further. If that be the cafe, I have been miftaken in my judgment, and you are not the men I once thought you. .Neither confcience, nor the fear of infamy, ought to terrify you : for thofe that fucceed in their attempts (let them have ufed what means foever) are never upbraided with them, or called by ignominious names : and as for confcience, you have no reafon to give yourfelves any trouble about it. When famine, and racks, and dungeons, are fure to be our portion, what greater terrors can there be in Hell? confider the courfe of this world ; you will find the rich, the great, and the powerful, have arrived at all their wealth, and grandeur, and authority, either by violence or fraud : and·

Y

laws, againft which they have offended: they continue therefore in their crimes, becaufe they think men will not be fatisfied with their repentance."
* This is a conftant topic with ringleaders of tumult and fedition ; we find it urged by the famous Gabrini Rienzi, in the revolution he occafioned at Rome, by Maffianello to the rabble of Naples, and Wat Tyler's Chaplain in the Kentifh infurrection, during the reign of Richard II. who was fo ingenious to verfify it in the following manner :
When Adam delv'd and Eve fpan,
Who was then a Gentleman?

when

when once they are in poſſeſſion of them, you ſee with
what oſtentation they gild over the foulneſs of their
uſurpations, with the unjuſt, but glorious titles of
conqueſt and good policy. Obſerve, on the other
hand, what generally becomes of thoſe who are either
too ſtupid or too puſillanimous to follow their examples : they are buried in poverty and obſcurity, or
wear away their lives in ſlavery and contempt. Honeſt ſervants are ſervants for ever, and good men
are always poor: whilſt the bold and reſolute ſoon
free themſelves from bondage, and the fraudulent
and rapacious from indigence and diſtreſs. God and
Nature have given every man the means of making
his fortune : and it is ſooner and more eaſily done by
force or circumvention, than by honeſty and plain
dealing. Hence it is, that we ſee mankind in general
is more prone to rapine than induſtry, to evil than
good. Hence it is that we devour each other,
and he that is weakeſt is at all times ſure to come off
with the worſt. Force, therefore, is always to be
uſed, when there is an opportunity : and what fairer
opportunity than the preſent, can we ever hope for
from the hands of Fortune? The Citizens are divided, the Signiory irreſolute, the Magiſtrates frighted : ſo that before they can come to any determination, the matter will be over, and we ſhall either
be maſters of the whole City, or of ſo great a part
of it, as will not only procure us pardon for what is
paſt, but enable us to keep our enemies in ſufficient awe for the future. I confeſs the reſolution is
bold and dangerous* ; but where the neceſſity is ur-

* In this ſpeech, which is otherwiſe in Character, there is, however, this inconſiſtency, that in the former part of it, the Plebeian
having repreſented the enterprize " as eaſy, and the ſucceſs not to be
doubted of ;" now ſays, he confeſſes the reſolution is " bold and
dangerous." This may either be an overſight in the author, or purpoſely put into the mouth of the Speaker, who is not to be conſidered as an orator, but an illiterate rough man, provoked by oppreſſion, and blinded by his paſſions to ſuch a degree, that whilſt he
is earneſtly recommending revenge, he forgets what he has ſaid before, and contradicts himſelf, as it generally happens upon ſuch oc-
caſions. The latter perhaps, may be the caſe; ſince Machiavel ſays,

gent, boldnefs becomes prudence, and danger, in great undertakings, is always defpifed by brave and courageous men. Thofe enterprizes that are begun with peril, for the moft part are crowned with glory; and men feldom extricate themfelves from one danger, but by rifquing a greater. Befides, as we have nothing but prifons and tortures, and death before our eyes at prefent, we have lefs to fear in behaving ourfelves like men, than from defpair, and giving up all for loft: for in one cafe our deftruction is certain, and in the other, there is a poffibility of fuccefs. How often have I heard you curfe the infatiable avarice of your Tafk-mafters? how often groan under the injuftice of your Magiftrates? now is your time, not only to fhake off the yoke, but to retaliate their oppreffions. Time has wings, opportunity flies away, and when once paft, are never to be recalled. You fee what preparations they are making; let us be before-hand with them. If we ftrike the firft blow, we are fure of victory, to the ruin of our enemies, and the exaltation of ourfelves; for it is an enterprize that will honour many of us, and fecure us all."

This fpeech fo inflamed his hearers, who before were fufficiently ripe for mifchief, that they determined to rife as foon as they had drawn a proper number of accomplices into the confpiracy: and in the mean time, they bound themfelves by an oath, to affift and ftand by each other, when any of them fhould be oppreffed by the Magiftrates.

But whilft they were confpiring in this manner againft the government, the Signiory had fecret information of their proceedings, and caufed one Simone della Piazza, and fome others, to be apprehended, who confeffed the whole plot, and that the very next day was defigned for the infurrection. Upon

in the Dedication of this hiftory to Pope Clement VII. "That the fpeeches and harangues to the public, as well as his own private reflexions and obfervations, are always delivered without reftraint or referve, and in a manner confiftent with the actions, character, and temper of the perfon that fpeaks, or is fpoken of." The reader is left to judge.

this,

this, confidering the danger they were in, they immediately fummoned the Colleges, together with the Syndics of the Arts, and thofe Citizens that had been appointed to ufe their endeavours for the re union of the City. But, before they could be got together, it was late at night, and the Signiory were advifed by them to confult with the Confuls of the Arts, who were inftantly fent for, and unanimoufly agreed, that all the Militia of the City fhould be raifed, and ordered the Gonfaloniers of the people to appear early the next Morning, at the head of their feveral Companies under arms in the Piazza before their Palace. At the time that Simone was under torture and the Citizens were affembling, one Niccolo da St. Friano, who took care of the clock, happened to be in the Palace, and being aware of what they were about, he ran home as faft as he could, and raifed all the Neighbourhood; fo that above a thoufand men were prefently got together in arms at the Piazza di Santo Spirito. Upon this, the reft of the confpirators took the alarm, and the Piazzas of St. Pietro Maggiore and St. Lorenzo, (places which had been appointed before-hand for their rendezvous) were likewife foon filled with armed men. It was now day-light in the morning of the twenty-firft of July, and not above eighty of the militia were affembled to fupport the Signiory; and of the Gonfaloniers, not fo much as one appeared; for as they were informed, that the whole City was in arms, they durft not ftir out of their houfes. The firft of the mob that entered the Piazza of the Signiory, were thofe that had affembled at St. Pietro Maggiore, and not being oppofed by the Militia, they were foon followed by the reft, who likewife meeting with no refiftance, began to call upon the Signiory in a furious and threatening manner, to deliver up their prifoners: but as no regard was paid to their threats, they determined to ufe other means to force them to a compliance, and immediately fet fire to the houfe of Luigi Guicciardini: upon which, the Signiory, to prevent greater mifchief,

chief, ordered the prifoners to be difcharged. When they had thus got their accomplices fafe into their hands again, they took the Gonfalone, or Standard della Giuftizia, from the Effecutore; under the cover and authority of which, they burnt feveral of the Citizens houfes down to the ground, and wreaked their malice upon many others, againft whom they had taken any pique, either on public or private accounts. For if any one of the Plebeians had been injured or affronted by a particular Citizen, he led the Mob directly to his enemy's houfe: nay, it was fufficient barely to mention the perfon's name, or to call out, *to fuch a man's houfe*, or *to fuch a one's fbop*, and immediately the new Gonfalonier carried the Standard that way. They burnt all the books and accounts of the Clothier's company, and after they had done a great deal more mifchief, to crown their proceedings with fome action of merit and *eclat*, as they thought, they knighted fixty-four Citizens: amongft whom were Sylveftro de' Medici, Benedetto and Antonio degli Alberti, Tomafo Strozzi, and others of their friends; though fome of them fubmitted to it with much reluctance. Their levity, indeed, was very remarkable upon this occafion, for they conferred the honour of knighthood on fome of thofe very perfons whofe houfes they had burnt down but a few hours before; particularly upon Luigi Guicciardini, the late Gonfalonier: fuch is the caprice of the multitude, and fo foon are their difgufts changed into favour and affection!

The Signiory being thus abandoned in this perilous conjuncture by the Militia, the heads of the Arts, and even by their Gonfaloniers, were not a little difmayed when they faw nobody come to their affiftance, as they had ordered: for out of the fixteen companies, only thofe of the *the Golden Lion*, and *the Squirrel*, under the command of Giovenco della Stufa and Giovanni Cambi, made their appearance; and they did not ftay long in the Piazza; for not being joined by the reft, they thought it moft prudent to draw off

VOL. I.   O   again.

again. Some of the Citizens of their party, feeing
the Multitude fo outrageous, and the Palace deferted,
durft not ftir out of their doors ; others mixed with
the Mob, and went along with them, hoping thereby
to fave their own houfes, and thofe of their friends : by
which means the number of the people was much increafed, and the Signiory left almoft alone to defend
themfelves. This ferment continued all the day ; and
at night they fat down, to the number of fix thoufand,
near the palace of Meffer Stephano, behind St. Bar-
naby's Church ; from whence they fent, in a threat-
ning manner, before day-break, to demand the Colours from the Heads of the Arts. The next morning, as foon as it was light, they proceeded with the
Standard of Juftice, and the Colours of the feveral
Arts, to the Palace of the Podefta, and demanded
pofleffion of it ; which being refufed, they broke
down the doors, and forced their way into it. The
Signiory, therefore, being defirous to come to fome
compromife with them, fince they were not able to
quell them by force, fent four of their body to them,
at the Palace of the Podefta, to know their demands :
but upon their arrival there, they found that the
Ringleaders of the Plebeians had already fettled the
terms which they expected from the Signiory, with
the Syndics of the Arts, and fome other of the principal Citizens : fo that they returned with four Deputies from the People, who made the following demands : That the Clothiers Company fhould no longer be fubject to the jurifdiction of any Magiftrate
who was not a Florentine by birth. That there fhould
be three new companies of Arts added to the others ;
one of Woolcombers and Dyers ; another of Barbers,
Taylors, Shoemakers, and other fuch mechanics ;
and the third, of the Trades that were inferior to
thefe : out of which Companies, two of the Signiory
fhould always be chofen, and three more out of the
other fourteen minor Arts. That the Signory fhould
provide Halls where thefe new Companies might meet
for the difpatch of bufinefs. That no perfon that was
incor-

incorporated into thefe Arts fhould be compelled to
pay any debt under the fum of fifty * Ducats, before
the expiration of the two next enfuing years, at which
time the Principal only fhould be paid to the Creditor,
and the intereft into the Bank, or publick Stock. That
all fuch as were in banifhment, or under any fentence,
fhould be recalled and pardoned : and that thofe who
had been admonifhed, fhould be made capable of enjoying any dignity or poft of honour. Many other
articles were added to thefe, in favour of their particular friends, and to the prejudice of their enemies,
fome of whom they infifted fhould be fent into exile,
and others admonifhed. All which demands, grievous and difhonourable as they were to the government, were yet deliberated upon by the Signiory, the
Colleges, and the Council of the People, who were
apprehenfive of ftill greater mifchiefs, if they did not
comply with them. But, before a Law could be
paffed for that purpofe, it was neceffary it fhould
have the affent of the Common Council, which could
not be obtained immediately, as it was contrary to
eftablifhed cuftom to hold two councils on the fame
day. However, as they were told that was the only
obftacle, the Arts feemed pretty well contented, and
the people fo well fatisfied, that they promifed to lay
down their arms, and give no further difturbance, as
foon as the Law they demanded fhould be paffed.
The next morning, whilft the Common Council were
deliberating upon it, the Multitude, naturally vo-
luble and impatient, got together again under the
fame Colours, and returned into the Piazza before the
Palace ; where they made fuch a dreadful clamour,
that the whole Council, as well as the Signiory, were
not a little terrified : and Guerriante Marignuoli,
one of the Signiors, being more frighted than any
of the reft, ran down ftairs under a pretence of fhut-
ing the gates, and. fneaked away to his own houfe.
He was difcovered, however, by the Mob; but they

* The Silver Ducat is worth about 4s. 6d. fterling, the Golden one
about 9s.

did

did not offer any fort of violence to him ; and contented themfelves with crying out, as he páſſed thro'
them, "that if all the Signiory did not immediately
quit the Palace, they would murder their Children,
and burn their houſes." In the mean time, the Law
had paſſed, the Signiory had retired into their proper apartment, and the Counſellors being come down
ſtairs, were walking in the Portico and Cloyſters;
expecting the immediate deſtruction of the City, and
afraid to ſtir out, conſidering the baſeneſs of the
Mob *, and the perverſeneſs, or rather the puſillani-
mity of thoſe, in whoſe power it was not only to have
curbed, but utterly ſuppreſſed them. The Signiory
were in no leſs diſtraction, and gave up the City for
loſt, ſeeing themſelves deſerted by one of their col-
leagues, and that nobody had the courage either to
aſſiſt or even ſo much as to comfort or advife them.

Whilſt they were in this diſtreſs, and knew not
what courfe to take, Tomaſo Strozzi and Benedetto
Alberti, either out of ambition, and a deſire of remaining alone in poſſeſſion of the Palace, or perhaps
becauſe they thought it the beſt expedient to allay
the fury of the populace, adviſed them to give way
to it, by reſigning the Magiſtracy, and retiring to
their own houſes. This advice, though given by
thoſe that had been the chief fomentors and abettors
of the inſurrection, would have been immediately

---

* Livy's remark is moſt true. *Hæc natura multitudinis eſt ; aut ſervit
humiliter, aut ſuperbe dominatur : libertatem quæ media eſt, nec ſternere
modice, nec habere ſciunt ; & non ferme dejunt irarum indulgentes mi-
niſtri, qui avidos atque intemperantes Plebeicrum animos ad ſanguinem &
cædes irritent.* " Such is the nature of the multitude ; humble and
abject even to baſeneſs when they obey ; but inſolent to the laſt degree, when they command. They are neither conſent with liberty,
nor without it, nor know how to keep any medium. And for the
moſt part, there are perfons ready enough to indulge their paſſions,
and irritate their greedy and intemperate minds to plunder and blood-
ſhed." Livy, lib. xxiv. c. 25. As Milton ſays of them ;

" They bawl for freedom in their ſenſeleſs mood,
And ſtill revolt when truth would ſet them free.
Licence they mean, when they cry Liberty ;
For who loves that, muſt firſt be wife and good ;
But from that mark how far they rove we fee,
For all this waſte of wealth and loſs of blood."

com-

complied with by all the rest of the Signiory, if
Niccolo del Bene and Alamanno Acciaivoli, who had
a little recovered their spirits, and were moved with
a just indignation, had not made answer, "that if
other people had a mind to retire, it could not be
helped; but for their own parts, they were determined rather to die like men, than quit the Palace,
or lay down their authority before the usual time.
This opposition increased the perplexity of the Signiory, and the rage of the People, to such a degree,
that at last the Gonfalonier, chusing rather to resign
his office in a dishonourable manner, than to maintain it at the peril of his life, recommended himself
to the protection of Tomaso Strozzi, who led him
out of the Palace, and conducted him to his own
house. Upon which, all the rest of the Signiory
thought fit to follow the example of their Gonfalonier, and were led away one by one: so that Niccolo and Alamanno seeing themselves left alone, and
thinking it would be rather fool-hardiness than prudence to stay there any longer in their circumstances,
likewise retired and left the Palace in the hands of the
people, and the Eight that had been appointed to act
as Secretaries at War, who had not yet laid down
their offices.

When the people first entered the Palace, one Michael di Lando, a Woolcomber, but a bare-footed
ragged fellow, carried the Standard of Justice before them; and after he had got up to the top of the
steps, near enough to be heard by the Signiory, who
were then sitting, he turned himself round to his followers, and said to them, "You see, my friends,
not only the Palace, but the whole City is in your
hands; how would you have them disposed of?"
Upon which, they unanimously cried out, "that he
should be their Gonfalonier and chief Magistrate, and
govern the City as he pleased." Michael, therefore,
who was a shrewd sensible fellow, and much more
obliged to Nature than Fortune, readily accepted of
the government, with a design, however, to compose
the

O 3

The City, and put an end to all disturbances as soon
as possible. For this purpose, and to keep the people
employed, that he might have a little time to digest
his designs, he sent them to search for * Ser Nuto,
who had been appointed Provost Marshal, or rather
Hangman, by Lapo da Castiglionchio. And to begin
his administration with an appearance of Justice, as
he had acquired it by favour, he caused a Proclamation to be issued, that nobody should dare to burn
or plunder any man's house for the future: to enforce the observance of which, he ordered a Gibbet
to be erected in the great Piazza. After this, in order for a further reform of the City, he immediately
turned all the Syndics of the Arts out of their offices,
deprived the Signiory and Colleges of their authority,
and burnt the old Imborsations. In the mean time,
the Mob had brought Ser Nuto into the Piazza,
where they hung him up by one leg upon the Gibbet; and as every one tore away a joint, or a piece of
his flesh, in two or three minutes, there was nothing
left of him but one of his feet. On the other hand,
the Eight Secretaries at War, thinking the government of the City devolved upon them, since the ab-
dication of the late Signiory, had already appointed
a new one: but Michael being informed of it, sent
them word to quit the Palace immediately, for he intended to let every one see that he knew how to govern Florence without their advice or assistance. He
then called together all the Syndics of the Arts, and
appointed a new Signiory, consisting of Eight members: four of which were chosen out of the Plebeians, two out of the greater companies, and two
more out of the less. He likewise reformed the other
branches of the Magistracy, and divided it into three
jurisdictions, one of which was to administer justice

---

* The Italian word *Messere*, or *Messer* (which is a contraction of
it) is a title of respect prefixed to the proper name of a man, and
answers to our *Mr*. But the word *Ser*, which is still a further ab-
breviation, is rather a term of diminution and inferiority, and
sometimes of contempt, as we say in English, *Master* such a one.

to the new Companies, another to the greater, and a third to the lefs Arts. He gave the rents of all the fhops upon the old Bridge to Sylveftro de' Medici, and took the Podefteria, or Bailiwic of Empoli, him-felf: befides which, he was very liberal to many other Citizens, who had befriended the Plebeians, not only out of gratitude for paft favours, but to engage them to fupport him in future againft envy.

But in this reformation of the State, the Plebeians thought Michael had been too partial to fome of the principal Commoners, and that they themfelves had not fuch a fhare in the government, as was fufficient to defend, much lefs to maintain them in it ; where-fore, according to their ufual infolence, they again took arms and ran in a tumultuous manner under their Colours into the Piazza, calling to the Signiory to come out upon the Ringheria, there to deliberate upon new matters, which they had to propofe to them for their own fecurity, and the good of the public. But Michael being well acquainted with their arro-gance, and not caring to exafperate them too far, be-fore he knew what their demands were, gently repri-manded them for applying in fo clamorous a manner, exhorting them to lay down their arms, and affuring them, that they fhould find the Signiory ready to com-ply with any thing that was reafonable; but that it was not confiftent with their dignity to fuffer it to be extorted from them by compulfion. This anfwer fo enraged the multitude againft thofe in the Palace, that they drew off to a place near St. Mary's new Church, where they appointed eight heads over them, with other fubordinate Officers and Magiftrates, to give them more dignity and reputation : fo that the city had now two Tribunals, and was governed by two diftinct adminiftrations. Thefe heads refolved amongft themfelves, that eight perfons, to be chofen by their own new Companies, fhould always refide with the Signiory in the Palace, and that whatfoever was refolved on by the others, fhould not pafs into a law, till it had their affent. They took away all ho-

nours and emoluments which had been granted to
Sylveſtro de' Medici, and Michael di Lando, in their
former deliberations; and aſſigned places and penſions
to ſeveral of their own partiſans, the better to ſupport
the dignity of their reſpective offices. After they had
come to theſe reſolutions, to make them more effectual, they ſent two deputies to the Signiory, who
were to inſiſt upon having them confirmed by the
Councils, and to threaten them with violence in caſe
it ſhould be refuſed. Theſe deputies, accordingly,
delivered the ſubſtance of their Commiſſion to the
Signiory, with much boldneſs and preſumption, reproaching the Gonfalonier with the authority they had
conferred on him, the favours he had received from
them, the ingratitude, and ſupercilious manner in
which he had ſince behaved; and concluded their
ſpeech with ſuch menaces, that Michael, not able to
bear with ſo intolerable a degree of inſolence any longer, determined (with a reſolution more ſuitable to
the dignity of his new office, than the meanneſs of
his birth) to chaſtiſe this height of audaciouſneſs in
an exemplary manner; and having drawn a ſword
which he had by his ſide, after he had given them ſeveral cuts with it, he ſent them tied neck and heels
to priſon.

As ſoon as the Plebeians heard of this, they were
enflamed to the laſt degree, and reſolved to uſe violence to obtain their ends, now other means had failed: for which purpoſe, they moved forwards in a
furious and diſorderly manner, directly towards the
Palace with a deſign to force their way into it. Michael in the mean time, apprehending the conſequence
of what he had done, determined to be before hand
with them, thinking it more honourable to ſtrike the
firſt blow, than to ſtay cooped up within the walls of
the Palace, till he was attacked by the enemy and
forced to ſneak out of it, as the late Gonfalonier had
done to his great mortification and diſgrace. He
therefore aſſembled a conſiderable body of the Citizens, who now began to repent of their folly, and
put;

putting himfelf at the head of them on horfeback, he proceeded towards St. Mary's with an intent to engage the Multitude. The Plebeians likewife, as we have juft faid, had already determined to attack him, and were moving forward towards the Palace at the fame juncture for that purpofe; but as each fide happened to take a different route, they did not meet by the way. Upon which, Michael turning back again, and finding the Mob had got poffeffion of the Piazza and were going to make an affault upon the Palace, inftantly fell upon them and difperfed them, driving fome of them quite out of the City, and forcing the reft to throw away their arms and hide themfelves. This victory put an end to the tumult; a victory gained entirely by the magnanimity and good conduct of the Gonfalonier, who upon this occafion, fhewed himfelf in valour, generofity, and prudence, far fuperior to any other Citizen, and well deferves to be numbered amongft thofe few that have been real benefactors to their Country. For if he had been of an ambitious or felf-interefted difpofition, the Republick muft have totally loft its liberty, and relapfed into a more intolerable degree of fervitude than it was under the tyranny of the Duke of Athens. But his integrity would not fuffer him to cherifh any defign that might be prejudicial to the good of the public, and his prudence taught him to conduct himfelf in fuch a manner, as not only gained him the firft place and confidence of his own party, but enabled him to triumph over that of his enemies. Thefe proceedings ftruck a terror into the Plebeians, and opened the eyes of the better fort of people, who could not help wondering at their own ftupidity, that after they had fuppreffed the pride of the Nobility, they could fo patiently fubmit to be infulted by the very dregs and refufe of the city.

When Michael obtained this victory over the Plebeians, the new Signiory was already appointed, two of whom were of fo bafe and abject condition, that every one feemed defirous to rid themfelves of fuch
infa-

infamous Magiftrates : fo that on the firft of September, when the new Signiory entered upon the Magiftracy, and the others were coming out of the Palace Gate, there began to be an uproar in the Piazza, which was full of armed men, who fhouted out with one voice, " that they would have no Plebeians in the Signory." The reft of the Signiory therefore, in order to appeafe them, degraded their two affociates, one of whom was named Tira, and the other Baroccio, and chofe Georgio Scali and Francifco di Michaele in their room. They likewife diffolved the Plebeian Companies, and deprived all thofe of their offices that had any connexion with them, except Michael di Lando, Ludovico di Puccio, and fome few others of the beft of them : and in the laft place, they divided the fubordinate Magiftracy into two feparate jurifdictions, one of which was to prefide over the greater Arts, and the other over the lefs. For the Signiory, it was only provided in general, that five of that body fhould be drawn out of the lefs Companies, and four out of the greater ; and the Gonfalonier alternately out of each.

In this manner the tranquillity of the city was re-eftablifhed for that time : and though the government of the republick was taken out of the hands of the Plebeians, yet the lower Companies had more power than the chief Commoners, who were forced, however, to be content with what they had, in order to fatisfy the Arts, and to deprive the Plebeians of their countenance and affiftance. Several others likewife that wifhed to fee thofe kept down, who, under the name of the Guelph party, had treated many of their fellow Citizens with fuch infolence and indignity, rejoiced at this regulation; and as Georgio Scali, Benedetto Alberti, Sylveftro de' Medici, and Tomafo Strozzi were the principal of thofe who favoured and promoted it, they became in a manner the chief governors of the city. Thefe proceedings, however, and this new model of government revived the old divifions betwixt the more confiderable Commoners and

and the lower fort of Mechanicks, which had firſt been occaſioned by the ambition of the Ricci and Albizi : and becauſe they afterwards produced terrible conſequences, and we ſhall often have occaſion to ſpeak of them in the courſe of this hiſtory, we ſhall henceforward diſtinguiſh theſe two factions by the Names of the *Popular* and the *Plebeian.*

This conſtitution of government laſted three years, a period which, though ſhort, abounded with Executions and Baniſhments: for as thoſe that were chiefly concerned in the adminiſtration well knew there were great numbers of Malecontents both within the city and without it, they lived in perpetual fear and alarm. The diſaffected within the walls, either actually did, or were ſuppoſed to cabal daily againſt the State; and thoſe without, being no longer under any reſtraint, were continually raiſing diſturbances abroad by the aſſiſtance of foreign Princes or Republics, ſometimes in one part, ſometimes in another.

There was then at Bologna one Giannozzo da Salerno, a commander employed in the ſervice of Carlo Durazzo (a deſcendant from the Royal Family of Naples) who deſigning, if poſſible, to wreſt that Kingdom out of the hands of Queen Giovanna, kept this general in pay at the expence of Pope Urban, betwixt whom and the Queen there had lately been great conteſts. There was likewiſe a vaſt number of the Florentine exiles in Bologna at the ſame time, who held a cloſe correſpondence with him and his maſter Carlo, which gave great uneaſineſs to the governors of Florence, as they were the more eaſily prevailed upon thereby to give credit to the malicious reports that were raiſed of ſuch Citizens as they ſuſpected before. In the mean time, whilſt the Magiſtrates were under theſe apprehenſions, they received intelligence that Giannozzo was actually to march towards Florence at the head of the exiles, and that many within the Walls were ready to take up arms at his arrival there and deliver up the city to him. Upon this information, numbers were accuſed; the chief of whom

I   were

were Pietro degli Albizi, Carlo and Philippo Strozzi, Cipriano Mangioni, Jacopo Sacchetti, Donato Barbadori, and Giovanni Anfelmi, who were all committed to prifon, except Carlo Strozzi, and he fled. Befides which, the Signiory ordered Tomafo Strozzi and Benedetto Alberti to patrole the city with fome Companies of the Militia, in order to deter any one from rifing in favour of the enemy. After the Prifoners had been examined and nothing criminal could be proved againft them, the Magiftrate was going to acquit and difcharge them : upon which, their enemies immediately called the people together and raifed fuch a ferment by their clamours and calumnies, that he was forced to pafs fentence of death upon them. And though Pietro degli Albizi had been more honoured and refpected in Florence for a long courfe of years than any other Citizen of his time ; yet neither the clearnefs of fuch an eftablifhed reputation, nor the fplendor of his family availed him any thing. It happened not long before, whilft he was regaling his fellow Citizens one day at a great entertainment which he had made for them, that fome perfon unknown (perhaps a true friend with a defign to put him in mind of moderation in fo remakable a degree of profperity, or very likely it might be an enemy, who did it to terrify him with the apprehenfion of fome fudden change, when he confidered the volubility of fortune) fent him a falver of fweetmeats and amongft them a large nail, which being obferved and handed about the table from one to another, was whimfically interpreted as an admonition to nail down the wheel of fortune now he was got to the top of it * ; as it muft

---

* In the confulfhip of L. Genutius, and L. Æmilius Mamercus, the plague continuing to afflict the Romans, they had recourfe to the ceremony of driving a nail, which had never been done before, but to keep an account of the years, (quia raræ per ea tempora literæ erant, fays Livy) according to an ancient Law, " that the Great Prætor fhould drive a nail on the third day of September.' From that time this political ceremony was turned into fuperftition, and fimple people were made to believe, that this action would be effectual to avert public calamities, or at leaft to nail them down,

of neceſſity happen, if the rotation continued, that he would ſometime or other be whirled to the bottom : and this prognoſtication was indeed fully verified by his ſudden fall and unfortunate end.

Theſe executions occaſioned freſh murmurs and diſcontents in the city : ſo that both thoſe that had got the upper hand, and thoſe that were depreſſed, lived in continual fear and ſuſpicion of each other. Dreadful indeed were the conſequences which flowed from the apprehenſions of the former ; as every little accident furniſhed them with a handle to trample upon their fellow Citizens ; ſome of whom they daily either put to death, admoniſhed, or ſent into exile. They likewiſe made ſeveral new laws to ſtrengthen their hands, and keep thoſe down of whom they entertained the leaſt ſuſpicion : beſides which, they appointed forty-ſix Commiſſioners, who by the authority of the Signiory were to purge the Commonwealth of all diſaffected perſons. Theſe Commiſſioners admoniſhed thirty-nine Citizens, degraded ſeveral of the higher rank, and exalted many of the lower : and to defend themſelves againſt any danger from abroad, they took † John Aguto into their pay, an Engliſh

and retard their progreſs. This nail was of braſs, and driven into the wall behind the Chapel of Minerva, in the Capitol, on the right hand of the Temple of Jupiter Capitolinus : and to perform this ceremony, a Dictator was purpoſely created. Vid. Danet in voce Clavus, and Livy, lib. vii. c. 3. Probably this might be a cuſtom amongſt the Italians when this tranſaction happened, and derived from the ancient Romans ; ſince they have been forward enough to imitate them in many other rites and modes of worſhip, as the late Dr. Middleton has fully ſhewn in his letter from Rome.

† This John Aguto, or Augut (as he is corruptly called by the Italians) before-mentioned in the firſt book of this hiſtory, was Sir John Hawkwood, an Engliſh Knight ; who was ſo highly eſteemed in Italy for his courage and military conduct, that the Senate of Florence honoured him for his extraordinary merits, with an Equeſtrian Statue, and a magnificent monument, as a perpetual teſtimony of his valour and fidelity. The Italian hiſtorians are full of his great exploits, and Paolo Jovio celebrates them in his Elogies. I ſhall only quote the four following verſes concerning him out of Giulio Ferroldo.

Hawkwood, Anglorum decus, et decus, addite, genti
  Italicæ, Italico præſidiumque ſolo ;
Ut tumuli quondam Florentia, ſic Simulachri
  Virtutem Jovius donat honore tuam.

Com-

Commander of very great reputation, who had been many years in the service of the Pope and other Italian Princes. Their apprehensions from abroad chiefly arose from the intelligence they had received that Carlo Durazzo was raising a powerful army to invade the Kingdom of Naples, as it was given out, and that he had a great number of the Florentine exiles under his banners. But to guard against the danger

Hawkwood, whom England boasts her stoutest son,
And glad Italians their Preserver own;
A stately tomb as grateful Florence gave,
So learned Jovio does thy picture save.

This renowned Knight thus celebrated abroad, was neglected and had no honours paid to his memory at home; except that some of his fellow soldiers and followers in the foreign wars, founded a chauntry for him at Castle Henningham, in Essex, the place of his birth, and for two of his Companions, John Oliver, and Thomas Newington, Esquires. Vid. Camden's Britannia, Vol. i. p. 240. Second Edit. by Bishop Gibson.

The account given of him by Collier, is as follows: " He was born at Sibble Henningham, in Essex, in the reign of Edward III. His Extraction was mean, his Education suitable, but his improvement in arms wonderful. His father was Gilbert Hawkwood, a Tanner, who bound him apprentice to a Taylor, in London. But being pressed into the King's service in his French wars, he behaved himself so valiantly, that it was not long before he got a company of Foot, and was afterwards knighted for some good services. However, as a peace was concluded soon after betwixt the two Crowns, and his estate was not sufficient to maintain his Title with dignity, he went into Italy with some English forces to advance his fortune. There he served first, with good success, under John, Marquis of Montferrat; next, under Galeazzo, Duke of Milan, at the sollicitation of Bernabo, the Duke's brother; with whom he was in such esteem for his successful valour, that he gave him Domitia, his Daughter, in marriage, with a dower suitable to her birth. This alliance spread his fame far and near, chiefly throughout Italy: yet either upon further hopes, or some disgust, he quitted the service of his father-in-law, and went over to the enemy. Afterwards he went to Rome, where the Pope made him commander in chief of his forces, in an expedition for the recovery of part of Provence, which had revolted from him. When he had effected this, he entered into the pay of the Florentines, whom he served so successfully, that he was looked upon as the best soldier of that age. He died at Florence in a very advanced age, Anno 1394, and in the 18th of Richard II. The Florentines, to perpetuate the memory of his great exploits, and faithful service to their state, honoured him with a Statue and a sumptuous Monument. His friends also raised him one of Stone at Sibble Henningham, arched over with a representation of Hawks flying in a wood, in allusion to his name. But it is now utterly destroyed by time. He had a Son named John, born in Italy, who was Knighted, and naturalized in the reign of Henry IV.

with

with which they were threatned from that quarter, they not only put their Militia in good order, but raifed a large fum of money; and when Carlo had advanced as far as Arezzo, they made him a prefent of forty thoufand Ducats, upon a promife that he would not moleft them. He accordingly proceeded in his march to invade the territories of Queen Giovanna, and having made himfelf mafter of the Kingdom of Naples, he fent her prifoner into Hungary. But this fuccefs alarmed the governors of Florence ftill more, who could not flatter themfelves that the new King would have a greater regard to their bribe, than the alliance which had always fubfifted betwixt his family and the faction of the Guelphs, whom they had fo grievoufly oppreffed.

Thefe fufpicions growing ftronger and ftronger every day, made them behave with more rigour to the other party: a manner of proceeding that only ferved to multiply their difcontents, and to increafe, inftead of allaying their own fears, which were not a little heightened by the infolence of Georgio Scali and Tomafo Strozzi, whofe authority was much fuperior to that of the Màgiftrates; and therefore they all ftood in great awe of thofe two Citizens, as they knew it was in their power, if they fhould join the Plebeians, to turn them entirely out of the adminiftration. This intemperate and tyrannical manner of governing began to grow intolerable, not only to all good Citizens, but even to the feditious themfelves; and it was not poffible that the arrogance of Georgio Scali in particular could be long fupported. It happened accordingly foon after, that fome of his informers accufed one Giovanni di Cambio of confpiring againft the State: but as he was found innocent of the crime that was laid to his charge, the Magiftrate, who was then the Captain of the people, adjudged that the accufer fhould fuffer the fame punifhment that would have been inflicted upon Cambio if he had been proved guilty. Georgio therefore perceiving that all his authority and interceffions for

him

him were in vain, went together with Tomaſo Strozzi
at the head of a Mob which they had raiſed, and
having reſcued him by force, they plundered the Captain's Palace and obliged him to hide himſelf for fear
of being murdered. This outrage ſo highly diſguſted
the whole city, that his enemies thought they had
now a fair opportunity not only of wreaking their own
private revenge upon him, but of delivering the
Commonwealth out of his hands and the hands of
the Plebeians, who had ſo unmercifully tyrannized
over it for the ſpace of three years. And this deſign
was not a little promoted by the Captain's behaviour,
who went directly to the Signiory as ſoon as the tumult was over, and told them, " that, as they had
done him the honour to confer that office upon him,
he had accepted it with pleaſure, upon a preſumption
that he was to ſerve good and virtuous men, and who
would have taken arms, if neceſſary, to favour the
courſe of juſtice, and not to obſtruct it. But ſince
he had ſeen enough of their manner of governing the
city and behaving themſelves, that poſt which he had
ſo chearfully accepted in hopes of advancing his own
fortune and reputation as well as ſerving the Commonwealth, he ſhould much more chearfully reſign,
to avoid further danger and ſave himſelf from utter
ruin." Upon this, ſome of the Signiory, after they
had perſuaded the Captain to continue in his office, by
giving him fair words and promiſing they would
take care that he ſhould not only be indemnified
for the loſs he had already ſuſtained, but that he
ſhould live in ſecurity for the future, immediately
entered into a conſultation with ſuch of the Citizens
as they thought wiſhed well to their country and
were the leaſt ſuſpected of diſaffection ; in which it
was concluded that now or never would be the time
to deliver the city from the yoke of Scali and the
Plebeian faction, as he had alienated the affections
of the generality by this laſt enormity. They reſolved therefore to make uſe of the opportunity before the paſſions of the people ſubſided, well knowing

ing that the favour of the multitude is foon loft and
as foon regained by any little accidental circumftance.
And to conduct the affair to a happy iffue, they
thought it abfolutely neceffary to draw Benedetto Alberti into a concurrence with their defign, without
whofe affiftance the undertaking feemed too rafh and
dangerous.

Benedetto, tho' a man of immenfe fortune, was yet
very humane, ftrict in his morals and principles, a
fteady friend to the liberties of his country, and fufficiently difgufted at the tyrannical proceedings of the
government : fo that it was no difficult matter to engage him in any meafures that might contribute to the
downfall of Scali. For as the infolence and oppreffion of the principal Commoners and the Guelph
faction had made him their enemy and a friend to the
Plebeians : fo, when he faw the latter purfuing the
very fame meafures, he quickly detached himfelf
from them, and had not the leaft hand in any of the
late injuries and violences that had been offered to
his fellow Citizens ; the fame motives, that at firft
inclined him to take part with the Plebeians, afterwards determining him to leave them. Having thus
brought Benedetto and the Heads of the Arts into
their defign, they feized upon Georgio Scali ; but
Tomafo Strozzi made his efcape. The very next
day he was beheaded, which ftruck fuch a terror
into his party, that not fo much as one of them offered to ftir in his favour, though they crowded in
great numbers to fee his execution. When he came
to fuffer death in the face of that very people which
had fo lately worfhipped him with a degree of ido-
latry, he could not help complaining of the hardnefs
of his deftiny and the wickednefs of thofe Citizens,
who, by their oppreffions, had forced him to court
and carefs a Rabble in which he found there was
neither honour nor gratitude. And feeing Benedetto
Alberti at the head of the guards that furrounded the
fcaffold, he turned himfelf towards him and faid,
" Can you too, Benedetto, ftand tamely by, and fee

me murdered in this vile manner? I affure you, if you was in my circumftances, and I in yours, I would not fuffer you to be treated fo : but, remember that I tell you, this is the laft day of my misfortunes, and the firft of yours." He then bewailed his own folly in having trufted to the fidelity of the Plebeians, which he might well have known is ever liable to be fhaken and feduced by any little fufpicion, mifreprefentation, or blaft of envy. With thefe lamentations he ended his life in the midft of his enemies to their great exultation : after which, fome of his chief Confidants were alfo put to death and their bodies dragged through the ftreets by the people.

His death threw the whole city into a ferment : for, during the execution, many of the Citizens had taken arms in favour of the Signiory and Captain of the people ; and many others to gratify their own revenge or private ends. And as the city was full of different humours, almoft every one had a feparate view, and was eager to accomplifh it before he laid down his arms. The ancient Nobility, now called Grandees, could not bear to live any longer without fome fhare in the public honours, and exerted their utmoft efforts to recover them : for which purpofe, they endeavoured to have the Captains of the Arts reftored to their former authority. The Heads of the popular faction and the greater Arts were difgufted that the government of the ftate was fhared in common with them by the inferior Arts and Plebeians : the inferior Arts, inftead of giving up any part of their authority, were very defirous to increafe it : and the Plebeians were afraid of having their new Companie diffolved. From thefe different views and appreher fions it came to pafs, that there was nothing to b feen in Florence but tumults for the fpace of a who! year : for fometimes the Grandees, fometimes th greater, fometimes the lefs Arts, and fometimes th Plebeians were in an uproar ; and it often happene that they all took arms at the fame time in differer

par

parts of the city. So that there were frequent fkirmifhes and frays betwixt them and the guards of the
Palace : for the Signiory fometimes by oppofing, and
fometimes by giving way to them, endeavoured by
all poffible means to find fome remedy for fuch diftractions. At laft however, after two Conferences
had been held, and two Balias inftituted for the reformation of the city, after many mifchiefs and more
dangers and troubles, a form of government was
eftablifhed for the future ; by which it was provided,
that all fuch fhould be recalled as had been banifhed
fince Sylveftro de' Medici was Gonfalonier. That all
offices and appointments which had been conferred
by the Balia of 1378 fhould be abolifhed : That the
two new Companies fhould be diffolved, and their
individuals reincorporated into their refpective Arts :
That the inferior Arts fhould not chufe any Gonfalonier di Giuftizia : That inftead of enjoying one
half of the public honours, they fhould now be limited to one third, and thofe too of the lower rank.
So that the Popular Nobility and the Guelphs re-
affumed their fuperiority in the Government of the
State ; and the Plebeians were utterly difpoffeffed of
it, after they had held it from the year 1378 till *1378*
1381, at which time this revolution happened. *1371*

The new adminiftration however was no lefs grievous and oppreffive to the Citizens at firft than that
of the Plebeians had been : for feveral of the Popular
Nobility, who had fhewn themfelves the forwardeft
in fupporting the people, and many of the Heads of
the Plebeians were banifhed : amongft the reft was
Michael di Lando, whom neither the remembrance
of his former great merit and authority in reftraining
the fury of the populace when they were fo licen-
tioufly plundering the city, nor any other confideration, was fufficient to protect from the refentment of
the governing party. Such was the gratitude of his
countrymen for his former fervices ! and from this
impolitic manner of proceeding in Princes and Governors of Commonwealths, it happens that men naturally

turally growing difgufted at their ill-timed feverity and ingratitude, often incur their difpleafure before they are aware of it. Accordingly, as fuch executions and banifhments had ever been difapproved of by Benedetto Alberti, he could not help blaming the authors of thofe that had lately happened, both in pub· lic and in private company. Upon which the government began to grow fufpicious of him as a favourer of the Plebeian party, and one that had confented to the death of Georgio Scali, not out of any real difapprobation of his conduct, but that he might the more eafily get the reins of government into his own hands. His daily converfation and behaviour increafed their fufpicions to fuch a degree, that they kept a ftrict watch over him, and refolved to take the firft opportunity of ruining him.

Whilft they lived in this manner at home, they did not fuffer much from abroad, though indeed they were not altogether without their alarms. For about this time Lewis of Anjou came into Italy with an army to drive Carlo Durazzo out of the Kingdom of Naples and to reinftate Queen Giovanna. His arrival threw the Florentines into no little perplexity : for Carlo as their old friend and Ally demanded their affiftance; whilft Lewis on the other hand, infifted upon their ftanding neutral if they expected any future favour or good offices from him. That they might feem willing therefore to oblige Lewis, they difcharged Sir John Hawkwood from their fervice : and at the fame time, to affift Carlo, they prevailed upon his Ally Pope Urban to take that commander into his pay. This double dealing was exceedingly refented by Lewis, who eafily faw through it : fo that when frefh fuccours arrived in Tufcany from France, to enable him to carry on the war againft Carlo in Puglia, he joined the exiles from Arezzo, and having forced his way into that town by their affiftance, he drove out the governing party there which adhered to Carlo. He likewife determined to have changed the government of Florence, but was prevented by death, which

which gave a new turn to affairs in Puglia and Tuſcany ; for Carlo then firmly eſtabliſhed himſelf in a
Kingdom which he had in a manner given up for
loſt : and the Florentines, who were ſomething du-
bious, whether they ſhould be able to defend their
own city, reſolved to make themſelves maſters of
Arezzo, which they bought of the garriſon that Lewis
had left in poſſeſſion of it.   After Carlo had thoroughly ſettled himſelf in Puglia, he left his wife
there with his two children, Ladiſlaus and Giovanna
(as we have elſewhere related) and went to take poſſeſſion of Hungary, which Kingdom had devolved to
him by right of inheritance, but died there ſoon after
he was crowned.

Greater rejoycings never were ſeen in any city, even
for a victory of their own, than there were in Florence, both in public and in private, upon this acquiſition; many families keeping open houſes, and
vying with the public in the pomp and extravagance
of their entertainments.   But none of them were to
be compared to thoſe made by the family of the Alberti, the ſplendor and magnificence of which were
ſo far above the condition of any private perſon, that
they would have done honour to a Prince.   This
oſtentation excited much envy amongſt their fellow
Citizens, which, added to the ſuſpicion that the government had already conceived of Benedetto, at
laſt proved his ruin : for they could not quiet their
apprehenſions, whilſt they thought he was taking
theſe ſteps to reconcile the Plebeians to him, in order
to drive them out of the city whenever he thought
proper.

Whilſt they were indulging theſe jealouſies, it happened, that he was drawn Gonfalonier of the Companies, and his Son-in-law Philippo Magalotti, Gonfalonier of juſtice at the ſame time ; an accident that
redoubled the fears of thoſe in the adminiſtration,
who thought Benedetto had now much more power
than was conſiſtent with the ſafety of the ſtate : and
as they were deſirous to find ſome means of averting

the

the danger they apprehended themfelves in, without noife or tumult if poffible, they fecretly encouraged Befe Magalotti, his enemy and competitor, to reprefent to the Signiory, that Philippo not being fo old as the Law required in the perfon that filled that office, neither ought nor could be admitted to it. Upon this, the affair was brought before the Signiors, part of whom out of hatred, and the reft for the fake of peace and quietnefs, adjudged him unqualified to hold that dignity: after which, Bardo Mancini was drawn in his room, a bitter enemy to the Plebeian faction, and no lefs inveterate againft Benedetto. No fooner was this man in poffeffion of his office, but he called a Balia for the reformation of the State; by the authority of which, Benedetto was fent into exile, and all the reft of his family admonifhed, except Antonio. Before his departure he called all his friends together, and feeing them very forrowful and dejected, he took his leave of them in this manner:

"You fee, my dear friends and fellow Citizens, in what manner fortune has contrived my ruin, and how fhe ftill threatens you: at which, neither you nor I ought to be at all furprized, fince it is almoft always the Lot of thofe who endeavour to maintain their integrity, in wicked and corrupt times, and to fupport that which the generality are defirous to pull down. The love of my Country firft induced me to join with Sylveftro de' Medici; and afterwards to feparate myfelf from Georgio Scali. From the fame principle I could not forbear cenfuring the proceedings of thofe that are now at the Helm, who, having nobody to chaftife them, are likewife defirous to get rid of every one that dares to reprehend them. I cheerfully fubmit to banifhment, if I am doomed to it, only to free them from the awe they ftand in of me, and not of me only, but of every one, who, they are confcious, has an eye upon their tyrannical and licentious proceedings. On my own account I am not much concerned; for that reputation with which I was honoured whilft my Country was free, can-

cannot be taken away from me now it is enflaved; and the review of my paft life will always afford me more fatisfaction, than the difgrace of my exile can give me regret. It fills we with concern, I confefs, to leave my Country a prey to the avarice and oppreffion of a few particular men. It grieves me, when I reflect, that this day, which puts an end to my misfortunes, in all probability will give birth to yours, and that the malevolence of fortune may fall ftill more heavy upon you than it has done upon me. Let me exhort you however, not to defpair, but to bear up againft her frowns, and to behave yourfelves in fuch a manner, that whenever you fall into adverfity, which you may daily expect from the prefent fituation of things, the world may bear witnefs that it is not owing to any demerit of your own." After his departure, he ftill kept up the fame reputation of piety and goodnefs abroad, that he had ever maintained at home; and going to vifit the Holy Sepulchre, he died in his return at Rhodes. His bones were brought back to Florence and interred there with the higheft honours, by thofe very people who had perfecuted him whilft alive with fo much rancour and injuftice.

The family of the Alberti were not the only fufferers in thefe diftractions, for many other Citizens were either admonifhed, or fent into exile: amongft thofe that were banifhed were Pietro Benini, Matteo Alderotti, Giovanni and Francifco del Bene, Giovanni Benci, and Andrea Adimari, befides a great number of the lower fort of people: amongft thofe that were admonifhed, were the Covoni, the Benini, the Rinucci, the Formiconi, the Corbizi, the Mannelli, and the Alderotti. It always had been the cuftom to empower the Balia to fit for a certain determinate time; but the Citizens, who were members of this, having done what they were deputed for to the fatisfaction of the State, were going to break up before the expiration of that term, as they thought it would have an appearance of modefty and difintereftednefs.

P 4   But

But the people hearing of their refolution, ran in arms to the Palace, and infifted that they fhould banifh and admonifh feveral others before they refigned their authority : at which, the Signiory were exceedingly offended, though they thought proper to amufe the people with fair words and promifes, till fuch time as they had got their guards together, and were ftrong enough to make them lay down their arms by force. However, to give them fome fort of fatisfaction, and to diminifh the authority of the Plebeians ftill more, they made a Decree, by which the third part of the public honours which they before enjoyed, fhould now be reduced to a fourth. And that there might be always two at leaft in the Signiory of approved fidelity to the government, they gave the Gonfalonier di Giuftizia, and four other Citizens, authority to make a frefh Imborfation, and to put the names of a felect number of Citizens into a particular purfe, out of which two of every new Signiory fhould always be drawn.

1381.   Every thing being thus fettled in 1381, after a feries of troubles and convulfions, which had lafted fix years, the Florentines enjoyed tranquillity at home till the year 1387 : at which time, Giovanni Galeazzo Vifconti, commonly called the Conte di Virtu, imprifoned his Uncle Bernabo, and thereby became fole Lord of all Lombardy. This Conte di Virtu thought he could have made himfelf King of Italy by force of arms, as he had made himfelf Duke of Milan, by treachery : for which purpofe, he began fo vigorous a war upon the Florentines, in the year 1390,

1390   and conducted it in fuch a manner, that he would certainly have ruined them, if he had not died foon after. However, they made a courageous and indeed a wonderful defence, confidering their State was a Republic * ; and the conclufion of the war was not

* What other advantages foever the advocates for a republican form of government may alledge in its favour, when compared with monarch'c l power, it is certain that the former cannot exert itfelf with the fame vigour as the latter, efpecially in time of war. And the

fo

fo fatal as the fury with which it was conducted
feemed to threaten. For after the Duke had taken
Bologna, Pifa, Perugia, and Siena, and was making
preparations to be crowned King of Italy at Florence, he was prevented by fudden death from enjoying the fruit of his victories, and the Florentines
delivered from the calamities, which otherwife muft
have fallen upon them.

During the time of this war with the Duke, the
office of Gonfalonier di Giuftizia was fallen into the
hands of Mafo degli Albizi, whom the remembrance *Mafo*
of Pietro's unfortunate end had made a bitter enemy
to the Alberti, though Benedetto was now dead.
And as the animofities of the Factions were not yet
extinguifhed, he refolved to be revenged on the reft
of that family before he went out of office. For
which purpofe, he availed himfelf of a depofition,
that had been made by a certain perfon who was accufed of holding a fecret correfpondence with the exiles, in which Alberto and Andrea degli Alberti were
named as his accomplices, and immediately taken into
cuftody. Upon this, the whole city was in fuch an
uproar, that the Signiory having fufficiently provided
for their own defence, called the people to a con-

more any governments have of democracy in their conftitution, the
weaker they generally are in that refpect   Their deliberations are
flow, their councils divided, and the refult of them too public. Befides which, they are fo fubject to tumults and faction and civil diffenfion, that they muft of neceffity be more feeble and tardy, either
in defending themfelves, or annoying the enemy.   They have often
been fo fenfible of thefe inconveniencies, upon fuch occafions, that
they have been forced to create Dictators, Stadtholders, &c. and
put themfelves under the government of one fingle Prince, or other
perfon vefted with abfolute power and authority for a certain ftated
time, as the only means to clofe the wounds of faction, and to give
more life and vigour to the State.   A prince is to the community what
the fpirit and foul are to the body.

Spiritus intus alit, totamque infufa per artus
Mens agitat molem, & magno fe corpore mifcet.
Virg. Æn. VI. 726.
One common Soul
Infpires and feeds and animates the whole.
This active mind infufed thro' all the fpace,
Unites and mingles with the mighty mafs.   Dryden.

ference,

ference, appointed a new Balia, (by the authority of
which many Citizens were banifhed) and caufed a
frefh imborfation of Magiftrates to be made. Amongft
thofe that they banifhed were almoft all the Alberti;
befides which many of the Artificers were either admonifhed or put to death. This tyrannical manner
of proceeding fo enraged the Arts and the lower fort
of people, who now faw their lives and honours fo
wantonly taken away, that they rofe in arms, fome of
them running to the Piazza before the Palace, and
others to the houfe of Veri de' Medici, who after the
death of Sylveftro was become the Head of that family. In order to footh thofe that were in the Piazza,
the Signiory fent Rinaldo Gianfigliazzi and Donato
Acciaivoli (two Commoners that were more acceptable to the Plebeians than any others) with the colours of the Guelph faction and thofe of the people
in their hands. The other party that had repaired
to the houfe of Veri de' Medici earneftly intreated
him to take the government into his hands, and deliver them from the oppreffion of thofe Citizens who
were daily endeavouring to deftroy the Commonwealth
and every good man in it.

All writers that have left any memoirs of the tranfactions of thofe times, unanimoufly agree, that if
Veri had been as ambitious as he was virtuous, he
then might eafily have made himfelf abfolute Lord of
the City : for the violence and grievous injuries that
were indifcriminately offered both to the good and
bad, had provoked the Arts, and all thofe that favoured them, to fuch a degree, that they only wanted fomebody to lead them on to fatiate their revenge.
Amongft feveral others that advifed him to take the
fole government of the Republic into his hands, Antonio de' Medici was the moft importunate, though
they had been long at open enmity together : but
Veri, inftead of paying any regard to him, only faid,
" that as he had always defpifed his threats, whilft
he was his profeffed enemy, fo he would not be ruined
by his counfel now he pretended to be his friend;"
and

and turning to the multitude, he exhorted them not to defpair, for he would fecure them, if they would follow his advice. After which, he advanced in the midft of them to the Piazza, and from thence, went by himfelf into the Palace, where he told the Signiory, " he was far from being forry, that his manner of life had been fuch as to procure him the love of his fellow Citizens; but he could not help being concerned, that they had formed an opinion of him, which he trufted his converfation had not at all deferved: for as he had never fhewn the leaft fign of an ambitious or turbulent difpofition, he could not imagine what induced them to think he would either favour fedition, or entertain any defign of ufurping the government. That he prayed their Lordfhips, however, that the error and ignorance of the multitude might not be imputed as a crime to him, fince he had delivered himfelf up into their hands as foon as it was poffible. That he exhorted them to ufe their power with moderation; and for the prefervation of the City, to be content with the fuperiority they had already obtained, rather than endeavour to make their victory complete by its utter ruin."

The Signiory having highly commended Veri's behaviour, defired him to make the people lay down their arms, and then they would comply with any thing whatfoever that he and the other Citizens fhould advife. Upon this, he returned into the Piazza, and having called together his followers, and thofe that were under the Colours of Rinaldo and Donato, he told them all, that he found the Signiory very well difpofed to give them any manner of fatisfaction: that many things had been already granted, but that the fhortnefs of the time, and the abfence of fome magiftrates, had prevented their being put in Execution. That in the mean time, he conjured them to lay down their arms, out of reverence to the Signiory; affuring them, that inftead of menaces and infults, obedience and a refpectful behaviour were more likely to prevail upon the government to gratify their

re-

requests : and that if they would follow his directions, both their liberties and honours fhould be fecured to them. Upon thefe affurances and a reliance
on Veri's word, they all returned to their own houfes.

As foon as this tumult was compofed, the Signiory,
in the firft place began to fortify the Piazza, and then
immediately inrolled two thoufand Citizens, well affected to the government, whom they divided into
Companies, with orders, to be ready to affift them
whenever they fhould be called upon ; ftrictly prohibiting all others at the fame time, from bearing arms
upon any occafion whatfoever. After they had taken
thefe fteps to fecure themfelves, they put many of the
Artificers to death, and banifhed others that had been
the moft active and clamorous in the late infurrection.
And that the Gonfalonier della Giuftizia might have
the more reverence fhewn him, they ordained, that no
one fhould be capable of being admitted to that dignity, before he was five and forty years of age. They
likewife made feveral other provifions to ftrengthen
their hands, which were not only intolerable to thofe
againft whom they were particularly defigned, but
odious to all good Citizens of their own party ; who
could not help thinking that a bad adminiftration,
and built upon a fandy bottom, which ftood in need
of fo much feverity to fupport it. Thofe of the Alberti that were ftill left in the City, and many others,
particularly the Medici, who thought themfelves, as
well as the people, abufed and deceived, were extremely difgufted at thefe proceedings ; but the firft
that had courage enough to oppofe them, was Donato, the fon of Jacopo Acciaivoli. This Donato,
though he was one of the Grandees of the City, and
rather fuperior than equal to Mafo degli Albizi
(who by the fteps he had taken whilft he was Gonfalonier, was become in a manner the Head of the
Commonwealth) could not live quietly himfelf in a
city where fo many were difcontented ; and difdained
the common practice of making a private advantage of public misfortunes. He therefore refolved to
                                                    ufe

ufe his intereft, in the firft place, that all fuch as had
been fent into exile, might be recalled, at leaft th t
thofe who had been admonifhed fhould be requalified
to hold their former honours and employments. For
this purpofe, he infinuated firft to one Citizen, and
then to another, that there was no other expedient
left to quiet the people, and allay the rage of faction;
and that if he was one of the Signiory, he made no
doubt, but he could bring the matter to bear. But
as delay is irkfome in all things, and too much precipitation is commonly attended with danger; to
avoid one extreme, he ran into the other. There
were them in the Signiory Michael Acciaivoli, his
near relation, and Niccolo Ricoveri, his intimate
friend : and as he thought this was an opportunity
not to be loft, he entreated them to propofe a Law
to the Councils for the reftoration of their fellow Citizens. At his perfuafion, they accordingly moved it
to the reft of the Signiory, who were all of opinion,
that it would be imprudent to attempt any change
of Government in which the advantage would be
doubtful, and the danger very great and certain. Donato, therefore, having firft tried all means to no
purpofe, began to grow outrageous, and fent them
word, " That fince they would not fuffer the City to
be reformed by other methods, it fhould be done by
force :" at which they were fo incenfed, that after
they had communicated the affair to thofe that were
in the adminiftration, Donato was cited to appear before them, and being convicted of fending that meffage, by the Evidence of the perfon who carried it, he
was banifhed to Barletta. They likewife banifhed *Medici.*
Alamanno and Antonio de' Medici, and all thofe that
were of Alamanno's family, together with many of
the inferior Arts, who had any intereft amongft the
Plebeians. All thefe things happened within two
years after Mafo degli Albizi had affumed the government.
In this fituation of affairs, whilft many were difcontented at home, and many impatient under their
banifh-

banifhment abroad, there happened to be amongſt
the Exiles at Bologna, Picchio Cavicciulli, Tomaſo
de' Ricci, Antonio de' Medici, Benedetto degli Spini,
Antonio de' Girolami, Chriſtofano di Carlone, and
two others of much inferior condition; but all young
and ſpirited men, and determined at all events to return to their Country: eſpecially as Piggello and Baroccio Cavicciulli, who were in the number of thoſe
that had been admoniſhed in Florence, had found
means to ſend them word, that if they could get ſecretly by night into the City, they would receive them
into their houſes, from whence they might take ſome
convenient opportunity of ſallying out and killing
Maſo degli Albizi, and afterwards call the people to
arms, who would be ready enough to riſe, as they
were ſufficiently diſaffected to the Government, and
ſure of being ſupported by the Ricci, Adimari, Medici, Mannelli, and many other conſiderable families.
Fluſhed with theſe hopes, they privately entered the
City at a place appointed, on the 4th of Auguſt 1397,
and immediately ſet ſpies to watch the motions of
Maſo; as they deſigned to begin the tumult by diſ-
patching him. Not long after, Maſo came out of
his Houſe, and went to an Apothecary's, not far from
the Church of St. Pietro Maggiore: upon which,
the perſon that had been ſent to watch him, ran to
acquaint the conſpirators, who immediatly took their
ſwords and haſted to the Apothecary's, but found he
was gone from thence. They were not diſcouraged,
however, at this diſappointment, but turned aſide towards the Old Market Place, where they killed one
of their enemies party, and proceeded towards the
New Market, ſhouting, and calling upon the Citizens
to arm for the recovery of their Liberties, and put
the Tyrants to death. From thence they advanced
towards a Street called the Calimara, at the end of
which they killed another man: but ſeeing that nobody regarded their cries, nor offered to take arms
and join them, they retired into the Loggia Nighit-
toſa, from the garrets of which they again called out
to

to a great mob (which by this time was got round
them, more out of curiofity than with a defign to
give them any affiftance) conjuring them to take
arms, and fhake off fo deteftable a Yoke; and affuring them, " that the groans of their fellow Citizens had moved them more than any private injuries which they had fuftained themfelves, and were
the only occafion of their making that attempt to
refcue them out of flavery : that they had often heard
that many of them were continually wifhing for fome
opportunity of revenging themfelves, and were determined to do it whenever they could get any body
to head them. But now that opportunity was come,
and they had leaders to conduct them, they ftood
gazing upon each other, till they would fee the af-
fertors of their Liberties maffacred, and their oppreffions redoubled. That they were aftonifhed to
fee thofe who formerly ufed to take arms upon any
little grievance, now crouching under fo intolerable
a burden, and tamely fubmitting to have fo many of
their fellow Citizens admonifhed, and fo many fent
into exile, when it was in their own power both to
reftore the Exiles to their Country, and thofe that had
been admonifhed, to their former honours." Thefe
exhortations and reproaches, ftinging as they were,
had yet no effect upon the people, who either durft
not ftir out of the awe they ftood in to the Government, or would not, out of the prejudice they had
conceived againft the Exiles from the death of thofe
two Citizens, whom they had killed. So that when
thefe Ringleaders of the tumult perceived that neither
their words nor actions made any impreffion upon the
multitude, they were at laft convinced, when it was
too late, how dangerous a thing it is to attempt the
deliverance of a people who are willing to continue
in flavery : and defpairing of fuccefs, they fhut themfelves up in the Church of St. Reparata, not with
any hopes of faving their lives, but of deferring their
death for a little while.

Upon

Upon the firſt rumour of this tumult, the Signiory had armed themſelves, and fortified their palace; but when they heard the event, who they were that had been the occaſion of it, and whither they had retired, they recovered their ſpirits, and ordered an officer to take a party of the guards with him, and ſeize them. The doors of the Church were eaſily forced, but the others defended themſelves ſo reſolutely, that many of them were killed : the reſt being taken and examined, it did not appear that any other of the Citizens had been privy to the Conſpiracy, except Baroccio and Piggello Cavicciulli, whom they put to death with their accomplices.

This conſpiracy was hardly quaſhed, when another and more dangerous one was diſcovered. The Florentines, as we have ſaid before, were then at war with the Duke of Milan ; who not being able to conquer them by dint of arms, had recourſe to other methods ; and having engaged many of the Citizens in his deſign, by means of the Exiles, (of whom there were numbers all over Lombardy) it was agreed amongſt them, that upon a certain day appointed for that purpoſe, all the Exiles who lived neareſt to Florence, and were able to bear arms, ſhould advance towards the City, and endeavour to force their way into it by the channel of the Arno. In which attempt, if they ſucceeded, they were to be joined by their friends in the City, and then proceed to the houſes of the chief governors, whom they had determined to put to death, and afterwards to reform the State as they thought proper. Amongſt the Citizens within the walls, that were concerned in the conſpiracy, was Samminiato de' Ricci ; and as it often happens in ſuch undertakings, that a few perſons are not ſufficient to put them in execution, and it is dangerous to truſt a great number, whilſt he was endeavouring to engage as many in it as he could, he unluckily met with one that betrayed him. For having communicated the affair to Sylveſtro Cavicciulli, whom he thought the remembrance of his Kinſman's death, and the ſuffer-

ings

ings of his family, would infpire with a thirft of revenge, he proved to be miftaken in his man : for
Sylveftro being moved by fear more than any other
confideration, immediately went and informed the
Signiory of it, who ordered Samminiato to be taken
into Cuftody, where he confefſed himſelf guilty, and
acquainted them with every particular circumftance of
the defign. None of the other Confpirators, however,
were taken, except Tomaſo Davizi, who coming from
Bologna towards Florence, without knowing what
had happened there, was arrefted upon the road : all
the reft, when they heard what had befallen Samminiato, were ſo terrified, that they fled out of the
City.

Samminiato and Tomaſo being puniſhed according
to the nature of their crimes, a new Balia was inftituted, confifting of many Citizens, with authority to
proceed againft Delinquents, and to provide for the
Safety of the Commonwealth. By this Council, fix
of the family of the Ricci, fix of the Alberti, two
of the Medici, three of the Scali, two of the Strozzi,
Bindo Altoviti, Bernardo Adimari, and many others
of lower condition, were proclaimed Rebels. All the
reft of the Alberti, Ricci, and Medici, except fome *Medici,*
very few, were rendered incapable of holding any
office for the ſpace of ten years.

Amongft thoſe of the Alberti that were not admoniſhed, was Meſſer Antonio, whom they ſpared, as a
man of a very quiet and peaceable diſpofition. But,
before the Signiory had thoroughly got over the apprehenfion they had been in from the late danger, a
prieft was taken up, who had often been ſeen to go
backwards and forwards betwixt Florence and Bologna, whilft the confpiracy was upon the anvil :
and upon examination, he confefſed that he had
feveral times brought letters for Meſſer Antonio.
Upon which, he was immediately taken into cuftody;
and though he pofitively denied it at firft, yet being
convicted by the prieft, he had a fine laid upon him,
and was baniſhed to the diftance of three hundred

miles from the city. And to free the government from the continual apprehenfions they had lived under, from the practices of the Alberti, they banifhed all of that family that were above fifteen years of age.

1400 Thefe things happened in the year 1400; and about two years after, Giovanni Galeazzo died, which, as we faid before, put an end to a war that had lafted ten years. After a refpite of thefe two years from foreign troubles and domeftick feuds, the government having drawn a little breath, and in fome meafure recovered its ftrength, it was refolved to attempt the reduction of Pifa; in which enterprize they fucceeded, and not only gained great reputation abroad,

1433 but continued quiet at home, till the year 1433, ex-
1412. cept that in the year 1412, fome of the Alberti having returned from banifhment, another Balia was appointed, which made new laws for the fecurity of the State, and inflicted other penalties upon that family. During this period, the Florentines likewife engaged in a war with Ladiflaus, King of Naples,

1414 which ended in the Year 1414, upon the death of that Prince, who finding himfelf not able to cope with their forces, was obliged to cede Cortona to them, a City which had been fome time in his hands. But afterwards gathering frefh ftrength, he renewed the war with much more vigour: and if he had not been prevented by death (as the Duke of Milan was likewife in his defigns) he certainly would have reduced them to great diftrefs, and perhaps as much danger of lofing their liberties, as ever they were in from that Duke. So that their efcape was no lefs remarkable at the end of this war, than at the conclufion of the other; for after the King had taken Rome, Siena, all la Marca d'Ancona, and Romagna, he had no impediment left but Florence, to obftruct his progrefs with all his forces into Lombardy, he fuddenly died. In this manner, the death of others was more than once of greater Service to the Florentines, than any Friend, or Valour of their own.

After

After the deceafe of this Prince, the State continued in tranquillity both at home and abroad for the fpace of eight years, at the end of which, the wars that enfued with Philip, Duke of Milan, revived the fpirit of domeftic faction, which never fubfided again till the fubverfion of that Adminiftration, which had ruled the State from the year 1371 till 1434, main- *1434* tained many wars with great glory, and added the Cities of Arezzo, Pifa, Livorno or Leghorn, and Monte Pulciano, to their own Dominions ; and would have done ftill greater things if the City had continued united, and the rage of faction had not flamed out afrefh, as we fhall more particularly relate in the next book.

END OF THE THIRD BOOK.

Q 2   T H E

THE

HISTORY

OF

FLORENCE.

BOOK IV.

ARGUMENT.

The importance of one honeſt, wiſe, and powerful Citizen.
The chief cauſe of changes in a Commonwealth. The
family of Medici, having been depreſſed, at laſt, in
ſome meaſure, recover their authority. Philip Viſ-
conti, Duke of Milan, enters into a treaty with the
Florentines; which he breaks, and ſeizes upon Furli
and Imola, and defeats the Florentine army. Rinaldo
degli Albizi endeavours to quiet the clamours of the
people, and adviſes a continuation of the War. Uz-
zano's opinion. They try to bring over Giovanni de'
Medici. His anſwer to Rinaldo. The factions of Uz-
zano and Medici. The remarkable courage and fide-
lity of Biagio del Melano. The perfidy and cowardice
of Zanobi del Pino. Niccolo Piccinino, the Florentine
General, goes over to the Duke of Milan. The Vene-
tians enter into a League with the Florentines, and ap-
point Carmignuola their Commander in chief. A new
taxation, called the Cataſto. The conſequences of it.
How Carmignuola conducted the war in Lombardy. A
peace concluded betwixt the Duke and the Allies The
conditions of it. The advice of Giovanni de' Medici to
his two ſons, at his death. His character. Volterra
rebels.

7

*rebels against the Florentines; but is soon reduced to
obedience. Rinaldo promotes a war with Lucca. Uzzano opposes it, but to no purpose. The cruelty of
Astorre Gianni, the Florentine Commissary, to the Seravezzans, and their complaints of it. He is cashered
for it. Rinaldo, the other commissary, is likewise accused of misconduct. His speech to the Council of Ten.
The project of Philip Brunelleschi, a celebrated Painter
and Architect, to lay Lucca under water, is defeated.
The tyrant of Lucca is deposed by the people. The Florentines are defeated by Piccinino, the Duke's General.
A peace ensues between them and the Lucchese. Uzzano is persuaded by Niccolo Barbadori, to join him in
endeavouring to drive Cosimo de' Medici out of the City.
His answer. His death. Rinaldo becomes head of
that faction. He garbles the Magistracy, and impri-
sons Cosimo. Malavolti's generous behaviour to him in
prison. Cosimo is banished. Rinaldo's advice to his
party is neglected. He, with many others, rise in arms
to depose the Signiory ; but lay them down again, at the
mediation of Pope Eugenius IV. The Signiory banish
Rinaldo, and recall Cosimo.*

ALL Republics, especially such as are not well
conſtituted, undergo frequent changes in their
laws and manner of government. And this is not
owing to the nature either of Liberty or Subjection
in general, as many think, but to downright oppreſſion on one hand, or unbridled licentiouſneſs on the
other, For the name of Liberty is often nothing
more than a ſpecious pretence, made uſe of both by
the inſtruments of licentiouſneſs, who, for the moſt
part, are Commoners, and by the promoters of ſlavery, who generally are the Nobles, each ſide being
equally impatient of reſtraint and controul. But
when it fortunately happens, which indeed is very
ſeldom, that ſome wiſe, good, and powerful Citizen,
has ſufficient authority in the Commonwealth, to
make ſuch laws as may extinguiſh all jealouſies betwixt the Nobility and the People, or at leaſt ſo to

mo-

moderate and reftrain them, that they fhall not be able to produce any bad effect; in fuch cafe, that State may properly be called free, and its conftitution looked upon as firm and permanent. For, being once eftablifhed upon good Laws and Inftitutions, it has no further occafion, like other States, for the virtue of any particular man to fupport it. On fuch laws and principles, many of thofe ancient Commonwealths, which fo long fubfifted, were formerly conftituted: and for want of them, others have often varied, and ftill vary, their form of government from tyranny to licentioufnefs, and from licentioufnefs to tyranny. For as each of thofe ftates always has powerful enemies to contend with, it neither is, nor can be, poffible they fhould be of any long duration. All good and wife men muft of neceffity be difgufted at them; fince much evil may very eafily be done in the former, and hardly any good in the latter: the infolent having too much authority in one, and the ignorant and unexperienced in the other; and both muft be upheld by the fpirit and fortune of one man alone, who yet may either be fuddenly taken off by death or overpowered by adverfity. I fay therefore that the model of government which took place in Florence after the death of Georgio Scali in the year 1381, was at firft folely maintained by the conduct of Mafo degli Albizi, and afterwards by that of Niccolo Uzzano.

1414

The city continued in tranquillity from the year 1414 till 1422: for as King Ladiflaus was now dead *, and Lombardy divided betwixt different mafters, the Florentines had nothing to fear either at home or abroad. Thofe that had the greateft authority in it next to Niccolo da Uzzano, were Bar-

---

* He was poifoned at Perugia by a Phyfician's daughter of that city, of whom he was paffionately enamoured Her father having been bribed by the Florentines, to get him difpatched, prevailed upon her, to give him poifon in a Philter, or love-potion. He was a brave and generous Prince; but his virtues were obfcured by many vice. He died in 1414, and was fucceeded by his fifter Giovanna, or Joan. Collenucio. Hift. Neap. l. v.

tolomeo

tolomeo Valori, Nerone di Nigi, Rinaldo degli Albizi, Neri di Gino, Capponi, and Lapo Niccolini.
The animosities however, which were at first kindled
in the city by the quarrel betwixt the Albizi and the
Ricci, and afterwards blown up to such a height by
Sylvestro de' Medici, were not yet extinguished : and
although that party which had the largest share in the
affections of the people, continued only three years
in the administration and was turned out of it in
1381, yet as they were favoured and supported by the *1381*
greater part of the Citizens, they could not be totally
suppressed It is true, indeed, that frequent admonitions and the continual persecutions that were carried on against the Heads of it, from the year 1381
to 1400, had brought them very low. Those that
suffered most by these proceedings were the Alberti
and the Medici, several of whom had their estates
confiscated, others were either banished or put to
death, and those that were suffered to continue in the
city, were deprived of all their honours and employments; by which their party was much depressed and
almost reduced to nothing. They retained however a
sharp resentment of the injuries they had received,
and determined to take the first opportunity of revenge ; which they thought proper to dissemble in
these circumstances.

This administration, which was composed of the
most considerable Commoners, or popular Nobility,
and had kept the city so long in peace, at last was
guilty of two errors in point of conduct which proved
its ruin. For in the first place, they grew insolent
and supine ; and in the next, they began to quarrel
amongst themselves, instead of taking proper care to
guard against their enemies : so that whilst they were
daily provoking their fellow Citizens by fresh op-
pressions, and become so jealous of each other, that
they rather encouraged plots and cabals against their
associates in the government, than used any means to
defeat the revenge of those whom they seemed to de-
spise, the Medici in a great measure recovered their *Medici*

for-

former power and authority. The firſt of this family that began to lift up his head again, was Giovanni the Son of Bicci de' Medici; who being a man of great goodneſs and humanity, and grown exceeding rich, was admitted to a ſhare in the government of the State: at which there was ſuch extraordinary re-joycings amongſt the people, that many of the graver ſort of the Citizens were not a little alarmed when they ſaw the old humours began to ſhew themſelves again. Upon this, Niccolo da Uzzano took the op-portunity of repreſenting to his Collègues, how dan-gerous a thing it was to promote a man of ſo ge-neral a reputation to ſuch a degree of power: that it was an eaſy matter to get the better of ſome diſorders in the beginning of them, which afterwards would admit of no remedy: and that he knew Gio-vanni was a perſon of much greater influence and abilities than ever Sylveſtro had been. But theſe remonſtrances made little or no impreſſion upon the reſt of the Governors, who envied Niccolo's repu-tation, and were glad to avail themſelves of any aſ-ſiſtance, which they thought might contribute to ruin him.

Whilſt theſe ſparks of diſcord were ſecretly re-kindling in Florence, Philip Viſconti, the ſecond Son of Giovanni Galeazzo, becoming ſole Lord of all Lombardy by the death of his brother, had ſet his heart upon recovering the State of Genoa, which then lived free under the government of their Doge Tomaſo da Campo Fregoſo. But he was diffident of ſucceſs in this or any other enterpriſe except he could firſt engage the Florentines to enter into an Alliance with him; the credit of which he imagined would enable him to accompliſh his deſigns. With this view, he ſent Ambaſſadors to propoſe it to the Ci-tizens of Florence; many of whom thought it better to continue upon the ſame amicable terms they had been with him for many years, than to enter into any particular treaty: as they plainly ſaw how much re-putation he would acquire thereby, and how little

ad-

advantage their own city was likely to reap from it.
Others were of a different opinion, and voted for a
treaty with him upon certain conditions; which if
he did not obferve, he would manifeft his evil defigns to the whole world, and juftify them in making
war upon him. After long debates, an agreement
was at laft concluded, in which Philip engaged not
to interfere in any affairs on this fide the Rivers *
Magra and Panaro. But foon after this ftipulation,
he firft feized upon Brefcia, and then upon Genoa,
contrary to the expectation of thofe in Florence that
promoted the convention; who thought the Venetians
would have protected Brefcia, and that Genoa was
able to defend itfelf. And as Philip was to keep poffeffion of Serezana and fome other towns on this fide
the Magra, by the capitulation made betwixt him
and the Doge of Genoa, (on a promife that if ever
he alienated them, the Genoefe fhould have the refufal) he confequently was guilty of infringing the
articles of the Convention he had fo lately made with
the State of Florence. Befides which, he had entered into another treaty with the Legate of Bologna.

Thefe proceedings alarmed the Florentines to fuch
a degree, that they thought it high time to provide
fome remedy, left worfe confequences fhould enfue.
Upon which Philip, who was aware that he had
rouzed their apprehenfions, immediately fent Ambaffadors to Florence, in order to juftify himfelf and
feel the pulfe of the Citizens; and at the fame time,

---

* The former of thefe Rivers arifes in the Parmefan, and taking
a fouth-weft courfe by Pontremoli, waters a Valley that is likewife
called Magra, and at laft falls into the Mediterranean a little below
Sarzano. Lucan makes mention of it, Pharfal. l. ii. The Panaro
rifing in the Apennine mountains on the confines of Tufcany, runs
northward into the Modenefe, and divides that State from Romagna:
then turning eaft-ward it runs by Ferrara, through the Ferrarefe, and
empties itfelf into the Gulph of Venice at Valona, where it is called
the Podi Valona. As the fources of thefe two Rivers are not far afun-
der, and their ftreams run different ways, they almoft cut Italy in
two, from the north-eaft to the fouth-weft, and were therefore pitched
upon, very likely, as proper boundaries betwixt the contending
parties.

if

if poſſible, to lull them into ſecurity, by repreſenting
how much he was ſurprized at the unkind opinion,
he heard, they had conceived of him; and that he
was ready to cancel any thing he had done, which
might give them the leaſt umbrage or ſuſpicion of his
ſincerity. But this Embaſſy ſerved only to raiſe diſcord and diviſions in the city: as ſome of the moſt
conſiderable of thoſe that were in the adminiſtration,
thought it would be adviſeable to arm themſelves,
and take proper meaſures to fruſtrate the deſigns of
the enemy: for when ſuch preparations were made,
Philip perhaps might think it his beſt way to remain
quiet; and thus by preventing a war, the peace
that ſubſiſted betwixt them might be eſtabliſhed upon
a ſurer and more ſtable foundation. On the other
hand, there were many who, either out of oppoſition
to the government, or the dread of a war, alledged,
" that it was unreaſonable and unjuſt to entertain
ſuch ſuſpicions of an Ally upon ſo ſlight an occaſion;
as he had not yet done any thing that could juſtify
them in treating him after that manner: that raiſing
forces and appointing officers, they muſt ſurely know,
was the ſame as declaring war, which could not be
carried on againſt ſo powerful a Prince without bringing inevitable ruin upon their city: that there was
not the leaſt proſpect of any advantage which might
accrue from it: for as Romagna lay betwixt their
Dominions and thoſe of the Duke, they muſt not expect to remain in poſſeſſion of any conqueſts they
ſhould make; nor could they hope to penetrate even
into Romagna, when they conſidered that the forces
of the Church were ſo near at hand." The former
opinion, however, prevailed at laſt, and they accordingly appointed ten ſuperintendants of the war,
raiſed ſoldiers, and impoſed new taxes upon the Citizens; which being laid heavier upon the poorer
ſort of the people than the rich, occaſioned great
murmurs in the city; every one exclaiming againſt
the oppreſſion of their Governors, who had wantonly
embroiled them in an expenſive and unneceſſary war,

only

only to gratify their own private interefts and ambition, and to eftablifh themfelves in their tyranny.
They had not yet, indeed, proceeded to an open rupture with the Duke, but their fufpicions grew ftronger
and ftronger every day; efpecially as he had fent
fome troops to Bologna at the requeft of the Legate, who was under no little apprehenfions from the
practices of Antonio Bentivogli, one of the exiles in
that city. Thefe forces therefore lying fo near the
territories of Florence, gave the governors of that
State great uneafinefs: but what ftill increafed it,
and more fully difcovered the Duke's defign to commence hoftilities againft them, was his manner of
proceeding at Furli.

Georgio Ordelaffi, Lord of Furli, died about that
time, and left his Son Tibaldo to the care of Duke
Philip. And though his widow, who looked upon
fuch a Guardian with a very fufpicious eye, had fent
the Child to her father Ludovico Alidoffi Lord of
Imola, yet the people of Furli obliged her to comply with the will of her hufband, and to put him into
the Duke's hands again. Upon which, the better to
avoid fufpicion and difguife his own defigns, he got
the Marquis of Ferrara to fend Guido Torelli as his
Lieutenant, with a body of foldiers to feize upon
Furli in his name; and in this manner that Town fell
into the hands of Duke Philip. When this event
and the arrival of his troops at Bologna came to be
known in Florence, it fully determined the majority
of the Governors to declare war, notwithftanding that
refolution ftill met with great oppofition, efpecially
from Giovanni de' Medici, who publickly protefted
againft it, and faid, " that although they were fufficiently convinced of the Duke's defigns, it would yet
be more prudent to wait till he attacked them, than
to be the aggreffors: for otherwife the Duke might
fairly juftify all his fubfequent proceedings to the
other Princes of Italy; and for their own parts, they
could not in that cafe expect fuch effectual affiftance
from them, as they might do when his ambitious and

en-

enterprising spirit came to be more generally known; since experience shewed that all States act with much more vigour when their own safety is concerned than in the defence and protection of others." To this it was replied, " that it would be much better to march boldly out and meet the enemy, than to stay till they were attacked by him at home : that fortune in general was more favourable to the Invader, than to those that are invaded : and though perhaps it might be more expensive, it certainly would prove less detrimental in the end, to carry the war into the territories of their enemy, than to have their own depopulated." This advice was approved of, and it was resolved, that the Ten should use their utmost efforts in the first place to wrest the City of Furli out of the Duke's hands again. But Philip seeing the Florentines so earnestly bent upon the recovery of a town which he was resolved to maintain, now thought it high time to throw off the mask, and immediately sent Agnolo della Pergola with a considerable force to Imola, to keep the Lord of that place so fully employed in the defence of his own State, that he should not be able to give his Grandson any assistance. Agnolo accordingly advanced almost to the walls of Imola, and finding the moats frozen over, (as it was then a very cold season) he took the town by surprize the same night, and sent Ludovico prisoner to Milan, though the Florentine army lay no further off at that time than Modigliana.

The Florentines, therefore, seeing Imola lost, and open war now publickly avowed, ordered their Commanders to go and lay siege to Furli ; which they did, and invested it on every side : and, to prevent the Duke from sending all his forces to its relief they took Count Alberigo into their pay, who made daily excursions from Zagonara, a town in his possession, to the very walls of Imola. But Agnolo, who perceived our army was so advantageously posted, that it would be impossible to raise the siege of Furli, without running too great a risque, determined to sit

down

down before Zagonara, rightly judging, that the Florentines would abandon their enterprize againſt Furli, and march to its ſuccour; which muſt oblige them to fight him at a great diſadvantage. In the mean time, Alberigo was reduced to ſuch diſtreſs by the Duke's army, that he was forced to capitulate, and agreed to ſurrender, if the town was not relieved in the ſpace of fifteen days. When this came to be known in the Florentine camp, and in the City, the eagerneſs which every one ſhewed to prevent that loſs, was the occaſion of their ſuſtaining a much greater. For having räiſed their camp before Furli, to go to the relief of Zagonara, they came to an engagement with Agnolo, in which they were utterly routed; not ſo much by the valour of the enemy, as the badneſs of the weather: for our forces having marched ſeveral hours, through very deep and miry roads, and continual rain, found the enemy quite freſh, and in ſo good order, that, as it might well be expected, they were not able to ſtand before them, but ſoon fled and were diſperſed. However, in ſo great a defeat, and which made ſo much noiſe all over Italy, there was nobody killed but Ludovico degli Obizi, and two of his men, who were thrown from their horſes, and trampled to death in the mire.

The news of this misfortune occaſioned great conſternation in Florence, and particularly amongſt thoſe of the governing party, who had been the chief promoters of the war; as they ſaw the enemy now ſo powerful and elated, and themſelves in a manner not only diſarmed and without allies, but hated to the laſt degree by the people, who inſulted them whenever they appeared in the ſtreets; complaining of the inſupportable taxes they had laid upon them, and upbraiding them with the heavy expences of an unneceſſary war. " Theſe are the men, ſaid they, who appointed ten ſuperintendants to ſtrike a terror into the enemy! how bravely they wreſted Furli out of the hands of the Duke! you now ſee, fellow-Citizens, the bottom of their hearts, and their villainous machinations!

chinations ! thefe are the *Defenders of our Liberty* forfooth ; a name that they inwardly hate, as their actions have fully fhewn, which never tended to any
other point than to eftablifh and increafe their own
power, which God has now, moft juftly indeed, been
pleafed to humble. This is not the only time they
have brought our city to the brink of ruin ; the expedition againft King Ladiflaus, and many others of
the fame kind, might be inftanced, if it was neceffary.
To whom will they now have recourfe for affiftance
in their extremities ? To Pope Martin, whom they
fo vilely abufed, only to gratify Braccio da Montone ?
To Queen Giovanna, whom they bafely abandoned,
and obliged to throw herfelf into the hands of the
King of Arragon ?" With thefe and other fuch taunts
as fury and defpair commonly fuggeft to an enraged
multitude, they purfued them wherever they went.

The Signiory, therefore, having called a meeting
of the principal Citizens, earneftly exhorted them to
ufe their good offices and endeavours to footh the people, and to appeafe the general indignation which their
clamours had excited. At this meeting, Rinaldo
(eldeft fon to the late Mafo degli Albizi) having fecretly entertained fome hopes of becoming fole governor of the Republic, by the merit of his own fervices, and the reputation of his father, made a long
fpeech ; in which he told them, " That it was neither generous, nor juft, nor good policy, to form a
judgment of fuch enterprizes from the event of them ;
for it happened fometimes, that the beft laid defigns
mifcarried, and the worft were crowned with fuccefs.
That if bad meafures were applauded, merely becaufe
they proved fortunate, it would give encouragement to
rafhnefs and prefumption ; which might one time or
other be the deftruction of the Commonwealth ; as
it did not always happen that they fucceeded. That,
on the other hand, it might be of great prejudice to
vilify defigns that were wifely planned, for no other
reafon than becaufe they failed in the execution, fince
that would deter fuch as were moft able, from giving
their

their advice, and delivering their opinion, without referve, in any exigency." He then fhewed the neceffity of entering into this war, and that Tufcany muft have been the feat of it, if they had not carried their arms into Romagna: that although it was the will of God their forces fhould be defeated, the lofs was not fo great as it would be, if they abandoned themfelves to defpair: that if they would exert themfelves as they ought to do, they would find no great reafon to be fo dejected at their overthrow, nor the Duke to triumph in his victory. That they might make themfelves eafy about the taxes, which would not be fo heavy by a great deal for the future, as they had been; fince a defenfive war could not be attended with fo much expence, as an offenfive one. He laftly conjured them to imitate the noble example of their anceftors, whofe magnanimity even in the loweft ebb of their fortune, had at all times fupported the State againft the moft powerful enemies."

Upon thefe exhortations, enforced by the authority of fo popular a man, the Citizens began to recover their fpirits, and took Count Oddo, the Son of Braccio da Montone, into their pay, under the infpection of Niccolò Piccinino, who had learnt the art of war from Braccio himfelf, and was efteemed the beft foldier that had ever fought under his banners: to whom they likewife joined feveral commanders of their own, and remounted fuch of the cavalry as had loft their horfes in the late defeat. They alfo gave a commiffion to twenty of the Citizens, to raife further fupplies for the maintenance of the war; who feeing the governing party now humbled by their misfortunes, took courage, and laid the chief burden of the tax upon their fhoulders; at which they were not a little mortified in their turn. However, as they could not for fhame remonftrate againft it as a particular hardfhip, they only complained of it in general, and faid, it was too heavy, and ought in fome meafure to be remitted. But when this came to the ears of the council, they took effectual care to prevent it; and

in

in order to make all impofitions appear the more
grievous and hateful to the people for the future,
they gave a ftrict charge to their officers to collect
this with the utmoft rigour, and to kill any one that
fhould dare to oppofe them, or refufe to pay it. In
confequence of thefe orders, fo many were either murdered or grievoufly wounded, that it was apprehended
the two parties would come to blows, and that much
mifchief would enfue: for thofe who had been fo
long in power, and ufed to be treated with fuch reverence and diftinction, could not bear the thoughts of
being infulted in this manner; and the other fide
were refolved, that every man in his turn fhould
equally feel the fting of thefe oppreffions.

Certain of the principal Citizens, therefore, had a
private conference, in which they determined to refume their former authority, and to fupport it with
more vigour for the future; feeing their remiffnefs
had emboldened private men to cavil at their conduct,
and given frefh courage to thofe who were wont, upon
every occafion, to put themfelves at the head of the
populace. After many of thefe meetings, and much
confultation, they agreed to have a more general one
in St. Stephen's Church; where they accordingly affembled, to the number of feventy, by the permiffion of Lorenzo Ridolphi and Francifco Gianfigliazzi,
who were then in the Signiory. But Giovanni de'
Medici was not there; either becaufe he had not been
invited, as a perfon in whom they could not thoroughly confide, or refufed to come, becaufe he did
not approve of fuch cabals. When they were all
met, Rinaldo degli Albizi took the chair, and reprefented to them, in a pathetic manner, the prefent
circumftances of the City, and how the government
of it, by their too great fecurity and inadvertence,
had again fallen into the hands of the people, from
whom their fathers had recovered it in the year 1381.
He reminded them of the tyranny of thofe that were
in the adminiftration from 1377, till that time; in
which interval, either the Father, or Grandfather, or
some

fome near relation, of almoft every one that was then prefent, had been unjuftly put to death. That the City was now going to relapfe into the fame ftate of confufion and oppreffion, as the multitude had already taken upon them to impofe taxes ; and, if they were not either curbed by force, or reftrained by fome other more defirable expedient, would certainly, in the next place, proceed to appoint fuch officers as they thought fit : after which, they would turn the prefent magiftrates out of their feats, to the utter de-ftruction of an adminiftration which had governed the City with fo much glory and reputation, for the fpace of forty-two years. The confequence of which would be, that Florence muft either be blindly go-verned by the caprice of the multitude, (and then one party would live in continual danger and appre-henfion, whilft the other rioted in all manner of li-centioufnefs) or it muft fall under the fubjection of fome one perfon, who would make himfelf abfolute Lord, and perhaps Tyrant over it. It was the duty, he faid, of every man that had any affection for his Country, or regard for his own reputation, to exert himfelf at that time, and to follow the example of Bardo Mancini, who delivered the City from the im-minent danger it was in, by the extirpation of the Alberti : and as the audacioufnefs of the multitude was in a great meafure owing to the largenefs of the Imborfations, and the little care that was taken in them, (which had filled the palace with new and mean men) he thought the only remedy that was left for fuch diforders would be, to reftore the authority of the Nobility, and diminifh that of the Minor Arts, by reducing them from fourteen to feven : which would leffen the power of the Plebeians in the Councils, both by retrenching their number, and by throwing more weight into the fcale of the Grandees, who would be fure to ufe all poffible endeavours to deprefs them, out of revenge for old injuries. That wife men always availed themfelves of different forts of people at different feafons ; and if their fathers had made ufe of the affiftance of the Plebeians, to humble the infolence of the Grandees, now the latter were brought fo low, and the former become fo audacious, it would be no bad expedient to join with one to lower the other: to effect which, if artifice was not fufficient, they muft have recourfe to forcible means; as they had that in their power, now fome of them were in the *Commiffion of Ten*, and might fecretly bring a few companies of foldiers into the City."

This fpeech of Rinaldo's was much applauded, and his advice approved of by every body; and Niccolò da Uzzano, in the name of the reft, made anfwer, " That what he had faid was very true, and the remedies he propofed efficacious and certain, provided they could be applied without making an open divifion in the City; which yet he thought might be done, if they could draw Giovanni de' Medici into their defigns: for if he concurred with them, the multitude being deprived of their head, would not be able to make any oppofition: but if he could not be brought over, they could not effect it without force; and in that cafe, it was doubtful whether they fhould prevail; and if they did, they probably might not long enjoy the fruits of their victory. He then modeftly reminded them of the advice he had before given them, and of their contempt of thofe warnings, at a time when they might eafily have prevented thefe difficulties: but it was now too late to do that, he faid, without great peril and hazard, except they could gain Giovanni de' Medici."

They deputed Rinaldo, therefore, to wait upon Giovanni, and try, if he could make any impreffion upon him; which he did accordingly, and ufed all the arguments he could think of to perfuade him to join them; and not, by foftering and indulging the multitude, at laft encourage them to rebel, to the utter fubverfion of the Government, and ruin of the City at the fame time. To which Giovanni replied, " That he had always thought it the duty of a good and

Uzzano

Medici.

and wife Citizen to endeavour to prevent any change in the eftablifhed laws and cuftoms of the State he lived in, as nothing gave greater offence to the generality, than alterations of that kind; and where many are difcontented, it is but natural to apprehend fome fatal event. That this their defign, in all probability, would produce two very pernicious effects: for, in the firft place, they would be obliged to confer honours and employments upon fuch, as having never enjoyed any before, did not know how to fet a due value upon them, and confequently would have the lefs reafon to complain, if they were not admitted to them; and in the next, by depriving others of fuch emoluments as they had long been ufed to tafte the fweets of, they would provoke them to fuch a degree, that it would be impoffible ever to appeafe them again till they were reftored: by which manner of proceeding, one party would think themfelves much more aggrieved, than the other benefited. So that whofoever fhould be hardy enough to purfue fuch a refolution, would foon find he had gained but few friends, and many enemies; the latter of whom would be more eager to do him a mifchief than the former to defend him: mankind being naturally more prone to revenge than gratitude; fince the one puts them to the expence of refunding, and repaying paft favours; the other always feems attended with fome degree either of pleafure or profit."
Then addreffing himfelf in a more particular manner to Rinaldo, he told him, that if he would be pleafed to recollect what had already happened, and confider how bafely and perfidioufly the Citizens of Florence commonly dealt with each other, perhaps he might not be altogether fo fanguine in his prefent undertaking: for that as foon as the promoters and advifers of it had fufficiently depreffed the people by the help of his authority, they would certainly fall upon him next with the whole force and affiftance of the Plebeians, whofe affections he muft have loft by fuch a conduct; and then he would be utterly deferted

ferted

ferted and ruined. That he could not help remembring the fate of Benedetto Alberti, who, at the inftigation of fuch as confpired his deftruction, confented to the fevere proceedings againft Georgio Scali and Tomafo Strozzi; and foon after, was fent into exile himfelf, by the very perfons who had inveigled him into thofe meafures. He advifed him, therefore, to think more coolly of the matter, and to tread in the fteps of his father, who, amongft other Benefactions, had made himfelf fo dear to his fellow-citizens, by lowering the exceffive price of falt; by leaving it to the option of every one, whofe taxes did not amount to the value of half a Florin, whether he would pay them or not; and by procuring a law to be paffed, that no body fhould be arrefted for debt on fuch days as the Councils were affembled. He told him in fhort, that for his own part, he fhould never agree to have any alterations made in the laws or conftitution of his Country *.

When the fubject of thefe deliberations came to be publickly known, it ftill added to the reputation of Giovanni, and wonderfully increafed the hatred which the people had already conceived againft the other Citizens; with whom he broke off all manner of commerce, that he might not feem to give them any encouragement to purfue their defigns under his countenance and authority. On the contrary, he took great pains, to convince every one in his daily converfation, that it was fo far from his intention to blow up difcord and faction, that he fhould ufe his utmoft endeavours to extinguifh them; and that he defired

---

* Nothing can be more difguftful to a free people, that have lived in peace and fecurity under the protection of good Laws, (the neceffity, utility, and comfort of which, have been fully evinced by a long courfe of time) than an attempt to annul them. Nor has any thing been more fatal to Princes: of which, every one muft remember many inftances, that would be tedious, and perhaps invidious, to recite. Hence the celebrated faying, Nolumus Angliæ leges mutari: and, old ways are the beft ways: the latter of which was formerly engraved upon the walls of the Houfe of Commons. Hence the juft attachment and regard that has always been fhewn to them.—The learned Sir John Fortefcue, Chancellor of England, in the time of

no-

nothing more than the union of the City. At which declarations, many of his followers were not a little difappointed, as they expected to have feen him act with more vigour in fuch a conjuncture; efpecially Alamanno de' Medici, who being a man of a warm difpofition, was continually urging him to take this opportunity of humbling his enemies, and exalting his friends; reproaching him with his coldnefs and phlegmatic manner of proceeding, which, as he faid, emboldened thofe that wifhed him ill, to form daily confpiracies againft him, without any fort of fear or referve, and would one time or other prove the ruin of all his family and dependants. They were feconded in this by Cofimo his fon; but he was deaf to *Cofimo* all their remonftrances and prognoftications, and determined to purfue his own meafures: the defigns of the faction, however, were now plainly difcovered, and the City began once more to divide itfelf into parties.

There were at that time, two Chancellors prefiding in the fupreme Court of Juftice under the Signiory, whofe names were * Martino and Paolo: the former was of Uzzano's party, the latter followed that of the Medici. Rinaldo, therefore, perceiving that Giovanni continued inflexible, and would not come into their meafures at any rate, refolved to turn Martino out of his office, as he thought that court would then be wholly at his devotion. But the other fide being aware of this, were before-hand with him, and contrived matters fo well, that they got Martino continued and Paolo difcharged, to the great mortification and prejudice of his party. This would certainly have occafioned great commotions in the City, if it

Henry VI. fpeaking of this kingdom in his treatife, De dominio politico & regali, fays, " Regnum hoc in omnibus nationum & regum temporibus, iifdem quibus nunc regitur legibus & confuetudinibus, regebatur." " The laws and cuftoms by which this Kingdom is now governed, are the very fame with thofe by which it was governed in the times of all former Kings, and the feveral nations that have come into it." A rare example! See State 'Tracts, Vol. III. p. 269, 270. concerning the right of Subjects to petition, &c.

* The furnames of thefe two Magiftrates are wanting in the original.

had not happened in a time of war: for the people had not yet recovered their spirits since the defeat before Zagonara; and whilst things were in such confusion at home, Agnola della Pergola, the Duke's General, had taken all the towns in Romagna, that were in the possession of the Florentines, except Castracaro and Modigliana; some of them being so ill fortified, that they were not in a condition to sustain a siege, and others given up through the pusillanimity or treachery of their governors.

In the reduction of these towns there happened two remarkable circumstances, which may serve to shew how much true valour and fidelity are admired, and with what detestation, cowardice and perfidy are looked upon even by an enemy. Biagio del Melano was then Governor of the Castle of Monte Petroso, which was invested on every side by the enemy; and as they at last set fire to it, and he saw there was no possibility of saving the fortress, he threw a parcel of straw and bedding over the walls, on that side where the fire had not yet spread itself, upon which he let down two of his Sons who were but infants, and told the enemy, " they were welcome to them and all his other worldly goods, which indeed were now in their hands; but his honour and reputation, which he had always esteemed his only real treasure, he would never give up, nor was it in their power to ravish them from him." The besiegers, struck with admiration at his Magnanimity, immediately ran to take up the children, and threw him ropes and scaling ladders to save himself; but he would not make use of them; and chose rather to perish in the flames, than owe his life to the enemies of his country *. An example of

---

* An instance of the same kind happened at Præneste, when it was taken by Sylla. He ordered his soldiers to plunder the town, and put all the inhabitants to the sword, except one man, who had formerly entertained him with great hospitality. This man, however, when he heard of it, said, he disdained the thoughts of being obliged for his life to one that had ruined his country; and disguising himself, he mixed in the crowd with his fellow-citizens, and was killed. But are not these instances of madness rather than true valour? and if they are not, have we not many of the same in modern history, and some in that of our own nation, without recurring to antiquity?

fortitude that may vie with the heroifm of Antiquity ; and the more remarkable, as fuch were but very rare in thofe times. What effects could be faved from the fire were generoufly reftored to the children, who were likewife fent home to their relations : and the Republick, out of gratitude to the bravery of their father, made a handfome provifion for them as long as they lived. Very different was the behaviour of Zanobi del Pino, governor of Galeata, who not only fhamefully gave up that place without making any defence, but advifed Agnolo to leave the mountains and faftneffes of Romagna, and defcend into the plains of Tufcany, where he might carry on the war with lefs danger and greater advantage. But Agnolo, detefting his bafenefs and cowardice, delivered him up to his own men, who, having treated him with the contempt and abhorrence he deferved, fhut him up in a dungeon, with nothing but a pack of cards to eat ; telling him " *that* would foon make him a good Ghibeline, fince he had chofen to leave the Guelphs :" but he died in a few days of hunger *.

In the mean time, Count Oddo and Niccolo Piccinino had entered the Vale of Lamona, to try if they could prevail upon the Lord of Faenza to join the Florentines ; or at leaft to curb the excurfions of Agnolo, if poffible, in Romagna. But as that Vale is naturally fortified with ftrong paffes, and the inhabitants inured to arms, the Count was flain and Niccolo taken prifoner and fent to Faenza. Fortune however fo ordered it, that the Florentines gained by

---

* As Machiavel has honoured Biagio with faying, that ' his fortitude might vie with the heroifm of antiquity,' he ought in juftice to have diftinguifhed Zanobi too by comparing his bafenefs with that of old times. For there were very eminent Poltroons and Traitors in thofe days as well as in thefe later ages, bad as they have been : though Machiavel, like many others, feems to fpeak as if the world was inhabited only by Heroes and Demi Gods at that time of day. There have always been good and bad, brave men and cowards, and mankind feem to have been pretty much the fame from the firft accounts we have had of their actions to the prefent times. Complaints of their prodigious wickednefs and degeneracy are not peculiar to our own : the moft antient poets and hiftorians, both facred and prophane, abound with them.

R 4

the

the confequence of this defeat what they could not perhaps have obtained by a Victory : for Niccolo negotiated fo effectually with the Lord of Faenza and his Mother, that they confented to enter into an alliance with the Republick of Florence ; in confequence of which he was fet at liberty. Yet he did not think fit to purfue thofe meafures himfelf, which he had recommended to others : for when he had received the arrears that were due to him from the Florentines, he either thought their pay too inconfiderable, or that he could have better elfewhere : upon which, he fuddenly left Arezzo, where he then refided, and went to Duke Philip in Lombardy, who took him into his fervice. The Florentines, difmayed at this unexpected defertion, and the great expence they had been at to no purpofe, began to perceive they were not any longer able to bear the burden of this war alone ; and therefore fent Ambaffadors to entreat the Venetians to take a fhare in it, and prevent the farther progrefs of a Prince, whofe growing power, if not timely checked, would be as prejudicial to them as to the State of Florence. The Venetians were likewife advifed to it by Francifco Carmignuola, a Commander of very great reputation in thofe times, who had formerly ferved under the Duke, but afterwards left him upon fome difguft. They were doubtful, however, for fome time what part to act in this matter ; as they did not thoroughly confide in Carmignuola, and fufpected the mifunderftanding betwixt him and the Duke was only a pretended one. But whilft they were in this ftate of fufpence, it happened that the Duke had found means to bribe one of that General's Domefticks to give him poifon ; which, though it did not prove mortal, very much impaired his health. Upon this, the Venetians laid afide all fufpicion of Carmignuola's fidelity ; and the Florentines ftill continuing to follicit their aid, they entered into a League with them, in which it was agreed betwixt the two States, that the war fhould be profecuted at their common expence ; that the Venetians fhould hold what they
might

might happen to conquer in Lombardy, and the Florentines enjoy fuch towns as they could reduce in Tufcany and Romagna; and that Carmignuola fhould be appointed Captain General of the League. In confequence of this confederacy, the war was immediately carried into Lombardy, where it was conducted with fuch bravery and integrity by Carmignuola, that in the courfe of a few months, he took many towns from the Duke, and at laft made himfelf mafter of Brefcia; a city which, according to the method of making war in thofe times, was thought impregnable.

This war having now lafted five years, that is, from 1422 to 1427, the Citizens began to be fo grievoufly impoverifhed by the heavy and continual impofitions which had been laid upon them, that it was thought proper to make fome alteration in them. In order, therefore, to proportion them according to every man's circumftances, it was provided that perfonal eftates fhould be taxed as well as real; and that whofoever had effects of that kind to the value of an hundred Florins or more, fhould pay one half as much for every hundred as a perfon that had land or houfes of the fame worth. And as this tax was regulated by a Law made on purpofe, and not left to the Arbitrement of partial or interefted perfons, it was likely to fall fo much the more heavily upon the richer Citizens. Upon which account, it was vehemently oppofed by them all before it paffed into a Law, except Giovanni de' Medici, who publickly expreffed his approbation of it; fo that it was carried againft them. And becaufe every man's goods were rated in this affeffment, which the Florentines call Accaftare, it went by the name of Catafto. By this law the more powerful Citizens were in fome meafure reftrained from oppreffing the inferior fort, and influencing their votes in the Councils, as they had been ufed to do, by the threats of taxing them according as they gave their fuffrages. This tax, therefore, was very cheerfully fubmitted to by the generality, though highly difguftful to the government.

vernment. But as it is the nature of mankind to be ever reftlefs and difcontented, and when they have gained one advantage, to be ftill grafping at a higher, the people not fatisfied with this equality of taxation, eftablifhed by the Law, demanded a retrofpect, by which it might appear how much lefs the rich Citizens had paid before, than they ought to have done according to this regulation, and every one be made to account for deficiencies; that fo they might be put upon the fame level with thofe who had been obliged to fell their goods and inheritances to difcharge impofitions fo arbitrarily laid upon them. This demand feemed ftill more grievous than the Catafto itfelf, to thofe that had lately been in power, who, to evade the force of it, made heavy remonftrances, and faid, " it was a moft unjuft diftribution; as the tax was laid upon moveables, which often changed hands and were daily fubject to perifh: that there were many who had concealed treafures, the knowledge of which could not eafily be come at: that it was hard upon thofe who were loaded with the care of the public affairs, (to the great detriment of their own private concerns) to be equally taxed with the reft of the Citizens; and that it might reafonably be hoped, whilft the Republick was fatisfied with only the pecuniary contributions of fome, it would not be fo rigorous to exact both the labours and fortunes of others." To this it was anfwered by thofe who approved of the Catafto, " that as moveable goods changed hands, the tax might be varied accordingly; that no account was to be made of fuch as had concealed treafure, or money locked up in their coffers; for as wealth of that fort did not yield any profit or intereft, it would be unreafonable to tax it; and whenever it was otherwife applied, it muft of neceffity be known: that if any one was tired of his labours for the good of his country, he was at liberty to refign his employment, if he pleafed, and to give himfelf no farther trouble about it; fince it was hoped, other well-difpofed Citizens might be

found,

ound, who would not grudge to affift the Republic both with their fortune and counfels : and that when fo much honour, and fo many other emoluments were the conftant reward of fuch as filled the great offices of State, they might think themfelves very well paid for their fervices, without being exempted from the common taxes.   But this, they faid, was not the real caufe of their murmurs ; they were mortified that they could no longer carry on a war folely at the expence of others, but were now obliged to fhare in it themfelves : that if this courfe had been taken before, there neither would have been any war with King Ladiflaus in times paft, nor at prefent with Duke Philip ; both which were fet on foot, without any neceffity, and only to enrich fome particular Citizens."

Thefe difcontents, however, were in fome degree allayed by the authority of Giovanni de' Medici, who reprefented to the people, the bad confequences of retrofpects : " That it behoved them rather at prefent to look forward, and provide for the future : that if the late taxes had been heavy and unreafonable, they ought to thank God that a way had been found to alleviate them, and to ufe their endeavours to unite, and not divide the City, as they certainly would, if they perfifted in their demand of reducing former taxes to the level of the prefent : and that a wife General was fometimes very well content with a victory, that was not altogether complete ; fince experience fhewed, that men, by grafping at too much, often loft what they had gained before."   With thefe, and other arguments of the like nature, he foothed the refentment of the people in fuch a manner, that they dropped their demand of a retrofpect.

Soon after this, a peace was concluded with Duke Philip at Ferrara, by the mediation of a Legate from the Pope : but as it was not long before he broke the conditions of it, the League took up arms again, and came to an engagement with his forces at Maclovio, where they utterly defeated him.   After which,
he

he propofed frefh terms to them, which were accepted by the Florentines, becaufe they grew jealous of the Venetians, and thought, that they were throwing their money away only to aggrandize others. The Venetians likewife, for their part, were no lefs ready to come into the accommodation; as they found Carmignuola proceeded but very flowly, and made little advantage of his victory, after he had routed the Duke's army: on which account, they thought it unfafe to truft him any farther. A peace therefore was figned betwixt them in the year 1428; by which, the towns that had been taken from the Florentines in Romagna were reftored to them, and Brefcia ceded to the Venetians; befides which, the Duke gave them the city of Bergamo, and the Territory belonging to it. This war coft the Florentines three millions and five hundred thoufand Ducats; a war, which only ferved to give the Venetians an opportunity of extending their power and dominion; whilft it produced nothing but poverty and diffenfion amongft themfelves. For a peace was no fooner concluded with the Duke, but frefh Commotions began amongft their own fubjects. The late Governors not being able to bear the Catafto, and feeing no other way to rid themfelves of it, endeavoured to raife a fpirit of difcontent in the reft of the Citizens; that fo they might avail themfelves of their co-operation to procure a repeal of it. For this purpofe, they reprefented to the Commiffioners that were appointed to levy the tax, " that they ought to fearch all the houfes of the neighbouring towns; as the inhabitants of Florence might, perhaps, convey fome part of their effects thither." In confequence of which, all towns that were fubject to the Florentines had orders to deliver inventories of their goods to them in a certain time. But the people of Volterra would not comply with this order, and fent fome of their townfmen to complain of it to the Signiory, as an act of oppreffion: at which the Commiffioners were fo provoked, that they fent eighteen of them to prifon.

. The

The Volterrans likewife were exceedingly enraged at this treatment; but durft not rebel at that time, for fear of bringing a heavier punifhment upon their Deputies.

In this juncture, Giovanni de' Medici fell fick, and *Giovanni* finding there was no hope of recovery, he called his two Sons, Cofimo and Lorenzo, to his bed-fide, and fpoke to them in this manner: " I perceive that I am now approaching the limits which God and Nature have prefcribed to my days. I fhall die with pleafure, as I leave you both, my dear children, in health and profperity, and in a condition to live with honour, and beloved by every body, if you follow my example and inftructions. For indeed, nothing gives me fo much confolation in this extremity, as the reflexion that I have never injured any man; but, on the contrary, have always endeavoured to do good to every one to the utmoft of my power. Let me advife you to do the fame. If you would live with fafety and comfort, be content with fuch a fhare in the government as your fellow-citizens confer upon you; by which you will avoid envy and danger. For as it is that which a man arrogates to himfelf that makes him odious, and not what is voluntarily given him: fo you will always be upon a much fecurer bottom, and obtain more than they, who, by attempting to invade the rights of others, often lofe their own, and in the mean time live in continual anxiety and difquietude. By obferving this conduct, I have not only preferved, but augmented my fortune and reputation in this City, amongft fo many enemies and inteftine broils: and by the fame manner of life, it is in your power both to maintain and increafe yours. But if you take a different courfe, you may depend upon it, your end will be like that of feveral others, who, in my memory, have ruined both themfelves and their families." He died not long after, extremely lamented by the whole City, as he well deferved to be, confidering his excellent qualities. For he was very charitable and compaf-

fionate,

sionate, and not only gave liberally to those that were in want, but prevented their asking. His universal benevolence taught him to love good men, and pity the evil. He never sollicited any Honours, though he obtained the highest. He never went to the palace, but when the rest of the Signiory sent for him. He was always averse to war, and recommended pacific measures. To those that were in adversity, he was a kind friend, and promoted the welfare of such as lived in prosperity. Disdaining to plunder the public, his sole aim was to serve his Country. When in power, he was affable and easy of access to every one; exceeding wise, though not a man of much eloquence. He had a melancholy countenance, but was pleasant and facetious in conversation. He died possessed of immense riches, and full of glory and reputation; leaving his son Cosimo heir to his fame and fortune; both which he not only maintained, but augmented.

The Volterran deputies being tired of their imprisonment, at last promised to comply with the order before mentioned : upon which, they were set at liberty, and returned to Volterra, just at a time when they were making an Imborsation for new Magistrates there : and as it happened, one Giusto *, a Plebeian, but a man in great credit with the people, and one of those that had been confined at Florence, was drawn amongst the rest. This man, though already sufficiently irritated at the Florentines, both on account of the private injury which he himself had sustained, and the indignity that was offered to the whole town, became still more determined by the instigations of Giovanni di †, a man of a noble family and his associate in the Magistracy, to make use of his interest and authority, to wrest the town out of the hands of the Florentines, and take the government of it upon himself. Upon this encouragement, Giusto took

---

* The Surname is wanting in the original.
† The Surname is also wanting here.

arms,

arms, made himfelf mafter of the town, feized upon
the Governor, and, by the confent of the people,
took the reins into his own hands. The Florentines
were not a little mortified at the revolt of Volterra.
However, as they had concluded a peace with the
Duke of Milan, they thought they fhould have nobody to difturb them in attempting to recover it;
and therefore immediately appointed Rinaldo degli
Albizi and Palla Strozzi their * commiffaries to conduct the expedition. But Giufto expecting to be molefted in his new fovereignty by the Florentines, fent
to defire the aid of the Lucchefe and Sienefe; the
former of whom would not fend him any, as they
were then in amity with the State of Florence: and
Paolo Guinigi, who at that time was Lord of Lucca,
in order to regain the friendfhip of the Florentines
(which he feared he had loft by inclining to the intereft of Duke Philip) not only flatly refufed to give
him any affiftance, but fent the perfon under a guard
to Florence, who came to follicit it. Thefe commiffaries refolving to come upon the Volterrans before
they could form any alliances, prefently drew together all their horfe, and raifed a large body of infantry
in the lower part of the Vale of Arno and the territory of Pifa, and advanced towards Volterra.
Giufto, on the other hand, was not wanting to himfelf; and though he faw the great preparations which
the Florentines were making againft him, and that
he muft expect no fuccour from the neighbouring
States, yet he trufted to the ftrength and fituation of
the place, and manfully provided for his defence.
There was at that time in Volterra, one Meffer' Arcolano, a man of good intereft amongft the moft

---

* Commiffaries, in the foreign fervice, are officers that mufter the
army, fettle the procuration, conveyance, and diftribution of provifions, ammunition, and pay, take a particular account of every
regiment, fee that they are complete, that the horfes are in good order, and the men well armed and accoutred. They likewife fometimes regulate the conduct of the General, and are a check upon his
proceedings, and fometimes command the forces themfelves, acting
as Intendant of the army and Lieutenant General at the fame time.

confiderable of the townfmen, and brother to that Giovanni, by whofe perfuafions Giufto had been prevailed upon to take the government of it himfelf. This Arcolano having affembled feveral of his moft trufty friends, reprefented to them how fair an opportunity Providence had now given them of advancing themfelves and delivering their city out of its prefent troubles : for if they would take up arms to depofe Giufto and deliver up the city again into the hands of the Florentines, they would not only preferve its ancient privileges, but become the Governors of it. To this they all readily confented, and going directly to the Palace where Giufto refided, fome of them ftaid below ftairs, whilft Arcolano and three others went up into his apartment; and finding him there with fome of the Citizens, they took him afide, as if they had fomething of importance to communicate to him; and having drawn him by degrees, in the courfe of their converfation, into another room, they fhut the door and fell upon him with their fwords. He had the courage however to draw his own, and defperately wounded two of them before he fell : but not being able to deal with fo many, he was killed at laft, and his body thrown out of the window. After which, the reft of Arcolano's accomplices took arms and delivered up the city to the Florentine commiffaries; who prefently brought in their whole army and took poffeffion of it, without any Capitulation or terms granted to the inhabitants. So that the city was ftill more humbled and fell into worfe circumftances than it was in before : for befides other marks of their indignation, the Florentines took away the greater part of their territory from them, and reduced the reft into a Bailiwick.

Volterra being thus happily recovered, it was hoped a lafting tranquillity would have been eftablifhed both abroad and at home. But ambition foon kindled a new war. Niccolo Fortebraccio, the Son of a Sifter to Braccio da Perugia, had long ferved the

Flo-

Florentines in their wars with the Duke of Milan. But after a Peace was concluded betwixt them, this commander was difcharged from their pay, and had his quarters at Fucecchio : from whence the commiffaries fent for him and his troops to employ them in the reduction of Volterra. It was therefore generally believed that whilft Rinaldo degli Albizi was engaged with him in that enterprize, he perfuaded him to pick a quarrel upon fome pretence or other with the Lucchefe, by infinuating to him that if he did, he would fo order matters, that war fhould be declared againft Lucca, by the Florentines ; and that he fhould be appointed their commander in chief. Accordingly, as foon as Volterra was retaken, and Niccolo had returned to Fucecchio, (either at the follicitation of Rinaldo, or in confequence of a defign, which he himfelf had formed) he marched away in November 1429, at the head of three hundred *1429* horfe, and the fame number of foot, and furprized Ruoti and Compito, two Caftles belonging to the Lucchefe ; from whence he daily made excurfions into their other territories and there committed great depredations.   When the news of thefe proceedings arrived at Florence, the whole city was divided into little meetings and cabals of all ranks of people ; the generality of whom were for commencing hoftilities againft the Lucchefe. Amongft the more confiderable Citizens that favoured this undertaking, were all the followers of the Medici family, who were joined by Rinaldo degli Albizi, either becaufe he really thought it would be for the good of the Public, or that he fhould thereby effectually ferve his own private intereft and ambition, and become more popular if the expedition proved fuccefsful, by having been the advifer and promoter of it.   Thofe that oppofed it, were chiefly Niccolo da Uzzano and his Party.

It feems almoft incredible that there fhould be fuch a change of opinions in the fame Citizens, on this occafion, concerning the expedience of a war.   And yet thofe very perfons who, after a Peace that had lafted ten years, oppofed a war againft Duke Philip, which was undertaken in defence of their own liberties, now ftrenuoufly infifted upon one againft Lucca, to invade the rights of others; and at a time too when the city was exhaufted and impoverifhed to the laft degree, by the heavy expences of the laft. And on the contrary, thofe Citizens who had been the moft active and forward in promoting that war, were now as vehement in diffuading this. From hence we may obferve, what a wonderful alteration time ufually makes in the judgment of mankind; how much more ready they are to ufurp the property of others, than to defend their own; and how much ftronger the hope of gain is, than the fear of lofing; the latter feldom operating except when the danger is imminent; but the former at all times, even when the profpect of fuccefs is moft precarious and at the greateft diftance. And it muft be confidered likewife that the Florentines were at this time exceedingly elated with the hopes of enjoying thofe acquifitions, which Fortebraccio had already made and was daily increafing; and from the Letters they received from the governors of their fortreffes that lay near the confines of the Lucchefe: for thofe of Pefcia and Vico wrote to defire commiffions to take fuch towns as furrendered, under their protection; fince they might affure themfelves they would foon be mafters of all the territories belonging to the Lucchefe. And thefe expectations were ftill heightened by an embaffy fent from Paolo Guinigi Lord of Lucca to the Signiory of Florence, to complain of the depredations made by Fortebraccio, and to entreat them not to join their enemy in making war upon a neighbouring State, which had always lived in ftrict amity with them.

The name of this Ambaffador was Jacopo Viviani, a man, who not long before had been thrown into prifon by Paolo Guinigi for being concerned in a confpiracy againft him: and as Guinigi had pardoned
him,

him, though he was found guilty, he thought he might reasonably expect his best endeavours to serve him. But the remembrance of the danger he had escaped, making a deeper impression upon him, than the sense of the favour he had received, when he came to Florence he secretly advised the Citizens to pursue their designs. Flattered by this encouragement and the hopes they had already conceived, the Signiory assembled the Common Council, where the matter was debated by some of the leading men of the Republic, in the presence of four hundred and ninety-eight Citizens. Amongst the chief of those that promoted the enterprize, was Rinaldo degli Albizi (as was said before) who shewed them the advantages that would result from making themselves masters of Lucca : that they could never have a fairer opportunity than the present, as that State was then abandoned both by the Venetians and the Duke of Milan, and could not be relieved by the Pope, who was sufficiently embroiled in the affairs of Naples: that the success was certain, as the government of Lucca was then usurped by one of its own Citizens, and had lost much of its ancient vigour and alacrity in defending its liberties ; so that it was more than probable it would be delivered up into their hands, either by the people, to get rid of their tyrant, or by the tyrant for fear of the people. He then recited many instances of Guinigi's malevolence and of the injuries he had done their Republic ; assuring them they would find him a thorn in their side, and a very dangerous enemy, if they should chance to be engaged in a fresh quarrel with the Duke, or the Pope ; and concluded with saying, " that no war was ever entered into by the State of Florence with more justice on its side, or more likely to be attended with success and advantage to the public."

In answer to this, Niccolo da Uzzano said, " that on the contrary, he could not help being of opinion that they had never engaged in any undertaking that was more unjust, more hazardous, or more likely

to be of fatal confequence to the State. That in the
firft place, they were going to declare war againft a
city of the Guelph party, which at all times had
been a friend to the Florentines, and had often received the Guelphs with open arms, and with great
peril and prejudice to itfelf, when they were not fuffered to live at peace and fafety at home. That there
was no inftance to be found in the annals of the Commonwealth of any offence that the Lucchefe had ever
given them : that if thofe who at different times had
ufurped the government of their State, as Caftruccio
formerly, and Guinigi at prefent, had done them any
injury, it ought not to be imputed to the Citizens,
but to the Tyrant that ruled over them. That if
they could make war upon one, without hurting the
other, he fhould not be againft it : but fince that was
impoffible, he thought it moft cruel and unjuft, that
a people with whom they had always lived in amity
and alliance, fhould be plundered and ftripped of
their goods and territories without any caufe or offence : that however, as they lived in an age when
little account was made of juftice, he fhould drop
that confideration, and confine himfelf chiefly to
what regarded common utility and the welfare of
the Republic. Thofe meafures, he faid, might be
efteemed good and fafe, and therefore profitable,
which were not liable to be attended with lofs or damage : but he did not fee how any one could call
that undertaking profitable, where the lofs was certain, and the gain precarious. The certainty of lofs
proceeded from the expence it muft occafion ; the
greatnefs of which was enough to alarm even a city
that had long lived in tranquillity, but much more
their own, which had already been fufficiently harraffed and exhaufted by a tedious and devouring war.
The profit they might expect to reap was the acquifition of Lucca, which he confeffed, was confiderable : but the difficulties and uncertainty of fucceeding in the enterprize ought likewife to be remembered, and appeared to him fo great, that he
thought

thought it impoſſible. For it was not to be imagined that either the Venetians or the Duke of Milan would ſuffer them to make ſuch a conqueſt, though the former perhaps might conceal their deſigns at preſent, not to ſeem ungrateful to the Florentines, at whoſe expence they had lately enlarged their dominions ſo conſiderably: and the latter would be glad to ſee them entangled in a new war, and impoveriſhed with freſh expences, that ſo he might fall upon them again with greater advantage. That in the mean time, when they vainly thought themſelves ſureſt of ſucceſs, he would find ſome means or other, of ſupplying the Luccheſe with money either publickly or privately; and if that was not ſufficient, he might pretend to diſband his troops and ſend them as ſoldiers of fortune into their ſervice. Upon which account, he would adviſe them to give up the enterprize, and rather endeavour to excite the people of Lucca to riſe againſt their Tyrant; for if nothing elſe would ſatisfy ſome perſons but the acquiſition of that city, he thought there was no way ſo likely to effect it, as to ſuffer them to live under the oppreſſion and inſolence of the uſurper. For if the matter was conducted with prudence, things might ſoon be brought to ſuch a paſs there, that the tyrant would not be able to ſupport himſelf in his government, and the Citizens not knowing how to govern of themſelves, muſt of neceſſity give it up to them. But that he ſaw the Council in a manner already determined, and that his advice was not liſtened to. However, he would take upon him to propheſy, that the war would be attended with a very grievous expence and much danger; that, inſtead of making themſelves maſters of Lucca, they would only enable it to ſhake off its preſent yoke; and from a weak and oppreſſed city that was in amity with them, it would become a free State, and an enemy too; which in time might prove no inconſiderable obſtacle to the aggrandizement of their own Republic."

After

After both sides of the question had been thoroughly canvassed, they proceeded as usual to * a ballot, by which it appeared, that out of so great a number, there were only ninety-eight against a war. It was therefore resolved upon; and ten Citizens being appointed to conduct it, they raised both horse and foot, made Astorre Gianni and Rinaldo degli Albizi their commissaries, and agreed with Niccolo Fortebraccio to be their Commander in chief, on condition that he should be suffered to keep possession of the towns and fortresses he had already taken. When the commissaries arrived with their troops in the territories of Lucca they divided their army; Astorre marching with one part through the plains towards Camaggiore and Pietro Santa; and Rinaldo towards the mountains with the other; imagining that when all communication was cut off with the Country, the city must soon fall into their hands. But this expe-

---

* A manner of voting in elections, debates, or criminal causes by dropping black or white balls, called *Balotes* by the French, into a box or bag or something of that kind; the white ones signifying assent, the black ones dissent: by which every man is at liberty to vote according to his conscience, not being in awe of any one, or fear of having it known which way he gave his vote: the majority of white balls determining *for* the question, of black bal's *against* it. This seems to be a very equitable manner of proceeding, and is of great antiquity. In the trial of criminal causes at Rome, an *A* upon the Balots which the Judges threw into an Urn, signified the whole word word *Absolvo*. or, *I absolve the person accused*: whence Cicero calls *A*, *Litera salutaris, a saving letter*. They had other Balots with a *C* upon them which signified *Condemno, I condemn the person accused*: and others likewise marked with the letters *N* and *L*. *Non Liquet*, to order that the matter should be further enquired into: as the Judges hereby declared, that it was not sufficiently plain, and that they would not decide it whilst it remained so. This was also sometimes expressed *viva voce*, by the word *Amplius*, as we may learn from the following passage in Cicero: " Caufem pro Publicanis dixit Cælius. Confules re auditâ *amplius* de Concilii fententiâ pronunciârunt. Cælius pleaded for the publicans. The consuls, after they had heard him, by the advice of the Senate, pronounced, *let this matter be further enquired into*." The Greeks likewise used this custom in their criminal causes, banishments or oftracifins, so called from writing the sentence or acquittal upon oyster-shells, or by throwing black or white beans into a covered Urn. It is a pity it is not still continued in all great assemblies, as it seems so well calculated to prevent corruption. Some interpret the saying of Pythagoras, *abstine a fabis*, as an admonition not to meddle in public affairs, especially in sentences.

dition

dition proved unfortunate to them both in the end:
for though they took feveral towns, yet their conduct
was highly cenfured by the Public; and Aftorre's indeed with great reafon.

There is a Vale near Pietra Santa called Seravezza,
which at that time was very rich and full of inhabitants, who hearing of the commiffary's approach, went
out to meet him, and entreated him to receive them
into his protection, as faithful fubjects to the State of
Florence. Upon which, Aftorre feeming to accept
their fubmiffion with pleafure, ordered his forces to
feize upon all the paffes and ftrong places in the
Vale: and having affembled them all in their principal Church, he kept them prifoners there, and
caufed his foldiers to plunder and ravage the whole
Country, with unheard of avarice and barbarity;
not fparing even the confecrated places, or women of
any degree or profeffion whatfoever. When the news
of thefe proceedings arrived at Florence, not only the
Magiftracy but the whole city was exceedingly offended. And fome of the Seravezzans, who had
efcaped from the commiffary, flying directly to Florence, made fuch grievous complaints and lamentations to every one they met in the ftreets, that many
of the Citizens, who either thought Aftorre deferved
to be feverely punifhed for thefe mifdeeds, or hated
him becaufe he was not of their party, advifed them
to apply to the Council of Ten, and defire an audience; which being granted, one of them thus addreffed himfelf to the Council. " We humbly truft,
Magnificent Lords, that you will give credit to our
report, and compaffionate our unhappy condition,
when you fhall have heard in what manner your
commiffary has feized upon our Country, and how
we have been fince treated by him. Our Vale, as
the records of your city will amply teftify, has ever
been of the Guelph party, and often afforded a fecure
retreat to fuch of your Citizens as fled to it from the
perfecution of the Ghibelines. Both our anceftors
and ourfelves have at all times fhewn the higheft re-

gard

gard for this renowned Commonwealth, as the head
and fupport of our party: and whilft the Lucchefe
continued to avow the fame principles, we voluntarily
fubmitted to their government: but fince they are,
fallen under the dominion of a Tyrant who has for-
faken his former allies, and gone over to the Ghibelines, we have obeyed him indeed, but it has been,
out of conftraint, and not any good will or inclination,
of our own.   We call God to witnefs how often we
have prayed his Divine providence to give us an opportunity of fhewing our affection to our ancient,
friends.   But how fallacious are the hopes of men !
what we thought would have been our redemption,
has proved our utter ruin.   For when we had intelligence that your Standard was advancing towards
our Vale, we came out to meet the commiffary, not
as an enemy, but as a fervant of our ancient mafters,
and delivered up our Country, our fortunes, and our
perfons into his hands, recommending ourfelves to
his protection, upon a prefumption that he had the
foul, if not of a Florentine, at leaft of a man.   But
pardon our freedom, we befeech you, Magnificent
Lords, (fince the reflection that our misfortunes are
already fo great that they cannot be increafed, infpires
us with this degree of confidence) your commiffary
has nothing of a man but the fhape, nor of a Florentine but the name.   He is a Peftilence, a wild
Beaft, and fuch a monfter of luft and cruelty, as was
never let loofe upon any people before.   For having
drawn us all together into one of our Churches under the pretence of a conference, he firft made us
prifoners, and then carried fire and fword through
the whole Vale, plundering and murdering the men,
violating the chaftity of the married women, and
tearing thofe that were unmarried from the arms of
their mothers, to deliver them up to the brutality of
his mercilefs foldiers.   If we had provoked him to
thefe barbarities by any injury done either to himfelf
or the Republic of Florence ; or if we had fo much
as taken up arms in our own defence, we fhould
have

have had the lefs reafon to complain ; nay we fbould.
have juftly condemned ourfelves, for bringing hem
upon our own héads, and confidered them as a pnifh-
ment due to our arrogance. But as we deliverd up
ourfelves, freely and unarmed, into his hands ; to be
afterwards treated in this inhuman manner, exceeds
all patience and juftifies our bittereft lamentations.
And though we might have made not only Lombardy but every part of Italy ring with a rectal of
our forrows, to the great difgrace of this city ; we
did not think ourfelves at liberty to do fo owever,
for fear of ftaining the reputation of fo benefient and
honourable a Republic with an imputation of crimes
committed by the malevolence and villany of private fubject ; whofe unexampled avarice (if w had
known the man before) we would have endeavored
to fatiate if poffible (though indeed it feems to ave
no bounds) by facrificing one part of our eftates to
preferve the other ; that fo we might have efcapd
irretrievable ruin. But fince that is now too la,
and we have no refuge left to fly to but your com
paffion, we befeech you, Magnificent Lords, to pi
the miferable condition of your poor and deftitu
fubjects ; left others hereafter may be deterred by ou
example from putting themfelves under your pro
tection. If the greatnefs of our fufferings is not fufficient to move pity, let the fear of God's vengeance,
however, excite you to punifh the wretches who have
fo impioufly dared to rifle and burn his churches,
and to maffacre the people, whom they had fo bafely
betrayed, before his very altars." And having thus
faid, they threw themfelves at their feet, weeping and
imploring them to caufe their goods and eftates to be
reftored ; and fince their honour could never be repaired, that they might at leaft have the confolation
of feeing their wives returned to their hufbands, and
their daughters to their parents.

The enormity of thefe facts, fupported not only
by common fame, but the teftimony of the fufferers
themfelves, enflamed the Magiftracy to fuch a degree,

gree, that Aftorre was not only recalled immediately,
but afheered, and rendered for ever incapable of.
being employed again in the fervice of the Republic.
A ftrict fearch was likewife made after the effects of
the Sravezzans, and what could be found was reftored to the owners; for the reft they were afterwards indemnified at the expence of the Republic.

Rinaldo degli Albizi was alfo accufed of carrying
on the war in fuch a manner as tended only to his own
private advantage, without any regard to that of the
Commowealth. They faid, that after he was appointed commiffary, he thought no more of the reduction of Lucca, but employed himfelf in plundering the Country to ftock his own eftate with the cattle, and furnifh his houfe with the fpoil of others.
Tha he was not content with the booty he had amaffed
himfelf, but bought up all that had been taken by
the common foldiers: fo that inftead of a commiffary,
he was become a Pawn-broker. Thefe calumnies exceedingly mortified his pride, (for he was a haughty,
though an honeft and upright man) and raifed his
paffions to fuch a height, as was not confiftent with
the character of his gravity and wifdom. He therefore took poft full of rage and indignation againft
the Magiftrates, and without waiting for their leave,
immediately returned to Florence, and prefented himfelf before the Council of Ten; whom he told without any ceremony or referve, " that he well knew,
how difficult and dangerous a thing it was, to ferve an
unbridled People, and a divided State; fince the one
was carried away with every rumour; the other, put
a malicious interpretation upon actions that were
doubtful, and always punifhed the evil, but never
rewarded the good. So that if a commander fucceeded in an expedition, he had no praife at all; if
he was guilty of an error, his conduct was cenfured
by the generality; but if he mifcarried, he was fure
to be condemned by every one: for in one cafe, his
own party would envy his fuccefs, and his adverfaries
not fail to infult him in the other. That, however,

he

he had never been difcouraged by the fear of idle
flander and undeferved reproach, from purfuing any
undertaking, that he was convinced would be of real
advantage to his Country. That indeed, the afper-
fions fo unjuftly thrown upon him at prefent, had
overcome his patience and difcompofed his ufual temper. That he advifed them to be more ready to defend the reputation of their fervants for the future, if
they expected to be cheerfully and effectually ferved
by them : and fince it was not the cuftom of the Florentines to honour their Citizens with Triumphs, it
might be hoped at leaft they would protect them
againft calumny and unjuft accufations. That they
ought to remember that they themfelves were likewife
officers in the fame Republic, and liable at any time
to be traduced in the fame vile manner, and then
they would find how grievous fuch treatment was
to men of honour and integrity."

Upon thefe remonftrances, the Council endeavoured
to appeafe his refentment as much as they could at
prefent; but gave the further care of conducting that
expedition to Neri di Gino and Alamanno Salviati;
who, inftead of ravaging the Country, determined to
advance directly to Lucca with their forces; which,
as it was then very cold weather, had retired into
winter quarters at Capannole. But the commiffaries
who defigned to draw nearer, and inveft the town
without further lofs of time, having ordered them to
march out and encamp before it, the foldiers flatly
refufed to ftir in that fevere feafon of the year; tho'
the Council of Ten had likewife fent them ftrict orders to advance, and faid they would admit of no
excufe.

There was at that time in Florence, one Philip
Brunellefchi, a celebrated Painter and Architect,
many of whofe paintings and buildings are yet to be
feen in Florence * : and for which the Citizens thought

---

* At length (fays Voltaire) wealth and liberty excited the genius
as well as the courage of the nation. In Florence Brunellefchi began

them-

themselves so much obliged to him, that after his death, they erected a marble statue to his memory in the principal Church, with an inscription upon it setting forth his great merit and excellency in those arts. This Philip having reconnoitred the course of the river Serchio and the situation of Lucca, informed the Council of Ten, that he would undertake to lay that city under water; and so far convinced them of the practicability of his design, that they gave him a Commission to put it in execution. But this project had a very different effect, and occasioned such disorder amongst the Florentine troops that it saved the city. For the Lucchese being aware of it, immediately threw up a strong bank, quite across the meadows through which they were diverting the current of the River upon them. After which, they cut a sluice one night in the bank of the Channel which the enemy had made; through which the water presently took its course, and being opposed by the Dam, began to rise in such a manner upon the plain above, where the Florentine army had at last encamped, that instead of advancing any further, they were forced to raise their Camp and abandon the enterprize for that time.

This expedition having proved unsuccessful, the new Council of Ten which had lately been appointed, sent Giovanni Guicciardini to supersede the late com-

to revive the ancient taste of Architecture. Giotto was remarkable for his Paintings, and Boccaccio ascertained the Italian language. Guido of Arezzo invented the new method of musical notes. In Petrarch and Dante there is a great number of passages wherein we admire the vigour of the Ancients joined to the freshness of the moderns. What gave modern Rome some superiority over the ancient, was the Cupola of St. Peter's. There were only three antique monuments of this kind extant in the world; part of the dome of the temple of Minerva at Athens, the dome of the Pantheon at Rome, and that of the great Mosque at Constantinople, formerly St. Sophia's, built by Justinian. But these Cupolas, though sufficiently raised on the inside, were too flat without. Brunelleschi, the restorer of Architecture in Italy in the fifteenth century, remedied this defect in the cathedral of Florence, by building two Cupolas one within the other; but those Cupolas had something of the Gothic, and were not in just proportion. Vol. ii. part iii. p. 5. and Vol. iii. part vi. p. 104.

missaries;

miffaries; who fat down with his army as near the town as he could. The Lord of Lucca therefore, feeing himfelf clofely befieged, fent Sylveftro Trenta and Ludovico Bonvifi to follicit relief from the Duke of Milan, by the advice of Antonio del Roffo, who at that time refided with him as envoy from the Republic of Siena. But thefe Deputies finding him unwilling to fend any fuccour to their mafter, affured him privately in their own name and that of the people of Lucca, that if he would fend a body of troops to their affiftance, they would feize upon the Tyrant, and deliver both him and the town into his hands: but if he did not, the Tyrant would certainly give up the town to the Florentines, who had offered him very advantageous terms. This fuggeftion wrought fo effectually upon the Duke, that he immediately laid afide all referve, and ordered Count Francifco Sforza, his General, publickly to demand a paffage for his troops through the territories of Lucca, into the Kingdom of Naples: which being granted, he advanced with them to Lucca; though the Florentines, who faw through his defign, fent to defire their common friend Boccacino Alamanni, to diffuade him from it. But upon the arrival of Sforza at Lucca, they withdrew their forces to Librafatta, and the other went to lay fiege to Pefcia, of which Paolo da Diacetto was then Governor; but he bafely abandoned it and fled to Piftoia; fo that if it had not been better defended by Giovanni Malavolti, Commander of the Garrifon there, it muft have fallen into the enemy's hands. The Count, however, not being able to carry it by affault, marched away to Buggiano, which he took, and burnt the Caftle of Stiliano, a neighbouring fortrefs. Upon which, the Florentines not a little chagrined at thefe devaftations, refolved to have recourfe to a remedy that had often been of great fervice to them in times of danger and diftrefs; knowing by experience, that mercenary foldiers might generally be corrupted, when they could not otherwife be oppofed. For this purpofe, they offered the

Count

Count a sum of money, provided he would give Lucca up to them and quit the Country: and the Count finding he was not likely to squeeze any great matter out of the Lucchese, soon began to lend an ear to those that could better feed his avarice. He therefore agreed with the Florentines, not absolutely to deliver Lucca into their hands, which he could not for shame comply with, but to draw his forces from it, upon payment of fifty thousand Ducats. After which treaty, in order to engage the Lucchese to excuse his proceedings to the Duke, he determined to assist them in deposing their Tyrant.

Antonio del Rosso, the Sienese envoy, was then in Lucca, as we have said before; and by the Duke's authority began to enter into measures with the Citizens for that purpose: the principal of whom were Pietro Cennami and Giovanni da Chivizano. And this they did the more freely, as Lanzilao the Tyrant's Son, was then with Sforza, who lay encamped upon the banks of the Serchio, at a little distance from the town. The Conspirators therefore, taking arms, to the number of forty, went directly to Guinigi's house in the dead of the night; who being awaked by the noise they made, came down to them trembling and frighted, and desired to know what they wanted. To which Cennami made answer, " that, as they had been so long oppressed by him within the walls, and reduced to such straits by an enemy without, that they were every day in danger of perishing either by famine or the sword, they were now resolved to govern themselves; and therefore demanded the Keys and treasure of the city to be delivered to them." Guinigi replied, " that the treasure was all spent, but the keys and himself were at their service: that he hoped however, as his reign had both begun and been continued till that time without blood, there would be none shed at the conclusion of it." Upon which submission his life was spared for that time: but Sforza took both him and his Son along with him to the

the Duke at Milan, where they died not long afer in prifon.

At the departure of the Count, the Lucchefe being freed from the yoke of their Tyrant, and the Florentines from the fear of the Duke's forces; onefide began to prepare for their defence, and the othr to renew hoftilities. The latter having appointed the Count of Urbino their Commander in chief, laid clofe fiege to the town, and reduced the Lucaefe to fuch extremities, that they were obliged to rake frefh application to the Duke, who under the ame pretext that he had before fent Count Sforza, 10w fent Niccolo Piccinino to their fuccour. But the Florentines refolving to difpute his paffage ovei the Serchio, as he was advancing to relieve the town, came to an engagement with him upon the banks of the River; in which they received fo great an over-throw, that only the commiffary and a very few of his men efcaped the hands of the enemy, and fled to Pifa. This defeat threw the city of Florence into *defeat.* the utmoft confternation; and as the expedition had been undertaken almoft by general confent, the people not knowing againft whom elfe to turn their rage, began to abufe thofe that had conducted the war (fince they could not well tell how to blame thofe who by their own inftigation had firft advifed it) and revived their old calumnies againft Rinaldo degli Al- *Rinaldo* bizi. But the perfon whom they fell upon with the greateft virulence was Giovanni Guicciardini, who, they faid, might eafily have put an end to the war after the departure of Count Sforza, if he had not been bribed: nay, they went fo far as to charge him with fending a horfe-load of money to his own houfe, and particularly mentioned the names both of thofe that carried, and thofe that received it. Thefe clamours and accufations made fuch a noife, that the Captain of the People could not help taking cognizance of fo public a charge; efpecially as he was likewife impor-tunately called upon fo to do by Giovanni's enemies. Having cited him therefore to clear himfelf of this

impu-

imputation, he made his appearance, but with much feeling indignation, and contempt of their malice, and his relations exerted themfelves fo ftrenuoufly forthe honour of their family, that the Captain was obliged to ftop all further proceedings againft him.

The Lucchefe after their late victory not only recovred the towns they had loft, but poffeffed themfeles of all the territories of Pifa, except Bientina, Cazinaia, Livorno (or Leghorn) and Librafatta : and if confpiracy had not been difcovered, which was formed in Pifa, that city would alfo have been loft amonft the reft. The Florentines however recruited their army, and put it under the Command of Michdetto *, who had been bred up under Sforza. The Duke on the other hand, did not fail to purfue his advantage; and in order to defeat all future attempts of the Florentines more effectually, he prevailed upon the Genoefe, the Sienefe, and the Lord of Piombino, to enter into a league for the defence of Lucca and to take Piccinino into their pay : which laft circumftance fo plainly difcovered his defigns, that the Florentines likewife renewed their confederacy with the Venetians. Upon this, open hoftilities were immediately commenced in Lombardy and Tufcany, where the war was carried on, and feveral fkirmifhes enfued with various fuccefs on each fide: till at laft they were both fo tired, that a general Peace was concluded in the Month of May 1433 : by which it was agreed, that whatfoever towns had been taken by the Florentines, Lucchefe and Sienefe fhould be mutually reftored to their former poffeffors.

During the courfe of this war abroad, the factious humours began to ferment again at home; and Cofimo de' Medici, after the deceafe of Giovanni, began to act with greater fpirit in public affairs, and with more opennefs and zeal for the good of his friends, than ever his father had done: fo that thofe that rejoiced at the death of Giovanni, were not a little

1433

osimo

* The furname is wanting.

damped

damped at the proceedings of his Son. Cofimo, was a man of very great prudence, of a fedate and agreeable countenance, exeeding liberal and humane : never entering into any meafures that would be pernicious to the State, or even the party that he oppofed; but taking all opportunities of doing good to every one, and of conciliating to himfelf the affections of his fellow Citizens by his goodnefs and generofity. So noble an example of benevolence, greatly increafed the hatred which the public had already conceived againft the governing party, and at the fame time was the beft method he thought he could take, to enable himfelf either to live with reputation and fecurity in Florence, or to get the better of any perfecution that the malice of his enemies might raife againft him, by the intereft he had with the people, and even, if neceffary, by force of arms. There were two Citizens that contributed more than any of the reft to promote this intereft, whofe names were Averardo de' Medici, and Puccio de' Pucci: the one by his boldnefs and activity, the other by his great wifdom and experience, which added much reputation to his party. And indeed the judgment and authority of the latter were fo generally revered, that he gave name to the party, which was not called Cofimo's, but Puccio's party.

In this divided ftate of the City, the expedition againft Lucca was undertaken; which, inftead of extinguifhing the rage of faction, ftill added fuel to it. For though Puccio's party had promoted and advifed a war, yet thofe of the other fide were chiefly employed in conducting it, as they had greater power in the government. And fince Averardo de' Medici and his friends could not by any means prevent this, they took every opportunity of defaming them and calumniating their actions: fo that when they met with any misfortune (as they did with feveral) it was not imputed to the fuperior ftrength or better management of the enemy, but to the mifconduct and imprudence of the Commiffary. This was the oc-

cafion that the enormities committed by Aftorre
Gianni, though very great indeed of themfelves,
were ftill exaggerated.   It was this fort of treatment
that provoked Rinaldo degli Albizi to fuch a degree,
that he left his command without permiffion.   This
was the true caufe of Giovanni Guicciardini being
cited to appear before the Captain of the People.
From hence proceeded all the charges and complaints
that were exhibited againft other Magiftrates and
Commiffaries : and whilft thofe that had any foundation were always aggravated, and fometimes fupported by downright falfehood, the people greedily
fwallowed all, whether true or falfe, out of the hatred
they bore to them.   And though Niccolò da Uzzano
and the other heads of that party, were fufficiently
aware of thefe bafe artifices, and had feveral private
meetings to confider of proper means to prevent the
effect of them, yet they could not fix upon any expedient.   It was very dangerous, they knew, to connive at them, and not lefs fo to proceed to open violence.   Uzzano himfelf was averfe to any remedies
of that kind.   But Niccolò Barbadori, feeing they
were harraffed in this manner with war abroad, and
faction at home, took an opportunity of going one
day to vifit him at his own houfe, where he found
him very thoughtful and alone in his ftudy ; and as
he himfelf wifhed to fee the ruin of Cofimo, he left
no method untried to prevail upon Uzzano to join
with Rinaldo degli Albizi to drive him out of the
City.

Uzzano   After fome paufe, Uzzano replied, " It would be
much better for yourfelf and your family too, Barbadori, and for the Commonwealth in general, if
both you and all others that propofe fuch meafures,
had * beards of filver inftead of gold, as your name

---

* Barba d'oro, in the Italian, fignifies *a beard of gold.* This is
therefore one of thofe little puns, or *concetti,* from which the very
beft authors that wrote in Machiavel's time, and long after, are not
altogether free.   They were not peculiar to Italy ; for we find them
fcattered in great plenty (the more is the pity) through the works of
the firft rate Genius's of our own country.

im-

imports : for then every one might hope for wife and
wholefome counfel from grey hairs and long experience. Common prudence, however, I fhould think,
would be fufficient to induce thofe that advife the
expulfion of Cofimo, in the firft place, to compare
their own ftrength with his. Our party, it feems, is
now diftinguifhed by the name of the Nobility, and
the other, by that of the Plebeians. And fuppofing
there was any juft reafon for that diftinction, fuccefs
in fuch an undertaking would ftill appear very du-
bious ; and we ought rather to fear the worft, than
hope for any good from it, when we remember the
fate of the ancient Nobility of this City, who at laft
were utterly fuppreffed in their contefts with the Plebeians. And we have ftill fewer advantages on our
fide than they had : for our party is divided, whilft
that of our adverfaries is compact and entire. Neri
di Gino and Nerone di Nigi, two of the chief men
in the City, have not yet declared themfelves; and
it is uncertain what fide they will take. Several families are divided amongft themfelves; and many
there are that hate us, and favour our adverfaries,
merely out of envy or malice to their own brothers,
or fome other near relations. Some of the moft confiderable of whom, I fhall mention ; the reft will naturally occur to your own memory and obfervation.
Amongft the fons of Mafo degli Albizi, Luca, out
of hatred to Rinaldo, is gone over to the other fide.
In the family of the Guicciardini, Pietro, the fon of
Luigi, is a mortal enemy to his brother Giovanni,
and joins our adverfaries. Tomafo and Niccolò Soderini openly oppofe us out of picque to their uncle
Francifco. So that if we confider the quality of
thofe that conftitute their party, and of whom our
own confifts, I fee no reafon why one fhould be called
the Nobility in preference to the other. If it is becaufe they are followed by the whole body of the
Plebeians; that very circumftance makes them fo
much fuperior to us, that if ever we come to an open
trial of our ftrength, we fhall not be able to ftand

be-

before them. And if we ſtill continue in poſſeſſion
of the firſt places in the Commonwealth, it is entirely owing to the eſtabliſhed credit of an adminiſtration, which has now ſupported itſelf for the ſpace
of fifty years. But if things ſhould come to extremities, and our preſent weakneſs be diſcovered, you
may depend upon it, we ſhould be forced out of the
Magiſtracy, perhaps to our utter deſtruction. If it
be ſaid, that the juſtice of our cauſe will increaſe our
reputation, and diminiſh that of our enemies; I anſwer, that it is neceſſary the people ſhould firſt be
convinced, that it really is a juſt one: and how can
that be done, ſince it muſt plainly appear, that the
motives of our proceedings are founded merely upon
a jealouſy that Coſimo may attempt to uſurp a ſo-
vereignty over this Republic. If we entertain ſuch
ſuſpicions of him ourſelves, others are ſo far from
doing it, that they accuſe us of thoſe very deſigns
with which we charge him. What reaſon is there for
theſe apprehenſions, they will ſay, except that he
freely lends money to every one that wants it; not
only to private people, but to the public, upon any
exigency, and to foreigners as well as Florentines;
that he is a friend to ſuch as ſtand in need of protection; or becauſe he ſometimes helps to advance an
acquaintance to a reputable employment in the Commonwealth, by the intereſt which his univerſal benevolence has gained him amongſt the people? What
then ſhall we be able to plead as an excuſe for endeavouring to expel him the City? Shall we accuſe
him of being charitable, friendly, liberal, and beloved by every one? Tell me, I pray you, what law
prohibits or condemns charity, liberality, and bene-
ficence. Indeed theſe virtues are ſometimes counter-
feited to cajole the vulgar, by ſuch as aſpire to dominion; but they do not appear in that light at preſent, nor is it in our power to make them; we have
loſt our reputation by our late miſconduct; and a
people naturally prone to faction, and corrupted by
continual diviſions, will no longer put any confidence

7   in

in us, or give credit to fuch accufations. But fuppofe we fhould fucceed fo far as to get him banifhed
(which indeed might poffibly be done if the Signiory
would concur in it) how fhould we prevent his return,
when he has fo many powerful friends left in the
City, who would never reft till they had got him recalled? This would be to no purpofe therefore,
whilft his intereft is fo great, and the remembrance
of his benevolence fo frefh upon the minds of the
people; and the more we fhould banifh of his declared friends, the more we fhould augment the number of our own fecret enemies. So that when he returned, as he certainly would do in a fhort time, we
fhould find, that we had done nothing more, than
banifh a good man, and bring back a bad one, as
his difpofition would be altered by thofe that had
procured his reftoration; to whom he would think
himfelf under fuch obligations, that he could not oppofe them in any thing. But, if it is intended to put
him to death in a judicial manner, that can never be
effected; for as he is rich, and the magiftracy corrupt, he will be fure to efcape all punifhment. But
let us fuppofe he fhould be condemned, or perhaps
never return from exile; I cannot perceive what the
Commonwealth would gain by that: for no fooner
will it be free from the apprehenfions it was under
from Cofimo, but it will be liable to the fame from
Rinaldo. For my own part, I am one of thofe that
never defire to fee one Citizen exceed another in authority. And if one of thefe two muft feize the reins,
I know not any reafon that fhould induce me to prefer
Rinaldo to Cofimo. I have nothing further to add,
but that I pray God to preferve this City from ever
falling under the dominion of any one man; but, if
a time fhould ever come when our fins fhall bring
that judgment upon us, I pray ftill more earneftly,
that we may not become fubject to Rinaldo. Let
me exhort you, therefore, not to perfift in a defign
that is every way fo full of danger, nor to imagine
that you fhall be able to get the better of the multi-

tude

tude by the co-operation of fo few affiftants as you will have : for take my word for it, the far greater part of the Citizens, fome out of ftupidity, and others out of malice, are thoroughly difpofed to fell their country ; and fortune has been fo favourable to them as to provide a purchafer. Take my advice then for once ; endeavour to live quietly ; and as to any invafion of our liberties, be affured, that you have as much to apprehend from our own party, as the other, When troubles arife, take no fide *, for by ftanding neuter, you will be upon good terms with every one, and advantage yourfelf, without prejudicing your Country."

Cosimo

Thefe diffuafions, in fome meafure, cooled Barbadori's refolution : fo that the City continued tolerably quiet, till the war with Lucca was over. But a peace being concluded, and Uzzano dying foon after, there was nobody left of fufficient authority to fupprefs the ill humours that began to fhew themfelves again without referve, when all reftraint was at an end. Rinaldo degli Albizi in particular, who now looked upon himfelf as the Head of that party, was continually teazing and importuning fuch Citizens as

* " It is a man's duty, faid a celebrated but unhappy Prelate of our Church, to keep himfelf always from embarking in parties and factions, and falling with vehemence into all the interefts and defigns of them. This will neceffarily, in time, embitter his fpirits, and four his humour, make him like and diflike men implicity, and lead him into many refentments which he hath nothing to do with." Bifhop Atterbury's Sermons, publifhed by Dr. Moore, vol. ii. p. 335. This paffage occurs in that upon Rom. xii. 18. The author of Dr. Afheton's Life (an eminent Divine, who died at the beginning of this century) fays, p. 39. " That he had narrowly obferved the conduct of all parties in every reign, during the courfe of his life : that he faw the madnefs of the people, and how defigning men can feduce them to proclaim Hofannas at one time, and demand crucifixion at another: that he was aware of the mean felfifhnefs, ambition, and violence of the beft parties ; which gave him the fame idea of parties in general ; and confequently was fenfible of the expedience of thofe precautions recommended by Archbifhop Dawes, in his Sermon upon the 30th of January, " That we ought to take care not to lift ourfelves as thorough members of any party."—It is no extraordinary thing, fays a very celebrated author, to fee perfons die in that party, which they declared for, at the rife of a faction, or the beginning of a revolution.

he

he thought were likely to be the next Gonfaloniers,
to take up arms and deliver their Country out of
the hands of a man, who, taking the advantage of
the ſtupidity of ſome, and the malice of others, would
certainly enſlave it.   Thus Rinaldo, by endeavouring
to ſupplant his adverſaries, and they to ſupport themſelves, kept the whole City in continual alarm and
ſuſpicion : ſo that when new magiſtrates were appointed, it was preſently known how many there were
on one ſide, and how many on the other: and at the
Imborſations for the Signiory, there was nothing to
be ſeen but tumult and uproar.   Every trifling affair
that was brought before the Magiſtracy, created a
diviſion amongſt them : all ſecrets were divulged ;
they had no regard to juſtice ; the good and the evil
were treated alike ; and there was not ſo much as one
Magiſtrate that did his duty.

The City being in this confuſion, and Rinaldo impatient to lower the authority of Coſimo ; conſidering
with himſelf that Bernardo Guadagni (though a man
very fit for his purpoſe) could not be admitted to the
office of Gonfalonier, even if his name ſhould be
drawn, except the arrears he was in to the public
were firſt diſcharged, he paid them himſelf.   And as
fortune (the conſtant enemy of our City) would have
it, in the Imborſation for a new Signiory, Bernardo
was actually drawn Gonfalonier for the two enſuing
months of September and October.   Upon which,
Rinaldo immediately went to congratulate him, and
told him, how much the Nobility, and all honeſt men
who deſired to live in peace and ſecurity, were rejoiced to ſee him in poſſeſſion of that dignity ; and
that it was hoped he would behave himſelf in ſuch a
manner as would give them no cauſe to repent of it.
He then repreſented to him the danger they were in
from their diviſions ; that the ſureſt way to reſtore
union amongſt them, was to rid themſelves of Coſimo, who was the only man that ſtood in their way :
that the popularity he had gained by his immenſe
riches, had given him ſuch an aſcendancy, that, if

T 4   timely

timely care was not taken to prevent it, he would
certainly make himfelf abfolute Lord over them : and
therefore it was his duty, as a good Citizen, to provide againſt the danger, by calling the people together in the Piazza, to reinſtate the adminiſtration
in its former power, and fecure the liberties of his
Country. He defired him to remember the example
of Sylveſtro de' Medici, who (even without any appearance of juſtice on his ſide) was able to check the
over-grown power of the Guelphs, though they certainly had the faireſt claim to govern the city, as a
reward for the blood which their anceſtors had ſo generoufly ſhed for the defence of it : and that what
he alone could effect without any juſt pretenſions,
and in ſpite of ſo many powerful adverfaries, might
ſurely be done again in a juſt caufe, and when there
was but one man to oppofe them. He exhorted him
to act with vigour and refolution, as all his friends
would immediately take arms to fupport him ; to
make no account of the mob (though they feemed to
adore Cofimo at prefent) for in time of need, he
would be ferved by them juſt as Georgio Scali had
been formerly : nor to ſtand in awe of his riches ; for
when once he was in the power of the Signiory, his
wealth would fall into their hands. He concluded,
with faying, that when this was done, the Republic
would become united and fecure, and his own reputation eſtabliſhed for ever." Bernardo made anfwer in a few words, " that he was fully convinced
of the expedience and neceſſity of what he had urged :
but as it was high time to proceed to execution, he
defired him to prepare their friends to take arms as
foon as pcſſible, ſince he was perfuaded they ſhould
be fo well fupported."

As foon as Bernardo had entered upon his office,
their friends being in readinefs, and every thing fettled
betwixt him and Rinaldo, he fummoned Cofimo to
appear before the Signiory ; which he did, trufting
rather to his own innocence, than to their mercy ;
though he was diffuaded from it by many. But he
was

was hardly got into the palace, before he was arrefted. Upon which, Rinaldo inftantly fallied out of his houfe, with a body of armed men, and all the reft of the party at his heels, and came into the Piazza; where the Signiory affembled the people, and appointed a Balia, confifting of two hundred Citizens, to reform the State. The firft thing that was debated, after they met to confider of a reformation, was, whether Cofimo fhould be put to death or not. Some argued for it, others thought banifhment fufficient, and many fat filent, either out of affection to him, or fear of the other party : fo that in fuch a diverfity of opinions, nothing was determined upon.

In the turret of the palace there is an apartment, called Alberghettino, to which Cofimo was committed prifoner, under the cuftody of Frederigo Malavolti. From this place he could hear the clamours of the armed men that were below in the Piazza, and frequent outcries for a Balia; which made him apprehend that his life was in danger, but much more, that his particular enemies would take fome extraordinary method to difpatch him. For that reafon, he would eat no meat for the fpace of four days, except a mouthful or two of bread. Of which Malavolti taking notice, addreffed himfelf to him in this manner : " Whilft you are afraid of being poifoned, you will ftarve yourfelf to death, to my great difhonour; for certainly you muft have a vile opinion of me, to fufpect I would be concerned in fo bafe a deed. In my opinion, your life is not in any danger, as you have fo many friends both within the palace and without it : but if there is any fuch defign in agitation, you may affure yourfelf I will not be employed as an executioner, nor ever ftain my hands with the blood of any man, much lefs yours, who never did me any injury. Take courage then, eat your meat, and keep yourfelf alive for the good of your friends and your country : and that you may have no further fufpicion of that kind, I will eat with you myfelf." Upon this encouragement, Cofimo em-

braced

braced him with tears in his eyes, acknowledging his generofity and gentleman-like behaviour in the moft thankful manner, and affuring him, he would amply recompence his kindneffes, if ever fortune fhould put it in his power again to fhew his gratitude.

His apprehenfions therefore being in fome meafure quieted, and his fate yet undetermined by the Balia, it happened that Malavolti, to entertain his prifoner, invited one Farganaccio a friend of the Gonfalonier's, and a man of humour and pleafantry, to fup with him. Upon which, after fupper was almoft over, Cofimo hoping to make fome advantage of this vifit (as he himfelf was well acquainted with him) gave a hint to Malavolti to leave the room, who, pretty well gueffing at his intention, immediately went out to order fomething that was wanting, as he pretended. When they were alone, Cofimo after many fair words and promifes of a greater reward, gave his gueft a draught upon the Governor of St. Mary's new Hofpital for eleven hundred ducats, defiring him to keep an hundred himfelf, and to prefent the other thoufand to the Gonfalonier, from whom, he faid, he fhould be glad to receive the favour of a vifit, if he could find a proper opportunity. This he willingly undertook to perform, and gave the money to Bernardo, who then began to grow cooler and more moderate in the profecution : fo that after all, Cofimo was only banifhed to Padua, though Rinaldo ufed his utmoft endeavours to have him put to death. Averardo de' Medici and many others of that family were likewife banifhed at the fame time, and with them Puccio and Giovanni de' Pucci. And to keep thofe in ftill greater awe that feemed diffatisfied at Cofimo's exile, the Balia was reduced to eight (who were called wardens) and the Captain of the people. After thefe regulations, Cofimo was brought before the Signiory, *1433* on the third of October in the year 1433, who pronounced the fentence of banifhment upon him, and exhorted him to fubmit to it with patience, left he fhould provoke them to proceed with greater rigour

both

both againſt his perſon and eſtate. He received the
ſentence with a chearful countenance, and aſſured
them he would ſtay with content wherever they ſhould
be pleaſed to ſend him; praying them however, as
they had ſpared his life, that they would protect his
perſon, ſince he knew there were ſome in the Palace
that thirſted after his blood. He then took his leave
of them with ſaying, " that in what part of the world
ſoever he ſhould ſojourn, his perſon and fortune
ſhould always be at the ſervice of the Republic, the
People, and the Signiory." In anſwer to which, the
Gonfalonier told him " he would take care his life
ſhould be in no danger;" and having detained him
in the Palace till night, he then conducted him to
his own houſe to ſup with him, and afterwards ordered a party of the guards to eſcort him to the confines of the Florentine dominions. Wherever he
came he was received with great honour, and publicly viſited by the Venetians, who treated him not
as an exile, but as a perſon of the firſt rank and conſequence in the State.

Florence being thus deprived of ſo great a man,
and ſo univerſally beloved, both parties had their apprehenſions: Rinaldo therefore, who ſaw a ſtorm
riſing, reſolved not to be wanting either to himſelf
or his friends: and having called ſeveral of them together, he told them, they had now ruined themſelves, as they would ſoon find, beyond all redemption, by giving way to the tears, ſupplications, and
bribes of their enemies, not foreſeeing that it would
quickly be their own turn to weep and implore compaſſion from thoſe who would be deaf to entreaties
and tears: that they would be forced to refund the
principal ſum of the bribes they had taken, with the
heavy intereſt of tortures, executions, and baniſhments. That it would have been much better for
them to have remained content in their former circumſtances, than to ſuffer Coſimo to eſcape with life,
and leave ſo many of his friends in Florence; as great
men ought either never to be provoked, or, if they

are,

are, to be entirely crushed. That he saw no remedy now left but to collect their strength and fortify themselves; that so, when their enemies should rise upon them (which was daily to be expected) they might be able to clear the city of them by dint of force, since, it seemed, they could not do it in a judiciary manner. That for this purpose, they must endeavour to regain the affections of the Grandees by restoring them to their honours and authority (as he had often advised) and to strengthen themselves by their assistance, as the other party had done by that of the Plebeians. That by such a junction they should considerably increase their strength, and might possibly recover their former power and reputation: but if this last and only expedient was not made use of, he knew of no other, for his part, that could preserve them, and indeed the Republic itself, from the imminent ruin it was threatened with amidst so many enemies." In answer to this, Mariotto Boldovinetti said, " that the insolence and tyranny of the Grandees, always had been, and always would be insupportable: and that it would be madness to run headlong into a certain and slavish subjection to them, when the danger that was apprehended from the Plebeians might only be imaginary." Rinaldo therefore seeing his advice rejected, could not help lamenting the misfortunes that he foresaw were going to fall upon himself and his party; but modestly imputed them rather to the malevolence of their destiny, than to the blindness and perverseness of men.

Whilst things were in this situation and no manner of provision made for their security, a letter was intercepted from Agnolo Acciaivoli to Cosimo, in which he informed him of the good disposition of the Citizens in general towards him, and advised him to stir up a war from some quarter or other, and to make Neri di Gino his friend; as he thought the people would then be in want of money to carry it on, and finding no body else that was able to supply them, they would naturally turn their thoughts upon him,

him, and be fo much the more impatient for his return. To which he added, " that if Neri could by
any means be detached from Rinaldo, his party
would be fo much weakened that it would not be able
to fupport him." But this letter falling into the
hands of the Magiftrates, Agnolo was taken into
cuftody, and afterwards brought to a trial, and fent
into banifhment; which in fome meafure reftrained
the ardour of thofe that favoured Cofimo.

It was now almoft a year fince Cofimo had been
banifhed; and at the end of Auguft 1434, Niccolo
di Cocco was drawn Gonfalonier for the two next
months, and with him eight new Signiors, all friends
to Cofimo; at which Rinaldo and his party were not
a little alarmed. And as, according to cuftom, the
new Signiory could not enter upon their office till
three days after they were drawn, Rinaldo once more
applied to the other chiefs of his party, and reprefented to them the certainty and nearnefs of the danger they were in, and that there was no refource left
but to take arms immediately and oblige Donato Velluti, who was then Gonfalonier, to affemble the people in the Piazza, to appoint another Balia, and depofe the new Signiory: after which, they might get
others drawn more fit for their purpofe, by burning
the old Imborfation, and making a frefh one, in
which the purfes might be filled only with the names
of their friends. This refolution was thought proper
and abfolutely neceffary by many; and by others too
violent and odious. Amongft thofe that difapproved
it, was Palla Strozzi, a man of a peaceable and humane difpofition, and rather given to ftudy than inclined to concern himfelf in the intrigues of faction.
He faid, " that all fchemes that were either too finely
fpun, or too bold, appeared likely to fucceed at firft
fight, but generally proved difficult in the management, and pernicious in the end. That he thought
the fear of new enemies abroad (as the Duke's army
was then in Romagna and near their confines) fhould
make the Signiory turn their attention to them, ra-

ther

ther than bufy themfelves in domeftic feuds: that however, if they fhould actually fee any fteps taken to raife a commotion (which could not well be with-out their notice) it would then be time enough to take arms, and make fuch regulations as fhould feem neceffary for the public fafety, which being done for their own defence, would alfo occafion lefs wonder and difguft amongft the people." It was therefore refolved to let the new Signiory enter peaceably upon the Magiftracy; but to keep a ftrict watch upon their conduct, and if they fhould attempt any thing to the prejudice of their party, then to rife immediately and affemble in the Piazza of St. Pulinare (a place near the Palace) from whence they might proceed to act as occafion fhould require.

With this refolution they parted; and the new Sig-niory having taken poffeffion of the Palace, the Gon-falonier, to begin his office with fome action that would give him reputation and ftrike a damp into fuch as might think of oppofing him, immediately committed his predeceffor Donato Velluti to prifon, upon a pretence that he had embezzled the public money. After which, he began to found the reft of his affociates about Cofimo's return; and finding them well difpofed to it, he communicated their defign to thofe that were reputed the Heads of the Medici party; who all encouraging him to attempt it, he cited Rinaldo degli Albizi, Ridolpho Peruzzi, and Niccolo Barbadori, as the principals of the other party, to appear before him. But Rinaldo feeing there was no more time now to be loft, inftead of obeying the citation, rufhed out of his houfe with a great number of armed men, and was inftantly joined by Peruzzi and Barbadori with feveral other Citizens and many difbanded Soldiers that were then in Flo-rence, and drew up in the Piazza of St. Pulinare, as they had before agreed. And though Palla Strozzi and Giovanni Guicciardini had affembled a good many men, they did not think proper to ftir out of their houfes; upon which, Rinaldo fent to haften

them

them and upbraid their tardinefs. But Guicciardini
fent him word back again, that he thought he fhould
do his party better fervice by ftaying at home and
preventing his brother Pietro from going to the relief of the Signiory : and Strozzi after many preffing
meffages, at laft came to St. Pulinare on horfeback ;
but with only two attendants on foot, and all three
without any arms, When Rinaldo faw him come in
that manner, he could not help reproaching him bitterly with his backwardnefs to join his friends; as he
faid, " it muft be owing either to perfidy or cowardice, the very appearance of both which ought to be
moft carefully avoided by fuch a man as he pretended
to be. That if he thought to efcape death or exile,
in cafe their enemies fhould get the upper hand of
them, by not fulfilling his engagement with his party,
he would find himfelf fatally difappointed. That for
his own part, let what would happen, he fhould at
leaft have this confolation, that he had done his duty,
not only in warning them of the danger before hand,
but in prefcribing remedies to prevent it, and laftly,
by behaving himfelf like a man when it did come :
that, on the contrary, he and his trufty companions
muft furely reflect with horror, that they had betrayed their country three different times : firft in
letting Cofimo efcape ; next, in not liftening to his
advice ; and now, in not fupporting him in the manner they had promifed." To this Strozzi muttered
fomething by way of anfwer, but in fuch a manner
that it was not underftood by the reft; and turning
his horfe about, he rode directly back again to his
own houfe.

The Signiory being informed that Rinaldo and his
party had taken arms, and feeing themfelves unable
to make head againft them, caufed the doors of the
Palace to be barricadoed, as they knew not what
other courfe to take in fo fudden an emergency. But
as Rinaldo ftaid waiting to be joined by others who
never came near him, inftead of advancing immediately to the Palace, as he ought to have done, he loft

his

his opportunity, and gave the Signiory time to provide for their defence. Upon which, many of the
Citizens reforted to them, and advifed them in the
firft place to ufe their endeavours to prevail upon the
other party to lay down their arms. They fent fuch
of their friends therefore, as were leaft obnoxious, to
acquaint Rinaldo and thofe that were with him, " that
they could not conceive what was the caufe of fuch a
commotion ; efpecially, as they had never defigned
to do them any injury : that if it was upon Cofimo's
account, they could affure them they had no thoughts
of recalling him ; for which they would give them
any fecurity, if they would come into the Palace;
where they fhould be honourably received, and have
fatisfaction in all other refpects." Thefe promifes,
however, made but little impreffion on Rinaldo, who
faid, he would take care to fecure himfelf by turning
them all out of their offices, and then the State
fhould be reformed in a manner that would be more
for the advantage of every one. But it feldom happens that any defign fucceeds, where the authority of
the conductors is equal, and their opinions different.
Ridolpho Peruzzi replied, " that for his part, he defired nothing more than that Cofimo might not be
fuffered to return : and fince that had been promifed,
he was very well contented, and inftead of infifting
upon any thing further, which might involve the city
in blood and confufion, he would accept of the invitation which the Signiory had given him ;" as he
immediately did, and went with all thofe that had
followed him, directly into the Palace, where he was
joyfully received. So that all hope of fuccefs being
defeated by the delay of Rinaldo at St. Pulinare, the
pufillanimity of Strozzi, and the defertion of Peruzzi,
the reft of the party began to lofe their fpirits and
grew much cooler in the undertaking than they had
been at firft : to which the interpofition of the
Pope's authority did likewife very much contribute.

Euge-

Eugenius IV. having been driven out of Rome by the people, was then at Florence *; and seeing these tumults, he thought it his duty to compose them, if possible. For this purpose, he sent Giovanni Vitellēschi, the Patriarch of Alexandria, who was intimately acquainted with Rinaldo, to desire he might speak with him, as he hoped he had credit and authority enough with the Signiory to procure him all reasonable security and satisfaction, without effusion of blood, or prejudice to any of the Citizens. Upon which Rinaldo, at the persuasion of his friend, went with all his followers to wait upon his Holiness at St. Maria Novella, where he at that time resided. After he was introduced into his presence, the Pope informed him that the Signiory had given him their word that all differences should be left to his arbi-

* Philip, Duke of Milan, having made an incursion into the Pope's territories, the cavalry which he sent thither, were commanded by Niccolo Fortebraccio, who had quitted the Pope's service in disgust: for when he demanded his pay, Eugenius answered, "that he ought to think himself amply paid by the booty he had amassed in plundering several towns." Exasperated at this answer, he went into the Duke's service, and being employed by him against this Pope, he made such dreadful havock in the places adjacent to Rome, that the whole City was in the utmost consternation, and the Pope himself for some time in doubt whither to-retire. The people resorted to him in crowds, to complain of the losses they had sustained: but, as he was then in an ill state of health, and did not know which way to turn himself, he referred them to the Cardinal his Nephew and High-chamberlain, an indolent and voluptuous man, who used to shuffle off the complaints of the people who had lost their cattle (as Platina says in the life of Eugenius) with this answer, "You really set too great a value upon your cattle; the Venetians live much more genteely without such encumbrances" " Eos nimiam spem in pecoribus collocasse: Venetos quidem sine gregibus & jumentis longe urbaniorem vitam ducere." At which they were so enraged, that they cried out, To arms! Liberty, Liberty! and not only removed all the magistrates from their employments, who had been appointed by Eugenius, but created others in their room, and seized upon the Cardinal his Nephew. The Pope being reduced to such extremities, put on the habit of a monk, and went on board a bark, in order to fly to Ostia, where he arrived safe, notwithstanding the vollies of stones and arrows that were discharged at the vessel as it fell down the river. From Ostia he went to Florence, and resided there some time. But the Romans did not long enjoy this liberty: for the Pope's authority was restored at Rome in his absence by John Vitellefchi, Patriarch of Alexandria, who proceeded with great severit against the mutineers.

tration, and that every thing fhould be fettled to his own fatisfaction, as foon as he and his party had laid down their arms. Rinaldo therefore, feeing the coldnefs of Strozzi and the levity of Peruzzi, and having no other refuge left, put himfelf under the protection of the Pope, whofe authority he thought was fufficient to fecure and defend him. In confequence of this, the Pope ordered Niccolo Barbadori, and the others that were waiting for him without doors, to lay down their arms, as Rinaldo would remain with him till he had made terms for them with the Signiory: upon which, they difperfed, and every man returned to his own houfe.

As foon as the Signiory faw their adverfaries difarmed, they began to treat with them through the mediation of the Pope, and, at the fame time, fent privately into the mountains of Piftoia for a body of foot foldiers, which, being joined by all the horfe they had in the adjacent territories, were brought into Florence by night; and having taken poffeffion of all the paffes and ftrong places in the city, they called the people together in the Piazza before the Palace, and appointed a new Balia, which at their firft meeting recalled Cofimo, and all the other Citizens that had been banifhed with him. On the other hand, they not only fent Rinaldo, Peruzzi, Barbadori, and Strozzi into banifhment, but fuch numbers of others, that moft parts of Italy, and fome other countries, were crowded with them, to the great impoverifhment of Florence both in regard to its wealth, its inhabitants, its trade and manufactures. But the Pope feeing that party entirely ruined and diffipated, which had confented to lay down their arms upon his affurances and interceffion, was exceedingly enraged; lamenting with Rinaldo the grievous misfortune that had befallen him through his means, and in violation of the moft folemn engagements: exhorting him however, to patience under his fufferings, and to hope for a fpeedy change in his favour, from the inconftancy of fortune. Rinaldo made anfwer in a few words,

words, " that the little regard his friends had paid
to his advice, and the too great confidence he had
put in his Holinefs, had been the ruin both of himfelf and his party: but that indeed, he ought to condemn himfelf rather than any other perfon, for fool-
ifhly imagining that a man, who had been driven out
of his own Country, fhould have intereft enough to
protect another any where elfe. That he was no
ftranger to the viciflitudes of fortune, and as he had
never been elated with profperity, he fhould not be
dejected in adverfity; fince he knew that when it
was her humour, fhe would favour him again with
her fmiles. But if fhe fhould not, it would give
him no great degree of regret to be banifhed a
city where private men had more authority than the
Laws: for any Country was certainly more defirable,
where a man could enjoy his property and truft to
his friends, than that where the one was fo eafily
taken away, and the other always deferted him, out
of fear and mean felf-intereft, in the day of diftrefs.
That all wife and good men thought it more grievous
to be fpectators of the calamities of their Country,
than to hear of them at a diftance; and more honourable to be an honeft exile than an abject flave."
After which, he turned himfelf about, and leaving
the Pope with great contempt and indignation, he
went into banifhment; often bewailing his own credulity, as well as the bafenefs of his friends, and
their blindnefs in rejecting his counfels. Cofimo, *Cofimo*,
on the other hand, having notice that he was at liberty to come home again, immediately repaired to Florence: and it has feldom happened that
any commander, though returning in triumph from
fome extraordinary Victory, was received with fuch
acclamations and univerfal joy, as Cofimo was at his
return from banifhment by his fellow Citizens, who
ran in multitudes to meet him, and faluted him with
one voice, *the Benefactor of the People, and the Father
of his Country.*

B O O K V.

A R G U M E N T.

*The soldiery of Italy divided into two parties, under Count
Francisco Sforza and Niccolo Fortebraccio. The Duke
of Milan promises his Daughter in marriage to the
former. Rome is assaulted by Sforza, and la Marca
d' Ancona invaded by Fortebraccio. Pope Eugenius IV.
makes an ignominious peace with Sforza, and being
driven out of Rome by the inhabitants, flies to Florence.
A war in Romagna betwixt the Duke of Milan on one
side; and the Venetians, the Florentines, and the Pope,
on the other; who enter into a league against the Duke.
Sforza commands the forces of the league; and Piccinino those of the Duke. A new government in Florence. Their severe proceedings. Alphonso of Arragon
attempts to make himself King of Naples. His fleet is
defeated by the Genoese, and he himself taken prisoner
and brought to the Duke of Milan. The authority of
the Doge in Genoa. Francisco Spinola having betrayed
that City into the hands of the Duke, repents of it,
and is the author of recovering its liberty. Rinaldo
degli Albizi's speech to the Duke, persuading him to
make war upon the Florentines, which he does. His
General Piccinino commits terrible ravages in their*
terri-

territories, and takes up his quarters at Lucca, to the great offence of the Florentines. Count Sforza gives him battle, defeats his forces, and lays waste the Country of the Lucchese. The speech of a Citizen of Lucca to animate the inhabitants of that City to defend themselves against the Florentines. Count Sforza is made General of the League. The Venetians are jealous of his proceedings. The disputes betwixt them about his passing the Po. He leaves their service and retires into Tuscany. A quarrel betwixt the Pope and Count Poppi accommodated by the Florentines. A controversy betwixt the Greek and Roman Churches, determined at Florence by the submission of the former. The Pope deluded, and his territories invaded by Piccinino, who takes all the towns in Romagna from him. Count Sforza earnestly persuaded by the Florentines not to desert the Venetians, at last consents to pass the Po. Neri Capponi's speech to the Venetian Senate. Count Sforza makes an unexpected march and relieves Verona, which was besieged by the Duke's forces. He attempts to relieve Brescia also. Piccinino defeats and takes most of the Venetian gallies upon the Lake di Garda. One part of his army is worsted by Count Sforza, and he himself escapes in a strange manner to the other. He surprizes Verona, which is recovered by the Count. The Duke of Milan is encouraged by Piccinino and the Florentine Exiles to invade Tuscany. The Patriarch of Alexandria, General of the Pope's forces. His character. He is suspected of endeavouring to betray the Pope: is committed to prison, and dies there. Differences betwixt the Venetians and Count Sforza about relieving Brescia, adjusted at last to his satisfaction. The Duke of Milan's forces invade Tuscany, under the command of Piccinino, who plunders the territories of the Florentines, and takes several towns and castles from them. The cowardice of Orlandini. Count Poppi revolts from the Florentines. The Duke's army is defeated in Lombardy, and Brescia relieved by Sforza. A remarkable battle at Anghiari, in which Piccinino is routed by the forces of the Florentines, in conjunction

with

with thofe of the Pope. Poppi is befieged and taken.
Count Poppi's addrefs to the Florentine Commiffaries
upon that occafion. Neri Capponi's anfwer. The
Count is ftripped of his dominions for his perfidy.

IN the changes that are incident to all governments,
they often degenerate into anarchy and confufion;
and from thence emerge again to good order and re-
gularity. For fince it is ordained by Providence that
there fhould be a continual ebb and flow in the things
of this world; as foon as they arrive at their utmoft
perfection, and can afcend no higher, they muft of
neceffity decline: and on the other hand, when they
have fallen, through any diforder, to the loweft degree that is poffible, and can fink no lower, they begin to rife again. And thus there is a conftant fucceffion of profperity and adverfity in all human affairs. Virtue is the mother of peace; peace pro-
duces idlenefs; idlenefs, contention and mifrule; and
from thence proceed ruin and confufion. This occafions reformation and better laws; good laws make
men virtuous; and public virtue is always attended
with glory and fuccefs. It has therefore been well
remarked, that arms are prior to letters, and that in
new States and governments there always have been
warriors and foldiers, before the rife of Scholars and
Philofophers. But the former being once fecurely
eftablifhed in their dominion by dint of arms, have
generally encouraged the ftudy of Letters, as an honourable relaxation in time of peace, and the moft
likely method to foften the ferocity of men inured to
war. And it is certain that indolence and effeminacy
cannot be introduced into any ftate in a more fpecious and dangerous difguife. Of which, Cato the
Cenfor feemed to be fo well apprized, that when he
faw the Roman youth eagerly liftening to the Lec-
tures and philofophical difcourfes of Diogenes and
Carneades, (who were fent Ambaffadors from Athens
to the Senate of Rome) and confidered the prejudice
which the Commonwealth might receive from fuffering

fering its subjects to employ themselves in those spe-
culative matters, he procured a law to be passed,
that no Philosopher should be permitted to come into
that city. These and other such causes sometimes
bring States to the brink of ruin: but when they are
at the lowest ebb, and grown wiser by their fall, they
frequently recover their strength, as we have already
said, by making new laws and institutions; unless
they are either totally overwhelmed, or prevented by
some forcible and extraordinary means.

Such were the Vicissitudes that Italy experienced;
first, under the dominion of the ancient Tuscans;
and then, under that of the Romans; sometimes
flourishing and powerful, and sometimes reduced to
misery and distress. And though no fabrick was afterwards erected upon the ruins of the Roman Empire, that could in anywise pretend to vie with it in
its ancient splendor, (which yet might have been effected by a brave and wise Prince) there arose such
a spirit, however, in some of the new States and cities that were founded upon those ruins, that if no
one of them usurped a Dominion over all the rest, they
neverthelefs were at first so well governed and united
amongst themselves, that they delivered their country
from the yoke of Barbarians, and defended it for a
while against any further invasions. Amongst these
States, the Florentines (notwithstanding their territory was of less extent) were not inferior to any other
either in power or authority: on the contrary, as they
were situated in the middle of Italy, exceeding opulent, and ready to turn their arms to any side, they
not only bravely supported such wars as were waged
against themselves, but generally threw the victory
into the scale of those allies with whom they thought
fit to confederate. From the warlike disposition of
these new States, it was not possible indeed that they
should long continue at peace together: but their
wars were not attended with much danger.' For as
those times cannot properly be called peaceable, when
they stood ready armed and watching all opportu-

nities

nities to attack each other; fo neither does that deferve the name of war, in which no men were killed,
no towns were facked, nor any State was fubverted :
their enterprizes being conducted in fo feeble a manner, that they were commenced without fear, carried
on without peril, and ended, for the moft part, without any material lofs on either fide. From whence
it came to pafs that all martial ardour, which in other
countries is fometimes damped and abated indeed by
a long interval of peace, was at laft utterly extinguifhed amongft the Italians, even in the midft of
wars; by the bafe and fpiritlefs manner in which they
were profecuted; as will plainly appear in the courfe
of thofe that happened betwixt the years 1434 and
1494: wherein we fhall fee a new inlet opened
to the incurfions of * Barbarians, and Italy once more
become fubject to their yoke. And though the actions of our Princes both at home and abroad during
this period, may not fill the reader with fo much admiration of their magnanimity, as the noble exploits
that were performed in ancient times; yet it may
occafion no lefs wonder, when he fees how many
brave people were bridled and kept in fubjection by
dint of arms fo weakly and pitifully conducted.
And if in the account of that corrupted age he
fhall find neither valour in the foldiers, nor fkill in
the commanders, † nor any love of their country

1434
1494.

---

* The Italians are pleafed to beftow this name, not only upon the
Goths and Vandals, and fuch other northern nations as are particularly mentioned in the beginning of the firft book of this hiftory,
but upon all Tramontanes, or people that live on the other fide of the
Alps. The French, Spaniards and Germans are here meant.
† Thefe *Condottieri*, or *pitiful Commanders*, as Machiavel juftly calls
them in the latter end of the firft book of this hiftory, were commonly either younger brothers and foldiers of fortune that had nothing to truft to but the profeffion of arms; or rebels and outlaws or
traitors, who having collected a parcel of Banditti in as defperate circumftances as themfelves, ufed to hire out their fervice, fometimes to
one State, and fometimes to another, (as beft fuited their own intereft) to fight their battles. So that their mafters were likely to be
finely ferved; as indeed they often were. For upon any little difguft, or offer of higher pay, they always deferted them and went over
to the enemy. They had at that time, as Machiavel fays, reduced

left

left in the Citizens, he may obferve however, what little fhifts and tricks, and low artifices, both the Princes and Commanders and governors of Commonwealths then made ufe of to maintain a reputation which they did not deferve. And this, perhaps, may be of equal utility with reading ancient hiftory : for as the great examples that occur in one will naturally infpire generous minds with a defire to imitate them ; fo the other may ferve to excite their abhorrence and difdain.

Italy therefore was reduced to fuch a condition by thofe who governed it, that a Peace was no fooner agreed to by the contending Princes, but it was prefently difturbed again by the foldiers who ftill continued in arms : fo that they neither gained any glory by their wars, nor tranquillity by a peace. Accordingly, after a peace was concluded betwixt the Duke of Milan and the League in the year 1433, the fol- *1433* diery being difcontented at it, refolved to turn their arms againft the Church. They were at that time divided into two parties, the Braccefcan and the Sfor-

---

their manner of making war to a fort of a trade or fyftem ; and thofe that employed them were fure to be lofers in the end, even if they were victorious : whilft their Condottieri always took care to fecure fome part at leaft of the bone in difpute for their own fhare, either by making themfelves arbitrators, or threatening upon one frivolous excufe or other, to go over to the enemy and leave their mafters difarmed. Thefe hirelings generally gave themfelves terrible names to infpire the enemy with fear, one calling himfelf Havock, another Hamftringer, and a third Fortebraccio or Strong-Arm, which laft has been adopted amongft the French under the name of Fierbras, and by the Englifh under that of Armftrong. They made but little account of Infantry in thofe times, and feldom ufed any artillery in their field engagements. They were afraid of lofing their men. For which reafon they endeavoured to bear down the enemy by the weight of their gens d' armes or heavy armed horfe, and did not often come to blows. Thofe that were driven out of the field were faid to be vanquifhed. There was more blood fhed in private quarrels and confpiracies than in battles. For as their horfemen were all covered with armour, it fometimes happened that not fo much as one man was killed on either fide, and fometimes not above two or three at the moft, in an engagement that lafted feveral hours ; and thofe too by being thrown from their horfes and trampled to death. This ftrange account of the military prowefs of that age, is however very far from fupporting what the Hiftorian juft before intimates refpecting the power, authority, and fpirit of the Florentines.

cefcan :

cefcan: Count Francifco Sforza being Head of the one, Niccolo Piccinino and Niccolo Fortebraccio the Chiefs of the other. To thefe two parties all the reft of, the foldiers in Italy then joined themfelves. But the Sforcefcan was in the greater credit, both on account of Francifco's valour, and the promife that the Duke of Milan had made of giving him his natural daughter Madonna Bianca in marriage; the profpect of which alliance gained him very great reputation. Both the parties, however, when they faw a peace concluded in Lombardy, immediately fell upon Pope Eugenius, though for different reafons. Fortebraccio did it in confequence of the ancient enmity that Braccio da Montone had ever profeffed againft the Popes; but the Count out of ambition alone. The former therefore bent his forces immediately againft Rome; and the latter poffeffed himfelf of la Marca d' Ancona: fo that the Romans in order to avoid a war, were obliged to force Eugenius out of the city, who made his efcape from the enemy with much difficulty and fled to Florence. Upon his arrival there, feeing the danger he was in, and that none of thofe States which had lately been fo forward to lay down their arms, now cared to take them up again merely to fupport his caufe, he came to an agreement with the Count and ceded the territory of la Marca to him; though the Count had not only feized upon it before without any manner of claim, but treated him with the utmoft infolence. For in the letters which he wrote to his correfpondents, he dated them in Latin (according to the cuftom of the Italians * *Ex Girifalco' noftro Firmiano, invito Petro & Paulo*; 'From Girifalco near Fermo, where I refide at prefent in fpite of St. Peter and St. Paul.' He was not content with this ceffion however, but infifted upon being created † Gonfalonier of the

* *Girifalco* or *Girfalco* in the Italian fignifies a fort of a Hawk called a Gerfalcon: but here I fuppofe it is the name of a place.

† The Gonfalonier or Standard-bearer of the Church was an officer created by the Popes to conduct their forces and protect them againft the Emperor, after they had ufurped his authority at Rome.

Church,

Church, which was likewife granted; as the Pope, it feems, prefered an ignominious peace to a dangerous war. Upon thefe compliances, the Count took part with his Holinefs and made war upon Fortebraccio with various fuccefs, for the fpace of feveral months, in the territories of the Church; but always with much prejudice to the Pope and his fubjects (which fide foever prevailed) and advantage to thofe that conducted the war. At laft, by the mediation of the Duke of Milan, a fort of truce was agreed to betwixt thofe two Chiefs; by which they both became mafters of feveral towns that belonged to the Church.

This war was hardly extinguifhed at Rome, when another was kindled in Romagna by Battifta Canneto; who having killed fome of the family of the Grifoni at Bologna, had driven the Pope's Governor, and fome others whom he fufpected to be his enemies, out of that city. And in order to keep forcible poffef- fion of it, he applied for aid to Duke Philip; whilft the Pope, on the other hand, follicited the affiftance of the Venetians and Florentines to enable him to recover it: and each party being furnifhed with fupplies, two powerful armies foon appeared in Romagna; the Duke's forces being commanded by Niccolo Piccinino, and thofe of the Venetians and Florentines by Gattamelata and Niccolo da Tolentino. Not far from Imola they came to an engagement, in which the Venetians and Florentines were defeated; and Niccolo da Tolentino being taken prifoner, was fent to the Duke at Milan, where he died in a few days after his arrival, either by poifon, or out of mortification at his difgrace. The Duke however, not purfuing his advantage, either becaufe his finances were too much exhaufted by the late wars, or that he thought the league would remain quiet after fuch an overthrow, gave the Pope and his confederates time to recover their fpirits in fuch a manner, that they appointed Count Sforza their General, in order to drive Fortebraccio out of the territories of the Church if poffible, and put an end to a war, which had

had been commenced in favour of his Holineſs. The Romans therefore ſeeing the Pope once more in the field with freſh recruits, endeavoured to make their peace with him ; which being effected, they ſubmitted to receive a commiſſary whom he ſent to Rome. Amongſt other places which Fortebraccio had ſeized upon, were Tivoli, Montefiaſconi, and the cities of Caſtello and Aſceſi ; into the latter of which he had retired when he found he was no longer able to keep the field. But being beſieged there by the Count for a long time, for he made a brave defence, the Duke began to perceive that it behoved him either to prevent the Allies from making themſelves maſ-ters of that place, or to provide for his own ſecu-rity, in caſe it ſhould fall into their hands. To make ſuch a diverſion therefore as might oblige the Count to raiſe the ſiege, he ordered Piccinino to force his way, if he could, through Romagna into Tuſcany: and the Allies judging it more neceſſary to defend Tuſcany, than to reduce Aſceſi, ſent inſtructions to the Count to oppoſe his paſſage through that pro-vince, though he had then advanced with his army as far as Furli. The Count, on the other hand, hav-ing raiſed the ſiege, marched with his forces directly to Ceſena, leaving the management of the war in la Marca, and the defence of his poſſeſſions to the care of his Brother Lione. But whilſt Piccinino was thus endeavouring to force a paſſage into Tuſcany, and the Count to prevent it, Fortebraccio boldly attacked Lione, and not only took him priſoner but diſperſed his army ; and, purſuing his victory with the ſame rapidity, took and plundered ſeveral towns in la Marca : at which the Count was not a little cha-grined, as he thought he ſhould now loſe all he had ſo lately acquired. Upon which account, he left part of his army to hold Piccinino at bay, and advanced with the reſt againſt Fortebraccio, whom he brought to an engagement ; in which the latter being routed and taken priſoner, died not long after of the wounds he had received in the battle. By this Victory the

Pope

Pope regained all the territories that Fortebraccio had taken from him, and forced the Duke of Milan to fue for a peace, which was at laft concluded by the meditation of Niccolo d' Efti Marquis of Ferrara: and it was agreed that all the towns that had been feized upon by the Duke in Romagna, fhould be reftored to the Church, and his forces withdrawn into Lombardy. Thefe conditions being complied with, Battifta da Canneto, not being able to maintain himfelf in poffeffion of Bologna by his own ftrength (as it generally happens to thofe that depend upon the power of others to fupport them in their ufurpations) was forced to fly from thence and leave the city open to Antonio Bentivogli, the former Governor, who immediately returned thither.

Thefe things happened during the exile of Cofimo de' Medici; at whofe return, thofe Citizens that had been his chief friends, and fome others who had been injured and oppreffed by the late Adminiftration, were determined, at all events, to take the government of the State into their own hands. The Signiory therefore, that was drawn for the two enfuing months of November and December, not content with what their predeceffors had already done in favour of their party, prolonged the term, and changed the refidence of feveral that had been banifhed, and fent numbers of others into exile. And this was done, not only out of party rage, but likewife on account of their riches, alliances, and private connexions: fo that this profcription, except in the article of blood fhed, might in fome meafure be compared to that under Sylla and Octavius. There were, however, fome executions; for Antonio the fon of Bernardo Guadagni, was beheaded: and four other Citizens, amongft whom were Zanobi Belfratelli and Cofimo Barbadori, having left the place to which they had been banifhed, and gone to refide at Venice, were fecured by the Venetians as fetting a greater value upon Cofimo's friendfhip than their own reputation, and fent prifoners to Florence, where they

were

were put to death in an ignominious manner. These examples greatly increased the strength of Cosimo's party, and struck a terror into that of his enemies, when they saw such a powerful Republic as Venice so meanly prostitute its honour to the Florentines: though some thought this was not done so much to oblige Cosimo, as to revive the spirit of faction, and create more dangerous divisions in Florence by such executions; as the Venetians plainly saw, that peace and union in that city, was the only obstacle to their further aggrandizement. When they had thus pretty well cleared the City of their enemies, and such as they thought disaffected to their government, they began to strengthen their hands, by caressing and heaping favours upon others. For this purpose, they recalled the family of the Alberti, and all the rest of the Exiles that had been formerly banished: they reduced the Grandees (except some very few) to the rank of Commoners: and divided the possessions of those whom they had banished, amongst themselves. After this, they fortified themselves with new laws and ordinances, and made a fresh Imborsation, taking the names of all suspected persons out of the purses, and filling them up again with those of their own friends. But remembering the supineness and neglect that had been so fatal to the late administration, and considering that even such an Imborsation as they had already made, might not be sufficient to establish them firmly in the government, they likewise took care, that such magistrates as had the power of life and death entrusted to them, should always be chosen out of the most eminent of their party; for which purpose, they ordained that the Syndics who inspected the Imborsations, in conjunction with the old Signiory, should have the power of appointing a new one. They left the cognizance of capital offences, to the eight Wardens, and enacted, that no Exile should return, even after the term of his banishment was expired, till he had obtained the consent of the Signiory, and thirty-four of the Colleges, though the
whole

whole number of them amounted to no more than thirty-feven. All perfons were prohibited to write to or receive any letters from them ; every word, or fign, or gefture, that difpleafed the governors, was punifhed with the utmoft feverity : and if there was any fufpected perfon left in Florence, who had not fallen under their lafh for fuch offences, they took care, however, to load him feverely with new taxes and impofitions : fo that one part of their adverfaries being driven out of the City, and the other depreffed and over-awed by thefe means, they in a fhort time fecured the government to themfelves. And to fupport their power with foreign aid, and deprive their enemies of all affiftance, if they fhould offer to difturb them, they entered into a defenfive league with the Pope, the Venetians, and the Duke of Milan.

Whilft things were in this fituation at Florence, Giovanna Queen of Naples and Sicily died, and by her laft will, declared Regnier, Duke of Anjou, her fucceffor. Alphonfo, King of Arragon, was at that time in Sicily, and had fuch an intereft with the Nobility there, that he was taking meafures to make himfelf fovereign of that Ifland. The Neapolitans in general, and many of the Nobles in particular, adhered to Regnier : the Pope, on the other hand, was not willing that either Regnier or Alphonfo fhould become mafter of it, as he wanted to get poffeffion of it himfelf and to govern it by a Lieutenant. But Alphonfo making a fudden defcent upon the coaft of Naples, was received there by the Duke of Seffa, and took the forces of feveral other Princes into his pay ; with a defign (as Capua was already in his poffeffion, and governed by the Prince of Taranto, in his name) to compel the Neapolitans to fubmit to him : for which purpofe, he ordered his fleet to make an attack upon Gaieta, which was then in their hands. Upon this, the Neapolitans fent to defire the affiftance of Duke Philip : but he recommended them to the protection of the Genoefe, who, (in fubmiffion

7   to

to the commands of the Duke their fovereign, and in hopes of fecuring the great quantity of merchandize which they had lodged at that time in Naples and Gaieta) immediately fitted out a powerful fquadron for their relief. Alphonfo hearing of this armament, thought proper to reinforce his own, and went to Sea with it in perfon, with a refolution to fight the Genoefe; and the two fleets happening to meet near the Ifle of Ponzio, came to an engagement, in which the Arragonefe were not only defeated, but Alphonfo himfelf, and many other Princes that attended him, were taken, and fent Prifoners by the Genoefe to the Duke. This victory ftruck a panick into the Princes of Italy (who before were under great apprehenfions of the Duke's power) as they thought he had now a very fair opportunity of making himfelf abfolute fovereign over them all. But, contrary to the expectation of every one, he took a very different refolution.

Alphonfo was a Prince of great wifdom and addrefs, and as foon as he had an opportunity of a private converfation with Duke Philip, he reprefented to him, " how little he confulted his own intereft, in fupporting his competitor Regnier: for if Regnier fhould become King of Naples, he would certainly endeavour (he faid) to make the Duchy of Milan a Province to the King of France; that fo he might have a fpeedy recourfe to him, and a door ready opened for fuccours upon any emergency; which could not be effected without introducing the French into that Duchy, to the utter deftruction of it. That for his own part, he thought the cafe would be very different, if he himfelf fhould fucceed to the crown of Naples and Sicily: for as he fhould not be afraid of any enemy but the French, he muft of neceffity be obliged to court and carefs, and fhew the moft profound obedience to thofe who only had it in their power to fuffer his enemies to invade him. That the name and title of King of Naples would then indeed devolve to Alphonfo, but the power and authority to

Philip

Philip Duke of Milan. So that it behoved the Duke much more than himself, to confider the danger of proceeding in that manner, and the advantages that might refult from a contrary refolution; unlefs he chofe rather to give way to his paffions than to fecure his State. For in one cafe he would continue free and independant; but in the other, (as his dominions lay betwixt two powerful Princes) he muft either entirely lofe his Duchy, or live in perpetual apprehenfion and flavifh fubjection to them both." Thefe remonftrances made fuch an impreffion upon the Duke, that he changed his refolution, and not only fet Alphonfo at liberty, but fent him in an honourable manner to Genoa, and afterwards to Naples; from whence he went to Gaieta, which city had been feized upon by fome Lords of his party, as foon as they heard that he was releafed. But the Genoefe feeing the Duke had thus fet him at liberty, without any regard to them, and not only reaped all the glory of a war, which had been carried on folely at their rifque and expence, but had the merit of releafing him, and left them to his refentment for having defeated and taken him prifoner, were exceedingly enraged at it.

In the city of Genoa, when it has the full enjoyment of its liberty, a chief Magiftrate is chofen by the free fuffrages of the people, whom they call the Doge; not invefted with the power of an abfolute Prince, nor to determine upon any thing himfelf, but only to propofe fuch matters as are to be debated and confidered in council. The Nobility, however, were fo powerful in this city, that they ftood in very little awe of the Magiftrates: and amongft them, the two families of Fregofo and Adorna, were at that time the moft eminent. From hence it came to pafs, that there were frequent divifions, and but little civil order obferved amongft them; and as their contefts for power were oftner decided by arms than the laws, fometimes one party was depreffed, and fometimes the other. Sometimes it happened, that thofe who had been excluded from a fhare in the government,

called in foreign Princes to their affiftance, and facri-
ficed the State to ftrangers, when they could not ufurp
it themfelves.   From hence it likewife generally happened, that thofe who were mafters of Lombardy,
had alfo the command of Genoa; as Duke Philip had
at the time when Alphonfo of Arragon was taken
prifoner.   One of the Nobles that were the chief inftruments in fubjecting that city to the Duke of Milan, was Francifco Spinola; who, not long after he
had been the caufe of enflaving his country, became
fufpected (as it often happens in fuch cafes) and very
odious to Philip *.   Upon which, he was fo difgufted, that he retired to Gaieta, as a voluntary exile,
where he was when the engagement happened betwixt
Alphonfo's fleet and that of the Genoefe; and having behaved with great bravery in their fervice upon
that occafion, he thought he had fo far regained the
Duke's favour by it, that he fhould at leaft be fuffered
to live quietly at Genoa, as a reward for his merit.
But perceiving that the Duke ftill looked upon him
with a fufpicious eye, and feemed to think that a man
who had betrayed his country, could never be faithful to any one elfe, he refolved to make an attempt
to reftore Genoa to its former liberty, and to retrieve
his own reputation, that fo he might hereafter live in
fecurity at home; as he found there was no other
way left to make his peace with his Fellow-citizens,
but by healing the wound which he himfelf had given
them.   Seeing therefore, the univerfal indignation
which the releafe of Alphonfo had excited againft
the Duke, he thought it a very opportune conjuncture to proceed to the execution of his defigns.   For
which purpofe, he communicated the matter to fome

---

* It feldom happens that they who raife either a ufurper or a lawful Prince to the throne, enjoy his favour long.   This, however, is
not always owing to the maxim, "that men love treafon but hate
traitors;" nor becaufe men imagine, that they who laboured to dethrone their firft mafter, will not fcruple to dethrone their new fovereign.   It is chiefly becaufe thefe men think they are never rewarded as they deferve; and that a Prince who owes his crown to
them, ought to grant them whatever they requeft of him.

of

of his friends, who, he knew were equally impatient to regain their liberty, and earneftly exhorted them to affift him in the attempt. Accordingly, on the Feftival of St. John the Baptift, as foon as Arifmino, their new Governor for the Duke, had made his entry into the city, attended by Opicino the former Governor, and many of the Citizens, Spinola without further delay, rufhed out of his houfe with his confederates ready armed, and having drawn them up in the ftreet before his door, cried out, Liberty, Liberty. At this found, the people ran together with fuch eagernefs, that thofe who adhered to the Duke, either out of felf-intereft or fome other motive, were not only unprepared to make any refiftance, but hardly had time to run away. Arifmino and fome of the Citizens that were of his party, retired into the citadel, which was garrifoned by the Duke's foldiers. But Opicino endeavouring to get to the Palace, where he thought he fhould be able to fecure himfelf, and animate his friends to make a vigorous defence (as there were two thoufand foldiers in it under his command) was flain before he could reach it, and torn limb from limb by the populace, after they had dragged his body through every ftreet in the city. The citadel and other forts that were in the Duke's poffeffion, likewife furrendering in a few days, the Genoefe in this manner recovered their liberty and entirely fhook off his yoke.

The Princes of Italy, who fometime before had been under great apprehenfions that the Duke would grow too powerful for them all, began to hope they fhould be able to make a ftand againft him when they faw things take this turn; and the Florentines and Venetians, notwithftanding the league they had fo lately made with him, now entered into a confederacy with the Genoefe. Rinaldo degli Albizi therefore, and feveral others of the greateft diftinction amongft the Florentine Exiles, feeing the face of affairs fo changed, and further difturbances likely to enfue, did not defpair of prevailing with the Duke

X 2   to

to come to an open rupture with the Florentines; and for that purpofe, they went to wait upon him at Milan, where Rinaldo addreffed him in the following manner: " Neither your Highnefs, nor any other perfon, who confiders the coufe of human affairs and the mutability of fortune, will think it ftrange that we, who formerly have been your enemies, fhould now have the confidence to follicit your affiftance to reftore us to our Country; efpecially as we truft we can give a fatisfactory account of our paft actions to yourfelf, and prefent conduct to our fellowcitizens. No reafonable man will ever reproach another with defending his Country, by any means whatfoever; and in fo doing, it never was our defire or intention to do you the leaft injury, but merely to fecure ourfelves. For the truth of this, we appeal to yourfelf; as you muft very well remember, that in our higheft career of victory and fuccefs, whenever we found you fincerely difpofed to peace, we have promoted it with ftill greater ardour than you did: fo that we cannot accufe ourfelves of ever having done any thing that might give us reafon to doubt of your Highnefs's favour and protection; nor can our Country with juftice complain of us, for now inciting you to take up thofe arms againft it, which we have often fo vigoroufly exerted in its defence. For that State alone can duly claim the reverence and love of its fubjects, which equally beftows its favours upon them all: and not that, which fmiles only upon fome few minions, and frowns upon all the reft. Nobody, furely, will affirm, that it is unlawful in all cafes to bear arms againft one's Country: for every State, being of a compound nature, in fome meafure refembles the human body; and as one is fubject to feveral difeafes, which cannot effectually be cured without cauftics and amputation; fo, in the other, many diforders and inconveniencies arife, which if a good and dutiful Citizen did not endeavour to remedy, even by the fword, if neceffary, he would become highly culpable. What greater mi-

mifery then can there be in any Republic, than flavery? What remedy more expedient than that which
will certainly put an end to it? Thofe wars are always efteemed juft that are neceffary; and it is but
charity to our Country to take up arms, when there
is no other hope of redrefs for the injuries it fuftains.
For my own part, I know not what neceffity can be
more preffing than ours, nor any higher degree of
charity, than to refcue our Country out of the jaws
of flavery. Without doubt, we have a moft juft
caufe, and very well worthy of being maturely confidered and attended to by your Highnefs, as well as
ourfelves; and you, likewife, will be fully juftified
in making war upon the Florentines, by their fhamelefs behaviour in confederating with your rebellious
fubjects the Genoefe, in open violation of the folemn
engagements into which they have fo lately entered
with your Highnefs. But if our fufferings are not
fufficiently grievous to move pity, certainly the in-
dignities that have been offered to yourfelf fhould
excite your refentment, and prompt you to take a juft
revenge; efpecially, fince it is fo eafy to be effected.
Let not the remembrance of paft times difcourage
you, in which you have feen them defend themfelves
with fo much vigour and obftinacy: though indeed,
if their courage was now equal to what it was formerly, it would be much to be dreaded. But the
cafe is far otherwife at prefent; for what ftrength
can you expect in a city that has expelled the richeft
and moft induftrious of its inhabitants? What refolution in a people diftracted with frefh broils and
quarrels amongft themfelves, which will naturally prevent the little money they have left from being applied as it ufed to be? For men chearfully open their
purfes, when they fee it is for the reputation and fecurity of their Country, in hopes of regaining that
by an honourable peace, which they have expended
in fupporting a neceffary war: but with great reluctance, when they find themfelves equally oppreffed,
both in war and peace, and are plundered by the out-

X 3

rages of an enemy in one, and the rapacity of their
Governors in the other. It is certain, that the avarice of Governors is of much greater prejudice to any
State, than the depredations of its enemies: as the
latter, it may be hoped, will ceafe in time; but of
the former there feldom is any end. You formerly
waged war againſt the whole Republic; but now
againſt a very inconfiderable remnant of it: you then
had great numbers of good and worthy Citizens to
oppofe you; but at prefent very few, and thofe bad
men: you came at that time to deprive our City of
its liberties, but now to reſtore them: and furely,
from fuch a contrariety of circumſtances, you may
well hope for a very different event; nay, you may
certainly depend upon fuccefs. We leave your Highnefs to judge of the advantage you will reap from it,
in ſtrengthening your hands by a ſtrict alliance with
the Tuſcans, whom you will firmly attach to your
intereſt, by the merit of fo great a deliverance; an
alliance from which you may avail yourfelf of more
effectual fupplies in any future undertaking, than
even from Milan itfelf: and though fuch an enterprize, at another time, might have been imputed to
injuſtice or ambition, it will now be regarded as equitable and compaffionate. Permit us, therefore, to
exhort your Highnefs, not to let fo fair an opportunity flip away, but to confider, that although your
former attempts againſt that State were attended with
great difficulty, expence, and diſhonour, you may
eafily fucceed in this, and gain infinite reputation and
advantage."

The Duke did not require much follicitation to
induce him to make war upon the Florentines, as he
entertained an hereditary hatred to them, and was
prompted to it by the blindnefs of his ambition, which
governed him in all his actions: befides, he was not a
little provoked at their confederacy with the Genoefe.
But when he confidered the vaſt expences he had
been at, the rifque he had run, the loffes he had fo
lately fuſtained, and the vain and ill-grounded hopes
of

of the exiles, his ardour was something abated. However, as foon as he heard of the revolt of Genoa, he
ordered Niccolo Piccinino to advance towards that
City with all his Cavalry, and what infantry he could
raife in his own territories, to try if it was poffible to
recover it, before the Citizens had eftablifhed any new
government, and made neceffary provifions for their
defence; as he depended much upon the ftrength of
the Citadel, which he thought was ftill maintained by
his garrifon. And though Piccinino not only drove
fome of the Genoefe up into the mountains, but took
the Vale of Ponzeveri from them, where they had
fortified themfelves, and forced them into that town,
yet they defended it fo obftinately, that he could
make no further progrefs, and was obliged to draw
off again with his forces. Upon which, the Duke,
at the inftigation of the Florentine Exiles, fent him
inftructions to make an incurfion towards the Sea-
coaft near Leghorn, and harrafs the confines of Pifa,
as much as poffible; imagining he fhould be better
able to judge from the fuccefs of thefe expeditions,
what courfe it would be moft proper to take next.
In confequence of this, Piccinino made an affault
upon Serezana and took it; and after he had committed great ravages thereabout, in order to alarm
the Florentines ftill more, he proceeded towards
Lucca, giving out that he would march into the
Kingdom of Naples to the affiftance of the King of
Arragon. In the beginning of thefe new commotions
Pope Eugenius left Florence and went to Bologna,
where he endeavoured to bring about an accommodation betwixt the League and the Duke, to whom
he caufed it to be fignified, that if he did not confent
to it, he fhould be obliged to give Count Francifco
Sforza leave to go into their fervice, who was then
his General and Ally. And though his Holinefs took
great pains in the matter, it was to no purpofe: for
the Duke would not liften to any agreement, except
Genoa was reftored to him; and the League infifted
that it fhould continue in the enjoyment of its liber-

ties:

ties : fo that all hopes of peace being at an end, both fides prepared for war. Upon the arrival of Piccinino at Lucca, the Florentines beginning to be apprehenfive of new difturbances from that quarter, ordered Neri di Gino to march directly with their forces to cover the Country about Pifa, where he was joined by Count Sforza, according to the Pope's directions, and both of them took poft at Santa Gonda. On the other hand, Piccinino, who lay at Lucca, fent to demand a paffage through that Country into the Kingdom of Naples; which being refufed, he threatened to force one.

The ftrength of the two armies, and the abilities of the commanders were nearly the fame : fo that neither fide being very defirous to come to an engagement, efpecially in the depth of winter, (as it was then December) they lay many days in their quarters, without proceeding to further hoftilities. The firft that moved was Piccinino, who being informed, that if he made an affault upon the town of Pifano, he might eafily carry it. But failing in that, he laid wafte all the adjacent Country, and not only took St. Giovanni alla Vena, but plundered it and burnt it down to the ground. The fuccefs of this enterprize (though he failed in his main defign) determined him to attempt fomething further; efpecially when he faw that neither Gini, nor the Count ftirred out of their quarters to oppofe him. He therefore made an attack upon St. Maria in Caftello and Filetto, and took them both. Yet even this did not provoke the Count to put himfelf in motion; though he was not afraid to face the enemy; but becaufe the Government of Florence had not yet fully refolved to declare war, out of reverence to the Pope, who was ftill negociating a peace. But this manner of proceeding, which was the effect of moderation and prudence in the Florentines, being imputed to pufillanimity by the enemy, fo elated them that they marched forward and fat down with all their forces before Barga, This new provocation, how-

however, determined the Florentines to lay afide all
refpect, and not only to relieve Barga if poffible, but
to invade the territories of the Lucchefe. For
which purpofe, the Count advancing directly towards Piccinino, engaged and routed his army, almoft under the walls of that town, and forced him to
raife the fiege. In the mean time, the Venetians
perceiving the Duke had broken his engagements
with them, fent Francifco da Gonzaga, their commander in chief, to Ghiaradadda, who made fuch
devaftation in the Duke's territories, that he was
forced to recall Piccinino out of Tufcany. This
retreat, and the advantage which the Florentines had
lately gained over him, encouraged them to make an
attempt upon Lucca, and not without great hopes
of reducing that city; in which expedition they proceeded without either fear or ceremony, as they faw
the Duke, who was the only perfon that could inter-
rupt their defigns, was likely to be fufficiently employed by the Venetians; and the Lucchefe could
not with any face complain of hoftilities being commenced againft them by a people whofe enemies they
had received into their bofom, and giving them an
opportunity of invading their dominions. In the beginning of April therefore 1437, the Count put his
army in motion again: but being defirous of recovering what the Florentines had loft, before he invaded others, he firft retook St. Maria in Caftello,
and all their other towns which Piccinino had made
himfelf mafter of: and then directing his march towards the territories of the Lucchefe, he laid fiege to
Camajore, the inhabitants of which, though very
well affected to their mafters, being terrified at the
fudden arrival of the enemy before their gates, forgot their loyalty, and furrendered to the Count.
With the fame facility he reduced Maffa and Serezana, before the end of May; and then carried his
arms into the confines of Lucca, where he laid wafte
all their corn-fields, burnt the Villages, cut up their
Vines and fruit trees, drove away their Cattle, and

spared

ſpared nothing that his ſoldiers could lay their hands on. The Lucccheſe on the other hand, ſeeing themſelves abandoned by the Duke, and in no condition to defend their Country, retired into the city, which they fortified with redoubts and other works in ſuch a manner, that they were not without hopes of defending it for ſome time; eſpecially as they had a ſtrong garriſon within the walls, and remembered how often the Florentines had miſcarried in their former attempts upon it. The only thing they had to fear, was the baſeneſs and irreſolution of the common people, who being wearied out with a ſiege, would moſt likely prefer their own private ſafety to the liberty of the public, and force them to ſome ignominious capitulation. To encourage them therefore to make a reſolute defence, one of the oldeſt and moſt experienced of the Citizens, having called them together in the great Piazza, harangued them in the following manner:

" Ye need not be told, fellow-citizens, that whatſoever is the effect of neceſſity, deſerves neither cenſure nor applauſe. So that if ye ſhould accuſe us as the occaſion of a war which the Florentines have now commenced againſt our State, by admitting the Duke's forces into this city, and giving them a more convenient opportunity of invading their dominions, ye certainly do us much wrong; ſince ye muſt all but too well remember the many attempts they have formerly made upon us, which have not been owing to any injuries that we have done them, or any juſt apprehenſions from us on their ſide, but to our weakneſs and their ambition; both which, from time to time, have continually incited them to conſpire our ruin. Let us not flatter ourſelves therefore, that any merit on our part will ever divert them from their purpoſes, or any offence that we may give, can more fully determine them in ſuch a reſolution: and ſince it is their deſire to deprive us of our liberty, let it be our endeavour manfully to defend it. We have ſufficient cauſe indeed to lament, but not to be ſurprized,

at

7

at their prefent manner of proceeding : for how is it
poffible to fupprefs our grief, when we fee our country invaded, our towns taken from us, our houfes
burnt, and our fields laid wafte ? but can any man
be fimple enough to wonder at it, when he confiders
that we fhould treat them in the fame manner, and
perhaps worfe if it was in our power ? And though
the arrival of Piccinino amongft us has furnifhed
them with a pretence to begin this war upon us, yet
they would certainly have found-out fome other, if he
had not come hither : the evil might have been deferred for a while, but it would in that cafe very likely
have fallen fo much the heavier upon us at laft. So
that we ought not, in reality, to impute thefe misfortunes to his coming, but to our own evil deftiny and
the ambition of our enemies : for we could neither
refufe admittance to the Duke's forces, nor reftrain
them from committing hoftilities when they were here.
Every one muft needs know that we cannot poffibly
fupport ourfelves without the aid of fome powerful
Prince; and that no one is either more able or more
willing to defend us than the Duke. As he reftored
our liberty when it was loft, we may reafonably hope
he will ftill maintain us in it; efpecially againft enemies fo implacable, that he himfelf has always looked
upon them with abhorrence. If then we had offended
him for fear of difobliging the Florentines, we fhould
have loft a firm friend, and made our enemy ftill more
powerful and ready to attack us. 'It is furely therefore much more eligible to be at war with them, under his protection, than to incur his difpleafure by
patching up a peace ; as we may depend upon it he
will deliver us out of thofe dangers to which he has
expofed us, provided we are not wanting to ourfelves.
Ye very well remember with what a degree of inveteracy the Florentines have often invaded us, and
with how much reputation we have always defended
ourfelves, even when we had no other hope but in
God, and in time; both which have hitherto conftantly preferved us. And fince we were enabled to
do

do fo in thofe exigencies, why fhould we defpair of
it at prefent? At that time we were left to their mercy
by all the States of Italy, but now the Duke efpoufes
our caufe, and we have good reafon to hope the Venetians will not be very forward to annoy us; as they
look with a jealous eye upon the growing power of
our enemies. When the Florentines attacked us before, they were not fo much embarraffed in their affairs as they are now; they had alfo greater depend-
ance upon foreign affiftance, and were more powerful
themfelves: on the contrary, we were every way
much weaker than we are at prefent: for we then
were obliged to defend a Tyrant; but now we fight
for ourfelves: at that time he reaped the glory of
defending us; but now the reputation is our own:
the enemy was then united and entire, but now fo
divided and difmembered, that every part of Italy
fwarms with their Exiles. But if we had none of
thefe motives to animate us, certainly we ought to
exert our utmoft efforts to defend ourfelves in fuch a
conjuncture as this. Every enemy indeed ought to
be juftly dreaded by us, as they are all ready to take
advantage of our weaknefs to aggrandize themfelves
with our fpoils; but the domination of the Florentines is much more to be feared than that of any
other people. Tribute and obedience, and the government of our city will not content them; they
will feize upon our very perfons and houfes, to fatiate
their cruelty with our blood, and their avarice with
our poffeffions: fo that it behoves every one of us, of
what rank or condition foever, to guard againft them
above all others. Let us not defpair however, tho'
we fee our Country laid wafte, our towns reduced to
afhes, and our lands in the hands of the enemy; for
if we can fave our city, thofe of neceffity muft return into our poffeffion; but if we lofe that, it will
avail us nothing to preferve the other: if we maintain our liberty, they will hardly be able to continue
mafters of our eftates; but if we are to be flaves, it
fignifies but little what becomes of them. Let us
take

take arms then, and in the day of battle, let every man remember that he is fighting not only for his country, but for the prefervation of his wife and children and private fortune."

The latter part of this fpeech excited fuch a fpirit in the people, that they unanimoufly promifed to fhed the laft drop of their blood, rather than fail in the duty they owed to their Country, or liften to a peace, that fhould be in any wife prejudicial to their liberty; and immediately began to make all neceffary preparations for the defence of the City.

In the mean time the Florentine army was not inactive: for after they had committed great devaftation in the adjacent country, they took poffeffion of Monte Carlo by capitulation, and then laid fiege to Uzzano, in order to diftrefs the Lucchefe on every fide in fuch a manner, that when there was no hope of relief from any quarter, they might be compelled by famine to fubmit to them. The Citadel however, was very ftrong and had a numerous garrifon in it, fo that it did not prove fo eafy a matter to reduce it as the reft. The Lucchefe feeing they were thus ftraitened, had recourfe to Duke Philip (as might well be expected) and recommended themfelves to his protection in the moft preffing terms; fometimes reminding him of their paft fervices, fometimes of the infults he himfelf had received from the Florentines, and fometimes reprefenting to him " how much it would animate his other allies, when they faw him thus ready to interpofe in their defence: and on the other hand, how greatly it muft difcourage them, if they fhould be left to the mercy of their enemies. That in cafe they fhould lofe their lives or liberties, he would alfo lofe his friends and his reputation at the fame time, as well as the confidence of all others who fhould at any time expofe themfelves to the like dangers to ferve him. To thefe remonftrances they added tears and entreaties befeeching him to have compaffion on them at leaft, if he had no remembrance of former obligations." The Duke therefore,

not

not only confidering the late merit of the Lucchefe,
and the ancient enmity of the Florentines to him, but
being likewife very defirous to prevent them from
growing ftill more powerful by frefh acquifitions, refolved either to fend a confiderable army into Tufcany, or to make a vigorous war upon the Venetians;
that fo the former might be neceffitated to abandon
their prefent enterprize, in order to march to their affiftance. As foon as the Florentines had intelligence of this
refolution, they began to grow fick of their undertaking; and therefore, to find him fufficient employment at home, they earneftly follicited the Venetians
to fall upon him with all their forces in Lombardy.
But the Venetians being daunted at the defertion of
the Marquis of Mantua, who had quitted their
fervice and gone into the Duke's; and feeing themfelves in a manner difarmed thereby, made anfwer,
" that they were fo far from being able to become
principals in the war, that they could not take any
fhare at all in it, except they would fpare them Count
Sforza to command their army; and upon condition
too, that he fhould be obliged to pafs the Po with
it in perfon: otherwife, they would not embark in
the war (notwithftanding any former engagements)
fince they could neither carry it on without a General, nor hope for fuccefs from the conduct of any
one but the Count; nor even from his, unlefs he
would engage to ferve them with equal vigour and
fidelity in all parts." The Florentines faw very
plainly that it was neceffary to make a powerful di-
verfion in Lombardy; but confidered that if they
parted with the Count, their enterprize againft Lucca
muft fall to the ground: and they were likewife
aware that the Venetians made that demand, not out
of any real occafion they had for him, but to prevent them from becoming mafters of that State.
On the other hand, the Count did not refufe to go
into Lombardy to ferve the Confederates there, but
was refolved not to violate the obligation he lay under not to pafs the Po; for fear of forfeiting the advantages

vantages he expected from his promised alliance with
the Duke.   So that betwixt the defire of reducing
Lucca, and the apprehenfion of being embroiled in
a war with the Duke, the Florentines were in no
little perplexity.   But fear at laft prevailing over ambition, as it generally happens, they confented that
the Count, after he had taken Uzzano, fhould march
into Lombardy.   There ftill remained another difficulty however, which feemed much harder to be fur-
mounted, and gave them more trouble and vexation
than the former.   For the Count would not be obliged
to pafs the Po; and the Venetians would not take
him into their pay upon any other conditions.   But
as there was no way to accommodate thefe differences,
without making fome conceffions on one fide or the
other, the Florentines prevailed upon the Count to
promife them in a letter to the Signiory, that he
would pafs that river; telling him, that a private
promife could not diffolve a public engagement, and
that he would be under no neceffity of obferving it:
from whence they fhould gain this advantage, that
when the Venetians had once begun a war, they
would be obliged to perfecute it; which perhaps
might divert the ftorm they were then threatened
with themfelves.   On the other hand, they reprefented to the Venetians, "that as fuch a letter was
fufficiently binding, they ought to be fatisfied with
it:' that it was but reafonable to fkreen the Count, as
much as they could, out of regard to the expectations
he might have from his future father-in-law: and
that it was both their intereft and his, not to divulge
the letter without a manifeft occafion."   The Venetians appearing fatisfied with this expedient, it was
accordingly determined to fend the Count into Lombardy; who having taken Uzzano, and thrown up
fome works round Lucca to keep it ftill blocked up,
recommended the fuperintendance of that war to
Commiffaries, and paffing the * Apennines advanced

---

* The original fays, *paffo l' Alpi*, he paffed the Alps.   But it is
plain, the Apennines are here, meant.   And though the word Alps

to Reggio. But the Venetians fufpecting his fincerity, and defirous to difcover his real intentions, fent him orders thither to pafs the Po immediately and join their forces: which being peremptorily refufed by the Count, much ill language paffed betwixt him and Andrea Mauroceno, who brought him thofe orders, each upbraiding the other with pride and infincerity: fo that after much altercation, one infifting that he was not obliged to pafs the River, and the other protefting he fhould receive no pay if he did not, the Count returned into Tufcany, and Mauroceno to Venice.

After this, the Count encamped in the territories of Pifa, by an order from the Florentines, who expected he would ftill have conducted the war againft the Lucchefe; but in that they were difappointed. For the Duke being informed, that he had refufed to pafs the Po, out of refpect to him, began to entertain fome hopes that he might preferve Lucca by his mediation, and therefore defired him to ufe his endeavours to make a peace betwixt the Lucchefe

is generally appropriated, by way of eminence, to that vaft ridge of mountains which divides Italy from France, Germany, and Switzerland, yet the Latin, Greek, and Italian writers (and Machiavel in particular) very often apply it to other mountains, and in both numbers. The French ufe it only in the plural. The fingular is chiefly found amongft the poets. And indeed it fignifies any high mountain. Antonini fays, " *Alpe* fignifica in generale ogni altiffima montagna, come in Greco e in Latino; i Francefi non l'hanno in quefto fentimento: particolarmente fignifica quella che fafcia l'Italia da tramontana. Gl'Italiani l' ufano nel fingolare e nel plurale; come, *di neve in Alpe fenza vento; e, giafu l' Alpi neva d'ogni intorno.*" The Englifh ufe it in the fame manner. Milton makes his Sampfon Agoniftes fay, l. 628.

" No breath of vernal air from fnowy Alp."

Which muft be meant of the mountains of Paleftine; as it could not without great impropriety be fpoken of any other, efpecially of thofe in Italy: For what breath of vernal air could he expect from mountains that were at the diftance of fo many hundred leagues from him; if indeed he conld be fuppofed to know there were any fuch in being? The Appennines run the whole length of Italy, from the north weft to the fouth-eaft, and may, perhaps, be deemed a ramification of thofe mountains that are particularly called the Alps. They lay directly in the Count's way from Lucca into Lombardy, whither he could not poffibly get without paffing them, and are at a great diftance from the other.

and

and the Florentines, and get him included in it if poffible; ftill buoying him up with the promife of his
daughter in marriage at a more convenient opportunity: which made no flight impreffion upon the
Count, who was in hopes, that by fuch an alliance,
he might likewife fometime or other become Lord of
Milan, as the Duke had no fons. He therefore ufed
all means to prevent the Florentines from profecuting
the war, protefting that, for his own part, he would
not give himfelf any further concern about it, except
the Venetians would firft pay him the arrears that were
due to him, and fulfil their other engagements: for
that the payment of his arrears alone, was not fufficient to maintain him in the quiet poffeffion of his
State, without fome other fupport befides that of the
Florentines. So that if he was abandoned by the Venetians, he muft do as well as he could for himfelf;
hinting, at the fame time, that he would go over to
the Duke.

The cavils and double dealings exceedingly chagrined the Florentines, who faw that they muft
not only give up all thoughts of making themfelves
mafters of Lucca, but provide for the fafety of their
own dominions, which would be in great danger if the
Duke and the Count fhould join forces againft them.
They fent Cofimo de' Medici, therefore, to Venice,
in hopes that a man of his reputation would be able
to prevail upon the Venetians to perform their engagements with the Count. But after the affair had
been thoroughly difcuffed in the Senate, and he had
reprefented to them at large the ftate of affairs in Italy
at that time, the greatnefs of the Duke's power, the
reputation of his arms, and fhewed them, that if he
was reinforced by the Count, they would be driven
back again to the Sea, and the Florentines in the utmoft danger of lofing their liberties; the Venetians
made anfwer, " That they knew their own ftrength,
and that of the other Italian States, and trufted they
fhould be able to defend themfelves upon occafion.
That it was not the cuftom of their Republic to pay

foldiers who fought for others; and therefore, they thought the Florentines ought to pay the Count, as they had employed him. That in order to enjoy their dominions with fecurity, it was more neceffary to humble his pride, than to fupport it by penfions: for as his ambition had no bounds, if they now paid him his demands, when he had done them no fervice, he would foon make others, which perhaps might be more dangerous and difhonourable to them. That it appeared of the laft confequence to them, to curb his infolence in time, and not fuffer it to become incorrigible: but if they were defirous to continue him their friend, either out of fear or any other motive, they would advife them to pay him by all means."

With this diffatisfactory anfwer, Cofimo returned to Florence. The Florentines however, earneftly follicited the Count not to abandon his confederates: which indeed, he was not very defirous to do: but his impatience to be married to the Duke's daughter, kept him in fuch fufpence, that every little accident fhook his refolution. He had left the care of his poffeffions in La Marca, to Furlano, one of his principal officers; who being tempted by great offers from the Duke, quitted the Count's fervice, and went over to him; which fo alarmed the Count, that he laid afide all other confiderations, and entered into a treaty with the Duke; in which, amongft other articles, it was agreed betwixt them, that the Duke fhould not, for the future, interfere in the affairs of Tufcany or Romagna. After this agreement, the Count took great pains to perfuade the Florentines to come to an accommodation with the Lucchefe; and, indeed, in a manner compelled them to it: for as they faw there was no other hope left, they made a peace with them in the month of April 1438; by which the Lucchefe were left in the enjoyment of their liberties; and the Florentines kept poffeffion of Monte Carlo, and fome other fortreffes they had taken from them. But not fatisfied with this, they wrote letters into all parts of

Italy,

Italy, full of murmurs and complaints, that, since God and man had not been pleased to suffer them to reduce the Lucchese under their dominion, they had been forced to make a peace with them. And it has very seldom happened, that any other people has shewn so much regret at the loss of their own territories, as the Florentines expressed, when they found they were not able to usurp those of their neighbours.

Notwithstanding they were so busily employed at this time in their own affairs, yet they found leisure to attend also to those of their friends, and to beautify their City. Niccolo Fortebraccio, who had married a daughter of the Count de' Poppi, being dead, and Poppi having got possession of the Bourg and Citadel di San Sepulchro, during the life of his son-in-law, still held them in the name of his widow (pretending they had been settled upon her) and refused to deliver them up to the Pope, who demanded them, as usurped from the Church. Upon which, his Holiness sent the * Patriarch of Alexandria, with an army, to wrest them out of his hands: and the Count finding he was not able to maintain them, made an offer of them to the Florentines; which they refused to accept; and at the Pope's return to Florence, endeavoured to accommodate matters betwixt them. But as the treaty was attended with many difficulties and delays, the Patriarch made an assault upon Casentino, took Prato Vecchio, and Romena, which he likewise in his turn offered to the Florentines, who would have nothing to do with them, except the Pope would consent that they should restore them to the Count; to which, after much wrangling, he at last agreed, upon condition that the

---

* A Patriarch is a great Dignitary in the Church, above an Archbishop. A Bishop presided only over the territory of the City whereof he was Bishop. A Metropolitan superintended a Province, and had the Bishops of it for his Suffragans. A Primate was the chief of a Diocese, and had several Metropolitans under him. A Patriarch had under him several Dioceses, the Primates themselves were subject to him.

Flo-

Florentines would ufe their intereft with the Count, to reftore the Borgo di San Sepulchro to him. After his Holinefs was thus fatisfied, the Florentines being defirous to have Divine Service performed in their Cathedral Church of St. Reparata, (which had been many years in building, but was now finifhed) en-treated him to oblige them fo far, as to confecrate it himfelf: to which he willingly confenting, a gal-lery was built (to heighten the folemnity, and fhew greater honour to the Pope) from St. Maria Novella, where he refided, to St. Reparata, eight yards in breadth, and four in height, under a very richly em-broidered Canopy, and hung on the fides with cloth of gold, through which his Holinefs only and his Court was to pafs, with fuch of the Magiftrates and principal Citizens, as were deputed to attend him; all the reft of the people crowding into the ftreet, the windows of their houfes, and every part of the Church, to entertain themfelves with fo magnificent a fpectacle. When the ceremony was over, the Pope, as a further inftance of his refpect for the City, con-ferred the honour of Knighthood upon Giuliano d' Avanzati, then Gonfalonier of Juftice, and a Citizen of very great and long eftablifhed reputation : and the Signiory, out of regard to a man whom his Ho-linefs had been pleafed to diftinguifh, likewife made him governor of Pifa for one year.

About this time, certain difputes arofe betwixt the Roman and Greek Churches, concerning their modes of Divine worfhip; in fome particulars of which, they did not altogether agree. And as much had been faid upon that fubject by the Prelates of the Weftern Church in the laft Seffion of the Council held at Bafil, it was determined to ufe all means to bring the Emperor and the Greek Bifhops thither, to try if matters could be accommodated betwixt the two Churches. And though it feemed deroga-tory to the Majefty of the Eaftern Emperor, and mortified the pride of his Prelates to fubmit to the Roman Pontif: yet as they were diftreffed by the
Turk,

Turk, and not able to defend themselves, they
thought it the best way to comply; that so they
might with greater confidence demand the affistance
of the western Christians. The Emperor therefore,
together with the Patriarch of Constantinople, and
several other Grecian Prelates and Barons, in obedience to the order of the Council, came to Venice
with a design to proceed to Basil: but as they were
frighted at the news of the plague being there, it
was resolved that their differences should be discussed
and decided at Florence, where they accordingly af-
sembled: and after many long debates, which lasted
several days in the Cathedral Church of that City, the
Greeks submitted, and were reunited with the Church
and Pontif of Rome *.

After a peace was concluded betwixt the Lucchese
and the Florentines, and betwixt Count Sforza and
the Duke of Milan, it was thought all disturbances
would have subsided in Italy, especially in Lombardy
and Tuscany: for as to the war which was still carried on betwixt Regnier of Anjou, and Alphonso of
Arragon, there was no likelyhood of its being ended,
but with the ruin of either one or the other of those
two competitors. And though the Pope was not a
little exasperated at the loss of so many towns as had
been taken from him; and the ambition of the Duke

---

* The Council of Basil, was only a prolongation of several others,
which had been summoned by Pope Martin V. sometimes at Pavia,
and sometimes at Siena: but as soon as Eugenius IV. was elected, in
1431, the fathers there assembled, began with declaring, that the
Pope had neither a right to dissolve, nor even to transfer their af-
sembly; and that he himself was subject to their jurisdiction. Upon
this declaration, Eugenius issued out a Bull to dissolve the Council.
The contest lasted a long time, and both the East and West were engaged in it. The Greek Empire was no longer able to support itself
against the Turks, without the assistance of the Latin Princes; and
in order to obtain a weak and very precarious supply, the Eastern
Church must submit to that of Rome. The Græcian Clergy were not
at all inclined to this submission; nay, as their danger increased, they
rather grew more stubborn. But the Emperor John Paleologus resolved to comply, that he might secure some assistance at least; and
addressing himself at the same time, both to the Pope and to the
Council, they vied with each other, who should have the honour of
converting the Greeks.

and

and the Venetians were sufficiently known to every
one; yet it was imagined his Holiness would be
forced to be quiet out of necessity, and the others,
out of downright weariness. But it happened quite
otherwise: for neither the Duke, nor the Venetians
could rest in peace; but soon took up arms again,
and raised fresh wars in Lombardy and Tuscany. The
Duke's pride was piqued that the Venetians should
still keep possession of Bergamo and Brescia, and so
much the more, as he saw them continue armed and
making excursions every day to harrass and ravage
his other dominions; and at a time too, when he
thought himself able, not only to curb their insolence,
but recover the towns they had stripped him of; especially, when they were deserted by the Pope, the
Florentines, and the Count. He therefore resolved,
if possible, to take Romagna from the Pope, imagining, it would not be in his power to molest him, when
he was once in possession of that; and that the Florentines seeing the fire so near them, would not dare
to move, for fear of being burnt themselves: or, that
if they should, they could not easily do him any mischief. He likewise was no stranger to the resentment
which the Florentines harboured against the Venetians, for their late behaviour to them in the affair
of Lucca, and thought they would upon that account be less inclined to take up arms in their favour.
As for Count Sforza, he concluded that the treaty he
had so lately made with him, and the hopes of marrying his daughter, would keep him still attached to
his interests. And to avoid the imputation of perfidy, and give others the less occasion to arm against
him, he contrived matters so, that Niccolò Piccinino
should invade Romagna, (as if it was solely to gratify his own ambition) since he could not openly embark in that enterprize himself, without being accused
of violating the engagement he had entered into with
Sforza.

At the time when that treaty was concluded, Piccinino was in Romagna, and pretended (as it had
been

been concerted betwixt him and the Duke) to be fo
highly difgufted at the alliance he had entered into
with his profeffed enemy the Count, that he retired
with his forces to Camurata, a town betwixt Furli
and Ravenna; where he fortified himfelf, as if he
intended to ftay there till he could be employed by
fome other State. The report of his difguft being
induftrioufly fpread abroad, he took an opportunity
of reprefenting to the Pope, how ungratefully the
Duke had requited him for his long and faithful fervices : that he knew it was his defign to make himfelf mafter of all Italy, and that he thought he fhould
be able to accomplifh it, as he had got two of the
moft experienced Commanders, and confequently all
the beft forces of it in his fervice. But that, if his
Holinefs pleafed, he would point out means to him,
by which he could make one of thofe Commanders,
upon whom the Duke fo much depended, become
his utter enemy, and the other entirely unferviceable :
for if his Holinefs would furnifh him with money to
pay his troops, he would fall upon the territories
which the Count had taken from the Church, and
find him fuch employment there, that he would have
no leifure to affift the Duke in his ambitious defigns.
Thefe propofals feeming feafible enough, the Pope
eagerly liftened to them, and not only fent him five
thoufand ducats, but promifed to provide largely
both for him and his Children. And though his Holinefs was warned by feveral to beware of Piccinino,
yet he gave no credit to them, nor would bear to hear
any thing faid againft him.

Oftafio da Polenta was Governor of Ravenna for
the Church ; and Piccinino now thinking it high time
to proceed to the execution of his defigns (as his fon
Francifco had taken and plundered Spoleto, to the
great difhonour of the Pope) refolved to make an attempt upon Ravenna ; either becaufe he thought he
was more likely to fucceed in that enterprize than any
other, or had a private correfpondence with the Governor : whatever might be his motive, it furren-

dered

dered upon terms, after a fiege that lafted but a few days. After which, he feized upon Bologna, Imola, and Furli, and which was ftill more unexpected, out of twenty fortreffes that were garrifoned with the Pope's troops in thofe parts, there was not one that did not fall into the hands of Piccinino; who, not content with bafely robbing him of thofe poffeffions, added infolence to his perfidy, and told his Holinefs in a letter which he wrote to him, " that he thought he had ferved him very right for attempting in fo fhamelefs a manner, to break the friendfhip that had fo long fubfifted betwixt the Duke and him; and for writing letters into all parts of Italy to make people believe he had abandoned that Prince, and was gone over to the Venetians.

After Piccinino had thus made himfelf mafter of Romagna, he left the defence of it to his fon Francifco, and marched himfelf with the greater part of his forces into Lombardy, where he joined the reft of the Duke's army, and falling into the territories of Brefcia, foon reduced all that part of the Country, and then fat down before the city itfelf. But the Duke, who earneftly wifhed to fee the Venetians deferted by their Allies, and left alone to his mercy, took great pains to clear himfelf to the Pope, the Florentines, and Count Sforza from the fufpicion of being in any wife acceffary to Piccinino's proceedings in Romagna; and faid that what he had done there was exceedingly difpleafing to him, as it was fo contrary to his engagements: fecretly affuring them, that at a proper time and opportunity, he would not fail to make him fmart for his difobedience. The Florentines and the Count, however, paid little regard to thefe proteftations; and thought (which indeed was the cafe) that the late outrage had been committed upon the Pope with a view to check and over-awe them, whilft he himfelf fell upon the Venetians; who thinking they were fufficiently able of themfelves to cope with him, were fo lofty that they difdained to afk affiftance from any other State, and

trufted

trufted folely to their General Gattamelata to conduct the war.   Count Sforza was defirous to have gone to the relief of Regnier of Anjou in the Kingdom of Naples, if he had not been prevented by the difturbances which happened in Lombardy and Romagna; and the Florentines were very well inclined to have affifted him in that enterprize, out of the amity which had always fubfifted betwixt their Republic and the Crown of France.   The Duke, on the contrary, would willingly have protected Alphonfo of Arragon, as he had contracted a friendfhip with him whilft he was his prifoner.   But they all had fuch employment at home, as would not fuffer them to concern themfelves in foreign affairs.

The Florentines, therefore, feeing Romagna in the hands of the Duke, and the Venetians hard preffed by him, began to apprehend that the depreffion of their neighbours might perhaps conduce to their own ruin.   Upon which, they follicited Sforza to come into Tufcany, that they might concert meafures to prevent the Duke from making any further progrefs; fince he was now become much more powerful than ever he had been before: adding, that if his ambition was not effectually curbed by fome means or other, all the States in Italy would foon feel the effects of it.   The Count was fenfible that the Florentines had fufficient reafon for thefe apprehenfions: but the earneft defire he had to conclude the match with the Duke's daughter, ftill kept him in fufpence.   And the Duke, who was well aware of it, continually flattered him from time to time that it fhould fpeedily be confummated, provided he did not take up arms againft him, as the lady was now of a marriageable age.   Nay the farce was carried on fo far, that fometimes great preparations were made for the wedding; when all on a fudden, fome frefh excufe or other was found out td protract it.   However, to keep him quiet and prevent all fufpicion, he fent him the fum of twenty thoufand Florins, which was to be her dower by the articles of

mar-

marriage. In the mean time, the war began to wax hot in Lombardy, and the Venetians every day loſt ſome town or other; the Veſſels which they fitted out to cruiſe along their coaſts, were continually taken; the country about Breſcia and Verona, entirely in the enemy's hands; and thoſe two Cities ſo cloſely inveſted by the Duke's forces, that it was generally thought they could not hold out long. The Marquis of Mantua, who commanded their forces for many years, had unexpectedly left their ſervice, and gone into the Duke's: ſo that in the progreſs of the war, fear at laſt compelled them to do that, which their pride would not ſtoop to in the beginning of it. For when they began to perceive there was no other hope left but from the ſuccour of the Florentines, and Count Sforza, they condeſcended to aſk it, though not without much diffidence and ſuſpicion that the Florentines would return them ſome ſuch anſwer, as they had given the Florentines in the affair of Lucca and the Count's arrears. But they found them much readier to comply with their demands than they expected, or indeed deſerved, conſidering their late behaviour to them: ſo much more powerful was the enmity of the Florentines againſt an old inveterate enemy, than the reſentment of a ſlight they had received from an old Ally! for having long foreſeen the extremities to which the Venetians muſt of courſe be reduced, they had repreſented to the Count " that his ruin was inſeparable from theirs; that he would find himſelf deceived if he thought the Duke would treat him with ſtill greater regard, if he ſucceeded in his deſigns, than he did at preſent: that he had promiſed him his daughter, only becauſe he ſtood in fear of him; and ſince neceſſity compelled people to make promiſes, that alone could enforce the performance of them: for which reaſon, it behoved him to keep the Duke low: and that could not be effected without ſupporting the power of the Venetians. That he ought to conſider therefore, that if the Venetians ſhould be

driven

driven out of their poffeffions upon the * Terra firma, he would not only be deprived of all the conveniencies which might accrue from their alliance, but of thofe alfo that he might hope for from others, out of refpect to them. That it he would reflect upon the condition of the reft of the Italian States, he would find fome of them very poor, and others ill affected to him. That the Florentines alone, as they had often given him to underftand, were not able to maintain him : fo that he was obliged, by every motive, to ufe his utmoft endeavours that the Venetians fhould retain their territories upon the Continent.

Thefe arguments, joined to the refentment which the Count had now conceived againft the Duke for duping him, as he thought, in the match with his Daughter, at laft determined him to enter into a confederacy with them (though he would not be obliged to pafs the Po) and the articles were accordingly figned in February 1438 : by which the Venetians were to bear two thirds, and the Florentines one third of the expences of the war; both of them engaging to defend the Count's poffeffions in la Marca, at their own charges. . But the League thinking they had not yet fufficient ftrength, brought alfo the Lord of Faenza, the fons of Pandolpho Malatefta da Rimini, and Pietro-gian-paolo Urfini into the confederacy : and though they tempted the Marquis of Mantua with large offers, they could not detach him from the Duke. The Lord of Faenza alfo (though the confederacy had agreed to his demands) finding he could have better terms, foon deferted them, and went into the Duke's fervice ; which made them defpair of putting fo fpeedy an end to the troubles in Romagna as they had vainly promifed themfelves.

---

* So they call their dominions that lie upon the Continent, which formerly were confiderable; but at prefent they are very much reduced, as well as their commerce and naval power. They have particular magiftrates to fuperintend the affairs of what poffeffions they have ftill left upon the Terra firma, who are called *i favii della terra :* and there are yet feveral orders of Nobility, as Counts, Marquifes, &c. in that part of their dominions; but they are not treated with any great regard at Venice.

Their

Their affairs in Lombardy also were in a bad situation ; for Brescia was blocked up in such a manner by the Duke's forces, that it was daily expected to be obliged to surrender for want of provisions. They were under the same apprehensions for Verona : and if either of those Cities should be taken, they thought any further preparations for war, would be to no purpose, and all the expences they had hitherto been at, entirely thrown away. But there seemed to be no remedy, except the Count would march into Lombardy ; and in this, there were three obstacles to be surmounted. The first was, to prevail upon him to pass the Po, and carry the war whithersoever they commanded him. In the next place, they thought they should be left too much exposed when the Count was gone : as the Duke might easily retire into some of his strong places, and whilst he kept the Count at bay there with one part of his forces, he might send the other, in conjunction with the exiles, into Tuscany ; of which the Government of Florence was in very great apprehension. And lastly, to find a secure route by which the Count might march with his forces into the territories of Padua, where the Venetians had assembled theirs. Of these three difficulties, the second, which chiefly concerned the Florentines, seemed to be the most important. However, as the necessity was pressing, and they were tired with the importunities of the Venetians, who earnestly sollicited them to put the Count and his forces in motion, without whose aid they could not pretend to do any thing, they postponed their own danger to the necessity of their Allies. The last point, which was a safe route for the Count, they left to the care of the Venetians. And since it was judged convenient by the Signiory to send Neri, the son of Gini Capponi, to concert measures with the Count and persuade him to pass the Po : they likewise determined that he should go on to Venice, to make the favour appear still greater to the Senate, and to expedite necessary provisions there for the security of the Count's march. Neri accordingly

em-

embarked at Cefena, and went by Sea to Venice,
where no Prince was ever received with greater honour by the Senate, and as they thought the prefervation of their dominions entirely owing to his arrival
and the refolutions that would be taken upon it, he
was immediately introduced into the Council, when
he addreffed himfelf to the Doge in the following
manner: " Our Signiory have always been of opinion, Moft Serene Prince, that the ambition of the
Duke of Milan, would fome time or other be the ruin
both of your Republic and our own, except it was
prevented by their mutual defence and fupport of each
other: and if this Senate had likewife been of the
fame opinion, our affairs would have been in a better
fituation, and yourfelves fecure from the danger which
now hangs over your heads.   But fince you have neither been pleafed to put any confidence in us, nor to
lend us the aid you ought to have done in our necef-
fities, we could not run with fo much eagernefs to
your affiftance, nor you fo well tell how to demand it,
as both fides might have done, if you had dealt
with us either in your profperity or adverfity, like
the men we really are, or known that whom we once
love we always love, and thofe that we hate we hate
for ever.   Our ancient affection for this illuftrious Senate, yourfelves can witnefs, who have feen Lombardy
fo often filled with our forces, and what loffes we have
fuftained there to ferve you: and all the world knows
the hatred we bear to Philip; which we likewife fhall
continue to his family; for with us, the remembrance
of former friendfhip is not extinguifhed by recent injuries, nor that of ancient enmity, by modern favours.   We are very certain that if we had ftood
neuter in this war, the Duke would have thought
himfelf much obliged to us, and that it could not
have been of any great prejudice to ourfelves: for if
he fhould drive you out of Lombardy, and become
fole Lord of it himfelf, there would ftill be fuch re-
fources left in Italy, that we fhould have no occafion
to defpair of our own prefervation: fince the more

any

any Prince increases his power and dominions, the more envy and hatred he draws upon himself; which give birth to wars that generally end to his disadvantage. We likewise know very well, what heavy expences and what dangers we might have avoided, by not taking part with you in the war, and that by acting otherwise, we may probably remove the seat of it out of Lombardy into our own Country. All these considerations however, weighty as they are, cannot make us forget the affection we have so long borne to your State; and we have resolved to support it with the same vigour that we should defend ourselves if we were invaded. Our Signiory therefore judging it highly necessary, in the first place, to relieve Brescia and Verona, which cannot well be effected without the assistance of Count Sforza, sent me to persuade him to march into Lombardy, and carry the war into what part soever he shall be directed, though ye need not be informed, illustrious Senators, under what obligations he is not to pass the Po: and yet I have prevailed upon him to do it by the same motives that influence our own conduct. And as he is invincible in arms, he is unwilling to be outdone in point of courtesy; nay, he has even endeavoured to exceed us, if possible, in that frankness and generosity which he saw were the rules of our behaviour to you. For though he was sensible to what dangers, not only his own possessions, but all Tuscany would be exposed in his absence, yet when he saw that we had postponed all private interest and considerations to your safety, he freely did the same. I come therefore, illustrious Senators, to make you an offer of the Count's service at the head of seven thousand horse, and two thousand foot, all ready to march whithersoever they shall be commanded. But it is the expectation of our Signiory, and indeed of the Count himself, that, as they have sent a greater number of forces to your assistance than they were obliged to do by treaty, you will not be wanting on your part, to make him a liberal provision; that so, neither he

may

may have any caufe to repent of entering into your fervice, nor our Republic, of having perfuaded him to it."

This fpeech was liftened to by the Senate with as much attention as if it had been dictated by an Oracle, and made fuch an impreffion, that without waiting for the Doge to make an anfwer to it (as it had always been cuftomary) the whole affembly rofe from their feats, and with hands lifted up and tears in their eyes, returned thanks to the Republic of Florence for their affectionate regard to them; and to Neri for having executed his Commiffion with fo much addrefs and difpatch. They vowed that the fenfe of fuch an obligation, fhould be for ever engraved, not only upon their own hearts, but upon the hearts of their pofterity; and that for the future, they would always look upon the interefts of the Florentines and their own to be the fame.

When thefe emotions began to fubfide, they proceeded to deliberate upon the route which the Count fhould take; and upon the number of pontoons and pioneers and other provifions that would be neceffary to facilitate and fecure his march. There were four different routes. One from Ravenna along the fhore: but that being for the moft part ftraitened by the Sea on one hand, and Moraffes on the other, was not approved of. The next, was the direct high road; but obftructed by a fortrefs belonging to the Duke, called Uccellino, which muft be reduced before they could proceed any further, and that would take up more time than they could poffibly fpare, as the neceffity was urgent, and the utmoft expedition required. The third was through the foreft of Lugo: but as there was then a great flood upon the Po, it made the paffage that way altogether impoffible. There was, therefore, only one road left, which was through the plains of Bologna, and over the bridges at Puledrano, Cento and Pieve, and fo betwixt Finale and Bondeno to Ferrara; from whence they might tranfport themfelves, partly by water and

partly

partly by land, into the territories of Padua, and join the forces of the Venetians there. This way had likewise its difficulties, and they were liable to be attacked by the enemy in several places. However, as it was thought the best upon the whole, the Count had orders to take that route: upon which, he instantly began his march, and proceeded with such expedition, that he arrived near Padua on the 20th of June.

The arrival of this commander in Lombardy revived the drooping spirits of the Venetians in such a manner, that they, who but a little before seemed almost to despair of their own preservation, now began to think of invading others. But the first thing which the Count attempted was the relief of Verona: to prevent which, Piccinino moved with his army to Soave, a fortress situated betwixt the territories of Vicenza and that City, where he intrenched himself, and threw up a Fosse that reached from Soave to the Marshes formed by the river Adige. But when the Count saw his passage obstructed through the plain, he resolved to march over the Mountains, and to push on that way to Verona; imagining the other would not at all suspect his attempting any passage that way, because it was exceeding rough and difficult; or if he should, that he would not have time to prevent it. Having provided his army therefore with provisions for eight days march, he passed the Mountains and arrived in the plains beyond Soave. And though Piccinino had raised some forts to cut off his passage even this way, yet they were not strong enough to stop it. So that when he found the Count had actually passed the mountains, contrary to all expectation, he retired beyond the Adige, that he might avoid being forced to an engagement with him upon disadvantageous terms: and the Count still advancing, entered Verona without any opposition.

The first difficulty being thus surmounted, Brescia was in the next place to be relieved. That City stands

ſtands near the Lake di Garda, and though it was
blocked up by land, it might at all times be ſupplied
with proviſions whilſt the Lake continued open. But
the Duke being aware of this, had poſted troops
along the banks of it, in the firſt career of his ſucceſs, and ſecured all thoſe towns that might ſend any
aſſiſtance thither by water. The Venetians had alſo
ſome Gallies upon the Lake, but they were not of
ſufficient ſtrength to drive off the Duke's forces.
Upon which account, Sforza reſolved to act in concert with thoſe Veſſels, in order to make himſelf
maſter of ſuch towns, as kept the City blocked up
in that ſtarving condition: and for that purpoſe, ſat ·
down before Bandolino, a Caſtle ſituated upon the
Lake; hoping, when he had taken that, the reſt
would ſoon ſurrender. Fortune however was not pro-
pitious to him in this undertaking: for great numbers
of his men falling ſick, he was obliged to raiſe the
ſiege and retire to Zeno, a fortreſs belonging to the
Veroneſe, where there was a better air and greater
abundance of proviſions for them. No ſooner had
the Count retired, but Piccinino, reſolving not to
loſe ſo fair an opportunity of making himſelf maſter
of the Lake, left his Camp at Vegaſio, and proceeded with ſome of his choiceſt troops to the banks
of it, where he made ſo furious an attack upon the
Venetian Veſſels which lay there, that he took the
greater part of them, and got poſſeſſion of moſt of
the neighbouring Caſtles. At this misfortune the
Venetians were in great conſternation; and fearing
Breſcia muſt now likewiſe of courſe fall into his hands,
they ſent very preſſing and repeated meſſages to deſire the Count would uſe his utmoſt endeavours to
prevent it. Seeing, therefore, all hopes of ſuccour-
ing it by water were now at an end, and that it was
impracticable to do it by land on that ſide, conſidering the ditches, redoubts, and other obſtacles that
Piccinino had thrown in the way, which would ſo
embarraſs his forces, if he ſhould engage the enemy
there, that they muſt inevitably be defeated, he de-

termined to try whether it was not poffible to pafs
the Mountains and relieve the town that way, as he
had done Verona.   With this defign he quitted Zeno,
and marching through the Vale of Acri to the Lake
of St. Andrew, he proceeded to Torboli and Penda
upon the Lake di Garda; from whence he advanced
to Tenna, which he laid fiege to, as it was neceffary
to reduce that fortrefs before he could get to Brefcia.
But Piccinino having intelligence of his march,
moved with his army to Pefchiera, where he joined
the Marquis of Mantua, and having picked out a
body of his very beft troops, he advanced to give
the Count battle, and the Count not declining it,
Piccinino's forces were entirely routed, fome of them
being taken prifoners, others flying to the main body of
their army, and the reft to the Gallies upon the Lake.
Piccinino himfelf retired to Tenna the fame night,
and confidering with himfelf that if he ftaid there
till morning, he muft certainly fall into the hands of
the enemy, he refolved to run the laft rifque to avoid
fo imminent a danger.   Of all his followers he had
only one German fervant left with him, who was a
very lufty ftrong fellow, and had always been exceeding faithful to him.   This man he perfuaded to
put him into a Sack, and to place him on his fhoulders, as if he was carrying his mafter's baggage, and
by that means convey him to fome place of fecurity.
And as the enemy's army lay round Tenna after the
Victory they had gained, in a carelefs and fecure
manner, without pofting any guards, or obferving the
leaft order, the German found no great difficulty in
effecting it.   For having put on a futler's coat, he took
his mafter upon his fhoulders, as if he had got a
fack full of baggage or plunder, and carried him
through the whole camp fafe to his own army, without any moleftation or interruption.

If this Victory had been improved with the fame
good conduct that it was obtained, Brefcia might
have been effectually relieved, and the Venetians have

reaped

reaped greater advantages from it. But for want of that, the rejoycings of the one were very short, and the other was left in the same distressful circumstances. For as soon as Piccinino had got safe back again to his forces, he resolved to go upon some new enterprize; the success of which, might wipe off the disgrace of his late defeat, and prevent the Venetians from throwing any succours into Brescia. He was well acquainted himself with the situation of the Citadel of Verona, and had been informed, by some prisoners whom he had taken in the beginning of the war, it was so carelesly guarded that he might easily make himself master of it. He therefore determined not to neglect an opportunity, which fortune seemed purposely to have thrown in his way; of retrieving his own honour, and putting an end to the exultations of the enemy upon their Victory, by a stroke that might give them occasion to alter their note. Verona is in Lombardy, and situated at the foot of those Mountains that separate Italy from Germany, in such a manner, that one part of it stands upon the skirts of the Hills, and the other upon the Plain. To the North of this, in the Valley of Trent, the river Adige has its source, and at its entrance into Italy does not immediately take a strait course along the plains, but turning to the left and winding about the bottom of the Mountains, passes through that City; which it divides, but not into equal parts; for that next the plain is much larger than the other. Above the latter are the two Forts of St. Pietro and St. Felice, which seem better fortified by nature than art, and standing upon the heights command the whole town. On the other side of the River, in the part next the plain, there are also two Castles joined by the wall of the town, and at the distance of about a thousand paces from each other; one of them called the *Old*, and the other the *New Citadel*. From the former, there runs a wall in a strait line to the latter, that may be resembled to the string of a bow, which the wall of the town forms in its range betwixt the

two

two fortreffes : and the fpace betwixt one wall and
the other, commonly called the Bourg of St. Zeno,
is full of houfes and inhabitants.   Thefe two fortreffes and the Bourg, it was Piccinino's defign to furprize ; and he thought it would be no difficult matter to effect it, confidering the negligence and fecurity of the Garrifon, which in all probability would
be ftill increafed by the late Victory ; and becaufe he
knew by late experience that no enterprize was more
likely to fucceed than one that was judged impracticable by the enemy.   Having, therefore, drawn out
a picked body of men for this purpofe, he advanced
with the Marquis of Mantua in the dead of the night
to the walls of Verona, and making a fudden Sca-
lado upon the new Citadel, he carried it almoft before the enemy knew any thing of the matter.   From
thence he defcended with his men into the town, and
broke open St. Anthony's Gate, through which he let
in all his Cavalry.   But the Centinels of the old Citadel hearing the out-cries of thofe that had been furprized in the new one, and the noife that was made
at the breaking down of St. Anthony's Gate, at laft
perceived the enemy was upon them, and immediately began to beat their drums and ring the alarm
bells, to raife the people.   Upon which, thofe of the
Citizens that were moft courageous took up arms,
and ran in great confufion to the Piazza before the
Palace of the Magiftrates.   In the mean time, Piccinino's forces had taken poffeffion of the Bourg of
St. Zeno, and were pufhing forward into the town,
when the Citizens finding they were the Duke's troops,
and that there was no poffibility of defending themfelves againft them, advifed the Magiftrates to retire
into the Forts, to fave their own lives, and the City
from being plundered ; as it would be much better to
do that, and wait for a change of fortune, than to
be murdered themfelves, and provoke the enemy to
fhew no mercy to the City.

   The Magiftrates therefore, and all the reft of the
Venetians, took fhelter in the fort of St. Felice ; and
                                                        fome

fome of the principal Citizens going to wait upon
Piccinino, and the Marquis of Mantua, intreated
them to receive the City into their hands, rich and
flourifhing as it then was, which would very much increafe their reputation; rather than fuffer it to be
rifled and facked, to their great infamy and difgrace:
efpecially as they had not taken much pains to oblige
their former Mafters, nor deferved to incur the difpleafure of their new ones by an obftinate refiftance.
Upon this fubmiffion, they were favourably received
by Piccinino and the Marquis, who endeavoured to
reftrain the licentioufnefs of their foldiers as much as
they could, and prevent the City from being plundered: but as they were certain Count Sforza would
ufe his utmoft endeavours to recover it, they took all
poffible means to get the reft of the ftrong places
into their hands; and fuch as they could not make
themfelves mafters of, they feparated from the town,
and furrounded with foffes and other works, to prevent the enemy from throwing fuccours into them,
and thofe that were already there from annoying the
town.

Upon the firft rumour of this lofs, Count Sforza;
who then lay with his army at Tenna, could not give
credit to it: but when he was convinced of the truth
of it, from more certain intelligence, he determined
to make fpeedy amends for his paft negligence. And
though it was the opinion of all his principal officers,
that he ought to poftpone the relief of Verona and
Brefcia, and march directly to Vicenza, for fear of
being furrounded by the enemy, where he was; yet
he would not liften to their advice, but refolved to
ufe all means for the recovery of Verona: and addreffing himfelf, in the conclufion of the debate
(which had been occafioned by fuch a difference in
their judgment) to the Venetian * Proveditores, and
Bernardetto de' Medici, the Florentine Commiffary,

* A Proveditore is the fame in the Venetian armies, as a Commiffary in the Florentine.

he

he affured them, that he would certainly retake that town, if any one of the fortreffes there ftill held out for him. For this purpofe, having put his army in good order, he marched with all expedition towards Verona. At the fight of his vanguard, Piccinino imagined he had been going to Vicenza, as his officers had advifed him : however, when he perceived that he ftill advanced and bent his courfe towards the fort of St. Felice, he began to prepare for his defence. But it was too late; for he had not yet finifhed the barricadoes and entrenchments : and his foldiers being difperfed, and bufy in plundering, could not be got together to oppofe the Count's forces before they entered the fort. So that having gained a paffage into the town, they foon retook it, to the great dif-honour of Piccinino; who, after moft of his men were cut to pieces, retired with the reft into the citadel, and from thence made his efcape, in company with the Marquis, to Mantua; where he collected the remains of his army, and joined the other part of it that lay before Brefcia. In this manner Verona was taken and loft again in the fpace of four days, by the Duke's forces : and the Count feeing the winter now approaching, and the feafon very cold, after he had with much difficulty thrown fome fupplies of provifions into Brefcia, took up his quarters at Verona ; where he gave orders for the building feveral Gallies at Torboli, during the winter, that fo he might be ftrong enough to relieve Brefcia more effectually, both by land and water, when the fpring came on.

The winter having thus put an end to hoftilities for a while, the Duke, who was aware that he had been defeated in his hopes of making himfelf Mafter of Brefcia and Verona, chiefly by the affiftance which the enemy had received from the Florentines, whom neither the ill ufage they had met with from the Venetians could detach from their alliance, nor the offers he had tempted them with could gain over to himfelf, refolved to invade Tufcany, in order to make them more fenfible of the evils they were drawing upon them-

themfelves. In this defign he was likewife abetted
by the inftigations of Piccinino, and the Florentine
Exiles; the former of whom, much wanted to get
poffeffion of the ftates that were held by Braccio, and
to drive Count Sforza out of la Marca; and the latter to return to their own Country: both of them
urging fuch motives to prevail upon the Duke, as
feemed moft fpecious, and beft flattered his own ambition. Piccinino reprefented to him, " that he
might fend him with an army into Tufcany, and ftill
keep Brefcia blocked up; as he was mafter of the
Lake, had fo many ftrong and well garrifoned towns
round about it, and would have both Commanders
and foldiers enough to face the Count, if he fhould
make any further attempts in thofe parts; which yet
it could hardly be fuppofed he would do before he
had relieved Brefcia, and that he thought was impoffible: fo that he might fafely venture to carry the
war into Tufcany, without being obliged to difcon-
tinue it in Lombardy. For the Florentines, he faid,
muft either recall the Count when they faw their own
Country invaded, or fuffer it to be totally ruined: in
either of which cafes his advantage would be certain."
The Exiles affured him for their parts, " that if he
would fend Piccinino with an army to Florence, the
people there, who at laft were become defperate under the oppreffion and infolence of their Governors,
would inftantly take up arms againft them and revolt.
That nothing was more eafy than to march up to the
very gates of the City; as Rinaldo degli Albizi had
fufficient intereft with the Count of Cafentino to procure him a free paffage through his territories." So
that though the Duke was at firft inclinable enough
to engage in fuch an undertaking, he became thoroughly determined upon it by thefe perfuafions.

The Venetians, on the other hand, were very importunate with the Count to attempt the relief of
Brefcia with all his forces, though the winter was un-
commonly fevere: but the Count faid, " it was not
poffible at that time, and that he muft wait for a

milder

milder feafon; that however in the mean while, he would be getting his Fleet in readinefs to fuccour it both by land and water." At which anfwer, the Venetians were much diffatisfied, and afterwards proceeded fo flowly in making the neceffary provifions for their forces, that they began to dwindle away very faft. The Florentines alfo, when they had intelligence of their enemy's defigns and the tardinefs of their friends, were not a little alarmed; efpecially as they faw the war upon the point of being carried into their own dominions, and that their arms had met with fo little fuccefs in Lombardy. Nor were they lefs perplexed with the fufpicion they entertained of the Pope's forces; not that they thought his Holinefs himfelf was ill-affected to them, but becaufe they faw his troops under the command and direction of the Patriarch, who was their declared enemy, and that the foldiers fhewed much greater deference to him than to the Pope.

Giovanni Vitellefchi da Corneto, having firft been * Apoftolic Notary, then Bifhop of Ricanati, and next, Patriarch of Alexandria, was at laft created Cardinal, with the title of *Cardinal of Florence*. He was a fubtile enterprizing man, and had found means to infinuate himfelf into the Pope's confidence to fuch a degree, that he made him Commander in chief of his forces, and entrufted him with the fole management of all his affairs and undertakings in Tufcany, Romagna, the Kingdom of Naples, and even at Rome: fo that he had gained fuch an afcendant both over the army and the Pope himfelf, that the one was afraid to command him, and the other to obey any one elfe. This Cardinal happened to be at Rome with his forces, when the report was fpread that Piccinino was meditating an invafion upon Tufcany. A circumftance that redoubled the apprehenfions of the Florentines, as he had ever been their enemy fince

---

* An officer whofe bufinefs it is to expedite beneficiary matters at the court of Rome.

the

the banishment of Rinaldo degli Albizi ; becaufe they had not only abufed him in not obferving the agreement which had been promoted betwixt them at Florence by his mediation, but deceived Rinaldo, who had laid down his arms at his perfuafion, and furnifhed his enemies with the means of fending him into exile : fo that the government began to be afraid that Rinaldo and his friends would certainly be reftored and indemnified for all their fufferings if they fhould join Piccinino in his expedition into Tufcany.   And fo much the more, as that Commander had fuddenly departed out of Lombardy, and left one undertaking that feemed almoft fure to be attended with fuccefs, to go upon another, the event of which muft be very precarious : which they thought he would not have done, if he had not had fome fecret defign or invitation.   Thefe fufpicions they communicated to the Pope, who at laft began to be fenfible of the error he had been guilty of intrufting too much authority in the hands of another perfon.   But whilft they were under thefe apprehenfions, an accident happened that put an end to them.

The government had Spies in all parts that kept a ftrict watch upon fuch as carried Letters, in order to detect any confpiracy that might be formed againft them : and it chanced that one of thefe intercepted a Packet at Monte Pulciano, fent from the Patriarch to Piccinino without the knowledge of the Pope, which was immediately carried to his Holinefs by the Magiftrate, who had the charge of conducting the war. And though the letters were written in an unufual character, and the fenfe of them fo obfcure that they were difficult to be interpreted with any certainty ; yet thofe very circumftances, and the holding a correfpondence with his enemy, made the Pope fo jealous that he determined to fecure him, and gave a ftrict charge for that purpofe to Antonio Rido (a Paduan lately made Governor of the Caftle of St. Angelo at Rome) who readily undertook to execute his orders as foon as he had a convenient opportunity,

which

which prefently occurred. For the Patriarch intending to have gone into Tufcany the next day, fent word to the Governor of the Caftle, that he defired he would meet him in the morning at a certain hour upon the Bridge, for he had fomething to fay to him before he left the City : and as Antonio thought this was too favourable an opportunity to be neglected, (after he had made a proper difpofition for the execution of his defign) he went at the hour appointed to the bridge, which being near the caftle, was fo contrived, that it might eafily be drawn up or let down, as occafion required, for its greater fecurity. He had not waited long there, before the Patriarch came ; and having led him by degrees in the courfe of their converfation to the other end of the bridge, he made a fignal to have it drawn up : which being inftantly done, he, who but the moment before had been General of the Pope's forces, now became Antonio Rido's prifoner in the caftle of St. Angelo. His attendants, indeed, at firft began to raife an out-cry ; but when they were informed, that what had been done was by the Pope's orders, they were foon quieted ; and the governor, to comfort his prifoner in the beft manner he could, told him, " he hoped he would come to no further harm." To which the Patriarch made anfwer, " that perfons of his rank were feldom arrefted, only to be difcharged again ; and that thofe who deferved to be imprifoned, did not deferve to be releafed." Not long after his confinement, he died in the caftle ; and the Pope appointed Ludovico, the Patriarch of Aquileia *, Commander in chief of his forces. For tho' his Holinefs had been always unwilling before to embroil himfelf in the wars betwixt the Duke of Milan and the Confederates, he now promifed to affift the

---

* This Lewis (fays Volaterran, lib. xxii.) who was a native of Padua, having been promoted firft to the fenatorial dignity, for fervices done in the field, and afterwards to the Purple, grew fo proud, that, forgetful of his birth, he was the firft Cardinal who prefumed to keep horfes and hounds, and to introduce a greater degree of magnificence, in feafting, furniture, and equipage, than became that Order.

latter

latter, if Tufcany fhould be invaded, with four thoufand horfe and two thoufand foot.

The Florentines, though now delivered from the
fear of the Patriarch, were yet very fufpicious of Piccinino's defigns, and fo uneafy at the confufion in
which they faw their affairs in Lombardy (occafioned
by the difference of opinion betwixt Count Sforza
and the Venetians) that they fent Neri, the Son of
Gini Capponi, and Giuliano d'Avanzati to Venice, in
order to reconcile them, if poffible, and to fettle the
operations of the next campaign ; inftructing Neri in
particular, to found the refolution of the Venetians :
after which, he was to go to the Count, and perfuade
him to comply with fuch meafures as fhould appear
moft neceffary for the fecurity of the League. Thefe
Deputies had not got fo far on the road as Ferrara,
when they heard that Piccinino had paffed the Po
with fix thoufand horfe, which made them haften
their journey ; and when they arrived at Venice, they
found the Senate there fully determined to have the
relief of Brefcia attempted without further delay ;
fince that City, they faid, could not otherwife hold
out, for want of provifions, till the return of the
fpring, nor till the gallies were built, but feeing no
hope of fuccour, muft of neceffity be obliged to furrender to the enemy ; which would entirely anfwer
the Duke's purpofes, and occafion the lofs of all their
dominions upon the Terra Firma. Upon which,
Neri proceeded to Verona, to hear what the Count
had to fay, in anfwer to this ; who made it fufficiently
appear to him, that any endeavour to relieve Brefcia,
muft not only be ineffectual at that juncture, but of
great prejudice to their future undertakings : for confidering the time of the year, and the fituation of that
town, no fuccefs could be expected, and he fhould
only harrafs and fatigue his troops in fuch a manner,
that when a proper feafon for action came, he muft
be forced to return with his army to Verona, to fupply himfelf with fuch provifions as the winter had
confumed to no purpofe, and other neceffaries for the

fer-

fervice of the enfuing fummer: fo that all the time that ought to be employed in action, would be thrown away in fruitlefs marches and countermarches betwixt the two towns.

To obviate thefe objections, Orfatto Juftiniani and Giovanni Pifani, were fent to wait upon the Count at Verona; and after long debate, it was at laft agreed amongft them, that the Venetians fhould in-creafe the Count's ftipend for the next year to eighty thoufand Ducats, befides an allowance of forty Du-cats for every private foldier: and that he fhould not only take the field as foon as poffible, with his whole army, but endeavour to penetrate into the Duke's dominions, that fo he might be obliged to recall Pic-cinino into Lombardy to defend himfelf; after which agreement, the deputies all returned to Venice. But the Venetians finding fome difficulty in raifing fo large a fubfidy, proceeded very flowly in making the ne-ceffary provifions: whilft Piccinino, on the other hand, diligently purfued his march, and had already got into Romagna; where he tampered fo effectually with the fons of Pandolpho Malatefta *, that they deferted the Venetians, and went over to the Duke. This was very unwelcome news at Venice, and much more fo at Florence, as they had chiefly depended upon the Malatefti, to obftruct the progrefs of Pic-cinino; but when it came to be known that they had revolted, it occafioned great confternation in the City; efpecially as it was likewife apprehended, that Pietro-gian-Paolo Urfini, their commander in chief, who was then in the territories of the Malatefti, muft cer-tainly be betrayed and defeated; by which they would be in a manner difarmed, and deprived of all means of making any defence.

The Count himfelf likewife was not a little alarmed at this event. He was afraid of lofing his poffeffions in la Marca, if Piccinino advanced into Tufcany: and being refolved to attend more particularly to that

---

* They were Lords of Rimini, a town upon the Gulph of Venice, which now belongs to the Pope.

point,

point, he took poft and went to Venice, where he immediately demanded an audience of the Senate; which
being granted, he reprefented to them how neceffary
it was for the fervice of the League, that he fhould
march with his forces into Tufcany. "That the
main ftrength of their arms ought to be directed
againft the enemy's Commander in chief and the
place where he had collected his principal force; and
not to be diffipated in fruitlefs fkirmifhes with Garrifons and attacks upon particular towns. That if the
Duke's army could once be broken, there muft be
an end of the war; but if that was fuffered to remain
entire, the war would ftill be carried on with greater
vigour, even after his fortreffes were reduced, as it
almoft always happened in fuch cafes. That if Piccinino was not refolutely oppofed, both la Marca and
Tufcany muft inevitably be loft; after which, their
affairs in Lombardy would become defperate. But
if there fhould be any hopes left of retrieving them,
he thought it could not reafonably be expected that
he fhould abandon the care of his own fubjects and
friends; for as he was a Prince when he came [into
Lombardy, he did not defign to ftay there till he had
nothing left but the title of a private Commander."
To which the Doge made anfwer, "that if he left
Lombardy, nay, if he fhould only repafs the Po with
his army, all their dominions upon the Terra firma
would moft certainly be loft, and therefore, they
fhould not throw away any more money to defend them;
as it would be fimple to ufe any endeavours to fave
what could not poffibly be maintained, and lefs prejudicial and difhonourable too to lofe thofe territories
only, than to lofe both them and their money together. And if that fhould be the cafe, it would then
plainly appear, though perhaps too late, of what importance the prefervation of the Venetian dominions
in thofe parts, would have been for the protection of
Tufcany and Romagna. Upon which account, they
could not by any means approve of the meafures he
recommended, fince they very well knew whofoever

was

6

was mafter in Lombardy would be mafter every where elfe : and in that there could not be much difficulty ; for now Piccinino had withdrawn his forces out of it, the Duke's dominions were left fo expofed that they might be wholly over-run before that Commander could poffibly return, or any other remedy be provided. That if any one would maturely confider the matter, he would find that the Duke had fent Piccinino into Tufcany with no other view but to divert the Count from his prefent undertaking, and to remove the war out of his own Country into another. So that if the Count fhould follow him, before there was any abfolute neceffity for it, he would fall into the fnare, and fuffer him to gain his ends : but if they ftill kept their forces in Lombardy, and made the beft provifion they could in Tufcany, he muft foon be aware of his error, and find that he had entirely loft every thing in one, and gained nothing in the other." After the matter had been thoroughly difcuffed, and every one had given his opinion, it was concluded to wait a little while to fee what effects the new alliance betwixt Piccinino and the Malatefti would produce ; what Pietro-gian-Paolo Urfini, the Florentine General, would be able to do ; and whether the Pope really defigned to perform the promifes he had made to the League. A few days after this refolution, they had intelligence that the Malatefti had entered into that alliance by downright compulfion, and not out of any difaffection or ill will to the Florentines ; that Urfini was gone with his forces towards Tufcany ; and that the Pope was better inclined to affift the confederates than ever he had been before. Upon which, the Count was fo well fatisfied, that he confented to ftay in Lombardy, and that Neri Capponi fhould return to Florence with a thoufand of his horfe and five hundred others. That if affairs fhould take fuch a turn as to make his prefence neceffary in Tufcany, they fhould let him know, and he would immediately repair thither. Neri therefore proceeded with thofe forces towards Florence, and arrived there

in

in April, on the fame day that Urfini likewife returned to that City.

In the mean time, Piccinino having made all neceffary difpofitions in Romagna, defigned to have
proceeded in his march to Tufcany over the Mountains of St. Benedetto and through the Vale of Montone, but he found thofe defiles fo well guarded by
Niccolo da Pifa, that any attempt to force a paffage
that way muft be to no purpofe.   And fince this invafion was fo fudden, and the Florentines were but
ill provided with Officers and Soldiers, they had fent
only a few companies of new raifed foot to defend
the other paffes in thofe Mountains, under the command of fome of their own Citizens : amongft whom
was Meffer Bartolomeo Orlandini, who had the charge
of defending a Fort at Marradi, which fecured the
paffage that way.   The pafs at St. Benedetto therefore, being fo bravely maintained that Piccinino had
no hopes of fucceeding there, he determined to try
what might be done at Marradi, where he knew the
Commander was not a man of any great courage.
Marradi is a fort fituated at the foot of thofe Mountains that feparate Tufcany from Romagna, but on
that fide of them which lies next to the latter, and
at the entrance of the Vale of Lamona.   And tho'
it has no walls, it is otherwife pretty well fortified
by a river that runs clofe to it, as well as by the
Mountains and the valour of the inhabitants, who
are very courageous and faithful : for the banks of
the river are fo high above the water, that it is impoffible to get that way into the Vale, provided a
little Bridge that ftands over the river be well defended : and on the other fide the rocks are fo fteep
and craggy that it is inacceffible.   But the cowardice
of Orlandini ftruck a panic into his men and made
the fituation of no fignificance : for he no fooner
heard of the enemy's approach but he quitted the
place and ran away as faft as he could with all his
men, and never ftopped till he came to the Bourg of
St. Lorenzo.   Piccinino at his arrival was not a little

fur-

furprized to find a pafs of fuch importance fo meanly
abandoned, and overjoyed that he had got poffeffion
of it. For he immediately marched down into the
Vale of Mugello, where he feized upon feveral Caftles, and at laft took up his quarters at Puliciano ;
from whence he made incurfions into the neighbouring territories, as far as the Mountains of Fiefole;
and grew fo bold at laft, that he paffed the Arno,
plundering and ravaging all the Country till he came
within three miles of Florence.

The Florentines however were not at all difmayed
at thefe proceedings, but in the firft place began to
ftrengthen the hands of the Government, which yet
ftood upon a pretty good bottom, confidering the
popularity that Cofimo de' Medici had gained by his
benevolence, and that the fupreme Magiftracy was
vefted in a very few of the principal Citizens, who
kept a ftrict hand upon fuch as they thought difaffected or defirous of a change. They knew that
Neri Capponi was bringing back with him a good
body of horfe, and depended upon the Pope's affiftance; the hopes of which kept up their Spirits till
the return of Neri: who at his arrival, finding the
City under fome apprehenfion, refolved to take the
field, in order to check Piccinino's career and prevent
him from making fuch terrible devaftation in the
Country. For this purpofe, having raifed what number of foot he could in the City to join his horfe, he
marched out and retook Remole, which the Duke's
forces had got poffeffion of: after which, he encamped near that place, and fent the Citizens word,
that he had already put an end to the enemy's depredations, and hoped in a fhort time to drive him
entirely out of their territories. But Piccinino finding that every thing was quiet at Florence, and nobody offered to raife any commotion there, (as he expected) though there were now no forces left in the
city to over-awe them, determined not to throw away
his time to no purpofe, but to go upon fome other
undertaking that might provoke the Florentine troops

to

to follow him, and give him an opportunity of coming to an engagement with them, in which he made
no doubt of routing them, and then he thought he
fhould be able to carry every thing before him.

Francifco Count of Poppi (though he entered into
the League with the Florentines) had revolted from
them when the enemy penetrated into the vale of
Mugello, and was at that time with Piccinino's army.
And as the Florentines had always fome fufpicion of
his fincerity from the firft, they endeavoured to attach him more firmly to their intereft by augment-
ing his ftipend, and making him intendant over all
their towns that lay near him. Yet (fuch is the pre-
valence of party fpirit in fome men) neither the
fenfe of paft favours nor the apprehenfion of future
danger, could make him forget his connexions with
Rinaldo degli Albizi, and thofe that had formerly
been his affociates in the government of Florence.
So that as foon as he heard of Piccinino's approach,
he not only went and joined him immediately, but
advifed him to leave the neighbourhood of Florence,
and march towards Cafentino ; acquainting him with
the faftneffes of that Country, and reprefenting to
him, with how much eafe and fecurity to himfelf, he
might from thence more effectually harrafs and diftrefs the enemy. Piccinino followed this advice, and
advancing into the territory of Cafentino, firft took
Romena and Bibiena, and then laid fiege to the Caftle
of St. Niccolo. This Caftle ftands upon the fkirts
of the Mountains that divide the State of Cafentino
from the Vale of Arno ; and as it was fituated upon
. an eminence and well garrifoned, it was not eafily
reduced, though he battered it day and night with
fuch engines and * artillery as he had. This Siege

* The original fays, *ancora che Niccola continuamente con briccole e
fimile artiglierie lo combatteffe.* Machiavel fays, in the latter end of
the firft book of this hiftory, that great guns were firft ufed in the
wars that happened betwixt the Venetians and the Genoefe, about
the ifland of Tenedos, in the year 1376, or thereabout. But we
don't find the leaft notice taken of them in any of the field engage-

had lasted twenty days; during which time, the Florentines assembled more forces, having got together about three thousand horse at Fegghine, and taken several other Officers into their pay under the command of Ursini their General, Neri Capponi, and † Bernardo de' Medici their Commissaries. At that place they received intelligence of the distress to which the Castle was reduced, by four different Messengers who were sent from thence to desire immediate relief. But the Commissaries having reconnoitred the Country, found it impossible to send the Besieged relief any other way than over the Mountains that extend themselves from the Vale of Arno; the heights of which, perhaps, might be occupied by the enemy before the succours could get thither, as they were so much further from them, and could not conceal their march: so that there was no hope of succeeding in such an attempt, and their army must otherwise be entirely ruined by it. They sent the Messengers back again therefore to the besieged with high commendations of their fidelity, and instructions to capitulate when they found they could defend themselves no longer.

After a siege of two and thirty days, Piccinino at last took the Castle; but he lost so much time in making such a trifling acquisition that it was in a great measure the ruin of his main design: for if he

---

ments or sieges that have hitherto been mentioned in this history, and it is much to be questioned, whether they were used in the siege of this castle. For *Broccole*, which is a very old word, does not signify *cannon*, but other warlike engines, or *tormenta bellica*; the *arbalestra*, the *catapulta*, the *balista*, and other machines of that kind, to batter and throw great stones and darts. Nor is the word *artillery* confined to great guns alone, but is often used to signify other machines and weapons of war. Thus, 1 *Sam.* xx. 40. *Jonathan gave his artillery to the lad, and said unto him, go carry them into the city*; where *arrows* are plainly meant. The same (*calaju*) occurs again, 2 *Sam.* i. 27. but is differently translated. *How are the mighty fallen, and the weapons of war perished!* or *lost*. That is, the arms and armour, which had been taken from Saul and his sons, and placed as trophies in the temple of *Ashtaroth*, after they were slain by the Philistines. The Septuagint in both places says, τασκευη πολεμικα, *military apparatus.*

† The author sometimes calls him Bernardo, and sometimes Bernardetto de' Medici.

had

had continued nearer Florence with his army, the Governors of the City would have found much greater difficulty in raifing money and forces and making other neceſſary proviſions, whilſt the enemy was in a manner at their gates, than they did after he had retired: and many of the difaffected party would have inclined to ſome accommodation with Piccinino, to prevent the expences of a war, which they ſaw was not likely to be ſoon ended. But the impatience of Count Poppi to be revenged of the go-vernors of thoſe fortreſſes, with whom he had long been at enmity, induced him to advife thoſe mea-ſures; and Piccinino took them to gratify him; which proved the deſtruction of them both in the end. And indeed it generally happens that private intereſts and paſſions are highly prejudicial to public under-takings.

Piccinino purſuing his ſuccefs, took Raffina and Chiuſi; in the neighbourhood of which, Count Poppi perfuaded him to fix his quarters, as he might extend his forces from thence to Caprefe, and from Caprefe to Pieve; by which he would become maſter of all the paſſes in the mountains, and might then make incurſions at his pleaſure into the territories of Caſentino, the vales of Arno, Chiana, and Tevere, and be ready to attack the enemy, if they ſhould offer to move. But Piccinino conſidering the rough-neſs and barrenneſs of thoſe parts, told him, *his horſes could not eat ſtones*; and proceeding to the Bourg of St. Sepulchro, where he was received as a friend, he then began to treat at a diſtance with the people of Caſtello, to ſee if he could corrupt them; but they were too firmly attached to the Florentines to be moved by his offers. However, as he was deſirous. to engage the Perugians in his intereſts, he went to Perugia with forty horſe, where he was honourably received on account of his being their fellow-citizen. But they ſoon began to look upon him with a ſuf-picious eye, when they ſaw him tampering with the Legate there, and ſome other Citizens, to whom he

made

made several proposals; all which being rejected, he
returned to his army with a present of eight thousand
ducats, which they had made him. After this, he
formed a design of taking Cortona from the Florentines, by a conspiracy, in which he had engaged some
of the inhabitants: but this also miscarried, as it was
discovered in good time. For the evening before it
was to have been put in execution, Bartolomeo di
Senso, one of the principal Citizens, going to mount
guard by the Governor's order, at one of the gates
of the town, was warned by a friend not to go thither, except he had a mind to be slain: and upon
asking what his friend meant by that advice, he was
informed of the whole affair, and immediately communicated it to the Governor. But the Governor
having secured the chief conspirators, and doubled
the guards at that gate, waited there for the arrival
of Piccinino: who, according to agreement, came at
a certain hour in the night: but finding his design
was blown, he returned to his former quarters.

Whilst things were thus circumstanced in Tuscany,
where the Duke's arms made but a feeble progress,
his affairs in Lombardy were in a still worse situation.
For Count Sforza had begun the Campaign there as
soon as ever the season permitted him: and the Venetians having got a new fleet in readiness, he determined in the first place to make himself master of
the Lake di Garda, and to drive the Duke's forces
entirely away from it; imagining when he had done
that, he should easily succeed in his other designs.
For this purpose, he attacked them with his gallies,
and not only defeated them, but took the castles they
had got possession of: and the rest of the Duke's
army, which invested Brescia by land, hearing of this
overthrow, immediately raised the siege, and left that
City at large, after it had been blocked up three
years. Upon this success, the Count marched after
the enemy, who had retreated to Soncino, a castle
upon the river Oglio; from whence he dislodged
them, and obliged them to retire to Cremona, where
they

they made a ftand, and refolved to defend that part of the Country. But as the Count now diftreffed the Duke more and more every day, he began to be afraid of lofing fome part of his dominions at leaft, if not all: and being fenfible of the error he had committed in fending Piccinino into Tufcany, he refolved to remedy it if he could, as foon as poffible; for which purpofe, he wrote to acquaint him in what condition his affairs were; ordering him to quit Tufcany immediately, whatever progrefs he might have there, and return into Lombardy.

The Florentines in the mean time having collected all their forces under their Commiffaries, were joined by thofe of the Pope at Anghiari, a Caftle at the foot of the mountains which part the Vale of Tevere from that of Chiana, about four miles from the Bourg of St. Sepulchro. The Country round about was plain and even, and the fields large and fit for horfe to act in, if they fhould come to an engagement. But as the Commiffaries had heard of the advantages which Count Sforza had gained, and that Piccinino was recalled, they were in hopes of putting an end to the war without drawing the fword or any further trouble; and therefore fent them orders to avoid an engagement by all means, fince that Commander could not ftay many days longer in Tufcany. Piccinino having intelligence of thefe orders, and finding himfelf obliged to leave the Country, refolved to make his utmoft efforts at the laft, and to give them battle; hoping to take them unprepared, as it was not their intention to fight him. To this, he was likewife earneftly perfuaded by Rinaldo degli Albizi, Count Poppi, and the reft of the Florentine exiles, who faw they fhould have no hopes after Piccinino abandoned them; but that if they came to an action, they probably might gain a Victory and fucceed in their wifhes; and if they loft the day, they fhould not be in worfe circumftances than they were before.

With

With this refolution, he moved with his forces
from the place where he then lay, which was betwixt Caftello and the Bourg, and arriving at the latter before the enemy had any notice of it, he drew
two thoufand men out of that town, who, confiding
in the valour of their General, and allured by the
promifes he made them, followed him in hopes of
enriching themfelves with plunder. From thence he
proceeded with his army in order of battle directly
towards Anghiari, and had advanced within lefs than
two miles of that place : when Micheletto Attendulo
perceiving a great cloud of duft raifed at a diftance,
fufpected the enemy was approaching, and immediately gave the alarm. Great was the confufion in
the Florentine Camp upon this occafion. For though
indeed very little order or difcipline was ever obferved by armies in their encampments in thofe days,
yet the fupinenefs of the Florentines was at this time
greater than ordinary: and as they thought the enemy
had been not only at a much greater diftance, but
rather inclined to retreat than hazard an engagement,
moft of them had laid afide their arms and ftraggled
away to places at a diftance from the Camp, either
to enjoy the fhade (as the weather was then very hot)
or indulge themfelves in fome other pleafure. Yet
fuch was the diligence of the Commiffaries and the
General in getting them together, that they were all
mounted and ready drawn up to receive the enemy
before they arrived. And as Attendulo was the firft
that difcovered them, he likewife fuftained their firft
fhock ; having pofted himfelf with the men under
his Command on a Bridge that lay upon the road at
a little diftance from Anghiari. Upon the approach
of the enemy, Urfini had caufed the banks and
ditches to be levelled, which lay on each fide of the
way betwixt Anghiari and the Bridge ; and Attendulo having taken poffeffion of the Bridge itfelf, the
Cavalry were placed to the right of him, under Si-
moncino Commander of the Forces of the Church,
and the Pope's Legate ; and to the left, under the
Flo-

Florentine Commiffaries and their General Urfini; the Infantry extending themfelves on each hand along the banks of the River. The enemy therefore, had no way to come at them but over the Bridge; nor could the Florentines be forced to engage in any other place. Upon which account they ordered their foot to ply that of the enemy brifkly with their Crofs-bows, if they fhould quit the high road and fall to the right and left of their own gens d'armes; that fo they might be prevented from taking their horfe in flank, as they paffed or repaffed the Bridge. Thofe that made the firft attack were bravely received and repulfed by Attendulo: but Aftorre and Francifco Piccinino * advancing to their relief with a picked body of men, charged him fo furioufly, that they obliged him to quit the Bridge, and purfued him to the bottom of the hill upon which Anghiari ftands, from whence they were driven back and forced over the Bridge again by the Infantry that attacked them in flank. The difpute lafted in this manner for the fpace of two hours; during which, fometimes Piccinino's forces, and fometimes the Florentines were Mafters of the Bridge. And though the fuccefs of each party was nearly the fame upon the Bridge, yet Piccinino had much the worft of it on both fides of the River. For whenever his forces poffeffed the Bridge, they found thofe of the enemy well drawn up and ready to act as occafion required; (an advantage that was gained by the precaution they had taken to level the banks and ditches on their fide) fo that when any of their men were hard pufhed and began to faint, they were immediately relieved by a frefh party. On the other hand, when the Florentines paffed it, Piccinino was fo embarraffed with the banks and ditches on his fide, that he found it very difficult to relieve his troops: and though they often gained the Bridge, they were conftantly driven back again by the enemy. The Flo-

* He was fon to the General, Niccolo Piccinino.

rentines

rentines therefore having once more got poffeffion of it, and pushing forward into the road on the other fide with great fury, Piccinino found himself ftraitened in fuch a manner by his fituation, that he had neither time nor room to fuccour his men that were giving way: fo that thofe who were in the front recoiling upon the rear, his whole army was thrown into fuch confufion, that they at laft turned their backs and fled with the utmoft precipitation towards the Bourg of St. Sepulchro. Upon which, the Florentine Soldiers, inftead of purfuing them, began to plunder and ftrip the prifoners they had taken, of their horfes, arms and accoutrements, and what elfe they had : and indeed the booty was not inconfiderable : for there were not quite a thoufand horfe that efcaped with Piccinino. And the inhabitants of St. Sepulchro who had followed him for the fake of plunder, being all taken, with the lofs of their baggage and colours, were not only ftripped themfelves, but afterwards forced to pay a ranfom for their liberty. This Victory was of great confequence to the Florentines, though not very prejudicial to the Duke's affairs : for if *they* had loft the day, all Tufcany muft have fallen into his hands. But as *his* forces were routed, he loft nothing but their arms and horfes ; a damage that might be repaired at no confiderable expence. Indeed it never happened that invafions were made with lefs danger and flaughter on the fide of the invaders, than in thefe times : for in a battle that lafted four hours, and in fo total an overthrow, there was but one man killed ; and he too, not by the edge of the fword, or in any honourable attempt, but by a fall from his horfe to the ground, where he was trampled to death in the rout. With fo much fecurity did they make war in thofe days ! for moft of the foldiers being mounted on horfeback and covered with armour, had but little occafion to fear death in any engagement : and if they were defeated and furrendered, they commonly had their lives fpared.

This

This battle, and what immediately happened after it, may serve to shew the weak and pitiful manner in which they made war in those times. For as soon as Piccinino was routed and had fled to St. Sepulchro, the Commissaries, to make their Victory complete, intended to have pursued and shut him up there : but there was not so much as one of their officers, nor even a private soldier that would follow them, till they had laid up their plunder in some place of security, and got cured of the wounds they pretended to have received. And, which was still more remarkable and audacious, they went off the next day, openly in a body, and without asking any leave either from their Commissaries or General, to Arezzo; from whence, after they had secured their booty, they returned to Anghiari. A manner of proceeding so contrary to all military rule and order, that the smallest remnant of a well-disciplined army, would easily and deservedly have recovered a Victory out of their hands which they so little merited. Nay they presently released all the gens d' armes or heavy armed horse they had taken prisoners, in spite of the Commissaries who would have had them detained in order to deprive Piccinino of their service. Certainly it must seem astonishing that such an army should ever gain a Victory, and still more so, that another should be found vile and dastardly enough to be beaten by so contemptible an enemy.

Whilst they were thus taken up in going to Arezzo and back again, Piccinino marched away with the remainder of his forces from St. Sepulchro towards Romagna and took the Florentine exiles along with him, who now falling into despair of ever returning to their own Country, dispersed themselves into different parts of Italy and other States, every man providing for himself as well as he could. Rinaldo degli Albizi retired to Ancona; and having lost all hopes in this world, he went a pilgrimage to the Holy Sepulchre, in order to prepare himself for a better. Soon after his return from thence he died suddenly at dinner,

ner, whilft he was celebrating the marriage of one of
his daughters: fortune feeming favourable to him in
this at leaft, that he was taken away in one of the
happieft days of his exile. He was a man truly refpectable in all the different conditions of his life, and
would have been ftill more fo, if he had been born
in an united City: for many of his good qualities
which excited envy and jealoufy amongft his fellow-
citizens in a factious Commonwealth, would have
been admired and rewarded any where elfe.

After the departure of Piccinino and the return of
the Florentine forces from Arezzo, the Commiffaries
advanced with them to St. Sepulchro, the inhabitants
of which place offered to furrender to them, but upon terms that they did not think fit to grant. And
whilft they were yet in treaty, the Pope's Legate * beginning to grow fufpicious that the Florentines were
not willing that town fhould revert into the hands of
the Church, was fo enraged, that very high words
paffed betwixt him and the Commiffaries; and the
troops commanded by each would certainly have come
to blows if the treaty had continued much longer:
but that being ended at laft to the fatisfaction of the
Legate, their differences were compofed. Whilft
thefe things were in agitation, they had intelligence
from fome quarters that Piccinino was marching towards Rome, and from others that he was gone into
la Marca d'Ancona. Upon which, the Legate determined that Count Sforza's troops fhould advance
towards Perugia, in order to relieve either la Marca,
or Rome, to which foever of the two he had bent
his courfe, and that Bernardo de' Medici fhould go
along with them ; whilft Neri Capponi went with the
Florentine forces to reduce Cafentino. Upon this
refolution, Neri marched away for Raffina, which he
prefently took ; and foon after, Bibiena, Prato Vecchio, and Romena: after which, he fat down before
Poppi, and made proper difpofitions for two different

---

* Piccinino the Patriarch of Aquilea before mentioned.

affaults

aſſaults upon that town at the ſame time ; one on the
ſide that looks towards the plain of Certomondo ;
and the other from the hill that extends itſelf from
thence to Fronzoli.   Count Poppi ſeeing himſelf now
abandoned and deſtitute of all ſuccour, had ſhut himſelf up there ; not in hopes of any relief, but to gain
time and make the beſt terms he could for himſelf.
So that when Neri drew cloſe to the town to make an
aſſault, he demanded a parley, and had as good terms
granted him as he could poſſibly expect in his circumſtances ; which were, that he ſhould be ſuffered
to depart himſelf with his children, and what effects
they could carry with them, and immediately deliver
up the poſſeſſion of the town and all his other dominions to the Florentines.   During the capitulation he
came out upon the bridge over the Arno which runs
cloſe by the town, and with tears in his eyes thus
addreſſed himſelf to Neri.   " If I had rightly conſidered my own ſituation and the power of your Maſters,
I ſhould now have come out as a friend to congratulate you upon your late Victory, and not as a van-
quiſhed enemy to implore your pity in theſe unhappy circumſtances.   Fortune indeed has given you
ſufficient reaſon to rejoice, and me to weep and lament my wretchedneſs.   I lately had horſes, and arms,
ſubjects and dominions and riches ; and who can wonder that it grieves me to loſe them ? But ſince your
Republic ſeems determined, and now has it in its
power, to reduce all Tuſcany into ſubjection, we for
our parts ſhall obey you : and it is ſome conſolation
to me, that if I had not been guilty of this error,
neither your generoſity nor my future gratitude might
perhaps have appeared in ſo fair a light to the world.
For if you ſhall be pleaſed to leave me ſtill in poſſeſſion of my dominions, it will be an illuſtrious and
indelible inſtance of your clemency.   My imprudence indeed has been great, but I ſubmit to your
mercy and compaſſion, not without hopes that you
will ſtill ſuffer me to enjoy this place of reſidence at
leaſt, which has deſcended to me from Anceſtors to
whom

whom your Republic has formerly lain under many and great obligations *." To this Neri made answer, " that the having placed his confidence in people that were never likely to do him any service, and being by that means in some measure the cause of the insults offered to the Republic of Florence; these considerations, added to the circumstances of the times, necessarily obliged them to deprive him of his dominions, and to turn him out of those places as an enemy, which he might still have enjoyed if he had behaved himself like a friend. That his conduct had been such as would not allow them to let him continue any longer in possession of a territory that gave him an opportunity of insulting a Republic upon any little change of fortune, which indeed had no occasion to stand in fear of his person, though his dominions were so situated that he might open a way at any time through them for an enemy to annoy it. But that if he thought he could by any means obtain another Principality in Germany, he was at liberty to withdraw thither, and the Republic desired he would do it; where they should not fail to shew him all manner of respect, in consideration of the favours which he said the Florentines had received from his Ancestors." The Count replied with great indignation, " that he would endeavour to get as far as possible from them;" and finding there was no good to be done by intreaties and supplications, immediately broke off all further treaty, and giving up the town and his other possessions, except his personal effects, he quitted it with his wife and children, bitterly lamenting his folly and the loss of a State which his family had governed above four hundred years. When the news of this success arrived at Florence, it occasioned very great rejoicings both amongst the People and the Magistrates. And as Bernardo de' Medici found that Piccinino had neither advanced

---

* This speech is almost wholly taken from that of Caractacus in the 12th book of Tacitus's Annals.

towards Rome nor la Marca, as had been falfely reported, he marched back again with his forces to rejoin thofe under the command of Neri Capponi; and both of them returning together to Florence, it was decreed that they fhould be received with the higheft demonftrations of honour and refpect that had ever been fhewn to any of their victorious Generals : and they accordingly made their entrance into the City amidft the public acclamations of the Sigª niory, the Captains of the Companies, and all their fellow-citizens.

END OF THE FIFTH BOOK.

THE

THE

HISTORY

OF

FLORENCE.

BOOK VI.

ARGUMENT.

What is, cr ought to be, the chief design of those that make war. The bounds they should prescribe to themselves. How the ancient Republics used to dispose of the booty taken from their enemies. The error of modern governments in that respect. The Duke of Milan proposes a peace to Count Sforza. The Count's answer to him. The ingratitude of the Venetians to Ostasio da Polenta. Micheletto Attenduli made General of the League. Sforza reduced to great distress by Piccinino. The insolence of the latter to the Duke of Milan. The Count marries the Duke's natural daughter. A peace concluded. Naples taken by Alphonso of Arragon. Baldaccio d' Anghiari, General of the Florentine foot, an able and experienced Commander, vilely assassinated by Bartolomeo Orlandini, a coward and poltroon. A reformation in the government of Florence. Piccinino disappointed of a certain victory by the Duke of Milan, and otherwise ill used by him, dies of grief. The Bentivogli and Canneschi, two powerful families in Bologna. The latter raise an insurrection there in favour of the Duke of Milan, and kill Annibal Bentivoglio, the head of that family; but are quelled and driven out of the City.

Reform

City. Santi, a baſtard Son of Hercules Bentivoglio, being made Governor of Bologna, and of Annibal's children, governs with great prudence. A new war in Lombardy. Count Sforza courted by all parties. The death of Pope Eugenius IV. who is ſucceeded by Nicholas V. The Duke of Milan dies. The Count in deſperate Circumſtances. The Milaneſe make him Commander in Chief of their forces. The Venetians aſpire to the Duchy of Milan. King Alphonſo invades the Florentines. A mutiny amongſt the forces of the latter for want of proviſions. King Alphonſo retreats out of Tuſcany, after he had loſt many of his men. A battle betwixt the Count and the Venetians at Caravaggio, in which the latter are totally defeated. The generoſity of the Count to a Venetian Proveditore, whom he had taken priſoner. A peace concluded betwixt him and the Venetians. He deſerts the Milaneſe. The Speech of their Ambaſſador to him. His anſwer. He lays ſiege to Milan, makes a truce, and draws off his army; but returns at the expiration of the truce, and reduces the City to great diſtreſs. Coſimo de' Medici befriends him *Coſimo* in his undertaking. The Venetians aſſiſt the Milaneſe. Count Sforza enters Milan, and is made Duke thereof; by the general conſent of the Citizens. He engages in a confederacy with the Florentines; and the King of Naples with the Venetians. The latter ſend Ambaſſadors to Florence. The anſwer of the Florentines to them, delivered by Coſimo de' Medici. The Florentines *Coſimo* prepare for war. Frederic III. Emperor of Germany, comes to Florence, and proceeds to Rome, where he is crowned. Tuſcany invaded by King Alphonſo's forces. Stephen Porcari, a Roman Citizen, conſpires to deliver his Country out of the hands of the Pope and the Prelates: but fails in the attempt, and is put to death. The Vale of Bagno, by the perfidy of Gambacorta, is upon the point of being delivered up to King Alphonſo, but prevented by the bravery of Antonio Gualdani. The Florentines take poſſeſſion of it, and reduce it to a Bailiwick. The fate of Gambacorta. The Florentines and Duke of Milan, invite Regnier of Anjou, into Italy.

Italy. He comes with supplies, but soon leaves them and returns to France; from whence he sends his son, John of Anjou, to Florence. Peace betwixt the Duke and the Venetians, Florentines, and other States. Alphonso accedes to it. New troubles raised by Giacopo Piccinino, privately encouraged by Alphonso. Pope Calixtus III. endeavours to raise a Crusade against the Turks. A prodigious tempest in Tuscany. The Genoese invaded by Alphonso. They put themselves under the protection of John of Anjou. King Alphonso dies and is succeeded by his Son Ferdinand. Calixtus dies, and Pius II. is chosen Pope in his room. The Genoese revolt from the French. The Kingdom of Naples invaded by John of Anjou, who routs Ferdinand: but the latter being reinforced by the Pope and the Duke of Milan, takes the field again, and drives his competitor out of the Kingdom.

IT always has been, and indeed ought to be, the main end and design of those that wage war, to enrich themselves and impoverish their enemies: nor is there any other reasonable motive to contend for victory and conquest, but the aggrandizement of one nation, and the depression of another. From hence it necessarily follows, that whenever any State is impoverished by its victories, or debilitated by its conquests, it has either proceeded too far, or fallen short of those purposes for which the war was undertaken. A Kingdom, or Commonwealth, may properly be said to be enriched by victory, when it extirpates its enemies, and becomes master of their possessions and revenues. On the contrary, they are weakened by their victories, when they cannot utterly extinguish the enemy (though perhaps they may in some measure have subdued him) and his possessions fall into the hands, not of the State itself, but its soldiery. Such a Government suffers much more from a victory than a defeat: for in one case, it is only exposed to the outrage of an enemy, but in the other, it is injured and oppressed by its own friends; which seem-
ing

8

ing more unnatural, is likewife the more infupportable, efpecially when it is thereby neceffitated to lay
frefh taxes, and other heavy burdens upon its fubjects.
And if the Governors have any humanity in them,
they cannot, furely, much rejoice at a victory which
fills all the reft of the community with murmurs and
dejection.   The beft governed Republics that we read
of in ancient hiftory, after they had obtained a victory, always ufed to throw the fpoil they had taken
from the enemy into the common Treafury, to diftri-
bute largeffes amongft the people, to remit their
taxes, and entertain them with magnificent fpectacles.
But the victories gained by thofe States, of whom we
are now writing, not only exhaufted their public treafure, but drained the purfe of every private man, and
after all, did not effectually fecure them againft any
further attempts from their enemies.   All which was
owing to the abfurd and ridiculous manner in which
they carried on their wars : for after a battle, the
conquerors generally contented themfelves with ftrip-
ing the enemy, and feldom put any of them to death,
or fo much as made them prifoners : fo that the vanquifhed always renewed the war, as foon as ever they
were provided again with horfes and arms by thofe
that had taken them into their pay.   And as the
booty and ranfom-money were claimed by the foldiery, the State, receiving no advantage from thence,
was forced to tear the fupplies it ftood in need of, out
of the bowels of its own fubjects *, who had the
mortification of feeing that inftead of reaping any
fort of benefit from a victory, it only ferved to make
their Governors proceed with lefs regard and compaffion in laying new burdens upon them.

Thefe foldiers conducting the war in fuch a manner, reduced both the conqueror and the conquered,
to the neceffity of raifing continual fupplies at home,
if they intended to maintain any authority or com-

* Does not this feem to be our own cafe, with regard to the cap-
tures made by our Ships of war ?

mand over their forces ; as one fide expected to be
new clothed and accoutred, and the other to be rewarded for their fervices : and fince thofe that had
been defeated could not take the field again till they
were remounted, and thofe that beat them would
fight no more till they had been rewarded, it generally happened, that the former did not fuftain much
lofs, nor the latter gain any confiderable advantage
by their victory ; for the conquered had, for the moft
part, put themfelves in a condition to make head
afrefh againft the conqueror, before he was in readinefs to purfue his blow. From this perverfe and
diforderly behaviour in the foldiery, it happened that
Piccinino had remounted his troops before the news
of his defeat had reached many parts of Italy, and
renewed the war with greater vigour than ever he
had done before. To the fame caufe it was owing
that he was able to furprize Verona : that after his
forces had been difperfed when Sforza retook that
town, he was in a condition to invade Tufcany with
a powerful army : and that after his misfortune at
Anghiari, he was grown ftronger, even before he got
into Romagna, than he was at the beginning of the
action that happened there : fo that the Duke of Milan now began to conceive fome hopes of being able
to defend Lombardy, which he had in a manner
given up for loft, during the abfence of that General. For whilft Piccinino was making fuch havock as he had done in Tufcany, his mafter was in
danger of being ftripp'd of his own dominions ; and
being apprehenfive that he fhould be totally ruined
before the other could come to his relief, though he
had fent to recall him, he refolved to try if he could
not in fome meafure check Count Sforza's career,
and divert the fury of a ftorm by artifice and addrefs, which he was not in a capacity to refift. For
this purpofe, he had recourfe to fuch expedients as
he had often availed himfelf of before in the like
conjunctures, and difpatched Niccolo da Efti, Prince
of Ferrara, to Pefchiera, where Sforza then lay, who

earneftly exhorted him to peace, and reprefented to him how prejudicial a continuation of the war was likely to prove to himfelf; fince if the Duke was reduced to fuch circumftances that he could not fupport his prefent power and reputation, the Count muft be the firft man that would fuffer by it, as neither the Venetians nor Florentines would have any further occafion for his fervice, nor of courfe any longer the fame efteem for his perfon. And to convince him of the Duke's fincerity in defiring a peace, he folemnly affured him in his name, that as foon as one was concluded, the marriage fhould be immediately confummated with his daughter, whom he would fend to Ferrara for that purpofe, and there in perfon deliver her into his own hands. To this the Count made anfwer, " that if the Duke was really defirous of a peace, he might eafily obtain one, as the Venetians and Florentines were no lefs inclinable to it: but that for his own part, he could put very little confidence in him, fince he well knew he would never make any peace, except he was compelled to it by downright neceffity; and that, as foon as the danger was over, he would inftantly renew the war : that he could not give much more credit to what he promifed concerning the marriage, as he had been fo often deceived by him before ; but if other things could be amicably adjufted, he would proceed in that matter as he fhould be advifed by his friends."

The Venetians, naturally apt to fufpect their Generals, even when they have no reafon, had fufficient caufe to look with great jealoufy upon thefe negotiations, as indeed they did : and the Count being aware of it, endeavoured in fome meafure to recover their confidence by a vigorous profecution of the war. But the ufual alacrity of the one was at laft fo abated by his ambitious views ; and the minds of the other fo enflamed with fufpicion, that no other enterprife worth notice was undertaken during the reft of that Summer : fo that when Piccinino returned

into

into Lombardy, the Winter being come on, the respective armies went into quarters, the Count retiring to Verona, the Duke's forces to Cremona, the Florentines into Tuscany, and those of the Pope into Romagna. The last, after the battle of Anghiari, made an assault upon Furli and Bologna, in hopes of wresting them out of the hands of Francisco Piccinino, who held them in his father's name: but they were so well defended by Francisco, that the attempt did not succeed. Their march into those parts, however, struck such a terror into the people of Ravenna, that, to avoid falling into the hands of the Church, they (with the consent of Oftasio da Polenta their Lord) put themselves under the dominion of the Venetians; who, as a recompence for that favour, and to prevent Oftasio from ever recovering by force what he had so simply given away, sent him and his only Son to spend the rest of their days in Candia. These different enterprizes had so drained the Pope of money, that notwithstanding the Victory gained at Anghiari, his Holiness was obliged to sell the Castle of Borgo di San Sepulchro to the Florentines for the sum of twenty-five thousand ducats.

Things being in this situation, and both sides thinking themselves safe from any attack during the winter, all further thoughts of peace were laid aside, especially by the Duke; who now looking upon himself as sufficiently secured, in the first place by the season of the year, and in the next by the arrival of Piccinino, had broke off his treaty with the Count, and applied himself with great diligence to furnish his General with Cavalry and all other provisions that were necessary to continue the war. The Count, on the other hand, having intelligence of these preparations, immediately repaired to Venice to concert measures with the Senate there, for opening the next campaign. As soon as Piccinino was in readiness to take the field, and perceived the enemy was yet in no capacity to oppose him, he did not wait for the approach of the Spring, but passed the Adda in

I   the

the depth of Winter, entered the territories of Brefcia, and making himfelf mafter of all that Country,
except Adula and Acri, furprized above two thoufand of Sforza's Cavalry, who, not expecting any
fuch vifit, were all taken prifoners and ftripped. But
what moft chagrined the Count and alarmed the Venetians, was the defection of Ciarpellone, one of his
principal Officers, who had mutinied and quitted their
fervice. Upon the news of which, he pofted away
from Venice to Brefcia, and finding at his arrival
there, that Piccinino, after he had committed the
above mentioned hoftilities, was returned to his former quarters and lay quiet there, he did not care to
provoke him to ftir out of them again at that time ;
but thought it more prudent to make ufe of the opportunity which the enemy gave him, to put his forces
in good order, that fo he might be able to take any
advantage that offered and wipe off his late difgrace
at a proper feafon. He therefore prevailed upon the
Venetians to recall the forces they had in the fervice
of the Florentines, and perfuaded them to take Micheletto Attenduli into their pay, in the room of Gattamelata who was now dead.

At the return of the fpring, Piccinino appearing
firft in the field, laid fiege to Cignano, a Caftle about
twelve miles from Brefcia ; to the relief of which
the Count likewife marched out with his forces ; and
the war was once more begun and conducted in the
ufual manner betwixt thofe two Generals. The
Count on one fide, being apprehenfive that Bergamo
would fall into the enemy's hand, fat down before
Martinengho, a Caftle fo fituated, that whoever was
mafter of it might eafily throw fuccours into Bergamo,
which City was very much ftraitened by Piccinino ;
who, on the other hand, being fenfible that he could
not be annoyed from any other quarter, had taken
care to furnifh it with all manner of provifions for
its defence ; fo that the Count was forced to bring his
whole army before it. Piccinino therefore pofted
himfelf with all his forces likewife in fuch a fituation,

that

that, he entirely cut off all supplies from Sforza's camp, and fortified his own so strongly with ditches and breast-works, that the Count could, not attack him without manifest disadvantage: so that the besiegers were in much greater danger than those that were besieged. In these circumstances, as the Count could neither continue the siege for want of provisions, nor raise it for fear of Piccinino falling upon him, every body concluded the Duke must certainly gain a complete Victory, and that Sforza and the Venetians would be utterly undone. But by the caprice of Fortune, who takes delight in shewing her power to exalt her minions, and ruin such as are not in her good graces, things took a very different turn: for Piccinino grew so intolerably insolent and ambitious, in full confidence of Victory, that forgetting himself and laying aside all due respect to his Prince, he sent him word, " that as he had fought his battles so many years without being requited with so much ground as would bury him when he died, he desired to know what reward he might expect for his services : for since it was now in his power to make him absolute Lord of Lombardy and deliver up all his enemies into his hands, he thought a certain Victory deserved a certain recompence; and therefore demanded that the city of Placentia should be assigned to him, whither he might retire to enjoy a little repose at last, after so long a course of labour and fatigue." Nay he proceeded so far in the end as to threaten the Duke that he would abandon the enterprize if his demands were not complied with.

But the Duke was exasperated at this audacious behaviour to such a degree, that he chose rather to give up so great an advantage, than meanly to submit to his insolence ; so that what neither the menaces of his enemies, nor the many imminent dangers he had been in, could ever move him to consent to, he was at last induced to comply with by the arrogance of his friends ; and immediately resolved to come to an accommodation with the Count. For

which

which purpofe he fent Antonio Guido Buona da Tortona to him, with an offer of his daughter, and fuch
overtures for a peace, as were eagerly accepted both
by him and the reft of the confederates.

. As foon as the articles were privately figned, by
all parties, the Duke fent orders to Piccinino to make
a truce with the Count for one year, pretending,
"that he was fo tired of the expences of war, that he
could not help preferring a certain peace, to a victory that was ftill doubtful." Piccinino was thunder-
ftruck at this refolution, not being able to compre-
hend what motives could induce the Duke to let fo
glorious a victory flip out of his hands; little imagining that the reafon of fuffering his enemies to
efcape, was only to avoid recompenfing his friends.
He oppofed it, however, as much as lay in his power,
and behaved in fo refractory a manner, that in order
to force him to a compliance, the Duke threatened
to give him up, to be treated by the foldiers of both
armies, as they pleafed, if he did not inftantly obey
his orders. Upon which he was obliged to fubmit,
but with the fame reluctance that a man may be fuppofed to do, who is compelled to leave his friends
and country; lamenting his evil deftiny, and complaining with much bitternefs both of fortune and
the Duke, who had confpired together to fnatch the
victory out of his hands. After the truce was concluded, the nuptials were celebrated betwixt Madam
Bianca and the Count, who received the City of Cremona with her in dower: and in November 1441. a
peace was agreed upon; at the figning of which,
Francifco Barbadico and Paolo Trono affifted as Plenipotentiaries for the Venetians, and Agnolo Acciaiuoli for the Florentines. By this treaty, the fortreffes of Pefchiera, Afola, and Leonato, in the
Marquifate of Mantua, were ceded to the Venetians.

Though the war in Lombardy was now at end, the
kingdom of Naples was ftill far from being in peace:
and as no means could be found of quieting the diftractions there, they proved at laft the occafion of

raifing

raiſing freſh combuſtions in Lombardy. For during the laſt, King Regnier had been ſtripped of every town that he had got poſſeſſion of in that Kingdom, except the city of Naples itſelf, by Alphonſo of Arragon; who now thinking himſelf ſure of the whole, determined, at the ſame time that he laid ſiege to that City, to ſeize upon Benevento *, and ſome other towns belonging to Count Sforza, in the adjacent territory, which he thought might eaſily be effected, whilſt the Count himſelf was ſo fully employed in Lombardy. And he actually ſucceeded in his deſign, making himſelf Maſter of all thoſe places with little or no difficulty. But, upon the news of a peace being concluded in Lombardy, Alphonſo grew apprehenſive, that the Count would ſoon march to join Regnier, in order to recover his own poſſeſſions; and Regnier not being without ſome expectations of the ſame kind, ſent to entreat the Count to come to the aſſiſtance of a friend, eſpecially as he might, at the ſame time, revenge himſelf upon an enemy. Alphonſo, on the other hand, earneſtly ſollicited Duke Philip, that out of regard to the friendſhip which had ſo long ſubſiſted betwixt them, he would cut out ſome work of greater conſequence to the Count, in order to divert him from this deſign. With this the Duke readily complied, not conſidering, that it would be a direct violation of the treaty he had ſo lately concluded. He, therefore, in the firſt place, ſuggeſted to Pope Eugenius, that he now had a fair opportunity of recovering the territories which Sforza had taken from the Church; and for that purpoſe, recommended Piccinino to him (who after the concluſion of a peace, had retired with his forces into Romagna) and ſaid, he would pay him out of his own purſe, as long as

---

* Benevento is ſituated at the confluence of the river Solato and Colore, which here form the Volturno, 130 miles ſouth eaſt of Rome, and 34 north eaſt of Naples. It is an Archbiſhoprick, ſubject to the Pope, who is ſovereign of this City. The greater part of it was demoliſhed by an earthquake, in the year 1688, and the Archbiſhop of it dug out of the ruins; who, being afterwards advanced to the Papal Chair, by the name of Benedict XIII rebuilt this City.

the

the war continued. Eugenius, out of the ancient hatred which he bore to the Count, and the defire he had of recovering the poffeffions he ufurped from him, liftened with great eagernefs to this propofal, and though he had formerly been duped by Piccinino, in the very fame manner, he thought, now the Duke of Milan was on his fide, he had no occafion to miftruft him; and therefore immediately joining his forces with thofe of Piccinino, he made an incurfion into la Marca d' Ancona. The Count, on the other hand, though not a little furprifed at fo fudden an invafion, having affembled what troops he could raife, marched out to face the enemy.

In the mean time Alphonfo had taken Naples; fo that all the kingdom was now in his poffeffion, except Caftel Nuovo, in which Regnier had left a ftrong garrifon, and was gone himfelf to Florence, where he was received with much honour: but after he had ftaid a few days there, and found he could no longer continue the war, he went to Marfeilles. During this fhort interval, Caftel Nuovo had likewife fallen into the hands of Alphonfo; and Count Sforza perceiving he was not able to cope with Piccinino and the Pope in la Marca, had recourfe to the Venetians and Florentines for fupplies both of men and money; reprefenting to them, that if they did not take proper meafures to check the ambition of the Pope and King Alphonfo, whilft he was in a capacity to affift them, it would foon behove them to look to themfelves, as they would afterwards certainly join with the Duke of Milan, and divide Italy amongft them. To thefe follicitations the Florentines and Venetians were for fome time in doubt what anfwer to return, as they did not care to break with the Pope and Alphonfo, and their attention was likewife at that time wholly turned upon affairs at Bologna *.

---

* Bologna, or Bononia, lies about 50 miles north of Florence, and 200 miles north-weft of Rome, on feveral little rivulets, and a navigable canal, in one of the moft fruitful plains of Italy, and is

Anni-

Annibal Bentivoglio had lately driven Francifco Piccinino out of that city, and to defend himfelf againft the Duke of Milan, (who fupported Francifco) demanded the aid of the Venetians and Florentines, who readily granted it : fo that whilft their forces were employed in that fervice, they were doubtful whether they fhould be able to affift Sforza. But afterwards, when Annibal had entirely got the better of his adverfary, and that affair was over, the Florentines determined to fend him relief. However, in order to fecure themfelves againft the Duke, they, in the firft place, renewed the League with him, to whch the Duke himfelf was not averfe : for though he had in fome meafure contributed to bring that war upon the Count at a time when Regnier had got footing in the Kingdom of Naples ; yet, when he faw him vanquifhed and utterly driven out of it, he did not care to have the Count alfo deprived of his dominions, and therefore not only gave his confent that others fhould fend him fuccours, but wrote himfelf to defire Alphonfo would return with his forces to Naples and give the Count no further difturbance ; which he feemed very unwilling to comply with : but confidering his obligations to the Duke, he at laft acquiefced, and withdrew with his troops to the other fide of the Trenta.

Whilft things were thus circumftanced in Romagna, the Florentines had fome difturbances at home. Amongft thofe that had the chief authority in the Government there, Neri the Son of Gino Capponi was *Cofimo* one of whofe reputation Cofimo de' Medici was more jealous than of that of any other perfon ; as he had not only very great credit in the City, but was ex-

therefore called *Bologna the Fat*. This City is about five miles in circumference, remarkable for its magnificent Churches and Monafteries, and the riches and fine paintings in them. The inhabitants are computed to amount to about 70,000. It is the See of an Archbifhop, and one of the moft confiderable Univerfities in Europe, fubject to the Pope, and governed by his Legate. There is an Academy of Literati here, who ftile themfelves *Gli Otiofi*, from their retirement and tranquillity.

ceedingly

ceedingly beloved by the foldiery, whofe affections he had gained by his bravery, humanity, and good conduct when he commanded the troops of the Republic, as he had done upon feveral occafions. Befides which, the remembrance of the victories that had been gained by him and his father (one of whom had taken Pifa, and the other defeated Niccolo Piccinino at the Battle of Anghiari) made him refpected by many, and feared by others who did not defire any more affociates in the Government. But of all their Generals Baldaccio de Anghiari was certainly the moft eminent; nor was there any man in Italy at that time who furpaffed him either in courage, or military fkill, or bodily accomplifhments : and having always commanded the Infantry, they had fuch an opinion of him, that it was generally believed he could influence them to execute any purpofe, and that they would follow him in any undertaking whatfoever. This Baldaccio was very intimate with Neri, for whom he had the higheft efteem on account of his valour and other good qualities, of which he had long been a witnefs : but it was a connexion that excited infinite jealoufy amongft the reft of the principal Citizens, who thinking it dangerous to let him enjoy his liberty, and ftill more fo to imprifon him, refolved to have him difpatched; in which, fortune feemed to fecond their defign. Bartolomeo Orlandini was then Gonfalonier of Juftice; who having been fent to defend the pafs of Marradi, when Niccolo Piccinino invaded Tufcany, had fhamefully deferted it, (as we have before related) and abandoned all that country to the fury of the enemy, which, from the nature of its fituation, was of itfelf almoft inacceffible. So flagrant a piece of cowardice, provoked Baldaccio to fuch a degree, that he could not help expreffing his contempt of him, both in public converfation, and the letters which he wrote to his friends, in terms that not only excited Orlandini's refentment, but made him thirft for revenge, and flatter himfelf that he fhould extinguifh the infamy of

the

the fact, by the death of his accuser. · To this resolution * some other Citizens were privy, who encouraged him in it, and said by so doing he would sufficiently revenge the injuries which he had suffered
himself, and at the same time deliver the government
from the fear of a man whom it was dangerous to
employ, and might be their ruin to dismiss. Orlandini therefore, being confirmed in his purpose to af-
fassinate him, shut up several armed men in his apartment; and the next day when Baldaccio came to attend at the Palace (as he did most days) to confer
with the Magistracy concerning the pay of his soldiers, he was ordered to wait upon the Gonfalonier
immediately; which he did, without suspecting any
danger. As soon as they met and had taken a turn
or two in the gallery which is before the chambers of
the Signiory, they began to talk about their affairs,
and at last coming near the door of the apartment
where the armed men were concealed, the Gonfalonier gave them a signal: upon which, they instantly
rushed out, and as Baldaccio had neither arms nor
attendants, they soon dispatched him, and threw him
out of the Palace window that looks towards the Do-
gana, or Custom-house, from whence he was carried
into the Piazza, and after they had cut off his head,
his body was exposed there all that day as a spectacle
to the People. He left only one Son, who was but
a boy, and did not long survive his father. His Widow Annalena, being thus deprived both of her Hufband and Child, resolved to have no further commerce with the World, and having converted her
house into a sort of Convent, she shut herself up in it
with several other Ladies of Noble families, and there
spent the rest of her days, in acts of piety and devotion, immortalizing her memory by endowing and
calling the Convent after her own name.

* This vague and indiscriminate manner of speaking, seems rather
a stroke of partiality in the author; as it is well known, that these
other Citizens were the Medici, on whose family Machiavel was dependent when he wrote this history. Compare this with what he says
of his impartiality in the Dedication to Clement VII.

This

This tragical event gave a confiderable check to Capponi's intereft, and diminifhed the number of his partifans. The governors however did not ftop here : for as they had now been ten years in the adminiftration, and the authority of the Balia was expired, many began both to talk and act with much greater freedom than they thought was confiftent with the fecurity of the State. In order therefore to eftablifh themfelves in their power, they judged it neceffary to revive that Court; by which they would have an opportunity of ftrengthening the hands of their friends, and more effectually depreffing their enemies. With this view, the Councils inftituted a new Balia in the year 1444, *1444.* which confirmed the prefent Magiftrates in their refpective departments, vefted the privilege of chufing the Signiory in a few hands, and new-modelled the *Chancery of Reformation*, depofing the Prefident Philip Peruzzi, and fetting another perfon at the head of it, who they were well affured would conform himfelf to their inftructions. They likewife prolonged the banifhment of fuch as they had before fent into exile, imprifoned Giovanni the Son of Simone Vefpucci, and deprived all thofe of their honours and employments, that adhered to their enemies; amongft whom, were the Sons of Pietro Baroncelli, the whole family of the Seragli, Bartolomeo Fortini, Francifco Caftellani, and many others. By fuch means they at the fame time regained their former authority and reputation, and quafhed all oppofition : and having thus got entire poffeffion of the Government at home, they now began to turn themfelves with more attention to foreign affairs.

Niccolo Piccinino, as we have already faid, was abandoned by King Alphonfo, and Count Sforza grown fo powerful by the affiftance of the Florentines that he attacked him near Fermo, and gave him fo total an overthrow, that he efcaped with but very few of his men to Montecechio; where however he fortified himfelf in fuch a manner, that being foon rejoined by almoft all his forces, he was able to defend

fend himself againft the Count; efpecially, as he was favoured by the approach of the Winter, which obliged them both to fend their troops into quarters.

During the courfe of the Winter, Piccinino's chief care was to recruit his army, which was alfo not a little reinforced by other fupplies from the Pope and King Alphonfo : fo that as foon as the Spring came on, both Generals took the field again : but Piccinino's forces being much fuperior, reduced the Count to fuch extremities that he would have been utterly ruined, if the Duke of Milan had not interfered, and once more fnatched the Victory out of his adverfary's hand, by fending him word that he muft inftantly repair to his Court, for he wanted to confer perfonally with him about fome affairs of the utmoft importance to himfelf. Upon this, Piccinino, eager to know what thofe affairs were, immediately pofted away to Milan, and left his Son Francifco to command the army, relinquifhing a certain Victory for vain and fallacious hopes. For the Count being aware of this, refolved not to neglect fo great an advantage, but to draw the enemy to an engagement if poffible in the abfence of their General ; in which he fucceeded according to his wifh, and not only routed Francifco's forces, but took him prifoner near Monte Loro. Niccolo on the other hand, finding himfelf decoyed by the Duke, and hearing of his Son's misfortune foon after his arrival at Milan, was fo affected with it, that he died of grief in the year 1445, at the age of 64, a more valiant than fortunate commander. He left two Sons, Francifco and Giacopo, whofe valour was by no-means equal to that of their father, and their fortune ftill more unfavourable ; fo that the glory of the Braccefcan party was now in a manner totally eclipfed, whilft the arms of the Sforzas, being more fuccefsful, daily increafed their intereft and reputation. The Pope therefore, now Piccinino was dead and his army diffipated, not expecting much affiftance from Alphonfo, refolved to come to an accommodation with Count Sforza, which at laft was

brought

brought about by the mediation of the Florentines; it being agreed betwixt them, that Ofimo, Fabriano, and Recanati, towns in la Marca de Ancona, fhould be reftored to his Holinefs, and that the Count fhould remain in poffeffion of the reft of that territory.

After this peace, all Italy would have been in tranquillity, if it had not been prevented by the difturbances that happened at Bologna. There were then two very powerful families in that City, the Cannefchi and the Bentivogli: Annibal was head of the latter, Battifta of the former. To create a mutual confidence betwixt thefe two families, and to avail themfelves of each other's affiftance, there had been feveral intermarriages betwixt them: but amongft people that afpire to the fame degree of grandeur, it is much eafier to contract an alliance, than a friendfhip. Bologna was in league with the Venetians and Florentines, a treaty having been made with them for that purpofe by Annibal Bentivoglio, after the expulfion of Francifco Piccinino; but Battifta Cannefchi knowing how defirous the Duke of Milan was to have an intereft there, had engaged in a confpiracy with that Prince, to difpatch Annibal, and deliver up the City into his hands. Accordingly, when they had concerted proper meafures for the execution of their defign, on the 24th of June, 1445, Battifta and his accomplices fell upon Annibal, and killed him: after which, they ran about the Streets, crying out, *Long live the Duke of Milan.* The Venetian and Florentine Commiffaries happening to be in the Town at that time, immediately retired to their houfes upon the firft rumour of the fact; but afterwards, when they faw the people run together in arms againft the murderers, and bitterly lamenting the death of Annibal, they took courage, and having joined them with their domeftics, attacked the Cannefchi and their followers, whom they foon got the better of, killing fome, and driving the reft out of the Town. Battifta himfelf not being able to make his efcape, nor his enemies to lay hold on him,

hid

hid himfelf in a vault, in his own houfe, where he
ufed to keep his grain: but the people, after they
had fought for him in vain all day, though they knew
he had not got out of the City, at laft came back to
his houfe, and fo terrified the fervants with their
threats, that one of them difcovered where he had
concealed himfelf; from whence they pulled him out,
covered with armour as he ftill was; and after they
had put him to death, they firft dragged his body
through the ftreets, and then burnt it to afhes. Thus
having vainly depended upon the Duke's victorious
arms to fupport him, he perifhed in the attempt, for
want of proper fuccour.

The death of Battifta, and the expulfion of his
whole family, put an end to that infurrection indeed,
but the City ftill continued in great confufion; for
there was nobody left of the houfe of Bentivoglio
that was capable of governing it, as Annibal had
left but one fon, a boy of only fix years of age, whofe
name was John: fo that it was apprehended fome divifions would arife amongft the friends of the Bentivogli, which might open a door for the return of
the Cannefchi, to the utter ruin, not only of their
party, but of the whole City. Whilft they were in
this perplexity, Francifco, who had formerly been
Count of Poppi, happening to be then at Bologna,
fignified to the principal Citizens, " that if they had
a mind to be governed by a perfon that was of Annibal's blood, he knew where to find fuch a one: for
about twenty years before, one Hercules Bentivoglio,
a Coufin of Annibal, being at Poppi, had enjoyed
a young woman of that place, who afterwards was
brought to bed of a fon, whofe name was Santi; and
that he had often heard him acknowledge the child
as his own: which feemed the more probable, as
there was a very ftrong refemblance betwixt them."
This fuggeftion was liftened to with much eagernefs
by the Citizens, who not only gave credit to the ftory,
but immediately fent deputies to Florence to fee the
young man, and endeavour to prevail upon Neri
Cap-

Capponi, and Cofimo de' Medici, to deliver him to them.

Agnolo da Cafcefe, the reputed father, was dead, and Santi himself at that time under the care of an uncle, whofe name was Antonio da Cafcefe. This Antonio was a rich man, had no children of his own, and lived in great friendfhip with Neri, who being informed of thefe circumftances, thought it was an offer not to be defpifed, nor yet to be rafhly accepted ; and therefore determined that Santi fhould be introduced to Cofimo, together with the deputies that came from Bologna, where they might hear what each party had to fay for themfelves. This being done, the deputies not only acknowledged Santi, and treated him with the higheft refpect, but were almoft ready to proftrate themfelves before him, out of the ancient love they bore to his family and friends. Nothing, however, was concluded upon at that time : but Cofimo taking Santi afide, faid to him, " Young man, there is nobody that is capable of advifing you fo well in fuch a cafe as yourfelf ; and I would have you follow the dictates of your own genius : for if you are really the fon of Hercules Bentivoglio, you will naturally afpire to fuch actions as will be worthy of your father and his family : but if you are the fon of Agnolo Cafcefe, you will of courfe incline to continue in Florence, and fpend the reft of your life in combing wool, or fome other fuch vile occupation." The young man, who before feemed indifferent about the matter, or rather unwilling to accept the offer, being ftung with the farcafm, made anfwer, " that he would leave himfelf wholly to the direction of Cofimo and Neri ; and as they thought proper to comply with the requeft of the Bolognefe, he was foon provided with rich cloths, horfes, and equipage, and a few days afterwards conducted, in the midft of a numerous attendance to Bologna, where he was appointed Governor, not only of Annibal Bentivoglio's children, but of the City, and behaved himfelf with fo much prudence in thofe charges, that, though moft

of his predeceffors had been murdered by their enemies, he, on the contrary, lived all his days in great
honour, and died a natural death.

After Niccolo Piccinino was dead, and a peace concluded in la Marca, the Duke of Milan, ftanding in
need of another General to command his forces, made
fome fecret overtures for that purpofe to Ciarpellone,
who had returned into Count Sforza's fervice, and
was one of his moft experienced officers; and Ciarpellone having accepted the offer, demanded leave of
the Count to go to Milan, that he might take poffeffion of fome Caftles, which the Duke had given him
in the late wars. But the Count fufpecting his defign, caufed him, in the firft place, to be arrefted,
and foon after, to be put to death, that the Duke
might not avail himfelf of his fervice, if any future
difference fhould happen betwixt them ; pretending,
that he had difcovered a confpiracy, in which he was
engaged againft him. The Duke, indeed, was thoroughly exafperated at the difappointment ; but it
was matter of joy to the Florentines and Venetians,
who were always jealous of any connexion that might
make the arms of the Count fubfervient to the power
and ambition of the Duke. It ferved, however, to
excite frefh troubles, and kindle new wars in la
Marca.

Gifmondo Malatefta * was at that time Lord of Rimini, and as he had married the Count's daughter,

---

* Sigifmund Malatefta, or Gifmondo, as Machiavel calls him, was
a Philofopher, an Hiftorian, a great Soldier, and one of the moft renowned Commanders of the fifteenth Century. But thefe accomplifhments were obfcured by many very bad qualities. For he was
exceeding profligate and prophane, ridiculed a'l Religion, denied
the Immortality of the Soul, and ftuck at nothing to ferve his private intereft and ambition : by which behaviour he fo offended Pius
II. that he excommunicated him in the year 1462. This Commander, in conjunction with Count Sforza, routed Antonio Ordelaffi,
Lord of Furli ; and afterwards making war upon his other neighbours, almoft always with good fuccefs, the Venetians made him
their General. He then pafled into the Morea, and took Sparta, and
feveral other places from the Turks. At his return, the Florentines
and Sienefe appointed him Commander in Chief of their forces, to
make war upon Pius ; but he was not fuccefsful in that. He died

ex-

expected to have obtained the government of Pesaro
from him : but the Count, soon after he had got
possession of that place, gave it to his own brother
Alexander, which was highly resented by Gismondo ;
and what exasperated him still more, was, that Frederic di Montefeltro, his declared enemy, had taken
Urbino from him, chiefly by the assistance of the
Count. Upon these provocations, he went over to
the Duke, and earnestly sollicited the Pope, and the
King of Naples, to make war upon his father-in-law ;
who, in order to give Gismondo a taste of the war
he seemed so fond of, resolved to be before-hand with
them, and attack him in the first place. This presently filled all Romagna, and la Marca with tumult
and confusion : for the Duke, the King of Naples,
and the Pope, all sent powerful succours to the aid of
Malatesta : and on the other hand, both the Florentines and the Venetians supplied the Count with what
Money he wanted, though they did not send him any
men. Nor was the Duke content with carrying his
arms into Romagna, he designed likewise, if possible,
to strip the Count of Pontremoli and Cremona * : but
the former was defended by the Florentines, and the
latter by the Venetians. From these sparks a fresh
war was kindled up in Lombardy, where, after some

October 6, 1467, at the age of fifty one, leaving many children ;
amongst whom was Robert Malatesta, a famous warrior in his day,
who was a General in the Venetian service, and afterwards commanded the army of Sixtus IV. against Alphonso, King of Naples,
and the rest of his allies, whom he routed in 1482. The Pope ordered an Equestrian Statue to be erected for him in St. Peter's
Church. The Malatesti were a very powerful family, and governed
both Pesaro and Rimini a long time ; in the latter they maintained
themselves above two hundred years. Clement VII. at last took it
from Pandolpho Malatesta, who died in poverty at Ferrara. Mar-
chesélli & Sanfovino Orig. di famig. Ital.

* Cremona is the capital of the Cremonese, in the Duchy of Milan, situated upon the Po, 45 miles south-east of that City. Here
Prince Eugene, the Imperial General, surprized the French General
Marshal Villeroy, in his bed, and carried him off in the year 1702,
and would infallibly have taken the City, if the troops, appointed
to support him, had not lost their way. The Prince entered the
town in the night by a subterraneous passage, which had been an
aqueduct, and returned the same way, with very little loss.

skir-

skirmishes in the Cremonese, Francisco Piccinino, the Duke's General, was totally defeated by Micheletto Attenduli, who commanded the Venetian forces, in an engagement that happened near Casal. This victory so elated the Venetians, that they began to conceive hopes of making themselves masters of all the Duke's dominions: for which purpose, they sent a commissary with an army towards Cremona, who took Ghiaradadda by assault, reduced the whole country round about it, except Cremona itself, and then passing the Adda, made incursions up to the very gates of Milan. In this exigency, the Duke had recourse to King Alphonso, for succours; representing to him the danger his own dominions would be in, if Lombardy should fall into the hands of the Venetians: upon which consideration, Alphonso promised to send him the succours he requested, though it would be a very difficult matter, he said, to find any passage into Lombardy, if the Count should endeavour to prevent it. He therefore likewise applied to the Count himself, whom he earnestly entreated not to abandon his father-in-law, now he was weighed down with years, and had lost his sight. The Count, indeed, was not a little enraged at the Duke, for taking part in that war against him; and on the other hand, he could not help looking with some jealousy on the power of the Venetians, and the deficiency of his remittances, as the league began to grow very sparing in furnishing him with supplies: for the Florentines were now freed from those apprehensions of the Duke, which had formerly made them so much caress the Count; and the Venetians wished to see him ruined, as he was the only man that could prevent them from becoming masters of all Lombardy. Nevertheless, whilst the Duke was thus endeavouring to draw him over to his interests, and offered him the command of all his forces, provided he would leave the Venetians, and restore what he possessed in la Marca to the Pope, they also thought proper to send Ambassadors to him, with a promise of Milan, if they took it, and the command of their troops for life, upon condition that he would continue the war in la Marca, and obftruct the paffage of the fuccours which Alphonfo was going to fend into Lombardy.

The offers of the Venetians were very tempting, and the favours he had received from them confiderable, as they had entered into the war merely to fecure Cremona to the Count : on the contrary, the injuries the Duke had done were frefh upon his mind, and he knew his promifes were always infincere, and not to be depended upon. He therefore was in doubt what refolution to take : for on one fide he confidered his engagements with the league, the forfeiture of his honour, the late good offices they had done him, and the promifes of further reward : on the other, he could not help being moved by the entreaties of his father-in-law, nor to fufpect there was fome latent poifon in the magnificent promifes that were made him by the Venetians; efpecially as he was fenfible, that if ever they gained their ends, he fhould then have nothing to truft to but their mercy and honour for the performance of them, and even for his own prefervation, and that of his dominions; a condition to which no wife Prince would ever fubmit, except compelled by downright neceffity. But the ambition of the Venetians, at laft, put an end to the Count's fufpenfe; for as they had formed a defign of feizing upon Cremona, by the affiftance of fome of the Citizens there, with whom they held a correfpondence, they caufed their forces to march that way, though upon a different pretence ; but their intention being difcovered by thofe that governed the City for the Count, they not only faiied in that attempt, but entirely loft the Count by it, who, without any further confideration, or regard, immediately went over to the Duke.

Pope Eugenius being now dead *, was fucceeded by Nicholas V. and the Count had already advanced

* The name of this Pontif, before his exaltation, was Gabrieli Condelmerio. He was born of a Plebeian family at Venice, and fuc-

ceeded

with all his forces as far as Cotignola, in order to pass into Lombardy, when he received an account of the Duke of Milan's death. This event, which happened on the last day of August, in the Year 1447, exceedingly embarrassed the Count; for in the first place he began to be apprehensive his men would grow mutinous for want of the arrears which were due to them: and in the next he was afraid of the Venetians, who were already armed, and he knew would resent his abandoning them and joining the late Duke. Alphonso was his ancient enemy; and he could put no confidence either in the Pope or the

ceeded Martin V. in the year 1431. His Pontificate was an unquiet one, as he was involved in wars, and disturbed with schisms and ecclesiastical sedition, during the greater part of it. Being forced from Rome by the arms and intrigues of the Duke of Milan, he fled to Florence; and refusing to go to the Council which he had summoned to meet at Basil, he was deposed for contempt (as has been said before, in a note, towards the latter end of the fourth Book of this History) and the Antipope, Amadeus, Duke of Savoy, or Felix V. set up in his room. At last, however, after ten years absence, he returned to Rome, made a vigorous opposition to his enemies, who were making great havock in the ecclesiastical State; and at the same time sent a fleet by sea, and an army by land, against the Turk, under the command of his Legate Juliano Cesarini. He was very inconstant and desultory in his actions at the beginning of his reign, and led away by evil Counsels; but afterwards, acted with prudence and resolution. But an indifferent scholar, though pretty well versed in history; very liberal, especially to men of learning, whom he favoured and preferred; a great benefactor to the Religious Orders, to some of which he granted several privileges and revenues, and increased the foundations of others. But he delighted so much in war, that besides those he was embroiled in himself in Italy, he instigated the Dauphin of France to march with a great body of horse against his enemies at Basil: and afterwards sent Ladislaus, King of Poland, with his Legate Cesarini, against the Turks, of whom they cut off thirty thousand, in a battle betwixt Adrianople and the banks of the Danube; but the King and the Legate were also killed at the same time. Platina adds, that he was accounted very strict to his word, *except when he had made a promise which it was better to revoke than perform.* Qu. Does he mean *better* for himself or others? He died in the 63d year of his age, after he had reigned almost 16 years. See Platina. Spondan. Annal.

The Reflection he made just before he expired, is remarkable, and a proof that those that possess the highest dignities find them to be mere vanity. When he was going to breathe his last, he turned towards some friers who stood by his bed-side, and said with a deep sigh, that it would have conduced much more to his salvation, if he had never been either Pope or Cardinal. Launoius Epist. ult. Part. i. p. 82. Edit. Cantab.

Flo-

Florentines; as he had taken many towns from the one, and the other were in league with the Venetians. He refolved however to face them all, and avail himfelf of fuch expedients as might afterwards occur; well knowing that fortune ufually favours fuch as are bold and active, and turns her back upon thofe that give themfelves up to indolence and defpair: befides, he was not without fome hopes, that the Milanefe would be obliged to have recourfe to him for protection againft the ambition of the Venetians. Taking courage therefore, he marched into the territories of Bologna, and having paffed Modena and Reggio, he encamped with his whole army upon the banks of the Lenza, from whence he fent to make an offer of his fervice to the Milanefe. After the death of the Duke, his fubjects divided into factions, one party being defirous of forming themfelves into a Republic, and another of living under the government of a Prince: and of thofe that chofe the latter, fome were for having the Count, and others King Alphonfo to reign over them. Thofe however, that refolved to live under a free government, being more united amongft themfelves, at laft prevailed over the other party and eftablifhed a Commonwealth upon their own model: which yet many Cities in that Duchy would not fubmit to, in hopes they fhould be able to become independant as well as Milan: and even thofe that did not afpire to be abfolutely free, refufed to be governed by the Milanefe. Of the latter, Lodi, and Placentia put themfelves under the protection of the Venetians: but Pavia and Parma * maintained their own liberties. The Count

---

* The Duchy of Parma was affigned to the Houfe of Auftria, after the death of the late Duke, who had no children, by a treaty betwixt the Emperor Charles VI. and France, in the year 1736, and the Houfe of Auftria took poffeffion of it accordingly; againft which, the Pope protefted, claiming it as a Fief of the Holy See. The Court of Parma in the reigns of the late Dukes of the Houfe of Farnefe, was one of the moft fplendid in Europe.—The late Queen dowager of Spain was a daughter of Parma, whofe eldeft Son Don Carlos, the prefent King of Spain, was to have fucceeded to this Duchy, and

be-

being informed of thefe divifions, removed to Cremona, where it was agreed betwixt Commiffioners on
his part, and others who were fent thither by the Milanefe, that he fhould be commander in chief of their
forces, upon the fame terms that had been offered
him by the Duke : and further, that he fhould have
Brefcia ceded to him, till he could make himfelf
mafter of Verona ; after which, the former fhould be
reftored to them *.

 Before the death of the late Duke, Pope Nicholas †
had taken pains to re-eftablifh peace amongft all the

that of Tufcany, by virtue of a treaty betwixt moft of the Powers
of Europe : but the Queen of Spain and her Son were content to re-
linquifh their intereft in thofe Duchies, in confideration of Don
Carlos's being confirmed in the Dominions of Naples and Sicily, by
the Houfe of Auftria, in the year 1736. But by the treaty of Aix la
Chapelle, in the year 1748, the Duchies of Parma, Placentia, and
Guaftalla, were ceded to Philip Duke of Parma, fecond Son of the
Queen of Spain, and Brother to Don Carlos.

* Philip Maria Vifconti leaving only a natural daughter, whom he
had given in marriage to Francis Sforza, feveral Princes laid claim
to the Duchy of Milan. The Emperor Frederic III. pretended it
was efcheated to the Empire, as the laft Duke left no legitimate
children. Alphonfo, King of Naples, founded his claim upon that
Duke's will, in which he had appointed him his heir. The Duke of
Orleans alledged the right of confanguinity ; he being the fon of
Valentina, the Duke's fifter. Sforza urged, that the fame Duke had
adopted him, and added to this, his wife's right. Spondan. Annal.
ad ann. 1447. No. vii. From thefe oppofite pretenfions, therefore,
the Citizens of Milan thought they had a fair opportunity of turning
their State into a Republic : for which purpofe, having elected twelve
Magiftrates, whom they ftiled " Confervators of the Peace," they
tore the late Duke's will to pieces, and appointed Sforza General of
their army. The laft part of their conduct was very imprudent,
and ill fuited to the defign they had of eftablifhing a republican government in their city. They did not confider, that no circumftance
can be more favourable to a man, who wants to get poffeffion of a
fceptre, than the putting a fword into his hand ; " ben convenendofi
la fpada a quella mano che vuole fcettro " Vianoli. Hift. Venet. tom. i.
p. 604. Spondanus obferves very juftly, that feveral cities fell into
flavery at that time, through an excefs of eagernefs to avoid it.
Factions arofe within thofe cities : fometimes they would have one
form of government, and fometimes another ; and when one of thefe
factions got the upperhand, it fhewed no mercy to the other. Was
not this paving the way for flavery ? Mediolanenfes fervandæ per fe li-
bertatis impotentes erant ; &, ut in his fieri mos erat civitatum Italicarum,
illam fueri quærentes, mutuis diffenfionibus crudelitatibufque faciliorem fer-
vituti viam fternebant. Spondan. Annal. ad ann. 1449. No. 7.

 † This Pontif obliged the Antipope Felix V. to renounce all his
pretenfions to the Papacy, celebrated a Jubilee in the year 1450, and

Princes

Princes of Italy. For which purpofe, he ufed his
endeavours with the Ambaffadors whom the Florentines had fent to congratulate him upon his exaltation
to the Pontificate, that a conference might be held
at Ferrara, in order to treat of a lafting peace, or
at leaft a long ceffation of arms. Accordingly a Legate was difpatched by his Holinefs, to meet the
Plenipotentiaries appointed to affemble at that City
by the Venetians, the Duke of Milan, and the Florentines : but King Alphonfo did not fend any thither. He then lay at Tivoli * with a great body both
of horfe and foot, ready to fupport the Duke in any
undertaking ; and it was generally thought that as
foon as they could draw the Count over to their interefts, they would openly attack the Venetians and
Florentines : and that they were only amufing them
in the mean while with talking of a peace at Ferrara, to give the Count time to get with his forces
into Lombardy. For though Alphonfo did not fend
any Ambaffador to the conference there, he gave
them to underftand he would ratify whatever the
Duke fhould think proper to agree to. It continued
many days, and there were warm debates whether a
truce for five years, or. an abfolute peace fhould be
concluded : at laft, all parties confented that it fhould
be left to the Duke of Milan's option to determine
upon either one or the other, as he liked beft : but

crowned the Emperor Frederick III. but being terrified with a confpiracy formed againft him and the Cardinals, by Stephen Porcari
(an account of which the reader will meet with towards the end of
this book) and the taking of Conftantinople by the Turks, he fell
fick and died, in 1455. He was a great reftorer and favourer of
learning. He gave many thoufand books to the Vatican Library, of
which, fome fay, he was the Founder ; and collected a vaft number
of Greek and Latin Manufcripts, at an incredible expence. Platina.
  * The ancient Tibur of the Romans. It is in the Campagna di
Roma, fituated upon the River Taverone, about 18 miles to the
Eaft of Rome. The Palace of the family of Efte, Dukes of Modena,
which was built here by Cardinal Hippolyto d' Efte, is much admired for its Architecture, Sculpture, Paintings, noble Gardens and
Waterworks. Tivoli is now a little town, but the See of a Bifhop,
and fubject to the Duke of Modena, proprietor of the magnificent
palace above-mentioned.

his Plenipotentiaries, who returned to Milan to
know his pleafure in that refpect, did not arrive
there till after he was dead. Upon which event, the
Milanefe were defirous to have a Peace : but the Venetians now refufed to ftand to their agreement, as
they began to entertain ftill greater hopes of making
themfelves mafters of all their territories ; and feeing
that Lodi and Placentia had immediately fubmitted
to them upon the death of the Duke, they made no
doubt of reducing all the reft of his dominions, either by treaty or dint of arms, before any body could
come to their fuccour ; efpecially as the Florentines
were at that juncture upon the point of being embroiled in a war with King Alphonfo.

That Prince was then at Tivoli (as we have juft
now faid) and being determined to profecute his defigns upon Tufcany, according to the plan that had
been concerted betwixt him and the late Duke, thought
the war, which was now begun in Lombardy, would
give him a fair opportunity of fo doing, and of getting fome footing in the Florentine dominions, before
he proceeded to an open rupture with them : for
which purpofe, having entered into a correfpondence
with fome perfons in Cennina, a fortrefs that lies in
the upper part of the Vale of Arno, he foon after
made himfelf mafter of it. The Florentines were
not a little alarmed at this unexpected ftroke ; and
feeing the King had now commenced hoftilities, they
immediately augmented their forces, created *a Council
of Ten*, and made all other neceffary preparations for
war, with the utmoft diligence and expedition. On
the other hand, King Alphonfo had already advanced
with his whole army into the territories of Siena, and
tried all the means he could think of to get poffeffion of that City * : but the Sienefe continued fo firm

---

* Siena is the capital of the Sienefe, in the Duchy of Tufcany,
fituated on an eminence, in a very fruitful and pleafant Country.
It is about four miles in circumference, encompaffed with a ruinous
old wall, and defended by a citadel. The town is thinly inhabited,
but elegantly built, and the Cathedral efteemed one of the fineft

to

to their alliance with the Florentines, that they would neither open their own gates to him, nor admit him into any other place under their jurisdiction. They condescended so far however, as to furnish him plentifully with provisions : for which, they thought, their own weakness and the strength of the enemy would be a sufficient excuse.

The King therefore gave up his design of invading Tuscany by the way of the Vale of Arno, as he had at first intended ; for the Florentines had not only retaken Cennina, but were pretty well provided with forces to oppose him in that part of the Country : upon which account, he suddenly turned off towards Volterra, and surprized many fortresses in that neighbourhood. From thence he advanced into the territories of Pisa, where by the assistance of Henrico and Fazio de' Conti, heads of the Gherardeschi family, he took several Castles ; which gave him an opportunity of making an assault upon Campiglia, though he did not succeed in it ; as it was resolutely maintained by the Florentines, and they were favoured in their defence by the winter season. The King therefore having left sufficient garrisons in the places which he had taken, not only to maintain them, but to make excursions into the neighbouring Countries, retired into quarters with the rest of his army in the territories of Siena. And the Florentines being now secured from all further danger by the season of the year, began to raise more forces with all possible diligence, and appointed Frederic Lord of Urbino, and Gismondo Malatesta Governor of Rimini, their Generals. For though there had been an inveterate enmity betwixt those two Commanders, yet their dif-

pieces of Gothic Architecture in Italy. It is the See of an Archbishop, and an University ; and here is an Academy likewise of Literati. The Sienese are said to speak the Italian language with greater purity than any other people. The City is at present subject to the great Duke of Tuscany, who has been sovereign of it ever since the year 1555 ; till which time it was a powerful Republic, and often contended with the Florentines for empire. The Emperor of Germany is now possessed of it as grand Duke of Tuscany.

ferences

ferences were at laſt ſo happily compoſed by the prudence of Neri Capponi, and Bernardetto de' Medici,
the Florentine Commiſſaries, that they took the field
even in the depth of winter, and having recovered thoſe
places that had been taken from them in the territories of Piſa, and Volterra, they ſo bridled the ex-
curſions of Alphonſo's garriſons, which before uſed
to ſcour all the coaſts that lay upon the Sea, that they
were hardly able to ſupport themſelves in the towns
they were left to defend.

At the return of the Spring the Commiſſaries aſſembled their whole army at Spedeletto, which con-
ſiſted of five thouſand horſe, and two thouſand foot;
and King Alphonſo advanced with all his forces likewiſe, amounting to fifteen thouſand, within a league
of Campiglia. But when every body expeſted he
would have ſat down again before that place, he ſuddenly turned aſide to Piombino, imagining he could
eaſily make himſelf maſter of it, as it was but indifferently provided for a ſiege : and he knew if he
ſhould ſucceed in the attempt, it would be very advantageous to himſelf, and of the utmoſt prejudice
to the Florentines : for being in poſſeſſion of that
town, he ſhould be plentifully furniſhed with all manner of proviſions by Sea, and have it in his power to
diſtreſs the Florentines to the laſt degree, by laying
the whole Country round Piſa under contribution,
and ſpinning out the war as long as he pleaſed. The
Florentines were not a little alarmed at this ſtep;
but having conſidered what was beſt to be done in
their circumſtances, they thought if their forces
could gain the thickets and woody defiles of Campiglia, they might oblige the King either to make a
ſhameful retreat, or fight them at a manifeſt diſadvantage. For this purpoſe, they armed four Galeaſſes * at Leghorn, and having embarked three

_____
* Galeaſſes, or double Gallies, are large, low built, heavy veſſels,
which uſe both ſails and oars, and are the biggeſt of all the veſſels
that go with the latter. They carry generally about twenty guns,
and a great number of ſmall arms, the latter chiefly in the ſtern or

hun-

hundred Soldiers on board of them, they found meant to throw them into Piombino : after which, their army pofted itfelf at Caldane, where it could not be attacked without much difficulty, judging that fafer upon fecond thoughts, than to lie amongft woods and thickets, or upon an open plain, where they muft of courfe be expofed to great danger. Their fupplies of provifions they drew from the neighbouring towns, which being few in number, and thinly inhabited, were not able to furnifh them with a fufficient quantity : fo that they were in great want, efpecially of wine : for as there was none produced in thofe parts, and they could not then get much from other places, it was not poffible there fhould be enough for every one. But the King's army, notwithftanding all the endeavours of the Florentines to cut off its communication with the Country, having the Sea ftill open, was plentifully fupplied with all manner of neceffaries, except forage. Of which the Florentines being aware, refolved to try if they could not likewife furnifh their troops with provifions in the fame manner : but having loaded their four Galeaffes with provifions, and fent them to Sea for that purpofe, they were met by feven of the King's Veffels which took two of them, and obliged the others. to return into port. This difafter having utterly extinguifhed the hopes which their forces had conceived of being fupplied with provifions by Sea, one of their foraging parties which confifted of above two hundred, deferted, and went over to the King, chiefly for want of wine ; and many others began to murmur. and faid they would ftay no longer in that hot Coun-

poop, with three mafts, and a bowfprit, which are never to be taken down or lowered, as they may be in Gallies. They have thirty two benches of rowers, and five or fix men to each bench, with three tires of guns in the head, one over the other, of two guns each, which carry thirty-fix, twenty-four, and ten pounders. The Venetians are now the only people that ufe Galeaffes : The French made ufe of them formerly. Scaliger is of opinion, that what Pliny calls Long Ships, were what we call Galeaffes, the firft whereof was that of the Argonauts.

try,

try, where there was no wine to be had, and the
water was fo bad they could hardly drink it.

The Commiffaries therefore, at laft determined to
quit that ftation, and endeavour to retake fome other
Caftles, which ftill remained in the hands of the
King; who perceiving that his army (though it did
not want any fort of provifion, and was much fuperior to that of the enemy) was likewife diminifhed
every day by the diftempers which are incident to
thofe fwampy parts that lie near the Sea (efpecially in
the heat of Summer) and which raged at that time
with fuch fury, that numbers fell fick, and many
died. Each fide being thus diftreffed, fome overtures
of peace were made, in which the King demanded
fifty thoufand Florins by way of indemnification for
the expence he had been at, and that Piombino fhould
be left to his mercy; which terms after they had been
canvaffed at Florence, many who were defirous of a
peace feemed inclinable to accept; alledging that they
could not fee any probability of coming off with advantage in a war that muft be fupported at fo vaft an
expence. But Neri Capponi going himfelf to Florence, ufed fuch arguments to diffuade them from it,
that the Citizens at laft unanimoufly agreed not to
make thofe conceffions; and not only took the Lord
of Piombino under their protection, but promifed to
fupport him effectually both in peace and war, provided he would be faithful to them, and defend the
town for the future in the manner he had already
done. Of which refolution, King Alphonfo was foon
informed, and feeing his army fo diminifhed by ficknefs, that he had no hopes of reducing that town,
he immediately raifed his Camp in as much confufion
and diforder as if he had been routed: and having
loft above two thoufand of his men, he retreated with
the reft of his army in a feeble and languifhing condition into the territories of Siena: from whence he
returned after fome time into his own kingdom, highly
enraged at the Florentines, whom he threatened with
a frefh invafion at the return of the fpring.

Whilft

Whilft things were upon this footing in Tufcany, Count Sforza being in Lombardy and now appointed Commander in chief of the Milanefe forces, endeavoured in the firft place, to make Francifco Piccinino his friend, who was likewife in their fervice; that fo he might be induced to favour him in his future undertakings, or at leaft not to oppofe him with much vigour: after which, he took the field with his whole army. The inhabitants of Pavia therefore, being apprehenfive they fhould not be able to defend themfelves againft fo great a force, and at the fame time very loath to be governed by the Milanefe, made the Count an offer of their City; provided he would not fuffer them to fall under the domination of that State. The Count was very defirous of getting poffeffion of Pavia, as he thought that would be an aufpicious beginning, and furnifh him with a colourable pretence to profecute his other defigns: nor was he at all reftrained either by fhame, or the fear of being reproached with breaking his word; for great men commonly think it a difhonour to lofe, but an honour to gain any thing, even by fraudulent and perfidious means. But he was afraid if he accepted the offer, he fhould exafperate the Milanefe to fuch a degree, that they would throw themfelves into the arms of the Venetians; and if he did not, he thought the Pavians would put themfelves under the protection of the Duke of Savoy, to which, many of them feemed very much inclined: and in either of thofe cafes, he plainly faw he fhould have no further chance of making himfelf mafter of Lombardy. However, as there feemed to be lefs danger in taking that City himfelf, than in letting it fall into the hands of another, he determined to accept of it; perfuading himfelf, that he fhould be able to find fome way or other, of pacifying the Milanefe. For which purpofe, he reprefented to them the extremities they muft have been reduced to if he had not acted in that manner; fince otherwife, the Pavians would certainly have given up their City either to the Venetians or the Duke of Savoy;

and

and then the State of Milan would have been utterly ruined : that it muſt therefore be much better for them, to have him for their neighbour, who was their friend and ally, than an enemy, and a very powerful one too, as either of the others would be. But the Milaneſe having now diſcovered the Count's ambitious deſigns, and the object he had principally in view, were not a little alarmed : they thought proper, however, to diſſemble for a time; becauſe if they broke with the Count, they did not know whom elſe to have recourſe to, except the Venetians, whoſe intolerable arrogance, and tyrannical manner of governing, they could not think of without dread and abhorrence. They reſolved therefore not to detach themſelves from the Count at that time, but to avail themſelves of his aſſiſtance for a while, to guard them againſt the dangers with which they were then threatened, hoping that when they were extricated from thoſe difficulties, they ſhould find ſome means to get rid of him. For they expected to be attacked not only by the Venetians, but by the Genoeſe, and alſo by the Duke of Savoy, in behalf of Charles of Orleans, who was Son to a Siſter of Philip the late Duke of Milan. But the Count having ſoon quieted the two laſt, had no other enemy left to deal with but the Venetians, who were determined to invade the Milaneſe with a powerful army, and had already got poſſeſſion of Lodi and Placentia ; the latter of which however, was now inveſted by the Count, and, after a long ſiege, retaken and plundered by his ſoldiers, whom he then ſent into quarters (as the winter was coming on) and retired himſelf to Cremona, where he ſpent the reſt of that ſeaſon in repoſe with his family.

Early in the Spring, both the Milaneſe and the Venetian armies appeared in the field ; the former being very deſirous to recover Lodi alſo, and afterwards, if poſſible, to come to ſome accommodation with the Venetians ; for as they found the expences of the war were likely to be very heavy, and grew

· more

more and more fufpicious of their General, they ardently longed for a peace; that fo they might guard againft the defigns of the Count, and afterwards enjoy themfelves in quiet and tranquillity after their troubles. They refolved, therefore, that their forces fhould lay fiege to Caravaggo, imagining, that if they could make themfelves mafters of that fortrefs, Lodi would foon be forced to furrender. The Count obeyed their orders, though it was his own defire to have paffed the Adda, and fallen into the territories of Brefcia: and having fet down before Caravaggio, he fortified his Camp in fuch a manner with ditches and ramparts, that the Venetians could not attack him but at a very great difadvantage. They advanced, however, under the command of their General Micheletto Attenduli, within two bow fhots of him, where they continued feveral days, and had frequent fkirmifhes with his forces. But he ftill carried on the fiege, and reduced the caftle to fuch extremities, that it could not hold out much longer: at which, the Venetians were exceedingly mortified, as they apprehended the lofs of that fortrefs would totally defeat all their other defigns in that expedition. After many difputes amongft the Commanders concerning the means of relieving it, there feemed no way left but to attack the Count in his trenches, which yet could not be done without extreme hazard: but they had fet their hearts fo much upon the prefervation of Caravaggio, that the Venetian Senate, though naturally timorous and averfe to any doubtful undertaking, chofe rather to run the rifque of a defeat, than lofe the Caftle, and with it, all further hopes of fuccefs in their grand enterprize. With a refolution, therefore, to attack him at all events, they got under arms very early next morning, and falling upon that part of his Camp which was the weakeft, they at firft threw his whole army into fome diforder, as it generally happens in fuch fudden and unexpected affaults. But the Count foon rallied his men in fuch a manner, that the enemy, after many attempts to force his trenches, were not only repulfed, but fo totally routed and difperfed, that out of twelve thoufand horfe, of which their army confifted, not quite one thoufand efcaped; and as all their baggage and carriages alfo fell into the hands of the Count's foldiers, it was the greateft defeat, and the heavieft lofs, the Venetians had ever fuftained before that time.

Amongft the reft of the prifoners that were taken, there happened to be one of the Venetian proveditores, who, during the whole courfe of the war, and particularly a little before the battle, had fpoken in very contemptuous terms of the Count, calling him *a Baftard and a Coward*; but when he found himfelf at his mercy, and recollected what he had done, making no doubt but he fhould be punifhed as he really deferved, he threw himfelf, trembling and weeping, at the Count's knees, and (as it is the nature of bafe fpirits, to be infolent in profperity, and abject in adverfity) humbly befought him to pardon his offence. Upon which, the Count lifting him up from the ground, bid him take courage, and fear no harm : but faid, " he could not help wondering that a perfon of prudence and gravity, as he affected to be thought, fhould be guilty of fuch ill manners as he had been, in fpeaking fo injurioufly of a perfon who had done nothing to deferve it from him : that, as to the things which he had reproached him with, he neither could poffibly know, nor prevent what had paffed betwixt his father and mother before he was born, and therefore ought neither to be applauded nor upbraided for their actions : but that he would venture to affirm one thing however, which was, that fince he was capable of acting for himfelf, he had behaved in fuch a manner, as not to merit reprehenfion from any one : of which, both he, and his Senate had many and recent proofs." And having advifed him to be more modeft for the future, in fpeaking of others, and to proceed with greater caution

and

and deliberation in the execution of military undertakings, he difmiffed him.

After this advantage, the Count marched with his
victorious army into the territories of Brefcia, and
having prefently over-run all the adjacent Country,
encamped within two miles of the City. The Venetians, on the other hand, after their late defeat,
having reafon to apprehend that it would not be long
(as indeed it happened) before he made an attempt
upon Brefcia, had fortified it as well, and with as
much expedition, as their circumftances would admit: after which, they began to raife frefh forces
with great diligence, and having collected fome fcattered remains of their late army, applied to the Florentines for the fuccours they were obliged by treaty
to furnifh them with, in cafe of neceffity. And the
Florentines, being now no longer embroiled in the
war with King Alphonfo, accordingly fent two thoufand horfe, and one thoufand foot to their affiftance:
all which reinforcements put them in a condition to
treat of peace.

It had almoft always been the good fortune of the
Venetian Republic to recover twice as much by treaty,
as they had loft in an unfuccefsful war; and they
now knew that the Milanefe were exceedingly fufpicious of the Count's defigns; that the Count was not
content with being merely the Commander of their
forces, but fecretly afpired to be abfolute Sovereign
of Milan: and that it was in their own option to conclude an alliance with either of them; as one fide
would naturally be prompted to join them by ambition, and the other by fear. But having maturely
confidered the matter, they determined to come to an
accommodation with the Count, and to offer him
their affiftance for the reduction of Milan, imagining,
that when the Milanefe faw they were betrayed by
the Count, it would provoke them to fuch a degree,
that they would throw themfelves into any other
hands, rather than fubmit to him; and that when
they were reduced to fuch circumftances, that they

could

could neither defend themfelves, nor put any further confidence in the Count, (having no other refuge) they muft of courfe fly to them for protection. Having come to this refolution, they began to tamper with the Count, whom they found very well difpofed to a peace, efpecially when he perceived that he himfelf fhould thereby reap the fruits of the late victory at Caravaggio, which would otherwife redound to the honour and emolument of the Milanefe alone. A treaty, therefore, was foon concluded betwixt them, by which the Venetians obliged themfelves to pay the Count thirteen thoufand Florins a month, till he had conquered Milan; and to furnifh him with four thoufand horfe, and two thoufand foot, as long as the war lafted; and the Count, on the other hand, engaged to reftore to the Venetians, all the towns and prifoners, and whatever elfe he had taken from them, during the courfe of the war: and to reft content with fuch places only, as were in the poffeffion of Duke Philip, at the time of his death.

When the news of this treaty arrived at Milan, the inhabitants of that City were much more dejected at it, than they had been elated with their victory at Caravaggio; the Governors complained, the common people were outrageous, the women and children wept bitterly, all of them exclaiming againft the Count, as *a traitor and perfidious wretch*; and though they had not any great hopes left of being able to prevail upon him, either by entreaties, petitions, or promifes, to change the refolution he had taken; yet they fent ambaffadors to him, to fee what he could fay for himfelf, and what face he put upon fo ungrateful and wicked a manner of proceeding. When they were introduced into his prefence, one of them thus addreffed himfelf to him:

" Thofe that feek to obtain any end, commonly make ufe either of fupplications, gratuities, or menaces, to thofe whom they have to deal with, in hopes that being either moved by compaffion, biaffed by felf-intereft, or terrified with threats, they may at laft

be

be induced to comply with their requeſts : but as
none of theſe three different methods of application
make any impreſſion upon hard-hearted and rapacious
men, and ſuch as are buoyed up with an opinion of
their own great power and ſignificance, thoſe that
endeavour either to ſoften them by entreaties, gain
them by preſents, or frighten them with menaces,
will ſoon have the mortification to find they are labouring to no purpoſe. As we have, therefore, at
laſt, though too late, diſcovered the cruelty, the ambition, and the pride of your heart; we are now
come, not to aſk any favour, nor with the leaſt expectation of obtaining it, if we ſhould aſk ; but to
remind you of the kindneſſes you have received from
the people of Milan, and to upbraid you with the
ungrateful manner in which you have requited them :
that ſo amongſt the numberleſs miſeries and calamities which you have brought upon us, we may at
leaſt enjoy the pleaſure of reproaching you with them.
Recollect the circumſtances you were in after the death
of Duke Philip. You were at enmity with the Pope,
and the King of Naples. The Florentines and Venetians, whom you had ſo baſely deſerted, could not help
reſenting the affront, though they had no further occaſion for your ſervice, and looked upon you as an
enemy. You were debilitated and exhauſted by the
war in which you had been engaged againſt the Church;
you were left in a manner without men, without money, without friends, or any hopes of being able to
preſerve your own dominions, and former reputation,
which muſt have been inevitably loſt, if we had not
been ſimple enough to take you into our boſom, out
of the reverence we bore to the memory of our late
Duke, with whom you had entered into ſuch treaties,
and contracted ſo near an alliance, that we had reaſon
to expect the affection you profeſſed for him, would
have deſcended to his ſubjects ; and that when you
conſidered how many favours we had added to thoſe
you received from the Duke, the union betwixt us
would have continued firm and indiſſoluble : upon

D d 3   which

which account, we not only punctually fulfilled all
his former engagements with you, but gave you the
actual poffeffion of Brefcia too, till you could make
yourfelf mafter of Verona. What could we either
give, or promife you more ? What greater favours
could you have received, or even hoped for at that
time, we do not fay from us, but from any other
State ?—For thefe unexpected kindneffes, you have
recompenced us in a manner, which, we muft own,
was likewife altogether unexpected and undeferved by
us. Nor was this the firft inftance of your perfidy :
for no fooner were you invefted with the command
of our forces, but you took poffeffion of Pavia for
yourfelf, contrary to all the laws of juftice and equity :
from which firft fample of your friendfhip, we might
well have learned, what we had to expect from you
for the future. This injury, however, we bore with
patience, in hopes that fo great an acquifition would
have fatiated your ambition : but alas! we find to
our forrow, that fuch as grafp at the whole, will never be content with a part.—You promifed, that we
fhould enjoy all the conquefts you afterwards made,
well knowing, that what you gave us at feveral times,
you could take from us all at once ; as it has happened in fact fince the victory of Caravaggio, which
being purchafed at the expence of our blood and
treafure, has been unhappily perverted to our ruin.
Wretched are the States that are obliged to be continually in arms, to defend their liberties againft the
attempts of ambitious invaders ; but much more fo
are thofe that are forced to employ mercenary and
perfidious foldiers, like you, for that purpofe. May
our fate, however, be a warning to pofterity, though
we ourfelves were fo infatuated, as not to remember
how the Thebans were treated in the like circumftances by Philip. of Macedon; who, after he had
been their General, and conquered their enemies, in
the firft place turned their enemy himfelf, and then
ufurped the fovereignty over them. We, for our
parts, cannot with juftice be accufed of any other
fault,

fault, but of having put too much confidence in a
perfon whom we ought not to have trufted at all ;
efpecially if we had called to mind his former behaviour, and been upon our guard, as we ought to
have been, againft his reftlefs and unbounded ambition, which was never fatisfied in any ftate or condition : a perfon who had betrayed the Lord of Lucca,
extorted fuch vaft fums from the Florentines and Venetians, treated our late Prince with contempt, infulted a King, and (which was ftill more heinous)
had rebelled againft God, and perfecuted his Church
in fo atrocious a manner.   We ought not, indeed, to
have flattered ourfelves, that fuch a man would treat
the Milanefe with more refpect than he had done
thofe great and powerful States ; nor to have expected, that one who had fo often violated his engagements with others, would ever be faithful to us.
The imprudence, however, for which others may
condemn us, can be no excufe for your treachery,
nor fkreen you from the infamy with which you will
be branded, when it is known to the world how
much reafon we have to make thefe complaints. Does
not your own confcience reproach you ? Do you feel
no remorfe when you reflect, that you have turned
thofe arms upon ourfelves, which we had taken up
to defend our laws and liberties againft the invafions
of others ? We appeal to your own breaft. Do you
not look upon *yourfelf* as a Parricide ? Can you deny
that you deferve the fevereft and moft exemplary of
all punifhments ? But if you are fo blinded by ambition, that you are not capable of judging yourfelf,
the whole world has been witnefs of your iniquities,
and will rife up in evidence againft you : God himfelf will open your eyes, and make you fenfible of
your mifdeeds, if the moft flagrant perfidy, if per-
jury and treafon are crimes in his fight : though, indeed, his Divine Providence fometimes permits the
wicked to efcape with impunity for a while (as the
cafe may be at prefent) to be the inftruments of his
vengeance, and to bring about fome great and good

D d 4

pur-

purpofe that is indifcernible to our eyes. Flatter not
yourfelf, therefore, with the hopes of certain victory. You have little reafon to expect the favour of
Heaven; and we, for our parts, are determined to
defend our liberties like men, and in cafe we cannot
preferve them, to fubmit to any other Prince, rather
than wear your yoke. But if, as a chaftifement for
our fins, and in fpite of our utmoft endeavours to the
contrary, we fhould have the misfortune after all, to
become fubject to you, depend upon it, that a dominion ufurped by fraud, and founded in violence,
will end with ignominy, and utter deftruction to
yourfelf or your children."

The Count, though inwardly ftung with thefe reproaches, did not fhew any extraordinary emotion, either in his countenance or geftures, but calmly replied, "that as they feemed blinded with paffion,
he fhould in fome meafure overlook their indifcretion
and ill language, and the high provocation they had
given him in fo injurious a charge; to every particular of which, he would, however, have returned
an anfwer, if there had been any body prefent that
was capable of judging betwixt them: as he could
make it plainly appear, that he had never yet injured
the Milanefe in the leaft degree; and that all his paft
endeavours had been only to prevent them from injuring him. That they could not help remembering
in what manner they had behaved to him, after the
battle of Caravaggio; when, inftead of rewarding
him for his fervices with the free gift of either Brefcia or Verona, as they had promifed, they were fecretly negotiating a peace with the Venetians; that
fo the odium of the quarrel might be thrown upon
him alone, whilft they ran away with the fruits of
the victory, the merit of concluding a peace, and
all the other advantages he had gained them in the
courfe of that war. They had no reafon to complain, therefore, he faid, that he had made his peace
with the Venetians, fince they had endeavoured to do
fo themfelves: and that if he had deferred it a little
longer,

longer, it muſt have fallen to *his* lot to reproach *them* with that ingratitude of which they now accuſed *him;* but with what truth, the ſame God, whom they had ſo ſolemnly called upon to avenge the injuries they pretended to have received, would not fail to ſhew, at the end of the war; when it would be ſeen, he made no doubt, which of them had juſtice on their ſide, and was moſt favoured by Heaven."

After the Count had thus diſmiſſed the Ambaſſadors, he began to make preparations for invading the Milaneſe; and they being determined to defend themſelves, took Franciſco and Giacopo Piccinino into their pay (who out of the ancient jealouſy that ſubſiſted betwixt the Bracceſcan and Sforzeſcan parties, had always faithfully adhered to the Milaneſe) in hopes of being able by their aſſiſtance to preſerve their liberties; eſpecially if they could find ſome means to detach the Venetians from the Count, who they thought would not very long continue ſo ſtrictly united. The Count was of the ſame opinion, and therefore judged it the beſt way to ſtrengthen the confederacy betwixt them, by motives of ſelf-intereſt, ſince other obligations and engagements did not appear to him ſufficient. For this purpoſe, in concerting their plan of operations for the proſecution of the war, he propoſed that they ſhould lay ſiege to Crema *, whilſt he with the reſt of their forces over-run the other parts of that State. The Venetians ſwallowed the bait, and continued firm to the Count till he had made himſelf maſter of all the territories depending upon Milan, and reduced the City itſelf to ſuch extremities by cutting off all communication with the Country, and preventing any proviſions from being brought into it, that the Citizens deſpairing of relief from any other quarter, ſent Ambaſſadors to beſeech the Vene-

---

* Crema is the capital of a little Country, called Cremaſco, upon the river Serio, which joins the Adda upon the borders of the Milaneſe. There is a fine Palace and a Caſtle, with other fortifications, which now make it ſomething conſiderable; though it was formerly but an ordinary town. It is the See of a Biſhop, and at preſent ſubject to the Venetians.

tians

tians to commiserate their condition, and assist them
in defending their liberties, as all good Republicans
ought to do, rather than support a Tyrant in his ambitious designs, whose career they would not afterwards be able to check at their pleasure, if he should
ever get possession of Milan: insinuating at the same
time, that they must not expect he would be content
with that part of the Duchy which was to fall to his
share by the treaty he had so lately entered into with
them; since it was well known he aspired to the
whole.

But the Venetians were not yet masters of Crema,
and being loth to change sides till they were in possession of it, they answered the Ambassadors in public, " that as they were in alliance with the Count,
they could not send the Milanese any succour:" but
in private they spoke in different terms, and desired
them to tell their masters, that they might depend
upon their assistance.

The Count had now drawn his forces so near Milan, that he made an assault upon the suburbs: and
the Venetians having at last taken Crema, thought it
high time to relieve the Milanese; for which purpose
they entered into a treaty with them, and engaged
themselves by the first article of it to maintain them
in the full enjoyment of their liberties. Accordingly,
as soon as the treaty was signed, they sent orders to
such of their forces as were with the Count to leave
his camp, and join the rest of their own army: acquainting the Count likewise at the same time with
what they had done, and allowing him twenty days
to accede to the treaty himself if he pleased. The
Count was not at all surprized at this event, as he had
long foreseen it, and daily expected it would happen:
nevertheless, when it did come to pass, he was no
less chagrined at it than the Milanese had been when
he deserted them. He therefore desired the Ambassadors who had been sent from the Senate of Venice
to notify the treaty to him, that they would give him
two days to consider of it, and then, he said, he
would

would return them an anfwer: during which time he refolved with himfelf to amufe the Venetians, and not to give up his prefent undertaking. With this defign, he publicly gave out that he would accede to the Peace, and fent Ambaffadors to Venice, with full power to ratify it; giving them private inftructions, however, not to do it upon any account whatfoever, but to protract the matter as long as poffible with all the cavils and artifices they could invent. And to make the Venetians believe that he was really in earneft, he not only made a truce with the Milanefe for a month, but drew off his forces from their walls, and fent them to quarter in the neighbouring towns which he had taken from them. To this feint was owing all his future fuccefs, and the ruin of the Milanefe: for the Venetians depending upon a peace, were more remifs in making preparations for war; and the Milanefe feeing a truce concluded, the enemy drawn off, and the Venetians their friends, were firmly perfuaded the Count had given up all further defign of molefting them. A delufion that was doubly prejudicial to them: for in the firft place, it lulled them into fecurity, and made them neglect to take proper meafures for their defence; and in the next, as the coaft was now clear of the enemy and it happened to be feed-time, they fowed vaft quantities of their grain, which put it in the Count's power to diftrefs them fo much the fooner. But he on the other hand, well knowing how to make an advantage of their overfights, took the opportunity of this interval to refrefh himfelf and his men, and to look out for other allies.

During this war in Lombardy, the Florentines had not taken any fide, nor fhewn the leaft favour to the Count, either when he took part with the Milanefe, or afterwards when he invaded them; for as he had no great occafion for their affiftance, he did not afk it with much importunity: they had indeed fent fome fuccours to the Venetians after the battle of Caravaggio, in confequence of the alliance which then

subsisted betwixt them. But Count Sforza being now deserted by the Venetians, and not knowing to whom else he could have recourse, earnestly sollicited the aid of the Florentines; for which, he applied both publicly to the government of Florence, and privately to his friends in that City; particularly to *Cosimo* Cosimo de' Medici, with whom he had always lived in great intimacy, and who had constantly not only assisted him with his advice, but furnished him with liberal supplies of money in all his undertakings. Nor did he fail him in this exigency; for he both gave him large sums out of his own private purse, and encouraged him to pursue his present enterprize: using all his endeavours at the same time that succours might be sent him by the public; but in this he met with some opposition. For Neri Capponi, who had then a very great interest in Florence, thought it would not be consistent with the safety of the Repub-lic to let the Count become master of Milan; and that it would conduce more to the tranquillity of Italy in general, if he acceded to the treaty of peace, in-stead of continuing the war. He was apprehensive in the first place, that the Milanese, in the height of the resentment they had conceived against the Count, might throw themselves entirely into the arms of the Venetians, which must be attended with the ruin of all the other Princes in Italy: and in the next, he thought if the Count should get possession of Milan, his arms, when supported by so powerful a state, would grow too formidable; and that if he, who was so troublesome whilst he was only a Count, should ever come to be a Duke, he would then be insup-portable. For these reasons, he said, it would be much better for the Republic of Florence and all Italy, that the Count should be left to live upon the reputation of his arms, as he had done before, and that Lombardy should be divided into two Common-wealths, which, it could hardly be supposed, would agree so well together as to unite for the ruin of any other State, and singly, they could hurt nobody. To
effect

effect which, he knew no better expedient, than to give a deaf ear to the Count's follicitations, and continue in league with their old allies the Venetians.

These fuggeftions, however, made very little impreffion upon Cofimo's friends, who thought Capponi *Cofimo.* did not give this advice out of any regard for the public good, but becaufe he was jealous that Cofimo would become too powerful by his friendfhip with the Count, if the latter fhould make himfelf Duke of Milan. And Cofimo for his own part took upon him to demonftrate, that affifting the Count would be fo far from being of any prejudice either to Italy in general, or their own Republic in particular, that it would be of the greateft fervice to both : fince it was folly to imagine that the Milanefe could maintain their liberties, confidering the temper of the Citizens, their manner of living, and the factions then reigning amongft them ; all which made it impoffible to eftablifh a Republican form of government in that City : fo that it muft of neceffity happen that either the Count would become Duke, or the Venetians abfolute Lords over it. And in that cafe, nobody could be fo blind as not to fee whether it would be more eligible to have a potent friend for their neighbour; or an enemy whofe power would then be overgrown and uncontroulable. Nor was it to be feared that the Milanefe would rafhly put themfelves under the dominion of the Venetians, merely becaufe they were at war with the Count ; for the Count had a party and friends in Milan, and they had none : upon which account, the Citizens, when they found they could no longer defend their liberties, would certainly be more inclinable to fubmit to the Count than to the Venetians.

This difference of opinion amongft the principal Citizens, kept the Florentines for fome time in fufpence : at laft, however, they agreed to fend Ambaffadors with inftructions to conclude a treaty of alliance with the Count immediately, provided they fhould find him in fuch circumftances, as made it

feem

feem probable that he would fucceed in his defigns ;
but, otherwife, to raife difficulties and objections, in
order to defer it.   Thefe Ambaffadors were got no
further than Reggio, when they heard the Count had
taken Milan : for as foon as the truce expired, he
had fuddenly invefted that City again with all his
forces, in hopes of carrying it very foon in fpite of
the Venetians, who could not fuccour it on any fide,
except from the Adda, and that pafs was eafily
guarded.   He knew very well, that, as it was the
winter feafon, the Venetians would not be able to lie
in a camp any where near him ; and therefore made
no doubt of reducing the town long before the return of the Spring, efpecially fince Francifco Piccinino was now dead, and his brother Giacopo left fole
Commander of all their forces.

The Venetians in the mean time had fent an Ambaffador to encourage the Milanefe to make a refolute
defence, with affurances alfo of fpeedy and effectual
relief : and   there actually happened feveral flight
fkirmifhes betwixt their troops and thofe of the Count,
during the courfe of the winter.   But as foon as the
weather grew more favourable, they took the field
under the command of Pandolpho Malatefta, and
encamped upon the banks of the Adda ; where they
held a Council of war to confider whether, in order
to fuccour Milan, they fhould attack the Count and
try the fortune of a battle.   Pandolpho their general,
who well knew the bravery of the Count and his
troops, advifed them not to run that rifque, and
thought they might obtain a more certain victory over
him by avoiding an engagement ; as the want of forage and other provifions, muft in a very fhort time,
oblige him to move his quarters.   Upon this confideration, he perfuaded them to continue in the Camp
where they then lay, which would keep up the fpirits
of the Milanefe and prevent them from furrendering
to the Count.   This advice was approved of by the
Venetians, becaufe they thought it a fecure manner of
proceeding, and were not without fome hopes that the
Mila-

Milanese, being still kept in great distress, would at last submit to them, rather than the Count, from whom they had received so many injuries. In the mean time the Milanese were reduced to extreme misery ; for as there was a great number of poor people in the City, many of them dropped down dead in the streets every day for want of bread : and this occasioning murmurs and complaints in every quarter of it, the Governors began to be apprehensive of an insurrection, and therefore took all possible means to prevent any tumult, or assembling of the people.

The Commonalty are not easily excited to mischief; but when they are at once so disposed, any little accident serves to put them in motion. It happened one day, that two persons of no very great consideration meeting each other near the Porta Nuova, fell into a conversation concerning the miserable condition to which the City was reduced, and what means were left to relieve it. This being over-heard by others, the people insensibly gathered about them till they were increased to such a number, that a report was spread through the town that the inhabitants about Porta Nuova were rising against the Magistracy. Upon which, the populace, who only waited for a proper opportunity, immediately ran to arms, and having appointed one Gaspar da Vico Mercato to be their leader, they made so furious an assault upon the place where the Magistrates were sitting, that all those that could not make their escape by flight were killed upon the spot ; amongst whom was Leonardo Veneto, the Venetian ambassador, who had laughed at their miseries, and was thought to be the principal occasion of them. When they had thus in a manner made themselves masters of the City, they began to consult what were the most proper means to be taken, in order to deliver them out of their present distress and restore their former tranquillity. At last it was unanimously agreed amongst them, since they could no longer preserve their freedom and independency, to put themselves under the protection of some Prince that

that was able to defend them. But they could not so readily agree about the person; some proposed King Alphonso, some the Duke of Savoy, and others the King of France, but nobody mentioned the Count; so strong did the resentment of the people run against him! however, as they could not unite in their choice of any other Prince, Vico Mercato at last ventured to propose the Count, and represented to them at large, that if they had a mind to get rid of the war, there was no other way left but to submit to him; as their necessities demanded a certain and immediate peace, and they were no longer in a condition to feed upon the hopes of future succour, which after all might possibly be very uncertain, and at a great distance. He excused the Count's conduct, and threw the blame upon the Venetians and other States in Italy, some of which out of ambition, and others out of jealousy and avarice, would not suffer them to live free; and said, that since they were now under a necessity of giving up their liberties, it behoved them to give them to a person who both knew how, and was sufficiently able to defend them; that so, when they had lost their freedom, they might at least have the consolation of enjoying peace, and not be plunged into a still more dangerous and destructive war.

This harangue was listened to with wonderful attention by the populace, who as soon as he had done speaking, all cried out with one voice for the Count, and immediately dispatched Vico Mercato to invite him into the City: which invitation being accepted with great joy by the Count, he made his entrance into Milan on the 27th of February in the year 1450, and was received there with incredible acclamations by that very people who but a few days before had detested even the name of him *.

* A late author compares the populace to a coquet, who upon some days, is not to be prevailed upon either by sighs, or presents, or sollicitations of any kind. The next day, perhaps, she falls into your arms.—Thus there are some circumstances of affairs in which the most plausible Manifesto's of those that take up arms against their

When

When the news of this revolution arrived at Florence, the Florentines fent orders to their Ambaffadors, who were yet upon the road, that inftead of treating with him as Count Sforza, according to their firft inftructions, they fhould now pay their compliments of congratulation to him as Duke of Milan. Thefe Ambaffadors were received with great honour, and treated with the higheft refpect by the Duke; who well knew that he could not have more faithful or more powerful allies in all Italy than the Florentines, to fecure him againft the ambition of the Venetians. For though they were at laft freed from all apprehenfions of the Vifconti family, it was generally thought they would foon be embroiled with the Arragonefe and the Republic of Venice ; as both the former, and the King of Naples looked upon them with a fufpicious eye, on account of the connexions they had always had with the court of France ; and the Venetians who perceived that the ftate of Florence was grown as jealous of them as it formerly had been of the Vifconti, and remembered with what inveteracy they themfelves had perfecuted that family, began to be afraid they fhould have the fame meafure now dealt out to them in their turn; and therefore determined to ruin them both if poffible. In thefe circumftances, the new Duke of Milan prefently refolved to enter into an alliance with the Florentines : and the Venetians, on the contrary, made a League with King Alphonfo againft their *common Enemies,* as they called them ; in which they agreed to take up arms at the fame time, and that the King fhould invade the Florentine dominions, whilft the Venetians attacked the Duke; who, being hardly yet fettled in

Sovereign, will not have the leaft effect upon the people's allegiance ; and at other times, one half only of fuch pretences will be fufficient to bring about a revolution.—This, however, is not altogether to be imputed to the levity of the people : for how fickle and inconftant foever they are reckoned, they feldom care to ftir, except impelled by fome exterior force, as oppreffion or famine (as in the cafe before us) or the harangues and ambitious intrigues of factious Demagogues.

his government, they imagined would not be able to
make head againſt them, either with his own forces
alone, or any other aſſiſtance he could procure. But
as the League betwixt the two Republics was ſtill in
force, and the King had made a treaty with the Florentines upon the concluſion of the war at Piombino,
they both thought they could not juſtify commencing
hoſtilities without ſome fair pretext for a war. Each
of them, therefore, ſent an Ambaſſador to Florence,
who gave the Signory there to underſtand, that they
did not deſign, by the engagements they had lately
entered into with one another, to act offenſively againſt
any State whatſoever; but merely to defend their
own. After which, the Venetian Ambaſſador, complained that the Florentines had given Alexander, the
Duke's brother, leave to paſs with his forces through
Lunigiana into Lombardy; and that they had been
the authors and adviſers of the agreement made betwixt the Duke of Milan and the Marquis of Mantua, to the great prejudice of their Republic, and in
open violation of the treaty of alliance then ſubſiſting
betwixt them : upon which account, he begged leave
to repreſent to them in a friendly manner, that whoever injures another perſon without cauſe, gives him
a juſt right to revenge; and that, if they broke the
peace they muſt naturally expect a war.

Coſimo   To theſe remonſtrances Coſimo de' Medici was ordered by the Signiory to return their anſwer; who
addreſſing himſelf with much temper and prudence
to the Ambaſſadors, recited at large the many ſervices
and good offices the Republic of Venice had received
from that of Florence, and the obligations they lay
under to it for the vaſt acquiſitions they had made by
the aſſiſtance of the Florentines, whoſe treaſure, and
arms, and counſel had ever been at their ſervice. After which he told them, " that as the Florentines had
been the authors and promoters of the union betwixt
them, they would not be the firſt to break it; for
having always been lovers of peace themſelves, they
they had nothing to ſay againſt the engagements the
Vene-

Venetians had entered into with King Alphonſo, provided they were not intended to diſturb the public tranquillity. That indeed they could not help being a little ſurprized that ſo wiſe and majeſtic a Commonwealth ſhould think it worth their while to be at the trouble of making complaints of ſuch trifling and inſignificant matters as the paſſage of Alexander Sforza through Lunigiana, and the agreement betwixt the Duke of Milan and the Marquis of Mantua: but if they thought they deſerved any anſwer, the Florentines took that opportunity of declaring that a paſſage through their dominions ſhould always be open to any friend: and as for the other point, the Duke was a Prince of ſuch abilities, that he did not ſtand in need of their advice or direction in the choice of his allies. That he therefore ſuſpected there was ſomething more at the bottom of theſe cavils than he could at preſent diſcover; but if that ſhould be the caſe, the Florentines would let the world ſee that they had it in their power, not only to be good friends but dangerous enemies." Things however were pretty well compoſed for that time, and the Ambaſſadors ſeemed to go away ſatisfied: but the concluſion of ſuch a treaty, and the ſubſequent behaviour of the Venetians and King Alphonſo, gave the Duke and the Florentines much more reaſon to expect the breaking out of a new war, than to hope for a continuance of the peace. The Florentines therefore having entered into a ſtrict confederacy with the Duke, the Venetians began to diſcover their hoſtile deſigns by driving all the Florentines and their dependants out of the territories of Venice: and ſoon after Alphonſo did the ſame, without the leaſt regard to the treaty he had made with them the year before, without any juſt cauſe, or ſo much as a ſpecious pretence. The Venetians likewiſe endeavoured to reduce the Bologneſe; and having furniſhed ſome of their exiles with forces, they marched towards that City in the night, and got into it through an old ſubterraneous aqueduct ſo privately that no body was aware of their entrance till

they

they gave the alarm themfelves: upon which, the Governor Santi Bentivoglio, who was awake though in bed, being informed that the City was furprized by the exiles, immediately got up and refolved to face the enemy. And though he was advifed by many that were about him to fave himfelf by flight if pof- fible, fince he could not fave the City if he ftaid; yet he put on his armour and having gathered together fome friends whom he encouraged to follow him, he attacked the enemy, and not only routed them, but killed many and drove the reft out of the City : by which courageous behaviour, every body acknow- ledged that he had given fufficient proof that he was really defcended from the Houfe of the Bentivogli.

Thefe proceedings fully confirmed the Florentines in their apprehenfions of a war, and determined them to make the ufual preparations for their defence: for which purpofe they created a *Council of Ten*, took new Commanders into their pay, fent Ambaffadors to Rome, Naples, Venice, Milan, and Siena, to de- mand fuccours of their allies, to know what they might certainly depend upon from thofe of whom they were doubtful, to fix fuch as were wavering, and to pene- trate into the defigns of their enemies.

From the Pope they got nothing but general de- clarations of his good difpofition towards them, and exhortations to peace. The King of Naples con- tented himfelf with making trifling excufes for hav- ing driven the fubjects of the Florentines out of his dominions, and offered fafe conducts to fuch as ftill remained behind if they pleafed to afk them. And though he endeavoured by all means to conceal his hoftile defigns, yet the Ambaffadors plainly difcovered them, and that he was making great preparations to invade their Republic. With the Duke they not only renewed their League, but ftrengthened it with feveral additional articles; and by his means all for- mer differences betwixt them and the Genoefe were compromifed with fo much fatisfaction on both fides, that they became good friends to each other, though

the

the Venetians left no ftone unturned to prevent their reconciliation, and went fo far as even to follicit the Emperor of Conftantinople to banifh all Florentines out of his Empire : with fo much rancour did they begin the war, fo infatiable was their ambition of rule, and fo fully bent were they upon the utter deftruction of thofe to whom they entirely owed all their power and greatnefs ! but that Prince paying no regard to their follicitations, the Senate of Venice forbad the Florentine Ambaffadors to enter their territories ; alledging, that as they were in League with the King of Naples and Arragon, they could not admit of any Embaffies without his participation. But the Sienefe received their A baffadors with much fhew of kindnefs and refpect; though it was only out of fear of being over-run by their Mafters before the other fide could fend them any fuccours : and therefore they thought it the beft way to amufe them for a time, as they were not then in a capacity to make any refiftance. The Venetians however and King Alphonfo defigned (as it was then faid) to have fent Ambaffadors to Florence, in order to juftify the war they were going to make upon that Republic : but as the Venetian Ambaffador was refufed entrance into the Florentine dominions, and the other did not care to take that charge wholly upon himfelf, that Embaffy fell to the ground ; and the Venetians had the mortification to fee themfelves treated with as much contempt and difregard as they had treated the Florentines but a little while before.

In the midft of thefe apprehenfions, the Emperor Frederic III. * came into Italy to be crowned, and on the 30th of January in the year 1451, made his entry

---

* This Emperor, furnamed the Pacific, began his reign in 1440, and reigned 53 years. He was a Prince of great generofity and prudence; and naturally abhorring war, he endeavoured to fupply in policy what he wanted in power. He bore the infults that had been offered him by feveral of the Popes, with fuch patience, that the Italians ufed to fay, *he had a dead foul in a living body*. It was in the 12th year of his reign that he went to Rome to receive his crown at the hands of the Pope.

into Florence with fifteen hundred horfe, where he
was received with the higheft honours by the Signiory,
and ftaid there till the Sixth of February ; at which
time he departed for Rome, to receive his Crown
from the hands of the Pope. After that ceremony
was over, and his marriage confummated with the
Emprefs *, who had come thither by Sea, he returned into Germany ; but came back again to Florence
the May following, where he was treated with the
fame demonftrations of refpect that he had been before : and having been magnificently entertained by
the Marquis of Ferrara as he was going back into
Germany the fecond time, he, in return for thofe ci-
vilities, made that Prince a grant of Modena and
Reggio. But the Florentines were not diverted by
thefe folemnities from making due preparation for
the approaching war : and to give reputation to their
arms, and ftrike a terror into the enemy, they and
the Duke entered into a League with the King of
France, for the mutual defence of each other's dominions, which they publifhed with great triumph
and oftentation all over Italy.

1454

  It was now the month of May in the year 1452,
when the Venetians refolving to defer the hoftilities
no longer, entered the Duke of Milan's dominions
with fixteen thoufand horfe and fix thoufand foot by
the way of Lodi : whilft the Marquis of Monferrat,
either moved by his own ambition or the inftigation
of the Venetians, at the fame time likewife invaded
him on the fide of Alexandria. The Duke on the
other hand, having affembled an army of eighteen
thoufand horfe and three thoufand foot (after he had
put fufficient garrifons, not only into Lodi and Alexandria, but into all other fuch places as he thought
were moft liable to be attacked by the enemy) fell into
the territories of Brefcia, where he made prodigious
havock ; laying wafte the country on every fide, and
plundering all the towns that were not well fortified,

  * Eleanora, Infanta of Portugal.

And

And the Marquis of Montferrat being alſo defeated by the garriſons at Alexandria, gave the Duke an opportunity of turning with all his forces upon the Venetians and attacking them with greater vigour.

Whilſt the war was thus carried on in Lombardy with various ſucceſs on both ſides, but in ſo feeble a manner that nothing was done worth relating on either, the flame likewiſe broke out in Tuſcany, but not with greater vehemence, nor more danger than it had done in Lombardy. Ferdinand the illegitimate Son of King Alphonſo, had marched into thoſe parts with twelve thouſand men commanded by Frederic Lord of Urbino; and their firſt enterprize was an attempt upon Foiano in the Vale of Chiana: for the Sieneſe being their friends, they entered the Florentine dominions on that ſide. That fortreſs was but a ſmall one, and neither ſtrong nor well garriſoned; the number of men which had been ſent thither by the Signiory for its defence not exceeding two hundred: but they were reckoned as good and faithful ſoldiers as any in thoſe times. Before this place Ferdinand ſat down: however, either the reſolution of the beſieged was ſo great, or the conduct of the beſiegers ſo bad, that it did not ſurrender till after ſix and thirty days: which gave the Florentines time to provide better for places of greater importance, to aſſemble their troops, and make more effectual preparations for their defence.

After the reduction of this fortreſs, the enemy advanced into the territories of Chianti, where they made an aſſault upon two other places that were defended only by the townſmen, but were not able to carry them. From thence they paſſed on to Caſtellina, a town on the confines of Chianti, about ten miles from Siena, neither well fortified by art, nor ſtrong by its natural ſituation: yet, weak as it was in all reſpects, they could not make themſelves maſters of it; ſo that after they had inveſted it on every ſide for the ſpace of forty days, they were forced to raiſe the ſiege and make a ſhameful retreat. For ſo con-

E e 4   temptible

temptible were their armies in thofe days, and their
method of making war attended with fo little danger,
that towns which now would be abandoned as incapable of being maintained, were then defended in
fuch a manner, as if they thought them impoffible to
be taken.

Whilft Ferdinand was in the Country of Chianti,
he made daily incurfions into the Florentine dominions, and not only committed terrible depredations there, but advanced with fome of his parties within fix miles of the City, to the great confternation and diftrefs of the Governors there; who
having affembled their forces to the number of eight
thoufand near the Caftle of Colle, under the Command of Aftorre da Faenza and Gifmondo Malatefta,
did not care however to come to an engagement, but
kept at a good diftance from the enemy: becaufe
they knew very well, as long as their army was entire,
they could not fuffer much by the war; as the little
places which might be taken from them, would be
reftored at the conclufion of a peace; and for thofe
of greater confequence they were in no pain, being
affured that the enemy would not then venture to
make any attempt upon them. King Alphonfo had
likewife a fleet confifting of about twenty fail of Gallies and other fuch veffels hovering upon the Coaft
of Pifa; and whilft he befieged Caftellina by land,
he made an attack upon the Caftle of Vada by Sea,
which he took through the negligence of the Governor. This acquifition gave him an opportunity of
infefting all the adjacent Country: but his excurfions
were at laft checked by fome forces which the Florentines fent to Campiglia, who put an end to thofe
depredations, and kept his men clofely confined to
the Sea Coaft.

The Pope in the mean time did not interfere in
thefe broils any further than in endeavouring to re-
eftablifh peace amongft the contending parties. But
whilft he had the addrefs to keep himfelf out of the
war abroad, he was in no little danger at home.

There

There was at that time in Rome one Stephen Por-cari, a Citizen by birth, of a noble family and great learning, but much more eminent for the generofity of his mind. This Stephen (like men that are am-bitious of glory) refolved to perform, or at leaft to attempt fome action of *Eclat* that fhould make him memorable to pofterity. And nothing feemed to him more honourable than an attempt to refcue his Coun-try out of the hands of the Prelates, and reftore it to its ancient liberty: in hopes, if he fucceeded, of being called *The fecond Founder and Father of Rome.* What animated him to this enterprife, was the cor-ruption, infolence, and diffolute lives of the Prelates; at which, both the Nobility and common people of Rome were highly difgufted. But his chief confi-dence was founded upon fome verfes in one of Pe-trarch's Sonnets, which begins thus, *Spirto gentile,* &c. The verfes are thefe,

> " Sopra il monte Tarpeio Canzon vedrai
>   Un Cavalier, ch' Italia tutta onora
>   Penfofo piu d' altrui che di fe Steffo."

> On the Tarpein Mount my Mufe fhall fee }
> A Cavalier ador'd by Italy, }
> Regardlefs of himfelf, to fet his Country free. }

Stephen was poffeffed with a conceit, that Poets are often infpired with a divine and prophetic fpirit; and taking it for granted, that what Petrarch had thus foretold, would certainly come to pafs, he looked upon himfelf as the man deftined for the execution of fo glorious an undertaking; as he thought he was far fuperior to all his fellow-citizens in learning, elo-quence, friends, and popular favour. Having taken this into his head, he could not contain himfelf within the common bounds of referve, but behaved with fo much indifcretion, both in his words and actions, and manner of living, that the Pope beginning to fufpect he had fome bad defign in agitation, imme-diately banifhed him to Bologna, in order to keep

him

him out of mifchief, and fent inftructions to the Governor of that City, to keep a ftrict eye upon his actions, and to fee him every day at fuch an hour,
Stephen, however, was fo far from being daunted at
this rebuff, that he purfued his defigns with much
more refolution and affiduity than before, holding a
fecret correfpendence with his friends at Rome, and
often going thither and back again himfelf, with fo
much expedition, that he was always in time to prefent himfelf before the Governor at the appointed
hour. So that when he thought he had drawn a fufficient number into the confpiracy, being determined
to defer the execution of it no longer, he fent orders
to his friends at Rome, to prepare a fplendid fupper
on fuch an evening, where all the confpirators were
to meet, and bring as many confidants with them as
they could fully depend upon, promifing to be with
them before fupper was over. When every thing
was fettled, therefore, according to his inftructions,
he came to the houfe where they fupped, and having
put on an embroidered mantle, with a chain of gold
about his neck, and other ornaments, to give him
the more majefty and authority, he entered the room
where the confpirators were affembled ; and after he
had tenderly embraced them all, made a long and
pathetic fpeech to them, wherein he exhorted them
to behave like men, and prepare themfelves for the
execution of fo glorious a purpofe. After which, he
gave every man his feparate charge, ordering one
part of them to feize upon the Pope's palace early the
next morning, and the other to run about the ftreets,
and excite the people to take up arms. But the plot
was difcovered that very night ; fome fay, by the information of certain of his accomplices, and others,
by his having been feen in the City himfelf. However that might be, the Pope caufed him, and the
greater part of the Confpirators, to be immediately
apprehended, and afterwards put to death, as they
might well expect. Such was the event of this undertaking ! and though, indeed, Porcari's intention

in

in it may feem worthy of praife to fome people *, yet his judgment and manner of conducting it muft be condemned by every one : for notwithftanding enterprizes of this kind have fome fhadow of glory in the projection, they are almoft always attended with the ruin of the projectors.

The war in Tufcany had now continued almoft twelve months, and in the Spring of the year 1453, when both armies had taken the field, Alexander Sforza, the Duke of Milan's brother, came to the fuccour of the Florentines, with two thoufand horfe; fo that their army being augmented, and that of King Alphonfo rather diminifhed, the Florentines refolved to ufe their endeavours to recover what had been loft, and without much difficulty retook feveral towns. After this, they fat down before Foiano, which being facked through the negligence of the Commiffaries, the inhabitants were difperfed in fuch a manner, that they could not be prevailed upon to return, till great rewards and exemptions were offered them. They likewife recovered the fortrefs of Vada; for the enemy finding they could not keep it, firft fet the Caftle on fire, and then abandoned it. But whilft the Florentine army was making this progrefs, the king's not daring to face them, had retreated towards Siena, and made feveral incurfions into their territories on that fide, where they committed great outrages, and filled all the Country with terror and confufion. The King alfo endeavoured to annoy them in another quarter, in order to divide their forces, and to harrafs and diftrefs them as many ways as he could, in hopes of humbling them at laft. Gerardo Gambacorta was then Lord of the Vale of Bagno, whofe Anceftors,

---

* Confpiring againft the State, Mr. Bayle fays, is the greateft crime a man can be guilty of, and yet fome perfons fuffer themfelves to be drawn into confpiracies by fuch motives as they think are morally good: fo true it is, that man's confcience is liable to the moft lamentable errors! Brutus, and feveral of thofe whom he prevailed upon to affaffinate Julius Cæfar, were men of the moft eminent probity and virtue.

as well as himſelf, having been under great obligations to the Florentines, had always lived in amity with them, and were conſtantly either in their pay, or recommended by them to others. With this man Alphonſo began to tamper, and offered him another State in the Kingdom of Naples, which was more than an equivalent, provided he would deliver up that territory to him. But when this came to be known at Florence, the Signiory ſent an Ambaſſador to ſee how he ſtood affected; who was likewiſe at the ſame time to remind him of the favours which he and his family had received from that Republic, and to exhort him to continue faithful to it. Upon which, Gambacorta ſeeming to be much ſurprized at the imputation, aſſured them, with the moſt ſolemn oaths and aſſeverations, that ſo wicked a thought had never entered his head, and proffered not only to go back again with them to Florence, but to reſide there as a ſecurity for his fidelity. But as he pretended to be in an ill ſtate of health, he ſaid, what he could not do himſelf at that time, without great inconvenience, his Son ſhould do for him, and delivered him up to the Ambaſſadors as an Hoſtage. Theſe aſſurances and proofs ſeemed ſo convincing, that they fully confided in him, and looked upon the charge as a mere calumny. Upon this, Gambacorta proſecuted the agreement with the King with more earneſtneſs; and when it was concluded, his Majeſty ſent Brother Puccio, a Knight of the Order of St. John at Jeruſalem *, with a good body of forces into the Vale of Bagno to receive ſuch Caſtles and Towns as were in Gerardo's poſſeſſion; though the inhabitants of that Vale, who were very well affected to the Republic of Florence, ſubmitted to the King's Commiſſaries with great reluctance. Puccio, however, made himſelf maſter of all that territority, except the Caſtle of Corzano: but when Gambacorta was upon the point of delivering up that fortreſs alſo into the enemy's

---

* Now called Knights of Malta.

hands,

hands, there happened to be amongst his attendants, one Antonio Gualandi, a native of Pisa, and a spirited young man, who inwardly detested the perfidious behaviour of his master. This man, who was well acquainted with the situation of the place, and perceived by the countenance and behaviour of the garrison, that they were much dissatisfied at such a manner of proceeding, seeing Gambacorta standing at one of the gates to admit the King's forces, laid hold of him with both hands, and having thrust him out of the Castle, called upon the garrison to shut the gate upon so vile a wretch, and preserve the fortress for the Republic of Florence. And no sooner was the news of this event known at Bagno, but the inhabitants there, and of all the neighbouring places, immediately took up arms against King Alphonso's garrisons, and hoisting Florentine Colours, drove them entirely out of all those towns. The Florentines also being informed of what had happened, committed their Hostage, young Gambacorta, to prison, and sending forces to defend that territory, in the Name of the Republic, they reduced it to a Bailiwick, dependant upon themselves, from a State, which, for a great number of years, had been governed by Princes of its own. The Father, in the mean time, having betrayed both his Allies and his Son, with great difficulty made his escape, and wandering about the world like a Vagabond, left his wife and family, and all his possessions, in the hands of the enemy. This sudden revolution was of the utmost importance to the Florentines; for if the King had been in full possession of that Country, he would have had it in his power to make incursions into the Vale of Tevere, and the Territories of Casentino, with very little difficulty, whenever he pleased; where he would have been a continual thorn in their sides, and obliged them to divide their forces in such a manner, that they could not have turned their whole power against his main army, which then lay near Siena.

Be-

Besides the steps which the Florentines had taken in Italy to stop the progress of the enemy, they likewise sent Agnolo Acciaiuoli as Ambassador to the King of France, to pray that his Majesty would let King Regnier of Anjou return into Italy to the assistance of their Republic and the Duke of Milan, his antient allies; where he might also take proper measures for the recovery of the Kingdom of Naples, in which undertaking they promised to furnish him both with men and money. Accordingly, whilst the war was carried on in the manner we have related in Lombardy and Tuscany, that ambassador concluded an agreement with King Regnier; in which it was stipulated, that he should come into Italy by the latter end of June at furthest, with two thousand four hundred horse; that upon his arrival at Alexandria, he should be immediately supplied with thirty thousand Florins in ready money, and ten thousand more every month, as long as the war continued. In consequence of this treaty, he had got his forces in readiness to march; but their passage was obstructed by the Duke of Savoy and the Marquis of Montferrat, who were in alliance with the Venetians. Upon which, Regnier was advised by the Florentine Ambassador to turn aside into Provence, and endeavour to pass by Sea into Italy with what forces he could, in order to give some reputation at least to his friends: and at the same time to try if he could not prevail upon the King of France to use his good offices with the Duke of Savoy so effectually as to obtain him a passage through his dominions. This being granted at last, to oblige the King of France, some part of Regnier's troops marched through Savoy, whilst he transported himself, with the rest, by Sea, to join them in Italy; where, upon his arrival, he was received with the highest honours by the Duke of Milan: and these two Princes having united their forces, attacked the Venetians with so much vigour on every side, that they soon not only recovered all the places which had been taken from them in the Cremonese, but made themselves

felves mafters of almoft all the territory of Brefcia,
with fuch rapidity, that the Venetian Commiffaries
not thinking their army fecure in the field, retreated
and took fhelter under the walls of that City. However, as the Duke was then at Verona, and the feafon of the year pretty far advanced, he thought it
neceffary, for the refrefhment of his men, to put
them into winter quarters ; and having configned Placentia to Regnier, for that purpofe, they ftaid all the
reft of the year 1453, and the beginning of the next,
in thofe places, without attempting any thing farther.
But as foon as the weather began to grow more temperate, and the Duke was preparing to take the field
again, in hopes of ftripping the Venetians of all their
dominions upon the Terra Firma, Regnier gave him
to underftand, that his own affairs laid him under an
abfolute neceffity of returning into France.

This fudden and unexpected refolution, greatly
chagrined the Duke: and though he immediately
took poft, and went to him at Placentia, to fee if he
could not prevail upon him to change it, yet all his
offers and entreaties were to no purpofe : he only promifed to leave part of his forces behind him, and to
fend his fon John to ferve the allies in his ftead. The
Florentines, on the contrary, were not at all difpleafed
at this event ; for as they had now recovered all the
towns that had been taken from them, they were no
longer afraid of King Alphonfo, nor did they defire
that the Duke of Milan fhould become poffeffed of
any thing more than what belonged to him in Lombardy. Regnier accordingly returned into his own
Country, but fent his fon, as he had promifed, into
Italy ; who did not ftop in Lombardy, but came directly to Florence, where he was received with much
refpect.

After the departure of Regnier, the Duke of Milan feemed difpofed to a peace ; the Venetians, King
Alphonfo, and the Florentines, being all tired of the
war, were likewife defirous of it ; and the Pope had
always taken great pains, and ftill laboured with much
ear-

earneftnefs to bring about an accommodation betwixt
the different parties : for Mahomet the Grand Turk
had taken Conftantinople that year, and made himfelf
Mafter of all Greece *; an acquifition that ftruck
terror into all the Princes of Chriftendom, but efpecially into the Pope and the Venetians, who imagined,
they already felt the weight of his arms in their dominions. His Holinefs, therefore, vehemently follicited every State in Italy to fend their refpective Am-

---

* Voltaire having at large recited the caufes that contributed to
the lofs of this great feat of the Eaftern Empire, fays, "Mahomet II.
was twenty-two years of age, when he afcended the throne of the
Sultans. From tnat time he bent his mind upon the conqueft of
Conftantinople, whilft that unhappy City was rent into factions and
fchifms, difputing and quarrelling whether they fhould make ufe of
leavened or unleavened bread in the facrament, and whether it was
better to pray in Latin or Greek. He began therefore, with block-
ading the City; and in the beginning of April, 1453, the adjacent
Country was covered with near three hundred thoufand Turks, and
the Strait of Propontis with about three hundred gallies, and two
hundred fmaller veffels. One of the moft extraordinary, and yet
beft attefted facts, is the ufe that Mahomet made of thofe fhips. They
could not get into the Port, the mouth of it being barricaded with
ftrong booms and chains of iron, and befides, in all probability, ad-
vantageoufly defended. One night, therefore, he ordered the ground
to be covered for the fpace of two leagues in length with fir planks,
greafed with tallow and oil, and laid like the manger of a fhip: after
which, by the affiftance of machines, and bodily labour, he caufed
fourfcore gallies, and feventy tenders or fmaller veffels, to be hauled
out of the Strait, and rolled away over thefe planks. All this great
work was finifhed in one night; and early in the morning, the befieged faw with aftonifhment, an entire fleet defcend from the land
into their harbour. The next day, a bridge of boats was built
within fight of them, and ferved for the erecting a battery of cannon.
After a fiege of forty-nine days, the Emperor Conftantine was
obliged to capitulate, and fent feveral Greeks to receive the Law of
the Conqueror, who granted them terms. But as thefe Deputies
were returning to the City, Mahomet recollecting fomething which
he had forgot to add, ordered fome of his people to ride after them.
Upon which, the befieged on the top of the ramparts, feeing a body
of Turks gallopping after the Deputies, imprudently fired at them.
The Turks were foon joined by a greater number, and juft as the
Deputies were entering the gate, the enemy rufhed in pell-mell along
with them, and made themfelves mafters of the upper town, which
is feparated from the lower. The Emperor Conftantine XIII. was
killed in the crowd, after he had fought to the laft, with incredible courage : and when the Sultan had made himfelf Mafter of one
half of Conftantinople, he granted the fame terms to the other half
that he had offered to the whole City, which were accepted, and
punctually obferved by him." Voltaire's Gen. Hift. vol. ii. part i.
p. 55. &c.

baffadors

baffadors to him at Rome, with full powers to conclude a general peace; with which they all complied.
But when they met, and their feveral pretenfions
came to be difcuffed, many difficulties and impediments occurred, which feemed infurmountable. The
King of Naples expected that the Florentines fhould
indemnify him for the expences he had been at in the
war; and the Florentines made the fame demand upon him. The Venetians infifted upon the Duke giving up Cremona to them; and the Duke would not
be fatisfied except they reftored Bergamo, Brefcia,
and Crema. So that thefe obftacles feemed impoffible to be removed. Neverthelefs, what appeared fo
difficult at Rome, where the matter was canvaffed by
fo many, was foon got over at Milan and Venice,
where it was conducted by fewer managers: for whilft
the treaty went very flowly forwards under the mediation of his Holinefs, the Duke and the Venetians
concluded one betwixt themfelves, on the ninth of
April, 1454; by which fuch towns were to be reftored to each other, as they were refpectively in poffeffion of before the beginning of the war; the Duke
was left at liberty to recover thofe places, if he
could, that had been feized upon by the Duke of Savoy, and the Marquis of Montferrat; and the reft of
the Italian Princes were to have a month given them
to accede to the treaty, if they fo pleafed. The Pope,
the Florentines, together with the Sienefe, and feveral
other inferior States, came into it within that time;
befides which, a peace was concluded betwixt the
Florentines, the Duke, and the Venetians, for the
term of twenty-five years.

Of all the Princes in Italy, King Alphonfo alone
was diffatisfied at the peace, as he thought it would
be a derogation to his Majefty to be admitted rather
as an auxiliary than a principal; upon which account
he continued fome time in fufpence, and would not
acquaint them with his refolution. At laft, however,
after feveral formal embaffies from the Pope and other

States, he fuffered himfelf to be prevailed upon, (chiefly at the inftance of his Holinefs) and both he and his Son acceded to the treaty, which was renewed for thirty years : at the fame time a double alliance was contracted betwixt his family and the Duke's; each of thofe Princes giving his daughter in marriage to the Son of the other. Neverthelefs as the evil deftiny of Italy would have fome feeds of future difcords and troubles ftill left, he refufed to ratify the treaty after all, except the reft of the contracting powers would fuffer him to make war upon the Genoefe, Gifmondo Malatefta Lord of Rimini, and Aftorre Prince of Faenza, without being in any wife impeded or molefted in his operations by them. This being likewife complied [with, Ferdinand his Son, who was then at Sienna, returned into the Kingdom of Naples, after he had loft a great number of his men, and gained no material advantage by coming into Tufcany.

A general peace being thus concluded, the only apprehenfion that remained, was, that it would foon be difturbed again by the enmity which King Alphonfo bore to the Genoefe. But it proved otherwife; for in all outward appearance the fubfequent troubles were not owing to that Prince, but to the ambition of mercenary Soldiers, which indeed had been the occafion of moft of thofe that had happened before. The Venetians (according to their cuftom at the end of a war) difcharged their General Giacopo Piccinino, who retired with fome other Commanders and forces into Romagna, but without having then formed any other defign. From thence Piccinino paffed into the territories of Siena, where he began a war upon the Sienefe, and took feveral of their towns. In the beginning of thefe broils, and of the year 1455, Pope Nicholas died, and was fucceeded by Calixtus III. This Pontif, in order to extinguifh a flame which he faw juft ready to break out again almoft at his own door, immediately affembled what troops he could, under the Command
of

of his General Ventimiglia, and fent them againft Piccinino, in conjunction with the forces of the Duke and
the Florentines, who likewife concurred with him in
their endeavours to prevent the growing evils. Near
Bolfena, they came to an engagement; in which, notwithstanding Ventimiglia was taken prifoner, Piccinino was routed and forced to fly in great diforder to
Caftiglione della Pefcaia, where if he had not been
fupplied with money by King Alphonfo, he muft have
been utterly undone : a circumftance which gave every
one reafon to fufpect this enterprize was undertaken and
profecuted by the order and direction of that Prince.
So that Alphonfo perceiving his defigns were difcovered, endeavoured to make up a peace, in order to
regain the confidence of his allies, which he had almoft loft by this feeble and pitiful attempt : and for
that purpofe he fet a treaty on foot, wherein it was
agreed that Piccinino fhould reftore all the places he
had taken from the Sienefe, and that they fhould pay
him twenty thoufand Florins ; after which, he received both him and his forces into his own Kingdom.

At this time the Pope, though very watchful over
Piccinino's motions, was making great preparations
for the Common fupport of Chriftendom, which he
faw in imminent danger of being over-run by the
Turk; and not only fent Ambaffadors, but Preachers
into every part of Europe to exhort all Chriftian
Princes and people to take up arms in defence of
their Religion againft the Common enemy, and to affift each other in fo laudable an undertaking with
their perfons as well as their purfes : in confequence
of which, great fums were raifed at Florence, and
many wore red Croffes to fhew they were ready to
ferve perfonally in fuch an Expedition. They likewife made folemn Proceffions to implore the bleffing
of God upon their arms. And all perfons, in order
to fhew the warmth of their zeal for the Chriftian religion, were eager in offering their advice, their for-

tunes

tunes and perfons, to forward this enterprize. But thefe apprehenfions and this rage of Crufading were in fome meafure abated when news arrived, that the Grand Signior, having laid fiege to Belgrade (a fortrefs in Hungary fituated upon the Danube) was not only routed, but wounded himfelf. So that the Pope and other Chriftian States, having now recovered themfelves a little from the panic which the lofs of Conftantinople had ftruck into them, proceeded afterwards with lefs vigour in their preparations for the profecution of that war, which feemed to be much damped in Hungary likewife by the death of their Waivode who had obtained that fignal Victory *.

But to return to the affairs of Italy. The difturbances which had been raifed by Giacopo Piccinino being compofed and arms laid down on every fide, it pleafed God to vifit Tufcany with a ftorm of wind that wrought fuch effects as had never been heard of

---

* This was the famous John Corvinus, or Huniades, Waiwode of Tranfylvania, General of the Hungarian armies, under King Ladiflaus, and one of the greateft commanders of his time. He was almoft continually engaged in wars with the Turks, whom he beat in two battles, one in the year 1442, the other in the year following, and forced them to retire from before Belgrade after a fiege of feven months. He was at the battle of Verna, fo fatal to Chriftendom: where Ladiflaus was killed in 1444. Afterwards he was made Governor of Hungary, and his name became fo formidable to the Turks, that they looked upon him as a fcourge fent to chaftife their nation, and called him *Jancus Lain*, that is, John the Wicked. He was beat by them, however, in a battle that was fought on the 17th, 18th, and 19th days of October, 1448. But he prevented them a fecond time from taking Belgrade, in 1458, when it was befieged by Mahomet II. with an army of two hundred and fifty thoufand men; forty thoufand of whom were killed, and the reft abandoned the fiege in a precipate manner, leaving all their baggage, artillery, and ammunition, behind them. He died the fame year at Zemplin, and Mahomet, who faid he was the greateft foldier in the world, is reported to have lamented his death, and thought himfelf unfortunate, becaufe there was no other warrior of equal eminence left, by defeating whom, he might retrieve the glory he had loft. Pope Calixtus wept, and all Chriftendom was in affliction when he died. Thurofius. in Chron. Hungar. The word Vaivode or Woiewoda, fignifies a Prince, Duke, Governor, or chief Magiftrate, and in the northern parts is generally a feudal dignity. There is in Selden's *Titles of Honour*, an inveftiture, folemn livery, or infeodation of Moldavia to Stephen—as Vaivode thereof in the year 1485.

before

before that time, and will feem marvellous to pofterity †.   About an hour before Sun-rife on the twenty-
fourth of Auguft, a dark thick Cloud which feemed
to extend itfelf about two miles every way, arofe out
of the Gulf of Venice near Ancona; and traverfing
the Continent of Italy from eaft to weft, bent its
courfe towards the Sea coaft of Pifa.   This cloud
being driven forwards (whether by a natural or fu-
pernatural impulfe I will not take upon me to determine) was broken at laft into feveral parts, which
fometimes were hurried up to a vaft height in the air,
fometimes precipitated themfelves towards the earth,
dafhing violently againft each other, and whirling
round in a fpiral manner with aftonifhing rapidity.
Thefe concuffions, attended with a furious Hurricane
of wind, inceffant flafhes of red lightening, and fuch
dreadful burfts as far exceeded the loudeft thunder
or the moft difmal crafhes of an earthquake, made
every man's heart fail within him; as they thought
the world was certainly at an end and the elements refolving into their original Chaos.

No lefs amazing were the effects of this tempeft
where ever it paffed; but moft remarkable in the
neighbourhood of St. Caffiano, a Caftle about eight
miles from Florence, upon the mountains which divide the Vale of Pifa from that of Grieve.   For
paffing betwixt that Caftle and the Bourg of St. Andrew, which ftands upon the fame hills, it never

---

† The new world was not difcovered at that time: if it had, Sai-
lors would have called this ftorm (terrible as it was) but *a cap-full of
wind*, in comparifon of thofe dreadful hurricanes which frequently
happen in the Weft Indies.   The Editor of this work had the misfortune to be an eye-witnefs of one of them in Jamaica, in October
1744.   There were at that time ninety-five merchant veffels, and
eight men of war, in Port Royal Harbour; of which, only his Majefty's fhip the Rippon, rode it out, all the reft being either wrecked,
or driven afhore, and fome of them a great way up into the Country; where they were left *high and dry* (as the fea phrafe is) when the
waters fubfided.   The damage which the Ifland likewife fuftained by
that calamity, was hardly to be computed: and the havock it made,
fo prodigious and uncommon, that a particular narrative of it would
be credited by few.

F f 3   reached

reached the latter, and brushed the former in so slight
a manner, that it only blew down some chimnies and
battlements : but in the space betwixt those two places
it laid numbers of houses flat with the ground. The
roofs of St. Martin's Church at Bagnuola, and of
Santa Maria della Pace were taken off and carried
away entire above a mile. A carrier and his mules
were hurried out of the road into a neighbouring valley and there found dead. Many of the sturdiest
Oaks and other huge trees that did not bend to the
fury of the blast, not only had their branches stripped
off but were torn up by the roots and carried to a
considerable distance. So that when the storm ceased
and day light began to appear, the inhabitants of the
Country stood in amazement as if they had been thun-
derstruck or stupified. The fields were desolated,
the Churches and houses entirely demolished, and
nothing to be heard but the cries and lamentations of
those that had lost their whole substance, and had not
only their Cattle, but their families also buried in the
ruins. A spectacle indeed, that must fill the hardest
heart with terror and compassion ! but God in his
mercy seemed to intend this calamity rather as a warning, than a chastisement to Tuscany in general : for
if such a storm had fallen upon a large and populous
City, instead of a Country where there was not any
very considerable number of houses and inhabitants,
and little else to spend its rage upon but trees and
thickets, without doubt the havock it must have made
would have been greater than can well be conceived.
The Divine Being was pleased however to restrain
his Vengeance, and to let this scourge suffice for that
time, to revive in mankind a due sense of his Al-
mighty power *.

---

* These reflections do not seem to favour much of Atheism, with
which Machiavel has been so liberally charged, and often by people
that never read any of his works. He speaks pretty freely, indeed,
of the Church of Rome, and its corruption ; which being reckoned
a Mortal Sin in one of that Communion, seldom goes without its

But

But to refume the thread of our narrative. King Alphonfo, as we have faid before, was diffatisfied with the peace; and as the war, which he had caufed Giacopo Piccinino to make upon the Sienefe without any reafonable occafion, was attended with no material advantage, he was refolved to try his fortune in that which he was allowed to commence with the Genoefe by the articles of the late treaty. Accordingly in the year 1456, he invaded them both by fea and land, with a defign to take the government of their State out of the hands of the Fregofi, who were then in poffeffion of it, and to reftore it to the Adorni. On the other hand, he fent Giacopo Piccinino over the Tronto, with a body of forces to fall upon Gifmondo Malatefta; who having put all his towns in a good pofture of defence, made fo vigorous a refiftance, that his Majefty's arms met with no fuccefs in that enterprize: and his attempt upon Genoa afterwards involved both him and his Kingdom in fuch troubles as he little expected. Pietro Fregofo was at that time Doge of Genoa, and being afraid he fhould not be able to cope with the King, refolved to give up what he found he could no longer hold himfelf, to fome other Prince that was able to defend him from his enemies, and perhaps might one time or other make him a proper recompence for it. For this purpofe, he difpatched Ambaffadors to Charles VII. King of France, with an offer of the State of Genoa: which Charles readily accepted of, and fent King Regnier's Son John of Anjou (who had left Florence not long before and was gone back to France) to take

---

punifhment in this world. The Jefuits, and other religious Orders, according as they are touched, never fail amongft the reft of their wiles, to brand fuch a one with a name that will be fure to ftick clofe to him. A fearful outcry is raifed of Atheift, Infidel, Heretic, mad dog, &c.

" Cape faxa manu, cape robora, Paftor,"

And then, bleffed is the Zealot that takes up a ftick or a ftone, and knocks out his brains. It is well other Churches have more charity and moderation.

poſſeſſion of that City : as he thought nobody more proper to govern it, than a perſon who was ſo well acquainted with the cuſtoms and genius of the Italians, and might at the ſame time have an opportunity of proſecuting his claim to the Kingdom of Naples, of which his father Regnier had been deprived by King Alphonſo. John of Anjou therefore immediately repaired to Genoa, where he was received like a Prince, and inveſted with the whole power both of the City and the State.

Alphonſo was not a little galled at this circumſtance, perceiving he had drawn an enemy upon his back that was much too powerful for him : however he boldly purſued his undertaking, and had already brought his fleet to Porto-fino, near Villa Marina, when he ſuddenly fell ſick and died *. By his death John of Anjou and the Genoeſe were freed from the apprehenſions of war : and Ferrando †, who ſucceeded his father Alphonſo in the Kingdom of Naples, ſeeing he had now ſo potent a rival in Italy, began to grow very doubtful of the fidelity of his Nobility : many of whom being fond of change, he thought would ſide with the French. He was likewiſe afraid of the Pope, whoſe ambition he was no ſtranger to, and imagined it would naturally prompt him to make ſome attempt to wreſt his Kingdom from him, before he was thoroughly ſettled in his throne. His only hopes were in the Duke of Milan, who was no leſs

---

* This Prince, ſurnamed the Wiſe and Magnanimous, was a very great patron, and encourager of literature and learned men. Amongſt many other inſtances of his particular regard to them and their memory, it is ſaid, that at the ſiege of Gaieta, when he was told, there were none of the large ſtones left, with which they uſed to load the mortars, nor any to be found, except at a Country Seat, which, according to an old tradition, had belonged to Cicero, he anſwered, " that he choſe rather to have his artillery uſeleſs, than to ſpoil what had been the property of ſo great a man." He uſed always to carry Cæſar's Commentaries with him in his voyages and journies, and never paſſed a day without reading ſome part of them, with great attention. His device was an open Book. Anton. Panormit. de dict. & fact. Alphonſi, l. ii. Num. 12.

† Or Ferdinand I. natural ſon of Alphonſo.

anxi-

anxious than himfelf for the prefervation of that
Kingdom ; apprehending that if the French fhould
make themfelves mafters of it, their next attempt
would be upon his dominions, which he knew they
looked upon as of right belonging to them*. The
Duke therefore, immediately after the death of King
Alphonfo, not only fent fuccours to Ferdinand to affift and give him reputation at that time, but wrote a
letter to him in which he exhorted him to take courage, and promifed that he would never abandon him
in any circumftances.

After Alphonfo was dead, the Pope defigned to.
have given the Kingdom of Naples to his own Nephew Pietro Ludovico Borgia : and to fet fo good a
face upon the matter as might induce the reft of the
Italian Princes to acquiefce in it, he gave out that it
was only his intention to reduce the Kingdom to its
former obedience to the Church ; in which cafe, he
fhould fecure fuch territories to the Duke of Milan
as were at that time in his poffeffion, or had ever belonged to him there ; and therefore hoped he would
not fend any fuccours to the affiftance of Ferdinand.
But in the midft of thefe new projects and preparations his Holinefs died, and was fucceeded in the
Papacy by Æneas Piccolomini, a Sienefe by birth,
who took the name of Pius II. † This Pontif, whofe

---

* The Duke of Orleans having married a Princefs of the Houfe of
Vifconti, who became entitled to the Duchy of Milan, upon the
failure of a male heir.

† This was the famous Æneas Sylvius, who, at the age of twenty-
fix, attended Dominico Capranico, Cardinal of Fermo, as his Secretary to the Council of Bafil. He afterwards ferved feveral other Prelates in the fame capacity, particularly Cardinal Albergoti, who fent
him into Scotland, to mediate a peace betwixt the Englifh and the
Scots. After his return, the fame council honoured him with the
Charges of Referendary, Abbreviator, Chancellor, General Agent,
and fent him feveral Times to Strafbourg, Frankfort, Conftance, Savoy, amongft the Grifons, and conferred upon him the Provoftfhip
of the Collegiate Church of St. Lorenzo in Milan. At that time he
compofed thofe pieces in favour of the Council of Bafil, againft Eugenius IV. in particular, and the Papal ufurpations and pretenfions
in general : for which he afterwards made an apology to that Pontif,

chief

chief ftudy was to promote the common good of Chriftendom, and maintain the refpect due to the

and afked his pardon, who not only forgave him, but made him his fecretary. After he was exalted to the Pontificate, he likewife retracted them in a Bull, dated April 26, 1463, which is prefixed to the Collection of his Works, and may be feen in Father Labbe's Collection of Councils, tom. xiii. p. 1407. It may not be unentertaining, perhaps, to fee in what manner he apologizes for his former conduct, and how much his fentiments were altered with his circumftances. He excufes himfelf for having written thofe pieces when he was young, and incapable of forming a right judgment of things. He owns, that he had been guilty of an error, and defires the Univerfity of Cologne, to which he addreffes his Bull, not to regard what he had faid in favour of the Council of Bafil, but to condemn Æneas Sylvius, and to follow the fentiments of Pius II. " We are men, fays he, and have erred as men. We do not deny that many things, which we have faid, or written, may juftly be condemned. We have been feduced like Paul, and perfecuted the Church of God through ignorance. We now follow St. Auftin's example, who having fuffered feveral erroneous fentiments to efcape him in his writings, afterwards retracted them. We do juft the fame thing; we ingenuoufly confefs our ignorance, being apprehenfive left what we have written in our youth, fhould occafion fome error, which may prejudice the Holy See. For if it is fuitable to any perfon's character, to maintain the eminence and glory of the firft throne of the Church, it is certainly fo to us, whom the merciful God, of his infinite goodnefs only, hath raifed to the dignity of Vice-gerent of Chrift, without any merit on our part. Upon all thefe confiderations, we exhort and advife you in the Lord, not to pay any regard to thofe writings, which in any wife injure the authority of the Apoftolic See, or affert opinions that the Holy Romifh Church does not receive. If you find any thing contrary to this in our Dialogues, or Letters, or in any other of our works, defpife fuch notions, reject them, follow what we now maintain: believe what we affert now we are in years, rather than what I faid when I was young; regard a Pope rather than a private man; in fhort, reject Æneas Sylvius, and receive Pius II. *Nec privatum hominem pluris facite quam fummum Pontificem; Æneam rejicite, Pium accipite.* That heathenifh name was given me by my parents at my birth; but this Chriftian name we affumed, when we were raifed to the Apoftolical Character: *Illud gentile nomen parentes indidere nafcenti; hoc Chriftianum in Apoftolatu fufcepimus.* And fince it might be objected, that his Dignity was the only reafon of his changing his opinion, he anfwers that, by giving a fhort account of his life and actions, and of the Council of Bafil, to which he went in the year 1431, when he was very young, without experience, and, as he fays, " like a bird juft out of its neft."

After he had filled many other great preferments, and difcharged feveral embaffies and negotiations, with much applaufe and reputation, he was made a Cardinal by Calixtus III. whom he fucceeded in the Papal Chair, in the year 1438, and reigned fix years within three days. Platina fays, he was not only the beft, but one of the moft learned Pontifs that had worn the Tiara for many ages before

Church

Church, laying afide all private interefts and paffions, crowned Ferdinand King of Naples at the follicitation of the Duke of Milan; thinking it would be more eafy to compofe all differences in Italy by confirming one that was already in poffeffion, than either by favouring the French in their pretenfions to that Kingdom, or attempting to feize upon it himfelf, as his predeceffor had defigned. Ferdinand, in return for fo great a favour, not only gave his natural daughter in marriage to the Pope's Nephew Antonio, with the principality of Melfi for her dower, but likewife reftored Benevento and Terracina to the Church. After which, the tranquillity of Italy feemed to be perfectly fettled, and the Pope was ufing his utmoft endeavours, as Calixtus the laft Pontif had done before him, to unite all Chriftian Princes in a league againft the Turk; when fome animofities, which broke out betwixt the Fregofi and John of Anjou, the new Governor of Genoa, gave birth to frefh wars, and fuch as were of much more importance than any that had yet happened.

him. His works are very numerous. A Catalogue of them may be feen in Mr. Henry Wharton's Appendix to Dr. Cave's Hiftoria Literarie, and in the General Dictionary, vol. i. p. 295. Among them, there is a remarkable letter (which is the fifteenth in the firft book of his Epiftles, and tranflated in the General Dictionary, vol. i. p. 290) wherein he gives his own father an account of an amour that he had with an Englifh Lady, when he was Ambaffadour at Strafbourg, and of the fruits of it. Upon which, Mr Wharton obferves, in the work above cited, " that he is fo far from lamenting his crime, that he even boafts of it there." Indeed it is written with an air of much gaiety.—He likewife wrote another very extraordinary letter to Mahomet II. which, as Mr. Bayle fays, has cut out fufficient work for dealers in controverfy, and occafioned a very warm difpute betwixt the famous du Pleffis Mornai and Coeffeteau, the particulars of which may be found under the article Mahomet II. Gen. Dict. vol. vii. p. 352. Where the reader will fee upon what *pious* motives this *great and good* Pontif perfuaded the Sultan to turn Chriftian.—Olearius fays, that he regretted three things at his death: ıft, that he had written, The Hiftory of two Lovers, Euryalus and Lucretia: 2. That he had canonized Catharine of Siena, who had been miftrefs to one of his Predeceffors. 3. That he had excited the Chriftian Princes to a war with the Turk. Bibliothec. Scriptor. Ecclef. tom. ii. p. 28. The two firft articles feem probable; the laft does not, and is directly contrary to what is faid of him by all other writers, who affirm, that he had that expedition very much at heart to the laft breath of his life.

Pietro

Pietro Fregofo was then at a Caftle belonging to him upon the Sea Coaft, whither he had retired in great difguft, that he and his family had not been rewarded according to their merits by John of Anjou; as they had been the principal inftruments in making him Lord of Genoa. So that at laft they came to an open quarrel; at which, Ferdinand was not a little pleafed, and imagining that nothing could more effectually conduce to his eftablifhment in the Kingdom of Naples, he fent him fupplies both of men and money, in hopes that he fhould be able by fuch means to drive his competitor entirely out of thefe parts. But John having intelligence of this, immediately fent into France for fuccours to make head againft his adverfary, who was grown fo formidable by the reinforcements he had received, that John did not think proper to face him at that time, but kept clofe within the walls of the City in order to fecure that; which yet he could not do effectually. For Pietro having found means to enter it privately one night, feized upon fome of the ftrong pofts: but at the return of day light, being engaged by John's forces, he was killed himfelf, and all his men either taken prifoners or flain upon the fpot.

Elated with this advantage, John now determined to make a defcent upon the Kingdom of Naples: for which purpofe he left Genoa in October 1459 with a powerful fleet, and fteering his courfe directly thither he came to an anchor at Baia, * and from thence proceeded to Seffa, where he was received by the

1459

---

* This City was famous for its hot baths and elegant buildings in the time of the ancient Romans; and here they ftill fhew the ruins of certain edifices, which they call the palaces of Cæfar, Pompey, Cicero, and other great men, who ufed to refort thither. Horace tells us, it was the moft delightful place upon earth.

" Nullus in orbe locus, Baiis prælucet amœnis."

The little plot of ground, called the Elyfian Fields, fo much celebrated by the Poets, lies about a mile from this place, but has not much to recommend or make it admired at prefent. It is parted from Puteoli by an arm of the Sea about two or three miles broad, over which the Emperor Caligula built a bridge. Suet. Tacit.

Duke

Duke of that place; and foon after his arrival, the Prince of Taranto, the people of Aquila, and many other Princes and Cities declared for him: fo that the whole Kingdom was in a manner loft. Ferdinand feeing this, had recourfe to the Pope and the Duke of Milan for affiftance, and that he might have the fewer enemies to deal with, he came to an accommodation with Gifmodo Malatefta; at which, Giacopo Piccinino (who was an avowed enemy to Malatefta) took fuch offence that he prefently quitted the fervice of Ferdinand, and went over to the French. He likewife endeavoured to engage Frederic Lord of Urbino in his interefts, by a confiderable fubfidy; and having affembled a pretty good army (for thofe times) with as much expedition as poffible; he advanced to meet the enemy: but coming to an engagement on the banks of the Sarni, he was totally routed, and moft of his principal officers taken prifoners.

After this defeat, all the reft of the towns revolted to John of Anjou, except Naples itfelf and fome few other places, which ftill adhered to Ferdinand. Piccinino advifed John to purfue his victory and march directly to Naples; for when that was reduced, he faid, the whole Kingdom would immediately drop into his hands: but he determined, on the contrary, to ftrip his competitor entirely of what little he had then left in thofe parts, before he attacked the Capital; out of a perfuafion, that when he had cut off all fupplies from the Country, he fhould eafily make himfelf mafter of the City: not confidering that the members follow the motions of the head more naturally, than the head is directed by thofe of the members. This refolution, however, proved fatal to his defigns, and overfet the whole expedition. For Ferdinand after his defeat had retired into Naples, where he received great numbers of his fubjects who had been driven out of their poffeffions; and having raifed fome money amongft the Citizens there by gentle and perfuafive means, he

by

by degrees formed a little army. He likewise follicited the Pope and the Duke of Milan for fresh
succours : each of whom sent him speedier and much
more effectual supplies than they had done before ;
as they both began to be under very great apprehenfions that the Kingdom of Naples would be utterly lost. Strengthened by these reinforcements Ferdinand marched out of Naples, and having retaken
several of the towns which the enemy had seized
upon, began in some measure to recover his credit
and interest.

But whilst the war was thus carried on with various
success on both sides in the Kingdom of Naples, an
event happened which robbed John of Anjou of all
his glory, and made him despair of any further success in that enterprize. The Genoese being thoroughly sick of the avarice and insolence of the
French, at last took up arms against their deputy-
governor, and forced him to fly for refuge into the
Citadel : and in this insurrection both the Fregosi and
Adorni concurring, were assisted with men and money by the Duke of Milan in their endeavours to recover and maintain their liberties. So that King
Regnier, who soon after came thither to the relief
of his Son with a body of forces on board some trans-
ports, in hopes of preserving Genoa, as the Citadel
still held out for him, was routed almost as soon as he
had landed his men, and forced to return with great
disgrace into Provence.

When the news of this overthrow arrived in the
Kingdom of Naples, John was not a little shocked
at it : yet he did not abandon his undertaking, but
carried on the war for some time, chiefly by the support of such of the Nobility as had revolted from
Ferdinand and despaired of ever making their peace
with him. At last, however, after many other occurrences, the two armies came to a general engagement near Troia in the year 1463, in which John
was defeated. But he was not so much hurt by
this overthrow, as by the defection of Giacopo Piccinino,

cinino, who went back again foon after into Ferdinand's fervice: fo that being now in a manner difarmed, he retired into * Iftria, and from thence into France. This war continued four years, and during the courfe of it, John of Anjou more than once loft that by negligence and fupinenefs, which had been honourably gained by the valour of his Soldiers.

The Florentines had not publickly taken either fide in thefe difputes; and when they were importuned by Ambaffadors fent from John King of Arragon (who was lately called to the government of that Kingdom, upon the death of King Alphonfo) to fuccour his Nephew Ferdinand, as they were obliged to do by their late treaty with his Father Alphonfo, they made anfwer, " that they had no connection with Ferdinand, and did not think themfelves under any obligation to affift the Son in a war which his Father had commenced, and as it was begun without their advice or concurrence, he might either continue or end it as he liked beft, fince he had nothing to expect from them." Upon which, the Ambaffadors having charged them, in the name of their Mafter, with a breach of the treaty, and declared that he would expect to be indemnified by them for any future loffes he might fuftain thereby, immediately left the City with much indignation and refentment. But notwithftanding the Florentines had not embroiled themfelves in thefe wars abroad, they were far from enjoying tranquillity at home, as fhall be related more at large in the next book.

---

* All the Italian Copies, that I have feen, fay Iftria; but it is a miftake: for it was not Iftria that he retired to, but Ifchia, a little Ifland in the Neapolitan Sea, fifteen miles Weft of the City of Naples.

END OF THE SIXTH BOOK.